THE BROKEN BLADE

THE
BROKEN
BLADE

No man can serve two
masters forever.

THE KNIGHT OF ELDARAN
—— Book 3 ——

Anna Thayer

LION FICTION

To
My wonderful husband, Justin, who has been my companion,
critic, and champion in the editorial process;
Proverbs 27:17 springs to mind!
And to our delightful son, Leo
– and his new sister, due to arrive at any time!
You are, and will always be, a blessing and a joy to us.

Published by Lion Fiction
an imprint of
Lion Hudson plc
Wilkinson House, Jordan Hill Road
Oxford OX2 8DR, England
www.lionhudson.com/fiction

ISBN 978 1 78264 105 6
e-ISBN 978 1 78264 106 3

First edition 2015

A catalogue record for this book is available from the British Library

Printed and bound in the UK, February 2015, LH26

CONTENTS

MAP OF THE RIVER REALM AND ITS WORLD

THE LAND
OF THE
SEVEN SONS

THE
MERCHANT
STATES

SKAANIA

LAMIGLIA

GALITHIA

ISTANARIA

KADI FTTI IA

ETRAIA

QUYOSHTANATE

JARMASARIQ

DIADOGUS

MARUKSOSHYK

LIBELSHA

NERBOCIA

SIB'LEMIA

THE SOUTHERN WASTES

THE RIVER REALM

GIBLIRIA

BREISLARIA

MARBORISTIA

RIATANIA

CALATIA

ANQ...

LUSARILIA

FUERIA

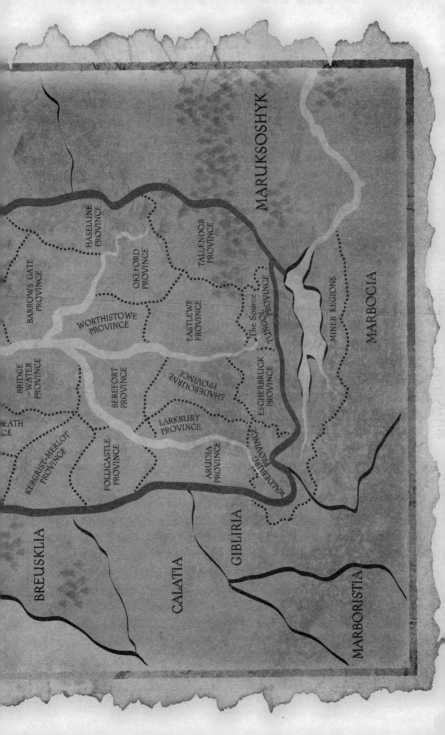

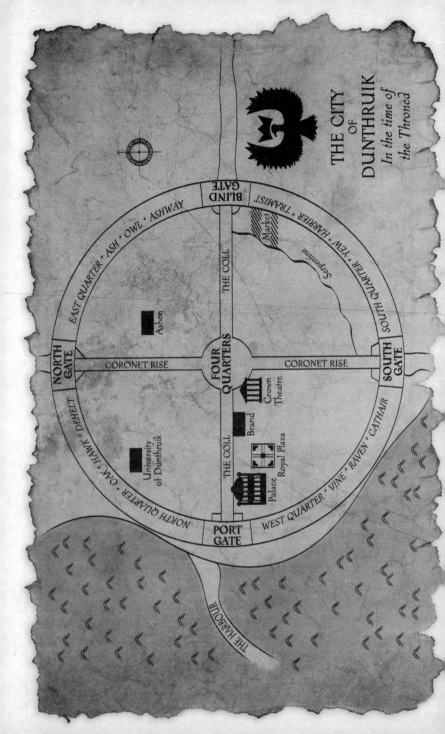

THE CITY OF DUNTHRUIK

In the time of the Throned

EDELRED'S PALACE - LOWER FLOOR

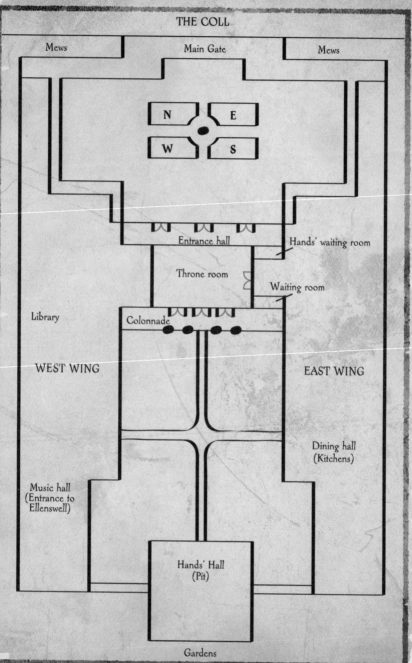

THE COLL

Mews   Main Gate   Mews

N   E
W   S

Entrance hall   Hands' waiting room

Throne room   Waiting room

Library

Colonnade

WEST WING   EAST WING

Dining hall
(Kitchens)

Music hall
(Entrance to
Ellenswell)

Hands' Hall
(Pit)

Gardens

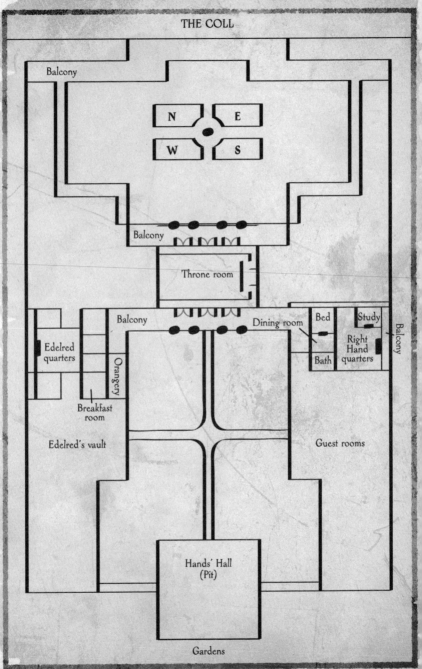

ACKNOWLEDGMENTS

This book is the culmination of long years of dreaming.

So many people have worked to support me in telling Eamon's story since I first began to pen it nearly a decade ago – too many to give them all the mention that they deserve.

Huge thanks must go once again to my old friends Esther and Jonathan, whose contributions of sound-boarding and encouragement have been immense; but, in this third book especially, I owe thanks to Esther for the moving words to Ilenia's song, and to Jonathan for his tireless and exhaustive dedication to all things military. It would have been far beyond my power to write a convincing – and logical – battle narrative without him.

Though he has already won himself the dedication to this book through his dedication to it, I am enormously indebted to my husband Justin, for his editorial acumen and plot-untangling skills – especially during the times that I have been suffering from Eamon over-exposure and baby brain! This trilogy would be much the poorer without everything he has given – and given up – to help me sculpt it to its final form.

Lastly, I must mention Tony Collins, Jessica Tinker, and Julie Frederick: the first for his willingness to take a risk on and build up an unknown author; the second for her unwavering enthusiasm and plot-combing; the third for her role as final gatekeeper of all things editorial. To each of you, my *heart*felt thanks!

Were the skies to be fretted with consuming fire and the mountains to devastate their roots beneath; were the seas to overpower their trembling coasts and every hill and vale and field to fall to wreck and ruin; were the world to be extinguished and go out before my very eyes, still would I know the promise – and still would I hold.

Fragment of the Bellwood Letters

CHAPTER I

At the Master's command, he rose. He stood before the throned, unwitting of darkling Hands and visions of death. He felt neither the weight of cloak and blade nor the malice of staring foes. Nothing could lay any hold on him.

How he had risen!

He had once been a Gauntlet cadet, struggling to find a lost dagger in the mud and wretched dark. He had laid his palm upon a mark of glory and swearing, become an ensign imbued with the power to breach. Then as a lieutenant he had delivered a hard-sought tome to his Master. And so he became a Hand. He had returned from the Serpent's lair bearing the head of his enemy, and by that triumph rose as a Quarter Hand whose deeds caused the whole East Quarter to pour praise upon his Master.

Rising from knees to feet in that ruddy hall, he ascended higher than most men dared. Now the whole of the River Realm held but one more powerful than he. Now he was second only to the one who had seized the throne from the mottled corpse of a King.

Rising, he became the Master's Right Hand. Rising, the hopes and dues of his bloodline came full circle. All that once tarnished his mocked and defamed house was unworked, the way to glory opened.

A Goodman stood before the throne, receiving all that the Lord of Dunthruik, of the River Realm, and of the world, could offer. No fawning wretch or treacherous slave was he; this Goodman's service was mastery.

In rising, he was everything.

Yet he was also nothing. The lieutenant who breached had also surrendered his sword, turned his back upon his marked palm, and given his oath to the King. The Hand who had so earnestly championed Edelred's glory had been no Master's man. All that he had done was done for the house of Brenuin, the true house. The King would soon return to his own.

These latter thoughts strengthened Eamon's heart as he stood before Edelred. Though the Master's gaze caressed him, Eamon subdued his fledgling arrogance.

In rising he had been named the Right Hand, but long before that day he had risen to his feet before another and answered to the name of First Knight.

He would not forget it.

The Master smiled at him. "Son of Eben, sheath your blade."

Eamon looked to the curved dagger in his hands. Its sinister writing glinted back at him. The blade was a symbol of his new authority; it was the same blade that had taken Eben's life. It felt terrible and binding as he pressed it into its scabbard.

"*The King's house will hold, Edelred!*"

Eben's cries sounded in his mind, as though from a faraway room. Eben could never have known it, but he had been right: the house of Brenuin had held.

So would the house of Goodman.

Eamon looked up. Edelred's bold, burning face was before him. The Master watched him with delighted intensity.

"Son of Eben," he commanded, "dismiss my Hands."

Slowly, Eamon turned to look across the hall at the other Hands, their faces grim with new and seething wariness. Not one of them could now gainsay him. Arlaith's black look might have crippled any other, but it could not land on him. The Master was behind him; who, then, could dare stand against him?

Eamon smiled. His voice came, fell and arrogant, to his lips: "Leave."

The Hands bowed, spoke to the Master's glory, and departed.

CHAPTER I

Eamon fixed his gaze upon them. How they went! Did they not go, cowed and trembling, before him and his might? For well they knew that he could pay them back for their black-hearted plots and harrying. Would he not delight in such a venture?

He closed his eyes and grappled to cast back the web-like trappings of pride and power. Vengeance was not his calling, nor was the power given to him to be used as its tool. To be an instrument of calculating wrath and spite could only bind him to the Master, as every other Right Hand had been bound before him. Such pursuit would never serve or honour the King whom he loved.

A light touch fell on his shoulder. He froze.

"Son of Eben." The Master's whispered words were close by Eamon's ear.

Eamon turned to face him. The throned surveyed him with a look of whimsy and affection that was more terrifying than any that Eamon had yet seen.

"My Right Hand." The Master ran his hand along Eamon's shoulder, straightening the folds and creases of the cloak upon it. "This raiment and this blade are birthrights long denied you."

"I will not deny them, Master," Eamon breathed. He scarcely knew what words he spoke.

"Many have said as much. Few have done so."

"I will be loyal," Eamon answered.

The Master laughed. "Loyal," he repeated. Then he smiled, and his hand strayed from Eamon's shoulder to his face; power and will were in those fingers. That same hand moved across his face and, in a gesture of unimaginable gentleness, smoothed the hair upon his brow.

"Will you be loyal to me, son of Eben?" the Master asked. "Or will you love me?"

Eamon gazed at him, over-awed. The piercing grey eyes looked through him at some other whom Eamon had never been, nor could ever be. Yet how he yearned to be the object of that look!

Eamon bowed his head away from the impaling force of the

Master's gaze. "I… I will undo what Eben did, Master. I will redeem my house."

Edelred smiled. "So Ashway said," he answered, withdrawing his hand.

With a tremor of joy Eamon looked up once more. But the Master's face was closed to him. It filled him with distress and then with doubled horror, for part of him ached to be all that Edelred sought.

"Come." With that word Edelred stepped away, turning his steps from the throne and along the hall towards the great north balcony. It was the balcony on which Eamon had first seen Edelred at the majesty.

It was where he had danced with Alessia.

The Master climbed the steps and Eamon followed him, catching a glimpse of the Royal Plaza through the drapes that framed the doors. As the Lord of Dunthruik passed out onto the balcony stones, all things shrivelled and shrank before him, as though before a column of flame.

Enthralled beyond measure, Eamon followed him. He lingered among the curtains as the Master swept forward to the ledge. The stones were red-veined.

Without turning to look back at him, the Master spoke. "Gird your blade, Eben's son."

"Yes, Master."

Trembling, Eamon attached the dagger to his belt. The Master did not look at him.

"Follow me," Edelred commanded. Then he crossed to the main sweep of the palace walls.

An archway, marked with red stones, separated the balcony from the walls. The Master stepped through it. Eamon trailed after him. He could scarcely walk, and yet he followed Edelred down the length of wall that bound the plaza. They came to stand above the palace gates.

The Master stopped. Eamon hung uncertainly behind him.

Chapter I

"Come and stand beside me, son of Eben."

Slowly, Eamon stepped forward. The Master's presence drove all other sense from his flesh.

"Tell me what you see, son of Eben."

"I see Dunthruik," Eamon answered. It took his breath from him.

The mist cleared, and beyond the plaza and palace walls the whole city lay beneath the sudden, piercing blue of the morning sky. It was a myriad wash of stones, of red and gold, of voices. The people in the Coll and in the streets below moved about their business; Gauntlet moved among them. The stone statues of the Four Quarters gazed back at him as crisply and clearly as though he stood beneath them. Before him lay the North Quarter and the tall, distinctive towers of the university, its spires gilt with eagles. To his left was the Port Gate, and beyond it, the sea; to his right the dome of the Crown Theatre, and far beyond it, the tip of the Blind Gate. The city walls embraced Dunthruik, the parapets dotted with men in red. Beyond those walls the mountains marked the northern border; their very valleys and crags seemed as clear as his reflection in a mirror. Below the mountains lay the hills and fields and plains and the River itself, the city's lifeblood. To the south, the River coiled its way like a mighty serpent through the plains towards the city, where its mouth met the unassailable sea.

Shaking, Eamon pressed his hands against the stone before him and stared. Dunthruik was a seat of awesome power. Even if he harried every region of the River Realm and mastered the southern stretches of the River, even if he had the help of the Easters and had taken Edesfield, even if he was the last true heir of the house of Kings...

Even if he had done all those things... against the whole host and might of Dunthruik, what hope did Hughan have?

None, son of Eben, the voice whispered. *He has none.*

Yet as he stood and gazed out from the very heart of Edelred's stronghold, for the briefest of moments Eamon saw the King beside him. The vision wakened the hope that slumbered deep inside him.

The throned watched him.

"You know well, son of Eben, that the Serpent closes upon us."

The Master's voice had taken on a strange tone: dark, burdened with emotion beyond his ken. As he met the throned's gaze he caught frayed glimpses of forgotten battles and of the Nightholt, raised high in the Master's hand.

He said nothing.

The throned gazed out across the city. "With my own hands I razed this land," he said, "and from ashes did I raise it again, setting my name and glory over it. The Serpent would take my realm and this city, tearing stone from mortar and shedding blood from vein."

Eamon swallowed. Surely nothing but destruction could follow when the King came?

He fixed his eyes upon the distant sky, filling them with its endless blue. Hughan was not a man of witless and unheeding violence. He was a man of compassion and justice. A man of valiance.

"The whole of the Serpent's heart is set upon the demise of my city." The Master's voice called him from his thought. "But, son of Eben, we will break it. When he comes against me we will take his heart in our hands and rend it. No graft of his house will remain.

"After he is slain there will be much for you to learn and do." The Master turned to look at him at last. "Until that day when the Serpent's blood has been trampled into the dust, your task, son of Eben, is to prepare this city to receive him and his sodden corpse."

Eamon met his gaze. Visions of Hughan's body – broken, torn, and humiliated beyond all imagining – harrowed his heart, rendering him speechless.

"You will begin this day," Edelred told him. "Take Lord Arlaith to the East Quarter and install him there. You will then be shown your quarters. And you will oversee this city as it prepares for our foe. You will report all things, and all manner of things, to me."

Anguish gripped him, but Eamon bowed his head. "Yes, Master."

"Lord Arlaith awaits you," Edelred told him. "Go."

Eamon bowed down low.

"Your glory, Master."

Edelred did not look at him again. Eamon withdrew.

He descended from the balcony gallery and left the throne room. As the great doors pulled shut behind him, Eamon shuddered and drew a gasping breath. He glanced down at his shaking hands; they seemed pale and feeble in the light, whilst his head was awash with fire. He touched at it feverishly; it was as though his frame was not enough to endure the Master's vision and... affection.

"Might I serve you, Lord Goodman?"

Eamon turned to see the doorkeeper. The man's face bore a knowing smile.

"I am well," Eamon answered. It took all of his strength. "Where is Lord Arlaith?"

The doorkeeper bowed. "He is here, my lord," he answered, gesturing to one side.

A figure grimly emerged from the Hands' waiting room, its face contorted into a clenched sneer thick with malice.

"Lord Arlaith."

"Lord Goodman."

"I will lead you to the East Quarter."

Arlaith bowed, shallowly and stiffly. "His glory, Lord Goodman."

As they left the palace gates, throngs of men bowed, all their eyes on Eamon. It only darkened Arlaith's mood.

They went in silence, exchanging neither word nor glance as they passed through the city streets. At last the Ashen rose before them and Eamon caught a glimpse of the Gauntlet ranks, drawn up to welcome their new master. In his mind his household huddled behind darkened windows to watch as the new Lord of the East Quarter arrived.

Eamon could offer no comfort to the house that was no longer his.

They reached the centre of the square and Captain Anderas's sword was the first of hundreds raised in formal salute. The lines of men, Gauntlet, and Hands of the East Quarter were faces that he knew, whose love and respect he had earned. As he halted in the square he knew that he could show them none of his former affection; Arlaith held them now.

Eamon surveyed them all.

"I come in the name of the Master," he began. "Let none gainsay me. I bring to you a man after the Master's heart, chosen by him."

He faltered, feeling Arlaith's thunderous presence at his side. Was he to entrust those that he loved to a man who hated him?

He had no choice.

"I declare that this man shall henceforth be Lord of the East Quarter."

Silence filled the Ashen.

"Declare yourself, lord," Captain Anderas called.

Eamon pressed his eyes briefly shut, resisting the urge to respond.

"I am Lord Arlaith."

There was a long pause as hundreds of men, men from the Quarter and from distant regions to whom the Quarter now played host, turned their gazes to the one who had once been the Right Hand. Eamon realized that for Arlaith it was a moment of utter humiliation.

"Lord Arlaith, choice of the Master, be his Hand among us." Anderas spoke primly, his every word crystal on the air as he led a second formal salute. Bar the sound of steel rising to attention, the Ashen was silent. Arlaith stared at the men before him, hatred in his bearing and his look.

"To his glory," Anderas called, a cry echoed by the men all around him.

"To his glory!"

It curdled Eamon's blood.

As the cries filled the square, Arlaith turned to him. The man's hatred was drawn into one long glare. Wrath writhed in every facet of Arlaith's being.

"Enjoy your little coup, Lord Goodman," Arlaith hissed. "While it lasts."

CHAPTER I

Was he not the Right Hand? As calls to the Master's glory filled the air, Eamon matched Arlaith's gaze.

"Speak to me in such a way again, Lord Arlaith, and it will go ill with you."

Arlaith raised one dark eyebrow. The chilling familiarity – and utter otherness – of the man pierced Eamon as never before.

"You would threaten me, Lord Goodman?"

"I make no threats, Lord Arlaith: I am a man of my word."

"So you are," Arlaith sneered. He glanced at the assembled college and at the doors to the East's Handquarter. Slater stood ready to welcome the new master of the house.

Arlaith looked at Eamon but said nothing. No smile or scowl or grimace crossed his face. He bowed once and then virulently crossed the Ashen.

Eamon watched him go, feeling oddly alone. Anderas stepped forward to greet Arlaith and presented himself faultlessly; the captain never once met Eamon's gaze. He could not.

"Lord Goodman."

A man stood by him. Gauntlet. He held his low bow.

"Rise," Eamon said quietly. In the corner of his eye Arlaith was speaking with Anderas. Weariness assailed him.

The man rose. He had a lean face, dark eyes, and a smile that Eamon disliked for no reason that he could place. The man had two flames at his collar.

"Your name, lieutenant?"

"Lieutenant Fletcher, my lord," the man answered. "Formerly of the South Quarter. I have been afforded the great honour of standing as the lieutenant to your office, while it is pleasing to the Master."

The words came as a blow to Eamon. "Congratulations on your appointment, Mr Fletcher. I am sure you will perform it well."

"Thank you, my lord."

"And what of Mr Kentigern?"

The man inclined his head respectfully. "I understand that he took ship this morning for Etraia. He will serve the Master in another fashion, henceforth, and I am sure he will serve well. He was very likeable."

Eamon reeled: Ladomer was gone.

He rounded on the lieutenant. "It is not your place to speak of your likes and dislikes to me."

Why had he not sought Ladomer out and spoken to him? He feared that his friend's prediction – that they would not see each other again – would turn true.

Fletcher bowed swiftly. "Forgive me, my lord."

Eamon blinked, forcing back the tears biting at his eyes. Perhaps it was his own mind, and his own grief, that made it so; the lieutenant's words sounded insincere to him.

"Mr Kentigern and I were close of late," Fletcher advised him. "He taught me my duties thoroughly. I will serve you to the fullness of my strength, to the Master's glory, Lord Goodman."

Eamon nodded once. He wished that there were someone who could do him the same service. "My first service to you is to be that of showing you your quarters in the palace."

"Then we shall return to the palace."

Fletcher bowed again. "I will procure you a horse, my lord."

"Procure it from the Handquarter stables," Eamon told him suddenly. "Ask the stablehands for my horse. It is a loyal beast, and I love it well. I will take it with me."

"Of course, my lord." Rising from his bow, Fletcher turned and moved across the Ashen.

Eamon stood alone. The Gauntlet filed from the Ashen and returned to their various duties. Lord Arlaith stood upon the Handquarter steps. Eamon looked at him. The Lord of the East Quarter gazed back. In that moment before he turned to enter his house, Arlaith met Eamon's look and smiled.

CHAPTER II

E amon felt, but scarcely heard, his footsteps as he walked through the palace halls into the East Wing; banners and faces whirled past him in a daze, and no man spoke a word to him. He recognized some of the passages; they threw his mind back many months to a cool September day when he and Mathaiah had followed Cathair and Ashway into the palace's ancient bowels, seeking Ellenswell.

Mathaiah was dead. Now, Eamon followed Lieutenant Fletcher.

As they passed through the passageways the clear light of that morning – the last morning in April – touched his flesh. He pressed it from his eyes.

Fletcher led him up an elaborately panelled stairwell in the East Wing into one of the highest parts of the palace. Following, Eamon paused to glance through a window; it gazed, like an eye, down over the complex of the Hands' Hall and across the long throes of the palace buildings and grounds. Wind played through the aperture. A flight of swallows wheeled past, their voices caught high in the air.

They passed on and the stairs spilt out into a wide landing. Two Hands stood at the stairwell, solemn in their black. They bowed low and did not rise until he commanded it.

The landing was thickly paved in red-veined marble, each streak flowing into the seamless joins of the stone. The walls that bound the hall were clad with elegantly grained wood and interspersed with arched windows that looked over the palace gardens. Great curtains hung to either side of these openings and sunlight struck through them to cast further traces of red into the high hallway.

At the far end of the hall stood a tall threshold. This, too, was flanked by Hands and by two tapestries, woven from the richest threads that Eamon had ever seen. Both showed the Master in battle dress, his flaming hair about his blazing face. In one hand he held aloft a book from whose open pages red light spilled. In the other he bore a sword. He was framed in clear skies and serpents crawled beneath his feet; they were bloody as they fled his might. The images chilled Eamon's blood.

Between the tapestries stood dark doors, richly crafted. Birds sat solemnly on the panels, their eyes fashioned from red jewels. Brass eagles in flight adorned the handles whilst a further obsidian eagle stood guardian over the doors themselves. Its sable feet gripped a scroll on which ran the same letters on the blade that now hung at Eamon's side:

CHAPTER II

Scarcely realizing that he did so he halted and gaped upwards, agog.

"What is this?" he breathed. The letters gripped him; he felt the Nightholt in his hands. The script stood openly before him and yet he could not read it, nor could he hope to. The archly formed words tormented him.

Fletcher seemed to take no notice of either the letters or his tone.

"This is the eyrie of the Right Hand, Lord Goodman," he replied. So saying, he turned and bowed to the two Hands at either side of the doors. Like sweeping harbingers, they drew the portals aside to reveal the quarters of the Right Hand.

"My lord," Fletcher said, and this time as he bowed he gestured to the open doorway with a grandiose undulation of his arm. Eamon nodded curtly to him and stepped forward.

The doors could never have prepared him for what lay inside. Before his eyes lay one of the most enormous rooms he had ever seen in private use. It was like Cathair's reception hall in the Hands' Hall, only larger, and its bounds went on and on.

The initial, circular entrance hall, its walls panelled in dark wood, spread back towards other doors. Mantelpieces, laced with intricate masonry, stood among the panels, and shields, bearing the black eagle of the Right Hand, stood above them. Gathered in the centre of the hall were a series of chaise longues, while behind these a group of steps led back to a raised platform, and to other sets of doors.

Eamon went up to each in turn. Through one he saw a study, large and neatly formed. Behind another was a room for washing and dressing. Behind a third, a room with a long dining table, and behind the last, a room showing itself to be a grand bedroom. The bed within – easily double the size of that in the East Quarter – was draped in black, and eagles flew at the posts and headboard. Red curtains embroidered with eagles sloped down from the posts. There was a balcony in the room also; it overlooked the palace gardens.

Returning to the circular entrance hall, Eamon saw another door, small and discreet, leading off from the side of the mantelpiece. He knew at once that it was the servants' door, connected to whatever stairs and corridors the palace held for those men and women who served the Right Hand.

He stopped and stared about the quarters – *his* quarters – in a daze. He stood in silence for a long time.

"Lord Goodman?"

Fletcher's voice stirred him. Silently he nodded, granting the man permission to speak.

"There is breakfast for you on the table."

At the words, Eamon looked once more to the dining room and its long table. Fletcher was right: there was a tray on the table. Breads, hams and cheeses covered it, while beside it stood an elaborate flagon whose handle was formed by eagle's wings.

"Whatever your command for your servants, whatever your commands for the city," Fletcher told him, "you need only speak to me, and I shall see them done."

Startled, Eamon realized then how powerful Ladomer had been.

"That is, of course, unless you wish to see to them yourself," Fletcher finished. "Lord Arlaith was, I understand, sometimes of that approach."

"I will eat."

"I will send some of your servants to attend you."

"I wish to be alone at present. You may send the servants when I have finished."

Fletcher did not look surprised. He bowed again. "Of course, my lord. You will not be disturbed."

"In an hour you will return," Eamon added. "We will go to each of the quarters. I will have reports from each of the Quarter Hands, detailing their readiness."

"With reverence, my lord," Fletcher began, "you need not trouble yourself with such a thing. I can easily send for them. They will come to you."

Eamon looked at him. For a moment, the thought tantalized him. He could have each Quarter Hand come to him, one black specimen after another, and they would answer him as he had been forced to answer to them. He could be rash and unforgiving, if he so chose it.

"I will go," he said quietly. "Send messages to them, advising them of my coming. I wish to meet with them and inspect their readiness in person. I will have their most recent reports, on Gauntlet and militia capacity, logistical flexibility, thresholder readiness. I will also survey the state of the city walls and the work that has been in progress on them."

Fletcher nodded. "Very well, my lord; it shall be as you command. By your leave, my lord."

"Mr Fletcher."

Fletcher bowed neatly and left. A strange quiet settled; once the doors were closed it was impossible to hear beyond them.

Drawing a deep breath, Eamon tried to relax. It was difficult.

Slowly he moved about the rooms, touching posts and lintels and feeling the smooth texture of the wood beneath his fingers. Every available space was decked with finery. From every quarter, the black eagle of the Right Hand stared back at him.

He stepped into his bedchamber and walked about the bed, trying to comprehend just how big it was. He wondered what use Arlaith might have put it to, and shuddered.

As he had seen before, the bedroom opened to a balcony. It adjoined the throne room's south balcony. The balcony spanned the length of that hall, joining East and West Wings of the palace together before ending at last by quarters opposite his own in the West Wing. They too bore an eagle, and Eamon knew at once whose rooms were connected to his own.

He shuddered.

He returned to the entrance hall and closed his eyes, but when he opened them the room was still there. He was still the Right Hand.

Had Hughan meant for this to happen to him? Had the King ever guessed that his First Knight would become Edelred's Right Hand?

Breathing deeply he drew the blade from his side. He rested it across his hands. Its shaft, etched with letters, gazed back at him. The weapon carried a faint red weave, as though it too bore the Master's mark.

Eamon looked at the eagle over the hall's mantelpiece. Its talons had been formed as hooks, so that they might hold a blade. It was the ceremonial hanging place for what he held.

As he looked at the eagle his vision changed.

The room became dark, lit only by the twisted candelabrum that stood in each of its corners. From every window – almost every stone – rang the sound of trumpets, triumphantly unfettered.

A man stood by the eagled mantelpiece. Fire burned in the hearth, flecking clothes and man with red. The man leaned against the mantelpiece's black ledge as he stared at the flames. The firelight revealed the dark sheath that hung at his side.

As the fire crackled, the man looked on. Then the cries of hundreds upon hundreds of ecstatic voices rent the air:

"To his glory! To his glory!"

Agony twisted the man's face. Eben Goodman buried his pale face in black-gowned arms, and wept.

Eamon staggered from the mantelpiece, retreating until his knees touched the edge of a chair. He sank into it.

Eben Goodman had been the last First Knight and the first Right Hand. Eamon wondered then if he did not at last understand some of the terrible grandeur, and power, that had drawn Eben from Ede to Edelred. Yet something had drawn Eben back to his first oath; something had driven him to endure terror and hardship in Dunthruik, to defy the throned and lose his life.

Eamon drew a deep breath. He served the house of Brenuin, just as Eben had done. But he had a hope that Eben, in his final moments, could scarcely have dared to believe: Eamon knew that the King returned. For long months Eamon had served Dunthruik, and he had done it for the King. Edelred was a terrible power, but the King was returning. Whether that day would bring good or ill he did not know, but it would soon arrive.

34

CHAPTER II

Suddenly he remembered the night when he had gone down into the Pit, the night when he had spoken freely with Mathaiah for the last time. He remembered the warmth and courage of his friend's embrace, and the young man's final words to him: "*Hold to the King.*"

Whatever came to him from that day forth, of one thing he was certain. Caged by the hatred of the Quarter Hands and the delight of the Master, now, more than ever before, he needed to hold – and hold fast.

He stirred from his thoughts. It could not be long before an hour passed. Setting the blade of the Right Hand back into its scabbard, he rose and passed into the dining room.

Fletcher returned promptly just as Eamon finished breakfast. He announced that he had sent messages to the Quarter Hands, or in their absence, their captains, and that Eamon was expected. Eamon thanked him. Not long after, they rode from the palace together.

It was mid-morning when the Right Hand and his lieutenant wound their way through the Four Quarters and down Coronet Rise into the South Quarter. Eamon was grateful for the narrow streets that they took towards the Handquarter. Tomorrow would be the first of May, and if the last day of April was anything by which to judge, the summer would come, sweltering and soon, to Dunthruik's streets. The South Quarter's tall buildings blocked the sun's glare from Eamon's tired eyes.

The South Handquarter was a grand affair carved from white stones which had been detailed in red. Two vast yew trees, not yet bearing their blood-like fruit, stood by the pillars to the hall, and crowns, flanked by birds, were etched into the white steps. Harriers for the South, Eamon recalled. The steps led up into a Handquarter's hall which, in shape and size, would not be unlike the one that Eamon had lost that morning to Arlaith.

Tramist's house expected them. Several servants waited in the cool shadows of the hall. As Eamon and Fletcher neared the

Handquarter's steps, the servants came forward as of one accord to meet him; one laid a mounting block on the ground. Though he did not need it, Eamon set his foot to it and entrusted his horse's reins to the nearest man.

"Where is Lord Tramist?" Eamon asked.

"In the hall," the servant replied. "He awaits you, my lord."

Eamon wondered wryly whether perhaps, though not as pale as Cathair, Tramist found strong sun troublesome.

After thanking the servants and bidding Fletcher to wait for him, Eamon swept up the sun-marked steps. The roof of the Handquarter's vaulted hall was painted red. Lord Tramist stood beneath the ceiling's gilded keystone, grim-faced.

"Lord Goodman." Tramist bowed. His voice was frosty and his eyes glinted. "You have come for some reports?"

"You know that I have," Eamon answered. To see the Lord of the South Quarter hiding in his hall made him feel more cheerful. "I thought it wise to put myself to work at once."

"Of course, my lord." Tramist paused as a couple of servants scurried by with lowered faces. "If you'll come with me to my study, we can speak there."

"Thank you."

Eamon followed him. The Handquarter was similar to the Ashen, but the corridor was lined with broad pedestals. As the hall was dimly lit Eamon barely distinguished them at first, but as they passed a window he caught a glimpse of one of them. A bird stood on it; its eyes were sinister and dead in the light, and Eamon realized that it was stuffed. The whole hall was lined with them, their empty eyes glinting in the dark. Eamon's cheer was dampened by a feeling of being watched. Whilst serving under Cathair as a Hand of the West Quarter, he had spent time with Tramist, and he reminded himself that, even if he did not like sunlight, the city's breacher was a formidable man.

Tramist opened the door to his study. This too bore various pedestals and stands. Of those in the room, the creatures that struck

Eamon the most were a wolf and some kind of great cat, the likes of which he had never seen. Its tawny jaws were drawn back in a fierce scowl.

It was as he looked at the stuffed creatures that Eamon was suddenly, and horrifyingly, reminded of the bookends that Cathair kept at Ravensill. Had the Lord of the South Quarter been party to that deed?

The study's desk was covered with ordered papers. Tramist selected a pile.

"These are the South's reports, Lord Goodman," he said. "Nothing out of the ordinary. All of the additional Gauntlet given to me have been housed. We still struggle a little to keep our horses and mules fully stabled, but most of the Quarter's remaining peasants have been persuaded to assist in that. My logistics draybant is handling the matter well."

"Good."

"We are yet to fully draft the South's thresholders," Tramist told him, "but in all other matters we are well prepared, as the reports show. The culling groups have turned out some impressive results of late," he added, "especially along the Serpentine."

For a moment Eamon froze, his thought suddenly on the innkeeper who had helped him escort Mathaiah's wife Lillabeth to safety. His troubled thoughts shifted to the East Quarter, on his servants and friends there, and to the cadets – now ensigns – in the West...

"Good news indeed," Eamon answered, resolving to drive down his sudden fear. "The Master has given me overall charge of preparing this city for any forthcoming hostility." A task, he realized, to which he did not feel entirely equal. Although he had learned much while serving the West and East Quarters he knew but little about defending a whole city, and Dunthruik had been placed in his hand as though it were some sweetmeat.

"Clearly," he added, "I will require your support in this matter. You will make your reports to me thorough and regular."

"Of course, Lord Goodman," Tramist answered, extending the group of reports towards him. As Eamon reached across to take them Tramist's hand suddenly faltered, and the papers dropped in a flurry to desk and floor.

Tramist hissed with quickly veiled annoyance. "My apologies, Lord Goodman," he said, stooping so as to gather the sheets. Eamon moved to assist him. "Do not trouble yourself, my lord," Tramist added.

"It is no trouble."

They both picked up the papers, Tramist concentrating on those upon the ground. Eamon stacked the others back together on the desk.

"Here are the others, my lord," Tramist said, setting them down upon Eamon's pile. Their hands brushed past each other.

At that touch Eamon felt a sharp and sudden pain run through him, so swiftly that he wondered whether he imagined it. He closed his eyes, and for the briefest of moments he was convinced that he saw the breaching plain.

It went as quickly as it had come. Before he knew it, Tramist's hand was far from his own, folding some other papers away. The Hand's gaze was lowered and unaffected.

Filled with gnawing misgivings, Eamon looked sharply at him. "Lord Tramist?"

Tramist matched his gaze with a querying look. "Are there papers missing, Lord Goodman?"

Eamon did not even glance down at them. He was sure that he had seen the plain. He held the Hand's gaze.

"You touched me," he said quietly. He knew that he could not prove it and realized that, even if he had the right of the matter, he did not know what the Lord of the South Quarter had done to him.

"I gave you the papers, my lord," Tramist answered levelly, casting one hand at them in a gesture. His fingers came near Eamon's own once more. Involuntarily, Eamon flinched.

Tramist looked at him with mock concern. "Is something the matter, Lord Goodman?"

Eamon continued to watch him. "You touched me."

Tramist assessed his manner for a moment, as though he did not comprehend Eamon's words.

"By the Master's own writ, Lord Goodman, you have been proclaimed this city's finest Hand," he said. "My lord, you are untouchable."

The statement unnerved him, for against such praise Eamon knew that he could not press the matter. He also knew, and knew too well, that Tramist had been a breacher since before he had himself been born. He wondered then what skills the Lord of the South Quarter had declined to teach him.

"Lord Tramist," he said, "I have no reason to bear you enmity. I would not have you give me one."

Tramist shook his head with a smile. "Why should you think such a thing of me?" he asked. "Lord Goodman, I have always admired you and it grieves me that you might think me your enemy. I have only fine words for you." He paused. "I think, my lord, that you are tired. Perhaps you should find some time to rest this afternoon?"

Unconvinced still, Eamon matched his gaze. "Thank you, Lord Tramist, for your concern. Good day to you."

Tramist bowed. "And to you, Lord Goodman."

Sweeping the papers up into his hands, Eamon left the office.

He handed the papers to Fletcher and the lieutenant tucked them securely away in a saddlebag. He did not speak to the man. As he mounted his horse, his thought returned over and again to the hand that Tramist had brushed against; it ached, but he was unsure whether the pain was a concoction of his imagination.

Breathing deeply, he resolved to cast the matter as far from his mind as he could.

They crossed the city from the South Quarter and into the North, passing the great gates of the university and lodges of some of the city's guilds, notably the armourers and drapers.

"You should have gone to the university!"

Ladomer's voice suddenly entered his mind, resplendent with loving mockery. For a moment the memory of Edesfield was so sharp that Eamon felt transported; then, like a shadow, it dissipated.

The North Handquarters were situated nearly on the Coll itself, so as to have easy access to the port – for Dehelt occupied himself not only with the quarter and the university or guild politics, but a large portion of the port's business. In that business the West Quarter was an assistant, seeing mostly to the roads and waterfronts. The West's main, and most noble, concern was with the palace.

Eamon left his horse with the stable hands and enquired after Dehelt from Captain Longroad, who happened to be passing through the hall.

"He's at the gate, my lord, inspecting portions of the north wall. He had hoped to return before you arrived. Would you have me send for him?"

"No, but send after him, and have him know that I will meet him there," Eamon answered. The captain bowed and hurried off to do as he had asked. Eamon recovered his horse.

They took to Coronet Rise once again; Sahu needed no urging to canter up to the North Gate. Eamon quietly advised the beast that he had best not get too hopeful; there would be no riding the plains that day. Whether the creature understood him or not, he did not know, but when they halted at the gate and Sahu was given over to the gate men, the horse cast a mournful look out beyond the great lintels.

The same men who took charge of his horse told him that Lord Dehelt toured the nearer part of the wall with some city engineers. Thanking them, Eamon made to climb the stair to the full height of the wall.

"Shall I wait for you here, my lord?" Fletcher's voice called after him.

"Do so, Mr Fletcher."

A strong wind whipped across the ramparts that day. As he reached the topmost part, Eamon was driven against the stonework by its force. Sentinels were posted at regular intervals along the long walls, splashes of red against the grey, and in the near distance a figure in black, accompanied by a couple of others. Eamon went towards them.

"Lord Dehelt," he greeted, arriving.

"Lord Goodman." Dehelt greeted him cordially and bowed. The men with the Lord of the North Quarter did likewise.

"His glory," they said in unison.

"I would speak with you a moment," Eamon said.

Dehelt nodded, then turned to the men with him. "Thank you, gentlemen," he said. "Please advise the quarter's architects of the necessary adjustments, as we discussed."

The men bowed once more to both Hands and then moved off along the wall. Dehelt turned to Eamon again.

"I am sorry that I could not meet you at the Handquarter, my lord."

Eamon smiled. "It was little trouble for me to come to you."

"But I should have come to you, Lord Goodman," Dehelt replied. He looked at the stones all around them, his eyes caught by something that only he could see.

"How is the wall?" Eamon asked him.

"It needs but minimal repair," Dehelt answered. "I have always been attentive to it. It will hold for the North. As for South, East, and West, I do not know. Doubtless, my lords the Quarter Hands will have seen to that." He looked up. "Have you ever seen the full might of these walls, Lord Goodman?"

"No."

"The South is weakest – I understand that it is not the original city wall. From what of it I have seen, it seems to have been too swiftly built when the city was taken."

"I am sure that Lord Tramist has such matters in hand."

"He has my trust also, Lord Goodman. These walls have repelled strong foes in their time, and this city has weapons that may do so yet." Dehelt laid gloved fingers to the stone. For a long time he gazed north across the plains, towards the foothills of Ravensill and, beyond that, the northern mountains. He breathed deeply, then turned to meet Eamon's gaze. "You also have strong foes, Lord Goodman. I would bid you to be wary of them."

Eamon tried to assess the man's quiet face; it betrayed nothing.

"Will you speak no more clearly, Lord Dehelt?"

"I am not a politic man, Lord Goodman," Dehelt answered. "I am a watcher. There are deep currents in these Four Quarters." He turned to look out across the city, and Eamon saw that the man's gaze encompassed it all, from Blind Gate to port breakers.

"The currents go back long years," Dehelt added at last. "You are but young, Lord Goodman, and yet to the currents you are like a long-forgotten stream, emerging from deep places and feeding into churning waters. You trouble them."

Eamon looked out at the sea, to where the River's mouth gorged on waves. The crests of the high waters swirled beyond the breakers, and the tall masts of the purple-bannered merchant ships were gliding into port.

"You would counsel me, Lord Dehelt?"

"I would not, my lord."

Eamon met his gaze again. The eyes that watched him were not hostile, but neither did they speak of that love and support which he had known from every man in the East.

"The quarter's reports?" he asked.

"Here." Dehelt drew them from a pouch beneath his cloak. "You will find everything in order. Were the Serpent to come tomorrow, Lord Goodman, the North would offer him fitting greeting."

"It pleases me to hear it." He held the man's gaze for a moment. "Thank you, Lord Dehelt."

"His glory," Dehelt replied, and bowed.

From the North they went into the East Quarter. It had been only a couple of hours since he had last been there, and yet years uncounted could have passed.

"I did not have the opportunity to say so this morning, but it is a lovely quarter, my lord," Fletcher commented as they passed into the Ashen. "You must have been proud of it."

"I am," Eamon answered.

Despite the messages that he had sent with Fletcher earlier that day, it was not Arlaith who met them. As they prepared to alight at the Ashen, a familiar figure came to meet them.

"Lord Goodman," it called.

Eamon smiled. "Good afternoon, Mr Lancer," he said, remembering in time not to call the man by his nickname of "Lieutenant Lackey".

"I've been asked to deliver these to you, my lord," Lancer told him, holding out a collection of reports, "though I daresay you know their contents well enough."

"Thank you," Eamon replied. It was true; he had written the papers himself, with Anderas's assistance. He had Fletcher stow them with the others. "Where is Lord Arlaith?"

"In a meeting with the captain," Lancer answered readily. "He charged me with giving these to you." Eamon could not help but glance up at the Handquarter with a flicker of fear in his heart. What kind of meeting did Anderas endure?

He could not allow himself to linger on it; he had to trust Anderas. Had he not done so before, even with body, life, and faith?

"Thank you, Mr Lancer. Please give my regards to Captain Anderas."

"And to Lord Arlaith?"

After only the slightest hesitation, Eamon nodded. "Even so."

The lieutenant bowed and, with Eamon's permission, returned to the college. Eamon breathed deeply and turned to Fletcher.

"Take these reports back to the palace."

"And those for the West Quarter, my lord?"

"I will bring them myself," Eamon told him. "I would like you to tally these together while I do so."

"Of course, my lord," Fletcher answered. After bowing he turned and spurred his horse back towards Coronet Rise.

Eamon sat for a while in the saddle, watching the East Quarter's college and Handquarters.

Sahu shifted beneath him and tossed his head to dislodge a fly resting on his nose. The movement called Eamon back to the present. Patting the horse's neck fondly he turned and prepared to go into the West.

He passed once more through the Four Quarters and there, at the heart of the city, he stopped. Dunthruik pulsed all about him, its strength drawn up the Coll towards the walls of the palace. The movement was in every stone, in every gesture, and every gaze.

How could Hughan hope to stand against it?

As he paused there he heard the sound of many approaching feet. A large contingent rolled down Coronet Rise, flanked by men from the North Quarter. To judge, both from their bearing and the wagons and mules that bore them, the group was being evicted from the city to make room for Gauntlet reinforcements, the last of which arrived from the north. As they approached, the officer at the column's head noted Eamon and paled.

The officer brought the entire column to an uneasy halt, bowed, and stood still. Calls and cries from further back in the grinding mass demanded to know why it had stopped.

Eamon gently urged his horse to the column and the sweating officer. Eamon counted the flames at the man's collar.

"Is something the matter, lieutenant?"

"My lord," the man stammered. "I had no wish to impede your crossing of the Quarters."

By reflex, Eamon laughed; it did nothing to aid the pallor of the man's face.

"Crossing!" Eamon said good naturedly. "I agree, lieutenant, that my horse is more impatient than I, but I rather think that I was stationary at the time you arrived. You would not have impeded a thing."

The lieutenant bowed again. "Yes, my lord." His knees shook.

"At ease," Eamon told him. "You may take your column on, lieutenant."

The man rose uncertainly. "Thank you, my lord." At a gesture he set the column moving again. It trundled back into motion like a weary ox at the ploughshare.

Eamon retreated back into the shadow of the Four Quarters and watched the column go. The pale faces in the line could not meet his gaze, though they knew he was there; murmurs of "*the Right Hand!*" ran through the line.

Manoeuvring the line through the Four Quarters was no easy business. Carriages and people had to hold back at each of the roads leading into it, which caused a great amount of confusion and an indeterminate number of bruised egos. Eamon watched as the Gauntlet herded the passing populace and drove back those waiting their turn to pass. Group after group went by.

Suddenly a face caught Eamon's attention; it belonged to a middle-aged man whose back was bent beneath a tattered wicker basket. His eyes watched Eamon. As soon as his gaze was met, he looked quickly away.

Eamon started. He knew the face. As the realization washed over him the man shuffled further into the belly of the line.

Eamon pressed his horse forward. He struggled to remember the man's name. He had served in Alessia's house. Eamon was sure of it. But what was his name?

"Mr Cartwright," he called at last.

The hunched, half-hidden man fell still. At Eamon's gesture the man came forward. He bowed low.

"How may I serve you, my lord?"

"You may do just that," Eamon replied.

The man looked confused. "My lord," he said, "I was bidden to leave the city –"

"And I bid you to stay in it." He was the Right Hand – he could do as he pleased; and here was a known face. His encounter with Tramist, Dehelt's words of warning, and the smile with which Arlaith had left him that morning had shaken him. "You served Lady Turnholt well," he added gently. "Now you will serve me."

Cartwright bowed. "As you wish, my lord."

"Go to the palace and ask for Lieutenant Fletcher," Eamon told him. "Tell him that I sent you and that you are to join my servants."

"My lord." The man hefted the basket onto his back and climbed the Coll. The line continued moving, and he was lost from view.

It was only then that Eamon realized he had not asked for service; he had commanded it.

He rode to the West Quarter and ascended the familiar steps into the college. He was told that Cathair had left the city early that morning for Ravensill on some business or other. Eamon was not sorry to learn that the West's reports had been left with Captain Waite.

The captain was in his office, crowded with perhaps the largest pile of papers that Eamon had yet seen. The reports that Waite gave him showed that the West's walls had been checked, the Gauntlet was prepared, the militia were ready, and Waite and Cathair had already appointed the thresholders, the units of citizens and militia who would form the last defence of the city in time of need.

"You'll find everything to your satisfaction, my lord," Waite told him. "Lord Cathair sends his apologies for his absence."

"I accept them," Eamon answered. He continued to skim-read the papers, then looked up at the captain with a smile. "I see that the West has not been idle."

"Today of all days, the West could not be idle," Waite answered, taking in Eamon's face with joy. Eamon wondered if the captain might have embraced him, had decorum permitted such a thing. It touched him deeply. "How could the West be idle? Its favourite son has not been. Rather, he has today won an accolade that graces us all."

Eamon swallowed, unsure of what to say. "Thank you for your work, captain," he managed at last.

Waite smiled broadly. "It is a pleasure to serve you, Lord Goodman."

CHAPTER II

Returning to the palace, Eamon sought out Fletcher. The man had been busily at work, and had made good progress on an initial report of the city's status. Eamon handed him the West's work and examined the draft of the report.

"This is good work, Mr Fletcher."

"Thank you, my lord."

"How long will it take to complete?"

"The rest of the day," Fletcher answered. "I will have copies drawn up for the Quarter Hands."

"Do," Eamon nodded. He knew that such copies would be made by the throned's own efficient scribes, word for word. "I will take some details from this draft to the Master this afternoon."

"Of course." Fletcher finished making a note on a piece of parchment and then looked up at him. "My lord, a man by the name of Iulus Cartwright reported to me not an hour ago."

Eamon looked at him blankly for a moment. "Iulus Cartwright?"

"He says that you sent him, my lord," Fletcher added.

"Yes," Eamon answered. Was he so dull that he could already have forgotten? "I did. I would have him serve me personally."

Fletcher's face coloured with disapproval. "With all due respect, my lord, you have a full complement of servants –"

"And I want this man, Mr Fletcher."

"Of course, my lord," he answered. "As you wish it. Perhaps, in future, you may wish to discuss such matters with me, prior to appointment? I must have the palace's permission to take on new servants."

Eamon raised an eyebrow. "My command is not permission enough?"

"It is, lord," Fletcher replied, and Eamon sensed reticence in his voice.

"Then do not dictate to me," Eamon retorted. As Right Hand he could do as he wished, but it was his lieutenant who had to sort the details. Perhaps the thought should have humbled him. "You will do as I ask, when I ask it."

47

"Yes, my lord, on those occasions when I do not foresee your desire," Fletcher replied. "I will ensure that your new servant sees to you from the morning. He must first be suitably inducted." He paused for a moment, gathering papers. "I will take these to the scribes," he said. "These you may take with you to the Master, if you wish it."

"Thank you, Mr Fletcher," Eamon answered and dismissed him.

He went on to study the papers Fletcher had left him at some length. Dunthruik had been preparing for war for many months; the papers confirmed it. More than this, as he read Eamon saw that the city was fully garrisoned, in places distinctly over-garrisoned. The walls, bar a small section along the South, had been or were being reinforced, and the city's many forges rang to hammer and anvil as thousands of weapons were produced and armour was strengthened and made. All the iron that the River Realm could afford had been impounded for it. The knights were ready and provided with full retinues of squires and followers to assist them. Wall and gate defences were strong and the gate towers were ready to repel anyone with a mind to breaching them.

The reports reaffirmed the terrible truth: the city was more than ready for its foe. What could Hughan possibly drum out of the valleys and mountains that could take arms against the Master's stronghold?

Both doubt and despair lurked in Eamon's thought when, in the late afternoon, he turned his steps towards the throne room. Though he could have gone down directly from the great balcony he did not dare – he preferred to follow the long corridors through the East Wing. Thought of the Master's touch and voice and gaze returned to him, making his stride unsteady as he followed the bannered hall to the throne room.

The doorkeeper bowed immediately.

"Lord Goodman."

The doors opened. Without a word, Eamon entered the throne room.

The Master was there. With a long smile upon his face he waited while Eamon crossed the length of the hall and then knelt in the stony lake of fire at his feet.

"Your glory, Master."

"Rise, Eben's son. You have seen your quarters."

"Yes, Master."

The Master rose and approached him.

"Do they please you?"

Eamon did not dare meet his gaze. "How could they not, Master? I received them from your own hand."

Edelred's fond touch alighted on him, pressing his face upwards. He could not refuse it; obediently, he subjected himself to the gesture that filled him with such yearning, disgust, and fear.

"You please me, son of Eben. Tell me of your doings this day."

"I have done as you asked me, Master."

He went on to speak at length on the state of the city, giving the relevant details from the reports that he and Fletcher had compiled. As he spoke the throned absorbed his every word, and every word increased his smile.

"The only difficulty the city has is in feeding these men and beasts," Eamon concluded. "But the North is finalizing the details of increased trade with Etraia to see to that need; a dozen extra loads of grain are due to dock in the next week, to be exchanged for arms."

Silence fell between them.

"Son of Eben, you have worked well today."

Eamon bowed his head. "To your glory, Master."

Edelred laughed. "Tell me, my Right Hand, how does my Left?"

Eamon blinked and looked up. "Forgive me, Master," he said, "your 'left'?"

The throned laughed again – a chilling, deafening sound – and he lifted both his hands before Eamon's face.

"You are my Right Hand," he said, holding out his right. With it he smothered his left. "Lord Arlaith is my Left."

Eamon started. "Lord Arlaith has been made Lord of the East Quarter, Master," he said. "It is as you willed."

"Does it grieve you, Eben's son?" The Master's voice plied him, seeking the intimacy of his deepest thought. "Seeing your pearls bestowed on swine?"

The freshness of Eamon's wound returned to him; the East was at Arlaith's mercy. How he feared for it! He checked himself in time. He could not allow the Master to draw that from him.

"Lord Arlaith is your chosen Hand over the quarter, Master," he said at last. "What matters is not who holds it, but that it glorifies you."

Edelred smiled. "Come, son of Eben. Follow me."

Eamon followed him.

The throned drew him past the throne and out through a doorway at the rear of the dais. Eamon had never before stepped through the thick drapes that bedecked the darkest recesses of the throne room; they felt thick and stifling about him as he followed.

The door led to a corridor lined in red, and eagles dashed down its walls. Eamon caught sight of a garden through the windows and, above it, dark-hewn arches and balconies. One bore the black eagle on a red banner, and he realized with a start that he looked at his balcony. The Master led him through the corridors of the West Wing and eventually to the royal suites themselves. Eamon felt the colour draining from him.

But they did not go to those rooms; the throned soon halted before a wide set of doors that were cast open for him by two men dressed in gold, red, and black. Eamon recognized them as members of the Master's own private guard.

Behind the door was a long reception hall, lavishly decked in the Master's colours. A small number of men waited inside it. The leading of these four or five wore a red apron over his clothes. Eamon understood the man to be another of Edelred's own servants, but what he did was something that he could only guess at.

As the Master entered, the men bowed down low. Papers and cloth lay neatly on a table behind them, accompanied by wide-eyed needles and crimson thread. There was also a cushioned stool, bearing the Master's eagle.

"Your glory, Master," spoke the man in the apron. His eyes burnt with ardour as he looked upon the throned. "Whom are we to fit?"

"Here is the man," the Master answered with a smile, and for a moment Eamon felt a pang of indescribable jealousy. The Master smiled at him alone!

With the thought he shuddered. He pressed his eyes shut, sending his thought back to Mathaiah, and to the Pit. He had to hold to the King.

The man with the apron bowed deeply. "We serve at your pleasure," he said. At his gesture the others brought forward the stool and positioned it in the centre of the rug on the floor, in the midst of a flood of light from the windows.

The aproned man looked up and caught Eamon in his gaze. "Lord Goodman."

Eamon started as though from a daze. "Yes," he answered uncertainly.

The man gestured to the stool. "If you would step up, my lord."

Bewildered, Eamon did as he was bidden. The light blinded him as he found his balance on the stool; even atop this perch he did not match Edelred's great height. The Master watched as a herd of men flooded forward with paper and quills. The men surrounded Eamon and, drawing out long measures, took the length of his limbs.

"What would you, Master?" asked the aproned man. He conferred quietly with the throned; every so often, the Master's eyes flicked towards Eamon as the tailors' hands covered Eamon with measures.

"Such garments as have never been seen on a Right Hand," Edelred replied. "Fit for a majesty, fit to enthral both Dunthruik and myself. Fit for an heir."

Eamon gasped; a tape was drawn constrictively about his breast, measuring his midriff. The Master smiled at him.

Moments later the flurry of tape-wielding hands about Eamon retreated to their papers. The master tailor lifted Eamon's arms up

51

and out to the sides, then paced about him, looking at him from various angles.

"To his advantage, Master, his form has no blemishes needing to be covered or compensated," the tailor said. "However, he also has no especially notable features that I may enhance. A very average kind of man." The tailor mused for a moment. "Nevertheless, he will not appear such, when I have done."

The throned nodded appreciatively. The tailor made another onslaught, this time with a dozen subtly varying sable fabrics in his hands.

"Black, Master?"

"Of course," Edelred replied. "And red."

The tailor nodded and held a few of the fabrics up against Eamon's face; they felt smooth against his cheek, like the Master's hand…

Eamon forced his mind to the King. And yet while the Master stood before him, watching him and webbing him with smiles, Eamon found that he could not keep the King's face in his mind's eye.

Maybe half an hour later the tailor gave a final nod and stepped back. "You may step down, Lord Goodman."

Doll-like, Eamon did so.

The tailor bowed towards the Master. "I will need some three days, Master, if you permit me leave to work on nothing else."

"You will work on nothing else until I am satisfied with this."

"Your glory, Master."

The tailors bowed in unison, and left.

Eamon stood still on the rug, blinking the light from his eyes. A voice, and a touch upon his cheek, called him from his confused thoughts.

"You have glorified me this day, son of Eben."

The touch of the hand was like that of the sumptuous fabrics with which the tailors had palled him. A small, but steadily growing, part of his heart urged him to surrender himself to both.

How could the indulgence of a single man so allure him from his resolve and King?

As Edelred smiled at him Eamon's tangled tongue suddenly loosed itself.

"I will not glorify you in such clothes as these will make me, Master!"

A chilling silence. Eamon knew in an instant that he had gone too far. He swallowed, not daring to meet Edelred's gaze.

"You refuse my gift?" the Master asked, coolly.

"No, Master," Eamon whispered. "I will love your every gift as much as I do you yourself. But how can I serve you in such finery?"

"Those upon whom I bestow tokens of my love show my glory by their finery."

"Then send these measurements after an armourer," Eamon cried, "and have him make for me such plate as has never been seen in all the long years of Dunthruik's craft. Then will I serve you, Master, proving your glory on my body, by my blade and with my blood."

"Both those things are already mine, son of Eben," the throned replied. "As to your body, I shall dress it in whatever way seems best to me."

Eamon faltered. Slowly, he sank down to one knee.

"Forgive me, Master," he said. "I spoke in haste. I am ill at ease with fine things; my only thought is for your service."

Though the Master smiled, there was dark thought behind his eyes. "Rise, son of Eben," he said, "and go to your rest. You have done much this day. Tomorrow you will take breakfast with me."

Eamon did not raise his head. "Yes, Master."

As the evening gave way to the night Eamon climbed the stairs towards his eyrie, the heavy tread of his boots his only company. He felt as though he bore a hundred years of toil.

How long had it been since he arrived in Dunthruik? He paused on the stair, trying to count the months. But every day was a blur in his deadened mind and he could no longer see where his road had begun. Still less could he see where it would end.

Was it not a simple task – to hold firm to Hughan? It had seemed so that morning. Yet, in that single day he had wavered more times than he could number.

The Hands at either side of his door bowed as he approached and then opened the great portal before him. As he entered and the doors shut behind him, he thought he heard the sound of footsteps retreating down the servants' stair.

Eamon went to his bedroom; its balcony stood open to the air and the moon gleamed down through the tall aperture. Quietly Eamon stepped out, letting the still air enfold him. Though lights burned in the palace, piercing the growing gloom, Eamon turned his head up to the night sky, towards the dark. The stars, mirrored far away in the crests of the distant sea, glinted back at him.

Leaning against the cold stone, he breathed deeply. When he exhaled, it came out as a shuddering, exhausted breath.

Dunthruik. The city lived in his very veins and he was a lord over its men and women. Its defence was entrusted to him. Could he not still be the King's Hand, even as he had been in the East Quarter? With Edelred so close by him, it seemed a distant hope.

He sighed. The stars filled his sight and he drifted into silent thought.

He did not know how long he stood there, engulfed by the high and distant starlight. After a while he shivered and looked back at the palace. Its lights, drapes, music, and laughter seemed gaudily abhorrent. As his eyes adjusted to the changing light he saw a shadow on the balcony opposite his own.

The Master stood there, broad hands clasped on the stonework; he watched his Right Hand with keen eyes.

Eamon stepped away from the wall. Slowly, he bowed low before withdrawing into his bedchamber. The Master's eyes followed him.

He allowed the drapes to fall over the window and shied back from them, his heart pounding. He was watched. The bed loomed behind him, a pit in which he dared not lie.

He eschewed it. Returning to the entry chamber, where veined candles and burning lamps cast their glow, he took instead to one of the chaise longues. The play of light over the eagle on the mantelpiece made it seem to shiver.

Casting aside boots, sword, and dagger, he lay down stiffly in the long chair, threading his arms along its edge as though he laid himself deep in a tomb. The thick cushions and his cloak moulded around him, swallowing him. He closed his eyes.

As he fell into shifting sleep, he heard a pall-song carried on the breeze.

CHAPTER III

"Lord Goodman?"

He had not heard the opening of any door, nor the footsteps that approached him. He barely knew the voice through the dimness of his groggy sleep.

"Lord Goodman?" it spoke again. It seemed timid in the grey morning.

"What hour is it?" Eamon croaked at last.

"About the second, my lord," his servant answered. Eamon remembered; it was Cartwright. "I am sorry to wake you," the man added hesitantly, "but you are desired at breakfast."

"Yes."

Eamon forced his eyes open and Cartwright's face came into focus before him. His muscles felt stiff. He remembered that he was lying in his chair.

"Is there something the matter with your bed, my lord?"

"No."

Eamon drew a deep breath to force the blood about his limbs, and looked at the servant again. The man carried a broad length of fabric that Eamon recognized to be a towel. He heard splashing nearby.

"Where is the water, Cartwright?" he asked blearily.

"Lieutenant Fletcher told me to see that you were properly refreshed before your breakfast. The maids are drawing a bath for you."

Eamon's face reddened. He remembered the scars on his back. "I will not be attended by them."

Cartwright's answer was pristine. "No, my lord. I shall attend you."

Slowly, Eamon rose. He felt lightheaded and stiff-necked. He wondered if he had moved once during the night, and doubted it.

Cartwright fell back a pace from him as he stood. "Come, my lord," he said. "I will help you undress."

Memory of Alessia flew into Eamon's mind. Angry, he pushed aside his longing.

"I have not needed such assistance before," he snapped.

"It is your due, my lord. Yet, as you will it."

Cartwright duly dismissed the maids before leading Eamon into the bathing area. The chamber held an ornate bath hewn of black marble. Its feet were like eagle's talons and it was filled with steaming water. Eamon wondered how long it had taken the maids to heat the water, let alone bring it to the vessel. He regretted then that he had dismissed them so quickly and without a word of thanks.

Reluctantly, he permitted Cartwright to assist him in undressing. As the last layers of clothes fell from him, he drew a deep breath, knowing his scars were exposed.

Cartwright paused uncertainly.

"You must not speak of them, Cartwright."

"I will not, my lord," Cartwright answered. "And I will be gentle."

Relief rushed through Eamon. "Thank you."

He allowed Cartwright to bathe him. It was a lordly service and yet it felt invasive to him. That, he reminded himself, was not the fault of his servant. The man barely spoke as he worked, being especially gentle when washing and rinsing Eamon's back. When he had finished, Cartwright wrapped Eamon in the long towel and then brought him robes and cloak. Eamon numbly let the man dress him. As his servant's hands passed over him, his thought turned first to Alessia and then, with growing horror, to the throned.

"Does something trouble you, my lord?" Cartwright asked.

Eamon broke abruptly from his thought. "What concern is it of yours?" he asked.

Cartwright did not falter or pause like a man rebuked. He continued speaking as steadily as a man sure of his words, as though unconcerned that his audience was the second most powerful man in Dunthruik. "You are a burdened man, my lord."

Eamon looked at him in surprise. "You speak boldly. These are not the words of a servant. Do these words belong to you, or to another?" he asked.

The servant faltered. "They are not mine," he said, lowering his gaze.

"Then whose words do you thus convey?" Eamon demanded.

Cartwright did not meet his gaze. "Forgive me, my lord. It was Lady Turnholt."

Eamon glowered. "You will not mention her before me!"

Cartwright flinched. Eamon forced himself to draw a deep breath. "I will not have her named before me," he said, more measuredly. "Do you understand?"

Cartwright bowed low. "Yes, Lord Goodman."

After a long moment, Eamon sighed. "Thank you, Cartwright," he said belatedly.

"You are summoned to breakfast, my lord," came his servant's reply.

Eamon went back into his hall and took up his belt and dagger; he drew the latter from its sheath. The jagged writing on the blade grinned foully at him.

There was a knock at the door. Fletcher strode in.

"Good morning, my lord."

"Lieutenant."

"I am to advise you, my lord, that when you go to breakfast you are expected to attend by means of the south balcony," Fletcher told him. "The Master's doorkeeper will be waiting for you there."

"Very well," Eamon nodded, standing still while Cartwright set his cloak over his shoulders.

"There was a small disturbance at the South Gate during the night," Fletcher added, holding out a sheaf of paper. "This is Lord Tramist's report."

"Am I to be troubled with every skirmish and dispute in the city?"

"No, my lord," Fletcher answered. "This was not a skirmish." With a sigh Eamon took the paper from him. "The disturbance occurred when two dozen stragglers came to the gate demanding entrance."

"For what reason?" Eamon asked, whilst skimming the report.

"The stragglers had been in a column, my lord – one of the ones that was evacuated for the billeting of the regional units," Fletcher told him. "They say that they came from the East Quarter. Initial checks seem to indicate that this is the case."

Eamon's blood cooled. "The East?" he repeated. He had sent wayfarers from the city in such columns; what cause could they have to return to Dunthruik?

"Yes." Fletcher looked down at some notes on a separate paper. "They're a splinter-segment from one of the first columns that you dispatched," he added. "They say that they were viciously attacked by wayfarers up River and that they lost almost half the column near Hightown. They felt that the only thing they could do was return to the city. They were harried further on the way."

Eamon looked at him. Why would wayfarers attack wayfarers? Could it be true? Why should he trust a report from Tramist? "Casualties?"

"Aplenty, I am given to understand."

Eamon glared. "Their names, Fletcher!" he cried. Cartwright stepped back from him.

Fletcher looked at the papers and then shrugged. "I do not know them, my lord."

"And the survivors?"

"In the report, my lord."

Eamon scoured it. The name of Grennil – whom he had entrusted to deliver his message to the King – was not listed. He realized that he could not hope to know whether any of them lived, nor whether they had delivered his message.

Fletcher watched him. "Lord Tramist thought that you might wish to know of it."

"Thank him," Eamon managed. "Have him send the returnees to the Crown Office in the East Quarter; Mr Rose and Mr Lorentide will re-house them."

"Such a measure will need Lord Arlaith's –"

"I command it, Fletcher," Eamon growled. "Lord Arlaith *will* obey me."

Fletcher bowed. "As you wish, my lord."

For a long moment there was silence. Eamon stood and stared at the papers.

"My lord?"

"Mr Fletcher?" Eamon snapped.

"Forgive me, my lord; you are awaited at breakfast."

Eamon sighed angrily. "So I am told," he retorted. Thrusting the papers across into Cartwright's astonished hands, he swept past Fletcher to the balcony.

Eamon shook as he stepped out. The sun struck him, blinding him for a moment. As he passed down the length of the balcony he could see down into the throne room. It looked like a chamber of fire.

He reached the far end of the balcony where it turned to follow the inner wall of the West Wing. The doorkeeper stood there beneath a curved archway. He bowed.

"Lord Goodman. I will lead you to breakfast."

Terrified, Eamon responded with only a nod.

The doorkeeper led him through the archway. Eamon expected to follow into a corridor or a passageway, but instead found himself in a long, light room filled with beautiful trees. Their branches reached up to twine overhead like beams and each tree was planted in an enormous pot.

The doorkeeper moved through the room at speed, but the trees forced Eamon to a standstill. He recognized the fruits that they bore.

They were western stars. The same fruit Anderas had once told him grew all around the city. The same fruit that the Master had destroyed when he claimed Dunthruik.

"Lord Goodman?"

Eamon looked back to the doorkeeper. Seeing that he was not followed, the man paused in the long gallery.

"This way, my lord."

Eamon followed him.

The chamber ended in another arch whose grand doors stood open so as to let in light. Eamon followed the doorkeeper to the threshold and the vast hall beyond.

"Lord Goodman," the doorkeeper announced. He gestured for Eamon to enter and bowed as he passed.

An enormous oak table was the room's centrepiece. It was decked with red cloth and bowls and platters. Men and women dressed in the throne's colours moved silently about the room, setting dishes and pouring wine.

At one end of the table sat the Master. A tall black chair was set to his right. As Eamon bowed in the doorway, Edelred smiled.

"Your glory, Master."

"Good morrow, son of Eben," the Master replied. "Come and break your fast with me."

Eamon walked the length of the room. The red-clad servants froze and bowed before him, all in absolute silence. One servant pulled the sable chair from the table.

At the Master's gesture, Eamon bowed once more and then sat; the servant set his chair closer to the table. Then another servant swiftly laid bread and cheese upon the plate before him whilst a third stepped forward and filled a chalice with wine, setting it by Eamon's hand.

Eamon watched them in astonishment, then managed to catch the gaze of the last.

"Thank you," he said quietly.

The young man froze and watched him for a moment with wide eyes. He said not a word. Eamon offered him a small smile.

"You serve well," Eamon told him.

The air rent with laughter.

"You waste your thanks, Eben's son!"

Startled – for he had almost forgotten that Edelred sat by him – Eamon looked back at the Master in surprise.

"Master," he began, "surely all service is worth some thanks –"

"Including ill service?" the throned asked, a baiting glint to his eye.

"Master," Eamon answered quietly, "I was not ill-served by this man."

"He cannot receive your thanks, Eben's son," Edelred replied, gesturing once to the servant. The man merely stood by them, watching. It disconcerted Eamon utterly.

"Nor does he," Edelred continued, "or any of these others, require it. You are so far above them as to be a flame at the mountaintop and they a carcass on the plain beneath. Even were that not so, still they would not receive your words."

Eamon drew cautious breath to speak once more, but the look on the Master's face silenced him.

"These about you neither hear nor speak, my Right Hand," the Master told him. "It was the first condition of their service."

Eamon looked up at the man at his elbow. His stomach sank.

The Master gave a sharp gesture and the servant bowed low before stepping away. Eamon watched him go, mouth ajar, and stared at another as a plate of cold meat was laid down at his right.

"I see that you would join my servants' silence, son of Eben," the throned laughed.

No words passed Eamon's mouth. Had all the men and women in that room been born unable to speak, or had they been made that way? His chilling heart told him that some would have chosen their silent world so that it might revolve around the man who sat at the head of the red-clothed table.

Edelred spoke again. "Your service is not so different to theirs, Eben's son, but you, a man worth many jesters, tend to ample use of your tongue." The Lord of Dunthruik looked down at him with an indulgent smile. "Use it now."

Eamon struggled to attend to Edelred's words. "What would you have me do this day, Master?"

"Always you turn your mind to my glory," the throned said, and laughed. "You are a rare man, Eben's son! It is that which makes the others loathe you so. But they do not see what I have seen." Suddenly the Master's hand was at his face, and the Lord of Dunthruik tilted Eamon's chin so that he might look into his eyes. Eamon quivered. The touch was liquid fire.

"Still I see it," the Master breathed.

The hand moved away. Eamon tried to steady himself as the throned leaned back. The Master gestured to another servant. This one, who was dressed more finely than the others, tasted the wine from the decanter on the table before carefully pouring some into the Master's chalice.

Eamon watched in terrified fascination as the Lord of Dunthruik drank, lowered his cup, and smiled.

"Eat, son of Eben," he said. "Eat, then speak out the whole thought of your arduous heart to me."

"Master, I am overwhelmed —"

"Then you must content yourself with eating!" the Master answered him wryly. "There will yet be time to speak, Eben's son. Much time."

Eamon bowed his head and gave his thanks. Then, under the Master's watchful eye, he ate. With every morsel or sip that he swallowed, Edelred observed him like a favoured child.

After Eamon had finished, a servant laid a dish of star fruit down beside them followed by a bowl of water.

The Master gestured to the dish.

"Is such fruit to your liking, son of Eben?"

Eamon's heart sank. "Yes, Master."

"Then you shall take of these."

He could not refuse. Eamon reached across to the bowl and chose the nearest fruit. It filled his palm. He placed it on his plate and took up his knife. Anderas had taught him what to do.

Slowly, he cut down through the fruit. The segments split apart, revealing the fibrous shape at their heart. Beneath the incision, the star seemed to bleed.

Edelred smiled. "My trees bear good fruit," he said. "You will do the same."

Eamon looked at the fruit lying open before him. "Yes, Master."

He ate in silence. The fruit cloyed in his throat as, engulfed by the Master's scrutiny, he swallowed. At his own table he might have taken wine to help him wash down the sickly mouthful, yet though his reddened cup glinted at him enticingly, he shunned it. He did not dare to take it. While he ate, Edelred did not; he only watched.

At last Eamon finished the fruit. He carefully dipped his fingers into the water and dried them. Not knowing what else to do, he lifted his head and met the Master's gaze.

"Thank you, Master."

Edelred smiled. Suddenly he made a circling gesture towards the servants with one hand; several of them darted forwards. They cleared the table. As they whirled about him, Eamon felt tempest-tossed; his head spun with the deftness of their silent world.

"Son of Eben."

The Master's voice was by his ear. Startled, he looked up.

"Master."

At another gesture from Edelred, a servant laid his hands to the back of Eamon's chair so as to pull it back. A little clumsily, Eamon rose from it and was swallowed by the Master's grey gaze.

"Follow," Edelred commanded.

Eamon bowed. "Your glory," he answered.

As the Master turned to leave, the servants bowed and froze. Eamon moved in Edelred's wake through the swathe of bent men.

They stepped out of the dining room into a corridor. Eamon shivered as cooler air drove past him. The corridor was carpeted and great tapestries hung from the walls. He guessed that the Master's own chambers were to the right and for a terrible moment he feared that he would be led there. But Edelred turned rather to the left, towards the deepest reaches of the West Wing. Eamon could not see where the corridor went, but he followed. They passed many windows and Eamon fancied that there might well be doorways hidden behind the tapestries. The windows to his left looked down over the palace gardens. He caught a glimpse of the Hands' Hall, a brooding edifice among a sward of green. Windows on the highest level of the East Wing looked back at them, and Eamon wondered whether he saw figures following in them, engaged in a ghostly mimicry of his onward step.

The corridor opened into a small antechamber. There were several chairs within, and at the far end, a monumental set of double doors boldly marked with red-eyed eagles. A sinister glint in the red stone indicated the passage was guarded by the mark of the throned; the doors were sealed. Eamon wondered whether only the Master could open them.

Edelred paused before the doors. The glint in the eagles' eyes grew stronger. Thrilling tension filled the air, throbbing and pulsing about the Lord of Dunthruik. The Master lifted one hand. The doors opened.

Eamon felt as though he watched the yawning aside of gates that guarded the cavernous lair of a hidden beast; the sight filled him with terror. Yet as the doors swung back his jaw fell in amazement, for all beyond the portal was drenched in a drowning wash of ruby and of gold.

Edelred crossed the threshold. Speechless, Eamon followed.

The rooms beyond were a realm of riches. Each part was filled with stands bearing every imaginable jewel or gem, some cast into settings more intricate than the filigree threads of fine laces. By these countless objects – necklaces, rings, medallions, clasps – were other stands displaying hosts of figurines, their faces a dazzling mosaic of precious stones. There were gowns tailored with golden threads and garments doused with jewels, each prominently displayed. In places tables held richly bound books and stands, which supported finely wrought lances, spears, or swords. Enormous paintings with gilded frames covered the walls, each more exuberant than its fellow in its attempts to show the Master radiant with glory, and statues of marble or alabaster lined the length of the room. One showed a man with an eagle on one arm and a serpent crushed in his other hand. In each corner of each room stood enormous candelabra, their golden boughs littered with rubies. From marbled floor to towering roof above, the solemnly bejewelled chambers showcased the Master's glory with all conceivable opulence.

Eamon had never seen such riches; they staggered him. He faltered in the heart of the first hall, gawking and overwhelmed. The treasures of the West Wing gazed silently back at him. Edelred strode among them, more terrible in flesh than any likeness.

Eamon was not sure how many chambers there were. Each one held more than he could comprehend, and those things that he did see and understand were nothing but poorly grasped details of the whole.

Edelred led the way through each chamber, never pausing to look at what surrounded them. In one, Eamon saw a wall strung with banners. There were emblems and heralds there with designs that Eamon did not know, and there were banners from the merchant states; Eamon recognized those of Galithia, Lamiglia, and Breusklia. There were banners from the east, some known to him, and one, showing a purple and crimson sun against a yellow background, that he had never seen before. Beside these were the emblems of the River's provinces – Eamon's heart soared as he recognized the lions of his home, Edesfield, among them – and of Dunthruik and its quarters, some showing only the quarters' leaf motifs.

But it was the banner hanging at the heart of these that struck Eamon dumb, for its frayed edges and dulled threads wove the shape of an eight-pointed star. Beneath this, clasped between the talons of great golden eagles, was a tarnished sword.

Tearing his sight away, Eamon looked back to Edelred. The Master pressed onwards. Eamon followed.

The chamber into which they went was a glut of gold as all the others; the austere glint of precious stones and metals stung Eamon's eyes. But in this chamber Edelred stopped.

Eamon halted but a pace behind him. Choked by the wealth around him, he struggled to focus as the Master gestured to the wall.

"Look," Edelred told him.

Eamon tried. His eyes sought the wall before him. It was different to the rest of the vault.

Although it was still richly hewn from marble and dark woods, the wall in front of him did not carry gold or gems. Rather, it showed an odd collection of objects: a leaf from a book, a great key, a curved sword, the torn fragment of a discoloured banner, a strangely shaped shield, a couple of small daggers, a ring, a cup, a small model of a holk, and three dark feathers pinned together by a clasp. Each object was carefully mounted and held in place by the talons of eagle-shaped clasps. But the eagles were not golden – they were black.

For a moment, Eamon simply stared. Though some of the objects were finely made they seemed utterly at odds with everything else that he had seen in the chambers. At a loss as to what to say or think, he looked up at Edelred.

The Master did not meet his gaze. Instead he stepped to the end of the line of objects. One additional set of eagle-clasps hung against the wall, empty. As Eamon looked at them, Edelred turned to him.

"This is my wall of Right Hands. Take this, son of Eben," he said. The Master held a frame, such as might encase a painting.

Trying to settle growing unease, Eamon reached forward and received it. As he weighed it into his hands he saw that the frame held a piece of parchment. It was a finely scribed sheet bearing the Master's eagle at its head. Eamon looked at it, his eyes racing across the words before him but unable to take in the meaning of any of them.

"Set it in the clasps," Edelred commanded.

Eamon stepped forward to the empty clasps. The back of the frame had hooks set into it, and these Eamon used to mount the whole into the eagles' claws. As he stepped back his mind at last caught up with his sight and he understood what the paper was: the writ – or perhaps a copy of it – by which the law of confession had been restricted to treason and the death penalty removed from property crimes.

"You glorified me on the day that this was writ, son of Eben," the Master told him. "In glorifying me you earned my love." With a laugh Edelred turned his grey eyes from the parchment to Eamon's face. He laid his hand on Eamon's cheek. "It is in your blood. More than any of them, son of Eben," he said, his voice a fervent whisper, "you will glorify me."

Eamon bowed down low. "Yes, Master."

Edelred withdrew his touch and walked back through the vaults. Quivering, Eamon turned from the wall of the Right Hands and followed him.

He kept his gaze fixed on the floor – he could scarcely bear the rooms which, in their grim and golden expanses, crushed and swallowed him. They had almost reached the doors leading out of the pageant of chambers when Eamon half-tripped. As he recovered, something on a distant wall caught his attention.

A painting. It had faded and its frame was worn with time, but Eamon dimly made out its content: a river running through a quiet, green valley. The river sparked blue and the valley was detailed with exquisite flowers.

Amid the red and gold, the trophies and the jewels, the dulled painting seemed otherworldly. Eamon stared at it.

Edelred's voice broke him from his stupor. "That work strikes you, son of Eben?"

Eamon turned. The Master had looked back to him and watched him. Fearfully, Eamon bowed.

"Yes," he answered.

"It was a gift." Edelred's voice seemed strange as he spoke

– pained almost. Eamon rose. For the smallest of moments, the Master's face was marked with wistful remembrance.

The moment passed. "Come, son of Eben."

Eamon obeyed.

Relieved to leave the choking vaults, Eamon staggered into the dining room, gulping air. The table in the room had been cleared and the servants were gone; the doorkeeper stood by the entrance to the gallery of trees.

Eamon bowed low to Edelred. "I do not deserve what you bestow upon me," he said. "I thank you, Master."

"And you delight me." Edelred smiled at him. "You shall eat with me every morning, son of Eben."

The words were crushing. Doubled over in his bow, Eamon forced speech to his trembling lips.

"To your glory."

CHAPTER IV

Eamon passed much of the rest of that day familiarizing himself with the palace, learning his way between the Master's rooms and his own, and where he might find his servants. He tried to keep himself from thinking about the vault that he had seen and the power that it held.

That afternoon he went to inspect the failing south wall and to give recommendation and authorization for its repair. He also spoke to the officers who had received the survivors of the East Quarter column, but they knew little. Eamon resolved to seek out the survivors themselves in the East Quarter if he could.

As he returned from the South Quarter, he met Cathair riding along the Coll. He would happily have avoided the man – but Cathair had never been one to afford his prey easy escape.

"Lord Goodman! Good day to you!"

"Welcome back, Lord Cathair," Eamon answered. "All was well at Ravensill, I trust?"

"Indeed," Cathair answered with a smile.

"I am glad. Forgive me," Eamon began, "but I cannot stay. I have business to attend –"

Cathair pulled a disappointed face. "Such business that would keep you from riding with me on such a day?"

"Even so," Eamon answered.

"Oh, but it cannot be!" came the melodramatic outcry.

"I fear it is."

Cathair smiled sadly. "Well, my lord, I must then leave you to tend to your misfortunes, whilst I tend to mine."

Eamon looked at him curiously. "Have you had misfortunes, Lord Cathair?"

"In part they are mine, in part Lord Dehelt's, I understand," Cathair answered. "There was an accident at the port this morning. See what happens, Lord Goodman, when I leave this city for but a moment?" He shook his head. "I understand that there have been losses, and damages."

It was the former word that caught Eamon's heart.

"Are you riding there?" he asked. Cathair nodded. "Then I will ride with you."

"As I am sure you know, the port's state is not a pressing matter, my lord," Cathair told him. "The Serpent may have allies, but they are Easters; such men will not come from over the sea."

"No," Eamon conceded, "but food for our garrisons will and that may yet be hindered by what you describe." If such were the case then he would have to rearrange all the logistics for feeding the city. It was not a thought that he relished.

He rode reluctantly with Cathair up the Coll to the port. The Sea Gate was busy, and even before they came close to it, Eamon saw dust in the air. A number of Gauntlet surgeons moved through it. As Eamon and Cathair approached, a cart passed into the city from the gate. A dusty, bloodstained doctor perched inside the cart with injured men – all of them militia – gathered about him like fledglings in a nest.

They rode closer. A merchant ship docked in the nearest berth bobbed rhythmically against the quay – or what remained of it. The winches and pulleys next to the boat were severed and tattered. Only half the gangplank remained; it ended abruptly in a mess of splintered wood. Gaps in the stonework revealed where massive boulders had fallen loose from the shattered quay. A group of men gathered at the water's edge, but dared not venture too close.

Nearby, the merchant captain was engaged in animated conversation with a man Eamon recognized to be Captain Longroad of the North Quarter. As Eamon arrived, both men stopped and greeted him.

"Lord Goodman, Lord Cathair," Longroad said. The merchant bowed in silence.

"I see we have been the victim of quite some misfortune this morning," Cathair mused.

"I fear so," the captain replied. "I am very sorry for you, Lord Cathair."

"What happened?" Eamon asked.

"The cargo ropes snapped," the captain explained, pointing up to the frayed and broken ropes swaying freely in the wind. "They were loaded with cases of arms."

"I had hoped to catch the fair tide." The merchant shook his head sullenly, raised his fist to the sky, and uttered a curse in his curious tongue.

Captain Longroad continued, "And now your haste has cost you both wine and arms, and you will of course be expected to pay restitution to Dunthruik for the lives of the Gauntlet lost to your recklessness."

Eamon looked up sharply. "Gauntlet? What were Gauntlet doing on this vessel?"

"With the increase in Etraian trade, and the reduction of portmen from the exodus, some Gauntlet have been assigned to loading and unloading the ships," Captain Longroad answered.

"How many men were lost?" Eamon asked, choking back a sudden fear that grew in his heart.

"Half a dozen," Longroad said, "perhaps more; the surgeons are still at work. Quite a few were on the gang when the casks fell; the ones that were hit by the falling cases were, I suspect, killed instantly. Others were drowned, at least one man in trying to pull others from the wreckage. There were injuries when the quay gave way."

"Do we know the names of the victims?" Eamon asked.

"The men lost were ensigns and militia from the West Quarter. The surgeons have made a list of the dead ensigns, my lord,"

Longroad answered. He offered a crumpled scrap of parchment to Eamon. "We're still working on the names of the militia."

Drawing a deep breath, Eamon took it and read. First horror, then grief, overcame him.

Ostler, Ford, Smith, Barde, Yarrow. He knew every one of the dead ensigns.

Eamon blinked hard. The names on the list didn't change.

"Has Captain Waite been advised of this?" he managed at last.

"Not yet, my lord," Longroad answered.

"Then send word to him. The West has lost fine men this day." Tears welled in his eyes as he said it.

Cathair peered over his shoulder at the names and clucked his tongue.

"I am quite in agreement, my lord," he said. "They were all good men." The Hand looked across at Longroad. "I am sure that you did your best, captain, to save them."

Longroad nodded. "My men and I did everything that we could, Lord Cathair."

"Good merchant, did your crew take any hurt?" Cathair asked.

"No, Lord Cathair," the merchant answered.

"Well," Cathair answered, offering Eamon a smile. "That, at least, is fortunate."

Eamon scarcely heard him, for his sight was drawn by a pile of bodies growing at the quayside. He recognized Ostler's pale, broken face among them. At the quay's steps, men worked to bring another mangled body up from the water. Eamon dared not try to recognize it, for he felt sure that he would.

The men laid the body with the others.

Cadet Manners was among the men performing the grisly task of clearing the wreckage. The cadet's eyes were red; his arms bore cuts and scars, and he was drenched with foul water.

Manners bowed once to Eamon and went back to the murky waters.

"Good men," Eamon whispered.

"I'm sorry, my lord," Cathair's voice slithered into his ear. "I was being inattentive, for which I crave your pardon. Did you say something?"

Eamon looked once at him and then back to the list of the dead in his hands.

"No, Lord Cathair," he answered. But as he read again, his heart grew cold.

"Good men": it was the name by which his old cadets, and the many men whom he had saved from the Right Hand's decimation, had called themselves. They had taken that name because a "Goodman" had redeemed them.

As he looked at the list, Eamon realized that every man upon it had been one of them.

The following days passed as a torturous nightmare, one punctuated by breakfasts, papers, and visits to the four Handquarters. Eamon was never left alone and even when he slept – which became more and more infrequent – he felt as though the Master watched, and caressed, him.

The repairs of the port were an ongoing nuisance. Because governance of the port fell outside the jurisdiction of any one quarter, it fell to Eamon to oversee the repairs. Three days after the accident, when the repairs were well underway, Eamon made a visit to the East Quarter Crown Office. He sought news regarding the survivors of the families evicted from the East Quarter.

Rose was there. He greeted Eamon in the hall.

"My lord," he said, bowing low. "It is good to see you once again. How fare you?"

"Well," Eamon answered, though he felt shaken and hounded. "Yourself?"

"Well, my lord." His pale face gainsaid him.

"I am pleased to hear it," Eamon replied. "How is the quarter's reconstruction work proceeding?"

"Well, my lord, well, but…" He faltered and bit down hard on his lip.

Eamon frowned at him. "Is something the matter, Mr Rose?"

"Yes... No..." Rose wrung his hands in his ample sleeves. "Some adjustments have been made to your list," he blurted.

"Adjustments?" Eamon repeated. "What kind of adjustments?"

"When I said 'some', my lord... you must forgive me. I would have done better to say that your list has been *altered*... In truth," Rose finished at last, "the priorities of the preceding list have been restored."

"Who gave this command?" Eamon demanded.

Rose cowered. "Lord Arlaith," he offered quickly. "I believe that he seeks the favour of the knights, my lord."

Eamon fell wrathfully silent. He could not countermand an order given under such auspices, for he knew, as did Arlaith, that the knights would be needed in any forthcoming battle.

For a long time he stood, still and silent, forcing his anger away. Rose seemed distracted, his eyes flitting from side to side and his hands trembling like the branches of an elm in the wind.

"We did complete some of the projects on your own list, my lord," Rose offered, his voice strained.

The words snapped Eamon from his mood. "I am sorry, Mr Rose," Eamon said at last. "I understand that this is not your doing. Is Mr Lorentide here?" he added. "I would speak with him, about what was completed before the change in the list was effected."

Rose's face grew paler. "Surely... you jest with me, my lord?"

"When have I jested with you, Mr Rose?"

"My lord, he..." Rose squirmed. "My lord," he said, "Darren Lorentide is dead."

Eamon stared at him. "Dead?"

"L-lieutenant Taine found him a night ago," Rose stammered. "I didn't hear about it until the morning..."

"But what happened?"

"He was stabbed for his purse. What with the grain prices being as they are in the quarter..." He buried his face in his hands, then tore them away again. "For his purse, Lord Goodman! He only ever carried less than a fifth of a crown! It was well known. His poor wife…" Rose bit back a melodramatic sob. "The Serpent's influence is growing, Lord Goodman, and it is everywhere!"

Swallowing back his own grief, Eamon set his hand on Rose's shoulder. "I am truly sorry for your loss, Mr Rose. Please… give my condolences to Mrs Lorentide, when you next see her."

Rose mopped at his eyes. "I will, my lord."

Eamon thanked him. Forgetting all else he left the office, lest he too should weep.

That evening Dunthruik was aflame with light, and the streets were filled with people. Swathes of them wore the Gauntlet's uniform, and they followed behind their officers and captains and Hands in a long and jubilant stream towards the Royal Plaza to stand beneath the Master's great balcony. Red cloth touched every post, and the light from the torches shook every shadow out of its solitary dark.

It was to be a majesty like no other.

Eamon stood in the throne room, his newly tailored robes gathered around him. The tailors' work made Eamon look like the Master's Right Hand and an embodiment of his glory. After helping Eamon dress that evening, Iulus Cartwright fell back in awe. Even Fletcher, who seemed imperturbable by nature, had genuflected to see the Master's favourite in such raiment.

Now the Master's favourite was little more than a lone figure huddled against a pillar just beyond the great balcony. Eamon listened to the crowds and music below and drew his arms tighter over his breast as he shook. Though he had been bathed and perfumed to perfection at the Master's command he felt haggard and harrowed. Each day brought new hurt and anguish. Each day, when he bowed, the touch of the Master's hand and voice threatened to draw him away from Hughan.

"Hold to the King."

Eamon closed his eyes and breathed deeply. He was not holding; through grief and fear and rage, in the very depth of his being, he

77

clung to the King as though for life itself – yet his grip loosened daily. He feared that the adulation of the majesty would claim one more part of his faltering heart for the Master.

Footfalls sounded behind him. He turned and saw the Master's shadow approach across the gallery. The Master's servants attended him and bore his long cloak off the ground as he walked. Eamon shrank before him.

"My tailors tell me, son of Eben, that they have excelled themselves." The Master's voice resonated through the air above all the cheering in the plaza below. "Show me."

Closing his eyes, Eamon stepped into the light before Edelred. As the Master's appraising smile rained down on him, vomit pressed the back of his throat.

"Does it please you, Master?"

"You, Eben's son, please me more each day." Then, leaning forward, he kissed Eamon's forehead with the peculiar tenderness of a cruel and fickle father. A sob escaped his lips as he received it.

Smiling, the Master gestured to the balcony door. "Glorify me," he commanded.

Eamon strode onto the platform of light. The whole of Dunthruik lay before him, shown forth as a swelling ocean of faces in the teeming plaza below. His head spun as he looked down at them. He steadied himself on the balcony's edge. A great roar filled the air.

"Long live the Right Hand! Long live Lord Goodman!" The storm of voices erupted into applause. "Lord Goodman, *to his glory!*"

Pride and fear, arrogance and humility shattered Eamon like a tempest-strike. The city of Dunthruik adored him.

"The city loves you, Eben's son." The Master spoke from the darkened gallery behind. "Accept their love as you accept mine."

Slowly, Eamon raised his arms; his black cloak fell down from them and the folds struck outwards, like the plumes of a great eagle in flight. The crowd clamoured ecstatically.

"The Serpent is defeated," Eamon called, "and the land is crowned."

"The land is crowned in glory!"

The liturgy had begun; never had Eamon heard it given with such passion.

"The glory is the Master's, for he cast down the Serpent's brood." Suddenly Eamon's voice rose to an unimaginable volume; something in him stirred to fervency by the ardour of the crowd. "Behold the majesty of him who delivers you from the broken and cursed house whose star has set. Behold him, Dunthruik!" he cried. "Behold him and rejoice!"

The balcony became awash with light that tore Eamon's sight from him. His ears were blasted with the cry from below.

"*To his glory! To his glory!*"

For the Master of the River and the Lord of Dunthruik stood on the shore of the city's adulation, and there he smiled.

"Dunthruik," he called. "Never has my glory had such a champion. I give you: my Right Hand."

And Dunthruik roared.

Eamon barely slept that night. His heart was full of the city's praise and his forehead tainted by the press of the Master's lips.

Cartwright woke him early. Eamon let the man prepare him for another day. The robes he had shed the night before had been removed from his quarters, to be laid out for him when the Master desired it. To dress once more in the general robes of his rank felt akin to donning a worn, pale doublet that had seen years of harsh service; it felt rough against his skin.

When had he grown accustomed to finery?

He went again to breakfast and barely noticed the mute servants in the hall as they fed him. He basked in the Master's praise and yet all the while it seemed hollow in his ears.

"You have yet to see to the theatre, Eben's son," the throned told him.

Eamon looked at him in surprise. "Master?"

The Master favoured him with a smile that broke his heart. "The Crown is yours," he replied. "It awaits its patron."

Eamon's mind flew back what seemed a hundred years, to the night when he had sat in the theatre with Lord Arlaith speaking softly in his ear and Alessia clinging to his hand, her treachery but a breath away.

"Yes, Master," he said. "I will attend to it."

He made another tour of the city that morning and saw that repairs at the port had gone well. Waite was there, his gaze tired and sullen. He greeted Eamon formally and accepted his condolences with gratitude.

"I am a hardened soldier, Lord Goodman. Death is part of my life. Yet some deaths are easier to accept than others. When men of the Gauntlet die, it should be in battle against the Serpent. Any death is tragic, but it is more so when the deaths of good men carry no meaning. Their deaths gained nothing," the captain murmured. He turned to Eamon and swallowed in a swollen throat. "Does that not seem grievous to you, my lord?"

Eamon looked at Waite; his heart wrenched.

"The manner of their death does not change the fact that they are dead," he answered at last.

Waite looked back at the quay and Eamon wondered whether the captain imagined the ensigns' last moments, squalled in stone and water.

"No," Waite breathed.

Fletcher brought Eamon a great number of reports that afternoon. Eamon was not happy when the lieutenant laid the pile of paper – a hand tall – before him, all of it to be signed and sealed.

"From the quarters," Fletcher told him. "There is one, however, that I believe warrants your urgent attention."

"Indeed?" Eamon replied, looking cheerlessly at the ream.

"One of your prior judgments has been called into question."

Eamon looked up sharply. "By whom?" he asked, though he knew the reply before his lieutenant answered him.

"Lord Arlaith." Eamon's face grew grim. If Fletcher noticed, he overlooked it. "It regards a certain Mr Fort. I have been advised that the matter is to be judged at the ninth hour."

It was but moments away. Eamon got to his feet.

"I will see Lord Arlaith at once," he said. "Where is he?"

"My lord, he is treating with the matter as –"

"Where is he, Fletcher?"

"I understand that the matter is to be seen to in his Handquarter office." As Fletcher answered, a dire look broke across Eamon's face; it was the same place where he had acquitted Fort himself – and Arlaith knew it.

"I will see him, and I will see him now," he growled. The mauled returnees, the West Quarter ensigns, Darren Lorentide, the reduction of the East Quarter building programme, his own tattered heart… all these whirled through his mind, and rightly or not, one by one, Eamon cast the blame for each squarely at the feet of Arlaith.

"Shall I summon –?" Fletcher began.

"No," Eamon answered hotly, and stormed from the room.

His horse was ready for him in the stables. In minutes he rode out of the palace gates. Rage and grief gripped his breast such as he had not known for a long time, and all of it, its every part, cried out against Arlaith. A bright May sun touched the streets as he charged into the East Quarter. The stable hands recognized him and fell back from the look on his face; they took his horse without question. Without a word Eamon took himself into the Handquarter, passing through corridors as familiar to him as his own palms. It was the ninth hour; he burst unannounced into Arlaith's office.

Arlaith was not alone. Cathair and Tramist were also there along with several Gauntlet ensigns, Captain Anderas, and Mr Fort himself. Fort was on his knees before the Hands. Tramist stood over him, palm stretched towards the howling man's brow.

In three angry strides, Eamon had crossed the room. Seeing him, the Hands halted. Eamon seized Tramist's wrist where it still hovered above Fort's forehead.

"You will not breach him," he said, casting the hand aside. "But you will answer me."

Silence fell. The three Hands looked at him; none of them looked terribly surprised to see him. It disquieted him.

It was Fort who called his mind back to the present. "Lord Goodman!" Fort sobbed, his wretched voice torn between relief and alarm.

"A pleasure to see you, Lord Goodman." Arlaith bowed as an afterthought and the faintest flicker of a smile passed over his face.

Eamon turned at once to Anderas. "Captain, you will take Mr Fort and your men from this room." Relief passed over Anderas's face, though whether it was at the command or at his presence, Eamon did not know. "Wait outside," he added.

"At once, my lord." Anderas drew Fort to his feet and shepherded him and the nervous ensigns from the room.

The door shut. Eamon turned to face the three Quarter Hands. As he did so, he belatedly realized how dangerous a situation he had created: he stood, *alone*, in a room with three of his greatest enemies. If they were in league against him…

He set his face towards them. He was the Right Hand. He would not fear them.

"I will be answered and I will be answered *now*," he said fiercely.

"Perhaps," Arlaith put in politely, "you will be answered more easily, Lord Goodman, if you ask a question?"

"Be silent," Eamon seethed. Arlaith almost flinched.

"Lord Goodman!" Cathair exclaimed. "What has happened to your legendary courtesy?"

"I rather think that I lost it when I discovered that my decisions were being questioned without my being consulted," Eamon answered wrathfully. "Do you think, Lord Cathair, that the Master would take kindly to the revelation of such a thing?"

Tramist laughed. "*Such* a man!" he jibed snidely. "He runs crying to the Master at every scrape, like a child."

Eamon glowered at him. "If you must sully matters with your tongue, Tramist, you may at least do so answering my question." He glared at them each in turn. "What are you doing?"

"I shall answer you, Lord Goodman." Arlaith stepped forward and offered him another mocking bow. "Mr Fort has been brought back for questioning not through any desire to spite you, as you so wantonly seem to think, but rather because new… *evidence* has come to light. As you so eloquently taught us but a fortnight ago," he added, "all evidence must be properly weighed and considered, especially in the absence of a second witness."

Arlaith's tone and manner unnerved him. "What evidence?" Eamon asked, trying not to let his sudden discomfort show. "And what reason have you all to be here? Surely this is an East Quarter matter?"

"Allow me to indulge in a touch of last-first, Lord Goodman," Cathair answered suavely. "The evidence came from the West Quarter, Mr Fort was taken in the South Quarter, and the East has jurisdiction over him."

Eamon looked hard at him. He didn't believe it for a second. "And this evidence, Lord Cathair?"

"Mr Fort has not been entirely honest with us, Lord Goodman," Arlaith replied. "Alleana Tiller and her family were not killed by the Gauntlet. Mr Fort knew this, and he withheld it."

"Of course, you were not to know, Lord Goodman," Tramist added. "You did not, after all, breach him before you had him acquitted."

"There was no need to breach him," Eamon replied coldly.

"Forgive me, my lord," Tramist answered, his words dripping insolence. "The evidence seems to suggest otherwise."

"Such a thing reflects oddly on you," Cathair added, "but perhaps, if you breach him now…?"

"He will not be breached," Eamon answered.

Cathair bowed. "I do, of course, defer to you, Lord Goodman." Eamon heard insincerity in every syllable. "Still, I must ask why you so insist upon not breaching him?"

"Lord Ashway's investigation of the matter was thorough enough," Eamon answered. "He judged this case and he acquitted this man. There is a formal East Quarter report. The matter has been dealt with on every level. Breaching is not required."

"I will not hold that opinion with you, Lord Goodman," Tramist hissed.

Eamon glared at him. He was about to speak when Arlaith lightly touched his arm.

"Perhaps you would like to hear Lord Cathair's account of the new evidence, Lord Goodman?" he said.

Eamon held his gaze for a long moment, then turned to Cathair. "What are these records?"

"You may be acquainted with the general account of the incident in question," Cathair told him. "Mr Fort maintains that his cousin, Alleana Forthay – or Tiller – and her family were killed by the Gauntlet on the twenty-fifth of October in 519. He also says that he was called upon to identify the bodies. The records in the East Quarter ratify this.

"However, a second set of records discovered in the West Quarter gives that Alleana Tiller was found dead in her home on the twenty-eighth – the same day that one Mr Tiller and child are recorded as leaving the city. The exit papers in question were later found to be improper," Cathair added.

Eamon's heart went cold.

"I have had the liberty of having the exit papers brought out of the Crown Office," Arlaith added, and scooped them up from his desk. They were yellowed with age. The Hand trailed them for a moment under Eamon's gaze.

Eamon froze with unfolding dread. He knew the shape of the letters upon them, remembered well the hand that had formed them. He remembered the day that his father, known in Dunthruik by the name of Tiller, had handed the papers to the Gauntlet on duty at the East Gate. They had been permitted to pass.

He drew a deep breath. "I will see the conflicting papers."

"Of course." Arlaith answered, genteelly handing him the two reports.

Eamon looked at them; they were exactly as Cathair had described them. The only substantial difference between them was that papers from the East Quarter had been signed by Lord Ashway in person, while those now produced from the West merely bore the signature of a quarter draybant. Eamon's brow creased.

He could only conclude that Ashway had lied.

Looking up, Eamon set the papers down on the desk. "Summon Mr Fort," he said.

"Of course, Lord Goodman." Cathair strode to the door to do so.

A moment later Anderas brought Fort back into the room. The man shook; he bowed wretchedly, the look of hunted prey on his face.

Eamon turned to Anderas. "Wait outside, captain."

"Of course, my lord." Anderas bowed and left.

Eamon looked down at the trembling man before him. "Mr Fort."

"M-m-my lord," the man quivered, bowing again.

"Tell me what happened on the twenty-fifth of October, 519."

Fort held his gaze fearfully for long moments. His eyes darted to the other Hands and then back to Eamon. "My lord, the records –"

"I have seen them, Mr Fort." Eamon looked at him sternly. "I charge you to truthfully tell me everything that happened."

Fort took a shuddering breath. "Alleana Forthay was my cousin," he said. "She was killed on the twenty-fifth. She was a proven wayfarer. I was the head of the family at that time – my own father had recently died. I had barely learned of her death when, having only the name of Forthay, Lord Ashway summoned me. I think it was the twenty-seventh that I was seen... He asked me about Alleana Forthay – he told me that she had been killed and that he was keen to hunt down any other snakes connected to her. I explained to his lordship that she had been married for nearly fifteen years, and that her name was Tiller."

Fort paused. Eamon watched as the man wet his lips nervously. "Lord Ashway dismissed me," he said, "but the next day I was summoned again. I was to be the official witness to identify Alleana's body. Then…" Fort faltered and looked up at Eamon. "Then he told me that I was also to sign documents witnessing to the deaths of her husband and her son. I was to spread the account that all three of them were wayfarers and that all three of them had been killed, which was what the official reports would also say." His face grew pale. "The truth was that her husband and son had already left the city. Lord Ashway was very clear: under no circumstances was I to speak of the truth unless the Right Hand or the Master himself called me to do so. If I did, then my own family would bear the consequences. As a grace to us, Lord Ashway allowed us to formally change our family name to Fort." Suddenly Fort dropped, shaking, down to his knees. "Forgive me, my lord," he said. "I lied to you, but I was bound to do only as Lord Ashway had commanded! I am sorry, my lord!"

Eamon's heart beat fast. Ashway had concealed the Tillers' flight from the city. Had Dunthruik's seer come to know of Elior Tiller's truer name, and come to know it too late to stop his escape?

"Captain Anderas!" he called.

The door opened and Anderas stepped in once more. "My lord?"

The other Hands stood about him in silence. Eamon gestured once to Fort. "Take Mr Fort out for a moment."

"My lord."

As Anderas stepped forward, Fort rose to his feet. He trembled, but he bowed.

The door closed behind them. Eamon looked back to the Hands but could not read their faces. He marshalled his thoughts.

"You have heard Fort's account," he said.

"His account merely explains the discrepancy in the papers," Arlaith answered. "It does not prove that he is not himself a snake."

Eamon stared at him in disbelief. "He was under commands from Lord Ashway."

"How are we to ascertain that?" Tramist asked bitterly. "Lord Ashway is dead!"

"The only way to be certain that the truth is being told is to breach Fort," Arlaith put in sagely.

"He will not be breached," Eamon thundered.

Cathair gave a clipped laugh. "Calm yourself, my lord!"

"Do you desire the Master's enemies to walk freely in the street, Lord Goodman?" Arlaith challenged.

Eamon's blood cooled at once. There was a baiting glint to Arlaith's eye. "No," he said, measuring his tone.

"Then this man must be breached."

"Not if it is proven that he was faithfully obeying the commands of Lord Ashway." Eamon snatched up the report from the East Quarter and pressed it into Cathair's hand. "Test this paper," he said, "and I am convinced that you will find that it is sealed with the Master's mark and Ashway's own hand."

Cathair held his gaze for a moment and then laid his fingers over the paper's seal. As had happened on the very first day that Eamon entered Dunthruik, red light answered him.

"It is as you say," Cathair told him, setting the paper demurely aside.

Eamon turned to Arlaith again. "As you see, Mr Fort is guilty of nothing but doing as Ashway ordered," he said. "Breaching him now would therefore be the same as saying that a family connection to a wayfarer is enough to warrant the incarceration and torture of a citizen of Dunthruik. This is a dangerous precedent."

Arlaith gave him a short smile. "We all know how strongly you feel on matters of the law, Lord Goodman," he said. Eamon glared at him. "However, you cannot deny that families are influential in such matters."

Eamon stared at him. Why should he not let Fort be breached? It would show the truth, and at no danger to himself.

But breaching was a tool of the throned, and if Tramist had anything to do with it, it would mean prolonged agony. Eamon swore angrily in his mind. Advocating on Fort's behalf would have been easier if he had not such a keen dislike for the man. Yet Eamon had already made a fool of himself before his enemies on Fort's behalf – what more could be expected of him?

He drew a deep breath. Fort had been made the plaything of Hands who cared nothing for justice. Eamon could not let them breach him.

A thought leapt to his mind and he seized it.

"A family's influence works both ways. I forbid you to breach Mr Fort."

Arlaith scoffed. "On what basis?"

"The law," Eamon replied with quiet resolve.

"The law? It is the very law of which you speak that requires this man be breached!" Cathair exclaimed.

Eamon swallowed in a dry throat. "A nobleman of Dunthruik is exempt from the prospect of being breached unless it is expressly commanded by the Master."

"*Pah!* Fort is no more noble than a rat!" Tramist sneered. "Men like him wind up dead in ditches, covered in their own stinking blood every day."

"What might you be thinking, Lord Goodman?" Cathair asked, an interested look on his face.

"If it were found that one of Fort's kinsmen was of noble blood, loyal to the Master, then Fort would by extension also have noble blood and be exempt from breaching," Eamon answered.

Arlaith nodded firmly. "I think we would agree with that, Lord Goodman," he said with a little smile.

"And yourselves, my lords?" Eamon asked. "Would proof of such a relation content you?"

Cathair assented, but Tramist threw his head back with a wild laugh.

"Are you a magician, Lord Goodman?" he asked. "It is impossible to do as you suggest. Let me breach the man and let matters be concluded with that."

"Lord Tramist," Eamon answered quietly. "I can produce this proof."

A triumphant, almost ecstatic, look passed over Arlaith's face. It was a trap. Arlaith had prepared it well. Eamon knew it, and had taken the bait like a fool. But he dared not back down.

Tramist leaned forward with mocking interest. "Really?" he snickered. "Well, then, where is it, Lord Goodman?" He peered over Eamon's shoulder as though he expected patents of nobility to be produced by some parlour trick from the folds of Eamon's cloak.

Eamon met his gaze. "He stands before you, Lord Tramist," he answered quietly.

There was silence.

Suddenly Cathair laughed, and laughed so hard he had to clutch his sides in mirth while tears rimmed his green eyes.

"I had forgotten, in my long and dreary abstinence from your company, how amusing you can be at times, Lord Goodman!" he cried.

"This is not one of them," Eamon answered. "By right of my title as Right Hand to the Master, I am a noble of Dunthruik. Alleana Tiller was my mother. And Mr Fort is the son of my mother's uncle."

Cathair fell silent and stared. Tramist did similarly. But the surprise on Arlaith's face was feigned.

"Well, Lord Goodman," Arlaith said. "It would seem that parlour tricks are a hidden *forté* of yours." Eamon fixed him with an appalled gaze, but Arlaith smiled.

Tramist gaped at him. "What power in the River Realm saw fit for *you* to join the Gauntlet!" he yelled at last.

Eamon rounded darkly on him. "You would question my allegiance?"

"You!" Tramist cried again. "The son of a wayfaring whore!"

Eamon could have struck him. "You will ask such questions of Captain Belaal, or of Lord Cathair, who was long my guardian and mentor," he seethed; Cathair squirmed. "Or you will ask it of the

Master himself. You will not ask it of me, and you will not," he added, "speak of me in such a way again. If you do, you will answer for it."

Tramist stared at him, open-mouthed. "You would not dare –"

It was then that Arlaith stepped forward. "I am satisfied," he said. "Lord Goodman, I am more than willing to let Fort go with a full pardon, and to let this matter drop. Your allegiance is utterly unassailable and I am sure that Lord Cathair and Lord Tramist will concur with my assessment."

The other Hands murmured their assent. Eamon did not trust them, but there seemed little else to do but accept their words. Feeling wearied as with a century of toil, he nodded.

"I am glad that we have resolved this matter. To his glory," he added.

"His glory."

Eamon left the office. The Hands stared after him and no doubt they spoke as soon as the door shut behind him, but he did not stay to hear it. He did not wish to know.

Anderas waited a little further down the corridor. Fort sat in a small chair beside him, his head hung pitifully between his bound hands. As Eamon looked at them he felt a pang of ire in his breast. Had he sacrificed himself to Arlaith for such a man?

Eamon. The other voice, so silent in the days since he had become Right Hand, washed through him in an instant. *For him, or any other.*

Eamon drew a deep breath and tucked his shaking hands inside his cloak. It was then that Fort heard his approach. He rose to his feet at once and bowed.

"Lord Goodman –"

"You shall go free, Mr Fort," Eamon told him heavily. Anderas watched him. How desperately he wanted to speak to the captain! But they could only exchange a glance. "The charges have been dropped."

Fort's face lit up with joy and he fell to his knees, clasping at the hem of Eamon's cloak. "My lord, you work miracles!" he cried. "How can I repay you?"

Eamon stooped and raised the man to his feet. He quietly met his gaze. "I would be grateful, Mr Fort," he answered softly, "if despite all that you have suffered for her actions, you would forgive your cousin, for her son has secured your release."

Silence met his words. It tore palpably across Fort's face. Both Fort and Anderas stared at him, the former warily, the latter astonished.

Slowly, Eamon drew the bindings from Fort's hands. The man looked at him again. A sliver of disgust touched Fort's erstwhile jubilant face.

"Yes, my lord," he said.

Eamon drew a deep breath. "To his glory, Mr Fort," he said.

Fort bowed. "To his glory, Lord Goodman." The words were coldly given.

Without waiting for Fort to rise, Eamon passed on down the corridor.

He came back into the Ashen where the bright sun stung his eyes. The square was full of people who bowed as he emerged. Eamon imagined that the crowds had seen him riding to the Handquarter and wondered at the wrath on his face.

At his command the stable hands swiftly brought him his horse. Eamon came down the steps to meet them. With curt words of thanks he climbed into the saddle and was about to spur Sahu on when a voice came after him. "Lord Goodman," it called. "Did you know, when you joined the Gauntlet, that your mother was a wayfarer?"

Eamon felt as though a more terrible silence had never fallen. The press of shocked faces all around him was like talons sinking into his flesh.

Slowly, he turned. Cathair stood about a stone's throw away. The Hand's face was creased in a scowl.

"Will you not answer?" Cathair called again. His green eyes flashed and the Lord of the West Quarter surveyed the Right Hand as though he had been made the victim of dire treachery. "The woman who bore you worked foully against the Master and against his glory and so I ask you, my lord Right Hand: did you know it when you took your oaths?"

Eamon received both words and look without flinching. The whole city hung dead in the air around him.

"I did not," he answered. "I was a child, Lord Cathair. I was told that my mother was killed for her purse."

"By your father?"

"Yes, Lord Cathair."

"It would seem that he lied to you, Lord Goodman."

"Perhaps he did not know the truth," Eamon answered, "or perhaps he sought to protect me from it." A wave of sadness washed through Eamon. He wondered whether his father had known the history of the name he had borne. "But as for my own oaths, Lord Cathair," he said gently, "they stand as they were made."

Cathair held his gaze for a moment and Eamon wondered whether the Hand's expression softened.

"The decisions a man makes for his house are binding, my lord, and must be well considered," he answered at last, "as I am sure yours are."

Eamon nodded once towards him. "To his glory, Lord Cathair," he said.

"To his glory, my lord."

As Eamon turned to urge his horse from the Ashen, the onlookers bowed once again. He could not see their faces, nor could he fathom what they now made of the Master's Right Hand. He knew then that the nature of his lineage would be all over the city within the hour.

What would the Master say? He could not think on it. All he could think, and that bitterly, was that he had held to the King. He had held, and sacrificed himself, for his mother's worm-like cousin.

In the long day that followed, Eamon could barely lift his head to meet the gaze of any that enquired after him. His own household, Fletcher, Cartwright, and the maids whom he saw in his quarters, said nothing of his lineage to him, but it did not encourage him. Other men watched him sidelong as he moved through palace halls, and Hands hushed their conversations as he passed, and bowed with over-formality.

Most terrifying of all, the Master said nothing about Fort; he only watched Eamon with his keen gaze and spoke of other things. But Eamon felt his disapproval and it cowed him into silence. He fully expected rebuke and knew that when it came it would be crushing.

It came the next morning. As the servants wove and moved in the silent dance of their service and Eamon took his chair to breakfast, the throned fixed him with a penetrating glare.

"A day, Eben's son, yet still you do not deem to speak?" The Master's voice was fierce and quiet.

Eamon painfully drew his eyes up from his hands. "Master," he began, "I –"

"You believed that I should learn it from Lord Arlaith, or from palace gossip?" Edelred spat. "Should not my Right Hand speak out such things to me the very moment that they occur?" The voice became a menacing roar. "You have dishonoured me, Eben's son."

Eamon felt as though a blade turned in his chest. "Master, I meant no dishonour –"

"Still you brought it."

"I cannot hide my roots, Master!" Eamon cried. "My mother's choices were not of my making!"

The throned laughed, that soft and indulgent laugh that Eamon both basked in and feared.

"Eben's son!" he cried. "Do you not think I know your heritage? Do you not think I have known it since before your mother bore you?" Eamon trembled. "I know every twisted root and branch, every fruit and stone, of the trees that led to you. It is not your blood that dishonours me; it is your silence."

Eamon could not look at him. Blood and roots; did not everything go back to those? Was it not in deeds and words that blood and roots were either cursed or exulted? Had he not added further perjury to the curses that clung to his own? He knew he had; yet in his heart dwelt the sick hope that he might somehow receive the Master's forgiveness.

The throned took a long look at him. "Tonight, Eben's son, there will be a feast at the palace. I will be there, as will you, at my side."

Eamon gazed at him in terror. "But the whole city despises me, Master," he cried, "I cannot –"

"I am the city, son of Eben." His voice was like thunder. "And I delight in you." Eamon's head spun as the Master's smile touched him. "Even so, do not be so foolish again."

Eamon left the hall awash with fatigue and gruelling fear. He was but a plaything in the Master's hands, to be built up and cast down at any moment. Now he had to go to a feast and sit at the throned's right hand while Tramist, Cathair, and Arlaith pierced him with their venomous gazes. He would endure their stares and those of all the lords and ladies of the city. He had to, for the Master he loved commanded it.

The thought drew him up short. Did he love the throned?

He went to inspect the Blind Gate, its wide lanes lined with the severed heads of Dunthruik's enemies in various stages of rot and decay. He searched the rotting faces in vain, seeking one face in particular: Rendolet's, the shapeshifting Hand. Rendolet, who had taken the shape of the Master's sworn enemy, the Easter, Feltumadas. Rendolet, whose shapeshifted head Eamon had brought back to Dunthruik as "proof" of Feltumadas's demise. But the head was missing.

Later that day he learned of a fire in the East Quarter that had destroyed the Horse and Cart and several buildings near it. The innkeeper, his family, guests, and neighbours had all been killed.

When Eamon returned to his quarters that evening he found robes set out for him. They were the robes that he had worn at the majesty, bearing the design of the Right Hand's eagle on their breast. He could barely stand the sight of them.

Cartwright helped him to dress; Eamon's mind was weighted and troubled, in desperate need of ease.

"Cartwright," he said quietly. Tears pooled in his eyes as the servant's diligent hands fastened the cloak about his shoulders.

"My lord?"

Eamon faltered. What good could it do?

"Did Lady Turnholt ever speak of me?" he asked at last. He did not know why he asked it, except that her name and thoughts had once been things that rendered him solace.

The hands at his shoulder paused for a moment.

"Forgive me, my lord," Cartwright replied. "You told me not to speak of her."

"Did she?" Eamon persisted.

After a long and reluctant pause, his servant nodded. "Often, my lord," he said. "And dearly."

Eamon allowed the words to settle on him, trying to take comfort from them.

Suddenly Alessia's face was in his mind and he heard her weep: *"They made me a painted doll, to be dressed and undressed at their leisure…"*

The words haunted him and he looked down at the clothes he wore. Was he any more than that? Was he not dressed and undressed, built up and cast down, caressed and struck, just as they desired?

In an instant he wished for her hand and for her shoulder and long, beautiful hair, and he longed to bury his face and sorrows in them both. How truly she had spoken!

But she had betrayed him. How could he forget that?

Slowly he regained himself. "Thank you, Cartwright," he whispered. "I will go down to the feast."

"I will await your return, my lord," Cartwright replied.

Eamon made his way down the corridors towards the sounds of music and laughter. He mused that, apart from lavish breakfasts and his sleepless nights, he seemed to spend little time at the palace. He wondered if such had been the case for Arlaith.

Red stones guarded some passageways but Eamon barely noticed them as he passed beneath the auspices of hanging banners and great paintings. He made his way to the Master's quarters using the secret links between the East and West Wings of the palace, then took the path from the Master's quarters to the throne room. The festivities grew ever louder as he approached.

The door to the throne room was small and inconspicuous – a service entrance – but tonight it had been set aside for the Master. Eamon approached slowly. He noticed a bent figure stooping to a peephole in the wood. He cleared his throat.

The figure straightened and turned towards him. The doorkeeper. He bowed.

"Lord Goodman," he said.

"Doorkeeper," Eamon acknowledged.

The man beamed at him. "You look splendid, my lord!"

"Thank you," Eamon answered nervously. He resisted the urge to fold his hands and arms deep into his cloak, and tried to stand as a Right Hand would stand.

"My lord," spoke another voice behind him: Fletcher's.

"What must I do, Mr Fletcher?" Eamon asked quietly.

"In a moment, the doorkeeper will announce the Master," Fletcher answered. "You will go in with him."

"And then?"

Fletcher smiled. "Then, my lord, you will wile the night away in whatever way best pleases you and the Master."

Eamon swallowed. "Thank you, Mr Fletcher," he said, doing his best to mask his aversion to the prospect of spending his evening in the Master's company. He watched light and shadow move across the peephole, and wondered what the doorkeeper saw through the tiny hole.

CHAPTER IV

Then the Master arrived. Those in the room bowed.

"Your glory!" said those assembled. Belatedly, Eamon did the same, for he had never seen the throned look as powerful as in that moment. There were no words that could describe the fire that dwelt that night upon the Master of the River, nor how the tailors had contrived to set it in such costly and stupendous raiment as he now bore.

Eamon bowed low. How drab and dour seemed the colour blue when all the world was aflame.

As he bowed, the Master stepped forward. There was a glimmer of gold as the throned wreathed Eamon's neck with an opulent chain. From the chain hung the red stone that Eamon had seen on Arlaith the first time that he had seen the Right Hand. Now he wore it. The eagle emblazoned there lay heavily over his heart.

The Master smiled. "Rise, Eben's son," he said, "and walk with me."

Eamon did so and stepped to the Master's side. The doorkeeper tugged a small cord near the hidden door. A moment later the sounds within dropped away and were reborn as a fanfare in the hall. The door opened as a voice called out:

"The Lord of Dunthruik and Master of the River Realm."

The Master stepped forward. Drawn by some terrifying magnetism, Eamon followed him.

"To his glory!" called the crier.

"To his glory!" answered the hall; Dunthruik's greatest bowed down before them.

The Master stepped forward and raised his head. A crown of flames twined his brow.

"My glory is not bound by shores or walls, or by earth or heaven," he called, "yet it is shown in men who rise above the weakness of their blood and glorify me." Eamon froze. The eyes of the hall were upon him and upon the Master. In particular, it was to the Quarter Hands that his eyes turned; their gazes made a fearsome spectrum of ambivalence, disgust, hatred, and pity.

"It is such a man," the Master continued, "whom you shall honour this night. This feast is given for my Right Hand."

There could be no hesitation; Eamon felt the Master's hand on his shoulder. As it alighted, he faced the throned, then dropped down to one knee before him. He pressed the Master's hand feverishly against his brow.

"Your glory ever and above all things, Master," he whispered.

The hall watched in silence, amazed by the sight of a Right Hand on his knee. Then the hall erupted into an ocean of wild applause.

The throned smiled. "Rise, son of Eben," he said.

The music began again in earnest, but it could not drown the clapping. The throned led Eamon to the high table. There, servants seated the lords of Dunthruik, Eamon among their number, a bewildered lamb among wolves. He sat alongside the Master at the head of the table; the other Hands sat to either side, their faces turned in varying shades of disdain. Eamon wondered if there was not a touch of jealousy to Arlaith's grim brow.

The Master sat. The assembled guests did likewise and the feast began. Eamon had never witnessed its like. As each service was brought to the table, the nobles and knights, the ladies and courtiers, the Hands and visiting merchants, the Gauntlet captains and their assistants, raised their glasses towards the high table and gave out cries to the Master's glory and to his Right Hand. With each cry the faces of the Quarter Hands grew progressively darker, all save Dehelt's, who raised his cup with a smile.

At length the meal concluded and the throned invited the hall to make use of the floor to dance; the hanging lights and standing candles summoned fire from the paving stones and the lords and ladies danced to hymns which spoke of the Master's glory. Eamon recognized some of the words and realized that they had been drawn from the Edelred Cycle.

The Master smiled and began a circle of the hall to greet his many guests and accept their praise and flattery. Eamon supposed that many of them never saw the Master except at such times. He stayed behind and watched.

As the high table rose, Arlaith descended the hall and met nobles from the East. They greeted him warmly; Sir Patagon bowed deeply before seizing Arlaith's hand and clasping it with profound affection.

"How fare you, Lord Goodman?" asked a voice.

Eamon turned to see Lord Dehelt standing by him. He wondered what to make of Dehelt's pleasantries. If he scratched beneath the surface, would Dehelt prove just as malicious and virulent as the others?

"Why are they so warm with him?" Eamon asked, gesturing with a discreet nod towards Arlaith.

"He has done the quarter great service," Dehelt replied, "or so rumour would have it. He speaks but little of his doings to me," he explained. "It ill beseems a neighbour."

"What service?" Eamon asked.

"Grain prices in the East have been substantially higher than elsewhere for some time," Dehelt answered carefully. "It had started driving up the price throughout the city, though the South seemed to have some to spare. Lord Arlaith has now alleviated this problem, I understand."

Eamon felt a tremor of horrified presentiment. "How so?"

"He released a great deal of grain back into the city this morning."

Eamon's blood curdled. "He did not buy it?"

"No, my lord," Dehelt answered. "He found it – throne alone knows where."

But Eamon knew. He stared down the length of the hall at Arlaith with utter hatred.

"If you will excuse me, Lord Dehelt."

Dehelt began to reply, but Eamon never heard it. He swept down the hall to where Arlaith stood, surrounded by fawning nobles in their feckless gaiety. Eamon, draped in black and a wrathful heart, surged forward like a murderous tide.

"Lord Goodman," the nobles chimed as he approached.

"His glory," Eamon answered thickly. They watched him with wariness. In that moment he did not care. Part of him wanted to seize Arlaith by the throat there and then, drive the man up against the wall and call fire and fury down upon him. But he knew he could not; Arlaith also knew it.

"Lord Arlaith," he said grimly, "I would speak with you."

"Your wits are evidently befuddled with Raven's brew," Arlaith laughed cheerfully, "for it seems to me that you do just that, Lord Goodman!"

"I will speak with you now," Eamon said, "and in private."

Arlaith raised an insolent eyebrow, then turned to the nobles who stood by them.

"Excuse me, gentlemen," he said and imposed his cup upon one of them. "As you see, the Hands never cease in working for you."

"Hear!" called the nobles, and laughed.

Arlaith turned to Eamon, who would have killed the lord with a look if he could. Instead, he gestured to the south balcony. Some of Edelred's own guards stood there.

It was to the balcony and its guards that Eamon led Arlaith. "None bar the Master are to disturb us," Eamon told the men as they passed. The guards bowed deeply.

Eamon strode onto the wide stone ledge. Arlaith sauntered after him. As soon as the red drapes fell behind them and the sound of revelry became but as a distant dream, Arlaith smiled – the deadly, insincere smile that he had always borne as Right Hand.

"I see you have become well accomplished in giving commands, Lord Goodman. I congratulate you."

Eamon rounded on him. "Where did it come from, Arlaith?" he demanded.

"There is no need to raise your voice, Lord Goodman," Arlaith told him with a click of his tongue.

"Do not bandy with me!" Eamon snapped. "Answer! Where did it come from?"

Arlaith feigned surprise. "Perhaps you have not seen the report? That would be strange indeed. I entrusted it to Captain Anderas to bring to you. You spoke highly of him, as a man of infinite reliability and character." He shook his head sadly. "Perhaps you were misled…"

"Do not lie to me," Eamon thundered. "You gave no report to Anderas; he would have brought it to me." Arlaith stilled a little. "Now speak clearly," Eamon growled, "else your tongue will be the next thing served in this hall."

Arlaith looked at him with amusement. "You have grown bold, Lord Goodman." A smile darkened his face. "You would dare to threaten me?"

"I will not fear a Left Hand," Eamon retorted bitterly; the words almost knocked Arlaith's composure. "Now speak!"

"Very well, if you insist upon it…" Arlaith paused, looked once across the gardens towards the Hands' Hall as though pondering for a moment where to begin, and then shrugged. "I was clearing out some very unseemly and untidy corners of the East Quarter College – no reflection, I am sure, on their previous keeper – when I stumbled on some grain. Imagine my surprise!" he added. "Well, the people had been plaining for food and so I asked myself: what would Lord Goodman do? I had to think but for a moment to find the answer." Arlaith spread his arms with a laugh. "Tonight, the East sups at last."

Eamon glared at him; he could not argue against the Hand's flattering insolence.

"Why did you not come first to me?" he demanded.

"You knew of this?" Arlaith asked innocently, then his eyes widened. "Ah! Perhaps that is what the draybant meant, before he was…" He looked up with horror. "Oh *dear*, Lord Goodman." And the horror on his face became once more his accustomed and mocking smile.

"Speak plainly," Eamon cried, "or I swear –"

"Do not swear, Lord Goodman," Arlaith retorted. "You are not very good at it."

"The grain was stored under my orders," Eamon hissed, "to be kept until my orders released it."

"There was no paperwork to that effect," Arlaith replied. "Obviously, without paperwork to sanction their actions, the men who resisted my release of the grain could not be taken at their word."

The words froze Eamon to the core. "Resisted?" he repeated.

"Their actions were against the state – deeds of treachery, no less – without papers to sanction them," Arlaith answered. "I had letters delivered to their families this afternoon. They were classed as wayfarers and sent to the pyres."

"Even in the letters?" Eamon gaped. A family could endure no greater dishonour than to have their menfolk branded traitors.

"Even so," Arlaith answered steadily.

"Who?" he whispered.

"There were several injuries, among them Cadets Grey, Locke, and Bellis – they have been remanded in the brig – and three fatalities. Two ensigns whose names escape me, and Draybant Greenwood."

Eamon sank back against the stonework in horror. Greenwood, dead? The grain was wasted and Greenwood was dead.

It was the price, his wretched heart cried at him, to be paid for serving the King.

Wrathful, bitter tears sprang up into his blinded eyes. He rounded on Arlaith.

"You bastard!" he yelled. "You know full well what you did!"

"You injure me, Lord Goodman!" Arlaith replied. "I acted in the interest of the East Quart –"

"The grain was stored in the interest of the East Quarter!" Eamon raged. "You went against my commands and you killed men loyal to the Master!"

"I knew of no commands, Lord Goodman," Arlaith told him, "and I took no arms against these men of yours."

Eamon turned and gripped the stone. He might be Right Hand but he could not touch Arlaith; he could bring down no vengeance on him. Tiny twists of law and bureaucracy kept him safe.

"It distresses me to see you thus, Lord Goodman," Arlaith said at last. "Are you well?"

"Get away from me!" Eamon spat.

"As you command, my lord." Bowing slickly, Arlaith left.

Eamon shook. Was he so powerless? He was Right Hand, but he could not protect those whom he loved. So many men were dead, and more would follow. He could not save the city. He had been foolish to try. He had tried. He had tried to hold…

Suddenly footsteps came across the balcony towards him.

"Lord Goodman?" It was Fletcher's voice, and it trembled as it spoke.

Eamon did not turn to face him. "What is it, Fletcher?" His eyes burnt with tears that he could not weep before his lieutenant.

"The Master asks why you will not come and dance, and join the festivities?" Fletcher sounded terrified, as though he feared to bring the message and feared the answer that he would have to take back.

"Tell the Master that I excuse myself most humbly, and that I am exceedingly grateful for this great feast he has given for me," Eamon replied. His hands shook violently. "But I cannot go in. I am not well."

"Shall I fetch a doctor, Lord Goodman?"

"No!" Eamon yelled, turning to him at last. Seeing his face, Fletcher blanched. Eamon rubbed a hand over his brow; it was covered with sweat. "I will go to my quarters," he said. "The Master may seek me there, if he desires it."

"Very well, Lord Goodman."

Eamon stormed away along the balcony. The light from the feasting hall coloured his skin as he went.

Rage caught in his throat as he flung open the doors that led into his quarters. He slammed them shut behind him but he could still hear the music. With a cry he turned and stalked from his bedroom to his entrance hall. As his chest heaved he felt the weight of the stone, and with a great cry of wrath he tore the heavy chain from him. This he hurled across the room, and after it he cast Eben's dagger. Both came to rest by the mantelpiece and lay, whole and unscathed, in the glinting firelight. Shuddering, Eamon pressed his back, hard, against the wall, and shook.

"My lord?" spoke a timid voice.

Eamon looked up and saw Cartwright standing in the doorway to one of the other chambers, a taper in his hands.

"My lord, are you well –?"

Eamon looked up at him through a veil of tears. He could not hear, could not think.

"I told you not to speak of her, Cartwright!" he thundered, and as he lay against the stone he wrung his hands together in grief. "I told you not to bring that treacherous whore before me!"

Cartwright's face grew grey. "My lord," he whispered, "I did not speak of Lady Turnholt."

Eamon felt Alessia's soft face in his hands; the name convulsed through him, releasing a torrent of memory and hurt which he had long sought to hide.

"Do not name her!" he yelled. "Perfidious, lying whore!"

His outcry was too much for her servant.

"You repay her with such names?" Cartwright asked incredulously. "She loved you."

"Loved me?" Eamon stared at him. "She betrayed me; may she reap all reward of that from Fleance's cursèd couch!"

"You *believe* that story?" Cartwright gaped.

"It is the truth!"

"Forgive me, my lord, but it is not." Cartwright stepped angrily towards him. "I served her house, Lord Goodman, and I knew her well, long before you did. Alessia Turnholt went to no man's court and no man courted her after you deserted her. You did not know her at all if you believe these lies of her."

"It is the truth!" Eamon howled. He knew it was the truth; Ladomer had told him so. And Mathaiah had died because of her. *That* was unforgiveable. "She betrayed me!"

"If she had gone with Fleance with the Master's favour would her house have been disbanded? Would it not have gone with her? Would not I have gone? Would I be here in your hall if her house had *not* been disbanded?" The servant's face was flushed with anger; only death could await a servant who dared to raise his voice against the Right Hand, but Cartwright courted it. "You are an intelligent man, my lord, and you can answer these questions as well as I can."

Eamon could bear it no longer. He surged to his feet and forward, bearing down on his servant with the wrath of storm-torn skies.

"You snake!" he screamed. "Lying snake! Get out!" His voice and hands rose as though to strike the man and then shook with inconsolable rage. He could not. "Get out!" he bawled. "Out!"

With shaking hands Cartwright fled the room.

Eamon heard the door close behind him. He sank down to his knees, his head pounding with the pressure of lost loves and mixed loyalties, of lies and betrayals, hatred and longing. He had been harrowed and harried and feasted on by grief, and now it broiled deep within him. Death and blood and flame; he was mired by them, with no way of escape, and nothing to cling to, except the indulgence of the Master for whom he must fawn and prance like a witless puppet.

Perhaps that was all he was.

CHAPTER V

"Cartwright?" Eamon croaked. His voice sounded pitiful between the caverns of the drapes. No answer came. "Cartwright!" he called again, trying to sit up. He could not.

"Lie still, my lord."

He fell back against the deep bed. It was warm and damp.

Slowly he drew open his aching eyes – they felt swollen and heavy, and it took time to work them – then started in surprise. A man wearing the uniform of the Master's servants stood nearby, peering at him. As he focused, Eamon made out Fletcher standing behind the first man; the lieutenant's uniform was like a continuation of the drapes that the first man pushed as he leant close.

Drapes... Eamon gasped sharply and sat up. He was in the bed of the Right Hand; he had never dared lie in it before. He had never wanted to.

"How did I get here?" he demanded. As he spoke, he realized that he was naked beneath the covers. He became acutely aware of the scars on his back and settled firmly against the pillow. "Well?" he barked.

"You were found on the floor in your hall, my lord." The servant reached out and took Eamon by the wrist; he held the pulse and counted a short while before he continued. "You were moved."

"Moved?" he queried.

"By the Master's servants and myself, Lord Goodman," Fletcher answered. The first man continued his strange count, beating the pulse absent-mindedly against the bed. "I was sent to ascertain in what way you were unwell."

Eamon shivered. *"The Master may seek me in my quarters..."* So, like a fool, he had told Fletcher before he fled the ball, and the Master – or, at least, his servants – had come. How had the Right Hand been found? Senseless on the floor, wracked with wrath and grief; Arlaith would have enjoyed the sight, had he the opportunity.

He shuddered, wondering what words had been spoken over him and who had undressed him and laid him in the bed, and whether they had laughed or looked on him with pity. He did not know; he remembered none of it.

As he tormented himself with those thoughts he returned at last to what he did remember – his servant, and his waking.

"Where is Cartwright?"

"Who is this Cartwright?" the counting man asked.

"A servant," Fletcher answered, then stepped forward to the bedside. "I have not seen him yet this morning, my lord." Fletcher did not look concerned. "Shall I send for him?"

Eamon winced. How could he ask for the man after what he had said? He sighed and leaned back heavily into the pillow.

"No," he said at last. The counting man set Eamon's wrist down and examined him thoughtfully, marking his breathing. Fletcher watched in silence for a while and then turned officiously to the other man.

"What news shall I send to the Master?" he asked.

"That the Right Hand is awake, Mr Fletcher," the man answered, "and perhaps in need of leech craft to calm his somewhat over-excited blood."

"What!" Eamon exclaimed. "I need no leeches!" he added hotly.

The servant raised an eyebrow at him. "If I say that you need leeches, Lord Goodman," he told Eamon severely, "then you need leeches."

"Who are you?" Eamon demanded.

"This is Mr Doveton. He is the Master's physician, my lord," Fletcher told him quickly. "He has come to you at the Master's personal request and is an expert in his trade."

"I will have no leeches," Eamon persisted. The thought of them made his stomach turn.

"Unless your temperament makes startling improvement before I am a minute older, Lord Goodman, there shall be leeches all over you within the hour," the doctor replied.

Eamon glared at him but knew that he had no sway over a servant serving him at the Master's behest. It was a disconcerting realization.

"I apologize," he said quietly. The doctor looked utterly taken aback. "But I am not overly fond of the idea, besides which fact there is nothing wrong with me; I was tired and overcome with emotion."

"I beg your pardon?" the doctor breathed. He looked astounded.

"I said," Eamon began again, as calmly as he could, "that I was overwhelmed by emotion and that this led to my collapse."

"No, my lord," the man said, shaking his head. "I beg your pardon, I meant the first part."

"My apology?"

"Yes," the doctor said with an air of amazement. He looked to Fletcher, then shook himself as though to clear his head. "My recommendation will be that you allow me to monitor you for a few days, Lord Goodman," he said. "If you improve, my leeches shall go hungry."

"You'll forgive me if I feel no compassion for them," Eamon answered. The doctor blinked again, then laughed.

"The Master asks if you will come to breakfast, my lord," Fletcher interrupted.

Eamon glanced across at the balcony window. The idea made him feel sick, but he had no choice. "Yes, Mr Fletcher," he answered, rising from his bed. "I will go. You may tell him so."

Fletcher bowed and withdrew. The lieutenant's footsteps retreated across the hall and the doors opened – then closed – behind him. The doctor drew to his feet and gathered up the few things he had brought with him, among them smelling salts and other bottles.

Eamon saw that one of them had been opened. He wondered what it was and whether it had been used.

He eyed the doctor carefully for a moment. The man met his gaze.

"I will help you to dress, Lord Goodman," the doctor told him. "Your own house has been asked to stay away for the present, so that I might treat you."

Eamon froze. The doctor looked down at him. "My lord, does that trouble you?"

"I do not care for unknown eyes... prying."

"I assure you, you suffered no indignity under my supervision."

"That is not it... I – I carry marks from my past that I should prefer remain hidden. A man of my station has enough rumours surrounding him without adding to them."

"You speak of your scars?" said the doctor.

Eamon nodded. "How many others saw them?" he asked quietly.

"Some of the Master's house," the doctor replied. "But none who can speak of it." Eamon felt sudden and guilty relief that the servants were mute.

"My lieutenant?"

"Was not present when the servants laid you in your bed, my lord."

"You will speak of it to no one," Eamon told him.

"No... except the Master, my lord," the doctor replied. He watched Eamon for another moment, then stretched out his hand. "Come, my lord. You may dress and go to breakfast."

Once dressed Eamon made his way across the balcony towards the Master's dining room. As he walked he dwelt on what must have happened the previous night. The more he pondered it, the more humiliated he felt. This time he had needed no assistance; he had betrayed himself. A fine figure he had made, the Right Hand who had collapsed on the night of his own celebration; and so his anger increased.

The doorkeeper greeted him impeccably and admitted him to the throned's company. The servants within bowed; Eamon

110

wondered how many of their silent faces now knew what he had so long endeavoured to keep hidden.

The Master sat at the table, his taster at his side. As Eamon approached, the Master appraised him critically.

"How fare you, Eben's son?" he asked, though there seemed little concern in his voice, merely cold interest. It shredded Eamon's heart.

"Well, Master," Eamon answered. Did he want the Master's pity? He drew a deep breath. "Forgive me," he said. "I was not myself last night. I hope only that I did not anger you."

"Anger me?" The throned laughed. "Yes, Right Hand, you did." The Master fixed him with a piercing glare; Eamon would rather have been pinned with a hundred daggers than endure that look. "I asked you to come in, Eben's son, and you refused me."

Eamon swallowed. How could he explain why he had acted as he did? As he felt the glint of the Master's eye upon him he realized that he must.

"I received ill news, Master," he said quietly, "and I received it badly."

"What news?" the Master asked, and gestured for food to be laid before himself. Eamon remained standing. He had not been invited to sit.

"When I was Lord of the East Quarter, Master, I took it upon myself to set aside a store of grain."

"Indeed?" The Master did not sound interested, but his keen eye roved across Eamon's face like a hunter seeking a hare hidden in the bush.

"This store, Master, I made for the quarter; I hoped that were the Serpent ever to come to our walls and lay siege to our city, the East would live."

"This is an initiative, son of Eben, which was not discussed with me," the Master told him.

"I was afraid to speak of it, Master," Eamon answered, "because such provisions might lengthen a siege, should one come. I therefore did not know how the measure would be received. My heart was to have the people of this city kept safe." He paused, hoping that the Master might somehow encourage or berate him; but the man remained silent, his concentration seemingly on what he ate and drank.

Chilled, he saw no choice but to continue. "The news I received last night touched on this," Eamon said. "I learned that Lord Arlaith had taken this store and distributed it to the people of the quarter."

"And this made you sick, Eben's son?"

Eamon heard the mocking tone of the Master's voice. It pricked anger in the place of his grief. "Lord Arlaith did this not for your glory, Master, nor even for his own." Eamon thought of Greenwood's body being taken to the pyres, just as Mathaiah's had been, and suddenly his rage grew greater. He abandoned all effort to hide it. "Arlaith did this to spite me, to bait me, and weaken me. In so doing he killed, and branded as traitors, men who were nothing but loyal to you and to your glory."

Silence followed his outburst. Still the Master ate, and the servants stood.

The Master took a long draught of his drink. He looked up at Eamon.

"Tell me, Eben's son," he said. "What is it that you have done that Arlaith would bait you so?"

Eamon tried to match his gaze. He felt like a child.

"I have done nothing to him, Master."

"And, following news of the release of your grain store, you returned to your quarters and fainted?"

Eamon lowered his eyes; the Master's tone shamed him. "Yes."

"Son of Eben! Is so little a thing enough to cast you down?"

Eamon did not answer him.

The Master laughed, and a whimsical smile rolled across his face. "You are yet young and fragile, son of Eben. You will grow, and such small matters will not burden you." The Master surveyed him a moment more. "I understand that you have many scars on your back, Right Hand," he said quietly. "How came you by them?"

Eamon looked up in surprise, but the Master's face was unreadable.

"Did…" he faltered. Edelred watched him in the silence. "Master," Eamon breathed. "Did Lord Arlaith not speak of them to you?"

"I speak with you, son of Eben," the Master answered, "not with Arlaith."

Eamon swallowed. Arlaith had known that he had been flogged; was it possible that the Master had not known it before the previous night? "I… I was flogged, Master."

"For what trespass?" The Master's tone was deceptively neutral.

"My own," Eamon answered quietly. For a moment Mathaiah's face flashed across his mind, along with those of the other two cadets. In horror, he realized that he no longer remembered their names. He closed his eyes. "I was flogged for a failure in my command, Master. I keep it hidden. It is shameful to me."

The Master did not speak, but seemed deep in thought.

"Sit and eat," he commanded, gesturing to the plate which the taster had sampled before laying it at the table. He did not know whether this was done for his safety or the Master's amusement. "Your strength is needed, Eben's son."

Eamon bowed and took his place at the table. His strength? He had no strength left; it had been stolen from him in thrusts and jabs, by dinners and ceremonies, in every moment since he had become Right Hand.

His plate was filled with food and his goblet with fine wine. The idea of eating seemed abhorrent to him, but he took bread, dipped it into his goblet, and ate. The whole hall watched him.

He left the hall at the Master's bidding, his stomach heavy and unwell, but he had no freedom to refuse the throned. He wondered if he had ever had.

As he crossed the south balcony he looked down upon the gardens. Unlike the palace's grim and endless corridors, the gardens were green and clear. Eamon ached to be in them.

He passed through his quarters and sought out one of the many stairs that led down to the ground level of the palace. Once there he took a door into the gardens. The Hands' Hall stood like a blemish upon the green, but beyond it, paths wound in and out of hedges and blossoms that spiralled up after the spring light.

He went past them all, past the blossoms and the hall. His steps carried him towards the palace's southern-most garden. There, not far from the palace wall, he found a fountain at the centre of the broad courtyard. He paused there, watching the light leaping from the water up onto the stony eagles that stood guard over it. The light flecked them with shimmering plumage.

There was a small path beyond the fountain. He paused to look at it and saw that it was well kept. Yet it seemed older and wilder than the neat stones of the eagled fountain.

Eamon turned and followed it. Trees lined the path. Behind him, Eamon caught glimpses of the high palace arches and chambers, framed by thick green.

The path opened out into a small space from which Eamon could neither see nor hear the noises of the palace. Tall, delicate frames, painted white, wove round it, and twisted into these frames were climbing plants which spun gracefully about the wood. Caught up among them were roses, red as blood, as large as his fist, and as beautiful as he had ever seen them. In the silence of the courtyard they had their own song, but he could not grasp it. He almost reached out to touch the petals of the flowers, but he did not dare; they were beyond his ken in beauty and in sorrow.

He stood still for a moment, drinking in their heady scent, then looked about himself again. In the centre of the rose garden was a small pedestal. Quietly he walked to it. The stone was an object of great craft, solemn and tranquil amid the hanging roses that inclined towards it. At the top of the pedestal was a broad basin, engraved with a motif of running plants. Eamon stepped up and peered down into it. Then his breath was stolen away.

In the still water he saw the high arches of the blue sky. Birds moved across it and there, above the reflection of his astonished face and hidden in a corner of the growing light, stood a shining star. It was faint, but he saw it.

"*Hold to the King.*"

Eamon rested his hand on the pedestal and turned his head up to the sky. The light grew, and as he watched, the star faded from his sight; its final rays filled his eyes.

When he looked back to the basin, the water moved as wind breathed across it. The roses whispered to him. Feeling a strange peace, Eamon left the garden.

He rode to the port that morning to inspect the final stages of the quay repair and meet with one of the throned's merchant allies. He brought valuable Gauntlet men from their postings in Etraia. Fletcher rode with him, maintaining a stony silence, but Eamon did not mind it. He listened to the horses as they clattered across the cobbles and the stones, then watched as the gates opened out onto the sheltered harbour. The waterfront was broad and encircled by a wide breaker that gave only a narrow, west-facing entrance and exit to the port. The throned's own fleet, a small affair, was decked in red and stood in the shallows to the southern end of the harbour, while those craft docking or awaiting entrance or exit moved through the waters by virtue of oars and sails. Beyond the circle of the breakers, a line of craft moved on the swaying waters, taking turns to make use of the port-mouth.

"There is no need for you to trouble yourself overly with this meeting, my lord," Fletcher told him as they rode. "It is, however, important that Etraia sees we hold them in high enough regard to send you to meet a captain."

Eamon nodded. Etraia was the staunchest of the Master's merchant allies and the supplier of the vast quantities of grain that Dunthruik needed after the winter. In exchange, Dunthruik supplied arms, cloths, and wines from Ravensill.

Fletcher looked up to the harbour, then back to Eamon. "The most important part in dealing with the Etraian seamen, my lord, is never to ask them how their journey was, unless it is absolutely necessary."

"Oh?" Eamon asked, surprised. It was not a warning he had been given before. "I would have thought it the very first question to ask a man of the sea. It is brave work that they do, even in the summer months."

Fletcher leaned towards him and lowered his voice a little. "These ships cross the Straits of Etraia, my lord. It is a narrow and dangerous sea path between the western-most point of the River Realm and the eastern-most part of Etraia. Making use of it greatly shortens the journey between the northern and eastern regions of Etraia and Dunthruik. But these captains…" he paused. "They enjoy spinning a story from such things."

"And this is a problem?"

"It is invariably a *long* story, Lord Goodman." Fletcher's eyes glazed over slightly and Eamon wondered how many of these stories his lieutenant had endured.

They reined in their steeds at the quayside and waited while a great ship docked. The port-hands called to one another as they tied down ropes and secured the moorings. The ropes strained as the ship moved with the tide, but this did not impede the docking and the lowering of the gang.

After a time, the vessel's captain sauntered down. He was broad-shouldered and tanned. But for his colourings, he reminded Eamon of Giles. The captain's step was heavy as he came aground.

Fletcher dismounted at once and greeted the captain. The captain smiled and bowed warmly.

"Mr Fletcher!" he called. "A pleasure to see you! What a crossing I have had!"

The lieutenant drew a deep breath of resignation, and asked about the captain's journey. The sailor launched into his tale with great gusto, while the lieutenant forced a grin and nodded sporadically throughout the telling.

CHAPTER V

As the tale continued, Eamon took pity on his lieutenant. He dismounted and approached the captain.

The captain halted. "My lord," he acknowledged with a deep bow.

"A fair tide, I trust?" Eamon asked. Fletcher shot him a pained look of warning.

"Indeed," the captain answered, drawing breath, "though at the straits –"

"I have come to express to you the Lord of Dunthruik's personal pleasure with the service and fealty which Etraia brings to us at this time," Eamon interrupted. "Mr Fletcher is well acquainted with the form that this thanks will take and will discuss it with you on my behalf." On this occasion, it was to take the form of a vast number of Ravensill's finest wines – which were highly valued in the merchant state – as well as timber and stone from Dunthruik's ample supplies.

The captain inclined his head grandly. "The Master's thanks mean much to us, my lord Right Hand."

"I leave you to Mr Fletcher, captain," Eamon said.

"Of course, lord."

Eamon mounted his horse again and turned back for the port gate, leaving Fletcher and the captain to make the requisite arrangements.

As he urged Sahu on to the gate, he caught sight of a group of Gauntlet working at the quayside to bring grain down off a merchant galley. This had become a frequent sight at the port in recent weeks, but Eamon paused as he heard a familiar voice calling orders for the workers.

"The next load to the West house!" the voice called. The men hauled the grain across to a storehouse on the waterfront, from which men from each quarter would collect it.

The man giving orders was Manners. The cadet wore full Gauntlet uniform once again and bore two flames at his collar. He was cadet no longer.

Manners looked up and saw Eamon staring. The lieutenant gave a few more orders to the men at work and then approached Eamon.

"Lord Goodman," he said and bowed.

"Lieutenant," Eamon answered. The word was cumbersome on his tongue.

Manners had been sworn.

"Can I be of any assistance to you, my lord?" Manners asked.

"No," Eamon breathed. He stared for a moment at the tall ship and its workers.

"There were new orders for the grain this morning," Manners said quietly, following Eamon's gaze to the ship. "They have taken everyone by surprise. We have been told that every quarter is to hoard grain, against a siege."

It took a long time for Eamon to understand what he said. Suddenly he gaped. "Every quarter?"

"We are to set it aside now, much as I am told Draybant Greenwood used to do on your behalf," Manners continued, "but, to make the storage quota commanded by the palace, much is being withdrawn from circulation in the city as well. Lord Arlaith was here earlier this morning," Manners added, "proclaiming that this command came from the palace on your initiative."

Eamon felt as though a blow took him from behind. He would be held to blame for the soaring grain prices once more, only this time not simply in the East Quarter, but in the whole city.

"Do they speak ill of me?"

"Mine do not," Manners answered firmly. "Not every man will understand this command, my lord, nor that it came from the Master and not yourself."

"They will curse me for taking the food from their plates, and be justified," Eamon answered quietly. The grain would go from the people to the Gauntlet. He could imagine Arlaith, riding through the East Quarter, tearing grain from those who sold or prepared their bread, and saying in a high and commiserating tone that the command had come from the Right Hand...

Eamon pressed his eyes closed a moment. He should rejoice that the reserves would go back, that the whole city, not the East alone, would now be prepared against a siege. It was more than he had dreamed when he had first begun the hoard… But he felt no joy; he felt sick. The hoarded grain would feed the Gauntlet. His service to the people of Dunthruik would be as a blow to Hughan, when he came.

He was silent for a long time.

"Do not take it to heart, my lord," Manners told him gently. "Rumour has trammelled many names, even your own, before, and no harm has come of it."

"This time she does rightly," Eamon answered miserably. Manners frowned at him. "The Master gave this order for my sake, cadet…" He paused and shook his head. "Lieutenant," he corrected himself bitterly.

Manners saw the look on his face and bowed again. "My lord, might I speak frankly for a moment?"

"Yes," Eamon replied dully.

Silently he dismounted. The quay was busy and Eamon felt as though every man stared at him, the hated grain-hoarder of Dunthruik; but as he looked about himself he saw that none watched the Right Hand as he held conference with a lowly lieutenant of the West Quarter.

"My lord, I know what you see," Manners began, "and I know why it should render you grief." He gestured discreetly to the flames on his uniform.

Eamon looked at him carefully. He remembered Manners' promise of long ago, to serve whom he served… Did Manners now speak truly?

He matched the lieutenant's gaze. Could he risk believing what he had said? What if Manners was simply another piece designed to hedge him round with treachery? He had to hold to the King…

Should that mean no more than static clinging? He had taken great risks every day since he had arrived in Dunthruik and yet, since he had become Right Hand, his courage had dwindled to near nothing.

Did he dare risk it all on Manners?

"Why should I be grieved at your appointment?" he asked at last.

"It is not yet a formal appointment," Manners replied quietly. "Captain Waite lost so many men at the quay, and in the collapse at college –"

"Collapse?" Eamon asked, aghast.

"Yes, my lord," Manners answered grimly. "One of the walls in the ensigns' dormitories collapsed early this morning." Eamon stiffened, knowing that was where newly sworn Banners had habitually been stationed for rest.

"You were there?" he asked.

"No," Manners replied. "My watch duties were changed late last night. Fielder was taken ill; Waite asked me to cover him." Manners paused heavily and Eamon watched as he brushed a wisp of hair away from his face where it struck at his eye. "Fielder is dead," he said bravely.

Eamon was crushed. Was there nothing but death in the city of Dunthruik?

"How could this happen?" he whispered.

Manners had no answer for him. "I do not know, my lord," he said. He drew a deep breath. "Captain Waite is looking into the matter, as is Lord Cathair, I believe. The architects maintain that there was no fault with the lodgings…" He trailed off, then looked up again. "Captain Waite needs to maintain college numbers and could not siphon any other man from any of the regional units stationed in the West. He asked me to assume lieutenant duties. He has no one else, my lord."

Eamon stared at him. If Manners had "assumed"…

"Then…" he paused. "You're not sworn?"

"No," Manners answered and a small smile touched his face. "My record still precludes that, I fear."

Relief flooded through Eamon. "I am glad, Lieutenant Manners," he whispered. He could have embraced the lieutenant with joy but had the sense to restrain himself. "I cannot tell you how glad." He drew a deep breath. "Mr Manners…" he began.

Manners cast a glance across to the workers. Following his glance, Eamon saw Lord Dehelt on the quay. The North Quarter Hand saw them and approached.

"Lord Goodman," he said, bowing.

Eamon swallowed down the words that he had meant to speak to Manners. "Lord Dehelt."

"The new grain edict comes at your insistence?" Dehelt asked quietly.

Eamon met his gaze. "Yes," he answered. There was no use in denying it.

"The city shall tighten its belt," Dehelt mused. Suddenly he looked at Eamon and smiled. "This edict was long overdue, Lord Goodman," Dehelt said and bowed his head. "The North thanks you for it."

Eamon stared at him, bereft of words. Bowing once more, Dehelt excused himself and moved along the quay. He soon joined a group of merchants at the waterfront and began to speak with them.

Eamon watched him go, feeling fear and joy clashing in him. Manners turned to him. When Eamon met the lieutenant's gaze he saw fire in the young man's eyes.

"Courage, Lord Goodman," he said. Then Manners bowed and returned to his work.

Returning along the Coll towards the palace, Eamon felt strangely lightheaded. His grief at the news of the college collapse was immense; he could only imagine how Waite was handling the matter. To keep the West encouraged in the face of such a bizarre disaster would be no easy task. But in the great bustle of men in Dunthruik, he supposed the city would count them only as numbers that could not be fielded at battle. What mattered to the quarter was maintaining its parade strength.

Against all odds Manners was safe – and he was not sworn. And Dehelt… he raised one hand to his head as he thought once again of the Hand's words. Dehelt had confidence in him. Both were sparks of hope, small glimmers as of the spring sun rising against the dark wall of the world. They spoke quietly to him of things he had forgotten.

Holding to the King was not simply about maintaining a grip, as a quarter sought to maintain its numbers, nor maintaining it so harshly that soon what was sought diminished and slipped from the man who grasped it. Holding fast to the King was about fearless, just, and loving service. They were things that Edelred could never command from him.

As he rode he caught sight of the high roof of the Crown Theatre, closed like the petals of a flower. With a start he remembered that he was its patron and had not yet appeared there, though the Master had encouraged him to. To know of his authority over the place and look at the tall walls, the eagled gates, and the splendid doors… was an odd feeling.

He remembered Mr Grennil speak of his love for the "commoner" theatrical performances that any citizen of Dunthruik could attend. Eamon knew that the theatre would throw an inaugural performance for its new patron. Indeed, Fletcher had told him that the theatre already prepared it.

He had no other duty to attend to that morning, so with a gentle tug he turned Sahu and directed the animal down the Coll to the theatre.

Rather than ascend the broad marble steps at the front of the theatre, where tall eagles bore serpent-twined talons, he took his horse down past the western sweep of the building to the passage that ran beneath it to the alighting area for carriages. This was a great stone hollow beneath the body of the theatre, designed to receive traffic coming from one direction and feed it back out onto the Coll in another. There was space for the keeping of horses set further back.

The carriageway was still and silent as Eamon halted in the hollow. The theatre's floor arched, roof-like, above his head; the ceiling was painted with a great portrait of the city of Dunthruik which was held at its corners by the feet of stone eagles, who soared outwards towards the branching stone arches that supported the roof.

As he stood marvelling at the work, footsteps rushed towards him. Several pale servants arrived.

"Lord Goodman," one panted, coming to a hurried stop and bowing. "We meant you no disservice or displeasure. If we had but known –"

"It's quite all right –"

"– you would have found more fitting welcome."

"I did not myself know that I was coming," Eamon laughed kindly, "and will not fault you for my vagaries."

The servant fell silent, though whether due to surprise or his heaving chest was hard to tell. One of his fellows brought a mounting block.

Eamon thanked him and dismounted. "May I go in?"

The servant looked astounded. "Of course, my lord," he replied. "Would you have me guide you?"

"I shall find my way, thank you." Eamon gazed at a tall, circular stairwell that wound up into the theatre's entrance hall. Smiling once at the gathered servants, he went in.

The stairwell had a handrail running up to its top, on which were carved a long line of animals caught in an endless run and, where the stair met a doorway, two birds with huge, colourful tails had been painted. Stepping beneath the fanned arch of their stony plumage, he entered a grand hall.

The hall was octagonal in shape and rimmed with dark wooden doors. The floor bore a grand mosaic and there were painted trees carved into the lintels between the doors. They alternated between vine, ash, oak, and yew, and their hewn boughs intertwined over each doorway. The doors bore alternating black and gold eagles whose brows were crowned with golden diadems pierced with red.

Eamon hazarded a guess as to which door he should take: the one across from him stood open. As he passed over the central stones of the chamber floor, his footsteps were magnified by the domed roof over his head. He paused and looked up into the ceiling. At the dome's cap, a shining painted sun dropped rays to the leafy arches of the doors.

Unable to resist, Eamon called up into the dome; his voice came back to him wondrously grand. Leaning his head back he dared to lift his voice in song, singing words and a tune that came unbidden to him:

> *Star beam of the heavens deep,*
> *Star-song strong and star-fire sweet,*
> *Rising, shining, ever true,*
> *Light these stones and make them new!*

The beams and arches of the dome sang back to him. He laughed; the whole hall filled with it.

The open door led into a reception hall lined with magnificent candelabra. As he strolled past its huge windows, Eamon caught a stunning glimpse of the Four Quarters. Each window in the hall was strung with red drapes and he saw himself, a moving shadow, pass before the elegant glass.

He turned and looked at the hall. It was made from wood and marble and to either side ran tall staircases. It was where he had entered the night he had come with Alessia. His eyes traced the stairs, following those that led up to the private boxes. He saw what marked the grand doorway: the keystone was embossed with a great black eagle, bearing a golden crown at its breast.

Eamon stared at it. The black eagle was the mark of the Right Hand. At its very door, the theatre proclaimed that it was in his keeping.

He heard sounds beyond the doors and fell still. Sounds of singing, stopping and starting, drifted in the quiet air, barely discerned incantations.

Another servant approached him. She curtseyed deeply.

"My lord," she said. "What a great honour it is to have you

here!" She clearly meant it, for she smiled warmly. "How may we be of service?"

"Is the master of the theatre here?" he asked.

The servant laughed. "He stands before me, my lord!"

Eamon smiled. "Its director, then?"

"Within," the servant gestured towards the auditorium. "What would you, my lord?"

"I would arrange a commoner. In fact," he added, a great smile flooding his face, "I would like my inaugural to be a commoner."

The servant watched him for a moment. "Your inaugural, my lord?"

"I too am a citizen of this city."

"Shall I have the director, Mr Shoreham, come to you?"

"Is he indisposed?"

The servant gestured to the doors of the auditorium. "They are rehearsing, my lord, but –"

Eamon nodded. "I do not wish to disturb them," he said. "Perhaps you would speak to him on my behalf?"

"Of course, my lord."

"Thank you." Eamon looked up at the closed doors and listened to the music that moved behind them.

"You can go in, if you wish it, my lord."

Eamon paused. It was tempting. "I should not disturb them," he said at last.

"There is a passage here that leads to the back of the auditorium, my lord. You may enter from there without disturbing them."

Eamon smiled. "I would like that."

He followed her as she passed across the hall to a passage beneath one of the sets of stairs. It wound about in a semicircle for a short distance until it reached a small wooden door. Voices and music sounded on the other side of it.

The servant quietly opened the door and bowed again as she stepped aside to grant him passage. "My lord," she said.

Eamon smiled gratefully. Without a word, he stepped through.

It was much cooler inside the theatre than in its hall. Eamon had forgotten how enormous a space it was; the crimson-clad seats rose in tiers towards boxed walls and the great ceiling. He knew that the roof could be opened, and indeed it stood partially open so that the stage and pit were lit by the May light. Musicians in the pit tweaked their instruments and followed on the words of a bearded man who moved his hand to demonstrate the melody of a passage of music. Eamon assumed this man to be Shoreham.

Gathered on the stage were a number of men and women. They spoke together in lowered voices and fell silent as the director moved into their midst. He indicated a spot at the front of the stage with radiated arms, then gestured up to the highest boxes. Eamon could not catch what he said, but guessed the director's meaning well enough.

He was certain no one in the rehearsal had seen him, a black shadow in the darkened recesses of the theatre. He slipped down the seating area towards the stage. When he was close enough that he could hear clearly, but far enough away to avoid being seen, he stepped to one side and sat down.

The director finished giving notes to the musicians, and turned to the actors and singers on the stage. "Ilenia, can we have your piece, please?"

One of the singers looked through her notes. "The third lyric?"

"No. I'm sorry. I meant the promise piece."

The singer stepped forward. She was an elegant woman with bright eyes. While she may have worn her hair long in her youth she now had her dark tresses drawn neatly back behind her head, accenting the features of her face. She wore no makeup or costume, simply her ordinary garb, and her figure did not seem imposing; but as she stepped up to the front of the stage a strange hush fell on those around her.

The director swooped by the lip of the pit to check a last-minute matter with the musicians. The conductor tapped the air with his hand. On the third tap the musicians began to play.

The music was low and gentle at first, barely audible, pitched through with notes of sorrow and melancholy.

Chapter V

Eamon's mind slowed, and in that slowness something deep within him stirred and answered the music as it lifted in an earnest passion before growing gentle again. Then the singer drew breath, and sang:

> As roses smell their sweetest after rain
> So is your love, so deep and high and wide,
> Most dear when all my other comforts wane,
> And to my errant heart both staff and guide.
> For snares have bound me like a coiling chain
> A storm o'erwhelms me as a wrathful tide
> And yet the thorn reminds me in my pain
> You too have suffered and have been denied.
> So when I see the rose I cast aside
> The treasures, empty riches, I have stored,
> What place have I for boldness or for pride
> When I behold your crimson robe, my lord?
>
> Pray have compassion in your mercies vast,
> Turn not your ear from this my earnest plea:
> Though faithless once, now faithful to the last,
> I'll wait beyond the wilting of the tree.
> Come forth! Let me behold your shining mast
> And carry me across the friendless sea!
> Exiled I am in homelands of my past
> For I am dead to them and they to me.
> Bound in your arms of love I shall be free
> And give you all I have; then my reward,
> My highest joy and only boast shall be
> That I am yours alone, my love, my lord.

The words poured through Eamon, touching every part of every sense he had, filling them with keen, heart-splitting sorrow. But there, the music formed a waxing hope that stole away his breath: to suffer, and yet to hold and strive, was not his lot alone.

He felt tears in his eyes. Suddenly they were free, and freely fell, flowing in silence down his cheeks. He did not seek to hinder them. For a blissful moment he sat in the darkness unseen, and the music replenished and comforted him. He too had but one lord.

The singer fell silent, the music faded. She stood for a moment, wrapped in fading song, then opened her eyes and smiled. The director beamed and clapped his hands with sheer delight.

"I have no words, Ilenia," he said, shaking his head. "That is marvellous. Why, the Right Hand himself would weep to hear you!"

Ilenia curtseyed.

The director called up a pair of other actors and took them through various spots on the stage, taking care to indicate where the light from the candelabra and braziers would fall. While he gestured, the singer descended the stage steps into the rows of seats. She walked a good distance into the seating area and as she came closer, Eamon could not help but smile.

Suddenly she stopped. Seeing him, she cocked her head at him.

"The master propsman has excelled himself!" she laughed; her voice was as beautiful in speaking as it was in singing. "You look just like a Hand! As good as true. Isn't the dress tomorrow?"

"I am afraid I do not know," Eamon answered her.

Hearing his voice, the singer peered forward at him.

"I am so sorry! I mistook you for Marcus," she said, watching him. "Are you the new singer for the chorus of Hands?"

"I would covet the opportunity," Eamon told her truthfully, "but alas! I am not."

Carefully, he rose from his seat and stepped into the aisle. She gasped.

"My lord," she said, and curtseyed deeply before him.

"Madam Ilenia," Eamon told her, "you have done me honour beyond my dues by your song." He reached out, took her hand, and pressed it in his own. "I thank you."

The singer stared. "Are you Lord Goodman?" Her eyes took in his features with surprise.

"I am, madam."

"Then the honour, my lord, is mine alone." She smiled. "I am glad if the song spoke to you."

Eamon felt a great laugh in his heart and beamed at her.

"Please tell Mr Shoreham that I very much look forward to the fruits of his labour," he said. "I have already spoken to one of the servants, but perhaps you would convey to him that I would have my inaugural performance made a commoner?"

"Of course."

"Thank you again, madam." Eamon let go her hand and walked down the aisle to the great doors. They opened before him, flooding the room with light, revealing him to the whole stage.

Not since he had sung with Mathaiah in the Pit had he felt such joy.

That evening he asked his servants to bring him supper in his quarters; as he dined, his only company were the papers from the day's work. Among the Hands' reports were also papers from two of the Master's generals: Rocell, who had charge of the knights, and Cade, who had responsibility for the thresholders – the non-Gauntlet men who would be called up from the Four Quarters to defend the city. Eamon had met neither general but suspected that would change in short order. Madam Ilenia's song went round and round his mind as he read, rendering the task more bearable.

As a maid raised a flask of wine Eamon looked up. "Excuse me," he said. The maid nearly dropped the flask in surprise.

"My lord?" she recovered swiftly.

"Are you able to tell me where Mr Cartwright is?"

"Iulus, my lord?"

"Yes."

"I shall send for him."

"That would be kind, thank you."

The maid filled his glass, curtseyed, and left the rooms. Her feet pattered away down the servants' stairs.

He read through another dozen pages of the reports, stopping to make notes in the margins on various things. Steps returned to the servants' door.

"You sent for me, my lord?"

Eamon rose immediately to his feet, set his papers down on the table, and strode across to his servant.

"Mr Cartwright," he said without preamble, "I have treated you appallingly." The man was amazed. "I poured scorn on you and your service when I howled at you last night – I will not call it speech – and it was ill of me to do so. I scarcely think to thank you for all you do for me, I repay you with rancour and harsh words, and yet still you do as I ask."

The servant looked overwhelmed. Eamon drew a breath and tried to speak more slowly. "This place can be no less terrifying for you than it is for me, and I have not aided you in bearing that burden."

"Terrifying?" Cartwright asked. "My lord, the walk of a servant and of a Right Hand can hardly be compared –"

"Even if they could, it would not cede responsibility for what I have said and done," Eamon told him, "for it is said and done. I would understand your reluctance if you would not forgive me for it."

Cartwright held his gaze for a long moment. "Are you well, Lord Goodman?"

Eamon nodded. "I am," he said. "When I spoke wrongly to you last night, Mr Cartwright, I was distraught by matters that were not of your doing. I had no right to offend you."

"What matters?" Cartwright asked, then stopped. "I am sorry, my lord. I do not mean to pry."

"You need not apologize to me," Eamon told him. "A great many things have happened in the city since I became Right Hand," he said at last. "People I care for have been injured and killed. I have seen work undone that I sorely laboured to achieve, and that grieves me all the more, knowing that it is the city that will suffer for that undoing.

"Every day there is news of some new malaise, of dead ensigns and lieutenants, of blood spilled needlessly, of people starving and going to the pyres. The Master looks to me to show his glory and the city looks to me to make it new." He trailed off, his voice catching.

Cartwright watched him with wide eyes. Eamon matched his gaze. "There are wounds I bear, Mr Cartwright, that go deeper than these, but I cannot burden you with them." He breathed deeply and his heart, tempered by the song that he had heard that day, began speaking words he had not thought he could say.

"Lady Alessia was dear to me," he whispered, "the dearest thing I had. Doubtless she did what she had to do, but she hurt me – more deeply than almost any other hurt I have borne. It is that hurt which spoke through me last night," he said. "I should not have permitted it to strike at you also. Your mistress was a noble lady," he managed, "and unswerving in her service to the Master."

"Yes, my lord." Cartwright watched him with suspicion.

"Mr Cartwright," Eamon began again, "from the very first I have mistreated you, for I commanded what I should have humbly asked." He met the servant's curious gaze. "I will not keep you here against your will. If you would leave my service, I freely give you leave to go. I will give you any aid or assistance that you require, be it horse or purse or lodgings. I presumed to set you in my house; that was wrong of me."

Iulus Cartwright was stunned. "You would let me go?"

"On me the city rests," Eamon answered. "How may I see to it when I cannot judge rightly in my own house? I have done you wrong. For you, for me, and for my house, I would amend it."

Cartwright was silent for a long time. Eamon feared that he would choose to go. What comfort would there then be for him? Yet, what comfort would the man be, if his staying were enforced?

"You bear all these things?" Cartwright asked. "All these woes and griefs?"

"Perhaps I make them sound more weighty than they are; that, or I bear them badly."

"Forgive me, my lord," Iulus managed. "I was not clear. I mean to say, you bear all this – all of this – and yet, you howl at a single servant?"

"To do so at even a single servant is to do so at one too many."

Cartwright shook his head in amazement. "You are not who people say you are, Lord Goodman."

Eamon looked at him in surprise, though he knew not why it should surprise him that the servants in the palace, or the men and women in the city, spoke of him. "Who do they say I am?"

"They call you the sword-ceder and pine-feller; head-winner and grain-hoarder; house-builder and plain-rider; glorious favourite of the Master, and base-born son of a vagabond house."

Eamon laughed. "I would not answer to any of those names – though perhaps to some of the deeds."

Iulus looked down at his hands, which he joined together nervously.

"Mr Cartwright," Eamon said quietly. "Who do you say I am?"

Iulus was silent for a moment, then drew breath. "I believe, my lord," he mused, "that in all the names they give you, and all the stories they tell of you, the men and women of this city, as they hear and speak of you, forget. They forget that, when all those names have fallen from their lips and all is said and done, you are simply a man."

Eamon smiled. "In fairness, I think that I forget it, too."

"But," Iulus added, looking up, "you are a good man."

"Thank you."

There was a long silence. Eamon forced himself to wait through it, to stand with patience, and determined to keep his word whatever choice the man made.

At last, Iulus looked up. "You mean what you say? I may go if I wish it?"

With difficulty, Eamon nodded.

CHAPTER V

Cartwright looked about the quarters then rubbed awkwardly at his arm. Then he crossed to the table where Eamon's unfinished meal lay.

"I am sorry; with all our talk your supper is growing cold, my lord. Would you take some fruit?"

"Mr Cartwright, I should like nothing better."

"I will arrange it, my lord." So saying, the servant left the room.

Feeling light of heart Eamon sat. The fruit brought before him never tasted better.

CHAPTER VI

Two days passed, during which time Eamon saw the repair of the quay completed and the fortifications at the south wall brought to their conclusion. Reports spoke eloquently on the matter of the new grain edict. Much of the East's grain store had been put into circulation, but the whole had not been exhausted. Eamon was relieved by this, and his hope and heart were strengthened. Even so, the Master's smile and touch unnerved him, perhaps never more so than when he thanked him for the grain edict. He wondered whether the command had been given less for the city of Dunthruik and more for the fraught sensibilities of the Right Hand. In either case, it was an indulgence and Edelred's indulgences were fickle and perilous.

The whole city was in a preparative mood, and the streets teemed with Gauntlet. Eamon received word from Shoreham at the Crown, saying that they would be delighted to hold an inaugural commoner. Performances would be ready for delivery on the tenth of May. The news encouraged him greatly, as did Cartwright's ongoing presence in his house.

The Master's doctor continued to monitor him and at last promised to drop the threat of leeches, seeing no need for them. Eamon thanked him wholeheartedly.

He returned once or twice to the rose garden, but always alone and in secret. The place was more enduring, it seemed, than the palace that surrounded it, and Eamon wondered how long it had stood in that secluded corner beneath the eagle's very wing.

On the afternoon of the ninth of May, Fletcher came to him. "Lord Goodman?"

"Mr Fletcher," Eamon acknowledged, looking up from his latest report. "How was your meeting with the Master's secretary?"

"It went well, my lord," Fletcher replied. "We ironed out a few of the quibbles in how the Master's house and yours interact."

"I am glad of it."

"He sends me word that the Master wishes to see you, my lord."

Eamon frowned; he had been with the Master not an hour before.

"I shall go at once. Please could you have these papers delivered to Lord Dehelt?"

"Of course. The Master is in his quarters."

Eamon tried not to blanch. When the Master summoned him it was usually to the throne room, or to the private dining room. The idea of going to the Master's own quarters…

He swallowed. "Thank you, Mr Fletcher."

He could have taken the south balcony but he feared to go that way. Instead he took the corridors to the West Wing with practised speed. Reaching the corridors where the tailors had measured him, Eamon followed all the way to a grand staircase at the end of the long passage. The steps were fashioned from red and black marble with banisters bound boldly with gold filigree.

Eamon paused at the foot of the grand case, his heart pounding, and gazed up into the darkness. He saw nothing but a tall window high above him. It looked out to the open sky.

He saw none in the hall. He set his foot to the first stair; his step echoed upwards with dreadful clarity.

He felt giddy as he climbed up to the high landing. There he found a long hallway stretching out before him, lit by streams from huge windows. The carpet showed a sea of snakes that were crushed beneath Eamon's feet as he walked the hall. He shuddered and hurried on.

Two of the throned's own house stood guard at his monumental chamber doors. These men did not incline their heads towards him nor make any gesture of respect; they simply opened the door. It parted back, opening into an enormous reception hall where every detail was red and gold. Eamon staggered; he had not eyes and brain

CHAPTER VI

enough to take in the opulence that lay before him in an endless
landscape of gilt blood.

He heard a noise as a servant, doubtless as mute as those who
served at breakfast, bowed then rose and walked to one of the hall's
many doors.

"Am I to follow?" Eamon asked.

The servant gestured along the corridor and moved on. Feeling
shaken, Eamon followed.

They walked silently into the corridor beyond. It led to another
grand door whose dark panels bore eagles. The carved creatures held
a book between them and the handles of the doors were like thickly
coiled snakes.

Eamon shuddered as the servant reached forward and knocked
three times on the door with a firm hand. He stepped back as the door
opened inward on a fiery room. The servant receded, then retreated.
The door lay open before him. Eamon recognized the floor, the walls,
and the light: he had been there before, in dark dreams of long ago.

"Come hither, son of Eben."

Girding on every ounce of courage, Eamon approached. The
doors closed behind him.

The Master stood by a great window, so high that Eamon felt
dizzy to see it. The sunlight streaked the Master with gold.

He turned to look at his Right Hand. "There is little that escapes
me, son of Eben."

"How could anything escape you?" Eamon breathed. In that
moment, surrounded by light and framed by the high window, the
throned seemed more powerful and unassailable than Eamon had
ever seen him. There was iron beauty in his face as he turned his
grey eyes towards his Right Hand.

The Lord of Dunthruik laughed softly. "You know this place,
son of Eben."

"Yes."

Eamon looked at the walls. They were red, but nothing adorned
them; there were no eagles and no twists of gold. They were simply

137

red, as was the floor. In the centre of the room stood a broad table made from dark, wizened wood. It was strangely carved in no style that Eamon had ever seen in Dunthruik, though the fluted edges reminded him of the ceiling in the East Handquarter.

On the table was an ornate glass orb in which rose ruddy light. Eamon stared at it. He assumed it to be a lamp but could not see how it burned and did not dare ask. The strange light illuminated the whole room and showed forth letters set deep in the wood of the table. Eamon shuddered at their rigid forms: the same letters hung on the blade at his side and those same letters marked a design on the paving stones beneath his feet. Everywhere the letters swirled around him. He stood at the centre of the great web of words where every stroke seemed aimed at him.

The Master came to him. "You have proven yourself sure in my service, son of Eben." It was a terrifying pronouncement. "I have seen the work of your hands and I have received it with joy."

"Ever to your glory, Master," Eamon answered. He bowed his head, fearfully reducing his gaze to some unmarked part of the floor on which he stood. Even so, from the corner of his eye he saw the throned. It was as though a roaring lion prowled about him, waiting for the moment to take him by the throat.

Yet never could a lion seem as majestic as the Master that stood before him, regarding him with a deeper gaze than he felt he could know or endure. Eamon tried to meet it but he could not equal the vastness of the Master's power; it was enthralling.

"What would you, Master?"

Those grey eyes looked at him, testing him, assessing him. He had to excel their every desire and command! Eamon's heart raced, his blood pulsed. He desired the Master's council, more than all else! This man, this very man, was the desire of his heart…

Eamon, be true. You have one lord alone. Hold to him.

He blinked. What caused this change in him? He looked at the Master with renewed fear, for he knew too well the sway that the throned held over the hearts of men. It had swayed Eben and it

sought to sway him. Heat grew in his palm and brow. The fire of
the throned's mark lived there. Even as he tried to stem the flames,
his soul issued from them as from open wounds. The letters on the
ground about him were on fire. They glinted evilly in the light.

Astounded, he leapt back; the fire subsided and the Master smiled.

"These letters know you, son of Eben. Do you know them?"

"I have seen their like, Master." Eamon's thought went to the
Nightholt and his hand strayed anxiously to the blade at his side.

"Yes, they are on your blade," the throned told him. "They are
on your doors and on your posts, in your heart and in your blood,
for in striking your blood was bound. But there is another place
where you will find them, one that you have not seen." The Master
reached out and traced Eamon's face. "It is of this which we must
speak, now that your loyalty to me is proven."

Eamon shivered. For a moment the Master seemed lost in
thought, but then his eyes returned to Eamon's own.

"Son of Eben, these letters are also to be found in a book."

Eamon gaped at him in alarm. The Master knew it.

"A – a... book?"

"At the time of its writing, it was known as the *Tierrascuro*,"
the throned told him. The air chilled about Eamon as the ancient
word tumbled from the Master's mouth. "In the tongue of the River
Realm, it is known as –"

"The Nightholt," Eamon breathed. He spoke out the name at
the same moment as the Lord of Dunthruik.

The Master glared. "How do you know of this?" he demanded.
His voice, festooned before with indulgence, now grew deathly.

"Master, I have seen it."

Silence. More terrible than any other.

"What did you say?" the Master hissed.

"I…" Eamon searched the Master's face uncomprehendingly. "I
have seen it, Master," he whispered. "That is how I know."

An ear-splitting roar rent the air and suddenly the whole room
seemed ripped in two with flame. Eamon staggered as the floor trembled

beneath his feet and the unfettered power of the Master's fury screamed across him with an intensity that might slash flesh from bone.

"You would mock me!"

Eamon shook his head in horror. "No –"

Then the red light came.

Eamon saw it leave the Master's hands, saw it striking across at him and knew even as it came that he could do nothing to halt it.

"Master!"

But it was too late.

The fire reached him and clawed into his body, arching through him and forcing him down to his knees in spasms of agony. Eamon tried to move his limbs, as though he might send the hideous power of the light from him, but his struggles merely gave it strength. The light careered through him and mauled him like ravening wolves; it moved like lightning between blood and bone, rocketing through him as though it meant to shatter him.

Suddenly it stopped.

The Master stood over him, rage in his grey eyes. Eamon wept in torment – did this man not love him?

"I have seen it!" he screamed.

The Master's face creased with hatred. "Vile liar!"

"I do not lie!" Eamon cried, but the light returned. He howled as it went back into him; his skin boiled at its touch and every nerve and tissue in his frail limbs jarred violently.

The Master stopped again. There were tears on Eamon's face and they seared down his cheeks and jowls like liquid fire as he sobbed.

"Master," he begged, "I held it! I brought it out of Ellenswell with my own hands!" The throned raised his hands. Eamon shrank back with sobs of fear. The letters on the ground beneath his palms scorched him like molten iron.

The light came again. It consumed him, searing and rending, lacerating and scouring to the unimaginable depths of his wretched, writhing body. Again and again it came, until Eamon felt that he could bear it no more.

What of the King's grace?

Somehow, in the throes of his torment, he remembered it. Of all the powers that he knew, the King's grace alone could stand against the hand and mark of the throned. It could save him.

In that very moment his thought and tongue clawed towards it, to beg it to release him from what he bore, and he felt supplicant howls rising to his lips.

"Hold to the King."

Mathaiah's dear voice washed through him, stilling the cries that clamoured to leave his mouth. It was then that he understood.

The King's grace could save him – and would if he asked it – but if he did, and it came, he would lose everything for which he had suffered, for the throned would see his heart.

That was why the King's grace had been silent. That was why it had not yet come. Eamon knew then that he was called to bear the anguish laid upon him by the throned's fury. He was called to endure it so as to serve the King.

In his roaring agony, while cracking flames lashed out again and again from hands that had caressed his face, Eamon summoned up the last of his ailing strength. With it, he held.

"I do not lie to you, Master!"

And the light dissolved.

Eamon did not know what prompted the sudden mercy. He could not see, could not hear, could scarcely feel. As he recognized the respite from the grip of the throned's power he shuddered and sobbed against the ground. Pain continued to dwell in him. Every breath he drew poured flame into his lungs while his blood was acid in his veins. He felt grisly blotches and burns all over his skin as he panted and wept.

Suddenly a hand reached down. It seized him by his gagging throat and drew him to his feet.

"This pained you, son of Eben?" Eamon could not answer him; all he could feel were his tears, thick about the Master's fingers and his own throat, like blood. "You will know pain far greater if you deceive me!"

With a baleful utterance the throned cast him to the ground. Eamon cried out at the burning stones. He tried to raise himself up, but his shaking hands had no strength. He coughed and vomited and the Master watched him with fury.

"Speak!"

"Cathair and Ashway took me." Eamon wrenched words from his throat; his sight returned to him and there was blood on his hands. He did not know whence it had come. Another spasm of pain vaulted through him. "They took me to Ellenswell." He staggered through each word, retching and gasping. "They took me to Ellenswell and I opened it – I had the key. My ward was with me. They told us to search the grave tunnel. I found the Nightholt."

"Where?" the Master demanded.

Eamon tried to splutter an answer but could not; his throat was scorched with bile.

"*Where!*"

Eamon's head spun, but he remembered.

"The tomb." He pressed his eyes shut and saw it. "In the tomb… I gave the book to Cathair; he said it was to go to the Right Hand; the Right Hand sent us…"

Suddenly he saw Mathaiah's face before his own, lit by the torches of the tunnels, and he remembered the odd look on that face as the cadet had breathed out words that had led to his death: "*I can read it…*"

He lost control and burst into choking sobs. "Mathaiah!" he wept.

"What has that snake to do with this?" the throned spat.

"They took him, Master. The Right Hand commanded it because…" Eamon could barely think. He was in Cathair's library, at the second case, eighth shelf up, left-hand side… He clutched his hands to the side of his head with a cry. "Because Mathaiah could read it!" he howled. "He could read the Nightholt. They killed him when he would not tell them what he read."

The silence was deathly. Eamon tried to restrain his sobbing, feeling nothing but the searing cruelty of the Master's gaze upon him.

He blinked hard. When he opened his eyes, he could see once more.

The Master strode the hall and tore back the door as though he would pull it from its hinges.

"Summon Lord Arlaith!" he commanded. Eamon froze as the Master cast his steely gaze across him.

"Get up," he hissed.

Clenching his jaw shut, Eamon rose. The marks on him melted back into his skin, as though he had never been touched. His head still swam, and he did not know where or if he bled. As he struggled to keep his feet, two servants scurried in; they cleaned the floor of his vomit and blood with efficient speed, then left.

The throned paced by the high window, pausing to look down from it onto the city below with irrepressible, impatient, sheer wrath. Eamon did not dare to meet his gaze as it alighted on him once again.

"Hold yourself like a Right Hand, Eben's son!" the Master fumed. Eamon straightened his shoulders and drew his head up.

"Your glory, Master." As he met the grey eyes he saw a flicker of a smile pass over the man's face. It chilled him to his quivering, ashen core.

He did not know how much time passed. He stood still in the centre of the hall and the Master ignored him. Fear and weariness mustered in his limbs and he struggled to contain himself. He did not understand the throned's rage. Surely Edelred had known that the Nightholt had been found?

He stole a glance at the Master's face, but it was utterly unreadable.

More time passed, then the Master suddenly strode towards him. Eamon quaked as the Master straightened his dishevelled robes.

"Stand by me, Eben's son." His voice was as gentle and untroubled as a spring breeze. Eamon turned and stood with the Master before the door.

Moments later Arlaith walked in. Eamon felt the man's sharp gaze fall on him, but Arlaith looked swiftly to the throned and bowed.

"Master," he said. "How may I serve you?"

"A well-asked question," the Master answered lightly, but then his face darkened. "Son of Eben, you will wait beyond."

Eamon saw Arlaith's eyes grow large with premonition. For a moment he almost pitied the Hand.

"Yes, Master." Eamon bowed and left slowly; walking was an effort.

Servants gathered him as soon as the doors closed and they led him, shivering, away. He barely noticed them; all his thought was on the room behind him. What wrath would the Master inflict on Arlaith? He did not like to think of it.

He was led to a wide side chamber that was lined with chairs. The silent servants had him sit. Eamon laid his shaking limbs down and exhaled. He felt ravaged.

Not long later one of the servants came up to him. The man held a large chalice of wine, which he held out. Eamon looked up; it was the servant whom he had thanked on the first morning that he had breakfasted with the Master. The servant's face was neutral, but he inclined his head as he held out the drink again.

Bereft of words, Eamon took it and drank. In that moment there seemed no kinder gesture to him in the world.

He waited and the servant waited by him. About him all was silent; it was as terrifying as the throned's fury.

Again, he did not know how much time passed; all was stillness. At last the servant looked towards him. The look was sure.

"Now?" Eamon asked.

The servant moved towards the door and Eamon followed.

They came back to the doorway and the eerie silence persisted. The doors opened; fear and wrath quivered in the air. His heart quickened and he went inside.

The Master was there, his face dire in the strange light. Arlaith knelt before him. The Hand looked wan, haggard; an almost imperceptible trembling wracked him.

The doors closed. Eamon looked at the throned and waited. The Master's swathe of anger was disturbingly lucid.

"Eben's son."

"Master."

"See this wretch?" The Master's baleful glance touched on Arlaith. Tears stormed in the Hand's eyes. "He is nothing but a Raven's dupe." The words sliced through the air with the force of sharpened steel. Arlaith knelt very still, as though his life hung upon a thread. Perhaps it did. Eamon did not dare speak. Both he and Arlaith waited on the Master's wrath.

"Cathair knew full well what you delivered to him, son of Eben," the Master spoke at last, "but your predecessor did not command that search. He had not the wit for it."

Eamon glanced silently at the Left Hand. Cathair was many things... could he really have betrayed the throned? Yet surely the Master would have breached Arlaith?

"Cathair has denied you praise which was justly yours," the throned continued, "and an artefact which is mine by right." His tone hardened. "Arlaith is lax and inept – but Cathair has knowingly, insolently wronged me. It will cost him dearly."

The throned gestured, curtly and disparagingly, at Arlaith. Stepping forward, Eamon touched the Hand's shoulder. The Lord of the East Quarter shuddered but endured him.

Slowly, gently, silently, Eamon raised Arlaith to his feet and steadied him as he sought his balance. Then the Master turned to them again.

"Son of Eben." The throned's voice cracked with authority.

"Master?"

"Go with Arlaith and reclaim what is mine. Bring it to me, along with Cathair's head."

Eamon blanched. "Master –"

"Bring me the treacherous vermin's head!" the throned roared. "Send his worthless body to the pyres and string his precious, wretched, blithering dogs at the Blind Gate!" The Master's eyes narrowed. "You will do it, son of Eben... and, to prove your worth, you will do it alone. Be sure that you serve me better than Arlaith."

Eamon bowed low. How could he possibly kill Cathair unaided?

But he could not gainsay the throned. "Yes, Master."

He and the Lord of the East Quarter left the room.

As the door closed behind them, Arlaith staggered. He gave a cry as his knees buckled and he crumpled to the floor. Eamon reached out to help him, but Arlaith recoiled.

"Don't touch me!"

Eamon looked at him. Arlaith was perhaps the man he hated most in the whole world, the man who had wronged him the most. Yet as he looked at him he thought suddenly of Hughan. His memory of the King's compassion washed over him and stole his breath away.

Was not Arlaith also a man?

"Are you hurt, Lord Arlaith?" Eamon asked.

Arlaith looked at him as though he were mad. "No," he hissed.

"Let me help you," Eamon answered.

"You have done enough," Arlaith spat. The Hand forced himself to his feet with an inhuman effort, then began a slow and unsteady walk down the corridor. A sheet of crumpled paper fluttered to the ground from his dishevelled robes.

"Is this yours, Lord Arlaith?" Eamon glanced up at the Left Hand, then stopped: Arlaith's face pallored to corpse-light.

"Is something the matter, Lord Arlaith?"

"No," Arlaith clipped. The Hand seemed fixated on the paper: every muscle and nerve was held in tension. "It does not concern you, Lord Goodman," he added, holding out his hand for the paper. His voice quivered.

It was the quiver that elicited his distrust. Holding Arlaith's gaze, Eamon turned the sheet to read it.

The paper bore a list of names. Some were grouped together, though there seemed to be little to associate them. Some weren't even names, merely titles or descriptions. Some of the names had marks by them, and some of those with marks had been crossed through; others had been underlined. Some had notes by them, but Eamon did not read them at first, for he did not understand.

The Left Hand stood motionless.

As he read the list a second time Eamon realized that he recognized the names; indeed, he knew every one. With a shocking start, he saw that many of those named were dead, and suddenly saw that the dead names were the ones that were marked through with a thick red line.

At the foot of the sheet was Lord Tramist's seal, and a note in his hand.

Eamon looked up slowly. "What is this?"

Arlaith did not move, did not breathe, did not answer. Horror and realization lurched to meeting, and Eamon turned incredulous eyes to the list again:

Serpentine keeper
~~Cart and Horse keeper~~
~~Lorentide~~
Grennils
Mr Fort
Patagon's servant
Stable hands – various
Seamstresses/maids – various
Slater
Cara
Callum
~~Marilio Bellis~~
Wilhelm Bellis
Not to be forgotten, All the 'Good Men'…
Cd. Manners, ~~Lieu. Ford,~~ Smith, ~~Ostler~~
~~Ens. Longham, Brighthall, Yarrow~~
~~Draybant Greenwood~~
Capt. Anderas
Ladomer Kentigern
Tureon
As required of me, T.

The nature of the list was suddenly, chillingly, all too clear to him.

"Bastard!" he yelled. "Conniving, murderous bastard!"

Arlaith said nothing. Eamon surged at him.

"You are behind their deaths! *Every one of them!*"

Arlaith trembled; the Hand would not meet his gaze. But Eamon's mind leapt from thought to thought: Tramist's hand. The glimpse of the breaching plain...

He knew it: Tramist had probed his thought as only breachers might. This list was the result.

"You did this... you did this to spite me!"

Arlaith's silence confirmed it. He glanced at the doors to the Master's chamber in terror.

Eamon seized him.

"The restoration list and the grain hoard! Holding my quarter! *Marilio!* It wasn't enough for you? You scheming bastard! What kind of man are you? These were good men! They were loyal to the Master – they served and protected this city!"

"I'm sorry!" Arlaith protested suddenly.

"What?" Eamon breathed.

Arlaith drew a shaking hand across his brow. "I was vindictive and petty. I am sorry."

There was a long silence between them. Eamon could only stare as Arlaith began to quiver uncontrollably.

For a moment he tried to forget his fury; all that remained of the Left Hand was a frightened man.

Eamon cast his predecessor aside and scoured the list again. "How many of these are in progress?"

"What?" Arlaith murmured distractedly.

"How many are threatened by your assassins?"

"I'll call them off," Arlaith told him. "I'll do it now, as soon as we leave the palace. You shall witness it."

Eamon watched him with restrained anger.

"If any of the men who have survived your schemes die of anything other than natural causes, Lord Arlaith, you will answer to me. Is that clear?" Arlaith nodded silently. "The men who were killed and arrested in the grain skirmish," Eamon added quietly. "Have they been cleared of treachery?"

"The survivors have been released, but there was a delay with the clearing orders –"

"You will organize funerals for Draybant Greenwood and the two ensigns who died," Eamon told him. "You will invite their families and the men who were falsely imprisoned. You will publicly clear all of their names and apologize for the deaths of men loyal to the crown."

"Yes."

"Have you commenced the re-hoarding?"

"No."

Eamon glowered. "There were commands from the Master, Arlaith!"

"I will put back thrice what you stored!" Arlaith cried earnestly. "I will cease being hostile to your house. I will run it in the way you would have it run."

Eamon blinked, then realized that Arlaith meant the servants in the East Quarter. He found his thought turning in horror to Cara, who had been the keeper of his room.

He turned to stare at Arlaith. The Hand seemed to follow his thought, for he matched Eamon's gaze.

"I have done nothing to the Handquarter's servants, Lord Goodman," he said quietly. "Neither will I."

Eamon believed him.

Silently, Eamon looked at the list again. Arlaith fidgeted, twisting at his cape-fastenings.

"You will not take this to the Master?"

Eamon looked up in surprise; the idea had not occurred to him.

Seeing his face Arlaith fell suddenly to his knees. "I beg of you, my lord!" The cry caught in the man's throat and he shuddered. "Do not take it to him!"

The supplication astounded him. Of course, he knew that if he were to take the paper and a lament to the throned then Arlaith would be killed. That death would be neither painless nor swift. He remembered the arching light that had struck through him.

He closed his eyes. He could not wish that on any man, even Arlaith.

Eamon folded Arlaith's papers into his own cloak. Then he leaned forward and touched Arlaith's shoulder.

"I would be within my rights to take it to him," he said. Arlaith looked up, ready to protest. Eamon gently shook his head. "But I will not do so."

Surprise flashed over Arlaith's face.

"I will not," Eamon said, simply, "unless it comes to pass that others listed here meet with an untimely demise. If I were you, I should see to it that you do everything in your power to protect them from harm lest some accident befall them and I be given cause to doubt the sincerity of your repentance."

Arlaith stared at him. "I do not think that I would have said the same in your place," he whispered.

They watched each other for a long moment. At a gesture from Eamon, Arlaith rose.

Before leaving the palace, they paused only long enough for Arlaith to set down and seal commands that his assassination orders be rescinded immediately. Eamon noted grimly that they were dispatched to Heathlode and Lonnam in the East Quarter, and resolved to be more careful of the two Hands in future.

They took steeds at the palace gates. Arlaith saddled uncertainly but, once there, seemed more himself. He exchanged neither word nor look with Eamon. As they reached Coronet Rise Eamon remembered the Master's commands. He looked across at Arlaith, whose face was stricken and jaded.

"Lord Arlaith, where will I find the Nightholt?" he asked.

Arlaith shivered, as though the words brought the Master's fire to his flesh again. "You were there when it was found?"

"In Ellenswell," Eamon nodded.

Arlaith could not disguise his ire. "Cathair told me that he kept some books that he found there that day. He claimed they were of no importance. Lying corpse-glut!"

It was convincing rage. Eamon reminded himself to be wary of the Left Hand. "Where will he have placed those books, Lord Arlaith?"

Arlaith scowled. "He will have them at his lodgings in the West Quarter. He likely has some kind of safe – if I were him, I would probably hide them in my library." His jaw set grimly. "If they are not there, then we must ransack his entire quarters."

Eamon raised an eyebrow. "'We', Lord Arlaith?"

"*We*. Cathair has played most foully with me, Lord Goodman," Arlaith hissed, "and he evidently intended some dishonest blow to the Master. Why else would he withhold the Nightholt? I will help you kill him, and return the book to the Master."

"No."

The curtness of his answer seemed to shock Arlaith, who gaped at him for a moment. "The Master has tasked me, and me alone, with retrieving this book and ending Cathair's life. I understand your wish to redeem yourself," Eamon added gently, "but you will understand why I cannot allow it."

"Yes, Lord Goodman," Arlaith growled.

They turned their steeds towards the West, and the Brand came into view. Eamon felt a weight shudder onto him, as though the Raven already watched for his arrival.

"Cathair's weakness, bar his arrogance, is his thrust," Arlaith told him suddenly.

Eamon shivered. "What do you mean?"

"He never stopped using the strange blade he brought back with him from Istanaria. But it is a strong weapon." Arlaith's voice intensified. "Don't let him strike yours with it; you shall come off the worse if you do."

Eamon looked at him suspiciously. "Why would you offer me such advice, Lord Arlaith?"

"We have a mutual enemy now, Lord Goodman."

"Besides the Serpent."

Arlaith laughed unkindly. "Besides the Serpent."

There was a long silence. "Cathair is a dangerous man. He will swiftly realize he is cornered. He is no fool. He will make no poetic mistakes." Arlaith spoke quietly now, sincerely. "He will cast flame and dog and blade at you, and they will be driven by his fury. I know of no man who has survived such an attack from him."

They approached the Brand. "Will Cathair be at the college?" Eamon asked. His mouth was dry.

"Yes." Cathair had Handquarter offices in the West Quarter College as well as at the Hands' Hall; they were just off the college's central courtyard. Eamon remembered the many times that he had walked beneath their shadow to the officers' mess.

"Have you ever been inside?" Arlaith asked.

Eamon nodded. Mathaiah had been made his ward within that building, and Eamon had often worked there as a Hand of the quarter.

"Then you already know that their layout is almost identical to the ones he keeps in the Hands' Hall," Arlaith told him. "His library, which also acts as his study, has a small side room which he uses for his dogs. They sleep there, I believe." He looked at Eamon earnestly. "He came out of the East. You must be cunning with him, Goodman. Once he discerns your purpose, he will not spare you. His enmity with your house goes back further than his hatred of you."

Eamon tried not to blanch. "But he can be killed?"

"He is but a man," Arlaith told him, "though he is strong and crafty. He is a terrible foe."

"You are one also," Eamon answered. He looked firmly and earnestly at Arlaith, scarcely recognizing the words as coming from his own heart as he spoke them. "Be my foe no more, Lord Arlaith."

Arlaith held his gaze for a long moment. In that moment, Eamon wanted nothing so much as peace with the man before him.

At last, Arlaith bowed his head. "Whether you live or die this day, Lord Goodman, I will keep the promises I have made to you."

CHAPTER VII

It was early evening when they arrived at the West Quarter College and dismounted. Waite arrived to greet them; the captain looked ten years older than when Eamon had last seen him.

"My lords. How may I serve you?"

"I have some business to attend to with Lord Cathair," Eamon answered.

"Of course," Waite replied, his careful tone showing he comprehended more than was said.

"Part of my task involves retrieving a book from Lord Cathair's library. If I should not succeed in what I must do, captain, you will accompany Lord Arlaith while he retrieves the book in my stead. You will recognize it by its foreign script. When it is found, you – and none but you – will take that book and you will deliver it, in person, to the hands of the Master," Eamon told him. "No other man is to receive it, nor lay a finger upon it."

Waite glanced in alarm between them. "Surely, my lord, Lord Arlaith would be a more fitting –"

"It shall be as Lord Goodman has commanded, captain," Arlaith answered, though Eamon thought that he saw the Hand's lip catch for a moment in an angry sneer.

Waite's eyes widened. He looked back to Eamon. "What task have you, my lord?" Did the captain view him as another cadet whose life might needlessly be lost?

"One from the Master."

"How shall I know if… if I must search for this book, and go to him?"

"You must go if you hear that I am dead. You will give that book to none but the Master – not even to Lord Cathair, if he should command it."

Waite blanched. "Very well, my lord."

Eamon gave him a nod and glanced at Arlaith's stony face. Then he crossed through the hall to the courtyard. Cadets and ensigns watched him from the colonnades. He thought he saw Manners' face among them.

He paused before the door to Cathair's quarters. There he unstrapped his scabbard, drawing it into his hand so as to carry it with him. He kept it well back beneath the cover of his cloak. He crossed the threshold.

Cathair's hall was well lit. Eamon followed the corridors towards the Hand's library. He knew, from long experience, that it was Cathair's accustomed haunt.

He knocked on the door. When no answer came, he went inside.

The library was a broad room lined with bookshelves, much like its counterpart at Ravensill. Cathair was at his desk. Reclined comfortably in his chair, he read by the dwindling light of the window behind him. The arches of the window frames were darkly painted. Where they soared towards their apex, they resembled the spread wings of a raven in flight.

Paws clattered on the floor and Eamon froze. Cathair's four hounds bounded up to him, their white fangs bared in stark snarls. As they had always done they sniffed and feinted at him, daring him to fear.

Cathair indolently turned another page of the book that he held. Steeling himself, Eamon spoke.

"Call off your dogs, Lord Cathair."

Cathair looked up, feigning surprise.

"Lord Goodman! Why, you'll never believe me, but I didn't hear you come in. You've the silence of… a snake."

The Hand set the book down, rose, and came down the long room. Eamon assessed the Hand's size, the confidence of his stride and gait, and the glint in his savage green eyes. Cathair bore his blade at his side – a curved blade out of the east, as Arlaith had said it would be.

Cathair paused before him with a broad, insincere smile. The dogs continued snapping at Eamon, but then fell back a little so as to surround their master. They formed an impenetrably loyal wall of claws and fangs.

The Lord of the West Quarter laid his hand to the head of the nearest hound and caressed it. "I do not believe that any reports were required of me this afternoon and so I must ask myself what I can do for you, Lord Goodman?"

"You may obey me! Call off your hounds."

"My hounds?" Cathair answered. "How cruelly you misname them, Lord Goodman! They are but pups!" he cried, fondling their heads and ears.

Eamon laughed. "Then send them to their nest, Cathair, but remove them from my feet."

For a moment he was worried that Cathair would refuse. How could he obtain the Nightholt and kill the Hand if dogs surrounded him? The anxious thought assailed him that, somehow, Cathair already knew why he had come. But Cathair had not seen how he bore his blade. It emboldened him.

The Lord of the West Quarter watched him with a measured gaze, as though trying to break into his mind, but he was no breacher. At last he smiled.

"Very well, Lord Goodman," he said. He made a shrill noise and the four creatures looked to him. The Hand gestured firmly to the small door at the side of the library and, almost as one body, the hounds raced towards it barking and yapping. Relief flooded Eamon as Cathair opened the door to permit them passage, then closed it behind them. The dogs bayed at their confinement.

"Is that better, Lord Goodman?" Cathair crooned.

"Yes."

"And how are you finding yourself at the palace, my lord? I hear that you were unwell the night of your feast. I trust you are recovered?"

"The Master's doctor saw to me."

"Indeed? Then the Master must be very fond of you," Cathair smiled. "That would be most poetic."

"How would it be poetic?"

"You would not be the first Goodman of whom he was… fond. Though perhaps," he added wistfully, and not a little spitefully, "you shall be the last."

Eamon tried to match his gaze. "What do you mean by that, Lord Cathair?"

"I am right in understanding that you have no heir?" the Hand enquired politely.

"Yes," Eamon answered, utterly bemused.

"Then, Lord Goodman," Cathair answered, "I mean that your blood is as limited as many a man's."

Eamon stared at him, trying to make sense of Cathair's words. "Always you speak in riddles, Lord Cathair."

"'Thus spake the Raven'," Cathair replied with an airy smile. "I have my reputation to think of, Lord Goodman."

"Then let me speak plainly."

"Please do." Cathair strolled back to his desk and took up his book once more. Eamon stared after him, steadying himself.

"Somewhere in this library, there is a place where you hide things of value to you. It is a command from the Master that you show me this place and its contents."

Cathair raised an eyebrow. "That is… an unusual command, Lord Goodman."

"A command it remains. Show me the safe."

Now the Hand eyed him suspiciously. "How am I to know that this command comes from the Master, Lord Goodman?"

Eamon matched his gaze. "I am the Right Hand. You are bound by my commands also."

"Indeed!"

"Indeed. And should what I seek not be in your possession, you will come with me to the Master; he will verify that my commands are his own."

Cathair sighed theatrically. "Very well, Lord Goodman. I will show you my safe, and its poor contents."

The Hand went to the western side of his enormous library, and spent a moment idling at his shelves. A red light appeared on his palm. This he set by the back of a leather-bound tome. Eamon watched, amazed, as a panel of the case blurred in a haze of red light and flickered away, revealing instead a recessed alcove.

Not bothering to look inside, Cathair indicated the opening with a grandiose gesture. "Be my guest, Lord Goodman."

It was a nonchalance that betrayed the safe's contents: even before he took a step closer, Eamon knew *it* was there. He could feel it, a pulsing evil, before he breathed another breath.

He approached the alcove in trepidation. There, among the books, scrolls, and trinkets, tucked to one side, lay the Master's tome. The binding seemed scarce enough to contain the lacerated script that had long tormented Eamon's nightmares.

Eamon did not reach inside to take it: he would need both his hands to deal with the Master's betrayer. And yet... why would a traitor reveal his treachery so easily?

He wet his cracked lips. "You should know, Lord Cathair, that Lord Arlaith wishes you dead."

"Oh?" Cathair looked up carefully. "Is that so? Why would that be?" He still had not seen what lay in his keep. Could he not sense it?

"You betrayed the Master and set the blame upon him."

There was a long pause. Cathair's eyes pierced him.

"And so you come?" he laughed. "Pray, Lord Goodman, what treachery have I committed?"

Without another word, Eamon gestured levelly into the alcove. Cathair looked; saw; froze.

"Do you know this book?" Eamon demanded.

Cathair could only stare. "Whence came this?" he breathed. Fledgling fear was replaced by anger. "Who told you that you would find it here?"

"Lord Arlaith," Eamon replied. Cathair raised his eyebrows. "He seeks your life for what you have wrought against him, for he has endured the Master's wrath for what you have done. He is not the only one who has expressed your life as their object this afternoon."

"Indeed?" Cathair answered curtly. "Who else has spoken so foully of me?"

"The one you serve."

Cathair froze. "The one *I* serve?" His eyes narrowed. Slowly, he stepped away from the alcove. "Do you come to me with this news as a courtesy, Lord Goodman?"

"No," Eamon answered quietly. "You stand accused, Lord Cathair, of withholding the Nightholt from the Master."

Cathair met his gaze calmly. "I entrusted the Nightholt to Lord Ashway. Ashway delivered it to Lord Arlaith. Now, it would seem that the Nightholt has made its way into my keeping, with neither my knowledge nor my consent."

Uncertainty trickled into Eamon's veins. Cathair had always been fiercely loyal to the Master. What reason could he have for withholding the Nightholt? Yet there it lay.

One of the Hands was lying… but which one – the poet, the seer, or the Left Hand?

"The evidence stands against you, Lord Cathair," Eamon persisted.

"So it would seem, Lord Goodman. Tell me, do you not find this entire affair to be conveniently incontrovertible?"

"Tell me, Lord Cathair, who would plot so against you?"

"Who indeed?" Cathair stared at him for a moment, then his face suddenly became a picture of unspoken, dire outrage. "A treacherous, pandering knave!" he hissed, striding to one of the shelves at the far end of the room. "A duplicitous bastard! Beware, Right Hand," he bellowed, "for you know not what the Left is doing!"

Eamon watched him, a black figure in the window-light. The Raven turned towards him. His green eyes glimpsed Eamon's scabbard. When Cathair next spoke, his tone was simple.

"Have you come to kill me, Eamon Goodman?"

"Yes."

For a moment there was a leaden silence. Dust drifted in the darkling air. Then suddenly Cathair raised his arms. His palms were surrounded with red light. A long smile appeared on Cathair's face; his green eyes twinkled. Cathair cast his hands forward. There was fire between them, a flaming orb of red that would rend flesh from bone. Eamon knew it; he had seen it done in the Pit.

The sphere spun unstoppably towards him. Despite Arlaith's warnings, Eamon was unprepared; he leapt just before the light struck him, but tripped on the rug and crashed heavily to the ground, taking the worst of the fall on his knees and knuckles.

Cathair howled with laugher and as he laughed another orb cracked through the air, hissing and sparking. It careered towards Eamon, who leapt up, impeded by his heavy cloak.

It nearly cost him his life. The light struck the floor, reducing half the rug to ashes.

Eamon was on his feet again. His feet were on the solid wooden floor. He tore away the fastening on his cloak and let the thing fall to the ground. Cathair came forwards, laughing.

"Sent to kill me?" he bayed. The dogs beyond the door roared with their master, and lunged against the wood with their heavy bodies. The vile red leapt between Cathair's hands. "A sparrow sent to fell the Raven? You have been sent to die, Goodman!" The sphere left his hand.

Eamon darted from the fire's path and only too late did he realize that it had not been aimed at him; Cathair's goal was the wooden case by which Eamon stood. As the flame hit the wall, the impact of the collision caused the case to crack and come away. With a great creaking and shattering and shower of splinters, the grand bookcase groaned forward and vomited wood and tomes.

Eamon just had time to shield his eyes as the case smashed down on him. The crack of the thick volumes of poetry and harsh beams of wood beat against him like the sea's wrath overtaking breakers.

Eamon crumpled to the floor with a cry, the weight of the whole, shattered case upon him. Dust and paper flew into his face and mouth. He was trapped. Cathair's laughter echoed in his ears; the Hand approached. Eamon tried desperately to lift the filthy maw of wood off his frame.

Suddenly Cathair's voice was upon him:

> So from that bloody lair the knight bewildered crept;
> Blind spawn of fleeing snakes that, in his fleeing, wept.

Cathair towered over Eamon through the jagged wood; the Hand seemed enormous in the dust. A flame hovered on his hand, waiting to be loosed.

Cathair looked down at him with a patronizing gaze. "Did you think to stand against me, boy?" he cooed. "Against the Raven who was here when Dunthruik was birthed in the Serpent's blood? Alone? You have long been a fool, Goodman. Now you have proven yourself one." With a snide laugh, Cathair let go the flame.

Eamon saw the ball, saw the searing flames and knew that he was lost. But as the fire came he felt a sudden shiver of blue washing through him.

Stand forth, First Knight! it cried.

He cast his hand forward, turning his outstretched palm towards the howling flame as it came down on him. The fire struck his hand, then dissipated along lines of shivering blue that curved protectively around him. With the light about him Eamon rose slowly, awkwardly, from the books and shards. Then he came out from the wreckage.

Cathair stared. "You snake!" he breathed. His voice became a roaring howl. "Snake! *Snake!*"

"I am no snake," Eamon answered, his voice strong and fearless. "Nor serve I one. I serve the King."

"Traitor!" Cathair screamed and in a flurry of rage he sent orb after orb of burning light screeching towards Eamon. But to every one Eamon answered with his palm, for the King's grace was with him and none of Cathair's rending arrows could touch him. Each one split as it reached the shield of blue and then bled into the air. Cathair screamed with rage. The dogs howled louder.

"Wayfaring slime! Belly-walker!" Cathair howled, hurling another orb. "There is no scale but a snake's fit to weigh your lying tongue!"

"You will not burn me, Cathair," Eamon told him.

"Then I shall drink your blood!" Cathair bawled. He drew his blade and tore down the length of the room towards Eamon.

Eamon's sword felt heavy and dull in his hand as it jarred with Cathair's blade. Cathair screamed at him in an unknown language. The words gripped like curses as the Hand cut at Eamon with the savagery of a beast. Eamon's arms and upper body shuddered with the force of each blow. He knew that he could not turn a single one of them and, realizing it, understood his peril.

With a sounding crack Cathair brought his scimitar down against Eamon's sword. The metal shivered on impact and gave way; waves of strength buffeted up Eamon's arm, threatening to break bone.

With a cry Eamon let go of his broken sword and stepped back. Cathair was on him in an instant; Eamon pulled back from a jab aimed at his throat. He dove for his fallen sword and caught the hilt in his hand. The edge of the broken metal was jagged. He wheeled to avoid a returning blow, and sliced Cathair's arm.

Cathair cried out in agony, then snatched his sword from his bleeding right arm with his left. Eamon drove his broken blade deep into the Hand's unguarded flank.

Cathair collapsed. Falling, he cast a bolt of red light towards the door. There was a crash. Eamon turned with horror: the door was broken. The incensed dogs charged him.

He tore the scimitar from Cathair's hand and swung it down across the neck of the leading beast. It fell beneath his first blow, but the other three, enraged by the smell of blood and their master's howls, were on him within moments.

Eamon fell back before their jaws, but the dogs were faster than he. They leapt and bore down on him not three paces from where he had downed the first. Eamon snatched up his cloak and hurled it at them. Suddenly the world was a mass of swirling black and crushing jaws as he slashed blindly at his foes. A second dog yelped as it fell beneath Eamon's blade. It crashed into the third dog and knocked it sidelong. Eamon slid his scimitar through the third dog's ribs. It collapsed in a heap as blood spurted from the wound.

Eamon scrambled to his feet, trembling. The fourth – where was the fourth? He looked wildly about and then stopped.

The fourth hound, bleeding from its foreleg, took up a protective stance over its master. It stood between Eamon and Cathair and growled. Cathair wheezed and choked, coughing up blood.

Swiftly Eamon drew up the tattered remains of his cloak and wrapped it round his arm, bracing it. He was covered in blood and knew that some of it was likely his. He nearly slipped in it as he strode forward from the dogs' grisly corpses towards Cathair's last defender.

When he was a yard away, the hound sprang. Eamon shielded himself with his left arm and the beast went for it, driving its long teeth down about his limb. They pierced through the thick cloak to his flesh. The dog bit down harder. As the hound fastened on to his left arm, Eamon thrust his sword into its throat.

The dog crumpled to the floor, dragging Eamon with it. Using the scimitar, Eamon prised the dog's jaws from his arm, its teeth sharp, slippery. He staggered to his feet and tugged the cloak tight over his wound. His forearm burned. He wriggled his fingers. Pain shot up his arm in an army of tiny knives, but his fingers moved. At last, he turned to Cathair.

The Hand had crawled towards the exit, leaving a long smear of blood across the floor. Gasping, he rolled onto his back and laid a hand at the muzzle of one of his dead dogs. Eamon drew Eben's dagger.

"Bastard son of the Betrayer!" Cathair wheezed through bloody lips.

"I was once a Master's man, Cathair," Eamon told him. "You made me one. I was loyal to him when I went to Pinewood. But when I returned, you broke me. In breaking me, and crushing those I loved, you caused me to remember whom it was I served, and who I was. Know me, Lord Cathair: I am the First Knight of Hughan Brenuin."

Cathair's eyes went wide with horror. "The blade shall break and turn true…" he whispered. His face became deathly pale as Ashway's prophecy spilled from his lips. "It will fall…" Cathair looked up at him with a wretched and violent look. "So be it!" he rasped. "But know that I killed your 'goodmen', your precious cadets and ensigns, and I killed your ward, Goodman! I tore the eyes from his face and broke the hands from his wrists, and gorged on his blood!"

"Then know, Cathair, that I forgive you." The words had been unthinkable to him, but still they came. "I forgive you for the wrongs that you have done me; Mathaiah's death is not the least among them."

Cathair stared, unable to comprehend. "You cannot forgive me!" he spluttered.

"I do."

The Hand fell silent. As Eamon looked at him, he felt new authority filling him.

Courage, First Knight.

"Cathair," Eamon said solemnly, "you willingly raised voice and hand in deeds of treachery and deceit against the house of Brenuin. You have troubled this land and its people with torment and toil, and you have joyfully served a usurper whose hands have shed blood, and been set to deeds to which yours were gladsome servants. What you have done against this land, by word and deed, deserves death."

Cathair's bloody face gaped at him. "You presume to pass judgment on me?" he seethed.

"No," Eamon answered. "But under the authority of the King, I come to deal it." Cathair watched him with shallow breath as Eamon paused, weighing Eben's dagger in his hand. "Cathair," Eamon said, seeking the Hand's gaze, "the King is willing to forgive –"

163

Cathair spat blood at him. "You would offer me the banner of your whore-son star? You would *dare* to try to turn me?" His face grew paler with each word. He paused to snatch his breath. "May your house be consumed by fire and torment and your Serpent fall in treachery upon his own sword!"

Eamon let the words pass through him: his heart was secure. He looked solemnly at his foe. The dagger was in his hand and Cathair lay obdurate and baleful before him.

"Cathair," he said quietly, "if that is your choice, then I have nothing more to offer you than the final mercy of a swift clean death – a mercy you withheld from Mathaiah and so many others. I do not seek vengeance. What I do, I do for the King."

"Then do what you must!" Cathair hissed through clenched teeth.

No further words passed between the Raven and the First Knight. In silence Eamon pierced the heart of the Lord of the West Quarter.

He cleaned his blade on the edge of his bloody cloak. Fatigue rushed through him.

Cathair was dead.

For a moment he stood and stared. The silence of the wrecked room overcame him.

He stepped over to Cathair's scimitar and took it up in his hand. His own sword, which he had carried since he had joined the West Quarter College, lay in shards.

He returned to the cooling body and cut Cathair's head from it, binding it up first in his cloak and then in Cathair's. He gathered up the ends of the second cloak into his fist, and easing the ring of the West Quarter Hand from the blanched fingers, he laid the scimitar down over Cathair's breast. Then he returned to the alcove.

The Nightholt seemed a grisly jewel in its hiding place. If Cathair had not put it there... then who had?

The time for such questions was past: he could let no other take the book to the Master.

He lifted the tome from the alcove, shuddering. Drawing a deep breath Eamon turned his back on Cathair's library.

Eamon emerged from the long corridors into the dying sunlight, the weight of the head in one arm and the burden of the Nightholt in the other. As he left the doors of Cathair's hall the college courtyard opened out before him with the walls of the palace and the bustle of Dunthruik beyond.

Men stood in the courtyard: Waite and dozens of Gauntlet ensigns and officers, and a small group of shaking servants. Arlaith paced among them. As Eamon stepped down, the watchers stared through the dull light, as though trying to see which Hand looked back at them.

Eamon descended slowly. He knew that he was bloody and torn; his arm raged where the dog had mauled him and there was dust and sweat and splinters in his hair. But his heart was clear.

As he reached the courtyard path, Arlaith blenched. Only Waite came forward. His eyes glanced at the bundle Eamon bore, then to the book, then back to Eamon's face with awed dread.

"Come you from victory, my lord?" the captain asked quietly.

Eamon matched his gaze, then looked at the gathered spectators. "It is the Master's will that I have performed this day, captain."

"My lord?"

"Cathair acted treacherously against the Master." He did not know whether it was true.

Waite paled. "I knew nothing of this, Lord Goodman," he whispered.

"You knew only of its effects," Eamon answered. "Cathair's treachery entailed the death of many at this college."

Waite's look grew grim.

"Cathair alone was at fault," Eamon told him consolingly. "No other man in the West will pay." Waite nodded, relieved, but the man shook. "The dogs' bodies are to go to the Blind Gate," he said quietly. "Cathair's will go to the pyres. I must go to the Master."

Arlaith was suddenly at his side. "May I accompany you, Lord Goodman?"

The Left Hand seemed a bird of prey circling the lost tome. Eamon met his gaze sternly. "You may not," he replied. "I will go alone."

He went through the streets of Dunthruik with Cathair's head in one hand and the Nightholt in the other. Men stopped and stared to see the Right Hand riding thus, a creature of blood. He halted for none of them. Resolutely, he rode to the palace and crossed the Royal Plaza, going directly to the throne room.

The doorkeeper was there. When he saw Eamon he grew pale.

"I will see the Master," Eamon told him. Wordlessly, the doorkeeper opened the door.

Eamon strode the length of the hall with confidence. He did not see the paintings or the fine mosaics, and barely saw the Master's secretary, who stood by the foot of the throne in conversation with the throned. Eamon passed him by and climbed the steps to the dais. Reaching the very floor of the throne, he dropped to one knee.

"Master."

"What do you bring me, son of Eben?" the throned asked. There was grim anticipation in his voice.

"I bring you the head of Lord Cathair," Eamon answered, laying the bloody bundle down before him. Suddenly he shook. "And I bring you the Nightholt." So saying, he held the book forward on his palms.

The throned rose to his feet; the air about him quivered. He lifted the dark tome with dreadful, ravenous eagerness. Fire sparked across the book's lettering; the Nightholt knew and rejoiced at the touch of its Master.

Edelred held the book for a long moment, caressing its cover, touching its pages. He looked back to Eamon.

"How I love you, son of Eben!" As he spoke he pressed a kiss hard against Eamon's forehead, a kiss made passionate by long years of grim and bloody searching. Eamon received its fire with quaking limbs, for it brought with it the vision of a battlefield strewn with corpses, over which the Master and his Nightholt rode.

"By this service to me, son of Eben," the Master told him in a thrilling whisper, "you redeem your line."

Only then did Eamon realize what he had done.

The Master watched him, his gaze radiant with a father's pride. But in his horror, Eamon could scarcely hear or feel, for his sight was the thrall of the Nightholt and he had delivered it into the hand of its Master.

CHAPTER VIII

Visions of fire and sword whipped through him, struck him, impaled him.

Eben fallen upon by Hands veiled in darkness. The broad wastes of Edesfield. The churning mud choked with corpses that emanated blood-light. Arlaith, begging clemency. Cathair, mired in his own blood. The fangs of dogs deep in his flesh where the throned's kiss still lingered. The Nightholt in the Master's hands from whence poured ubiquitous red light. His heart pulsed out the promises of his blood. Every token of those promises cast down in the dark letters that marked the Nightholt and his flesh.

Besieged on every side by vision, thought, memory, and dream, Eamon trembled as he knelt. He heard faint sounds of others moving in the room – perhaps the Master's secretary? – yet he could not turn to look at them.

He could not undo what he had done.

"Let the city ring with jubilation!" called the Master's voice, a raging torrent in his ear. "Let every household in this city, from servant to lord, from maid to mistress, receive a case of the Raven's brew. For that carrion fowl has been felled by my Right Hand, and I am the more pleased with him."

The Master's hand fell on his brow. Powerful fingers drew across Eamon in a gesture of terrible tenderness, then that same hand was beneath his chin, bidding him to rise. Unsteadily he obeyed its command; weariness flooded every limb.

"Your glory, Master," he whispered.

The throned's grey eyes searched his. "Have the Right Hand

taken to his quarters; send my physician to him," he commanded. The Master took in every line of sweat and blood and youth on Eamon's face. His tone became suddenly as soft and wistful as the touch with which he had caressed Eamon's brow. "His blood is precious to me."

Eamon's blood thrilled through his veins.

The secretary was soon beside him, guiding him to the doorway and entrusting him to two of the Master's own guard. Yet as he was escorted from the hall, Eamon saw the Nightholt. It remained in his thought with every trembling step.

Rumour flew swifter than a crow through Dunthruik. The corridors by which the Master's guards took Eamon to his own quarters were flooded with people, all of whom bowed low; as he passed they whispered the name of the one who had struck down the Raven.

He climbed the stairs to his halls, weak in limb and scarce in breath. The guards steadied him as he faltered and swayed in the stairwell. His head swam. He felt trammelled by blood and filth.

The doors to his quarters were opened; his strength left him and his knees buckled.

"My lord," said an alarmed voice. It was Fletcher's. Within moments he was at Eamon's side.

"Lieutenant." Eamon raised one hand to his head. "The doctor is coming…"

"He is here," spoke a voice from the doorway. Doveton strode swiftly in.

"May I sit?" Eamon asked quietly.

"I would encourage it," the doctor answered, dismissing the guards.

Eamon sank into the long couch. As he gave over his weight, his trembling increased. His breath came in gasps. He had delivered the Nightholt… and Eben writhed and screamed before him. Eamon put his hands over his eyes and a moan escaped his lips. He tasted blood on them.

The doctor turned to Fletcher. "Lord Goodman will be in need of a very long bath."

"I will have the maids draw it." Fletcher hurried off. Eamon scarcely heard them as they spoke; the world passed him by like distant rumblings, obscured by visions of darkness.

A hand touched his shoulder. "Where are you hurt, Lord Goodman?" Doveton asked.

Eamon forced himself to focus on the doctor's face. "I do not know," he rasped at last. "I do not think my life stands in any peril," he added as the doctor took hold of his arm. Eamon hissed with pain.

"I shall need a closer look at this at least. It would seem that you have rendered your shirt quite useless," Doveton mused. "I would not even send what remains of it to the scullery for swabbing the paving stones. I am going to remove it."

Eamon allowed the doctor to take his bloodied shirt, barely caring for the scars on his back. As the doctor put his shirt aside, dust and splinters fell from it. He felt sore and wearied, but as the doctor assessed him he realized that he had no severe injuries, bar one.

The doctor carefully examined the wounds that the dog had made on his left arm. "Were you fighting wolves, Lord Goodman?" he asked wryly.

"No, a raven."

"So it is true?"

"It is true," Eamon replied. He blinked hard to refocus his eyes.

"Move your fingers."

Eamon obliged, moving them one by one and then flexing them out flat before clenching them into a fist, each at the doctor's direction. He grimaced; the movements seethed in his flesh.

The doctor made him repeat the exercise several times with both hands, then breathed deeply. "You are a fortunate man, my lord," he said. "This is an unpleasant wound, but it was not deep enough."

"I had my cloak around it," Eamon murmured and made a

gesture as of rolling the garment about it. He once again heard the dogs leap at him and tensed.

The doctor smiled encouragingly at him. "You saved your arm in doing so. You are right-handed?"

Eamon nodded.

"Good, else I should have prescribed becoming so," the doctor continued. Eamon grimaced again. "You will have a very sore, very painful arm, for a very long time. There are also cloak threads caught in the wound. I will have to remove them – something I am sure you will not enjoy."

"Will there be leeches?" Eamon asked, eyeing him suspiciously.

"You fear them overmuch, my lord," the doctor told him. "Come, you must bathe."

The bath had been drawn. The doctor rose to his feet and Cartwright entered from the bathroom. The servant's face grew grey as he took in the bloodied remains of the shirt on the floor.

"My lord –" Cartwright began.

Eamon dimly felt the doctor's hand upon his arm.

"Your assistance, Cartwright," the doctor said. "Lord Goodman is well, but before I may proceed he must be bathed."

Cartwright and the doctor wrapped their strong arms about him and helped Eamon to the bathroom. As he crossed the threshold the inviting warmth of the great bath came at him like a wave. Cartwright and the doctor helped him undress and climb into the water. As he set his foot into the currents, their heat coursed through his nerves like fire. Suddenly there seemed to be red light in his skin...

Cartwright's hand was on his arm. "Gently, my lord."

Eamon set himself down into the water, letting it enfold him. It permeated every pore. He sighed deeply.

"I will wait outside," said the doctor. He bowed and left. Eamon shuddered as a first stream of water ran down his back.

Cartwright washed him. The water turned red. The servant soaped him, working it over every bloodied part; he delicately rinsed it away. At last he spoke. "My lord."

Eamon breathed deeply. "Yes?"

"The secretary is having wine distributed to the house." Cartwright faltered. "Is it true... that you bore Lord Cathair's head to the Master's feet?"

Eamon gazed down at the reddened water about him. "I did." His left arm burned.

He had killed Cathair. He had taken the life of Mathaiah's murderer, removed one of Hughan's enemies, and delivered justice in the King's name. And yet he was not now at peace.

He saw Cathair's face caught among the drifting currents and shook it away. He knew he had done rightly. Cathair had brought him from the Hidden Hall, had taught and preened him into a perfect Hand. Cathair had stood proudly over him as he breached and tormented wayfarers. Cathair had rounded on him after Pinewood, had killed Mathaiah, had killed good men, had been party to the hardships he had borne since he dared to stand against the Right Hand. Cathair had hated him, fiercely and utterly, and that hatred had been in his eyes when he cast the first flame at Eamon. Cathair had baited him, humiliated him – and, at times, respected him.

He shook his head, feeling the confusion deep in his heart. Cathair had been justly killed. And that was not all he had done that day.

He had made peace with Arlaith. The thought shuddered through him: *peace.* He had saved the lives of the men on Arlaith's list, had secured the good names of those who had been unfairly branded. But the other thing that he had done...

"By this service to me, son of Eben, you redeem your line."

He glanced at Cartwright. "It has been such a terrible day, Cartwright." Fire from the Master's hands, hands that now held the Nightholt, struck at Eamon's mind. His voice caught in his throat. "I am so tired," he whispered.

"Come, lord." Cartwright gently offered to help Eamon from the bath. "The doctor still has work to do."

Eamon let Cartwright wrap him in great swathes of black towel. They smothered him round like a choking beast.

Cartwright led him back to his bedroom where the doctor waited patiently. Various lengths of bandage had been brought while Eamon bathed, along with ointments and others of the doctor's tools; they lay neatly arranged on the bedside table.

With Cartwright's hand unswervingly on his arm, Eamon sat on the bed and lay back.

"You'll note I have no leeches, my lord." Doveton straightened Eamon's arm on the bed and peered at it.

"A mercy for which I thank you."

The doctor set to work, painstakingly drawing pieces of tattered cloth from the gashes on his arm with tweezers. Eamon winced as the metal touched his raw flesh like ice-shards. The doctor set a glass lens to his eye. As the tweezers returned again and again, Eamon marvelled at the man's steady hand and concentrated face. It helped him ignore the pain.

At last the doctor sat back, content, and bound the wound with ointment and thick cloth. As he rose, he looked at Eamon once again. "How is your back, my lord?" he asked, removing the glass from his eye.

"Well," Eamon told him. The doctor frowned and touched Eamon's shoulder; Eamon gasped in pain and surprise. Doveton nodded sagely, and helped him to turn on to his front.

"You bear a great deal, Lord Goodman," he said, setting his hand firmly on Eamon's shoulders. "Fortunately for you, no additional tools are required to ease your back."

"I am sure it will be nonetheless unpleasant," Eamon replied, then cried out as the doctor's hand kneaded his shoulders.

"Yes," Doveton told him. "It will."

It seemed an eternity before Doveton finished his work. Eamon was exhausted, though his back was suppler than he had known it for a long time. The doctor knew his trade well and had been firm enough to take out the majority of the tension in his back without disturbing its long scars. Eamon's arm still ached dully when the doctor took his leave.

"Have you concluded?" Eamon asked.

"For now. I shall see you again soon."

"I look forward to it."

"Brave words, Lord Goodman." Doveton smiled and bowed. As he turned to leave he crossed paths with Cartwright, who carried a steaming goblet of mulled wine. The doctor nodded approvingly. "Drink deep, Lord Goodman, and take some rest. I will check on you in the morning."

"Thank you," Eamon answered, slowly moving his back and shoulders. "The Master is fortunate to have so skilled a physician."

The doctor smiled again. "Good night, Lord Goodman."

The doctor withdrew. Eamon cradled the chalice Cartwright had brought him between his hands, letting the vapours cover his face. The smell, the colour, the very texture of the wine told him of its fine quality, and he knew even as he held it that it came from Ravensill.

His stomach turned. Looking up from the cup he saw the bed's thick drapes, the room's dark walls, and starlight on the balcony beyond. There was a glimpse of red caught across the stonework and he knew it to be light from the Master's chamber.

The memory of the Nightholt's dark letters chilled him and he shivered. "Mr Cartwright, would you draw the curtains?"

Cartwright did so at once. Eamon sat back heavily against the cushions and drank. The wine burnt as it went through him, warming his hands and brow.

He had not been afraid to kill Cathair any more than he had feared to kill Rendolet, though both had been trials of his strength and courage. But the Nightholt...

He rubbed one hand over his eyes. "What can I do now?" he murmured.

"My lord." Cartwright spoke quietly and Eamon jumped. He had forgotten the servant's presence. "Today was but one day, and though you accomplished much, I am sure that you have much left to do."

"I don't even know what it is," Eamon told him; the Nightholt danced grimly before his eyes. "I don't know what it is."

"See what the morning brings, my lord," Cartwright answered him. "Rest."

Silently, Eamon supped wine at the expense of a dead man. His servant put out the candles and lamps then bade him goodnight, and left.

Eamon stared up into the darkness. What could he do? What was there left for him to do? Endure the Master's words and touch, watch as the city was committed to battle against the King? Fall on the field beneath a black banner? Fall in the streets beneath a dagger?

He laid his head in his hands. Did it really matter what the Nightholt was or who had it? What was left for him now but darkness and fire?

First Knight, your place is here. Be true.

He wandered in and out of sleep during the long watches of the night, tossing and turning between his covers, feeling the drum of his pulse. Long before dawn unfurled her standard, Eamon rose and paced his chamber. His footsteps sounded solemnly in the still night.

He went to the window. Pushing the curtains aside he set his back against the embrasure; his arm ached and he held it quietly as he looked across the palace. Before him were the Master's chambers; light flickered between the stones. Cool air touched his face.

Hughan. In that twilit hour his thought turned to the King. It was for one man and his sake alone that he bore all. Every scar, every hurt, every tear, every fear, every fire. Flame, tempest, tooth, claw, blade, bile.

All of them for Hughan.

Why do you bear it, Eben's son? The words shivered through him. For a terrible moment he was afraid that the Master stood by him. *Why should you cede everything to him? He is but a man.*

"It is his right," Eamon answered wearily.

His right! The voice mocked him. *His blood is feeble, weak, dying. It has no right.*

"He is the King." With the words came a depth of feeling which in his guilt and pain and exhaustion he had nigh forgotten.

This land has a throne and one to sit on it, came the dark answer.

Eamon looked past the walls of the city towards the plains and the mountains. Suddenly he sensed forest and fen, river and sea, and knew that every part of it belonged to the King's house. He did not understand that authority, nor how the house had come to be entrusted with it, but guardianship over the River Realm had been given to the house of Brenuin. "This land belongs to Hughan," he whispered. "The house of Brenuin has held."

And the house of Goodman? sneered the voice. *The blood and heart of Eben's son? Has that held?*

He pressed his eyes shut.

Hold to me, First Knight.

Eamon breathed deep. His worth was not in the caresses and words of the throned; it was in his service to Hughan. That was what had brought him to Dunthruik, what had driven him to do every good he could in the East, and to take Cathair's life. Hughan was a true and noble man, fierce in justice and in love, and he was the King. That was why Eamon served him.

Never have you rendered your precious Serpent better service than you have this day! The voice crooned.

Eamon reeled. The Nightholt, the Nightholt… He could not drive it from his mind.

Do not be afraid, Eamon. You served the King today.

Eamon looked across the palace stones. The city gazed back at him, serene in the moonlight. As he looked, his heart stilled.

The King had sent him to Dunthruik; however much or little that there was left for him to do…

There is nothing left, Son of Eben.

"The King sent me," Eamon whispered, "and until he tells me

that my work is done, or until I have no breath left to render it, truly I will stay."

The voice of Edelred was silent.

Eamon stood and watched as the dawn touched the city's stones with its long rays, driving away the moon and striking all with ruddy gold. But how much longer could he stay true to Hughan when he was circled on every side by the deepest counsels of the King's enemies?

He lifted his eyes to the distant mountains and saw the shapes of craggy passes and purple ravines picked out in the dawn's majestic hue. They marked the way to the east, where the sun was steadily rising.

"Come swiftly, Hughan," he whispered. "Come *soon*."

The sunlight touched his face and Eamon breathed deeply. As surely as the day followed the night, as surely as the sun moved from east to west, the King would come.

Until then, he had to do what Hughan had sent him to do.

Eamon rubbed his chilled hands together and moved away from the window.

He went to breakfast. Everywhere the servants and the Hands bowed, and his name darted before him down every corridor like a loosed bird.

The doorkeeper admitted him through the leafy gallery to the breakfast hall with exceptional gallantry; the man noted the bandage on Eamon's arm with delight.

The Master rose from his table as Eamon entered and swept forward, his arms wide and his eyes exultant. "Eben's son!" he cried. "The whole city sings of you this morning."

"Sings it drunkenly?" Eamon answered wryly.

A look of delight crossed the Master's face.

"It is drunk with your success. This deed shall outlive you, son of Eben."

"Then may it outlive me only to prove the glory of him I serve," Eamon said. Reaching out forthrightly he took the Master's hand and bent down to one knee to kiss it.

The throned's face flushed with pleasure and pride.

"Your success has made you bold, Raven's Bane. Your boldness pleases me."

"Your pleasure has made me bold," Eamon replied, rising. "What service may I render you this day?"

Smiling, the throned drew Eamon across to the table where servants seated him; the Master's house would not meet his gaze that morning.

"You will name a Quarter Hand," the Master told him. His grey eyes sparked with fire.

Eamon watched him for a moment. "Forgive me, Master," he said, "but my wit does not match yours. What mean you?"

"The Raven has taken flight," the Master answered. "Another must be limed." He met Eamon's gaze. "You shall choose the Hand to go in Cathair's stead."

Eamon stared. The throned delighted in it.

"Master, I am not fit to name a man to serve you."

"Are not fit, Eben's son?"

Eamon pursed his lips together. "Master, I did not mean –"

"You demean yourself to speak so humbly," the throned told him. "And that demeans me."

Eamon was silent for a moment; he felt the weight of the Master's gaze. A name sprang to Eamon's mind, and it surprised him: Lord Febian. Febian had fought with him at Pinewood and had been witness to when he left Hughan's camp with Rendolet's head. Eamon had a hold over him – Febian had been sent to monitor him but had failed in allowing Eamon to see him – and nominating him might just bring him some kind of ally, albeit a forced one. The more he thought on it, the more the idea appealed to him. Any leverage he could gain might well help in the coming days. "I would nominate Lord Febian," he said at last.

"Lord Febian?" the Master repeated curiously. "Explain your choice to me." Eamon detected an odd tone to the voice.

"Febian is of the West, and knows Cathair's quarter well. He has often worked at the port, and at Ravensill, and knows both places and their business. At Pinewood and in returning from that field, he proved himself valiant and ferocious in serving your glory and performing your will. You rewarded such qualities in me, Master, and I myself would render out gifts such as those you have bestowed on me."

The Master smiled – and Eamon knew he had convinced him. Edelred gripped a jewelled chalice and raised it wryly to his lips.

"Lord Febian for the West," he said.

The dawn gave way to a striking morning, with air so crisp that the crest of a single wave in the harbour could be distinguished from its fellows, and the nearer valleys of the mountains were as clear as a man's hand before his face.

Eamon rode to the Ashen, keenly feeling his authority. For once, the burden did not feel toilsome or heavy.

The square was lined with sombre faces, all of which recognized him and bowed to him as he rode. Most of them were Gauntlet from the East Quarter; others were newcomers to the city who had simply been stationed there. The insignia of half a dozen other divisions and regions marked the men. As he passed, he reflected on how many men there now were in Dunthruik – men he had only considered as numbers in a Hand's report.

At the far end of the square stood another group: the Hands and captain of the East Quarter, arrayed formally by the college steps. Arlaith stood first among these men and greeted Eamon as he dismounted.

"Lord Goodman," Arlaith said with a bow. He extended his hand. "It is good to see you."

"Thank you." Eamon took the proffered hand and clasped it.

Arlaith led the group of men into the college and across to the courtyard, where the ceremony was to take place. Arlaith, Eamon, and the other Hands went to one side of the college's speaking platform while Anderas went to its head.

Eamon halted and turned to look back across the courtyard. The East Quarter ensigns, cadets, and officers had drawn up in neat ranks down one side. Down the other gathered a group of men and women without uniform, dressed in formal attire. The mothers, fathers, and relatives of the dead and disgraced men seemed grossly outnumbered by the red uniforms. Eamon's thought turned to all those others who had been forced to quit the city and he wondered if they would ever return to it.

A moment later a lone trumpet sounded. The courtyard, which had been hushed already, now fell silent as a slow procession of Gauntlet soldiers appeared in the doorway. The two leading men carried a banner between them, showing an eagle whose breast was marked with a sprig of ash. Behind the banner-bearers walked three more men, one for each of the men who had been slain defending the grain; each man bore a sword upright in his hands. Behind them came the other ensigns and cadets who had been discredited, their faces solemn. Eamon was glad to see Wilhelm Bellis walking among them.

The procession came to the foot of the captain's platform and there it paused. The banner-bearers went up the steps to stand before Anderas. There they set the banner onto the platform's broad table. The two bearers then stepped to either side of it, drawing with them the wings of the banner's eagle. These they spread wide.

The first sword-bearer came forward. He climbed the steps and walked to the eagle. Then he turned the sword and spread it flat across his hands and faced the crowd.

"Draybant Joel Greenwood." Anderas's clear voice pronounced the name into the silent yard. As his words hung in the air, the ensign turned and laid the sword down upon the banner's breast. Then he quietly left the platform, returning to the ranks of standing men. Two more swords were laid on the banner in the same way.

When all the ensigns had rejoined the ranks, Arlaith stepped forward to stand behind the eagle.

"These men served the Master and brought him glory," he said. "Let us bring him glory also."

181

"To his glory," answered the yard. The two banner-bearers slowly folded the eagle's wings in over the swords. They stood back and the remaining men from the procession – those who had survived – climbed the platform; each touched his hand once to the folded banner before forming a line before Arlaith.

"These men also serve the Master," Arlaith declared. "Let all taint of the enemy fall from their names. They are loyal to the Master and with joy is their service received, to his glory."

"To his glory," the yard echoed once again. The men bowed before Arlaith and he received them formally, clasping his hands about theirs before they went to rejoin their lines. As the last man did so, Eamon's heart eased.

The ceremony did not go on much longer; the folded banner was carried away across the yard and as it left, the trumpet sounded once more. The hanging hush lasted a little longer and then the ranks of Gauntlet filed out; the families of the men affected followed them. Soon the whole yard held little but the sound of marching feet.

It was then that Eamon found Arlaith beside him.

"The matter has been conducted to your satisfaction, Lord Goodman?" the Hand asked quietly. Eamon looked at him.

"My satisfaction is met," he answered.

Arlaith paused for a moment and watched as more of the guests left. Anderas stopped by a group of people. Eamon wondered whose family they were.

"My lord." Arlaith's voice called him from his thought. He looked back to the Hand. "I have arranged a meeting. Mr Slater and Captain Anderas are to attend; it would be of great pleasure to me if you were to attend also."

"What is the purpose of this meeting?"

Arlaith smiled. "I hope to set your house in order, and to keep my promise to you."

Eamon matched the man's gaze and a sudden smile came onto his face. He had never imagined that he and Arlaith would share a smile.

"My keeping of promises pleases you, Lord Goodman?"

"Yes," Eamon answered, "immensely. I would have one more brought to this meeting," he added.

"You need but name him," Arlaith responded graciously.

"Lord Febian."

Arlaith paused. "Febian?"

"I desire his presence."

Arlaith nodded slowly. "Of course; I'll send for him at once."

"Thank you, Lord Arlaith," Eamon answered.

Arlaith sent a messenger for Febian then took Eamon back to the Handquarter. They made their way to Arlaith's office. Arlaith closed the door with all the gallantry of a nobleman and gestured to the room with a grandiose sweep of his hand.

"My house is your house, Lord Goodman. Would you like to sit?" Arlaith indicated a tall chair. Eamon set it into the corner of the room before sitting.

"I shall observe more than I partake," he said.

"Very well. A drink, Lord Goodman?" Arlaith stepped across to a small cabinet bearing cups and bottles of dark liqueurs.

"I shall decline, thank you."

"As you wish."

Not long later, the door opened. Slater bowed.

"My lords," he said, "Captain Anderas is here and Lord Febian has arrived." Eamon caught a glimpse of the Hand; he looked flustered.

"Thank you, Slater," Arlaith answered. "Bring everyone in and we can begin."

Slater bowed, then held the door open before Febian and Anderas. The Hand looked pale and out of breath. Anderas glanced briefly across to Eamon; Eamon nodded in return.

Hand, captain, and servant bowed.

"Welcome, gentlemen," Arlaith began. Slater shifted uneasily. Febian scowled, but the expression faded swiftly when he saw

Eamon sitting in the corner. Eamon realized that the man was terrified of him.

"Mr Slater," Arlaith continued, "I have new directives for the running of this house."

"My lord," Slater acknowledged. A furtive glance to Eamon betrayed his wariness. "What would you?"

"First and foremost, every man, woman, and child serving in this house will eat fresh bread every day, and will eat at least one substantial meal in the day apart from that. This directive will be funded by the house and my own purse."

If the command surprised the servant, he kept it well hidden. "Yes, Lord Arlaith," Slater said.

"Further to this, the servants of this house are free to move about as best serves their business," Arlaith continued. "The preceding discretion directive is remanded. Servants will be disciplined for breaches in the rule of the house, and that rule will remain strict, but silence shall no longer form a part of it. Any servant who is maltreated is to bring their complaint to you, and you shall bring it to me."

"As you command, Lord Arlaith." Slater bowed deeply.

"Captain Anderas, these commands will likewise be used for the college servants. All are to be judged on the basis of their fidelity to myself and to the Master, as expressed in their conduct and discharge of their duties."

Anderas nodded. "Yes, Lord Arlaith." The familiar ring of the captain's voice was like dawn-songs.

There was a pause. After a moment Febian looked awkwardly about the room and then swallowed audibly. "Lord Arlaith?"

"Lord Febian?" Arlaith answered crisply.

"I was called away from urgent business to attend this meeting," Febian began. His voice grew tetchy as he spoke. "You will forgive me, but I fail to see what concern all this is of mine."

Like a master actor passing centre stage to his fellow, Arlaith looked across to Eamon. Every gaze in the room followed Arlaith's. Eamon rose.

"These matters concern you closely," he said.

Febian almost glared at him. "How, my lord?"

A long silence fell. Febian stared, a strange mixture of elation and dread on his face. Eamon strode to him and took his hand. Memories of the dead after the retreat from Pinewood and of the Hand's fury in that battle flashed through Eamon's mind. The palm that lay open in his had shed needless blood.

Quietly he laid a ring on Febian's palm. Febian looked at it; a raven glinted back at him. Arlaith's gaze narrowed on the ring and he bit his lip.

"Your house is to be directed in the same way," Eamon told him.

Febian gawked. "The Master is great and gracious."

"You will come with me to the palace," Eamon added. "The raven's hall will not lie empty long."

Febian bowed. "My lord. To his glory."

"One thing more," Eamon said, turning back to the others in the room. "The Crown is to hold a commoner tonight, in my honour. I am sure that the invitations have already reached you, but I reiterate my desire that you each attend, and ask that the invitation also be extended to the house and college."

"With pleasure, Lord Goodman," Arlaith answered.

Febian matched Eamon's pace as they went back through the streets to the palace. A light rain blew in from the north and skirted the sky, patching the cobbles and grand paving stones. As they rode, Febian's eyes dropped now and then to the ring; his eyes grew wide with it. Then, as though aware of Eamon's gaze upon him, he looked up.

"Something troubles you, Lord Febian?" Eamon asked.

For a moment there was no sound but the horses' hooves on the Coll.

"I have never distinguished myself before the Master," Febian answered at last. "Why, then, does he lay this honour upon me, when this city is full of his Hands?"

"You were not the Master's choice," Eamon told him, "but you were mine."

Febian grew pale. Fear appeared in his eyes.

"You are a fine Hand, Febian," Eamon told him, "and I have seen the strength of your ardour for the Master. You know the West Quarter well and its workings better than others. And I know you."

Febian's face set grimly. "You are a politic man, Lord Goodman."

Eamon matched his gaze. "You misunderstand me," he answered softly.

"I may not contradict you, my lord," Febian said. "It is as you say."

"A man contradicted me once, Lord Febian, and in so doing saved my life," Eamon answered.

"Was he honoured as I am to be honoured?" Febian asked.

Eamon smiled, thinking of Anderas. "I gave him the greatest honour in my power," he answered.

"Then, as I am sure he did, I shall thank you," Febian said coldly.

They rode on in silence to the palace. Eamon conducted Febian deep into it and entrusted him to the keeping of some of the Master's servants. Febian looked at him.

"You will come for me, my lord?" he asked.

"Yes," Eamon replied.

He went to wait for the other Hands in the Hands' waiting room. It was a small room but lavishly decorated with the emblems of the Quarter Hands on its four walls. These corresponded to the points of the compass, and on the ceiling a great, black eagle was painted for the Right Hand.

Eamon walked slowly round the room and the harrier, falcon, raven, and owl gazed back at him. He stopped before the owl in thought.

The doors to the room opened. Lord Dehelt entered.

"My lord," Dehelt greeted him, bowing.

"Lord Dehelt," Eamon answered warmly. "Good day."

"And to you, Lord Goodman." Dehelt rose and met his gaze.

"They call you the 'Raven's Bane' in the streets, my lord," he said quietly.

Eamon said nothing; his ears resounded with howls and Cathair's curses.

"You were injured?" Dehelt asked. Eamon nodded. "Cathair had long talons," Dehelt replied, then shook his head and sighed. "For long years, he was ever the most loyal of all the Master's Hands. It seems that times change." He looked up. "You are recovered from your hurts?"

"Some of them," Eamon answered with a small smile.

"May none of Cathair's curses come to land on you, Lord Goodman," Dehelt said.

Eamon looked up. Dehelt offered him a small smile.

"I am no seer, Lord Goodman," the Hand added, "but you have done in this city things which have never been seen since the time of its founding. It rejoices in you. Your coming here was meant and I am glad to see it."

Eamon was awed. "Thank you."

He might have said more but at that moment the doors opened again, admitting Tramist, and mere paces behind him, Arlaith. Other Hands of the quarters followed behind them. All bowed towards Eamon. He had to lead them to the throne room, where the Master waited. He looked to the Hands. One face alone looked upon him with open hostility: Tramist's. Dehelt supported him after a fashion, and Arlaith's rancour dissolved more with each passing hour. The other Hands of the quarters looked on him in awe.

Did he dare to think that he might one day lead any one of them to the King?

"We will go in," he said.

The ceremony was just as Eamon remembered it. He partook in it fluidly, finding the words in his mouth and the gestures in his hands as they were needed. The Quarter Hands each declared Febian's service as they had done for him, and Eamon ratified it. Cloak and ring were bestowed. The new Lord of the West Quarter rose to his feet in the palace halls.

The throned commanded Dehelt to take Febian to the West Quarter to install him. It was a gesture for which Eamon was grateful; he was not sure Febian would take kindly to being installed by a man who might discredit him at a word. The other Hands were dismissed and the doors to the throne room closed behind them. Eamon was alone with the throned.

"Thus the Raven," the Master said. There seemed to be a touch of nonchalance in his voice.

"He is not Lord Cathair," Eamon agreed, "but he will serve you to the fullness of his strength, Master."

"You shall know it if he does not," the throned answered.

An icy chill bit through him. Eamon resisted the urge to shudder.

Suddenly the throned spoke again: "Son of Eben, follow me."

They went into the corridors between the throne room and the throned's quarters. Eamon barely glanced at them as they passed – already they had become too familiar to him.

It was to the room where Eamon had first met the tailors that they went; the light fell once again from the windows, brilliantly illuminating the centre. The Master halted by the doorway and Eamon stopped behind him.

"Go in," the Master told him, a strange smile on his face.

Eamon looked at him uncertainly for a moment but could not disobey. With the Master's eyes upon him he stepped into the room.

There was a stand at its very heart. A heavy cloth covered what it held. Eamon paused before the stand, taking in its height and width.

"Take down the cloth," the throned told him, "and receive my gift."

Eamon reached forward. The cloth was silken in his hand, and as he drew it away with a flick of his wrist it billowed out like smoke, then fell gently to the ground. What lay beneath stole his breath.

A tall suit of dark grey armour stood before him, glinting austerely in the half-light. Its smooth rounded lames, broad pauldrons, curved greaves, its finely wrought vambraces, breast and back plate, gauntlet and helm… Each was solemnly faultless. Eamon's whole being yearned towards it. It conjured in his mind the clash of blade against blade and the look of fear on the stricken foe as the wearer of such plate as this bore down violently upon them, to deliver the killing blow.

He stood and stared at it. Behind him, he felt the Master's presence as a well of flame.

"Master," Eamon breathed, "I have no words."

"'Then will I serve you, proving your glory on my body, by my blade and with my blood'," said the throned. His voice was quiet, and close by Eamon's ear. He smiled. "From your own tongue springs this art, son of Eben."

"I have never seen its like," Eamon breathed, and he had not. Only the Master himself could have a finer suit.

"Touch it," the throned told him.

Eamon did not need encouraging. The plate was cool and thrilling beneath his hand.

"Surely this is too fine a thing for me," he whispered.

"At the sight of it alone shall snakes flee in fear from you. Your blood is mine and it will be protected."

Eamon looked slowly at the Master. "They will come?"

"They must come," the throned replied, and Eamon saw anew the anticipation in the Master's eyes and tone. It was the same with which he had received the Nightholt, and it terrified him utterly. "They must."

"This city is ready for that day, Master."

"We await only the Serpent." The Lord of Dunthruik surveyed him and smiled. "Let him come!"

Eamon quailed, but the Master reached out and touched his face.

"I am ready, Eben's son," he said quietly. "And so are you."

CHAPTER IX

It was a long-awaited night. The music and festivity of voices and singing carried even to the high windows of Eamon's chambers. Eamon stood at his balcony and listened, forgetting all else.

"Can you hear them, Mr Cartwright?" he laughed.

"Most assuredly, Lord Goodman," Iulus answered. "It has been many years since we had a commoner and never has one been the inaugural gesture of a Right Hand."

"Did Lord Arlaith never hold one?"

"No, my lord."

"How long did Lord Arlaith hold his position?"

Cartwright hesitated. "I am not sure, my lord. He took the office long before my time."

"How old are you, Mr Cartwright?"

"Forty-five with the winter, Lord Goodman."

Eamon knew that Cathair had been the last of the Hands who had been with Edelred at the beginning, but had somehow forgotten that Arlaith had been Right Hand for a long time. He could not guess how old Lord Arlaith was – the man barely looked Cartwright's age.

"My lord, you must dress."

"Yes," Eamon conceded. His formal attire for the evening lay on his bed. "It would not do to be late."

He dressed swiftly and Cartwright assisted him, drawing the heavy cloak over him and settling it on his shoulders.

"Do you look forward to the commoner, Mr Cartwright?"

Cartwright did not answer immediately – he was too busy fixing Eamon's cloak in place with an elaborate eagle-shaped brooch.

"My duties preclude it, my lord."

"Which duties are those?"

"The house must prepare for your return," Cartwright told him.

"The house may leave the theatre as the performance ends, and I will dally at the Crown as long as the house would deem necessary to return before me," Eamon replied. Cartwright stepped back from him, appraised the hang of the garment, and then met his gaze.

"It can be done, my lord," he said.

"Yes it can," Eamon answered with a smile, "and it will. I have already made Fletcher set aside passes for all of you."

Cartwright smiled warmly. "Thank you, my lord."

"Enjoy the evening, Mr Cartwright," Eamon answered, dismissing him with a gesture.

Cartwright bowed and left the room. Eamon paused a moment to glance at himself in the mirror then went into his hallway. Fletcher stood there and bowed as he approached.

"My lord."

"Mr Fletcher. All the invitations were delivered?"

"Exactly as you asked."

"Good."

"The Lords Arlaith, Dehelt, and Tramist exchange their greetings and will attend you."

"And the Master?"

"Will not be in attendance. The commoner is for you. Your event has caused quite a stir in the city, my lord."

"Indeed?"

"The general passes were gobbled up swifter than they might be handed out."

"Is the play so spectacular?" Eamon laughed.

"The one it honours appears to be."

Eamon smiled. "It will be a good evening, Mr Fletcher. Let us go down."

Fletcher accompanied him to the Royal Plaza. A carriage stood there. Its whole body was red and a great black eagle marked the doors. Eamon stared as the coachman descended and lowered the mounting step.

"I have a carriage?" Eamon asked, turning to Fletcher.

"Yes, my lord," answered his lieutenant, bowing. "Lord Arlaith made little use of it. It has been re-upholstered and painted in your honour. It will bear you to the theatre."

Eamon looked at it again; the black eagle had a scroll beneath its feet. *Goodman* was lettered in gilt across the door.

The coachman drew the door open with a bow. The coach's interior was draped with red and black, and golden crowns were etched boldly over the doorways, which themselves formed the fronts of painted golden eagles. The coach might be Eamon's, but it displayed the Master's colours.

Eamon climbed inside. The coachman closed the door and moved back to the driver's seat. Four enormous horses awaited his commands. Eamon sat back on the cushions, marvelling at the craft which covered every part of the carriage, wondering how long it had taken to paint each detail. The door had a window covered by a small set of curtains. He drew them aside and saw Fletcher through the window.

"I will also make my way to the theatre, my lord," Fletcher told him with a bow.

"I will see you there, Mr Fletcher."

"Yes, my lord."

Then the coach lurched into motion.

They went smartly from the palace gates and down the Coll. Eamon gazed through the window with a child's delight, watching Dunthruik become a series of pictures framed between the red curtains. The city passed. Men and women in the lantern-lit streets cheered as he went by.

Soon he caught sight of the Four Quarters. Its eagles glistened in the night. The streets were thick with people who parted before his passage.

The coach drew up before the theatre and stopped. A rush of cool evening air penetrated the carriage's cushioned interior, carrying promise.

Eamon rose and alighted. As his foot touched the ground, he looked up and saw the theatre. The steps of its front gate were lined with row upon row of smartly uniformed Gauntlet and Hands. The square behind him was the throat of the city, a sea of faces that, at his appearance, crested in cheers and applause.

Drawing a deep breath, Eamon walked up the steps. As he climbed, the applause grew louder. Hundreds and hundreds of faces smiled at him, the words on their lips lost in the noise. They bowed and laughed as they waved their entrance passes in adoration.

Eamon reached the top of the stairs. The theatre's great, black eagle gazed down at him, lit by enormous braziers. Servants stood at the doors, formally attired and ready to check the passes for the evening; a task which Eamon did not envy. As he approached, they bowed. He recognized one of them as the woman to whom he had spoken when last he had visited.

"Am I to be first in?" he asked her.

"It is traditional, my lord," the servant answered with a bright smile. "After you will go your guests, then the Hands, nobles, officers, Gauntlet, and people."

"The seats and standing room are all arranged?"

"With numbers, my lord," she told him. "You have no pass, but you would see the numbers if you had one."

"If all have numbers then let the people go first," Eamon said. The servants gaped at him.

"My lord?" asked one.

"Would that complicate things?"

The servants exchanged looks. "It might ruffle the feathers of a few birds, my lord," the woman answered.

"I have a reputation of the like, I am told." The servants smiled a little uncomfortably. Eamon laughed. "This is a commoner!" he cried. "Let the last go first."

"And the first?" the woman asked uncertainly.

"Shall go last," Eamon smiled.

The servants bowed. "It shall be done, my lord," the woman told him. A couple of the other servants hurried off, no doubt to give notice of his directive.

Grinning from ear to ear, Eamon turned to look at the cascade of people that lined step and quarters.

"Welcome!" he called. "A commoner this is, and so shall the people, the very heart of the city, enter before me."

There was a strange hush. The men along the steps – the nobles, Hands, and officers – fixed him with astonished, even outraged, glares. No man moved.

Eamon laughed. In a moment of exhilaration, he went lightly down the theatre's steps to its gates, where the men and women of Dunthruik stood and stared at him.

He came to a halt before the first man he saw. Aghast, the man fell into a bow.

"My lord," he breathed. All the men and women by him bowed as he did so.

"Do you have a pass?" Eamon asked.

"Yes, my lord." The man held up a small tile.

Eamon smiled. "Then go in."

The man looked at him uncertainly. Eamon laughed, stepped forward, and gently tugged the man, and several of his fellows, through the gate.

"Go in," he told them. Then, laughing once more, he turned to the astonished crowd. "Dunthruik," he called, "go in!"

At last the people understood his sincerity. Nervously, they came forward through the gates and, with some encouragement from the Right Hand, climbed the steps.

"His glory," breathed one man as he passed. It was not long before the whole crowd was awash with the cry:

"*His glory!*"

With a great smile, Eamon stood at the gate and watched while the people of Dunthruik went up the steps and into the theatre. The Hands, the knights and nobles, and the Gauntlet followed in their wake.

Eamon stood and waited until every man had gone in before him. Then he too climbed the steps.

The hallway was bright and richly adorned. The buzz of excited men and women welcomed Eamon into the auditorium.

A servant approached him. "Your reception hall has been prepared. It is behind your box, my lord, so that you and your principal guests may enjoy some private company before the performance."

"Thank you," Eamon replied. Those principal guests would be the Quarter Hands and captains, and Fletcher. Had Eamon had full choice he might have included servants and ensigns from East and West in that number, but he could not yet be so bold. "I will go up."

"Your guests felt that it would be inappropriate to go up before you," the servant added. "They are waiting in another room. Now that you are here, shall I send them up?"

"Please do," Eamon told him.

The servant bowed and Eamon passed from the hallway to the stairwell that led to his reception hall. The stair was grandly paved with marble in red and black, and a great set of dark wooden doors stood at its head. But Eamon passed rather into a side passage; his entrance to the hall was, he knew, from the other side of the corridor. Right Hands, he supposed, did not use the same doors as their guests, even when the hall was their own.

At last he came to his door and went into the reception hall. It was awash with dark wood, its seats were couched in red, and banners bearing the eagle of the Right Hand hung upon the walls. Before him was the room's main door, by which all guests were admitted. To his right Eamon saw a curtained doorway that led to the box.

He listened in delight to the sound of the people in the theatre below.

It was not long before the first of his guests arrived: Febian and Waite, the latter looking significantly more confident than the former. Fletcher was with them.

"Lord Febian, Captain Waite," Eamon called cheerfully. "A pleasure to see you both. I trust that the wait did not tire you at all?" He turned to his lieutenant. "Welcome, Mr Fletcher," he added.

"Thank you, my lord," Fletcher answered.

"The wait was entirely endurable, Lord Goodman," Waite said, bowing. A smile was on his face.

"Lord Goodman," Febian greeted civilly.

"I have always wanted to see this part of the Crown," Waite said as he rose. "Thank you kindly indeed for your invitation. May I be so bold as to offer the college's thanks also?"

"Of course," Eamon replied, "and I receive them with pleasure." He turned to Febian. The Hand fidgeted absently with the heavy ring on his finger. "How do you find yourself in the West, Lord Febian?"

"I find it well enough. As you are aware, I served many years under Lord Cathair, so I know well the duties required of the post." For all the Hand's bravado, the way he bit his lip and twisted the ring on his finger belied his insecurity. His eyes flashed. "Not that Cathair made me privy to any of his private dealings. You did well to dispatch him. Had I any suspicion of his betrayal I should have attempted to deal with him myself –"

"Good," Eamon answered, smiling. "I'm sure you would have."

It was then that the doors opened again, admitting Dehelt, followed by Captain Longroad, Lord Tramist, and the captain of the South Quarter – a man whom Eamon had not previously encountered. Eamon welcomed them and they gave their thanks for his invitation. On the matter of who had entered the theatre first, they remained silent.

Arlaith arrived last of all, with Anderas following behind him. The Lord of the East Quarter had barely stepped through the door before he tumbled into a bow. "Lord Goodman, my apologies for my tardiness," he said.

"That's quite all right. All is well?"

Arlaith smiled. "You will not believe it, gentlemen. It but drizzled yesterday – barely enough to wet a whisker – and yet I manage to find a puddle big enough to ruin a very handsome cloak. I was obliged to change it," he added, "thus waylaying me, and one or two servants."

The room laughed generously. As the laughter died away Fletcher and the captains congregated together at one side of the room, the Hands on the other. Eamon surveyed them, the lords and captains of Dunthruik garbed in black and red. As he looked at them he longed to see them in other colours and their hands turned to other service.

It was then that his eyes fell on Tramist. The Hand watched him with a dark look that was quickly veiled. Eamon resolved to ignore it, but even so he wondered whether Tramist, or any of the Hands, could become King's men.

You are foolish to think it, Eben's son.

Eamon blinked. Tramist's hating gaze still rested on him. Was he the only one who could see it?

"My lords, good captains," Eamon said. "Will you come with me to the box? I believe that the performance is soon to start."

"What work is it?" Febian asked.

"It's called *The Thorn*," Eamon answered. He was about to add that the work dated to a period after the founding of Dunthruik when another voice spoke before him.

"By Miller – a writer better known for his lively discussions on the period's law. The work is, however, a very fine piece indeed." The voice was Arlaith's, and he smiled as he spoke.

"I did not take you for a man of the arts, Lord Arlaith," Dehelt commented, surprised.

"I am not one," Arlaith replied, "but in my youth I had a well-read friend who fancied himself of that calibre." He offered Eamon a somewhat wistful smile and Eamon found himself wondering what the Left Hand had been like as a young man. Where had he lived and called home, whom had he known? What life had led him to Dunthruik and to the office of the Right Hand?

"Also, my lords, it has been my good fortune to discover the rich library of the East Quarter," Arlaith added. "There is good reason why it was the object of Cathair's envy."

The mention of the former Raven elicited an uncomfortable silence. Eamon was relieved when a servant came and bowed low beside them.

"Lord Goodman, Mr Shoreham advises that they are ready to begin, if you are content."

"I am content," Eamon answered. The servant bowed and scurried off. Eamon looked back to his guests. "Come, gentlemen," he said, gesturing to the box. "Everyone has their seats; let us take ours."

He led the way to the box. The great wooden doors were drawn open by two servants, granting admittance to places with a spectacular view across the theatre. As Eamon led his guests onto the broad balcony, the theatre erupted into applause. At every level of the great building men and women rose to their feet, looked up to him, and cheered.

Arlaith was beside him. "It would seem that Dunthruik is for the Right Hand," he commented quietly. "It is ironic, Lord Goodman, but Lord Cathair's death has won them all to you."

Eamon knew that he was right. He looked out across the deep well of faces. Then he raised one hand to them in greeting. The theatre hushed.

"Welcome!" he called. The theatre cheered; it poured infectious delight into his blood.

Eamon sat. Every seat in the theatre was filled after him.

The performance soon began; all went quiet as the great curtains drew back, revealing the Crown's enormous stage. Colossal scenery depicted the stone walls and ships of Dunthruik's port. It was remarkably detailed and realistic. The crowd gasped. From the corner of his eye, Eamon saw Dehelt smile.

A troupe of actors came onto the stage, dressed as port workers. Coming swiftly to the front of the stage, they bowed low.

"To his glory!" they called.

The theatre answered them. The troupe bowed once more and then began to sing. The sound of the voices stirred something deep within Eamon. How long was it since he had heard so many voices singing together? He realized that he had last heard such a sound in the Pit.

The play, which was a mixture of prose, poetry, and song, told the story of a Gauntlet captain stationed to a city in Etraia. There, he fell in love with the daughter of a prosperous merchant, but after clashing murderously with her kinsmen, he was forced to abandon her without explanation of his departure. At the end of the first part she, seemingly betrayed and alone, was betrothed to another man.

All too soon the curtains closed, marking the end of the first half. Eamon rose to applaud, as did the rest of the theatre. Eamon knew that the story ended well: the daughter learned what had driven her lover away and rejected the marriage to the captain's rival while she waited, hoping against hope for the captain to return – which he would do at the end of the second half, taking her back to Dunthruik to marry her.

The actors and singers were faultless in their telling of the tale and no charge could be laid against any aspect of costume. Eamon wondered how long it had taken the theatre to put together such a show. A small army of servants appeared in the wings and corridors of the theatre; they went with tapers and candles and adjusted the lighting during the break.

Eamon rose and left the box with his guests. As they went back into the reception hall, the servants laid out a lavish selection of sweets and wines. He invited his guests to help themselves, then approached one of the servants.

"I would speak with Mr Shoreham following the performance."

"I will bring him to you when it concludes, my lord," the servant answered, bowing.

"No," Eamon told him, "I would go down to him."

The servant bowed again. "Then I shall have someone lead you, my lord."

Eamon thanked him again. As the servant went to other business, Eamon found Arlaith at his side. The Hand held a tall chalice of wine while he nibbled on a biscuit. The sight seemed hugely comical to Eamon. As he restrained a laugh, Arlaith looked at him.

"May a Hand not eat, my lord?" he said.

"Are you enjoying the evening, Lord Arlaith?" Eamon asked.

"Indeed," Arlaith answered, and sipped thoughtfully. "Puts my own inaugural performance to shame, if the truth be told."

At once Eamon was reminded of the awkwardness of speaking to the Left Hand.

Arlaith saw the look on his face, and laughed amicably. "My predecessor had let the theatre go very much to waste," he said. "I authorized its repair and maintenance but confess that I had little interest in it beyond that and my obligation, as patron, to be present from time to time. I had other matters to attend to. I commanded some performances," he added, "but none so grand an affair as this. The effort seemed ill-rewarded to me."

"You are not a great believer in the arts, then, Lord Arlaith?" asked Dehelt. The Hand joined them. Febian and Tramist followed after him, while the captains and Fletcher engaged in a conversation of their own, at a respectful distance from their Hands.

"The arts distract," Arlaith answered. "I am afraid that story-telling, in whatever form, is always a distraction."

"A distraction?" Dehelt looked intrigued.

"Being a man of the arts was of no help to Lord Cathair, in the end," Arlaith answered. An awkward silence followed, but he seemed not to notice it. "Tales are of no great merit to any man, bar perhaps the very young," Arlaith insisted.

"Surely, my lord, there are some tales that merit the telling?" Dehelt asked.

"What of the Master's taking of the city?" Febian put in.

Arlaith laughed. "That is history," he replied.

"Surely, now that there are none from those times, it is reduced to the status of a story?" Tramist challenged.

Arlaith clucked his tongue in disagreement. "Do you see Dunthruik, Lord Tramist?" he asked. "It is the very fruit of history. It proves what is told. A book, a play, an opera – these things can be invented, woven about with words, and produced as though they were the very proof of the things about which they speak, but they are not. They are leaves of paper, utterances that are spoken once and then dissolve into the air, forgotten and unseen.

"History builds walls and lays foundations; story does not. Does story offer ground to till, grain to sow, stone to quarry? Will it feed a man, or keep him warm? Will it sharpen his blade? No, it fills his mind with nonsense until he neglects his field and house and loyalty. It will bring him to ruin and destroy him utterly."

Arlaith's words were met with a moment of silence. He laughed once more. "This being my view of the matter, you will little wonder, my lords, why I neglected the theatre in my time."

"Your view clarifies the matter considerably," Dehelt conceded.

"And you, Lord Goodman?" Tramist asked. As he spoke all eyes suddenly turned to Eamon. "Do you share Lord Arlaith's assessment?"

"I do not," Eamon answered simply.

"What is your view, Lord Goodman?" Arlaith asked, peering over the rim of his chalice with interest.

"I will agree that history is a vital part of who we are," Eamon began. "No man can claim that he made his own flesh or blood; he is made of what came before him, though what he does with the blood in his veins is another matter." He paused. "But we are wrought by more than history. I am not just flesh and blood – I am words." The Hands watched him curiously as he strove to express his thought. Arlaith smiled.

"Every time I speak," Eamon continued, "every time I listen, every oath I make; these make me and bind me to the world as surely as does my blood. A story, made from words, is the worked-for fruit of flesh and blood, just as the man who made it. Being, then, beings of words and blood, the telling of tales flows in our veins." Eamon met Arlaith's gaze. "A story may not sharpen my blade, but a tale of courage may strengthen my hand when I strike. It may not till my field, but it might turn my gaze to the land I walk in; then I might see it, and myself, with renewed eyes, remember things that in the press of flesh and blood and history I had forgotten."

Eamon finished speaking. The Hands watched him with varying expressions.

"Then you are enjoying the evening's entertainment, Lord Goodman?" Dehelt asked.

"Yes," Eamon answered truthfully. "And perhaps it is time we went back to it," he added. He gestured to the doors, which several servants drew open. The Hands and captains went back inside, though Eamon and Arlaith lingered for a moment.

Arlaith drained his cup and set it down. "From time to time you make good speeches, Lord Goodman," he said, touching Eamon's shoulder with a small smile. The gesture warmed Eamon's heart by its friendliness. "Did you ever consider the university?"

Eamon laughed, a little sadly. "You are not the first to ask me that."

"No?" Arlaith asked, surprised.

"No." Eamon paused, his sudden tension dissolving. "Your lieutenant, Lord Arlaith, was a good friend of mine."

"Mr Ladomer Kentigern?" Arlaith said with a frown.

"Yes," Eamon answered. "He often jested that I should have gone to the university."

"He was a man of mirth," Arlaith nodded with a smile. "A very fine lieutenant."

"Why did he go to Etraia?"

"No man ever serves as lieutenant to the Right Hand for long, Lord Goodman," Arlaith told him. His face and tone became serious. "It is a powerful position, and a man outside the ranks and disciplines of the Hands can be vulnerable to that power. He had already served in the post for long enough. Keeping Mr Kentigern to serve you would have entailed… unnecessary complications."

"Such as?" Eamon asked, restraining the harsh edge suddenly in his voice.

"Divided loyalties," Arlaith answered, "and the provocation of them. Mr Kentigern was a lieutenant before ever you joined the Gauntlet, Lord Goodman," he said. "I would have you consider the complications that might have rendered you."

"Ladomer Kentigern was a good man," Eamon answered. "He would not have spoken of it."

"Perhaps; even so, he could never have served you."

"Then… I suppose it was right for him to go."

"Yes," Arlaith nodded. "It was. And Etraia was in need of a solid representative from Dunthruik."

"Has he been recalled to the city?" Eamon asked.

"No," Arlaith answered. "Nor shall he be. He is needed there."

Eamon breathed deeply. At the mention of Etraia his mind wandered back to the play, and he suddenly remembered that the theatre waited for him.

"Let us go in," he said to Arlaith. They did so, arriving in the box just as a shrill fanfare marked the air.

The whole theatre rose to its feet. After Eamon had sat, they did likewise.

The curtains drew back and the play began again. It was not long before Madam Ilenia took the stage and Eamon again heard the deep, stirring strains of music that had so touched him but days before. He watched, enthralled, as she drew breath to sing. His blood ran clear as the words poured across him. He glanced once at Anderas; the man's face wore the awe he felt.

> And yet the thorn reminds me in my pain
> You too have suffered and have been denied.

Suddenly Eamon remembered Alessia; he almost felt her hand in his. He closed his eyes.

Some time later the play wound to its conclusion. Eamon watched as the Etraian lady and the Gauntlet captain were reunited and married in the port of Dunthruik. As the chorus and musicians gave their final note, there was a pause, and then the players trouped back onto the stage and broke into dance, which was matched by the delighted applause of the audience, beat by beat. As the dance concluded the audience applauded again. The players gathered at the front of the stage called at the tops of their voices:

"To his glory!"

Then, to Eamon's amazement, as the theatre's echoing call died away, the players turned towards his balcony and raised their hands.

"Lord Goodman, to the Master's glory!" they called. The theatre erupted with it. Eamon rose to his feet to accept their praise.

At last the players left the stage. The applause died down. As the guests dispersed, they sang snatches of the play which lifted through the theatre and hung in the air. Eamon turned to those with him.

"Thank you for your company, gentlemen," he said. "I hope you have enjoyed yourselves."

"Most assuredly," Dehelt answered, and the others all expressed a similar sentiment. "Thank you for your kind invitation, Lord Goodman."

Eamon smiled. "I bid you each good night," he said. "His glory," he added.

"His glory," came the reply. The Hands and captains shuffled out of the box one by one.

"I will return to the palace, my lord," Fletcher told Eamon with a bow.

"Of course."

Anderas hung back as the others left, his furrowed brow giving the impression of a man deep in thought. He cast his gaze up towards the intricate carvings on the ceiling. Seeing him do so, Eamon laughed.

"Do they intrigue you, captain?" he asked.

Anderas looked back to him. "They do, my lord," he answered. "Though you will be relieved to know that I can tell you little about these."

Eamon laughed. As he did so Arlaith passed and bowed.

"Lord Goodman," he said, "I take my leave."

"Thank you for your company, Lord Arlaith," Eamon answered him.

"And you for an exquisite evening." Arlaith looked once to Anderas. "You need not hurry back, captain," he said. "I will see you in the morning."

Anderas bowed. "Thank you, my lord."

Arlaith left the hall. Silence fell in the reception room. Eamon and Anderas stood alone in it.

"He is much changed," Anderas commented, looking quietly after the door where Arlaith had gone.

"He is," Eamon answered. "I hope that it is for the better."

"I hope that it will last."

"As do I." Eamon turned to Anderas with a smile. "It is good to see you," he said, reaching out to clasp Anderas's hand. "It has been a long time."

"Too long," Anderas replied. "You hold?" he asked quietly.

"Yes. By some grace, I hold. You?"

Anderas smiled – a wistful kind of smile that Eamon recognized. It was the smile of a dozen stories, thoughts, and adventures that could not be told in that moment, but that longed to be shared.

"I hold."

"Did you enjoy the performance?" Eamon asked.

"Yes," Anderas answered. "Particularly the one before the play began." He shook his head. "I suppose one might call that a kind of last-first poetry in the flesh."

"Do not say so in front of Lord Arlaith," Eamon told him. "He will summarily explain to you his view on the worth of poetry."

"I shall avoid the subject with him."

"How is your servant, Toriana?" Eamon asked.

"Very well," Anderas smiled, "and of invaluable support to me. Thank you."

"You're welcome," Eamon answered. The news pleased him. "And the college?"

"It misses you," the captain told him, "but Lord Arlaith has, as you have seen, grown less fearsome."

"I am sorry about what happened to Mr Greenwood," Eamon said, then fell quiet. "I sometimes wonder whether, if I had put him forward to the Hands…"

Anderas shook his head. "It would not have changed anything, Lord Goodman," he said. "He would still have had charge of the grain. And his death was not in vain; it has sown stores throughout the city. He would have been proud of that."

Eamon nodded. He knew it was true. He had missed Anderas's counsel and wise words.

"I know I have said it once already," Eamon told him, "but it is good to see you."

Anderas smiled. "And you, my lord."

A moment later there was a knock at the door. A servant, who bowed down deeply, followed it.

"My lord," he said. "Shall I convey you to Mr Shoreham?"

"That would be kind, thank you," Eamon answered. He looked once at Anderas. "Would you like to come, captain?"

A brilliant smile passed over the captain's face. "I would."

The servant led them from the box and back to the reception hall. From there, they followed down the stairs towards the nether parts of the theatre. As they walked Eamon relaxed. He realized that his thought had strayed too little to Anderas and to how the captain-turned-King's-man might be faring beneath Arlaith's eye and hand. He remembered the list and drove down a shudder. How close the captain had come to being a name with strikes through it, he did not know.

The servant took them through several corridors, less ornate than those that Eamon had seen elsewhere, to a series of rooms that were behind the stage. Some had doors and some did not, but all the rooms were filled with musicians, singers, and actors, dealing with the aftermath of the evening's work.

For a moment none of them noticed him. There were several bearing Hands' colours in the room, in various states of undress. Then one of the actors recognized him; he swiftly alerted those near him. A hush fell, and every man and woman in the room rose to bow.

"Lord Goodman," they said.

"Thank you all," Eamon answered, "for a wonderful evening. Is Mr Shoreham here?"

"I am, my lord," answered a bearded man from the centre of the room. He came across to Eamon and bowed again.

"Mr Shoreham," Eamon said, "thank you for your hard work in producing this event for me."

"It was a pleasure, my lord," Shoreham answered him. "Should you wish any such performance again, I would gladly do the same."

Eamon's mind suddenly filled with a picture of the Crown bannered in blue, of a sword and star standing over the doorway. He smiled.

"I will be certain to ask for you, Mr Shoreham," he said. "Please," he said, surveying the room, "continue with what you were doing. I am sure you have a great deal of celebrating to get to this evening!"

Some in the room laughed, and with a further bow the troupe went back to its work. As he surveyed the room, Eamon saw Madam Ilenia sitting in one corner. A young woman brushed her hair. Eamon went across to them and Anderas followed him. As they stopped by her, the singer rose to her feet and curtseyed beautifully.

"Lord Goodman; captain."

"Madam," Eamon said, "please allow me to thank you again for your part in the performance."

"I am but one part in a body of many," Ilenia answered with a smile. She rose from her curtsey. As she did so, Eamon caught sight of a small ring caught on a thin chain about her neck. He smiled.

"You are married, madam?" he asked.

An odd expression passed across the singer's face. "Yes, my lord," she answered heavily, "but my husband is far away."

"That must be very difficult for you," Eamon answered gently. Surprise erupted on her face. Eamon offered her a smile. "I hope that he will return swiftly to you, madam, as the captain in the play did tonight."

"Thank you, Lord Goodman," she answered.

Eamon thanked the actors again and went with Anderas from the rooms. Together they returned to the theatre's grand entrance hall, which stood still and quiet in the moonlight. Servants were busy inside the auditorium, tidying and dousing the lights.

They paused in the hall and Eamon breathed deeply. It was then that he noticed the grey look on the captain's face.

"Is something the matter?"

"Yes and no," Anderas answered hesitantly.

"You cannot say both yes and no," Eamon chastised.

"The singer," Anderas began. "You said something to her that I think you did not intend."

Eamon frowned at him. "I thanked her for her performance," he answered. "Was that amiss?"

"No," Anderas replied. "You asked after her husband."

"Yes." Eamon saw the look on Anderas's face grow serious. "I should not have done so?" he guessed uncomfortably.

"Like any arena, the theatre has its own language," Anderas told him quietly, "and its own euphemisms." He paused. "In Dunthruik, a Hand who asks after the husband of a performer is not genuinely concerned for him. Rather, his interest is in the performer, and his question enquires as to whether her husband, or any other man, is in a position to gainsay him in it."

"To gainsay?" Eamon repeated. The sound of the servants working moved in the air. Suddenly the formality of Madam Ilenia's response came back to him in full force. "*He is far away.*"

Eamon blanched. "Oh," he said. He felt his face going from white to red as he understood. "Anderas, I didn't know!"

"I know," Anderas answered quietly.

They fell silent for a moment. Eamon sighed. He felt ashamed, both of his ignorance and of any distress he might have caused the singer. The thought of her misunderstanding him was haunting.

Anderas laid a hand on his shoulder. "Do not let it trouble you, Lord Goodman," he said. "Dunthruik is a city that mothers strong daughters. She will endure."

"No woman should have to endure such a thing," Eamon answered, and suddenly Alessia was before him in his mind, kneeling and sobbing. She too had suffered and he had denied her…

He shook the thought from his mind, then looked back to Anderas. "I will apologize to Madam Ilenia."

"Perhaps you should leave it till tomorrow," Anderas answered. "She may already have left the theatre. It might be awkward to go seeking her now."

Eamon felt the moonlight on his face. He nodded. "You are right," he said. "You are very often right, captain."

"A cruel and oft misunderstood misfortune laid upon me by the stars at birth," Anderas answered with a smile.

"Perhaps we were both born under a strange, forgotten star," Eamon returned.

"And a good one." Anderas smiled at him, then bowed. "Good night, Lord Goodman. Hold fast."

"And you, captain."

CHAPTER X

Eamon descended into the theatre's bowels to the carriage area, where his coachman waited. The streets were quiet, and there were few to mark his passing – Dunthruik's denizens dwelt in taverns or in beds. As Eamon returned to his own quarters his thoughts turned again to Madam Ilenia. He grew hot and uncomfortable.

He climbed the stairs to his hall and greeted the Hands on duty. The doors opened before him. Cartwright awaited him.

"Good evening, my lord."

Eamon smiled. "Good evening, Mr Cartwright," he answered. "Did you enjoy the play?"

"Yes, my lord, very much." Cartwright beamed from ear to ear. "I've not seen such a thing since I was a very, very young man... and that was some time ago! May I offer you thanks, on behalf of all your servants?"

Eamon laughed. "Only if you will thank each of them on my behalf in turn."

"I will, my lord."

Eamon stepped further into the hall and attempted to undo the clasp on his cloak.

"Let me help you, my lord," Cartwright said.

Eamon brushed his hands away. "I shall see myself to bed this evening, Mr Cartwright. I require no more service tonight – and perhaps you, and the rest of the house, would benefit from not rendering more of it until the morning."

Understanding at once that he could not be swayed, Cartwright stepped back and bowed. "Very well, my lord."

"Good night, Mr Cartwright."

"And to you, my lord."

Bowing once more, Cartwright turned and left. With a cheerful sigh, Eamon went to bed.

The eleventh of May was a clear day. At breakfast the Master congratulated Eamon on the play and its success – leaving him exhilarated – and during the morning an unexpected invitation came to him from the East.

"Lord Arlaith asks if you would care to join him for lunch," Fletcher told him.

Eamon looked up from his desk in surprise. "Let him know I would be delighted."

So it was that he lunched with Arlaith.

"I must say, I do believe that you did yourself great credit last night," Arlaith told him as they sat down to their meal. "Great credit indeed."

"Thank you."

"The Master was pleased?"

"Yes."

"Good. Dunthruik can do nothing but sing your praises – and a couple of refrains – this morning." Arlaith paused as a servant laid food before them, thanked him, then turned back to Eamon. "Would you believe that when I went to the Crown Office this morning I found Mr Rose in a full fit of song?"

Eamon stared. "Mr Rose?"

"Mr Rose," Arlaith asserted.

They watched each other for a moment. Suddenly Eamon burst out laughing; Arlaith joined him. At that moment it seemed that there could be nothing funnier in the whole world than a Crown official singing. They laughed together until they nearly wept with mirth.

In the late afternoon Eamon took delivery of a new sword which Fletcher brought him. It was a simple blade meant for Gauntlet infantry use. Only the previous day, the sword smiths had offered him elegant blades fit for a Hand, but Eamon knew what kind of weapon he preferred. The hilt and point of this one were finer than the one he had owned before, and the dark scabbard was skilfully crafted. When Eamon drew the sword, the steel glinted in the sun. Its balance, as he held it in his hands, was next to perfect. With such a blade he felt as though he could down a hundred Cathairs.

"It's beautiful," he told Fletcher. "Will you send my compliments to the master smith?"

"Of course," Fletcher answered.

"And would you send word to the stables to prepare my horse?"

"Of course, my lord."

Eamon strapped the scabbard to his side, signed a few last documents, and left.

In the early evening he rode down the Coll. The Crown emerged before him, its great dome glistening in the westering sun.

He rode to the alighting point beneath the theatre and left Sahu in the care of some servants, advising them that he did not mean to be long. Then he took himself inside.

There were servants in the hallways, still cleaning the corridors and auditorium from the previous night. Eamon stopped one of them and asked after the troupe.

"In the back rooms, my lord," the servant answered.

Eamon made his way to the rooms where he had been the night before. As he arrived he found the actors once again, though now they were ordinarily dressed and devoid of makeup. They seemed just to have finished a meeting of some sort, for as he arrived they began to leave; each bowed to him as they went. Eamon eased his way into the room.

"Mr Shoreham," he said, spotting the bearded director. "I am looking for Madam Ilenia?"

"Lord Goodman," Shoreham said. "She was just going into the vestry." He gestured to it.

Eamon thanked him and followed his direction. The largest of the rooms gave way to several smaller ones, each filled with tidy stacks of props, costumes, wigs, and scenery. Some also held musical instruments. As Eamon entered, voices sounded through one of the open doorways. He followed them and saw Ilenia, accompanied by a younger woman. They were tidying dresses into a long trunk.

"Good evening," Eamon spoke courteously. Both rose and curtseyed on seeing him.

"Lord Goodman," they said in turn.

"Madam Ilenia," Eamon began, "might I speak a word with you in private?"

"Of course," Ilenia answered. Her companion gave her an odd look, but at a nod from the singer she curtseyed once more to Eamon and hurried away.

Eamon breathed deeply as he watched the singer across the room. He wondered whether she was frightened – the poise and grace of her posture showed no trace of it.

"What would you, my lord?" she asked.

"Apologize to you, madam."

Ilenia looked at him curiously. "I do not think that the Right Hand has need to apologize to anyone."

"Right Hand or no, a man must apologize when he has done wrong."

"You have done me no wrong, my lord."

"Would you tell me if I had?" Eamon countered. Ilenia did not answer him. "Madam, I wronged you yesterday evening, when I spoke words which I both meant and did not mean."

"You spoke in a manner well befitting your station, Lord Goodman," Ilenia answered.

Her impeccable formality frustrated him. "May I speak frankly?"

"As it pleases you, Lord Goodman."

He looked straight at her. "I neither had, nor have, any desire to violate the pledges that rightly remain between you and your husband," he told her. Ilenia blinked hard and looked at him with surprise. "I am told that the words I used last night can be taken to mean quite the opposite."

"They can," Ilenia nodded slowly. "May I speak frankly with you, my lord?"

"Nothing would please me better."

"Then I must say that it surprised me to hear you say what you said yesterday, and now it surprises me to hear you *un*say it."

Eamon laughed. "Unsay?"

"Many things can be undone, Lord Goodman."

"Not all things," Eamon replied.

"I thank you for your apology," Ilenia told him, "and I heartily forgive you for any wrong you feel you may have done to me."

Eamon smiled. "Then you have more power than I, madam."

Ilenia looked at him curiously. "How so, my lord?"

"Your forgiveness, not my apology, undoes what I did."

"If you had not apologized, I might not have known that there was a matter to be forgiven," Ilenia countered. "So, perhaps, unsaying or undoing is the work of two hearts?"

Eamon laughed again. "You are a wise lady, madam."

"I have lived many lives," Ilenia answered with a small smile. "Such is the nature of the stage."

"I imagine that you can speak long on that," Eamon answered. He paused. "I wonder," he said, "whether it would offend you if I were to invite you and your husband to dine with me this evening?"

Ilenia smiled. "That is most kind, Lord Goodman. I would accept. My husband would decline, I fear, for he truly is far away. He is a Gauntlet captain, stationed on the Galithian border."

"He was not recalled to the city?" Eamon asked.

"No," Ilenia answered sadly. "The north is still a dangerous place."

"Friends of mine are also stationed at distant borders, madam."

"I am sure that you think of them often, my lord, and that they take solace from that."

There was a moment of quiet.

"Madam Ilenia," Eamon said, "I do not detract my words. You would be welcome to dine with me if you so chose. But *only* if you so chose."

Ilenia smiled. "I would gladly accept your invitation, Lord Goodman."

Eamon rode back to the palace and, much to Fletcher's confusion, sent his carriage to the Crown to fetch Ilenia. The intervening time gave him ample opportunity to tell Cartwright that there would be a guest to dinner.

While the preparations were being made, Eamon returned cheerfully to the Royal Plaza, where he startled the guards at the gate by engaging them in conversation while he waited for Ilenia to arrive. He laughed when one ensign was bold enough to explain that although duty at the palace was a great honour, it could also be somewhat tedious. Eamon agreed with him, and for a moment he could have been a first lieutenant once more.

The carriage soon arrived and came through the palace gates. Eamon saw Ilenia's face through the window. As the carriage stopped, Eamon stepped up to open the door.

"Welcome!" he called. "Did you enjoy your journey?"

"Perhaps it was not long enough to be called a journey, my lord," Ilenia replied, "but I did."

"Have you ever been to the palace before?"

"I played in the theatre once," Ilenia told him.

"There's a theatre at the palace?" Eamon asked, surprised.

"Yes," Ilenia answered. "In some part of the West Wing, I believe."

"I have not seen it," Eamon answered. "But then, you must understand that I did not know I had a carriage until yesterday." Ilenia laughed and he held his hand up to her. "May I help you down?"

"Thank you, my lord."

She laid her hand in his. Suddenly Eamon saw a dark night of months before; he heard the crack of a broken axle. A ghostly Alessia passed through his arms and heart. It stunned him.

Ilenia stepped down into the plaza. "Are you well, Lord Goodman?"

"Yes." He forced a smile. "Just a memory." His breast ached with it.

Thanking the driver, he led Ilenia through the palace grounds. Each tall building, every archway, every stone was lit by braziers and framed by the hues of the twilit sky. It dulled the gaudy glint of the crowns and gems, making them imposing and austere.

They went into the palace by the grand steps. From the entrance hall they followed into the East Wing and to the corridors that led to Eamon's own quarters. Ilenia gazed at everything in wonder.

"After I saw the theatre I always wondered if the whole palace was like it," she said. "It seems that it is."

Eamon remembered the dusty corridors that had led to Ellenswell, filled with charred walls and tapestries. "Not all of it," he answered, "but a great deal of it, yes."

"I wonder if this is what the River Poet had in mind: 'High and deep those crimson walls, where eagles, palled thick in crimson or in sable, dared to nest, to rear in flame…'" She trailed off pensively for a moment.

"'And to enthral'," Eamon finished.

Ilenia looked at him with surprised delight. "You know the River Poet?"

"Better than some," he answered. "My father was a book-binder – as was I, when I was young."

"When you were young?" Ilenia repeated. Suddenly she laughed. "I mean no offence, my lord, but you cannot have reached my two-score years!"

"No," Eamon conceded. He was a good deal short of them.

"Then you are still young," she insisted.

"I suppose that I must be," he answered. He did not feel it.

They reached the colossal hallway, called the Round Hall, whose stairs and corridors led into varying parts of the East Wing, including the Right Hand's quarters. Suddenly Eamon heard the sound of approaching footsteps. He looked up to see the Master and his secretary moving through the hall. Seeing Eamon, the Master paused then turned towards them. Eamon bowed and Ilenia curtseyed deeply.

"Master," Eamon said. His veins pulsed hotly; he was terribly and awkwardly conscious of the lady at his side. "Your glory."

"Son of Eben," said the Master. Eamon saw the grey eyes flick to Ilenia and then back to him. "You go to dine?"

"Yes, Master."

"Good. Madam, are you to be my Right Hand's company this evening?"

"Your glory, Master," Ilenia answered. Eamon was stunned by the steadiness of her tone. "It is as you say."

"I know that you performed delightfully yesterday evening," the throned told her. "I trust that you will do as well for my Right Hand tonight."

Eamon reddened, but Ilenia did not falter.

"Your glory, Master," she said, curtseying still. "I will please him."

"You speak well." The throned looked to Eamon with a knowing smile. "And you choose well, Eben's son. I will not expect you to breakfast in the morning." He spoke the words as one who gave a great indulgence.

"Thank you, Master," Eamon replied.

Without another word the Master left the hall. Eamon quivered as he looked to Ilenia.

"Madam," he began.

"I am well, Lord Goodman," she told him, rising from her curtsey.

Eamon stared. "Not many can say as much when first they meet the Master," he managed.

"Not many meet him first in the company of the Right Hand," Ilenia countered.

"I do not know if you are fortunate in that," he replied. As he looked at her he spoke again. "Are they many?" he asked. At Ilenia's questioning look he continued: "The Hands that solicit their evening's company at the theatre, I mean."

218

"Yes," Ilenia answered simply.

"Have others solicited you?"

"Yes." The singer's voice was quiet, and she looked away. Eamon felt his heart go out to her.

"If any man apart from your husband asks you again, tell him that you keep company with me," he said firmly.

Ilenia looked at him uncertainly. "I will, Lord Goodman."

He watched her for a moment. "Are you hungry, madam?"

"Yes," she answered.

"Then let us go to dinner."

Supper was a light but ample affair; there was soup, followed by some cold meats and cheeses with bread, fruit, and wine. As they ate, Eamon and Ilenia spoke about the theatre.

"How long have you worked on the stage?" Eamon asked her.

"Very nearly always, my lord," Ilenia answered. "Mr Shoreham is a distant cousin and my parents both worked at the Crown. I was lucky that I enjoyed singing as I worked, that the director heard me, and that my parents had no objection to my joining the troupe."

"They might have objected?" Eamon asked.

"It is not an easy life, Lord Goodman," she answered. "My parents knew it well. My elder brother joined the Gauntlet," she added. "He was stationed up River."

"Whereabouts?"

"Clearwater, originally," she answered. "It's a small town in Barrowsgate province. He became a lieutenant very swiftly and was sent to command one of the Barrowsgate groups. I don't know where he serves now," she added. "It has been difficult to receive news since the wayfarers began harrying the countryside in earnest."

Eamon nodded. "What is his name?"

"Lieutenant Helm," Ilenia answered. "If he is still a lieutenant."

"And your husband?"

A sad smile flickered almost imperceptibly across Ilenia's face. "Captain Roe," she said. "He is a good officer – perhaps too good.

Were he a little less skilled, he might not have been sent to the north for so long. But the Master has needed good men to keep that border safe."

Eamon nodded. "It is a difficult border," he said. "I was stationed there for a short time when I was a Gauntlet cadet. I do not remember whether I ever heard of your husband, though," he added.

"I believe, Lord Goodman, that Gauntlet cadets care less for distant officers than for their own," Ilenia answered.

"That is true," Eamon laughed. "My own were far more pressing." He looked at her kindly. "If I hear news, of either your brother or your husband, I will tell you."

Ilenia smiled. "That is kind of you, my lord," she answered. "I daresay they will return to the city when they are able. They will know where to find me." She paused to drink, then looked at him. "And you, Lord Goodman?"

"As you may already have guessed, I joined the Gauntlet," Eamon replied. "I would have been content to serve in my province, but I was stationed to the city where I managed, all unwittingly, to distinguish myself. The rest you know," he said, "or can see."

"You are modest, Lord Goodman."

Eamon laughed. "To tell the truth," he answered, "there are many men who should have been handed in my place. It was because of such a man – a friend who now serves in Etraia – that I joined the Gauntlet. Were it not for him, I might have gone to the university."

"Or become a poet?" Ilenia asked.

"A poet?" Eamon laughed, surprised and delighted. "What makes you say that?"

"You are a man of many words, Lord Goodman."

"A good many of which need changing by some better hand," Eamon countered.

Ilenia looked at him through a disagreeing frown. "You speak with a measured tongue."

"A measured tongue? My tongue is a fountain that pours out saltwater one moment and fresh the next," Eamon answered passionately. It had sworn him to the throned and to the King. What two things could be more different?

"Yet you strive for measure," Ilenia answered.

"Yes," Eamon told her. For one measure of which he could not speak to her.

He drew breath and met her gaze again. "Were you in a meeting this afternoon when I came?" he asked, deciding to change the subject.

"Yes," Ilenia replied.

"Was it an interesting one?"

"Mr Shoreham was discussing various works we could bring out of the repertoire for performance in the following weeks," Ilenia told him.

"What were the choices?" Eamon asked, intrigued.

Ilenia offered him a wry smile. "Mr Shoreham is quite fond of tragedies," she said.

Eamon frowned. "Last night's performance was not a tragedy."

"Ah, but it had 'tragic potential', my lord," Ilenia told him, mimicking Shoreham's voice. She laughed. "He wanted a tragedy, like *Lord Coriol*, but the troupe thought differently."

"What did they want?"

"A comedy," the singer answered. "Maybe *The Daughters of Elmgrove* or *All for Love*." Eamon nodded; he knew both plays.

"What was your vote?" he asked.

"For a comedy," Ilenia admitted, "but a less well-known one."

"If it is less well known, how is it in your repertoire?" Eamon countered.

"It was in the repertoire of another company; I heard it, once."

"Which comedy?" Eamon asked curiously.

"*Brothers in Law*."

Eamon paused for a moment. "I don't know it," he said at last.

"It's the work of an unknown playwright," Ilenia told him, "a little earlier than the River Poet, and perhaps an influence on him. There are also fragments of a play thought to have been written by him, based on the Edelred Cycle. *Brothers in Law* is the only surviving comedy he wrote, though."

"What is it about?"

"Two brothers," Ilenia answered. "One dark, the other fair. They are both Crown officials in a small town up River. The town itself is never named, but several references are made to a tower. Players enjoy speculating which town it might be set in."

"Then I shall refrain from the like," Eamon laughed. "What happens?"

"Most of the town is part of an estate governed by a rich knight. At the beginning of the play this knight wills the estate to his only daughter and to her future spouse. She tells her father that she is in love with the fair brother and he with her in return. Pleased with his daughter's choice, the knight makes a bond with the fair brother. The brother must perform a duty for the knight in a distant province and, in return, will receive the hand of the daughter in marriage. Two copies of this bond are made, one kept by the knight and the second by the fair brother, who then goes on his journey." Ilenia paused to allow a servant to refill her goblet, nodding graciously to him by way of thanks. Taking a sip, she continued.

"While the fair brother is away the knight falls ill and dies. The knight's servant shows the remaining copy of the bond to the dark brother – who is also in love with the daughter – and incites his envy. In a fit of fury, the dark brother destroys the bond and the knight's will and is tricked by the servant into helping him to write a new will and bond.

"Of course, the servant nominates himself as the lord of the estate. He hires a group of men (the text seems confused as to whether there are three or four of them) to carry out his orders on the estate, binding them to himself by means of his will-bond. There is only one copy of this document."

Eamon set down his fork in surprise. "One copy?"

Ilenia smiled. "This, of course, means that he can alter the terms of the bond as much as he likes without being accountable to anyone. He does so, playing his men against one another and using them to intimidate the town and estate – they are comic characters, dull-witted and easily fooled.

"The servant announces that he will marry the knight's daughter. Hearing this, the dark brother finally protests and is evicted from the house. As he leaves he warns the servant to be wary of the fair brother. The servant becomes anxious that the fair brother will return with the surviving copy of the knight's original bond, and sends out some of his men in an attempt to stop him.

"The daughter happens to overhear the dark brother's warnings and realizes that she must stall the wedding. She and her nurse come up with various ways of doing this, which become progressively infuriating to the servant.

"During one of these attempts to delay her marriage the daughter meets the dark brother, who is living on the estate in disguise, trying to find a way to bring down the servant. Recognizing the daughter, he confesses to her how he helped the servant to deface the original bond and begs for her forgiveness. It is an interesting speech," Ilenia observed.

"How so?" Eamon asked.

Ilenia paused pensively. As she did so, the servants began to clear dishes from their table. "'All this my hands have done,'" she began. "'Mine alone is the fault, for it is I who tore the bond and went against your father's will. Nothing but fire remains to me, who have betrayed my brother and bound his estate to blood and darkness…'" Ilenia stopped with a frown. "That is not quite how it goes," she said, "and I do not remember the rest now – it has been a long time since the play was performed! – but the speech as a whole would work much better in a tragedy. It is full of remorse and grief – though very much out of tone with the rest of the play. I find it most moving."

"One tragic speech was not enough to convince Mr Shoreham?" Eamon grinned.

"Not quite."

"How does the play end?"

"The servant discovers that the daughter is stalling, and despite the dark brother's best efforts to help her, a date is set for the wedding. That is, of course, the very same day that the fair brother returns, bringing with him a copy of the original bond. He arrives during the wedding ceremony and is challenged by the servant, who claims that the fair brother cannot prove the validity of the bond. The people of the estate are uncertain which of the two to believe. This is the point where the dark brother, who is attending the wedding in disguise, reveals himself and denounces the servant's treachery. He highlights that there is only one copy of the servant's will-bond and that this makes it void. The fair brother (who is also able to produce evidence of the knight's original will) breaks the servant's bond, stating it to be unlawful, and the estate supports him. The servant is exiled while his lackeys are released from his service and kept on to work the estate. The fair brother weds the daughter, becoming lord of the estate, and the two brothers are reconciled."

Eamon blinked hard. "That sounds terribly complex," he said.

"The best comedies are," Ilenia smiled. "I have omitted a few details, but you get the idea." Eamon nodded dumbly. "Of course, this play has the mercy of not making the two brothers twins, which is comic-law."

"A mercy indeed!" Eamon laughed. "It sounds like a good play. Do you think Mr Shoreham will be convinced to try it?"

"Sadly, no," Ilenia smiled. "Mr Shoreham wants to commission a new one."

The evening wore on until the sky became thick and dark. Eamon had no idea what time it was when he dismissed the servants for the evening, and even less idea of the time when he finally felt sleep fill his limbs.

"It is late," he said at last.

"Yes." Ilenia had fallen quite still and her tone, so free while she discussed the play, had grown distanced and formal.

"Is something amiss?" Eamon asked.

Ilenia folded her hands into her lap. "I am to stay, my lord?" she asked quietly.

For a moment Eamon merely stared at her. His thought flew suddenly back to the Master's words in the Round Hall, and he understood.

He looked back at her. "Madam," he said, "the Master's pleasure was that you lend me company tonight. That you have done, and I have been better than well answered by it. Nonetheless, it would do me great honour if you would stay, and breakfast with me in the morning."

Ilenia lowered her gaze. "Yes, my lord."

"Mrs Roe."

The singer looked up, startled.

"I will sleep in my hall tonight," Eamon told her. "My bed shall be yours, and yours alone."

Ilenia stared.

"When you are asked if you slept in the bed of the Right Hand," Eamon said gently, "you shall be able to give a good answer."

Ilenia searched his face. Then she smiled. "Thank you, my lord."

Eamon rose and took her from where they had dined, through his quarters and to his own room. Between the open curtains at the broad embrasure he saw the reddened balcony opposite his own. As he stepped into the room he thought that he glimpsed a figure on that balcony, looking back at him.

Ilenia hung back while he strode to the curtains and drew them firmly across. Then he turned to her.

"I am afraid that I have dismissed my servants for the evening," he apologized. "If you require anything, wake me and I will serve you."

Ilenia gazed at him in wonder. "Thank you, my lord."

"Good night, madam."

Ilenia curtseyed. "Good night, Lord Goodman."

He left the room, pulling the door closed behind him. As he did so, he breathed out deeply.

He made his way across his darkened hall to the long, dark couch that stood in one of its corners. It had half a dozen thick cushions, which he diligently piled together at one end so as to pillow his head. Then he pulled off his cloak and lay down, drawing it over him. It was more than enough cover on such a night. As he settled down his eyes drifted to the closed door of his bedroom.

He did not know what his servants would think if they came in and found him sleeping in the hall in the morning. He resolved to wake before them.

As he lay there, he drifted into thought, reflecting on the play that Ilenia had described to him. Comedies written at about the River Poet's time usually ended with the marriage of the protagonists, and *Brothers in Law* was no exception to that rule. If Mr Shoreham truly did have a penchant for tragedy then Eamon could see why he would have turned down the work; the kind of comic plot that Ilenia had described tended to rely on word-play and on a good amount of physical humour – likely provided, for the most part, by the servant's men. Eamon imagined that the plot involving the knight's daughter and her attempts to stall the wedding was also a good source of comedy, no doubt with her twisting words and situations to double meanings and perhaps playing the servant's men to her best advantage as well. He wondered, though, whether there might not be tragic notes there: the daughter would surely be aware that, once her stalling was unveiled, she would be forced to marry the servant?

Eamon tried re-imagining a different version of the final scene; one where the fair brother did not return in time and the daughter was married to the servant. The story would have been very different – indeed, it occurred to him that at that point the daughter would have become a tragic heroine. What would she have done? Would she have taken the servant's life – or her own? Would the fair brother have returned just in time to hold the body of the woman who should have been his wife? Would he have returned at all?

He shook the thoughts aside with a shudder, feeling an odd relief that the outcome of the play was as it should be – the marriage of the daughter and the fair brother. Even so, the tragic outcome simmered just below the surface.

It seemed to Eamon that the tragic element in the play was maintained the most by the dark brother. Ilenia had said as much when she described his speech. Perhaps that was his role – to balance the likely comic outcome against the tragic alternative. Eamon had seen plays where other characters did similar things and knew that it took a very skilful playwright to correctly hold the two outcomes in tension. He tried picturing the dark brother in his mind. The character's story was certainly a distressing one: tricked into betraying brother, the knight's daughter, and estate into the hands of the servant. It was little wonder that his speech was tragic!

How had it gone? Eamon drew Ilenia's words back into his mind: "*Nothing but fire remains to me, who have betrayed my brother and bound his estate to blood and darkness.*"

Eamon paused. Of course the dark brother's speech was stricken – he had bound the estate to the servant – but fire, blood, and darkness?

As Eamon considered the dark brother's words empathy engulfed him. How often had he felt exactly the same – that only fire, blood, and darkness remained to him? Ever since he had sworn his oath and discovered the history of his house he had grappled with the anguish of blood, fire, and dark. Such was the hideous weight of treachery – one that even Arlaith, sitting by him in the Crown when he had returned from Pinewood, had acknowledged. That same burden – of knowing that he had betrayed the rightful holder of the estate – moved the dark brother in the play.

Had Eben Goodman felt it?

The thought came at Eamon like an unexpected blow. Blood, fire, and darkness – if Eamon felt the clawing press of them, then surely Eben had? Like the dark brother, Eben had betrayed one dear to him – perhaps as dear as a brother – and he had unlawfully helped to set another in that man's place. Indeed, the dark brother's words might almost have come from Eben's own mouth.

An odd stillness fell.

What if Eben *had* said them?

For a moment he didn't move, scarcely dared to think. The dark of the Right Hand's eyrie hung silently around him.

Breathing deeply, he tried to reason with himself. If the play had been written by an author writing only a little earlier than the River Poet, then it would have been written in the decades shortly following the fall of the house of Brenuin. It was conceivable that such an author had seen the fall of Allera and the founding of Dunthruik. Eamon knew that writers and poets at the time had tended to move either within or at the edges of the court's circles – and so it was just possible that the unknown writer had known Eben. If that was the case…

Was it possible that the dark brother represented Eben Goodman?

He turned his mind to the play and its characters again, testing what he had been told about the dark brother against what he knew of Eben. He thought at once of Ilenia's assertion that the dark brother had helped the servant to destroy the knight's bond before lending his hand to the creation of the replacement will-bond.

"… *who have betrayed my brother and bound his estate to blood and darkness.*"

Eamon let out a long breath. The dark brother had betrayed the fair, just as Eben had betrayed Ede. If the fair brother represented Ede…

If the fair brother represented Ede – or perhaps the house of Brenuin – then the daughter and estate given to him by the knight's bond had to hold another meaning. Eamon's mind whirled. The estate seemed obvious – the lands stood for the land, for the River Realm. But why should they be willed to the daughter? In marrying her, the fair brother took lawful possession of the estate. Perhaps, then, the daughter somehow symbolized the right to govern that land. Perhaps she stood for the kingship itself.

It was the daughter and estate that the servant wanted and what he had deceived the dark brother to attain.

The servant stood for the Master.

Chapter X

A creeping chill settled in Eamon's bones, for suddenly the allegory seemed terrifyingly obvious to him. *Brothers in Law* was no comedy – it was a play about Edelred's rise to power.

He turned back to the story again and again, trying to wring some other meaning from it, but the interpretation he had reached would not loose its hold upon his racing thought. What else could it possibly mean?

Then he remembered the lackeys with whom the servant had drawn up a second bond and used to control the estate.

"*So shall all those who are marked be bound in body, blade, and blood.*"

The line Eamon had read in Arlaith's papers flitted suddenly across his mind and he held it for a moment. How could he not have thought it before? The servant's men were bound to him, and the Gauntlet and Hands were bound to the throned. They were bound by the marks that they had received when they had sworn body, blade, and blood to him. In the play, the bond was ratified by the falsified will.

He quietly traced the mark on his palm with his fingers. It was dull beneath his touch. By what were the mark and fire in his flesh ratified? If the play's logic was to be followed then Eamon's own oath to the throned – signified by the lackeys' bond – was tied into some grander "will" of the servant's design. The servant used the same will to grant himself authority over the estate.

> *And in his hand aloft – Dark Tome!*
> *Great covenant to claim the throne!*

Eamon's blood curdled in his veins. He remembered the dire wrath with which the Master had struck him when he had given name to the long-sought Nightholt. He remembered the dreadful eagerness with which the throned had taken that same book into his hands when, bloodied and worn, Eamon had borne it to him from Cathair's lair.

There was only one Nightholt.

He lost his breath. Of course there was only one: why else would the Master have grown so angry losing, or spent so long seeking, it? Usurped though it was, Edelred's right to mastery was in that book. It was one that no other man could gainsay, for there was but one copy. By that tome, Eamon knew, the "Serpent's right" had been "made to yield".

He drew a deep breath. The Nightholt, then, was both the servant's will and bond. But in the play the will had been written to replace the bond by which the knight had granted his daughter and estate to the fair brother. In the same way, Edelred's Nightholt had to be an attempt to undo or invalidate some older bond – the "Serpent's right" spoken of by the Edelred Cycle.

Eamon frowned. It was clear that, in the play's terms, the knight's will remained uncontested, being greater than either the bond he had drawn up with the fair brother or the will-bond subsequently forged by the servant. In fact, the original will was the basis for both. Who, then, was the knight?

He silently searched the deepest parts of his thought and tried to summon forth some explanation, but none could be found. He did not understand who the knight might be or what exactly his will represented, but he understood that first will could not be overruled.

Even so, the servant had perversely mimicked it with his will-bond, and Edelred had done the same with the Nightholt.

Eamon understood then why Eben had sought so desperately to hide it and why Edelred had rejoiced so much to have it returned to him. He shivered. Everything came back to the Nightholt.

Troubled, he shook his head. If the Nightholt was a mockery of whatever was signified by the knight's will – by whatever truly granted power and kingship – then surely it could not hold? Or did it hold only so long as it could not be disproved and undone?

"*We await only the Serpent. I am ready, Eben's son…*"

There was sweat on his brow. Feverishly, Eamon brushed it away.

CHAPTER X

Dunthruik was fortified and prepared. The throned held his Nightholt, the book by which he had claimed and bound his stolen power. Since Ede's death that same tome had kept the Master's mark over the whole of the River Realm. There was only one thing left that could break it.

Edelred waited for Hughan.

CHAPTER XI

Eamon did not sleep that night.

As traces of light touched first the sky and then the dim walls of his hall he heard the faintest sounds of his servants moving about on their morning errands. After the long, waking dark, those sounds were sweet to him indeed.

It was not long before the servants' door opened and he heard footsteps approach. Belatedly he remembered that he was lying on the chaise longue rather than in his bed and that the servants should not know it, but even as he sat up, he realized that it was too late.

Cartwright passed through the hall towards the dining room. He carried a breakfast tray. As Eamon came upright, the servant froze in his tracks and stared in surprise at the Right Hand, whose cloak was still wrapped about him like a blanket.

"Good morning, Mr Cartwright," Eamon managed.

"My lord," Cartwright answered. "I have brought breakfast for you and your guest, my lord."

"Thank you," Eamon replied. "Please do continue."

Cartwright bowed and went on into the dining room to his work. With a deep breath Eamon rose and followed him. He watched as the servant set everything upon the table: a bowl and goblet for the Right Hand, another for his guest. Cartwright moved swiftly. Though he said nothing, Eamon knew the thoughts of Alessia's former servant were on the closed bedchamber door.

"Mr Cartwright," Eamon said softly. "I have need of your discretion."

Cartwright nodded silently.

"None must know that you found me sleeping this morning in my hall," Eamon told him. "There are some expectations of me that I will not keep, but which I cannot openly defy."

Cartwright hesitated.

"She is a married woman, Mr Cartwright," Eamon answered, "and I am not her husband."

There was a moment of silence. "Yes, Lord Goodman." Cartwright finished laying down what he had brought.

"Thank you," Eamon said.

Cartwright bowed then gathered his tray under his arm. He returned to the hall and, setting the tray down a moment, turned his attention to the chair where Eamon had lain during the night. He tidied it with swift, expert hands, and then beat the creases out of Eamon's cloak before setting it firmly over the Right Hand's shoulders. No word passed between them as he worked. As Cartwright stepped back, Eamon heard the sound of movement from the bedchamber.

"Thank you, Mr Cartwright," Eamon said quietly.

Cartwright bowed once. "My lord," he said, and left by the servants' stair.

Ilenia appeared in the bedchamber's doorway. She came gracefully down into the grey hall towards him.

"Good morning," he greeted her.

"Good morning, my lord." She curtseyed deeply.

"Did you sleep well?"

"Yes, thank you. And you?"

"Well enough," Eamon answered. He wasn't sure whether she believed him or not; her face remained pleasantly unreadable. "Will you join me for breakfast?" he added, gesturing towards the dining room.

Ilenia's eyes followed his hand to the breakfast table. She smiled. "It is not even dawn, Lord Goodman," she laughed. "Why is it that we are both awake and thinking of breakfast?"

"In fairness to my house, it is not I who thought of commanding breakfast at such an hour," Eamon offered. "But I seem to be more

234

of an eagle of the day than an owl of the night." He looked at her. "So, you see, I can explain my waking. And you, madam?"

"I heard you speaking," Ilenia answered.

"I am sorry if I woke you." Eamon wondered how much she had heard.

"I do not mind it, my lord."

Eamon smiled. "That is gracious of you," he told her. So saying, he led her to the table in the dining hall and invited her to sit. Taking a seat beside her, he poured her a glass of wine. His hand shook slightly, for the Nightholt still dwelt in his thought.

Ilenia watched him. "You are tired, Lord Goodman," she said quietly. "Perhaps, my lord, you are also troubled?"

Eamon set the jug down. "Yes," he murmured. "I am troubled. But I may not speak of it."

He dearly wanted to. As his desire to speak strove with his need for silence, his thought turned to Alessia. She had been such a comfort to him…

He felt a sudden touch on his hand and gasped, for when he looked up the touch was real. But it was not Alessia's – it was Ilenia's.

Slowly he pulled his hand away.

"Have I offended you, my lord?" Ilenia asked into the following silence.

"No," Eamon answered, earnestly meeting her gaze. "You have done nothing but delight me since I met you." He fell silent again. He could not guess where *she* was that morning, nor how she broke her fast, nor with whom, nor what she would rise to wear and do and say that day.

How he missed her.

"I remind you of someone," Ilenia guessed.

The words drew him out of himself. When he looked up, the singer searched his face; he could not guess how much she saw or read there.

He closed his eyes. "She is gone," he whispered.

"No." Ilenia's dark gaze assessed his face. "Forgive me, my lord. She is with you still. And you are grieved."

An angry furrow marred his brow. "She betrayed me," he said, "and not me alone." Alessia had betrayed Mathaiah. How could he forget it?

Ilenia still watched him carefully. "Did she speak to you of it?"

"When the hurt was done," Eamon answered bitterly.

"And did you hear her?"

Eamon stared at her. "I let her speak," he retorted, his bitterness increasing. "She could not undo the wrong that she had done me by mere words and tears."

Ilenia held his gaze for a moment. "Two hearts, Lord Goodman," she said quietly.

Eamon fell silent. His rage at Alessia fed on him.

He sat in silence for a long time then reached for his goblet and drank. Thoughts of the long night returned to him. They crossed in dark waves across his face.

"If I might be so bold, Lord Goodman, I wonder whether you lied to me before."

Eamon gaped. "You are bold indeed!"

"You said that you slept well enough," Ilenia explained. "I think that you did not sleep."

Eamon looked at her. He knew that she spoke the truth.

"If I slept badly, madam, that was not your doing," he told her. "The Serpent is coming," he added at last. "It troubles me."

"It troubles many."

"But I am not simply troubled, madam," he answered. "I am afraid." The confession seemed strange, but she received it.

"Why are you afraid, my lord?"

For a long time, he did not answer.

"When the day of battle comes," he breathed, "and the Serpent unfurls his banner on the field, I must keep the gate of this city." In his mind he saw the sword and star raised over the plains and groves and vines of Dunthruik, set against the Master's and the city's eagles. He shivered. "I fear that, on that day, all the things for which I have striven will come undone."

Ilenia gave him a compassionate look. "Why should they?"

Eamon met her gaze uncomfortably. "Mine is blood that has undone this city before. Perhaps," he whispered, "I have already undone it."

For a moment, Ilenia watched him in thoughtful silence. "Forgive me, Lord Goodman," she said, "for a second time, I fear that I must gainsay you."

Eamon looked at her curiously.

Ilenia was undeterred by his silence. "You are a noble man of great heart – so much is clear. I do not doubt that some things have been given to you to do, or to undo." She paused and her eyes searched his face. When she spoke again, her voice was quiet, but determined. "Though you may have the task of watching at the gate, the saving or undoing of this city is not your charge."

Eamon gaped, astonished. "How do you reach that?" he breathed.

"You are a watchman, Lord Goodman," she told him, "and you have been preparing this city for when the Serpent comes. Then your time of watching will be at an end."

Tears blinded him briefly. He blinked them away. She was right, and it terrified him.

"When all my watching is done," he whispered, "what will be left to me?"

Ilenia matched his gaze. "The test of your heart," she told him. "For then, you must come down from the watchtower and draw your sword beneath the banner that you serve."

There was a long silence.

"Where did you learn to see the hearts of men so keenly?" Eamon asked.

"It is your heart that I see, Lord Goodman," she answered. "Take courage. Take breakfast, too," she added, and lifted the basket of breads towards him.

Eamon stared dumbly.

"Thank you," he breathed at last.

For a few minutes they ate and drank together in silence. The sounds about them were those of the palace rising to another day, and the sun continued climbing beyond the rim of the world.

Eamon looked at Ilenia again. "You will remember what I said to you yesterday evening?" he said. "If any man asks after your company?"

"Yes, my lord," Ilenia answered. "Thank you."

"It is the very least that I can do."

Eamon paused to drink. As he set his goblet down, the doors to the hall opened. Seconds later a man burst into the room.

"Mr Fletcher," Eamon said in surprise. His lieutenant looked pale.

"Your pardon, my lord," Fletcher garbled breathlessly, throwing himself into an untidy bow, "but you must come at once."

"What has happened?" Eamon asked.

"The port," Fletcher cried, gesturing towards it. "It's under attack!"

Eamon sprang to his feet. "Cartwright!" he yelled.

Cartwright appeared at once. "My lord?"

"Have Madam Ilenia escorted home. Madam," he added, turning to her, "please accept my apologies."

He did not wait for either of them to answer. Stopping only to seize his scabbard and sword, he rushed through the door.

Eamon and Fletcher tore wordlessly down the steps and into the plaza. The stable hands were already there; Sahu was saddled and waiting. Fletcher's horse stood beside, flanks quivering from the ride it had already made.

Right Hand and lieutenant leapt into their saddles. Eamon grabbed Sahu's reins and wheeled towards the palace gates. The cobbles shuddered through the limbs of both horse and rider as Eamon drove his steed into a gallop, Fletcher close behind him. Men fled from their path.

They raced up the Coll towards the Sea Gate. Before they reached the quay stones Eamon heard the cries of battle and the smell of smoke thick in the air. They bolted through the gate onto the waterfront. There, Eamon drew his horse to a sharp halt and stared.

The port was a churning lake of fire.

The quarters' storehouses on the dockside poured violent, billowing smoke and leering flame into the harbour and the air. As the fire guttered, the South Quarter storehouses crumbled. The flames engulfed the wares awaiting transport. Almost half the city's cogs and a dozen smaller vessels burned; masts withered and prows buckled as voracious flame devoured them. One ship was deeply staggered in the water at the harbour mouth, men pouring over its sides in terror, some only to be caught and drowned by hissing wreckage. Long slicks lay on the water and these also burned, giving out choking smoke. Walls of fire enclosed the port, trapping those within.

Just beyond the flame of the dying ships in the harbour mouth were three ships and half a dozen small holks, much like the one which had borne him from Edesfield. The ship nearest the mouth was a great cog. In that whole terrifying expanse of fire and water it was to the cog's mast, and to its flag, that Eamon's eyes were drawn.

The flag was blue.

There were men on the harbour walls: attackers dressed in browns and greys and armed with flaming bows, shooting at ships, men, and wares. The waterfront, which had been filled with traders and civilians with the breaking of the day, was a mass of terror.

As Eamon threw himself down from his horse, reinforcements arrived. Uniformed Gauntlet raced into the port and onto the walls while the attackers harried the Master's fleet. Men from the North Quarter charged along the length of the harbour's north wall, and the attackers, seeing their danger, turned their bows from red-sailed ships to red-shirted men. One man fell as, with a wrathful hiss, the arrows loosed. Screams of warning were answered by anguished cries.

Having loosed their charge, the wayfarers retreated along the wall. Reaching its end, they scrambled into a waiting boat. The wounded Gauntlet prepared to follow them. One man in grey was struck by a bolt and tumbled from the wall into the churning water.

More cries sounded from the south wall. West Quarter troops charged the length of the wall towards the enemy. The wayfarers fell back rapidly before them. Struck by an arrow, a Gauntlet man toppled into the water. Encouraged by the retreat, the Gauntlet pressed on, but suddenly the air above them was riven with a volley of flaming arrows from beyond the harbour wall. Men stumbled with cries of pain.

As the remaining Gauntlet pursued their quarry, the wayfarers piled back into their boats and withdrew. The largest cog, itself surrounded by the remains of flailing, flaming ships and treacherous fire slicks, retreated from the harbour mouth to the open sea. Another hail of arrows flew from the south, pinning the Gauntlet behind the walls.

Suddenly sense returned to Eamon. "Fall back from the walls!" he commanded. He raced towards them to make his call heard. "Fall back!"

The Gauntlet heard and obeyed. As he ran, Eamon looked again to the harbour and saw that the cog had reached the safety of the open water. It left a river of flame and death in its wake.

It was then that a thick whoosh shuddered the air; a burning missile hurtled over the south wall towards another storehouse. The Gauntlet on the wall, retreating with their wounded in tow, saw it too. The air filled with their cries as the missile smashed into the waterside. The building blossomed into a flaming quagmire.

Horrified, Eamon turned to his lieutenant. "Fletcher!"

The lieutenant reached his side. "My lord?" he shouted above the din.

"Form fire-fighting crews – now!"

As Fletcher raced off, one of the nearby storehouses collapsed; Eamon covered his eyes against the barrage of smoke and ash that burst from it. He fled for the south wall. As he ran, he saw a group of bodies lying in the rubble on the blackened quay.

With a sick stomach he raced up to them. They were uniformed in red and pierced with arrows – all but one. He bore traces of black beyond the stinking flesh that hung in brittle flakes from limb and face. What was left of its charred hand bore a ring, unscathed by ash or flame.

Eamon's face twisted with horror. As smoke and rage caught in his throat, he knew that he could not stop to think on it.

He looked back to the waterside, searching for men amid the fire and wreckage. More troops arrived from the Sea Gate. They ran towards him, an officer among them.

"Lieutenant!" Eamon yelled.

"Lord Dehelt?" The screaming officer struggled to see through the moving columns of smoke. When his eyes at last found Eamon, his face turned pale.

"Dehelt is dead," Eamon answered. "I am Lord Goodman. Assign your men to fire fighting." Bodies bobbed face-down in the water. The Master's ships, and those of his merchant allies, crumbled in hissing pools of timber. "Do it now, lieutenant!" Eamon yelled.

The officer left, barking orders to his men as he went. They soon returned with water and buckets. More Gauntlet staggered down from the north wall covered in smoke.

Eamon looked again at Dehelt. Driving down the bitterness in his heart, he took the man's ring, turned, and made for the south.

There too men returned from the tattered wall. Ensigns and cadets piled back down to the quay. As Eamon arrived, Febian reached the quayside. The Hand's face was horror-stricken.

"Febian!" Eamon yelled.

The Hand turned to him. "Lord Goodman," he answered. His hands shook holding the reins. "What in the Master's name happened?"

"Call the surgeons!" Eamon retorted. "There are wounded as well as dead."

Febian snapped out of his shock. He nodded and charged off. Waite and more men from the West Quarter arrived through the Sea Gate.

Eamon reached the men returning from the south wall. "Report!" he yelled.

The nearest man looked up at him. "Eleven lost, at least two injured," gasped the ensign. "There were caltrops and arrows on the wall."

Eamon nodded. He was about to turn away when he saw the last ensigns come down from the wall. They bore the body of an injured man. He had an arrow in his side and was marred with blood and grime. Eamon gasped.

It was Manners.

He rushed forward as the ensigns brought Manners' bleeding body down from the wall. The men carried their lieutenant to a sheltered part of the broken waterfront and laid him down on the stone. Manners erupted into a fit of coughing that brought pools of blood through his lips which splattered his ashen face. His eyes were dull.

"Get a surgeon!" Eamon commanded the nearest ensign. "The rest of you fight the fires!"

The ensigns raced away. The docks filled with shouting men, cracking fires, and the rush of water poured by pump and bucket onto what remained of Dunthruik's harbour.

Eamon looked down at the lieutenant. "Manners?" he said. He pressed the young man's hand. "Manners?"

No answer. Eamon looked up desperately. The port was flooded with Gauntlet and militia fighting the fires – and he should be with them, commanding them. As he knelt there, the Gauntlet brought other injured soldiers and laid them next to him.

The surgeons arrived moments later. One looked at Manners, solemnly shook his head, and moved on to the next wounded man.

Eamon looked down at Manners again. The lieutenant was dying.

In terrible anguish Eamon touched Manners' face. There were men all around him and he knew that he could not heal the man before him. He closed his eyes, feeling tears, but whether the greater of them flowed from grief or smoke, he could not be certain.

What could he do?

Suddenly he was on the plain. It had been so long since he had seen it that he scarcely recognized it at first. It was dark and dim, and for a moment he struggled to find his balance as nausea wracked him.

"Manners!" he called.

"Lord Goodman?"

The voice that answered him was frail. His pale face looked afraid in the darkness. Then he saw Eamon.

"Lord Goodman!"

"I'm here, Manners," Eamon answered. As he spoke, the young man stopped, a look of awe and surprise on his face. He stared at Eamon speechlessly.

"Manners?" Eamon asked.

"What should I call you, sir?" Manners breathed.

It was then that Eamon realized that on the plain he was dressed not in the black robes of a Right Hand, but in sapphire splendour.

Eamon matched his gaze. "Manners," he began.

"Am I dying?" Manners asked him.

"Yes." Terror ran across the man's face. "You are dying, Manners, and though I have it in me, I cannot save you."

Manners steeled his face and nodded. "Yes, sir," he whispered. Suddenly he gave a cry of pain and staggered down to his knees. Eamon was at his side at once. There were tears on his face.

Surely he could do something!

Suddenly he remembered the strange half sleep under which Mathaiah had been borne to Dunthruik and understood that Manners could walk there until Hughan came, if he would trust the King.

He looked earnestly into the fading face before him. "Manners, whom do you serve?"

"I…" Manners' face twisted in shattering pain. "I serve the Master… No! I… the Lord of Dunthruik…"

Eamon reached out and seized Manners' hands. "Do you remember what you once said to me?" he cried. "You told me that you served the one I serve. *Do you remember?*"

Manners shook his head violently. "You are the Right Hand. You serve the Lord of…."

Suddenly Manners' eyes shone clear and he fixed Eamon with soulful determination.

"You serve the King," he said.

Eamon did not have time to feel joy. "I cannot heal you," he whispered, "but the King can and will, if you will wait for him. Will you wait for him?"

"How can I wait for him?" Manners asked.

"You must wait with all your heart and all your strength: he will save you."

"But – I'm – dying…"

There was a crash in the darkness about them. Eamon's eyes opened and he stared at the port; he swore. Another building shattered beneath the bulk of the flames; Eamon shielded the lieutenant's body as smoking rubble rained down on them. The air filled with screams and yells.

Eamon looked urgently down at the lieutenant again. Manners' breath was shallow and he struggled to open his eyes.

"Sir? Sir, I can't see you!"

Eamon pressed his hand. "I am with you. Do you trust me, and the one who sent me?"

For a long time the lieutenant did not answer. Then, against all the power of Eamon's despair, the young man found the strength to nod his head.

Eamon leaned his face down close by Manners' ear. "By the King's grace, be granted strength and life to wait for him," he whispered.

The roar of the port was all around him. Manners drew a deep breath and fell still.

Eamon looked anxiously at the young man's face. His own hands trembled as he drew them away and rubbed at his blackened eyes.

"Surgeon!" he called.

One of the Gauntlet surgeons hurried to him. "My lord?"

Eamon gestured to Manners. The surgeon knelt down for a

moment and searched for vital signs. "Alive, my lord," he answered, "but weak."

"Transfer him to the West Quarter infirmary," said another voice – Captain Waite's. The man's face was grey and sweaty.

"Yes, sir," the surgeon answered.

Eamon rose and looked around again. Many of the quay fires had been extinguished, though the ships and water-slicks still burned. Beyond the harbour walls the tips of masts flew blue flags. He stared at them.

How had Hughan gathered a fleet?

As Manners was borne away by the surgeons, Eamon looked at the obliterated port, pale stone, and charred bodies. They filled him with uncomprehending grief. Slowly, he looked across at Waite.

"What is this?" he breathed.

The captain grimly met his gaze. "It is the beginning, my lord."

CHAPTER XII

The mood was sombre in the chamber where the Quarter Hands awaited admittance to the throne. The day waned heavily. When the doorkeeper bade them to follow him, they entered in silence.

The Master sat calmly in his towering throne. The Quarter Hands knelt before him, Eamon at their head. The formation was unbalanced without the Lord of the North Quarter.

"Rise. Tell me what happened, son of Eben." There was an oddly eager note to his voice.

It should have been the task of the port master to give the report. But Dehelt was dead.

"The Serpent's vessel was flying a Giblirian flag," Eamon began. "It was thought to be stopping to resupply. Just after dawn, the cog ran up the Serpent's flag and moved to block the port mouth. There were other craft at sea, beyond the north and south walls; they launched boulders into the harbour and destroyed several smaller river holks. They put snakes onto the walls; the snakes set fire to half the ships in the port and destroyed many of the quayside buildings. They poured slick into the water and set it alight. The cog blocking the harbour destroyed several others. There was a battle on the walls, after which the snakes retreated.

"We lost a dozen galley defenders and fifteen others, another dozen civilians, and up to sixty men with the sinking of your warship, *The Eagle's Wing*, to say nothing of those lost on the merchant vessels nearest the harbour mouth." Their allies' cogs had taken the most severe losses; Eamon paused to drive images of sinking ships from his mind. "We also lost Lord Dehelt," he said quietly, "and yesterday's quarter stores, which were yet to be delivered, as well as a cargo of wines and wood going to Etraia. The enemy's craft have remained in our waters, blocking entry to or exit from the harbour. The River ferry has also been destroyed."

There was a moment of silence as Eamon's report echoed in the long hall.

"Repair the ships," the Master said. He sounded unperturbed by what he had heard. "Clear the blockages. Send word to Etraia and her allies; she is to send a force to break the Serpent's obstructions. He shall not harry our mouth."

Eamon bowed but Arlaith stepped forward.

"It will not be easy, Master, to send word to Etraia," he said.

The throned eyed him critically. "Speak."

"The movers... can no longer move."

The revelation shocked Eamon. How could that be?

The Master did not seem concerned. "Send the Gauntlet," he commanded.

"I had done so, but Gauntlet patrols with duties beyond the walls have begun returning in haste to the city," Arlaith explained. "There have been heavy losses to several divisions, and groups of land-workers have been stranded outside the walls."

There was a moment of quiet. "With what force were they so attacked?" the Master asked.

"Survivors were unclear of the nature or numbers of the attack, Master," Arlaith answered. "The last groups spoke of an ambush of unprecedented force." He paused. "The Serpent does not simply glide in our waters and at our mouth, Master; he is on the plains," he said. "There he conceals his numbers with ease."

Eamon thought of the land beyond the city walls, the buildings and forest, the vineyards, orchards, and olive groves to either side of the East Road. There was a whole host of places where the wayfarers could hide.

"Then you will discover them," the Master told him firmly. "Send the Hands at dawn."

Chapter XII

Arlaith bowed. "Yes, Master."

The throned turned to Eamon. "Eben's son, you will assume the North. I have no wish to lose time in choosing another falcon."

Eamon bowed his head. "Yes, Master."

"Lord Tramist, what does the south wall see?"

"Little, Master," Tramist answered.

"The Serpent will go to the South Bank," the Master told him. "See him when he does."

"Yes, Master."

The Master smiled at them. "He comes," he said, and laughed. It sent a chill down Eamon's spine.

The throned dismissed them, commanding their return on the following day with news. This put grim looks on all their faces, but on Arlaith's in particular – he hurried swiftly away. As they left the throne room, Eamon walked alongside Tramist.

"Lord Goodman," the Quarter Hand greeted him formally.

"Lord Tramist," Eamon answered, equally rigid.

"It was you who found Dehelt?" the Hand asked, then added with a sneer, "Or what remained of him?"

Eamon rounded on him. "That is no way to speak of him."

"Forgive me, Lord Goodman," Tramist answered. "I repeat only what has been told, which is to say that he came to a grisly end."

"He was a lord of Dunthruik," Eamon retorted, aggrieved.

"Whence this anger, Lord Goodman?" Tramist asked with odd interest. "Dehelt died in the Master's service. Surely that does not upset you?" His eyes took on a shrewd glint.

Eamon met his gaze. "Lord Dehelt was a loyal servant who did not deserve death. That grieves and angers me."

"I hear that one of Captain Waite's lieutenants was badly injured this morning?" Tramist continued.

"Many men were hurt."

"This lieutenant was near death, as I understand, and yet he lives."

"He is still near death," Eamon answered. "As are others that the surgeons saved."

"A surgeon saw to him?" Tramist turned to him with a look of surprise that swiftly became insincere. "That was not what I heard."

They had reached the palace entrance. Tramist paused before bowing low to him. "I take my leave," he said, and mounted his horse to return to the south.

Eamon watched him go.

Eamon returned wearily to his own chambers. Though it was late, Captain Longroad of the North Quarter was sent to him. The man was pale, nervous, and evidently daunted by the quarters of the Right Hand. Eamon went through an amount of paperwork with him, giving authorization to various orders. For a moment, as he pressed his seal down into the wax before him, he could have been back in the East Quarter. But when he raised the ring he saw no owl, and when he looked up, the face before him did not belong to Anderas.

He thanked the captain and dismissed him. Then he summoned Cartwright. The servant came at once.

"My lord?"

"Did Madam Ilenia return home safely?"

"Yes, my lord," Cartwright answered. "She asked me to convey her thanks to you once again."

Eamon smiled ruefully. "Thank you. Would you send word for a light meal? Breakfast feels as though it was a very long time ago."

"Of course." Cartwright bowed and left the room.

Eamon sighed and leaned back heavily in his chair, allowing his head to loll back. The wooden wings of the Right Hand's eagle curved about his head.

It had begun. He rolled images of the morning through his mind. Hughan had blockaded Dunthruik. The King was coming. As he sat in the depths of his study, that idea somehow filled him with fear.

You will have to give account of yourself, son of Eben. You know what you have done.

Eamon closed his eyes. "I have served him," he murmured.

And if the Serpent claims this city? The voice crawled through his skin. *In victory he will have no further use for you. You are tainted, son of Eben. There is no place for you beneath his banner. There can be no place for those whose blood is mine. In victory he will renounce you and cast you out, as you deserve.* The voice laughed and Eamon shuddered. *Where will you go then, son of Eben?*

Eamon tried to draw himself together, but the voice's hissings taunted him. He was the Right Hand. Surely Hughan would have no choice but to send him away?

His hands began to shake on the desk. He tried to steady them. It was too early to think of victory, or defeat, or of long lonely roads into darkness. He trusted Hughan. Why should he fear a man whom he trusted?

Cartwright returned with some food for him. Eamon thanked him as the servant nervously laid it down.

"Is something the matter, Mr Cartwright?"

After a moment's hesitation, Cartwright nodded. "There's rumour in the house, my lord."

"What kind of rumour?"

"That the Serpent has come, to break the city walls and devour us." The man sounded truly afraid.

Eamon's own fears fled and he looked at his servant with pity. "Do not be afraid, Mr Cartwright," he said gently. "He will not."

Cartwright watched him for a moment in silence then, at Eamon's nod, left him to his meal.

The following day Eamon was in his study, deep in thought, when there was a knock at the door.

"Come."

Fletcher entered and bowed low. "My lord, you asked to be advised when Lord Arlaith's patrol returned."

"Yes. Where is he now?"

"He is on his way to see the Master."

"I will go and see him."

Eamon hurried through the palace towards the throne room. It was as he was passing through the main hall that he encountered Arlaith. Eamon soon caught up with the Left Hand's hurried steps.

"Lord Arlaith."

Arlaith looked up. "Lord Goodman," he greeted.

"Is there any news?"

Arlaith looked at him sourly. "Do I look like a man bearing news, Lord Goodman?" he growled.

"How would you prefer me to answer?" Eamon asked. "Truthfully or tactfully?"

"I may choose?"

"Yes."

Arlaith looked at him oddly then managed a small laugh. "You are a strange man, Lord Goodman."

"I am glad that I humour you."

"Not as glad as I," Arlaith replied.

They met Febian and Tramist on the way to the throne room and went together to kneel before the Master. He bade them rise, then summoned Eamon to his side.

"What sees the South, Lord Tramist?" the Master asked.

"Men out of the Land of the Seven Sons," Tramist replied grimly. "Now that we have no ferry the Easters are building an enormous pontoon over the River. In a day most of it has been erected; by tomorrow morning the South will see a complete bridge." He paused. "Master," he said, "there is an army camped behind it."

The throned nodded. The news did not seem to trouble him. "Lord Febian?"

"Repairs have begun on your ships, Master," Febian answered, "but work is slow. Slower still are our attempts to clear the slick, which still burns. Messengers have been dispatched to Etraia; at least three that we know of have already been waylaid by the Serpent."

"Work more swiftly, Lord Febian," the throned told him. "And send more messengers."

Febian shuddered beneath his address. "Yes, Master."

At last, the throned turned to Arlaith. "I will have your news, Lord Arlaith."

"I dispatched two dozen Hands this morning, Master," Arlaith answered. "Eight returned."

A pause. "I said that I would have news," the throned said quietly. Eamon repressed the urge to shiver.

"The plains are pocked with mounted men that harry any who attempt to pass. My Hands were met by archers, many out of the east."

Eamon remembered the thundering charge of the mounted archers at Pinewood. The Hands were the closest thing that the River Realm had to such men, but it seemed clear to Eamon that the Hands were too few, and perhaps too little skilled, to match the Easters. It was little wonder that Hands had been lost.

"Did you break their line and learn their number?" The Master's voice was almost polite in its enquiry. Both Right Hand and Left knew its truer nature.

"No, Master."

"Then why have you returned to me?" Arlaith bowed his head but could not answer. "You will take the Hands," the Master told him, "and you will press the lines again."

Arlaith looked up angrily. "Master –"

"You would defy me?"

Arlaith stilled. "No, Master."

"Master," Eamon interrupted boldly.

The throned turned to him. "What would you, son of Eben?"

"Lord Arlaith's concern is for the lives of your servants," Eamon told him. "It is no defiance to show concern for those who glorify you."

The throned laughed and turned with whimsical triumph to Arlaith. "Do you see, Left Hand, what kind of a man has supplanted you?"

Arlaith looked grey. "Yes, Master."

"Had I sent the son of Eben to survey the lines in your place, think you not that he would have returned with news of all the Serpent's strength?"

"Yes, Master," Arlaith returned. Eamon saw an odd glint in his eye as he spoke.

"You will press the lines and you will tell me their strength," the throned returned. "You will do it yourself. Go."

"Your glory, Master."

Arlaith bowed low and turned to leave. The other Hands went with him. Eamon made to follow them but the Master's voice soon stopped him.

"Son of Eben."

Eamon looked back to the Master. The grey eyes chilled him. He was held captive by that glance until the Hands had left the hall. Then he was held in silence.

"How may I serve you, Master?" Eamon asked at last.

"An evening ago you had a guest, Eben's son. Did you spend a pleasant night?" The throned's smile flickered with the curve of a voyeur. Eamon swallowed back a sickened feeling, and bowed.

"Thank you, Master," he answered. "I did."

"Pity is a vile and creeping virtue, son of Eben." Suddenly the smile was gone and the Master's voice was on him like a heavy blow, grinding him to dust. "Do not intercede for Arlaith."

Eamon bowed low again. "Yes, Master."

"Go. See that he does as I have commanded."

Eamon went that afternoon to the Blind Gate. The city streets were awash with Gauntlet and with noise, for the attack on the port had struck hard. Eamon saw fear in the faces he met and knew it to be in the people's hearts also: the Serpent had come and ringed the city, by land and sea.

He arrived in the square by the Blind Gate. It towered high above him, and watchmen lined the walls. They gazed out over the plains towards the valleys and the coils of the River. Near the watchmen was a trellis, on which the heads and bodies of traitors hung. Some belonged to Cathair's dogs.

Eamon brought his gaze away and looked back to the gates

themselves, remembering for a moment the exodus from the East Quarter, the Grennils and the countless other families who had left the city to make room for its defenders. He wondered where those families were that day and whether they looked on Dunthruik from beneath the King's banner.

The square by the gate was filled with Hands and horses. The horses looked fresh, but the Hands did not. Their faces were tired and grim. Eamon wondered whether they had been out that morning, seeking to break the lines.

Arlaith stood to one side of the group, carefully adjusting the straps and harnesses on his horse. The Hand swore as he pulled angrily at the saddle.

Eamon dismounted and went to Arlaith's side. Without a word he reached out and loosened the strap that had so infuriated the Left Hand. Arlaith looked up at him, first with surprise and then with ire.

"Thank you," he hissed. It was by no means a civil pronouncement.

"You did not deserve the wrath laid against you," Eamon said quietly. "That is why I spoke."

"You would judge the Master?" Arlaith returned.

Eamon watched as Arlaith finished violent adjustments of the saddle. "No."

"Then do not speak against him. You make things difficult in doing so, Lord Goodman, both for yourself and for those whom you seek to aid." Arlaith stepped back from the horse with an infuriated sigh. Eamon saw that the sword set at the Hand's side was different from his own and that it was borne in an ornate scabbard. It reminded him of Cathair's.

"Why are you here?" Arlaith demanded.

"To see that you do as the Master commanded."

"I have no need of watching," Arlaith spat. "I was riding to war before you were conceived, Lord Goodman."

"Still, I have come to watch," Eamon answered. "And to wish you good fortune. I do not envy you your task."

255

Arlaith's face softened a shade. "Then I shall thank you for your wish."

Without a further word Arlaith climbed into the saddle. He grew to an enormous stature and Eamon gazed at him in surprise. Seated upon the beast, Arlaith seemed to hail from a bygone age.

"To horse!" the Left Hand commanded. The others did as he bade and the square filled with the noise of mounting men. Eamon stepped to the side to let Arlaith pass, watching as the horsemen drew up behind the gate. So many mounted Hands was a fearsome sight.

"Open the gate!" Arlaith cried. There was a flurry of movement in the gatehouse and then the gates began to swing open. The horses fretted while they waited, neighing and dancing upon their hooves as though upon hot coals.

The Blind Gate opened. Through it the road ran out into the plains. They seemed empty of anything but grass and mud. Yet the churned earth gave evidence of an earlier sortie.

Arlaith took the reins and turned to face the Hands. "Once again, gentlemen, we seek an impression of the Serpent's force, and we will not fall back for mere arrows. If the Serpent sheds a few scales by our outing, then so much the better."

With a cry Arlaith urged his horse forward. It leapt into a gallop and charged through the gate. The Hands tore after him.

Eamon watched them go, mesmerized by the sight.

The gates drew shut behind them. Eamon went at once to the gatehouse and up the stair onto the walls. The smell of rotting flesh assaulted his nostrils as he climbed past the traitors' ledge, but he went on until he had reached the wall-top. There he turned to look out across the plain.

The mountains, hazy with distance, gazed back at him. The River and its banks were shaded with light copses. The galloping Hands drew into formation and pressed out across the plain. Still Eamon saw no foe.

The field flashed green and a group of Easter archers appeared. They came as though from nowhere, summoned by the charging

Hands. More groups appeared from behind the edges of the plain. The thrill of the charge filled Eamon's veins, but on the city wall, all was mute. He felt wind in his face – wind that bore the scent of flowers in a distant valley.

The Easters bore down with ferocious speed. Arrows flew. One of the Hands was struck, but he kept riding. The Hands drew off from their charge as more foes appeared from their right; they wheeled about and began to return to the city. They could not break through.

As the Hands quit the field, the Easters and wayfarers returned to their previous positions. Eamon followed a group of them with his eyes as they passed off towards the River. He caught sight of movement to the south on the far bank.

Remembering Tramist's words about a bridge, he curiously peered south through the haze. There was movement there, on what was called the West Bank. A group of river holks, some of which he suspected had been involved in the naval attack the previous day, and beyond them groups of men, gathered at either side of a large pontoon bridge.

The sound of galloping hooves reached Eamon's ears. The Hands returned to the gate. Eamon went down the steps to meet them. He arrived in time to see Arlaith clatter into the square.

"Bloody Easters!" he yelled. "Bloody, bloody Easters!" He dismounted violently, handing his horse over to one of the many Gauntlet who awaited them, then stormed across to Eamon. He opened his mouth to speak but Eamon spoke first.

"'Bloody Easters'?" he guessed.

"*Bloody Easters!* What has the Serpent to do with them? How am I to assess their numbers?" he fairly howled it.

"How many riders were there?" Eamon asked.

"How should I know? They conceal themselves and their positions. Short of going up and clasping hands most politely with each and every bloody one of the scions of the Seven Bastards, I have no way to count them!"

"Lower your voice, Lord Arlaith," Eamon told him. The other Hands looked at them nervously. The injured were brought on stretchers and taken to the surgeons.

"I will not ride out again," Arlaith hissed. "Let the Master be content with my assessment that there are many of them."

"Let us assign a number to 'many'," Eamon answered. "You are an experienced man, Lord Arlaith. What is your guess?"

"That the Easters seem to be supporting the troops from the port raid," Arlaith replied after a small pause. "They're here to blockade the city while the main army arrives, which it has done."

"And how many men would it take to blockade this city?" Eamon asked.

"At least five hundred," Arlaith answered bitterly.

"Then let us guess that the Serpent has used your logic," Eamon replied, "and I will take that news to the Master."

Arlaith eyed him carefully. "Will you, Lord Goodman?"

"Yes," Eamon told him levelly. "And I will ask you to go to the south wall, to assess what can be seen on the bank. Dismiss these Hands," he added.

Arlaith assessed him for a moment. "Very well, Lord Goodman."

Eamon nodded once to him and then returned to his horse. He mounted and rode to the palace.

He came swiftly to the throne room. The doorkeeper met him and bowed deeply.

"Lord Goodman."

"I bring news for the Master."

"He is in his private garden." The doorkeeper's answer surprised him. "I will conduct you to him."

The doorkeeper led him to the Master's wing of the palace. Passing the grand staircase that led up to the Master's chambers, the doorkeeper took him down a corridor and to a tall archway Eamon had never seen before. It led between the hedges and into the afternoon sun in a walled garden.

The walls of the Master's buildings bound the garden round. High above, the tall windows of the Master's rooms loomed over him. The garden was filled with red: red vines and climbing plants and flowers of more types of crimson and scarlet than Eamon could imagine.

A small building stood in the centre of the garden, more ornate than anything Eamon had ever seen: delicate fluting was carved in spirals all about its dome, like the flourishes of a dancer.

The doorkeeper conducted him there. Inside was cool and dark. Eamon could barely make out the markings on the walls, but long benches lined them.

The Master was within. He stood looking at a great crowned eagle that adorned the wall before him.

"Master," said the doorkeeper.

The Master rounded on him. "Why do you disturb me here?" he hissed viciously.

The doorkeeper paused. "I bring Lord Goodman."

The Master nodded wordlessly, and bowing, the doorkeeper withdrew.

It was then that Eamon felt his vision change. As he gazed at the hollow of the building he thought that he saw a woman sitting on one of the long benches. She sat and watched the doorway where Eamon himself stood. A moment later he saw a brilliant smile blossom on her face as a striking young man entered before her. His hair shone like fire in the sunlight as she rose and rushed to him. He took her hands and she laughed as he kissed her.

Eamon blinked hard and stared, but the vision had gone. The throned was before him, and as Eamon watched, the Master turned to face him.

"Where is Arlaith?" he asked.

"The south wall."

There was a grim silence. "I did not send him there."

"I did," Eamon said boldly. "I have come bearing his news in his stead."

"Have you, Eben's son?" The throned's grey eyes stabbed keenly at him. "Come you to take his praise, or his punishment?"

"I will take whatever you deem to lay upon me."

The Master's gaze softened into a laugh. "Speak."

"There are about five hundred men blockading the city, Master," Eamon answered, "and the enemy can easily send more. There is evidence of further movement beyond the bridge; it is this which Arlaith has gone to investigate."

The throned glanced up at the walls. "They will be from the Land of the Seven Sons," he said. "The Serpent knew that he had to cross the River to reach my city, but he had not the wit to do it. And now he lies there, waiting for his bridge." He laughed. "Come swiftly, Serpent," he murmured. "*Swiftly*."

Eamon could only stand in silence as the Master wandered in his own thoughts. Then the fiery head turned towards him.

"You will take council for battle, son of Eben," the Master said. "Tomorrow you will preside over my Quarter Hands and my generals."

The idea terrified him. "Yes, Master."

"You will go to Captain Waite of the West," the throned continued, "and you will greet him as 'general' in my name. He will command the Gauntlet during the battle that is to come. He will elect his own successor to the captaincy."

"Yes, Master," he said. Eamon's heart grew, in fear and in pride, for the captain.

"Meet them at first light, Eben's son," he said. "I will hear your plan of war by dusk."

"Your glory, Master."

With Fletcher's assistance, Eamon sent out the summons for the war council. He watched with growing dread as his lieutenant departed, the papers firmly under his arm.

As the evening drew on he took to his horse once again, so distracted that it took him two attempts to mount. Sahu whinnied disapprovingly and he apologized, after which the horse deigned to carry him down the Coll.

Night settled in the eaves of the West Quarter as he arrived at the college. A couple of cadets lit the braziers on the college steps. It surprised Eamon at first, but he realized that since the exodus of the city's civilians, a large number of servants had gone, too. Only the palace, nobles, and Quarter Hands had retained them. The colleges found the servants' tasks useful for the occupation of numerous cadets and ensigns who had arrived with the external divisions.

Eamon dismounted and went into the college, greeting those on guard. They bowed to him in return. As he passed through the hall he saw Overbrook's map; it still hung on the wall, the most detailed map of Dunthruik that had perhaps ever been drawn. Eamon smiled for a moment, remembering the cadet's enthusiasm for the project and how he had complained that the West's Crown Office had seemed curiously uninterested in its drawing. Eamon wondered if copies of the map had since been made. He supposed that they must have been.

He made his way into the depths of the college itself. There was a tense feel to the air and Eamon knew that the cadets, ensigns, and officers could feel the battle brewing in the distance – none better than they.

He found Waite in the central courtyard. The captain stood on the steps watching the dark clouds as they passed overhead. Although the air was warm his arms were folded across his breast.

Eamon stepped up beside him. Waite bowed at once. "Lord Goodman."

"In the Master's name I greet you, General Waite," Eamon answered.

Waite turned to stare at him.

"It is an honour for me to bring this to you," Eamon told him. The general stood, dumbfounded, as Eamon reached out and pinned another flame to his collar. "General Waite," he said, "there is to be a war council at the palace in the morning. As you have charge of the Gauntlet and militia in this city, it is the Master's wish that you attend me there."

"Of course, Lord Goodman." Waite glanced at the flame on his collar, and then back to Eamon with a sad smile. "I never would have guessed that this might be brought to me – and by you."

"Nor I."

"It has a certain poetic rightness," Waite answered, then laughed. "You see, Lord Goodman, that the West is still moved by poetry."

Eamon smiled. "The Master would have you choose a captain in your stead."

"I will do so, my lord, this night."

They stood for a few moments on the steps. A flight of swallows dashed by.

"How are the injured?" Eamon asked.

"In the infirmary," Waite replied. "We lost another man this morning, but the others seem stable."

"And Lieutenant Manners?"

"Of the cadets who served under you when you were a lieutenant, he is the last," Waite mused. "The others…" He sighed deeply, and stared out across the darkening yard. "To a man, and before ever the Serpent came to these walls, they have lost their lives. Does that trouble you, Lord Goodman?"

"Yes."

"Lieutenant Manners has proved to have some luck over him in recent weeks," Waite answered. "Even now, though he does not wake, he lives." The general paused and shook his head with a small laugh. "Did he ever apologize to you for how he treated you, the day you arrived in Dunthruik?"

"*Oh cadet, is it? You had better hope that I have a dull memory…*"

Eamon laughed; it seemed a strangely fond memory to him then. "I don't believe that he ever did, general."

Waite smiled. "He is a good man – they all were," he said quietly.

The pad of approaching footsteps sounded through the hall behind them. A cadet ran up to them and bowed, the lamp-lighting torch still glowing in his hand.

"My lord; captain," he said. Waite allowed the mistake to pass. Eamon smiled to himself. It was difficult to see the new flame in the half-light.

"Cadet," Waite acknowledged.

"I beg your pardon, my lord. You are Lord Goodman?"

"Yes," Eamon answered. It was refreshing not to have been recognized instantly.

"There is a messenger for you," the cadet said. "He comes from the Crown Theatre."

"The Crown?"

"He says it is urgent that he speak with you."

"Thank you, cadet." Eamon looked to Waite. "I will see you in the morning."

"Good night, my lord."

By the time Eamon reached the college steps again it was nearly dark. A servant stood beneath one of the braziers, peering nervously into the doorway. As he saw Eamon, he leapt forward.

"Lord Goodman?"

"The very same," Eamon answered, stepping into the light. The servant's face was pale. "You have a message for me?"

"I know you are busy, my lord, but there's been an incident at the theatre," the servant began. "I was asked to find you – I am sorry it has taken me so long to do so." The man looked red in the face, and Eamon wondered how long, and in how many places, he had looked.

"What has happened?"

"One of the troupe has been badly hurt," the servant answered. "Mr Shoreham said that she is under your protection, my lord, and so he sends word to you."

Eamon's blood turned cold. "I'll go at once."

Quickly he gathered his horse and rode down the Coll to the Crown. He dismounted and hurried inside, making his way swiftly to the troupe's rooms.

Arriving was like coming among the panic of a rattled flock: the actors were pale, some weeping. Shoreham was there; the bearded man came across to him at once.

"My lord."

"I hear that there has been an incident?" Eamon answered.

The man nodded nervously. "A Hand came. He asked to see Ilenia. They had an altercation and he attacked her."

"Attacked?" Eamon breathed.

"We have done all we can," Shoreham told him anxiously. "As an attack on someone under your protection is an attack against you, I sent for you."

"Where is she?"

Shoreham gestured down the hall. Eamon hurried to the room he had indicated, aware of Shoreham and a few others following him. Fearful at heart, he entered, and then stopped in horror.

Ilenia was crumpled on the ground in a pool of blood. Servants and other actors crowded round her. A series of bandages had been wrapped tightly around her chest. Between the bobbing heads of those who tended her, Eamon saw a seeping red gash growing ever larger on her abdomen. A dagger lay discarded to one side. It was of standard Hand issue, with no distinguishing mark, bar the blood that splattered hilt and blade.

Ilenia's maid knelt at the woman's side with a tear-stricken face.

Eamon's heart raced as he surveyed them. "From the room, all of you!" he commanded. "Leave me water and bandages, and go."

The actors and servants obeyed at once; a bowl of water and lengths of bandage were brought to him. They hurried from the room but the girl who clutched Ilenia's hand remained. She wept.

"Miss," Eamon said, "you must go, too."

"Please don't let her die, my lord!"

"Leave the room," Eamon told her firmly.

Almost doubled over with grief, the girl staggered for the door. She drew it shut behind her. Anguished sobs filled the corridor beyond.

Eamon looked down at Ilenia. Her face was pale and her hands pressed feebly on the blood-mottled bandages bound across her stomach. Her breathing was laboured, shallow.

Eamon drew her hands away and cast the sodden bindings aside. He did not stop to think how he would explain the woman's recovery, did not stop to think of anything at all but of saving her life. As he had done when a cadet lay dying on the deck of a ship bound for Dunthruik, and again in the wreckage of Tailor's Turn, he pressed his hands into the wound. He closed his eyes, searching deep in his heart for the King's grace.

Almost at once he felt light washing through his hands. As it touched the singer, he opened his eyes and saw the light's reflection dance in the blood on the floor. Ilenia did not move, scarcely seemed to breathe. Eamon was grateful that she could not see what he did.

Almost as suddenly as it had come, the light ebbed and vanished. Eamon pulled his hands away and peeked under the bandage at the place of the wound. All that remained of it was a pale, jagged scar.

Just enough of a miracle that it could be explained.

Ilenia drew a shuddering breath and then fell into a steady rhythm once more. In silence, Eamon took the bandages and marked them with the singer's blood before re-binding her.

He rinsed his hands in the water and shook them out before rising. Crossing to the door, he opened it and leaned out.

"Mr Shoreham?" he called.

Shoreham looked up anxiously and came down the corridor. Dozens of others were behind him. "My lord?"

"She should be carried to some chambers to rest."

"She lives?" Shoreham cried.

"Yes," Eamon answered. "Bring some to carry her."

The doors opened and a small crowd of people came in, the maid first among them.

He caught a flicker of movement from the corner of his eye – whether the shape of servant or actor he did not know. A moment later it slipped from the room. The figure had not entered the room with the acting troupe.

Eamon froze. He had been seen.

Eamon ran towards the door, but Ilenia's carriers blocked the way with their painfully slow progress. As calls of gladness ran round him Eamon's stomach sank in terror.

He had been foolish.

Shoreham was at his side. The director turned and bowed to him.

"Thank you, Lord Goodman," he said earnestly. "This theatre could not have borne her death."

"If you had not taken action when you did, Mr Shoreham," Eamon answered, "there would have been little that I could have done. Thank you."

Shoreham smiled and Eamon forced himself to return it. But his heart was cold: he was certain that the incident had been staged.

Someone in Dunthruik suspected his allegiance and was following him to prove it.

Eamon was grateful that he had ridden to the Crown. By the time he mounted Sahu, his legs were trembling so much that he could barely walk.

Slowly he rode back to the palace, his brain stupefied. He had been seen, *seen*. The blue light could only be the mark of a King's man, and he had wielded it. He had come so far…

He could not resist glancing over his shoulder as he rode. Who had reason to suspect him? Arlaith? But Arlaith had changed, and there was the matter of the list. Eamon drew a deep breath. If Arlaith brought an accusation against his allegiance he would speak of the list and say that Arlaith was enviously spreading rumour that was debilitating to the city and the Master's glory.

His thoughts whirled. It had not been Arlaith or Febian – for Eamon also had a hold over Febian. Besides which, the Lord of the West Quarter had no reason to suspect him. Lord Dehelt was dead…

Only Lord Tramist remained.

Eamon began to quiver. It had to be Tramist. Dunthruik's breacher had always loathed him and had never been afraid to express it. Eamon had no power over Tramist, and if the Lord of the South Quarter knew… then he was betrayed.

The King's grace will not betray a King's man. Courage, Eamon.

The gentle voice came to his mind. As he returned to the palace and staggered back to his own chambers he tried desperately to cling to it.

If he had been seen, how could he not be betrayed?

He paused and tried to reason through his situation. He did not know who had seen him. The people of Dunthruik rarely saw the mark of the throned – and the blue light that went with a King's man was seen even less. Even if it had been seen, how could the spy have known what he saw? Was it not possible that his eyes had seen without seeing?

It did not matter. The spy would go to Tramist and report that the singer had been saved. The thought chilled Eamon. The King was but days away. Were Eamon to fall there, then… the throned's vengeance would be slow and terrible.

There was nothing he could do.

"Good evening, Lord Goodman."

He breathed deeply and looked up. He had entered his rooms and Cartwright waited for him. "Good evening, Mr Cartwright," Eamon said quietly.

"Shall I have supper sent to you, my lord?"

"Thank you," Eamon answered. "Has Fletcher left any other business for me?"

"No, Lord Goodman."

"Then I shall eat and rest," Eamon told him. "I do not wish to be disturbed until morning."

"Yes, my lord."

Supper was brought and the servants left. Eamon ate alone and then went restlessly to his bed. His command not to be disturbed was obeyed, so he was left to the torment of his thoughts until he drifted at last into a terrible sleep.

CHAPTER XIII

There was to be no breakfast with the Master that morning, for which Eamon was grateful. He dressed swiftly and did his best to wash the stains of wretched sleep from his face. He was not convinced by the result, but could do no more. Cartwright had provided a light breakfast for him of which he ate but little.

"Are you well, Lord Goodman?" the servant asked.

"I go to preside over a council of war in the Master's name, and the Serpent is at our gates," Eamon told him. It was answer enough.

He went down into the palace halls; the meeting would take place in a council room in the West Wing. As Eamon made his way there footsteps approached from an adjacent passageway; looking up he saw Arlaith. He froze. For a moment he hung back in the shadow of the doorway where he stood.

What if Arlaith knew? What if the Left Hand denounced him before the council?

Courage, Eamon.

Drawing a deep breath he stepped out into the light.

Arlaith saw him at once and bowed to him. "Lord Goodman," he greeted.

"Lord Arlaith," Eamon answered. The Lord of the East Quarter smiled at him as he rose and there was no trace of any strange news in his dark eyes.

"You seem tired, Lord Goodman," Arlaith said.

"I have never been to a council of war," Eamon answered carefully, "much less presided over one."

Arlaith smiled at him. "You have missed little," he answered. "It will take the whole day to discuss matters that could be resolved in a couple of hours. I know," he answered, "for I have been to many. As for you, you need only preside over the debate. Do not trouble yourself with it too much, Lord Goodman."

Eamon almost dared to let himself breathe. "I am sure you are right," he said, then looked up. "Has there been any news?" he asked.

"Lord Tramist sent a report late last night," Arlaith answered. Eamon's heart almost stopped, but he forced himself to hold Arlaith's gaze. "The Serpent's allies have completed their little pontooning pastime. The army on the bank looks formidable."

"Formidable?"

"Easters," Arlaith replied. "Fools, the whole race of them! With them go whatever rabble the Serpent has drummed out of the hills and valleys of the River Realm." He laughed. "They will not stand against this city."

They walked together to the council room in the East Wing; many others had arrived. The generals Rocell, Cade, and Waite were there, each accompanied by an aide armed with quill, ink, and paper. Febian and Tramist were present. The room bore a long table at its centre. Seats had been set round it and a map of the city and its surroundings lay on it. Eamon recognized it at once as one of Cadet Overbrook's.

As Eamon entered, the whole room bowed to him, then they moved to their seats. The Hands and their aides took one side of the table, the generals the other. To Eamon was left the table's head, and an enormous carved chair.

He sat and surveyed the long table, forcing himself to meet each gaze.

"I preside over this council in the Master's name," he said, "and to him I will present our recommendations at the end of the day." Tramist watched him strangely, but he matched that gaze with his own until Tramist faltered and looked away. "Please be seated; we have much to do."

The council sat. When the sound of shuffling chairs faded, Eamon looked to Arlaith. "Lord Arlaith," he began. "Present the council with your report of the plains."

"Of course, Lord Goodman," Arlaith answered, and turned to the table. "It is clear that we face a prepared foe. My force of Hands made two attempts to break the plain-line yesterday, riding even as arrows were loosed at them by counter-attacking wayfarer hobilars and Easters. Over both attempts we have lost nigh a score of Hands in total, while the enemy lost only two men that I saw. It is clear that the city is hemmed in from land and sea," he added. "Lord Febian has dispatched various messengers to our allies, calling on them to break the blockade from the sea – but even if one gets past the Serpent it will take several weeks for any such aid to reach us."

"What effect is the blockade having on the city?" Waite asked.

"We lost a good deal of ware in the harbour," Eamon answered. In the two short days since the naval attack he had been examining the North Quarter records and those of the city at large. "Our spring stocking was critically interrupted, not to mention the loss of trade. Clearly our summer provisions will not reach us for some weeks, assuming aid comes. Our logistical situation has been fragile for some time and shortages will become very swiftly apparent. Disturbances have already been reported in the South and North, regarding the distribution and sale of grain. We are fortunate to have set so much aside," he added quietly, "but we can expect these disturbances to grow in violence and frequency."

A discontented murmur ran about the table.

"Advise us as to the level of reserve that we have, my lord?" Cade asked.

Eamon did so, and wasn't sure how long they then spent discussing various methods of maintaining calm in the city while feeding its many mouths. After what seemed forever, a strange silence fell. The situation, laid out in terms of mouths empty, was grim.

"The city will endure this hardship," Eamon said at last. "What reports from our allies?"

"Etraia holds with us," Febian said, speaking up for the first time. His voice grew in confidence as he continued. "I received word this morning that Galithia has turned from us –"

"Again," Arlaith snorted.

Febian ignored the interruption. "She is driving out all River Realm forces stationed there," he added.

"Captain Roe had charge of them," Waite said heavily. The name startled Eamon: was Waite discussing Ilenia's husband? "He will attempt to lead his men back to the city, encountering the Serpent on his way."

"Yes," Febian acknowledged. "I do not think they will reach us before we go to battle. The Serpent's hand is certainly in this work, and there is rumour that other merchant states consider taking his cause."

Eamon nodded. "General Rocell?"

"My lord," Rocell answered. "The nobles and knights of this city are ever for the Master, but rumour has grown even among their ranks in these days. Some are showing disconcerting signs that they doubt his glory's capacity to endure this battle. Some may go across to the Serpent if they think that it will serve them."

"He may have them!" Tramist said derisively.

"They should be repaid according to their loyalty," Arlaith hissed.

Rocell looked at him angrily. "My lord, without the knights –"

Eamon gestured for him to be quiet and turned to Arlaith. "Our efforts, Lord Arlaith," he said, "should be towards ending this blockade. Striking the knights will only sow further discord."

Arlaith glared. "As you have seen, Lord Goodman, the Hands *cannot* and *will not* break this blockade."

"That is why we need the knights," Rocell said with irritation.

"We should consider committing our full force against this blockade," Waite said. "I am confident that we would be able to break through the Serpent's hobilars and scatter any reinforcements."

"What would the Serpent do then?" Tramist asked. Eamon thought the man glanced briefly at him as the sneering words slipped from his lips. "Fight, or run?"

There was a moment of silence. "We cannot forget the bridge," Febian said. "Without our ferry or any good number of working ships, I do not relish the notion of sending any kind of attack to the bridge."

Arlaith laughed. "We have no need of that, my lord!" he said. "The bridge is a minimal concern. This city has artillery; we are well capable of making the Serpent's position uncomfortably untenable."

A long silence fell. Eamon stared openly at Arlaith, along with every other man at the table.

"Artillery?" he repeated uncertainly. He had studied the principles of various siege engines while a Gauntlet cadet, but, despite many tours of the city to check its defences, he had seen no such engines at Dunthruik.

Arlaith paused. "You did not know, Lord Goodman?" he said curiously.

Eamon matched Arlaith's gaze. "Speak of it," he commanded.

"It was a project under my command when I was Right Hand."

"You do not mean catapults?" Eamon tested.

Arlaith smiled. "No, Lord Goodman: something rather more spectacular than that. I apologize not to have spoken of it to you. The Master will doubtless give you its particulars now that its use is near."

"Indeed." Eamon felt shaken.

"In brief," Arlaith continued, "if we can deploy it effectively, we can damage the bridge and harass their camp – and if we cannot, it will still give the Serpent a very warm welcome should he reach our gates. Perhaps warmer than he would like," he added with a long smile.

Eamon felt a terrible foreboding. What kind of artillery did Dunthruik have?

"Notwithstanding the advantage that the bridge grants the enemy, the River could also benefit us," Waite added, gesturing at the map on the table. "Once they have committed, if we can destroy their bridge and make them surrender the North Bank they cannot return to it without withdrawing and preparing for a new assault;

they cannot cross the River for miles." He smiled. "Withdrawing and recommitting would cost them the port blockade. They would have to move almost every ship there to enable them to come back over the River."

"I would like to see the Serpent's allies remain loyal to him at such a time," Tramist said crisply.

"And if he fights?" Febian asked.

"He will be crushed," Arlaith smiled. It chilled Eamon to the bone. "Don't you agree, my lord?"

"Indeed," Eamon answered.

"If he fights he has a great advantage in the fact that he will be able to deploy his men more swiftly across his bridge than we shall through the Blind Gate," Waite told them, his brow pursed with worry.

"All the more to kill," Arlaith replied in a sing-song voice.

"A great victory at our gates would, as well as ending the blockade, restore confidence in the Master's glory," Rocell mused.

"And bring our allies flocking back to us in droves," Febian added.

"And make the Easters rethink their reckless support for the whole venture," finished Tramist.

"The Serpent could not survive so massive a defeat," Arlaith grinned. "He would be finished."

"So we hope to fight," Waite said, sitting back.

There was a long moment of silence, in which only the aides' note-making could be heard. At last Eamon leaned across the table towards them.

"How, then, do we fight, and what can we commit?" he asked.

"Ten full-strength banners, my lord," Rocell answered at once.

"You have replaced your losses from earlier actions?"

"This city does not lack noblemen wishing to become knights," Rocell told him with a smile. The table laughed, and Eamon turned to Waite.

"General Waite?"

"Provisionally, we have one hundred groups from twenty-five of our regions," Waite answered, glancing down at a set of notes he had brought with him. "We cannot expect to receive any men from those outstanding. Of those who have come to us, not every region sent four groups, but after some reorganizing most groups are at parade strength. Dunthruik itself has fifteen groups per quarter." He looked up. "Full strength, my lord," he said firmly.

Eamon suppressed a shiver. "If there are illnesses before an attack?"

"I will be able to drum up a few spare men to maintain parade strength," Waite replied.

"Most of those spare men are currently reinforcing the thresholders," Cade put in.

"How many thresholders are there?"

"At least three thousand, my lord," Cade answered.

"And they will fight?" Arlaith asked, somewhat bitterly.

Cade looked coolly at him. "These men, Lord Arlaith, will stay in the city and fight for their homes. What greater incentive could they have? Besides," he added, "the thresholders will only engage if we are defeated on the plain, which present company leads me to trust is unlikely."

"Let us discuss deployment," Eamon said.

"Infantry in two lines, with cavalry on the wings," Tramist suggested flatly.

"Not by my advice, my lord," Rocell replied with a quick shake of his head. "The River is a better flank guard, besides which the ground by it is soft, ditched, and full of hedges, especially closer to the city walls. What if it were to rain? We would lose men and beasts in the quagmire." He shook his head. "No, the south is no place for cavalry. The place for cavalry – and full deployment of it – is on the north wing," he added, gesturing towards the map. "There, we hit hard, perhaps before the enemy is fully ready."

"Wouldn't that area be severely constrained?" Waite asked, gesturing to the small villages and farms on the map.

"We'll need two cavalry lines, but I do not believe that would be overly problematic," Rocell replied with a shrug. "The Serpent would deploy his cavalry at speed to meet us, leaving his infantry to hold the River flank."

"Meaning our cavalry won't go against formed infantry," Waite agreed.

"A most helpful thing," Tramist murmured, with a sidelong glance at Eamon.

Eamon knew that the Lord of the South Quarter was thinking of Pinewood. He answered the Hand with a glare so cool that the man flinched, before looking back to the table at large.

"So we must make sure that we can deploy our cavalry properly into the north. How many Hands will we have?" he asked.

"Two hundred and six," Arlaith answered, "counting Quarter Hands. Unless," he added with a small smile, "Lord Tramist deigns to ride with us? That would bring us to two hundred and seven."

"I will not ride," Tramist answered coolly.

"No?" Arlaith enquired. "You disappoint me, Lord Tramist!"

Tramist fixed Arlaith with a withering glare. "I have not ridden to war since before you joined the Gauntlet, Lord Arlaith," he answered, "and I do not ride. Perhaps, in your absences, you forgot this?"

"No indeed," Arlaith replied firmly. Tramist's glare grew suddenly wide. Eamon saw the South Quarter Hand look once to him and then back to Arlaith in surprise. It left Eamon feeling very uncomfortable, but when both Hands looked to him again they met his gaze unfalteringly.

"So, the Hands are two hundred and six," he said, trying to cover a disconcerting presentiment.

"Can they be relied upon to keep back the Serpent's forces while our deployment is still feeding out of the Blind Gate?" Waite asked.

"As long as there are no teary farewells at the city walls," Arlaith replied caustically.

"Gentlemen, we have a great number of men to filter out of the gates when we go to battle," Eamon told them. His head began to ache. "Let us arrange how they will go."

The meeting did, as Arlaith had predicted, go on for the rest of the day. Eamon watched as they arranged which Gauntlet group was to line up in which road. The Coll would not be long enough to hold every man who would march out to battle, and almost every side street would need to be employed to contain and feed the deployment out of the city gates.

The afternoon wore on into the early evening. Eamon's brain was saturated with nothing but talk of banners and divisions and denominations of the plains before the city where those men would go. The map on the table soon became a board filled with an army of tokens.

At last they drew to the end of their council. Eamon was about to sit back in his chair and breathe a sigh of relief when the doors to the chamber opened. They all looked up and then rose instantly to their feet before bowing deeply.

It was the Master who entered. He was followed closely by his secretary.

"Your glory, Master," spoke the council as one voice.

The Master looked down at the table and there was a long moment of silence, in which the Lord of Dunthruik seemed somehow to absorb every facet of every word that had been spoken in the room that day.

"Son of Eben," he said. The voice was terrifyingly loud in Eamon's ears, and for a moment he feared that he was undone.

"Your glory, Master."

"All is prepared?"

The Master could see their plan well enough. "Yes, Master. We will fight."

"Good," the Master smiled. He looked once to his secretary, who stepped forward with a long, golden canister. The roll bore the throned's emblem at its head and was beautifully made.

The secretary handed this to Eamon; it was heavy in his hands. He looked at it for a moment then looked up, an unasked question on his lips.

"Within are writ my terms for the Serpent's surrender," the throned said. "You will take two Hands and a standard bearer of your choice. You will deliver these terms to him tonight, son of Eben."

Eamon's heart froze. "Yes, Master."

"Why offer him terms, Master?" Tramist asked, mouth pulled in disgust.

"Because he will reject them," the Master smiled, "and then he will fight."

The Master left. As the echoes of "your glory" died in the room Eamon blinked hard.

"You have leave to go, gentlemen," he said.

The council dispersed to their duties. Aware of Arlaith and Tramist speaking together behind him, Eamon concentrated hard on thanking each of the generals for their time.

Soon the generals left. Eamon gazed down at the map and its speckled layers of counters and divisions. Each counter marked a number of men. How many of them would die in battle against the King? He did not know.

"An enjoyable manner in which to pass the day, wouldn't you say, Lord Goodman?" asked a voice from his side: Arlaith's.

"I am not sure I would choose that word," Eamon answered. He felt tired, and the roll of terms felt cumbersome in his hands. "I will take Heathlode and Lonnam from the East Quarter as my Hands tonight," he said. Since the matter of Arlaith's list, Eamon had kept an eye on the East Quarter's Hands. He knew that Heathlode and Lonnam were capable men and knew also that they both held him in good regard. "Have them meet me in the Ashen at dusk." That would leave him two hours to prepare himself.

"Of course, Lord Goodman," Arlaith answered. "And for the third man?"

Eamon paused. He would have chosen Manners, but he could not. "I will take Mr Bellis as my standard bearer."

"I am sure there will be no objection, but perhaps you should speak to Captain Anderas on the matter," Arlaith told him.

"I will," Eamon answered.

It was early evening as Eamon came heavily away from the conference. He felt burdened and not a little afraid. Dunthruik was prepared: it had a plan of attack and a way of striking the Serpent. Did Hughan have as much?

Why had no one spoken against a Right Hand who carried the King's grace?

He went quietly to the Ashen and on to the college. It was refreshing to have air in his face that had not been trapped for hours in the same room, breathed in and out by the lungs of enemies.

The college was eerily quiet. The preparations for deployment would not happen until after the parley. Until then the whole city hung in a state of prolonged suspense.

He was admitted to Anderas's office at once. The captain was there, his hands filled with papers which Eamon knew had come straight from the aides at the council.

"Good evening, captain," Eamon said.

Anderas looked up, then rose and bowed. "Lord Goodman," he breathed, his voice strained. He glanced again at the papers and then back to Eamon. "You have had a tiring day, my lord?"

"Yes."

"How may I serve you?" Anderas asked.

"I am taking terms to the Serpent," Eamon answered quietly. "I need a standard bearer. I would like to take Wilhelm, if he is recovered."

"His injury was slight; I will happily let him go."

"Have him meet me in the Ashen at dusk," Eamon replied. "Lonnam and Heathlode will also be there."

"Yes, my lord."

They stood in silence. Eamon's thoughts turned to all the young men in the East Quarter. He remembered the marks on the map that had shown where those men would go. All those men would be in danger, and so would the man before him. He looked to Anderas.

"Captain," he began.

The captain met his gaze. "I will go to the battle and to my assigned place in it, my lord. That is my duty." He paused. "And you?"

"I will go," Eamon answered. His heart grew cold. "I will declare my colours, Anderas," he said quietly, "and I will go to battle."

"As will I," Anderas answered. "I will bring as many as I can with me."

Eamon stared. "How can you?"

Anderas smiled. "I have not been idle in these days, my lord."

Eamon nodded dumbly. "You will send Wilhelm?"

"Yes." Anderas glanced at the papers, then gathered a few. "I have a meeting I must attend."

"The busy life of a captain?" Eamon asked with a smile.

"Well, I do enjoy excuses to leave the college," Anderas replied. "Lord Arlaith asked me to deliver some vital papers to the South. I would send Mr Lancer, but he has been very busy since we lost Draybant Greenwood." He drew a deep breath. "By your leave, Lord Goodman."

"Of course," Eamon answered.

They left the college together and rode to the Four Quarters. There, Anderas turned his horse to the south and disappeared into the greying light. Eamon watched him go and then returned to the palace. His thoughts were dour.

He was exhausted and afraid. Should it not be of comfort to him that he would see the King that night? But it made his stomach lurch: the end was coming. Had he done everything he could to prepare the way for Hughan?

As soon as he reached his own quarters, he called for Cartwright. He asked him to lay out his most formal attire. As he waited, he saw the heavy roll, the golden canister for the terms, lying nearby. An idea came into his head.

He asked a servant to summon Fletcher for him. His lieutenant came almost at once and bowed. "Lord Goodman?" he said.

"There are copies of the Overbrook Dunthruik map?"

"There are several, my lord," Fletcher answered.

"I want one delivered to me now. There are aspects of the deployment that I want to review tonight."

Fletcher went away. Eamon dressed. He drew his thick travelling cloak over himself, ready against the cold. There was a knock at the door.

"Mr Fletcher has brought you the map you required, my lord."

"Thank you, Mr Cartwright. Have him leave it in my study."

"Yes, my lord."

Eamon finished adjusting his cloak, then took up the roll of terms and crossed to his study.

The map was there. Eamon marvelled again at its detail. He traced his fingers over the roads and streets, over buildings and places that he knew and stones that he had walked for many months.

He took the map and carefully folded it. This done, he placed it deep inside his shirt, far from prying eyes.

He emerged from his study; Iulus and Fletcher waited for him.

"Is my horse ready?"

"Yes, my lord," Fletcher answered. Carefully Eamon slung the roll over his shoulders; it rested like a quiver on his back, its cargo as keen as arrows, its strap pressing the feel of the map under his shirt against his breast.

"Then I go to meet the Serpent."

He rode to the Ashen in silence and alone. There in the hanging dark he saw a small group of figures. Two were mounted Hands. The third was Wilhelm Bellis.

Wilhelm's red uniform stood in contrast to the black that surrounded him. The young man held himself well in the saddle, one hand on the standard that he would carry. The banner hung limp in the air, a red token bearing a black eagle whose beak was bent to rend the neck of a serpent. It was the emblem not of the Right Hand, but of the Master.

Eamon was to be the Master's voice.

"Lord Goodman," said Lonnam, bowing his head where he sat. The others followed suit. "We serve the glory of the Master."

"Perhaps you have gathered, or have been told, where we go," Eamon answered. He could see Wilhelm's careful eyes watching the roll at his shoulders as it glinted in the light. "I have been charged with delivering terms to the Serpent."

He saw a strange look go over Wilhelm's face. "We are emissaries of the Master," Eamon added, "and we will conduct ourselves according to the rules of war. None of you will incite or deliver any form of violence to any that we meet, and you will not respond to any similar provocation. You will answer to me if you do. Do you understand me?"

"Yes, Lord Goodman," came the unified response.

"Then come with me."

He turned his horse and led it to Coronet Rise. His companions followed him.

Theirs was a solemn procession as they reached the Coll and the Blind Gate. In the lanterned streets faces watched them, a reflection of worried eyes in the darkness. Though no proclamation had been made, his duty was clear – the banner Wilhelm bore and the golden canister on the back of the Right Hand rendered it thus.

Ensigns from the East Quarter guarded the gate that night. The shapes of watchmen on the high walls paused to look down at Eamon and those who rode with him.

One of the East's officers came from the gatehouse.

"Lord Goodman," he said with a bow. He was corpse-pale.

"Open the gate," Eamon told him gently.

Moments later the gate yawned open to reveal a looming field of falling darkness. The ghostly shapes of trees and road gazed back.

CHAPTER XIII

Eamon stared out at the plain, a vast expanse of uncertainty. A low wind whistled through the darkness towards them.

"Torches," he said quietly.

Several ensigns hurried forward and gave blazing torches to the two Hands. Heat billowed off them, causing strange shadows to shift on the banner.

"Lord Goodman?"

Eamon looked down at the officer's grim face. "Lieutenant?"

"The city goes with you, my lord."

Eamon let out a slow breath. How well he knew it. "Thank you."

Then he gathered the reins into his hand and rode out into the near dark.

CHAPTER XIV

The plain was still and silent. As the city and its lights receded, Edelred's heralds became inky figures that moved between the standing groves and whistling grass. The breeze came down from the north, blowing along the plain in whispers of mountain passes beneath starry skies. Eamon saw the watchful moon nestled behind the distant peaks, shedding an eerie light down on the plain as it rose.

Their horses' hooves were steady thumps on the turf, like that of a beating heart. The soft crackle of the torch-flames and the flutter of the Master's banner were the only other noises. Eamon felt the stir of the wind on his face, the roll of terms over his back, and the map of Dunthruik at his breast. Away to the south he saw the River, and beyond it lights in the dells and woodland of the West Bank. The Easters' bridge boldly straddled the water, a feat of engineering that was as miraculous as it was threatening.

It was towards the bridge that Eamon turned his horse. The others followed him, unquestioning and silent. Each man was hostage to the preying thoughts that circled him in the gathering dusk.

They drew closer to the bridge and Eamon nodded once to Wilhelm. His standard bearer went before them.

None opposed them as they rode. Indeed none could be seen until they were a few hundred yards from the bridge. Then Eamon saw a group of men – presumably some of Hughan's hobilars – by the bridge posts. They were dressed in dark hues. As Eamon grew accustomed to the changing light, he realized that more men, hitherto unseen, had drawn up to flank Edelred's term-bearers at a distance on each side.

He gestured slowly for his companions to halt; the bridge was but a hundred yards away. The men standing at it did not move and did not speak. Eamon saw more men in the darkness and guessed them to be archers.

"I am Eamon Goodman, Right Hand to the Lord of Dunthruik."

"State your business, Right Hand of Edelred," called a voice. Eamon realized with a start that it was known to him: Leon's.

"I come as Right Hand and as herald," Eamon replied, "to present the benevolent terms of my glorious Master to your Serpent for his surrender. I will speak to him, and to him alone."

"Come you in good faith, Right Hand," Leon asked, "agreeing to be bound by such rules as there are for parleys in war?"

Eamon sensed the Hands behind him shuffling uncomfortably. "I come in good faith."

"Then both you and your escort will dismount and surrender your swords to me," Leon told him, "giving your word for your faith. If you or they play treacherously, you will each pay with your lives."

Wilhelm paled, sweat beading his young face. Eamon looked firmly back to Leon. "These men answer to me and have pledged to abide by such rules as I have given them."

"Then, again, I ask for your sword, Right Hand."

Eamon dismounted and carefully unbuckled his sword from his belt. He also ungirt Eben's dagger and laid it, with the scabbarded sword, in Leon's hands. The man watched him with little trace of emotion and Eamon could not help but wonder whether Leon had forgiven him for their last encounter.

After Eamon, the Hands also dismounted, giving both torch and sword to Leon's men. Wilhelm did likewise but bore the Master's standard down from the saddle. It moved overhead as Eamon met Leon's gaze once again.

"We have given both pledge and blade," he said. "Lead us to the Serpent."

"Your horses will remain here," Leon told them. "You will find them upon your return."

"Very well."

Leon nodded once and then turned to the bridge. As they began to move, a small group of hobilars formed up about them. Eamon caught sight of Wilhelm's hands; they trembled about the banner. "Courage, Mr Bellis," he said quietly.

Wilhelm nodded.

They crossed the last stretch of grass to the River's bank and the awesome bridge that spanned the running water. Eamon had heard reports from the South Quarter that the Easters had brought the bridge to the River by land and water in parts and that, with the aid of men on each bank and holks on the water, they had completed their pontoon within a day of the attack on Dunthruik's port.

They set foot on the bridge. It had been lined to either side with two rows of tall stakes, about which the rushing water flowed out to the sea. Eamon could not help but smile grimly. The stakes were to keep flotsam and jetsam, natural or otherwise, from striking and destroying the bridge.

Against the sheer expanse of the River and the breadth of the bridge, the torches borne by their escort cast the dimmest of lights. As they crossed, the broad grey waters rushed by beneath them, with starlight caught between the churning currents. For a moment, Eamon felt as though he were caught on a bridge over a sea of stars, unable to see either the bank from which he had come or the bank to which he went.

They stepped down onto the far bank, and Eamon began to distinguish some of the ghostly shapes he had seen as distant lights from the plain. Coming down among them was like coming into another world. Fires dotted the bank for the warmth and comfort of man and beast. Gathered a little way back from the River were what seemed hundreds of tents and groups of guarded wagons. Banners showing stars and suns fluttered in the breeze, and from every side murmurs grew as men emerged to look upon the Right Hand of the Lord of Dunthruik alighting on the West Bank.

Fearing a chorus of jeers or curses, Eamon did not meet the watching eyes. But neither curse nor jeer met him. The men simply stared: the Master's eagle had reached their camp.

Leon led them firmly through the camp to a clearing. The sound of the River roared behind them. The breeze carried snatches of song. The wayfarers were in good spirits.

The clearing to which they went was filled with a long row of tents. Each was grander than those that stood near the River and they bore a host of different banners and flags. At the far end of that long line of pavilions hung a banner that showed the sword and star, and by it another, bearing a unicorn. The pavilion that they marked was made from great folds of blue fabric. As he looked up at it, Eamon's blood ran hot. The King was there.

They crossed the field swiftly. In the fallen dark Eamon could see the figures of men standing between the tents. More men stood on guard at the pavilion's entrance. One of them gave a start and stared at him in astonishment. As he passed by, Eamon realized the man was Giles.

Leon took them quietly inside, and the guards held open the entrance to the pavilion so that Wilhelm and his banner could pass unimpeded. As they entered, Eamon had to blink to adjust his eyes to the torchlight.

"The Right Hand of Edelred," Leon announced. As he did so Eamon gazed about himself in astonishment.

The whole tent was blue. Silver facings lined its edges. There was a table to one side and various trunks about it, each covered with blue cloth. It filled Eamon's eyes with the sting of tears. After so many long months of unending red and black and gold, the gentle touch of the King's blue was like waves of water coursing through a shrivelled land. The colour washed into his heart to cleanse him from weariness and toil.

Others were in the tent – men that he knew and who knew him. They stood together by the table. Eamon was overjoyed to see them, but he caught sight of Wilhelm and the red reminded him who he had to be and what he had to do.

"Greetings to you, Right Hand," said a voice – a trumpet of homecoming to his long benighted heart. "And greetings also to your escort."

"You would greet us?" spat Heathlode in surprise.

"Lord Heathlode," Eamon reprimanded sternly.

The Hand pressed his lips together and stared defiantly back at the one who had greeted them. That man smiled.

"Men of Dunthruik are always welcome here," he said.

Heathlode's jaw fell open and he turned to Eamon as though to speak again.

But Eamon did not meet his gaze. Instead he looked up and inclined his head formally towards the speaker.

"For your greetings we exchange our own, Serpent," he answered.

Hughan nodded graciously. Eamon felt a flood of joy pass through him as their gazes met.

"Lord Goodman brings terms from the throned," Leon told them.

"Indeed!" snorted Anastasius. The Easter lord stood near Hughan and wore an amused expression.

"We will hear the terms, Lord Goodman," Hughan said.

Eamon drew the roll from off his back and opened it. There was a thick scroll inside, and this he withdrew, handing the empty canister to Lonnam. As he unrolled the scroll, his eyes were met first by the great eagle which spanned the crown of the paper and then by the words, each pristinely but ornately scribed.

His blood chilled: how could he read what lay in his hand to Hughan? How much he wished that he could hurl the thing away! They were vile words and he could not lay them against the one he served.

He looked up and saw that Hughan watched him. The King knew his doubt. "Do as you came to do, Lord Goodman," he said. "I am listening."

Eamon drew a deep breath. The eagle peered at him, crying to him of his broken faith, as he read:

From the hand of the Crowned Eagle, Edelred, glorious Lord and Master of Dunthruik and all its realm; to the Serpent, who presumes to name himself heir to a broken house.

In this land he is both trespasser and recreant, base-born and unlessoned; this land and city and throne revile him, naming him foe and villain, devourer and slanderer. In his wickedness the Serpent has betrayed east and west, drawing them from our wing to his threadbare and barren banner.

In his foolish arrogance he has dared to come against us in war. For the sake of this land which he would claim, let the Serpent heed well these terms of peace that we, the Lord and Master of Dunthruik, magnanimously extend to him, one undeserving of our beneficence.

First, the Serpent shall cede all his claims to this land, disowning blood and gainsaying any oaths that he has made. All rights of blood and oath shall be rendered unto Edelred, Master of Dunthruik and the River, and shall be rendered by the Serpent's own tongue and hand, as a lasting ordinance.

Second, the Serpent shall give his binding oath to leave this land; neither he nor his descendants shall ever enter it again, and his followers shall lay down their arms and commit themselves to the service of the Master of Dunthruik.

Third, the Serpent and his allies will vow never again to take up arms against sovereign Dunthruik, its allies, its realms, and its glorious Master.

Fourth, the Serpent shall recompense in full for his hostility against this land, paying for every damage caused in the pursuit of his wrongdoing.

Fifth, the Serpent will himself bow his knee to the Master of Dunthruik, coming in person to ratify the terms of this concord within a day of its deliverance. He will send word of his acceptance by the Right Hand of Edelred before dawn on the fifteenth day of May, in the Five hundred and thirty-third year of the Master's throne.

Non-concordance with these terms will be interpreted as incitement for the Master of Dunthruik to defend his own by all means available to him, showing neither pity to the fallen nor mercy to the defeated.

Eamon finished reading; his throat felt dry and he fought to keep his hands from shaking. The Master's seal was at the foot of the page, and Eamon shuddered to touch it. Some terrible power seemed bound up in both that mark and the words, which filled the tent with silence.

Scarcely daring to breathe, he looked to Hughan. Of all the faces in the pavilion the King's alone remained calm and determined.

"I will discuss these terms with Edelred's Right Hand," he said. "Lord Anastasius, Lord Ithel, and Leon, I would have you remain also. Leon, please have Giles lead the Right Hand's escort to a place where they may wait. Then send Lord Feltumadas to me."

Leon bowed at once and stepped outside the doorway. Eamon looked back to the Hands and cadet. Lonnam looked pale, and Wilhelm bit his lip. Heathlode simply set his jaw. Eamon met each of their gazes in turn.

"Remember my words," he cautioned.

"Yes, Lord Goodman," they replied.

Leon and Giles returned, the latter leading a group of men. Hughan looked to Eamon's escort. "You will not be harmed." Then the King nodded to Giles, who led Hands, cadet, and banner away.

Eamon felt the weight of the terms as he looked back to the watching Easter lords and King. The King looked at him and smiled.

"Well met, First Knight," he said at last, "and well come."

Overwhelmed, Eamon sank down to one knee and bowed his head. No words came to him, but the one to whom he knelt crossed the distance between them and lifted him to his feet. Eamon tried to meet the King's loving gaze but his heart was both awed and shamed to be its object.

"How can you greet me thus," he whispered, "after what I have brought to you?" His tongue burnt with the names he had been forced to lay against the King; his heart churned with betrayal. The throned had known that he would read them. It filled him with bile.

Hughan watched him for a moment. "I know you," he answered, "and I have known you since long before you walked in Dunthruik." He looked down at the parchment in Eamon's hands. "There was no shame in your reading this to me, and I am not sorry that you brought it."

Eamon stared, bereft of words. Tears touched his eyes and he shook. To come, after long weeks of walking in Edelred's palace, into the star-wrapped pavilion of the King, and to be loved and welcomed by that man, was more than he could comprehend.

It was then that Hughan smiled, reached forward, and embraced him. "Eamon!" he said, and laughed.

Eamon had never known such relief as in that moment.

Hughan stepped back from him and pressed his shoulder encouragingly. Almost in a daze, Eamon became aware once more of the Easter lords.

"What means the throned by sending terms?" asked a voice.

Eamon looked up and for a moment his heart froze, for Feltumadas came storming into the pavilion, his voice full of outrage. Feltumadas was accompanied by three other Easter lords – two of whom appeared to be twins – along with two of Hughan's generals. Though Eamon remembered almost at once that the man sweeping past him was truly Feltumadas he felt a flicker of fear run through his veins.

"Terms, indeed!" Feltumadas spat.

It was then that the Easter lord suddenly stopped, looked once to Hughan and his allies, and then back to Eamon with an astonished stare. "You!"

"Me," Eamon offered.

"*You* are Right Hand?" Feltumadas asked. Eamon was about to reply when Anastasius spoke.

"He is without his colours," he said.

Eamon met their gazes. "I have my colours. Indeed, I promised you, Lord Anastasius, that when next we met, you would see me wear them truly."

"I see a good deal of black, Lord Goodman." Anastasius peered at him with interest. "What say you to that?"

"Little," Eamon answered. Gently he reached up to the fastening of his cloak and undid it, before setting his hands to his black robes. He pushed back the weaves of black to reveal what he wore beneath. He had had to search long among his things to find it, had feared even that it might be lost in one of the many changes of quarters he had made since he had first bought it, but he had found it. As the Easter lords looked at him, their eyes grew wide.

For beneath his thick travelling cloak and darkling robes, Edelred's Right Hand wore a shirt of blue. It was still torn where the King's emblem had been ripped away at a ball so long ago, but the shirt's colour shone unrepentantly in the torchlight.

Eamon looked up to meet Anastasius's gaze – he, Leon, Ithel, Feltumadas, and the remaining Easters and generals stared at him in surprise. Hughan smiled.

"You are a man of your word, Lord Goodman," Anastasius said at last, a delighted smile on his face.

"Are you the man who struck off my head?" Feltumadas asked.

"Yes," Eamon answered.

Suddenly Feltumadas's fierce face broke into a smile uncannily like his father's. "You excelled yourself in boldness that day, First Knight," he said, "and I thank you for it."

Eamon stared at him. Feltumadas nodded once, then looked to Hughan. "What is this I hear of terms, Star?" he asked.

"They are here," Hughan answered, gesturing to the paper still in Eamon's hands.

"The throned does not ask much," Ithel put in. But for the glint to his eye, Eamon might have taken his words seriously.

"The Star's withdrawal, humiliation, oath of service, and blood of his first-born child?" Feltumadas asked.

"He stops a little short of that, brother," Ithel replied. "But only a little."

Feltumadas turned to Eamon and took the terms. He read them quickly, his face turning from one shade of disgust and outrage to another. He soon looked up with an angry laugh.

"I don't believe it!" he cried, and looked to Hughan. "You would hear my counsel, Star of Brenuin?"

"I know your counsel, good Feltumadas," Hughan answered. He looked up to include each of his generals and allies in his gaze. "I believe I know what you would all counsel me."

"We will follow your command, sire," Leon told him, "whatever our counsel."

"You cannot take these terms!" Feltumadas insisted.

"They are not terms unless in name," Eamon told them. "He wants you to fight, Hughan. He is waiting for you with... with terrifying eagerness." He felt the eyes of the others on him and turned again to Hughan. "He has had me with him day by day, and I have seen him; I have heard his thoughts. All that matters to him is that you fight."

Silence fell. Hughan looked at them one by one. "We did not come here to be bound to Edelred," he said. "Nor did we come to let his desire for battle turn us from it."

Eamon matched his gaze. "Then, sire, you may have need of this."

Every eye was on him as he reached deep into his robes and shirt and quietly drew out the map that he had brought from Dunthruik. He unfolded it and laid it on the table with the terms, smoothing the creases and gazing down at the city. A strange feeling moved through his heart; of pity and sorrow that the streets and stones would have to bear the violence which he knew to come.

"This map was drawn by a fine cadet. It is the most detailed of the city that exists. When you prepare for battle – and that must be early, with the first light – you must beware an initial charge from the cavalry in the north. It will take us a long time to deploy our men onto the field; they will all come from the Blind Gate. Make as much use of that time as you can."

"And you are certain about all this?" Leon asked suspiciously.

"I am the Right Hand," Eamon answered quietly, "and I presided over the council where Dunthruik's plan of battle was decided. The cadet who drew this map served me while he lived. I have walked through the Blind Gate many times and know well its width. The city also has some form of artillery – something I believe to be beyond mere engines. I know no more of it than that and so I say: be wary."

An odd look crossed Anastasius's face, but Hughan nodded firmly. "Thank you, Eamon," he said.

"There is another matter that I must speak to you about," Eamon added, meeting the King's gaze. "It concerns the Nightholt."

Hughan watched him for a moment and then nodded.

"Would you have us leave you?" Anastasius asked.

"Thank you, Lord Anastasius."

Together the Easter lords left the tent and, at a nod from Hughan, Leon and the other generals went with them. Eamon watched anxiously as they left and then looked back to Hughan.

"Anastasius knows a little about the Nightholt," Hughan said quietly. "I received your message. Know that Mr Grennil and his family are safe, and delivered your message well."

A weight fell from him. "Thank you."

"Thank you for sending him," Hughan answered.

"You may not thank me for what I have done," Eamon spoke nervously. "The Nightholt was found. I found it, a long time ago, but some Hand withheld it from the Mast… the throned. I took it to him." He shivered, feeling its weight on his hands and fire in his flesh. "I gave it to him. Since then…"

"He has been waiting for me."

"Yes."

Hughan gently touched his shoulder. "Peace."

"It is the greatest treachery I have done you!" Eamon replied. "The curse of my blood came upon me in that hour, Hughan! How can I have peace? I made myself his in doing it."

"How long must you believe him? You know he is a liar set against you. You are not his, First Knight," Hughan answered firmly. "Your heart is true and your blood is not cursed."

"Don't you know what the Nightholt is?" Eamon yelled and then he fell awkwardly silent. "Hughan, I'm sorry."

Hughan measured and then calmly matched his gaze. "I know what it is," he said, "and what was perverted to make it."

Eamon breathed out in awe. "Then there *is* another?"

"There is no other Nightholt," Hughan told him. "That I see you know – or have guessed. But there is what is called the King's Covenant. It was made long before Edelred or I walked these lands, by the first King of the house of Brenuin. By it, and the promise that preceded it, the River Realm was granted to that house."

"This Covenant… granted the kingship," Eamon guessed in a whisper.

"Yes. It joined King and land and people together in faith and promise and service. The house of Brenuin held one copy, and the second was kept by the bookkeepers; any man could go to them to see and read it."

"What happened?" Eamon asked.

"When Ede was killed, one copy of the King's Covenant was destroyed – the Nightholt had been based upon it. With its destruction and Ede's death, Edelred used his Nightholt to claim the throne."

Eamon's heart sank. "Then… he has a rightful claim to the River?" Memories of Edelred's fond caresses almost choked him.

"No," Hughan replied. "For however hard he sought by the slaying of men and the penning of words to claim it, my house has not surrendered its authority to him – and the second copy of the King's Covenant still exists."

Eamon's eyes fell in horror to the broad scroll that he had delivered. "*'All rights of blood and oath…'*" The words murmured past his lips before he realized it. He looked up in horror. "That's why he wants you."

"I am the last of the house," Hughan answered. "He believes that if I cede to him, or if I am killed, then he will have his victory at last."

"Believes?"

Hughan looked at him. "There are things deeper than land or sea, higher than the soaring heavens and truer than light in a faithful heart, about which Edelred understands nothing, and of which a King is but a shadow. The King's Covenant is proof of those things, for it came from them. Even if he killed me and destroyed the King's Covenant, Edelred could not undo those things – or rewrite his Nightholt, as perhaps he hopes."

Eamon stood, stunned. "You knew all this?" he asked at last.

"About the Nightholt? Yes, although the bookkeepers didn't realize that it was an actual book until your message reached us."

"Why didn't you warn me?" Eamon gaped. "I could have done something!"

"What would you have done?"

"I'd have found a way to bring it to you –"

"You'd have lost your life doing so," Hughan told him firmly. "That was not a price I was willing to pay." Eamon was taken aback. "Suppose you had brought me the Nightholt when you and Mathaiah found it – what would it have changed? Edelred would still be hunting me. Destroying his book would not destroy his hunger for my blood or his belief that he could eradicate the Covenant. But you could have been discovered and killed. Who would then be bringing me vital information on the eve of battle? Who would have defended Dunthruik in these last months of darkness?"

Eamon couldn't answer. Had he not betrayed Hughan in delivering the Nightholt to Edelred?

Seeming to read his thought, the King looked deep into his eyes. "Eamon Goodman, take courage: you are the last heir of a house that has defended mine since the promise was spoken and there was a house of Brenuin to defend. You are my First Knight, the sword that goes before the star. You are the broken blade turned true."

Eamon's jaw dropped. Ashway's prophecy! How did Hughan know of it?

Heart pounding, Eamon swallowed. Hughan clasped his shoulder.

"I know you are true," the King continued, "and Dunthruik will see that when the battle comes."

Eamon breathed deeply. "When the battle breaks, I will come to you," he said. "I will bring as many as I can with me."

"I know."

He did not yet know how he would do it. "Is Lillabeth here?" Eamon asked suddenly.

"Yes."

"Does she… does she know about Mathaiah?"

"I have told her. Thank you for sending word of it."

Eamon laughed bitterly. "She cannot have thanked me. His death is of my doing. They learned that he could read the Nightholt because of me, and one whom I trusted."

"Lady Turnholt?" Hughan asked.

Eamon looked at him in surprise. "Yes," he said. "Alessia Turnholt." The name came ruefully from his lips.

"Eamon." Hughan's voice was quiet but arresting. "There is something that you must know."

Eamon looked at him. Though he loved the King and knew that the King loved him in return, he felt suddenly afraid.

"What must I know?"

"She is here."

His whole world stopped. "Alessia?" he repeated dumbly.

"Yes."

"But she… she… she went…"

"She was held and tortured by the Right Hand before being sent to the city's pyres," Hughan told him, "where she was found by men loyal to me. She is under my protection," he added, "and she is safe."

"How can this be?" Eamon breathed. Anger grew in his voice as he gaped at Hughan. "How can you keep her here? She betrayed –"

"She gave account to me of what she did," Hughan answered quietly, "and I gave her my forgiveness."

Eamon stared. "*Forgiveness?*"

"She has borne much, Eamon," Hughan told him, "and much for you. What she did for love of you, she did for me also."

Eamon's chest felt suddenly too small to hold his anger and anxiety. What had Alessia ever done out of love for him?

He trembled. Had she really been tortured and sent to the pyres? Or had she lied to Hughan, as she had lied to him?

Could Hughan have been deceived?

"I am not you, Hughan," he whispered, tired by grief and anger. "I do not know that I can forgive her."

"I understand," Hughan replied gently. "Do not let her presence here weigh on you, but know that she is here."

They watched each other for a long moment. Eamon felt the depth of the King's gaze upon him as though he looked into the starry sky, and marvelled at it.

"I am glad you're here, Hughan," he breathed.

"As I am glad of you," the King answered. "But you cannot linger, First Knight."

"I know."

Hughan moved across to one of the trunks nearby. He opened and drew an object out of it. It was wrapped in lengths of blue cloth. Coming back to Eamon, the King extended it towards him.

"Cover your colours," he said. Eamon did so. "Take this, and this answer, back to Edelred. Tell him," he continued, laying the bundled object into Eamon's hands, "that the Source has been taken. The Star is constant and does not yield. Neither shall I."

Eamon received the cloth. It was heavy, as though it held a weight of metal. "What is this?"

Hughan smiled. "Something that belongs to Edelred. He will not be enthused by my returning it to him."

Eamon nodded. "I will take your message, sire," he said, firming his hold on what Hughan had given him.

Together they went to the tent's doorway. Just outside it stood the Easter lords and wayfarer generals. They looked up as King and Right Hand exited – for Eamon was Right Hand once more.

"Well?" Feltumadas peered at them both.

"Our course was ever towards the gates of Dunthruik," Hughan answered, "and so it remains." Feltumadas nodded, pleased. "Leon," Hughan continued, "please escort the Right Hand and his men back to the bridge, and let them return to the city."

"Yes, sire."

Hughan met Eamon's gaze once more. "Look for me on the field of battle," he said.

"I will meet you there."

Leon led him away from the pavilion and down the line of tents to one that was unmarked. By its posts stood several watchmen. They stiffened as Leon led Eamon into the torchlight.

"Bring out the escort of the Right Hand," Leon commanded. One of the guards ducked inside the tent and a few moments later Wilhelm, Lonnam, and Heathlode emerged. Each of them searched Eamon's face, but he did not meet their gazes or speak any word to them.

Leon and the guards led them back to the bridge and over it to where, as had been promised, steeds and blades were returned to them.

"Ride straight to your city gates," Leon told them. "If you turn right or left, or falter, my men will ensure that you do not do so again."

Eamon looked to his escort. "Let us go."

Silently they rode away from the camp until its noise and light were lost behind them. The city grew before them. At last Lonnam looked to him.

"What said the Serpent, my lord?" he asked. His eyes fell uncertainly upon the bundle cradled in Eamon's hand.

"His message is for the Master."

"He rejected the terms?" Heathlode asked eagerly.

The Hand's enthusiasm was unsettling. "In every part," Eamon told him.

Wilhelm said nothing.

The gates boomed open as they approached, flooding their faces with torchlight and making the plain behind them seem darker than before. Dozens of faces were at the gates and gatehouse, each looking to his and seeking to know the outcome of his meeting.

Eamon spoke to none of them. His escort rode with him to the Four Quarters where he dismissed the two Hands back to the East.

"Mr Bellis, ride with me to the palace."

"Yes, my lord."

They rode on in silence. Eamon watched the young man's face from the corner of his eye; it was pale and troubled.

"Are you well, Mr Bellis?" he asked. Wilhelm shifted the weight of the standard in his hands.

"Yes, my lord," he answered at last.

"You may speak frankly, Mr Bellis," he said. "Are you well?"

Wilhelm swallowed. "No, my lord. I have seen something terrible tonight."

"What have you seen?" Eamon asked gently.

"The Serpent," Wilhelm breathed. He shook his head as though to clear it.

"He is not what you expected?" Eamon guessed.

"No," Wilhelm agreed. "That is what makes it terrible."

Eamon looked at him for a moment. "Mr Bellis, this city is going to war."

Wilhelm drew a deep breath and nodded firmly, as though to focus himself. "Yes, my lord."

"When it does, will you ride with me and bear my standard?"

Wilhelm looked up in awe. "I, lord?"

"Yes."

"To follow you into battle would have been great enough for me," Wilhelm told him. "To go with you is more than I could ask."

"I ask it of you."

"I will do it gladly, my lord," Wilhelm replied.

They reached the palace gates and were admitted into the Royal Plaza. Eamon alighted there and several of Edelred's own household came to retrieve the standard from Wilhelm. He seemed relieved to let it go. "Good night, Mr Bellis," Eamon called.

"And to you, my lord," Wilhelm replied. Then he bowed, turned, and left.

Eamon went straight to the Master.

The corridors leading to the throne room were curiously empty. His footsteps bounded ahead of him in echoes.

The doorkeeper was at the throne room door; he seemed to be waiting. As soon as he caught sight of Eamon he emerged from the shadows.

"Good evening, my lord."

"I bring news for the Master."

"He awaits you." The doorkeeper bowed low and then cast the throne room door open before him. Nodding once to him, Eamon entered.

The Master sat in the silent hall alone. Eamon walked the long chamber of fiery stones to the dais, and knelt.

"Your glory, Master."

"What news?" The throned's voice was impatient and eager. "Rise and speak."

Eamon rose and matched the Master's gaze. "The Serpent sends this message: 'The Star is constant, and does not yield. Neither will I.'"

A broad smile spread across the Master's delighted face. "He will have war."

"Yes, Master," Eamon replied. A tremor ran through him: all the comfort he had received from Hughan slipped away before that smile.

"Master, the Serpent bade me bring this to you," he said, raising the bundle which the King had given him. "He says, 'The Source is taken.'"

He did not know what the words meant, but as the bundle was taken from his hands, a grim flicker passed over the Master's face. As Edelred unwrapped the token, Eamon caught a glimpse of gold. It resembled part of an eagle's wing.

Edelred's face became one of dire wrath. "Dares he blithely send this to me to goad me?" he thundered. "And you would dare deliver it!"

Eamon looked from the golden fragment to the Master's face in uncomprehending alarm. The Master's wrath transfixed him and he trembled, for that gaze was filled with savagery.

"Master, I mean no deed of daring or offence. I do not even know what I have brought!"

The throned laughed derisively.

"You know but little, son of Eben," he hissed, "and the Serpent is all the more witless." He drew a violent breath. "But he will have war from me, son of Eben," he snarled. "No harrowing or affliction that this land has yet seen will be like that which I shall render unto him. From its very source to its mouth, I will make the River run with his woe, his blood, and his lamentations."

Eamon quivered.

Edelred stilled, looked upon him, and smiled. "The Serpent will have war from me," he said, laying his hand upon Eamon's cheek. "He will have war from us."

CHAPTER XV

The fifteenth of May dawned clear and crisp. The whole of Dunthruik rose with it, and every man within the city walls awakened to the perpetual hum of preparations as blades were set to grindstones and hammers to nails.

Eamon spent most of the day in the North Quarter overseeing its preparations. He inspected each of the quarter's fifteen groups, offering words of encouragement. Officers, ensigns, and cadets found hope in his words, but Eamon left with a heavy heart. He knew too well that every man who looked to him to see the Master's splendour was a man he would soon betray.

There was so much movement in the city that the Coll was brought to a near standstill. Even the smaller side streets, the more secret ways of going from quarter to quarter known only to those who lived there, throbbed with traffic. The tension of the air webbed around Eamon and clung to him.

Towards the late afternoon, content with the preparations in the North, Eamon left the quarter. He rode to each of the other quarters to speak to their Hands and enquire after the day's work. Lord Febian greeted him nervously, but assisted as he was by Captain Farleigh, the Hand seemed to have most matters under control.

"Lord Goodman," Febian said as Eamon prepared to leave, "I wish to ride with the main body of the Hands tomorrow."

"You would have the West go Handless to the battle?" Eamon asked.

"I may be its keeper, Lord Goodman," Febian replied, "but I cannot ride at the head of the West. I will serve the Master in better heart and fuller strength among the Hands."

"Captain Farleigh is happy to assume command in your stead?"

"He is, my lord."

"He is a highly capable man," Eamon answered. "I will inform Lord Arlaith that you will ride with the Hands."

Febian sighed with relief. "Thank you, Lord Goodman."

Eamon went to the South, but Tramist was not available to see him. Tramist's captain nonetheless assured him that preparations had gone smoothly.

"Lord Tramist has always been particular about the proper arming of this quarter, my lord," the captain told him. "He will be examining and testing the arms of every single man, quite possibly in person – at least that appeared to be his intention when we spoke last night. Shall I have him come to you when he returns, my lord?"

"Only if he is not content with the preparations," Eamon answered. "Thank you, captain."

He went last of all to the East. There the number of men in the streets was greater than anywhere else, for the Blind Gate was being assiduously prepared for the exodus it would witness the following morning.

As Eamon rode past he caught sight of Anderas in the crowd. The captain was speaking to another man, an officer from one of the many external divisions.

"Captain Anderas!" Eamon called.

Hearing his name, Anderas looked up, saw Eamon, excused himself, and threaded his way across the crowded road between them. He reached Eamon as swiftly as he could.

"My lord," he greeted, bowing. He looked pale and sleepless.

"Are you well, captain?" Eamon asked quietly.

"Yes, Lord Goodman."

"And is the East prepared?"

"I believe so," Anderas returned. "You may wish to check my assessment with Lord Arlaith," he added, seeming to shudder as he spoke.

"I mean to," Eamon told him. It was then that he looked carefully at his friend. "You seem shaken, captain," he said, and so Anderas did: there was a tremor to the man's hands and a haunted look to his shadowed eyes. "You are sure you are well?"

"I passed a difficult night," Anderas answered at last.

"Would you speak of it?"

Anderas looked up at him gravely. "Not here, my lord."

"Lord Goodman!"

Eamon looked up to see a black-clad figure upon the city wall. It was Arlaith.

"I will speak with Lord Arlaith," Eamon said, glancing back to Anderas. "But may we speak of what has troubled you, when we find a moment?"

"Yes."

Feeling disconcerted, Eamon dismounted. As he alighted, Anderas steadied him.

"I am firm to our purpose, my lord," he whispered.

Eamon matched his gaze for a moment. It was indeed firm. "Thank you, captain."

Leaving his horse he climbed the wall to Arlaith. The Hand stood observing the plain and the River. As Eamon reached his side, the Hand gestured to the bridge.

"Is it nearly as feeble-looking as it appears from here, Lord Goodman?" he asked.

"Hardly," Eamon replied. He discerned an odd excitement in Arlaith's eyes as their gazes met.

"It will go down in flames, Lord Goodman," Arlaith told him, then laughed. "*Flames*."

Eamon repressed a shudder.

"How was the Serpent?" Arlaith added, with mock politeness.

"He rejected the terms," Eamon replied.

Arlaith laughed. "That I know, Lord Goodman! How seemed he to you?"

Wary of the glint in the Hand's eye, Eamon carefully matched his look. "What kind of answer would you have me make, Lord Arlaith?" he asked. "I delivered terms which he rejected. I am in no position to detail his state of mind to you."

"My apologies, Lord Goodman," Arlaith said and bowed gracefully. "I meant no disrespect to you."

Eamon looked at him, feeling and then quelling a streak of suspicion. "Your eagerness is commendable," he replied. Turning, he looked back over the city and stood for a moment, listening to its work.

"How stand the preparations?" Arlaith asked.

"Lord Febian wishes to ride with the Hands tomorrow," Eamon answered. "I have said that he may."

"He is not comfortable with so newly won an accolade at such a time," Arlaith mused. "A quarter is not an easy burden to bear."

"No. But he has prepared the West; Captain Farleigh will have charge of it. The North is prepared."

"As is the East," Arlaith nodded. "How is the South?"

"The captain advises me that all is ready."

"You did not see Lord Tramist?" Arlaith asked curiously.

"No," Eamon replied. "He was not there. The captain believes him to be out in the quarter, single-handedly inspecting every blade to be used on the field tomorrow."

"Lord Tramist is very particular about such things," Arlaith agreed. "I am led to understand that he was a fine soldier."

"Yet he does not ride?" Eamon asked.

"To ride in a time of peace and in a time of war are, as I am sure you will appreciate, very different matters," Arlaith replied. "Lord Tramist was also accomplished in the latter, in his youth, but I would not now force him to a bellicose saddle."

"I will heed your advice."

For a long moment Eamon was silent. As he stared across the plain at the pontoon bridge, Hughan's words suddenly rushed into his mind: "*She was held and tortured by the Right Hand...*"

His look snapped back to Arlaith. The Hand's smiling face was also turned towards the south and the bridge, and perhaps his mind toyed with visions of it aflame.

"Do all the knights of Dunthruik ride out?" Eamon asked quietly. He had a sudden thought he wished to pursue.

"Yes."

"Then I presume the knight Fleance will ride among them?"

Arlaith's brow furrowed. "Fleance… Fleance… The name does not seem familiar, but if he is a knight, he will be here with the others of course. How else, my lord, could he ride with the knights if he were not?" Arlaith asked with a small laugh.

"Surely you remember Fleance? The one for whom Lady Turnholt abandoned and betrayed me?"

Arlaith looked slowly at him. For a long moment he was silent. His face became utterly unreadable.

Eamon matched Arlaith's look. His own hardened.

"What would you say if I were to order Fleance to ride out at the fore of our armies where he would surely be slain by the enemy?"

Arlaith bit his lip. "I should not think it prudent, my lord."

"Prudence has nothing to do with it," Eamon snapped back. "It would be an act of revenge. Of spite, if you will, to take from her what she has taken from me."

Arlaith paled slightly. "It would be your right, my lord, but I should not advise it."

"Indeed? Then I shall give the order… unless, of course, you have other information concerning Lady Turnholt's circumstance?"

Arlaith wrung his hands and looked once more out across the plain.

"What happened to Lady Turnholt?" Eamon said bluntly. He fixed Arlaith with a piercing stare. "I will be answered."

"It was a delicate matter, Lord Goodman," Arlaith answered, "and one with which you should not trouble yourself."

"Why should I not trouble myself, Lord Arlaith?" Eamon returned crisply. "This is the second time that I have asked; do not make me ask again."

"With due reverence to you, I do not believe that you should ask, Lord Goodman," Arlaith replied. "The eve of battle is not the best time for such questions."

"You would defy me?" Eamon asked coldly.

Arlaith turned a sorrowful gaze upon him. "Please, Lord Goodman," he said quietly. "Do not insist upon the matter."

"She did not go with Fleance," Eamon told him, his voice growing in anger as he spoke. "Her house was disbanded and I have learned that you held her. Another question I will ask, Lord Arlaith, and you will answer it. What did you do with her?"

Arlaith held his look uncomfortably for a moment. "When you left to seek the head of the Easter lord," he said at last, "she was arrested for questioning; her loyalty had proven troublesome. She was allied to the enemy. At the Master's will I held her. Some information she gave up willingly, some had to be obtained from her..." Arlaith's voice trailed away and he lowered his gaze. "Lord Goodman," he said quietly, looking up with a pleading look, "I have no wish to –"

"Answer me!" Eamon demanded.

"She hated the Master," Arlaith told him, shaking his head at the recollection. "How she hated him! But her hatred of him, Lord Goodman, was as nothing compared to her hatred of you."

Eamon recoiled. Alessia hated him... The knowledge of it fortified his anger.

"How great the bitterness and rage she bore against you!" Arlaith whispered. "I had never seen its like, and hope never to see it again."

Eamon turned his gaze towards the plain. She had hated him, yet even now she was under the King's protection. He closed his eyes hard, to clear his thought. Hughan had forgiven her... How could Hughan have forgiven someone who so hated his First Knight?

He felt Arlaith's sharp gaze upon him.

"This lady wanted nothing more than to strike against you," the Hand told him quietly. "I was too late to stop her, Lord Goodman, but I would have done, had it lain within my power."

"To stop her from what?" he asked, turning to Arlaith at last.

Arlaith looked at him with deep pity. "She tore out of herself your unborn child, my lord."

Eamon could not even gasp. Shock and witless horror froze his very being, fixing his eyes on Arlaith's sorry face. As he stared, he willed the Hand to smile, or laugh, or somehow prove that what he had spoken was untrue – but Arlaith's eyes remained upon his own, grieved by the news that he had delivered.

"You lie," Eamon whispered. Why should he believe Arlaith? They had long been enemies. Suddenly his voice grew to a yell. "*You lie!*"

Arlaith did not speak. Eamon searched his face. "Admit that you lie!" But rather than the forceful command Eamon intended, his accusation emerged like the imploring whimper of a child.

Slowly, the Lord of the East Quarter shook his head.

"I speak truth."

"Swear it! *Swear* that you speak true, or I'll throw you from these parapets myself," Eamon hissed through clenched teeth.

Arlaith raised his hands in submission and took a step back. "What could I swear upon that you would believe…? The Nightholt, perhaps?" He lowered his left hand but kept his right raised. "I, Lord Arlaith, do solemnly swear upon the Nightholt that I speak truly. I would as soon lie to the Master himself as to you."

Grief took hold of him, digging in its talons so deep he gripped his arms across his aching breast lest it should rupture.

Gently, Arlaith reached across and touched his shoulder. "I am sorry, Lord Goodman."

Eamon rounded on him. "Had I a child? Had I a child, and she –?"

"She murdered it. She did so in cold blood, crying down curses and vengeance on you with her bloody tongue. How could I bring that news to you?" Arlaith asked, his face rent with pity. "How could I lay such sorrow upon you? Yet you commanded me, and as a faithful servant, I obeyed."

Eamon barely heard him. Had Hughan known of this? Had Hughan known and not spoken of it? His mind filled with Alessia's face, her touch, and he shuddered with hatred and revulsion.

Arlaith reached across and took him firmly by the shoulders.

"Lord Goodman, you must bear it like a man."

"Bear it?" Eamon howled, trying to tear away, but Arlaith held him. "How can I bear what she would not?" He drove his hands to his head, pressing them violently against his brow, but he could not still the terrifying thoughts that dwelt within him. "It was a child, Arlaith! A babe… and it was mine!"

Eamon began to sob.

Arlaith pressed his shoulders. "You will have a time for vengeance and for anger, Lord Goodman. But the eve of battle is no place for them." Eamon felt Arlaith's grip on his shoulders growing as he shook, and tried to control his crippling tears.

"Take your hatred to the field tomorrow," Arlaith continued, "and work out her treachery on those she loved. Pay back the blood she spilled, more precious than any other, in unnumbered bloody corpses on the field."

Arlaith's words slunk into Eamon's flesh, stoking his anger.

How could Alessia have dared to take the life of his child? *His* child! What had given her that right? What cruelty had he ever done her, compared with hers to him, that she would think to do such a thing?

How had Hughan seen fit to forgive her?

"Lord Goodman." Arlaith's quiet voice drew him from his thought. Eamon looked up at him, feeling the sore red of tears about his eyes. Arlaith watched him with concern. "I must return to the East," he said. "Will you be well, Lord Goodman?"

"I will be well." Eamon's tone and voice seemed fell in his ears and on his lips as he spoke.

Arlaith held his gaze a moment more, then bowed deeply. "By your leave, Lord Goodman."

Eamon did not watch him go. Driving his arms deep into his

cloak, he turned and stared out at the plain. Had one betrayal not been enough for her?

Eamon.

As the gentle voice washed through him, he shook with fear, for it forced him from his vengeful thoughts and showed him how dark they were. He shuddered to see them in its light.

How could he know that Arlaith had told him the truth? Why would Arlaith tell him the truth about such a thing?

Arlaith had said he had not lied… and Hughan had not spoken of a child. No; Hughan had told him that Alessia loved him still! Twice, then, Alessia had lied to the King, and Hughan had been fooled.

How could the King be fooled?

Eamon shook his head and tried to reason with himself. It could be a lie. Alessia might not even have been with child…

But even as he sought that comfort, whether from a vision sent by the King, or another of the Master's premonitions sent to torment him, Eamon knew the truth of Arlaith's words: Alessia Turnholt had been bearing a child in her womb – his child – and it was dead. His hands ached at the thought of the tiny babe that he would never hold – or even see.

He pressed his hands to the walls as his limbs shook. The city was behind him and the battle before him, but as the sun sank into the western sky, Eamon could only grieve for what he had never known, and unknowingly had lost.

A heavy darkness fell on the city that night. The lights of the Serpent's camp across the River gave back bright answer to Dunthruik's grim walls.

The throne room was long and empty when Eamon knelt wearily in it. He hid his grief as well as he could, but he wondered whether, as they watched him, the Master's eyes discerned it.

"Rise, son of Eben."

Eamon rose. "The city is ready, Master. It will deploy at dawn."

"It is a long-awaited watch that comes this night, Eben's son," the throned told him, and then looked at him. He rose and crossed the dais to where Eamon stood before reaching out to touch his face. "You, too, were long-awaited."

Eamon searched the Master's face in confusion. Smiling softly, Edelred leaned forward and powerfully kissed his brow.

"Rest, Eben's son," he said. "Much will be accomplished with the dawn."

So it was that, as the moon rose, Eamon returned to his quarters. Supper had been laid for him but he could not face it. With all that he had lived through that day his heart felt terrible and empty, and all his efforts vain. His very self seemed lost in that vacuum and, as he gazed at the table before him, the weight of his long months in Dunthruik came to rest heavily on his shoulders.

Cartwright came to clear the table and started when he found the food untouched. He looked at Eamon with concern. "My lord?"

"I cannot eat." Eamon drove his hands over his eyes and then gazed accusingly at his servant. "Did you know it?" he demanded.

Cartwright blinked. "Know what, my lord?"

"Did you know that your lady Alessia was with child?"

Cartwright remained very still for a moment and his face paled.

"I did not know it," the servant said, "but I would believe it."

"Would you also believe, Mr Cartwright, that she…" Eamon's tongue stuck in his throat as fresh rage ran through him. "You were right, Mr Cartwright," he managed at last. "She stayed in this city. She was held by the Right Hand, and she…" He thought of her pale, beautiful flesh, prone before the torments of a Right Hand.

"What happened, my lord?" Cartwright whispered.

Eamon looked at him. The thoughts were too terrible for him to bear. His jaw quivered. Desperately he struggled with his violent tongue but he could not hold it.

"She killed it to injure me!"

With a cry of vile rage he tore up to his feet. He seized the table, and setting against it every force of muscle and of limb, he hurled it down. With a tremendous crack, all that was on the table was cast asunder and the stones of the Right Hand's chamber rang with a splintering roar.

Eamon did not hear it. His tongue, stirred past all endurance, fell to curses. To think of her, laid open before the Right Hand...

His curses dwindled to wrathful sobs and his knees lost their strength. Sinking back upon his chair, he laid his head in his hands and wept.

If she had been tortured, she had deserved it. All that she had done, she had done to spite him. It was to spite him that she had slaughtered his child.

"My lord," Cartwright dared at last.

Eamon scarcely heard him.

"My lord, I cannot imagine how this weighs on you, but I am sorry."

Cartwright's gentle words fell on him with a chill. Eamon struggled to recover his senses.

"It was not your doing," he answered at last.

Cartwright stood nearby. He held an elegant black napkin, which he had rescued from the floor. Wordlessly, the servant extended it to Eamon. Eamon used it to wipe his stinging eyes and face.

"Thank you."

Cartwright nodded.

"I am sorry," Eamon added, gesturing to the broken table.

"I will clear it." Cartwright began to gather debris from the floor. As Cartwright worked, Eamon's thought turned to what the morning would bring.

"Mr Cartwright."

Cartwright paused and looked at him. "My lord?"

"If the Master fails tomorrow –"

"My lord!"

"*If* the Master fails tomorrow, and the Serpent enters the city, I want you to gather my house. You will go to a room somewhere in the palace and shut yourselves inside. And, should the enemy find you, you will tell them that you serve me." He paused. "Refer to me by name."

"My lord?"

"Do not question my instruction. Only swear to me that you will do this."

He did not look convinced, but the servant nodded. "Yes, my lord." He continued gathering the fallen meal and then looked up to Eamon. "Will the Serpent come, my lord?"

"Yes," Eamon replied. "He will come."

"Then you, my lord, must eat," Cartwright said quietly, "for this city's hopes are pinned on you."

Caught between growing terror and the embers of his anguished rage, Eamon shuddered.

"Yes," he whispered.

It was long that night before Eamon retired to his bedchambersand lay down to rest. For a while he heard the servants tidying the dining hall. When even that noise stopped, he was left alone with the rustling sound of the drapes moving in the evening air.

He lay through the scant hours of darkness, trying to rest. But he could not sleep; his eyes were haunted and his thought was tainted, and when he tried to distract himself by watching the drapes about him, he saw shadows as terrifying as those that dwelt within.

For a moment, however brief, he had not been the last of his house, but before it had even been born, his child had been cursed by his blood. It was repayment for his broken oaths.

So much had happened to him since the day when he had begun taking and breaking oaths. It had not been even a year, yet it felt as though he had lived a hundred. With the dawn, he would face that for which he had fought and suffered.

All over the city men lay down to sleepless rest, or restless sleep. Dunthruik lay on the land like a hideous beast, ready by labours and groans to birth an army through the Blind Gate. The fighting would begin before most of that army had reached the field, and the field would be covered in blood before the sun had reached the third hour.

And all for what – a book and a crown? Would men die for that? Would *he* die for it?

He searched his heart. First Knight they called him, and Right Hand, and Raven's Bane, and Eben's son. He had so many names that he scarcely knew who he was or what he was to do. When he rode before the divisions and lines of men, before the whole city of Dunthruik, its first son and triumph of its Master, and spoke of his allegiance… would he not betray them all?

His arm ached. Slowly he rubbed his fingers across the place where the fangs of Cathair's hound had gripped him.

Whatever he did in the morning, he was to be a traitor. He had always been one. Was he not blind to think that he could come from the battle and have but one name, and one allegiance? Two oaths he had sworn and two marks he bore. The scion of treachery, the house of Goodman was a stillborn house; it did not deserve to live.

Eamon's mind reached after Eben's dagger. By Right Hands was it wielded – Eben and Cathair were not the least of those whose lives it had claimed.

In the darkness of his thought, Eamon rose from his bed and crossed the room to where the dagger lay. Slowly, he knelt down by it and drew it from its sheath, holding the curved blade before him in the pale moonlight.

The letters were there; they glared grimly back at him. He reached forward and quietly touched his fingers to them, feeling their cutting shape beneath his skin.

Surely his task was done? Battle would be joined, and there was nothing now that lay in his power to halt it, or to bring victory or defeat to either side. And what awaited him in victory or in defeat? There was no hope of peace, or rest, or life for him. His life was spent, worn out in deception and in tears, and his blood spent also in the child that had never lived to bear it. What hope had he for goodness or for clemency? What desire had he for life?

As Eamon gazed down at the blade an answer shivered down his spine: *none*. To live was to plunge himself ever more deeply in sorrow and in blood. To reach the dawn was to declare his treachery and incur the wrath and hatred of those who admired him.

You need not reach the dawn, Eben's son.

Stunned, Eamon looked at the blade in his hands. It glinted back at him and, as he held it, its weight and shape and form seemed good to him. That dagger seemed the only good thing to him in all the world. He had borne much: who could ask him to carry more? How could he carry more?

And why should he? It was not despair in his heart, but rebellion. Why should he suffer and bleed and die for any man, or beneath any hand but his own? Why should he live and risk the breeding and bleeding of his house?

He gazed at the dagger's guileful blade and saw his own eyes caged between the letters, as though he saw them in a dark and bitter glass. His last service to the city, the Eagle, and the Star could, should, and would be his death.

Eamon.

The blade was in his hands and turned towards him, leaning against his very heart as he prepared to cast himself upon it – but the voice, and a memory of Hughan, halted him. *"Your blood is not cursed…"*

With trembling hands he cast the blade from him; it clashed into the wall and fell with an angry clatter to the ground. Light flickered on the letters.

Shaking, Eamon crawled to the post of his bed. He pressed his hands and shuddering body against it and drove his face into his arms.

Coward! The voice seethed so loudly that it seemed to shake the room. *Miserable wretch!*

Eamon.

Tearfully Eamon looked up to see a weeping man. The vision seemed astonishingly clear, and the depth of the man's grief was so forceful that Eamon knew it in his own heart. It was in the closeness of their hearts that he knew the man he saw as Eben.

Suddenly a lady was there. She was fair, her shining eyes were blue, and as Eamon watched she knelt down at Eben's side. He recoiled from her with woe.

"*Come not near me!*" Eben cried, his voice raised in anguish. "*I am nothing but a curse!*"

With gentle, fearless hands, the woman reached forward and touched his face.

"*These ills will be undone,*" she breathed, "*and blessings will be wrought through you.*" The lady leaned forward to kiss his grieved and wearied brow, driving back his care and leaving awe upon him. "*Peace, Eben,*" she whispered. "*Peace.*"

It was then that Eamon knew her: Ede's sister, the root of Hughan's line, Elaina.

As the vision faded away he gazed again at his room. The queen's word of peace filled it, and the shadows shrank.

"My lord?"

The quiet voice stirred through his silent dreams. Eamon drew open his eyes. "Yes?"

"It is time."

"Thank you, Mr Cartwright."

He rose slowly from his bed. The sky hung dark outside without even the faintest trace of dawn. By lamplight Eamon went, shivering, to his hall and ate what Cartwright brought him. As he finished, Fletcher appeared.

"Lord Goodman," he said, his voice dry with the early hour. "We wait to arm you."

"Very well, Fletcher," Eamon answered. "Come."

Fletcher bowed and left the room. Moments later he returned with a group of servants. They carried with them the various parts of the armour that the throned had had made for him. As each splendid piece was brought and laid down on a long table before him, Eamon's stomach turned with dread.

At Fletcher's command all the servants left the room. Eamon was alone with his lieutenant and servant. The armour watched him in the darkness – armour fit for a Right Hand and for one beloved of the Master. It had been made to hold him, and him alone.

Eamon looked at Cartwright and Fletcher. "Let me be armed," he breathed.

They dressed him in a thick doublet and hose, lacing them together at his sides and back. Eamon felt the strength of the material on him; it was padded. Sturdy mail gussets covered the spaces under his arms where the armour would not protect him. Cartwright and Fletcher worked silently together and bound the arming points with expert hands. When the doublet was secured, they lay the armour on him.

He stood as sabatons and greaves were buckled onto his feet and legs, then the cuisses and poleyn, both tightly strapped away from any attacker's blade.

Are you ready for war, son of Eben?

He longed for peace. He longed for a peace that would fill his heart and the River Realm just as Elaina's kiss had renewed Eben. Such peace, and all his hope, lay in the King.

Cartwright lifted the breastplate and held it steady as Fletcher began strapping it closely to Eamon's body.

You long for peace? The desire of a righteous man! The voice scoffed at him. *Neither peace nor righteousness can be yours, Eben's son.*

He had striven to do right until his heart broke. Had it not been enough?

The plates and plackarts snapped closely together and the straps binding them were tied. Then Fletcher brought him his pauldrons, upper cannons, vambraces and couters, deftly sliding them over his outstretched arms and fixing them all in place with the arming points worked into his doublet. The pauldrons sat on his shoulders like a layer of finely articulated scales that moved as fluidly as he did.

"Your hands, my lord," Fletcher said quietly. Eamon extended them and Fletcher slid gloves and gauntlets over them. Then he brought Eamon's belt and sword.

"*The blade will break and turn true…*" Ashway's prophecy came back to him. As Fletcher girt the sword securely to his left hip, Eamon knew that this day, more than any other, was the day that his turning would be proven.

You turn to the words of a frenzied, witless seer for encouragement? They will not save you. You are but broken, Eben's son. I broke you. There is no truth left in you to turn.

Fletcher left his side and returned a moment later carrying Eben's dagger. As Eamon saw it, his blood ran cold.

In striking bound, son of Eben.

Fletcher reached up to set the thing at his side. Eamon summoned his courage and turned from the voice.

"Leave the dagger," he said.

Fletcher looked at him in surprise. "You will need it, my lord."

"I will have another," Eamon answered. "I shall not be bound to this one."

"It is the blade of the Right Hand –"

"And this Right Hand has no hand for curved blades," Eamon answered. "Leave it here. I will have another."

"Yes, my lord."

A simple dagger was set at Eamon's right hip and then his tabard was brought to him. It was black and bore Edelred's own eagle in red, just as the banner Eamon had borne to the parley. Fletcher set it over his breast and made sure that the sleeves hung correctly over the vambraces.

Last of all they brought him his helmet. It had no visor and offered no protection for his lower face, so that he might see. Three feathers, each of black and red, crested it, and a twisted cord of the same colours marked its rim. It was set on his head.

You are bound to me, Eben's son, bound by blood. You cannot undo a work of blood; the Serpent will not loose or save you from it. The voice's strength was overwhelming, and fire drove at his brow and hands.

But the queen's whispered peace was as a grace over his heart. In that peace did he answer.

"You do not understand," he laughed. *"I am a King's man, under the King's grace. No power of blood or scheme of yours can bind me!"*

In silence, the voice left him.

Fletcher stepped back and looked at him. "You are ready, my lord," he breathed.

"Thank you," Eamon answered; and he was.

Dawn began to mark the sky when Eamon left the palace. From his quarters to the palace gates, its corridors were lined with men and women who watched his departure. He saw hope and fear in their eyes. The battle weighed on them but it weighed on him all the more, for he knew that he had become the emblem and banner of their courage.

The streets of Dunthruik were filled with men. Everywhere, he heard the din and saw the eerie glint of arms and armour. Sahu had been armed no less awesomely than he; curved plates covered the small white star-mark upon his forehead.

He rode to the Blind Gate. The roads nearby were choked with Hands.

Arlaith was at the Blind Gate looking out over the walls. The Hand wore a full, dark tabard and a long cloak ridged with ochre. The feathers on his helmet showed the same colours.

Eamon climbed up to him, feeling the strange weight of his armour with each step. He wondered if Arlaith suffered from any similar impediment. The effect of the Left Hand's tabard and cloak was to lessen any impression of armour at all.

"Lord Goodman." Arlaith bowed before coming forward and clasping his hand. "Good morning. How fare you?" he added softly.

"Well," Eamon answered.

"You are well armoured," Arlaith commented.

"A gift from the Master," Eamon replied. He turned and looked out across the pre-dawn plain. There was not yet much to see; the plain lay still and silent. Somewhere in the near distance he heard birdsong. It seemed unearthly. "You will lead the Hands?" he asked, turning back to the Lord of the East Quarter.

"Yes, Lord Goodman," Arlaith answered. "We'll give the Serpent's hobilars a good fretting, and make space for the knights and infantry – and for yourself."

Eamon nodded. He was to ride out at the head of the army. "When do you go?"

Arlaith pulled a face as he assessed the colour of the sky. "Before dawn."

"Not long from now," Eamon murmured.

"No."

They stood in silence. Recollections of Arlaith's dire revelations – of *her* betrayal; had he learned of it just yesterday? – seeped into his consciousness. Eamon steeled himself against them: this was not the time for grief or anger. He had much to do.

As the dawn continued climbing to the sky, the square below them became saturated with Hands.

At that moment a Gauntlet officer came up the wall to them, and bowed low. Eamon recognized him as one of the East Quarter's first lieutenants. "My lords," he said. "I have enquired as you asked, Lord Arlaith."

"There is news?" Arlaith asked.

"Lord Tramist is nowhere to be found," the officer answered. "He has not been seen since he returned from the war council."

Arlaith's gaze flicked suspiciously to Eamon, then hardened. "I fear for his safety," he said. "Tramist would not willingly absent himself in Dunthruik's hour of need."

Eamon stared at Arlaith. "Can we not send out more men to search for him?"

Arlaith shook his head. "And which men would you send, my lord? All our forces are committed to the front. Which ones would you have me withdraw against the Master's orders to act upon an unfounded suspicion? I fear Lord Tramist must rely on his own resources for the time being – provided he still lives."

"Why should he be dead?"

"Why indeed?" Arlaith answered cuttingly. He looked back to

the first lieutenant. "Assign full command to his captain," he said, dismissing the officer with a curt wave of his hand. The officer bowed once more and left. Arlaith fixed Eamon with a disconcertingly full and penetrating gaze. "Why indeed."

"I do not care for your tone. Do you mean to charge me with his death?" Eamon demanded.

Arlaith shook his head as he looked down at the Hands below. "No, my lord," he replied. "My apologies."

Eamon was about to speak again when he caught a glimpse of another figure coming down the Coll. Stepping to the edge of the wall, he looked down upon a sight that stole all speech from him.

The Master rode towards the Blind Gate. He too was armoured, but his armour showed forth like flecks of golden fire in the dim half-light. Red was the tabard that he wore, red the long, gold-hemmed cloak that flowed behind him and red the flaming hair that spilled like tongues of fire from beneath the crown upon his brow. The horse on which he rode was like a steed that had come, flaming, from the very sun itself.

All those in the road fell back before him, some bowing in wordless wonder and others calling on his glory. The Lord of Dunthruik rode to the gate of his city.

It was by the steps that led up to the Blind Gate's walls that the throned dismounted. Robed in fiery splendour, he ascended to the wall's full height to the place where Eamon and Arlaith both stood. As he reached them, both Right Hand and Left dropped down to one knee.

"Your glory, Master," they said.

"Rise," the Master commanded. They did. Edelred looked out across the plain towards the River. He smiled.

"Take your Hands and lead them out, Arlaith," he commanded.

"Yes, Master," Arlaith answered. "To your glory." He bowed once more before descending the wall.

Eamon stood silently with the Master, enveloped by the hanging grey of the coming morning. He could see a great number of hobilars out on the plain, soon to be lit by the rising sun. Eamon sensed an odd feeling of nausea in his stomach, and wasn't sure whether it was the result of his own anxiety or the effect of doublet and armour bound about it.

It was then that the Master turned to him. "Once, son of Eben, your forebear and I stood on this wall and surveyed this plain." Edelred smiled. "I do not think he thought that one of his house would stand here with me again."

The Master's reverie chilled Eamon to the core. "It is my great honour to stand with you, Master, and to serve your glory."

The Master reached across and laid his fingers to his face. He said no word.

With a great sound as of a roaring river, the Blind Gate opened. Moments later a dark tide of Hands flooded out of it, Arlaith at its head. To their left, more poured out of the North Gate. The sound of rumbling hooves thudded in Eamon's ears, and with it a great cry:

"His glory!"

The Hands advanced to form a screen across the plain. Behind this sheltering cove of Hands, Eamon would soon ride, followed by the knights.

"Son of Eben." Edelred's voice was full of pride and quivering eagerness. "You were born for this day."

He could scarcely endure the gaze with which the Lord of Dunthruik held him, yet Eamon took the Master's gauntleted hand. He raised it to his lips and kissed it.

"To your glory, Master," he said.

Edelred laid a smile upon him. "Go forth in it, my son," he said. His grey eyes filled with anticipation and delight.

Eamon quitted the walls and descended to the gate. Sahu awaited him, armoured head tossing between red harnesses. Wilhelm was also there – the young man had been armoured and wore a tabard that bore a design reverse to Eamon's own. The pole of the great standard was black and gold and the Master's standard ran high at its top. By Wilhelm rode two trumpeters, and by them, two Hands, Heathlode and Lonnam.

Eamon looked at them as he mounted. He wondered whether his poor horse, which had borne him and borne with him through long miles, would live out the day. He touched Sahu's head fondly as he took the reins. General Rocell and the knights drew up in the streets, ready to parade out of the gates behind him.

He looked up to the city wall. The Master gazed down at him, a broad smile on his face.

With that face upon him, Eamon turned his gaze to the open gate. The plain was caught between it, a dun stage soon to be bloodied as the day's events played out. He wondered what the Blind Gate would see that day.

He touched his spurs to his horse's flanks. The gate was before him, the knights behind, and the crisp notes of his trumpeters heralded his going as he passed under the great threshold of Dunthruik. Every stone in the Blind Gate seemed vivid to him.

The sun rose before him as he rode out of the gates. Dunthruik, its voice raised up in a tumultuous cry, followed him.

"*His glory!*"

Though it was difficult to distinguish anything beyond the screen of Hands, Eamon could see movement across the plain. The arrow-formed lances of knights rode out behind him. He and his staff moved from their path. As each lance exited the city gates, they drew up into banners. Among the glinting sea of banners and crests Eamon recognized the emblems of the Patagons and the Albens; certainly he saw banners of men who had ridden with him to Pinewood.

Eamon watched in silence as the knights streamed from the Blind Gate, each one a grim and armoured harbinger of the morning. He commanded many men. Many of them rode to their deaths. And the reward that he would render them for their service?

He hoped for their defeat.

He caught movement in the screen of Hands to the north. The line fell back before a counter-attack. Some Hands fell, though not many; most simply rode back apace as the screen continued to protect the deploying knights. To the south, cavalry rode across the Easter bridge. By the glint of colour he spied, Eamon knew the coming men to be Easters. The King's infantry were not far behind them. The Hands, led by Arlaith, fell back to regroup.

As the cavalry moved north, a blast of trumpets sounded from behind. Turning, Eamon saw the first of the infantry, Dunthruik's precious Gauntlet, march from the gate. The men marched in crisp formation. The regional divisions came first, followed then by Dunthruik's own. General Waite and his staff marked where the River Realm's regional troops ended and Dunthruik's own began. Eamon thought that he caught sight of the East Quarter troops among the dense lines.

"*His glory!*"

As the Gauntlet marched on, the Easter cavalry and Hughan's infantry drew up behind the hobilars. The bridge had indeed allowed the wayfarers to deploy quickly. While they stood ready, Dunthruik's men still streamed from the Blind Gate. Yet it could easily be another excruciating hour, maybe two, before the battle began.

Some time later, Arlaith rode to Eamon's side. His face was flushed with exhilaration and his horse panted from the skirmishing work it had done.

"Lord Goodman," he greeted.

"Lord Arlaith," Eamon returned. "Good work, I trust?"

"Indeed!" Arlaith answered. "The bowmen are just going out."

Eamon looked up to see groups of crossbowmen going forward from their lines; they were met at once by men from Hughan's lines, and both sets of bowmen began what seemed to be a fairly ineffectual exchange of shots. The Easters also loosed, but Eamon could not distinguish the many-shaded banners of green, yellow, and orange apart into separate houses.

For a long time he and Arlaith merely watched the exchange, their ears filled with the marching sound of the last groups of infantry deployed from the Blind Gate.

Eamon looked up to the sky; it had to be near the second hour already. He felt hot inside his armour and his nerves were frayed.

At any moment he would have to make his move: he would have to choose the banner under which he would stand.

You will not have the courage, son of Eben.

"I must return to the Hands," Arlaith said. Eamon nodded. Arlaith watched him with a disturbingly keen gaze.

"Do so."

Arlaith rode back to the regrouped Hands. Eamon breathed deep. There were knights to the north and countless lines of deployed Gauntlet behind him. The Master stood on the walls. Edelred, betrayer of the house of Goodman and usurper of the house of Brenuin, watched him. It was the moment when he had to turn, and turn truly, for Hughan.

Quietly he turned to Wilhelm. "Mr Bellis."

"My lord?" Wilhelm was startled. Eamon realized it had probably been two whole hours since he had uttered a word to his standard bearer. Never had it been more important that he speak.

You will not speak, Eben's son. You will not turn from me. Your blood is mine.

Eamon shivered, shaking the voice from him. In the King's name he had come to Dunthruik; in the King's name he had served it, with his whole heart. He knew what he had to do.

He looked firmly, but kindly, to Wilhelm. "Give me the banner."

Wilhelm passed him the great, billowing banner. The trumpeters and Hands glanced at him with curiosity. Eamon fixed his armoured fist about his standard, felt its weight. Then he looked deep into Wilhelm's eyes.

"If you would follow me," he said quietly, "then follow."

Wilhelm gazed at him uncomprehendingly but Eamon did not say more.

Setting spurs to his steed, Eamon rode out before the lines. Eyes and faces turned to him. He watched them all, measured them all. Those gazes and his armour and tabard were like strong bonds upon him. But the courage of his heart was in him and neither voice nor gaze nor grief nor anger could keep him back from what he had come to do.

The banner was in his hand. He passed before the men in the lines, men from every part of the River Realm. Not all of them would hear him, for the lines were countless and immeasurable, and of those that heard him, not all would follow. He knew it well. But he would speak.

"Men of Dunthruik, hear me!" he cried. "This city is our home, these fields our patrimony, this River our lifeblood. They are written in my heart as deeply as they are in yours. For love of them we have given oaths and chosen to stand in war; for them we are prepared to sacrifice all that we are and all that we have."

The lines gazed back at him, hundreds upon hundreds of faces casqued in helms and bound in uniforms of red. It touched him to his very core, for he loved them, and he loved the walls and city before which they stood. The sight pierced him with joy and pride, with hope and fear, and with sorrows keener than any he had yet borne.

"Dunthruik," he called. "I have come this day ready to shed my blood and make the same sacrifice as every man of you. I have come to bring glory to my lord and hope to the city that I have always served and loved, with all my heart."

He paused. The Gauntlet looked to him. Eamon felt anew the Master's binding will. The unyielding strength of the grey eyes watched him from the city walls. They were eyes that held him with crushing, choking, hideous love; eyes that demanded his body, his blood, and his blade. Eamon looked up and met them.

To the dissolving glower of fire upon the city walls had he sworn himself; knowing it, the Master watched. In a moment of crystal courage, Eamon broke from the ashen eyes and fiery countenance that sought him. With the fullness of his heart, he turned.

"But you have been deceived, men of Dunthruik. Edelred, the man who sits enthroned, is not the rightful lord of Dunthruik. Its true Master is the King of the house of Brenuin."

A terrible silence assailed him. But he did not falter. There, before the gaze of the whole city, Eamon took Edelred's banner between his palms and inverted it, forcing down the eagle's wings so that they flapped limply against the sun-struck grass.

He tore his helmet from his head, letting his hair run free in the morning wind. Casting his helm upon the ground he looked up and met the staggered stares and mottled faces of the men before him.

"Dunthruik!" he cried. "I am a King's man! Follow him if you will!"

CHAPTER XVI

The plain was filled with the trappings and din of war: the clamour of marching men, the roar of beating drums and blast of strident trumpets, the thunder of distant cavalry, and, from every quarter, the baying of the men who drove on each sound.

Yet grim and stony silence dwelt before Dunthruik's gates, for there men of the city, and of the River Realm, beheld with awe the man who was Right Hand.

He could not know the tenor of those gazes, nor hope to judge between the awe, alarm, astonishment, and loathing which answered his words. He knew only that, as his words fell upon the city, the Lord of Dunthruik pierced him with a furious glare. He felt it upon him, just as he felt the wrathful tendrils of the Master's power snapping about his thoughts – but he would suffer neither.

The silence was suffocating. He alone dared to break it.

"The King is for you!" he cried. "If you would follow, follow!"

His words strove in the hanging air, seeking ears to hear them and hearts that would dare to answer.

Answer came.

"*Traitor!*"

"*Snake!*"

"*Wayfaring whore-son!*"

"*Debaucher!*"

"*Defiler!*"

"*Traitor!*"

For a moment, Eamon reeled. Dunthruik looked as though it would rend him to pieces given half a chance.

"*Kill him!*"

"*Gut him!*"

"*Death to the snake!*"

The Hands set arrows to their strings. The Gauntlet and militia alike turned their aim to him. Would they really break rank and mob him? It would spell disaster for the city's defence.

Someone else clearly thought the same. "Hold rank!" yelled a voice – was it Arlaith's? "*Hold!*"

The first arrow hissed past Sahu.

Eamon had no time to think. Seizing the reins, he wheeled Sahu about and clapped his spurs to the horse's flanks, urging it forward into a gallop.

"Traitor!" screeched a voice on his left.

Suddenly Heathlode was by him, his horse matching pace with Eamon's own. The Hand drew his sword. With a blood-curdling cry, both man and beast lurched towards him.

"Death to you, Goodman!"

Eamon drove his spurs harder against Sahu. He ducked down against the horse's neck as Heathlode's sword swung past him. The blade missed him by a hair.

A sudden clack rent the air behind him, followed by the gargling scream of a falling horse. He could not look back, but he knew that Heathlode's beast had been struck from behind – whether by city defenders or assailants, he did not know.

He realized that two others rode but a pace behind him; one was Wilhelm, the other Lonnam. Eamon could not tell their purpose. Fearing the worst, he pressed his horse even harder. He heard a cry of pain and guessed that an arrow must have struck one of the two. He did not dare to look back.

"*Hold!*"

The thud of the earth shuddered through Eamon's limbs and he urged Sahu to a neck-breaking gallop. Almost as soon as he reached the astonished lines of Dunthruik's militia, Sahu was past them, vaulting the fallen body of one of the militiamen as he went. Cries of "traitor" pursued Eamon like a furious wind across the plain. The voices of the Gauntlet were lost in the distance behind him.

In what felt both a heartbeat and a year, Eamon careered across the plain. There were more archers before him, but these were Easters and hobilars. He hoped they knew his mission and held their fire long enough for him to pass. His grip on the reins grew steadily more uncertain. Still he charged at the King's lines. He did not have time to think what would happen if he or his horse were shot down; all he could do was ride. He pressed his head down and grimaced against the fierce wind. There were standards ahead. One, blue, bore the sword and star.

With a cry, Eamon angled the reins and made for it. He clasped his knees firmly against the saddle and flanks of his horse as it sped on.

Suddenly he was past the lines. Groups of wayfarers gaped as he charged towards the blue banner.

"*The Right Hand!*"

Armed men rushed him. Panting and breathless, he hurled himself from his saddle. He was dimly aware of a voice commanding the wayfarers to let him pass, but he could not tell whose it was. As he stumbled down, the ground still seemed to thud in a gallop beneath him.

"Stand down!" the voice commanded again. "He is a King's man, and First Knight!"

The man who spoke rode a white horse and was dressed in blue. Tabard and shield bore the sword and star, as did the cloak that was clasped over his shining armour. On his head he wore a bronzed helmet, crested with a starry crown of silver, whose nosepiece was shaped like a sword. The pennant of a rearing unicorn flew by him.

Eamon strode unsteadily forwards. He knelt before the feet of the one who rode beneath the blue. Only then did he look up and find the King's face with his wind-burnt eyes.

"Sire," he breathed.

The heir to the house of Brenuin came down from his steed. With a smile, he raised Eamon to his feet.

"Welcome, First Knight!" he said, and Hughan embraced him.

The men about them gasped to see the King embrace the Right Hand, but the moment was short. Cries followed from behind. Eamon turned to see a group of wayfarers escorting the two riders who had followed him across the plain. The King's riders had deftly caught the followers' reins and tried to still the trembling horses.

Sense returned to him. With a cry, Eamon pressed forward. The wayfarers let him pass. Whether this was out of respect to him or to the King that went with him he did not know, and it did not matter to him. As he went forward his heart sank with grief.

The first rider was Lonnam. The Hand was slumped awkwardly over the neck of his horse. A long, red-feathered arrow pierced his thick cloak and his rigid hands were clasped unbreakably about his reins. The horse shifted nervously from foot to foot, resisting many attempts to calm it, for it knew the burden that it bore.

Lonnam was dead.

Eamon turned his eyes to the other rider: Wilhelm. The red-tabarded cadet was pale. As Eamon pressed forward he saw that the cadet had also been struck by a red-feathered arrow. The missile protruded from the young man's shoulder in an ugly fashion, and the cadet groaned with pain as he was brought down from his horse.

"I follow Lord Goodman," he managed as he came staggering down from the saddle. "I follow Lord Goodman!"

Eamon moved towards the young man's side but Hughan was already there. The King smiled kindly at the cadet.

"You followed him well," he said.

Eamon saw the young man's face grow wide with awe as he saw who spoke to him.

"Sire, is Lord Goodman safe?" Wilhelm asked at last. "I did not see him reach you –"

"I am safe," Eamon told him, reaching his side. "And so are you."

"Lord Goodman!" Wilhelm breathed, and smiled.

The King turned to some of the soldiers by him. "Take this cadet to the field hospital," he commanded.

Wilhelm looked anxious, but as he clambered to his feet, Eamon touched his arm in encouragement.

"All will be well, Mr Bellis," he said. "These men will take care of you."

Slowly, Wilhelm nodded. "Yes… my lord," he answered.

Eamon watched as the King's men led the cadet away. A moment later Lonnam's still form was brought down from his horse. Eamon watched the black-robed mass with a heavy heart. He knew it would not be the last death he would see that day. The reddened arrow protruding from deep in the dead man's flesh angered him.

"First Knight!"

Anastasius rode across to them. He wore a tabard and bore a shield, both of which carried the emblem of a green sun. A few other Easter lords followed him, each with their own colours.

"Welcome!" Ithel called.

"Thank you," Eamon answered.

Hughan's horse was brought, and Hughan rose to the saddle. Still breathless, Eamon did likewise.

Hughan looked to his allies. "The throned's cavalry forms up," he told them. "We must begin."

With nods, the Easter lords bowed and each rode off at once to take their posts at various points along the line. The sprawl of the throned's cavalry was before them. As he saw the horses, Eamon remembered the countless mornings that he had spent on Dunthruik's plain with Anderas, charging and galloping until it no longer frightened him.

"You rode well," Hughan told him.

Eamon let out a long breath. "Thank you."

Eamon looked at last to the King's men – there were hundreds upon hundreds of them. To the north, Easters and hobilars were ready to go against Dunthruik's horsemen. He reasoned that there would be many more dotted throughout the groves, shallow hills, and orchards where the throned's cavalry would ride. To the south, as far as the River, a long line of wayfarer infantry waited. At the centre of the line there was a great group of Easters. Easter and wayfarer were drawn up against the throned's infantry. The two lines stared grimly at each other across the plain while opposing bowmen fretted the other. Behind the wayfarer line, mounted knights formed up. Eamon realized that Hughan had kept his cavalry in reserve for now.

"This is real," Eamon whispered, scarcely believing his words. He had spent so long waiting for battle that, standing upon its edge, it seemed like a dream.

"Yes."

Eamon looked back to Hughan. For the first time he noticed that among the men who rode near the King, two dressed in dark blue went at either side of him. Bodyguards. It chilled him.

A trumpet call marred the air. Eamon looked up. He saw movement among the throned's cavalry in the northern lines. A great mass of mirrored sunlight blazoned the arms and armour of Rocell's knights as the first wave of banners began their advance towards the King's lines.

It was a spectacular sight. For a moment Eamon forgot everything else. The knights and hobilars engaged each other on the rolling terrain. The tall lances at front and rear fell. Eamon wondered what the knights would do when their steeds were cut from under them and the hobilars fell upon them with sword and dagger…

The throned's formation loosened. Eamon could not tell whether it was intended.

Not long later there was a second horn-call, this one much louder. The mounted Easters charged. The horse archers led, loosing arrows into the enemy and weakening his ranks. Eamon lost sight of all but the nearest part of the lines. Men and beasts clashed together.

He looked to the Gauntlet lines. They were perfectly, steadily formed. As Eamon gazed across the mass of red, he felt cold.

None had followed him.

Tears stung. He tried to brush them away, but his gauntlets impeded him. He became horribly aware of the armour he wore and the one who had bestowed it on him.

"Eamon?"

The King held Eamon gently in his gaze.

"Did none follow me?" Eamon asked. After all that he had done, and endured, it seemed the cruellest blow that could have been lain against him. What of Anderas, what of the East? What of the men who had always sung his praises in the city for the good that he had done? Did they not see? Had they not heard? How could they not now understand?

"First Knight," Hughan told him quietly, "what you did was dangerous enough – and you had a horse and a position at the front of the lines. How many of them could have followed you in what you did, even were it the nearest desire to their heart?"

Eamon looked back to the red lines. He knew that the city's quarter units were in the reserve lines by the city walls, just as he knew that those lines had been littered with Hands. Shocked and shaken by the words of their Right Hand, how many would have dared the wrath of the throned's dark and powerful servants?

"None," he answered.

In the silence that followed, Eamon imagined the officers and captains, the Hands – and Arlaith overall – prowling the Gauntlet lines with threat and fear and words to stand contrary to his own, bolstering morale, and quelling any streaks of rebellion in the men. How often did a Right Hand proclaim allegiance to the King? It must have been a terrifying thing to witness.

But had they seen him for what he was? Or had their heads and hearts been filled with the cries of "traitor" that had followed him?

"Courage, First Knight. They have seen the way prepared by you, and it lies open to them also." Hughan reached across and touched his arm. "Do not let it trouble you; the day is long, and you will yet see who followed you in their heart when you rode to me. Until that time," he added gently, "I need you to be with me here, in every part."

Eamon drew a shuddering breath. "I am here, sire."

To the north, the knights and Easters both pulled back. Eamon gave Hughan a worried look.

"What is happening?" he asked, wishing for not the first time that he had understood something about cavalry tactics.

"Another wave of banners comes," Hughan answered. Eamon followed his gesture back to the lines and saw that a second wave of Dunthruik's knights, no less impressive than the first, rode across to engage the King's men and bolster the struggling first wave. It seemed strange to Eamon that so much should be happening in the north, and yet the lines of Gauntlet and King's men before him should hold still in the warm morning light.

He saw Hughan, who had, like him, been watching the clash of the northern lines, nod. He seemed satisfied with what he saw and looked to Eamon once more.

"Ride with me, First Knight."

Though he felt oddly weighted in his armour, Eamon took a firm hold of his reins and followed the King as he turned to move down to the infantry lines in the south. The lines reached all the way to a sharp bend in the River, and Eamon remembered Waite's assertion that it would be a difficult place to stand. The banners all along the line shivered in the wind, mirrors of the blue River and the sun-struck sky.

As they went down the lines the wayfarers began to cheer. Voices joined together and men raised arms and tongues as the King passed by.

"*The King! Brenuin for the River Realm! The King!*"

The cries were joyful and spontaneously taken up by the whole line; Hughan accepted them with a gracious smile as he rode, and Eamon felt how every man – even the Easters in the central part of the line – loved and respected the King. It amazed him.

It was as they came near to the southern end of the line that Eamon heard another cry mixed in with the voices of the King's men:

"*Goodman for the King! The First Knight for the King!*"

Astounded, Eamon turned. As he searched the calling faces for those who called his name he suddenly saw one that he recognized. Amazed and delighted, he dismounted at once and went across to him.

"Goodman for the King!" the voices cheered. As Eamon approached they whooped and applauded. He knew their faces, though they knew his the better.

He reached the line and stood before it in wonder. Mr Grennil, and a score of the evacuees from the East Quarter, stood a little way back in the line.

Eamon laughed. He rushed forward and embraced Mr Grennil.

"I thought you were dead!" he cried. The line cheered to see his joy. "I thought you were all dead!"

"And we feared for you," Grennil replied with a smile. "Goodman for the King!"

"*Goodman for the King!*"

"The East for the King!" he answered. The men cheered him, delighted, and Eamon felt tears of joy on his face. The King smiled at him, and he wondered how he could ever have believed that the wayfarers had killed the men who even now stood before him.

"First Knight!" called another voice.

Feltumadas, resplendent in helm and armour, rode towards them. His banner stood not far from there, at the centre of the infantry line.

"Lord Feltumadas," Eamon greeted, trying to wipe the tears from his face. His armour was not conducive to the task.

The Easter lord smiled at him. "I had not the time to greet you before," he said, "though I had time aplenty to admire your spectacular folly. The Star tells me that you never considered yourself a rider?" he added politely.

"Never," Eamon agreed. "Nor am I yet, I fear."

"Then what a ride you made, no-rider!" Feltumadas answered. "They will tell tales of that before your days are done, and long thereafter."

"May we live to hear them," Hughan laughed.

Feltumadas watched Eamon for a moment, then turned to Hughan. "May I counsel your First Knight, Star of Brenuin?"

"As you would counsel me," Hughan replied.

"Battle will soon be joined. While men standing and cheering will recognize Lord Goodman as your First Knight, once they are striking at their enemies, a moment's error will put red on his tabard which he did not intend."

Eamon glanced down suddenly at his breastplate's ruddy and sable covering, and knew at once that Feltumadas was right. He could not stand in the King's lines wearing these colours.

Flexing his armoured fingers, he set his hands to the hem of his tabard and put his strength against it. After a moment a tear appeared, but the material was strong.

Feltumadas watched Eamon's efforts for a moment before turning to Hughan. "May I lend you my blade, Star?" he asked with a grin.

"Thank you, Lord Feltumadas," Hughan replied.

Feltumadas swiftly swapped his mace from his right hand to his left, and then drew his blade. It was much shorter than the swords used by the Easter cavalry or Eamon's own long infantry sword. Feltumadas handed it to the King with a graceful gesture.

Hughan deftly dismounted and came to Eamon's side. He set blade edge to the tear. With a bold stroke he drew the blade up through the tabard, shearing it in two. Though it weighed but little, a great weight lifted from Eamon as the tabard came away in Hughan's hands, no more than a ream of cloth.

Eamon laughed as he shed the black and red. The men watching him cheered riotously to see the First Knight liberated from his colours.

Hughan handed the blade back to Feltumadas, then he and Eamon both remounted. Leaving Feltumadas at its centre, Hughan and Eamon proceeded futher, inspecting the line. Everywhere they rode they were met with a continual roar of cheers, and of arms clashed joyously against shields.

"All these men serve you," Eamon breathed. He could only gape at their numbers.

"And they honour you; they know what you have done." And as Eamon surveyed the lines, they called:

"The Sword and Star! The First Knight and the King!"

They rode down the line and back. The Gauntlet waited across the plain. He wondered if they were anxious seeing the wayfarers lauding their King and their First Knight, the man whom Dunthruik had dubbed Right Hand. As they rode, the cavalry battle sounded to the north. Eamon looked towards it. He discerned many scores of fallen horses and men, but he could not tell what happened.

A trumpet blast sounded across the plain, followed by drums. Eamon glanced sharply back towards the city. The great ranks of Gauntlet drawn up against the King's men began to move.

"Sire," Eamon said, pointing.

"I see them."

The strike of the drums pounded into Eamon's chest. It pulsed with the beat and readiness of battle. He flexed his hands. Soon he would be called upon to wield his sword. As the drums came on, he heard the call with them that chilled him:

"*His glory!*"

They returned to the centre of the line where Feltumadas kept sunny watch over the advancing Gauntlet. The Easter looked at Hughan.

"You should withdraw to the rear ranks, Star," he said, "and your First Knight also."

"The rear?" Eamon repeated, heart sinking.

Feltumadas smiled at him. "You are eager to strike?"

"Would not you be?"

Feltumadas looked back at the oncoming crimson lines. "Yes."

Hughan reached across and touched Eamon's shoulder. "You will have your chance, First Knight."

"But at the moment the Star is more concerned with both your hides," Feltumadas added. "Think, First Knight, how many men dream of felling the man beside you!"

Eamon glanced at Hughan. "Many," he replied sombrely. He had heard many dreaming of it, or swearing that they would do it.

"Given your deed of this morning, I imagine that there are now as many who would happily garrotte *you*," Feltumadas told

341

him lightly. "Perhaps they are as many as those who rejoice to see you here."

The drums grew louder. Dunthruik's militia crossbowmen withdrew and grouped into the advancing Gauntlet line. The Easter bows directed a last volley at the red line. Very few men were struck and fewer injured, for the Gauntlet were well armoured. After the volley, the Easter bowmen also withdrew swiftly to their waiting line.

It was then that Hughan went before his men, his helm aflame with silver.

"You are the honour and glory of my house!" he called. "You are the pride and joy of my heart! You have ridden with me through fire and storm, through bog and fen, over mountain and River, and I have been amazed by your courage."

Eamon gazed at Hughan, for the King's words stirred something in him that was wide and deep.

"You are more than flesh and blood, than iron and steel; you are King's men. And whether we have victory or defeat I will count myself rich to have fought this day with you."

"*The King!*" the line roared.

As the shouts continued, Hughan returned to Eamon's side. "Come, First Knight."

Eamon followed the King and his aides; the line parted before them and closed behind them. As they went, Eamon fully appreciated the depth of the wayfarer line and the countless men who formed it. He could not guess at their number but he knew that each man he passed was a man prepared to give his life for the King. As they went back through the lines, the King's cavalry reserve drew up further back along the plain, and battle sounded in the north; for a moment it chilled Eamon's blood.

Then the drums came. Quiet they had been, and distant, like the beat of a man's heart when he worked at his daily business. But now the sound increased and the line advanced. The drum beat grew and grew and the Gauntlet called out their Master's glory, raising bill, axe, and sword with each cry. They were a fearsome gash of red across the plain, the city's blood marching for vengeance – against the King that had besieged them, the Right Hand who had betrayed them, and for the glory of the Master that they served.

The beat of the drum came on.

Strange quiet fell over the wayfarers. Eamon could taste and smell the tension of arms and spirits preparing for battle. His heart beat to the pace of the drum. As the Gauntlet lines came on, he felt a sting of flame in his palm.

Was he not sworn as they were? And as they called again on the Master's glory, their words bubbled up to his lips: *His glory…*

He pressed one gauntleted hand over another, rubbing at the unseen mark that burned him. He was not of their number, and yet the drum beat penetrated him, calling him to undo his foolishness and return to the men he loved and the fire he served.

"Eamon."

Eamon saw that Hughan watched him. Embarrassed, he let go of his hand.

"If you would rather withdraw," Hughan began, "you may do so."

Eamon swallowed hard. "My place is here."

The second Gauntlet line halted a few hundred yards away; the first was pressed on. Movement at the north end of the lines attracted Eamon's attention – some of Hughan's hobilars struck out at the Gauntlet from a grove. At once a group of the throned's men countered the harassment, disrupting the uniformity of their careful lines and forcing the hobilars to drop back. The Gauntlet advanced again, the beat of the drums driving them steadily on. Feltumadas – who rode a little way back from the front of the wayfarer line – gave a signal, and suddenly the thudding drums were matched by a blast of trumpets that stopped Eamon's heart with its intensity.

Moments later the air was rent with a great clack as more than a thousand wayfarer bows loosed a storm of arrows at the red line. The Gauntlet marched on, urged by drum and officer. Some of the men went down in the hail of arrows. The Dunthruik militia answered the volley with one of their own, but barely had they begun when a second, third, and fourth flurry of wayfarer arrows filled the air, a merciless rain that beat down on the line. A standard in the sea of red dropped and disappeared in the surge before it re-emerged, like the head of an ocean beast over the crimson waves, swelling with the tide and moving in the hands of its new bearer.

Still the Gauntlet came on.

Feltumadas gave commands that were echoed by horn calls all along the line. The front ranks lowered their spears. The ranks behind them angled their crop of steel against the blue sky to ward against any stray missiles launched by the enemy. Then the trumpets blared again. Like a river, the wayfarer line washed forward to meet the red sea. It was a swift and an unerring advance, the sound of the drums lost beneath the sound of marching. Feltumadas, now on foot but marked by his great orange standard, went with them, keeping the pace and formation of the advance. A final crossbow volley was launched by the Easters to devastating effect on the Gauntlet lines: swathes of men fell.

The advance of the two lines towards each other was a gracefully executed death-dance. The tension and anticipation of their meeting grew in Eamon's breast as the allied lines went down the slope to their enemy. He felt the long, slow agony of time as the two forces went on towards each other, drum and trumpet, bill and axe, crown and star.

And suddenly the lines met.

The clash was deafening as axes and swords, bills and shields engaged upon Dunthruik's plain. The lines rammed together and then moulded one against the other as smoothly as the meeting of plane and lathe.

Once the two infantries met, Eamon could not discern one side from the other. He raised himself up in his saddle and peered forward, but he could make nothing from the chaos of the front ranks. Orange, green, and blue drove forward. The cries of men sounded as they took their oaths in their hands and proved their fealty with their blood.

Eamon was not sure how long the initial attack lasted. After a time, wounded men appeared behind the ranks, pushing or crawling their way from the mêlée, marred with blood and broken flesh, red on blue. The wounded gathered together and helped each other to stagger back to the field hospital far behind the lines.

The King's ranks seemed to lose ground to the south. Feltumadas pushed through the press, his mace reddened, calling those men around him on to courage for the King. Eamon's blood pulsed at the thought, demanding that he join the fight.

A great cry sounded to the south. The line shuddered before a violent drive from the Gauntlet. The line of King's men gave back before it and vomited out wounded men. Eamon saw at once that if the line gave back too far, then the Gauntlet would take the River bend and be able to take the wayfarers' flank. It would be disastrous.

"Sire, the south –" Eamon began but stopped; drums again. The reserves behind the main Gauntlet lines marched fiercely towards the weakened southern flank of wayfarers.

Eamon looked to Hughan. The King had also seen the danger.

"I must command the cavalry." Hughan matched Eamon's grey look. "First Knight," he said, "I have need of your sword."

"You have always had it," Eamon answered.

"Take the south flank. It must hold until I can send the cavalry to it."

"It will hold," Eamon answered grimly. He would hold it single-handedly if he had to.

"Go!" Hughan commanded. He and his horse and aides turned and wheeled across the plain towards the cavalry.

The Gauntlet reserves marched on the wilting wayfarer flank. The men there cried out, as if sensing their danger.

Eamon drew his reins tightly into his hand. Scores of men followed him. Calling quick words of encouragement to them and to his steed, he clicked his spurs and rode down towards the River – a shining sea of fighting men, of shattered helms and swords, and screams of the dying.

He swiftly reached the ailing part of the line, which shuddered back beneath another blow. Eamon saw the standard of a wayfarer general back the way he had come. It pushed into the thick of the ranks. The Gauntlet reserve advanced. Eamon did not have much time.

Hurriedly he threw himself down from his saddle. He drew the reins forward over his horse's head as his feet touched the ground. Gripping the reins, he drew his sword then pulled off belt and scabbard to avoid tripping over them in the fight. His blood beat thick and fast in his veins. He was an infantryman by training. He would fight as he knew best.

He tied belt and scabbard to his saddle and then looked to the lines.

Eamon could see little of the wayfarers' front lines, but he could feel fear about him everywhere. If the line failed, they would be slaughtered by the searing red. A turned southern flank could mean defeat for the King.

Cries sounded all around him. The smell of sweat and blood beneath the May sun overpowered his sense. Sword in hand, Eamon pushed forward.

Support it if you wish, son of Eben; it will not hold.

As he and his men pressed forward, Eamon found wounded men and fallen helms beneath his feet. He looked at the wearied, frightened men about him, heard the drums of the reserve marching grimly towards them. A terrible quiet fell as both Gauntlet and wayfarers anticipated the coming blow.

Eamon raised his head and his voice.

"Hear me!" he cried. "You are more than flesh and blood! You are more than body and blade! Fear no arrow, fear no flame, fear neither terror, nor oath, nor bond, nor strike against you, for you are King's men."

His voice seemed louder than he expected. Indeed, even the din of battle did not seem to drown it out. All around him the wayfarers heard, and their grips on their weapons grew firmer. New hope birthed in their eyes as they looked to him.

"Courage, men of the King: stand!" he cried, and raised his sword high.

"The King!" The whole line took up the call so loudly that it drowned the drums. For a moment the Gauntlet line seemed to falter. "*The King!*"

Eamon turned towards the flank of the wayfarer line and pushed forward. The cry of the King's name followed him. As he reached the forward ranks, the Gauntlet reserve reached them. The first strike ran through the whole line, pressing men and blades together.

"Stand!" Eamon yelled. "Stand, King's men!"

He felt the pressure all around him as the line tried to hold. The noise of battle was deafening, the clash a terrible and continuous roaring groan.

There was another stomach-churning jolt; the whole line moved back. Eamon turned in horror to his left in time to hear the cry as the southern-most part of the line buckled. A stream of red broke through. A huge, solid, indefatigable mass of Gauntlet blades rose and fell in their bloody work. Blood and bodies were crushed into the sodden earth.

He yelled again for the King's men to stand. He charged the charging red. Men gathered round him. They called at the top of their lungs and raced forward with him. The weight of armour and blade seemed but nothing to him as he went on, feeling the full flow of blood in his hands and the King's name over him.

Before him was the Gauntlet, the red dotted with black, Hands in their midst. One of them raised a bow and moments later an arrow spun through the air. The man beside Eamon went down in a froth of blood.

As the Hand nocked another arrow, the King's men came against the reserve. Several standards swung over the heads of the charging Gauntlet, one belonging to General Waite. Eamon's heart ached as he saw the other, for it belonged to the West Quarter. The South Quarter came behind it.

Driving down his hurt, he drew breath once more. "King's men, to me!" he cried.

The lines collided. Eamon's sword turned crimson in the morning sun. His hands plied a bloody trade on the field before Dunthruik. He did not know how many Gauntlet he struck down before he realized what he did; having realized, he could not stop. Swinging his blade round he struck down another opponent and trampled forward over the fallen body.

Wayfarers were all about him. They assembled themselves into a new line. Eamon knew it was not enough: they would not hold. Scattered and isolated clumps of men drew together into circles to make their last stands. Behind every Gauntlet man they killed, ten more stood. The bold blue line staggered back under the press. The desperation of that knowledge drove Eamon forward with grim and vicious prowess.

"Stand, King's men!"

He heard more cries to his right. Risking an upward glance, Eamon saw the wayfarer general press south, calling on the men to hold. Looking to the men around him, Eamon saw the ragged line they formed. By falling back a little they could bolster the general and perhaps hold the line.

"King's men, to me!" he called. Those men still standing came to his side. They drove together towards the general, fending off the blood-charged Gauntlet who came at them.

It was as they reached the general's standard that Eamon heard a roar. He looked up to see the standard go down beneath a choking wave of red. His heart caved as the Gauntlet fell upon Hughan's general. Through the shuddering mass of the line Eamon saw men gutted and stabbed.

A Gauntlet ensign came for him with a howl. Enraged, Eamon turned the blade away and quickly downed the man.

"Stand, King's men!" he yelled. But beneath the screams of the Gauntlet and the rolling drums, the broken wayfarer line could not hear him. He drove away another attack. His sword was heavy in his hand as he gave back another pace before the onslaught.

"King's men!" he cried, his voice breaking.

Where were the cavalry? Where was Hughan?

There was a shriek by his ear; the man beside him went down. As Eamon turned back to meet his next foe he knew that he turned too late: the soldier lunged at him with a bill. Eamon dodged the first strike, but he could not avoid the second as the bill-butt swung back at him.

It struck his head. The blow sent him reeling round in agony; blood leapt from his lips. He sank to his knees, scarcely aware of a man stepping up to defend him. His head throbbed. His sight spun. Through the awful pain, he heard horns. The sound cracked through his skull like the blow he had received. As he struggled to keep his eyes open, he thought he saw the King's standard coming across the field at the head of the thundering cavalry. The whole earth shook beneath him.

CHAPTER XVII

Eamon awoke to find himself in a different plain, the sky above him darkened and traces of mist in the blood-soaked air.

There were men about him, dressed in clothes of red and blue, but they were not the uniforms familiar to him. They moved around him and through him, bearing arms and shields that he did not know, though he knew their devices – sword, star, and eagle. In the grisly distance a watchtower looked over a stream that ran red into a field strewn with corpses.

A man rode across the murky field. He was robed in blue, and his armour shone brightly in the dim light. His sword was high in his hand. Words that Eamon could not hear were on his lips. A trumpet called men on to war.

As the rider reached the stream, Eamon saw men in the darkness there. One knelt in hiding among the fallen, dressed in blue. The one in blue arose, sword in hand, towards the rider. He gave a cry and a killing blow to the steed. Behind him was a man with flaming red hair.

In striking bound...

Suddenly Eamon's eyes were his own again. He was on his feet with his sword in hand. A gap opened in the ranks before him, a tunnel that led to a blue-marked rider on a star-white horse. Eamon knew that his steps took him towards that rider to work again the treachery of his line.

What treachery? This was ever my plan for you, Eben's son, and you accepted it when you first knelt to me.

There was fire in his hands and at his brow. The King was before him, all his effort turned towards staging the cavalry against the oncoming Gauntlet.

Eamon had a clear run, a perfect strike. He would be unseen, unnoticed, until the Serpent's heir was a crumpled, gutted mass on the ground. Certainly he could never escape the cavalry, but what of that? The voice told him that their revenge on him would be swift, and he would die vested in the Master's glory…

Entranced, Eamon's feet went steadily towards the King. His hands were ready to strike. His head and eyes and blood all burned – his line would be redeemed and ended at one blow. The poetry of it was pleasing.

The King was before him, his blue gaze turned away as he gave commands. He would never know who had struck him…

Strike! Strike now, Son of Eben!

With agonizing effort, Eamon hefted the blade in his hands and turned to face the oncoming Gauntlet. He would heed this voice no more. It was as he stood and felt the thunderous tread of the crying cavalry all around him that he found his own voice lifted in a singing cry against the Lord of Dunthruik:

"*My true vow calls again to me, and in his service I am free!*"

The King's cavalry charged against the Gauntlet line. They smashed into it, tore holes through it. The sound and sight and smell of the charging horsemen was terrifying from the ground but Eamon followed it. Suddenly there were Gauntlet men around him. They screamed at him with the fierceness and anger of the Master whom Eamon had defied.

"I am a King's man!" he cried. He struck them. "A King's man till I die! The First Knight for the King!" The Gauntlet fell back before him and the King's horse in fear.

The cavalry rushed past him. One of Hughan's guards was struck by a bolt and went down to the thick earth. His horse struggled under the fall of its rider. The Gauntlet swarmed about them. As Eamon fought, the King's cavalry pressed hard at the enemy line and broke through with a triumphant cry. Hughan rode with them and was lost from Eamon's sight.

As the cavalry rode forward behind the Star of Brenuin, the Gauntlet's spirit cracked. The reserve line fell back.

Eamon fell still, his sword ruddy in his hands. For a moment there were no enemies by him, merely fallen and dying men. He stared at his hands – hands that, but for grace, had nearly killed the King. His limbs shook with terror and exhaustion.

The noise of falling hooves sounded behind him. Eamon turned to see Sahu galloping to him. The beast was running, unhurt and riderless, in the wake of the moving cavalry. With a cry of joy, Eamon received his black steed as it came to him, unlooked for, from across the field.

He took a spear from a fallen knight and climbed into his saddle. "Go!" he called, and he urged Sahu on in the wake of the King.

The movement of his horse beneath him was sure and steady as he rode on into the breaking lines. The standards of the Gauntlet, and of the Four Quarters, fell back before the King's cavalry and disappeared beneath the charge of the knights. The Guantlet streamed back to the city gates. Hands rode among the Gauntlet, trying to rally them against the wayfarers, but the line was broken. The south flank was lost to them.

As he rode, Eamon passed a bleeding man. The wayfarer was badly injured, but he bore a standard as a crutch as he quitted the shattered field. A crippling shudder ran down Eamon's spine – the standard was Waite's.

Eamon turned from it and looked instead to the cavalry. They went north along the line, the King's banner flapping above them. It lifted his spirits and he spurred on.

Straggling Gauntlet came at him as he made to join the cavalry but he struck them down. Sahu whinnied and then broke into a gallop. As he neared the King's horses, a red banner in the churning rage of the retreating Gauntlet caught Eamon's eye. The banner bore four golden lions. Eamon recognized it, just as he recognized the man who held it.

It was the banner of Edesfield, and the man who carried it was Captain Belaal.

All at once Eamon felt a flurry of rage. The captain incited the shredded remains of Edesfield's men against the King:

"On, you bastards!" Belaal yelled. "On, and reap the Master's glory!"

The captain's eyes fell on Eamon, and his face became a picture of hot-blooded wrath.

"Goodman!" he shrieked. Eamon turned to him. The captain surged forward, obstructed by neither corpse nor injured man as he plunged headlong towards the First Knight.

"You vile, whore-son bastard!" he screamed. "Turn-coated, thieving, perfidious, bloody traitor!" Vested with his rage, he dropped the banner and hurled himself at Eamon, screaming: "Death! Death in darkness to you and your heirs, on their own blood! *Traitor!*"

Of the charge of traitor Eamon was barely aware; his anger had been stirred long before then. With an awful cry, he raised his spear and charged the screeching captain. Eamon drove his horse forward into a gallop. The power of the horse's strong flanks filled his limbs and arm. Undaunted, Belaal came on, screaming. He drew up his blade.

He never landed the blow. As Belaal prepared to strike, Eamon thrust at the man's face where the helmet lay open. The spear's tip plunged into the howling mouth with the full force of knight and horse behind it. Eamon lost the spear as it lodged into the man's throat in a wash of gore and curses, cracking bone and striking helm.

It was a moment before he realized what he had done. Shaking, he drew his horse to a stop then wheeled about.

He turned and came back at once to the captain and his fallen standard.

Most of the Gauntlet nearby had fled, but five or six men remained. The last men from the Edesfield division stood, astounded, by their dead captain, their faces pale and witless. Eamon thought that he recognized one of them: the man had been a cadet when he had left the town but now bore the rank of lieutenant. There were wayfarers all around them but this man held out his arms.

"Grant me the lives of my men!" he cried, turning his bloody sword in his hands so that the hilt was towards his enemy. He took the town's standard in his other hand and sought Eamon's face. "I surrender Edesfield and my sword!" The men for whom he spoke stood terrified behind him. At the lieutenant's gesture, they cast their blades and axes to the ground. "Grant us our lives!"

Eamon approached the terrified, blood-stained man. He remembered – how he remembered! – the day when he had offered his sword to Giles…

He met the lieutenant's fearful gaze. "They are granted," Eamon answered, taking the sword from him, "and I accept your surrender."

The man stared at him speechlessly. Then he drew himself up. "Who takes Edesfield's surrender?" the lieutenant stammered.

There, on the field of battle surrounded by corpses, Eamon forced a smile. "One who knows it, and loves it well. My name is Eamon Goodman, and I am First Knight to the King."

"Goodman," the lieutenant whispered. Recognition hit the man's face with a blow keener than that of any blade. Then the man turned the standard in his hands and held it out. "We surrender to you, First Knight, and hope for your King's mercy."

The lieutenant laid the banner in his hands; it was heavy and blood-smeared. Eamon took it. Tears filled his eyes, and joy shook his heart. In Edesfield had Ede been betrayed; in Edesfield had he and Hughan found refuge for a time. Now the town's standard – and its Gauntlet – had been won back to the King.

"You shall have the King's mercy," he said.

Eamon discharged the men into the care of some of the wayfarers and looked again to the standard he had won. It moved steadily in the wind before him. The juddering spear in Belaal's open jaw had fallen still, though blood still issued from it.

Eamon turned away. The King and his cavalry were ahead, as were the Easter standards. They pursued the retreating Gauntlet.

He tapped his horse's flanks and went after the King, the banner an odd weight in his hand. Hughan looked up as he approached; the King bore a reddened spear. That image struck deep.

"First Knight," Hughan greeted. His remaining guard was with him, though the rest of the cavalry had run far ahead in their pursuit. Groups of Gauntlet persisted across the field, but many more, including mounted Hands, fled west towards the sea. There were signs of battle by the River, and Eamon wondered whether any men had fallen or drowned there. Given the terrain, he found it more than likely. He realized how perilously – and skilfully – Hughan had committed his cavalry. He could not see what had become of the hobilars and Easters to the north, but he saw that the Blind Gate closed as arrows rained down from the walls. Any man who had not withdrawn to the city would be pursued and killed, or forced to surrender.

As he looked up at the great gate, Eamon could not help but imagine the abject fear and terror that those inside – especially the thresholders, boys and men too young or too old to be grouped into Dunthruik's militia – would feel. His thoughts passed for a moment to his servants, to the theatre, to the East Quarter. Would they be safe?

He became aware again of the standard in his hand. He turned to the King.

"Though Edesfield is already yours, this I bring you," he said, holding the banner out across to the King. His voice trembled as he spoke.

Hughan accepted what he offered, his heart no less moved than Eamon's by what he held.

"Of all the banners on the field today," Hughan told him, "this was yours to take."

Eamon felt pain at the back of his head. His eyes drifted to Hughan's own standard. He shuddered.

"Hughan," he began, turning to search the King's eyes. "When you came with the cavalry, I…"

Hughan met his gaze. "You were singing," he said quietly.

Eamon stared at him. In the whole press of the battle, how had the King heard him singing? "Hughan, I saw… I nearly…" he tried again.

"But you didn't," Hughan answered, and a tired smile passed over his face. "Eamon; you turned, and *you didn't.*"

"Nor will I ever," Eamon told him.

"I know."

They watched each other for a long moment on the plain, then Hughan passed Edesfield's banner to an aide. As he did, a familiar face approached.

"I see that you live yet, Star!" Feltumadas called as he arrived. The Easter lord's tabard was marred and torn, but a grim smile was on his face.

"Yes, I live," Hughan replied. "This surprises you?"

"No," Feltumadas answered, "merely feeds the rumour that you are not destined for death on a field of battle. But then, Dunthruik's troops seemed to lack a certain amount of enthusiasm for their work." He turned to Eamon with a smile. "And you, First Knight? You live still?"

"Just about," Eamon told him.

"Perhaps you will learn not to discard your helm so readily in future!"

Eamon's hand went to his head in embarrassment, but he swiftly withdrew it from the nasty lump forming there. "Perhaps," he answered. It was then that he also tasted the blood on his lips. He counted himself lucky that he had not bitten his tongue in half when he had been struck.

"The Gauntlet and Hands have retreated. Some may surrender," Hughan said. "The cavalry are routing out the stragglers. I want to reform the lines and prepare to assault the gates."

Eamon glanced over Hughan's shoulder at the great mass of the Blind Gate. How did the King mean to do that?

"The men are exhausted," he breathed.

"If we do not move on the city, we will lose the advantage that the enemy is also exhausted," Feltumadas replied. Eamon realized that that was not all they might lose: delay would give the city time to fortify itself, to rebuild its morale and courage. And, whatever else happened, the throned was still within the city's heart and Edelred still held the Nightholt.

Feltumadas looked back to Hughan and gestured excitedly to the Blind Gate. "We will take the gates, Star, and you shall enter in triumph!"

"We will take the gate," Hughan answered quietly, "but I will not go that way."

Feltumadas looked stunned.

"You will not go through the gate?" he asked, then laughed. "It is your right – one taken from you when the usurper did so in your ancestor's place!"

"I will not go through the Blind Gate," Hughan replied. "Not this day. Victory this day will not be determined by the load of this field, nor by our banners flying in the city streets."

Eamon shivered as the King's words passed over him, for he understood. He looked across at the city, to the dim mass within its walls that he knew to be the palace.

The throned; the Lord of Dunthruik; Edelred. There could be no peace, no victory, until Hughan had met him and done… what?

He realized that he did not know and looked back at Hughan with renewed awe. The King still held Feltumadas's gaze. At last, the Easter lord nodded.

"Very well, Star, delay your entry if you wish," he said.

"Bring the ram to the Blind Gate," Hughan commanded. "We will take it first, then the ram will go to the South with myself, the southern wayfarer infantry, and the knights. The First Knight will go to the North with the hobilars and Easter cavalry." Eamon looked up in a daze. "We will attempt our own entries, but once you breach the Blind Gate, send men north and south. We will make use of the tunnels by the South Gate."

"Even so, I shall grant you admittance, Star," Feltumadas smiled.

"We will meet at the Four Quarters," Hughan continued. "From there we will press on into the West." Eamon glimpsed a vision of the Four Quarters running with blood and choked back sudden, terrible grief.

How could the city bear it?

The King drew a deep breath. "Draw up the lines, Lord Feltumadas."

Those men who had survived the first part of the battle regrouped. As he watched the men reform, Eamon glanced up at the sky; it was nearly midday. He felt as though he had spent a whole lifetime out on the field, but it had only been a few hours.

"How are you faring?" Hughan asked him. Eamon realized that in gazing up at the sun the King had a fine view of the swelling beneath his sweaty, matted hair. He drove his hair out of his face.

"I have been better," he answered truthfully, "but I have been worse."

Hughan laughed kindly.

Feltumadas returned to them. "The lines will be drawn as soon as we are able," he told them. "I have sent word for the ram to be brought across the River."

"Thank you," Hughan nodded to him.

Feltumadas inclined his head and rode away.

It took some time for the ram to be brought from across the River; men and oxen drew the huge engine. These were led on by drummers and accompanied by a hundred archers as the ram went up to the gate. Eamon could only watch it as it came, marvelling at its size and construction. He had never seen anything like it and expected that Dunthruik's defenders would be as astounded by it as he was. More so: it would threaten their gates and their lives.

He watched as, group by group, Gauntlet and knights who had surrendered outside the city walls were marched back to the far side of Hughan's lines, the wounded to the field hospital and the others to detention areas. Eamon scanned the files of passing men for faces familiar to him, and though he saw some – mostly ensigns from the North and East – in his heart he knew that he could not hope to know what had become of those he loved the most until the day was done. Still, he saw also that the number of prisoners or surrendering men taken from the field was not small – in fact, great swathes of the Gauntlet had surrendered – and although the injuries borne by some of them were severe and not all of them would live, the sight heartened him.

But when he turned his eyes again towards the city, he saw that the plain before Dunthruik was showered with the dead. He did not doubt that men whom he knew lay among them. As the Easters' ram worked its slow way across the field towards the Blind Gate, carrion birds gathered.

The King's men brought new arrows from the camp and scoured the field for any that they might reuse in their bows. As Eamon watched those who searched among the wreck of the field, he shuddered at the number of men who lay beneath the full heat of the May sun. He felt spent, and sweltered in his armour; he wished nothing more than for the day to be done and to return to his quarters to have the stuff taken off him.

His quarters: the thought brought him up short. He had no quarters now.

He rode to distract himself while he waited. Every now and then thresholders on the city walls let loose a volley of arrows at the King's men as they moved their battering ram, but the wayfarer lines were too far back from the wall to be in any real danger. One of the Easters at the ram whistled softly to himself as he worked.

All the same, a terrible anticipation hovered over the field.

As he rode over the stricken plain, avoiding much of its debris, Eamon's attention was caught by a glint of metal nestled in a tiny ditch. Riding closer he recognized it and smiled: his helmet. He dismounted to reclaim it, marvelling that, despite the number of men who must have passed over it, it was for the most part intact; only the strap was broken. He laughed quietly as he picked it up, brushing dirt from it and untangling the feathers from the twisted cord. He wished the same could be said for his head as for his helm.

He set the helmet back on his head and felt a sharp stab of pain in his left arm. Unable to press it he tried flexing his fingers to ease it, but to no avail. The marks of Cathair's hound were still on him and he wondered how many other marks he would bear by the end of the day. He had been fortunate – perhaps more fortunate than he deserved – that morning, and fighting through the streets of Dunthruik to the West Quarter and the palace would be harder and more perilous than battle upon the field. His throat went dry at the thought of it.

As he flexed his fingers, a man laughed behind him.

"Is that something they teach you to do when they make you Right Hand?" a voice asked.

"I can't tell you," Eamon answered, turning to the voice with a smile.

Before him stood Giles. The burly man was battle-worn but seemed curiously uninjured. His sword was sheathed at his side.

"Where did you learn to ride like that?" the man asked.

Eamon gestured across the plain at the groves that led to Ravensill. "About there," he answered.

Anderas. It was Anderas who had taught him to ride fearlessly across Dunthruik's plains, and where was he now? He could only hope that the captain, and the vast majority of the East Quarter, were alive and in a place of safety.

"The King sent me," Giles added. "He says they're about to begin the assault."

Eamon nodded and tried to daub sweat from his brow. It was no more than an hour after midday. They would begin what would be the most difficult part of the battle in the hottest and most wretched part of the day.

"I'm ready," he said.

He rode with Giles to the King. Hughan watched quietly as the Easter ram went up against the gate under a hail of arrows. But the ram was impervious to them and the Easters who went with it were well protected by a tortoise-shell of shields. The hail was met, shot for shot, by the Easter crossbowmen, much to the thresholders' peril. The surviving King's men had drawn up again on the field.

Hughan smiled as Eamon approached. "Come with me," he said.

Eamon followed a little way behind the King as Hughan made his way to the reformed lines. The King's men looked worn and battered, but they could see that they had won the morning and that gave them the strength to cheer their King as he rode before them.

"You have fought bravely," Hughan cried, "and we emerge from this field with a dear cost that can never be paid back to us. We will take this city, and though we have borne loss it will not be a place of vengeance." His tone and look hardened. "There will be no pillage, and there will be no rape. Any man who commits either will answer to me for his crime with his life."

As the King spoke, he seemed to reach every man with his words and gaze. Eamon understood that every man there knew well the King's heart.

"We go into this city in war but not for war," Hughan told them. "You are King's men; you are my men. Let every one of you love mercy and do justly. Let every one of you be humble and valiant men of peace."

Eamon felt the truth of the King's words renew his spirit. Along with the countless other men still standing on the field, he lifted his voice to cheer the King.

As the cheering continued, Hughan looked to Eamon. "You will take fifteen hundred men with you to the North Gate to take it."

Eamon nodded. In that moment there seemed to be nothing strange or difficult to him in Hughan's command.

"The Easters mean to send the ram South when they've finished here," Hughan told him. "Can you get into the North Gate without it?"

Eamon gazed north and thought for a moment. Perhaps he could. He turned to Giles. "Do you ride with me?"

"Yes," Giles answered.

"Get yourself a red jacket."

Giles didn't query the command, but went at once to recover a red coat from one of the fallen bodies. The wayfarers had gathered many such bodies from the field while they awaited the assault.

Hughan looked curiously at Eamon. "What do you intend?"

Eamon smiled softly. "Perhaps they'll still let me in."

To the side, hundreds of Easters and wayfarers by the ram began to loose arrows at the city walls, setting panic among the thresholders even if none were struck. The city's archers took aim and marked the arrow slits in the city's walls. Some crossbowmen were hit by returning shots.

A terrific boom shuddered through the air as the ram struck against the Blind Gate. Infantry prepared ladders near the walls as the ram struck again at the gate.

"Be careful," Hughan told Eamon.

Eamon matched his gaze. "And you." It was a solemn and frightening moment.

Hughan clasped his hand. "I will see you at the Four Quarters, First Knight."

Eamon breathed deeply. "At the Four Quarters, sire."

The King and his men went south towards the gate as the ramming at the Blind Gate continued. Eamon realized he was the captain of an enormous group of Easters and hobilars; all watched him attentively as Giles returned wearing Dunthruik colours and a broad smile.

Eamon turned to the waiting men. "Are you ready to ride with me?" he asked them.

"We await your command, First Knight," said another voice. Leon watched Eamon from among the hobilars. The man nodded to him.

Eamon swallowed, feeling a new wash of fear and anticipation run through him. How many times had he ridden to the Four Quarters, as lieutenant, Hand, Quarter Hand, and Right Hand?

Now he would forge a path to the Four Quarters as the King's First Knight.

"To the North Gate," he ordered.

CHAPTER XVIII

Eamon and the men entrusted to him went about the bound of Dunthruik's walls. The King's men and allies stayed well out of range of the thresholders and their arrows.

"Hold this position and wait for the gates to open," Eamon instructed his captains. "I will take the hobilars with me. They will need to follow some distance behind so as to avoid detection.

"There is a postern to one side of the gate. That is my goal. If I can convince them to open the postern, I will attempt to hold it open long enough for the hobilars to sneak through. Once they are through, we shall attempt to open the main gate. Once that gate starts to open, order your men to advance through it with all possible haste to secure it."

"And if they don't open the postern?" asked a captain.

Eamon grimaced. "Then we try to get away alive, and crack open this gate the hard way."

"And how will you convince them to open the postern, pray tell?"

Eamon turned to Giles. "That is where you come in, Giles. No doubt you wonder why I've asked you to dress in the colours of Dunthruik."

"The thought had crossed my mind, sir."

"Together we ride to the gate. You will ride as though injured. I shall invoke my authority as the Right Hand to have the gates opened."

"And we just ride in?"

"Yes."

"Just the two of us?"

Eamon nodded. It was a foolhardy plan, but it was the only plan he had. He was counting on the fact that the gate defenders were isolated enough from the plain not to know of his true allegiance, and that the ruse of bringing an injured soldier safely inside the walls was so much in character for Lord Goodman that they would not question his motives more closely. "Just the two of us. Then comes the difficult bit as we hold the gate open long enough for the King's forces to pass through." He looked at Giles sternly. "Are you up to the task? There is no shame in wanting to bow out. Speak now and I shall find another."

"I serve gladly," said Giles.

At Eamon's command, he and Giles went far ahead of the mass of men. Giles rode slumped over to one side as though badly wounded. Flushed with adrenaline, Eamon found that his weariness flowed out of his veins to be replaced by a surge of the strength which had carried him that morning to Hughan's lines.

Eamon caught a glimpse of Giles's face as they went; it was lit with the thrill of battle and Eamon remembered that the man was no easy foe. That was, in part, why he had chosen Giles to accompany him. The two of them would have to use all their guile, wits, and strength to hold open the door to give the hobilars time to pass through.

The field beneath them was scattered with fallen helms and bolts, but their horses, trained for the shattered fields of battle, passed easily over them. Eamon wondered whether the steeds felt as weary, or as driven, as their riders. The boom of the Easter ram against the Blind Gate echoed across the field as they rode. Another, much louder, crack followed the sound. It seemed to move the very ground.

It was then that Eamon's thought lightninged to Arlaith's face and laugh: "*This city has artillery.*" But he had not the time to see if it were true – he had to take the North Gate.

The great gate was closed and bolted. Eamon peered up. He could not see them, but he knew thresholders lined the upper walls.

As he and Giles came to a halt beneath the gate, men called to one another on the far side. Eamon wondered how long it would be before they hurled things other than curses down at their foes.

In the great expanse of the main gate there was a postern. It was to this that Eamon and Giles went, Giles now hunched forward over his horse's neck. Eamon knew that the gate guards – a small group of Gauntlet or thresholders with orders to hold the gate – waited behind the doorway. He also knew that most of Dunthruik's thresholders would be either at the Blind Gate – doing their best to stave off the battering ram – or at the port, ostensibly to assure the neutrality of the merchant vessels there, but perhaps seeking a means of escape. The latter thought encouraged him.

As Giles, affecting frailty, dismounted, Eamon also came down beside him and took firm grasp of his shoulders, as though shoring him up against a terrible injury. He led Giles to the postern and rammed his fist harshly against the door.

"Open!" Eamon yelled.

He heard voices on the other side that sounded uncertain and alarmed. It did not surprise him.

"I am the Right Hand!" Eamon cried. Giles leaned hard against him as he continued. "There is a wounded man with me. His injury will not brook delay – open the door!"

"The Right Hand commands the forces at the Blind Gate," the hesitant voice replied.

"So I did – but I was caught outside the Blind Gate during the retreat. It has taken me some time to make my way here unnoticed – even so, I am now pursued." He bit his lip and pressed on. "Do not let this man's life be the gate-price: open the door!"

For a long moment there was no sound, then the scraping of bolts and bars being drawn back sounded through the door. Giles stared at him.

"*Be ready*," Eamon mouthed. He knew that almost as soon as the gate opened, and certainly as soon as he and Giles were within, the keepers would realize their mistake. His heart pounded as they waited, shivering.

As the postern opened, Eamon caught sight of a pale face squinting into the shadow of the gate. He did not, and could not, permit the man to look for longer than a second. He pushed swiftly through the door. Giles was at his side, staggering a little to maintain the façade of injury.

They were inside the gate less than a few seconds before the guards prepared to close the postern again, and a couple of men came forwards to inspect Giles' injury. The first man grew pale.

"You're not injured —"

He did not have the time to say another word. Giles tore himself away from the thresholder's grasp, swung his sword, and downed the first man. Eamon hefted his blade. The yard echoed to the cry:

"*Snakes! Snakes at the North Gate!*"

Eamon pressed through the small group of men about him. Some attacked but were cut down at once as Eamon and Giles forced on; others fled while shouting that the gate was breached. That same cry echoed throughout the quarters of the city. Only the officer, a stout lieutenant, remained to face them. He yelled and hurled himself over the bodies of his fallen men towards Eamon. Eamon met the oncoming blow and twisted it into a lethal strike.

Before he had been inside the city half a minute he had beaten and killed half a dozen men.

"Giles?" he cried, whirling from his last opponent.

"Here." Giles came forward, grim and bloody, and Eamon supposed that did not cut a better figure himself. Giles arched one shoulder back for a moment and then looked at Eamon again. "Can I get rid of this, now?" he asked pointing to the jacket.

"Yes."

Their moment of respite passed; more thresholders poured into the street. They bore their weapons bravely. Whether this gesture came from their own will, or that of the Gauntlet and Hands behind them, was difficult to tell, but each man cried defiance at the Serpent.

Eamon and Giles tensed and prepared to receive the new threat. Even as the reinforcements lined up to defend the breached postern, arrows hissed from the gate.

A few thresholders fell at once, their scant jerkins no protection against the arrows of the hobilars. The hobilars streamed through the gate on foot. The first men went immediately into the gatehouse, and moments later the whole North Gate began to swing open. At Eamon's signal, fifteen hundred soldiers made for the gate.

It was too much for the thresholders: they turned and fled. Some were shot down, while others reached the safety of the adjoining narrow streets.

His men were pouring through the gate. "Secure the gatehouses and the walls!" Eamon commanded.

The Easters and hobilars knew their trade well. Dozens of men climbed the walls. The thresholders screamed as they fled. Eamon directed groups of men to swarm along the base of the walls and spread out along them into the city. Scouts ran ahead of them, calling as other men made their way up into the nearby buildings, securing them for the King.

After a few minutes the first scouts returned, giving news that they could press forward. Eamon dispatched groups out into the North and East Quarters. The men went through the side streets, claiming buildings and roads from what defenders remained.

Eamon looked ahead. Coronet Rise loomed before him, rising up into the heart of Dunthruik. Not long later he led his own men along it.

The broad paving stones met each beat of his feet as he went, driving him on like a drum. Every building they passed was quickly and vigorously searched. Men went along the rooftops and into each narrow alley and called to each other. Eamon's ears filled with screams and cries. All over the city the thresholders fled. Few remained to meet the King's men. Many doors and homes were blockaded but that presented the wayfarers with little difficulty.

They pressed on, cutting through the web of Dunthruik with their bright blades. Eamon knew that it was not far to the Four Quarters – he had made the journey hundreds of times. Yet somehow the city's heart had never seemed further from him than that moment where he charged through its streets to meet it.

There was noise ahead. At first Eamon could not imagine what it might be. When he at last discerned it clearly, he wondered if his mind played him a cruel jest. Soon scouts returned with confirmation on their lips of what Eamon had so incredulously surmised: knights.

Shapes appeared on the road before them; the riders deployed proudly. The cobbles rang beneath their horses' hooves. The whole breadth of Coronet Rise before them filled with knights. Their armour gleamed. It showed dinned and tainted by the battle they had already fought that morning, but still it shone.

Eamon stared at them. He knew but little about horsemanship and even less about the ways of Dunthruik's knights, but even he knew that it would be folly to attempt a cavalry charge in the city's narrow streets: the narrowness would be deadly to horse and man and both sides. It was suicidal. But he also knew too well the grim and injured pride of Rocell's knights, and knew that such arrogance would drive them on even into such folly as a charge.

He was not the only one who thought it. "They wouldn't!" Giles cried, his voice strained.

"They would," Eamon answered. "King's men!"

Eamon had the time to form his own men into a receiving line before the leading knight raised his hand. The man yelled something Eamon could not hear, then drove his spurs to his horse's blood-stained flanks. The knights' line, six men across, came on in a fury of swearing, shouting men, and champing horses. Eamon could not tell how deep they rode.

The knights' faces were lurid and fearsome, but their tight formation soon broke. Before the knights had come close, the King's men loosed several volleys of arrows into the churning ranks. The horses lost their momentum and some of the knights their chargers. Eamon saw one horse go down with a horrific scream. It should have taken others with it as it fell but was ridden over by the superbly trained beasts of the throned's cavalry. Nevertheless the creature's flailing body contributed to the agonizing dampening of the knights' intended glory. As they came closer some of the King's men took to the alleys and side streets to remove themselves from the brunt of the charge.

Whatever hope they had of spearing down the King's men was lost in the cramped confines of the streets. Unable to maintain their pace, and unable to manoeuvre or turn to the side, they had only one attempt to charge down on Eamon's troops, and it was feeble at best. Eamon easily ducked under a thrust as the first knight came at him. As he leapt back, Eamon turned his great sword into the horse's belly. The beast screamed and fell, throwing its rider. Giles leapt upon the knight and stabbed down into the exposed opening between the visor's slits as the rider struggled to his feet; a fountain of blood erupted about Giles's blade. Eamon did not know how many of his own men had fallen, but all over the narrow road knights were unhorsed and slaughtered.

Eamon turned just as a knight sprang at him and brought his sword down in a fierce strike at Eamon's helmet. Eamon stepped to the side and slashed through his visor.

Eamon wrenched his sword free and gave a sickened cry as he met his next assailant. He downed him as swiftly as he had the first.

No more came. Turning from his bloody work, Eamon saw knights unhorsed and panicked horses. The remaining knights were drawing together in a ragged mess in the road. They raised their hands and voices at once.

"Mercy!"

Eamon made his way to the knights. As he approached, one tore off his helmet and cast it aside before kneeling down among the bloody stones. "Lord Goodman, mercy!" he called. His face was plastered with sweat.

"Mercy?" Giles growled, disgusted. The man's hands flexed about his hilt. "*Mercy!* What mercy do you deserve?"

"Giles," Eamon said sharply.

As though startled from a dream, the man looked across at him. At a nod from Eamon, Giles stepped back.

Eamon turned to some of the hobilars with him. "Have them contained," he commanded. There were perhaps a hundred knights up and down the road, dozens dead. "They will be held as prisoners. The rest of us will go on."

Leaving the knights in the care of some of the hobilars, Eamon gathered together his men once more. Some had been lost in meeting the knights, but there was no time to tend to the fallen. Eamon wondered grimly whether the corpses of the knights and King's men would be looted or violated in the bloody wilderness of Dunthruik's streets.

Pausing only to clean some of the blood from his blade, he turned and led his force deeper along Coronet Rise.

They had gone but a short distance when he heard noises above him. Looking up, he saw the thresholders. They pelted arrows, bolts, pots, trunks, stones, tiles, and javelins – anything they could get hold of – down upon the King's men.

"Ware above!"

A piece of pottery glanced off Eamon as he yelled the warning. Men raised their voices in alarm as objects smashed down into the paving slabs around them. Still they pressed on. Eamon sometimes saw groups of thresholders or Gauntlet racing through the narrow streets, retreating westward, but unless they came directly past his force he let them go.

Easter archers took to the roofs and pressed the thresholders, giving Eamon and his men some reprieve.

They had made perhaps half of the distance from the North Gate to the Four Quarters when Eamon saw a great mass spanning the road from side to side up ahead. A dense line of carts and trunks and barrels blocked the Rise and its side streets. Eamon caught glimpses of men behind it and knew that he would not be able to take it swiftly.

"How shall we pass, First Knight?" called an Easter named Lord Ylonous.

"We will not go over it." Eamon would not lead his men into a battle against the block. The side roads led into the East Quarter. From there he would be better able to navigate other ways to the city's heart.

He turned back to Ylonous. "Have some of your men infiltrate the blockade from the roofs and the flanks." Ylonous's men went at once. It would be a lengthy process; Eamon felt restless and impatient. He had to reach the Four Quarters sooner than it would take to break the blockade. "I will go another way."

"We will come with you." The voice was Leon's. A group of twenty to thirty men was with him.

Lifting his sword high, Eamon took his men into the side street. It was narrow and dark, and there was no better place for them to be ambushed, but he went on resolutely. Eamon knew that the road led eventually to the Ashen.

Despite the unspoken fears of his men and the thick cries that echoed in the city streets, they met little or no resistance in the dark streets. Eamon wondered how many families hid in their homes, dreading the coming of the King.

They passed shops and buildings that Eamon knew; places where he had walked and talked and lived with the people of Dunthruik. At last they came to the Ashen.

He came into the heart of the East Quarter at the head of his men. A group of thresholders and Gauntlet stood there, held in a grim line by a mounted Hand who yelled at them as the King's men appeared. Arrows hissed as the thresholders loosed. The King's men returned shots.

Eamon stopped in his tracks. It was neither arrow nor hand that stayed him, but the sting and smell of smoke.

The East Handquarter and college were in flames.

For a terrible moment Eamon stopped and stared. He was vaguely aware of the Hand falling from his horse, and of the thresholders dispersing with cries of panic. Defenders fled to the darkened streets of the Ashen, pursued by King's men. Then more King's men arrived from the south – Feltumadas's force from the Blind Gate – poured into the Ashen, and took up the quarry.

But Eamon did not give chase. He ran towards the steps of the Handquarter.

The flames devoured the college and the rear of the Hand's residence. As Eamon raced to the steps, he was struck by a wall of heat.

Between fits of coughing and gasping, he looked through the smoke into the hall of the Handquarter. There he made out the faintest sound and sight of people gathered within, trapped by the encroaching flames and choking on the smoke.

Eamon drew a deep breath and charged up the steps. He could barely breathe. Moving his limbs was agony.

"Slater!" he yelled, coughing as he inhaled a lung-full of smoke and ash. He swore. "*Slater!*" Sweat poured off his face.

The servants were gathered, trembling, behind the smoke in a corner of the hall. Smoke poured out of the kitchens and servants' quarters. He raced across to the terrified forms huddled in the sooty darkness. Why did they not try to escape?

Eamon reached the group of servants. One of them raised a hand to strike him.

Eamon caught the master cook's arm before the knife reached his armour. The servant gave a frightened yell.

"You are a brave man," Eamon told him, "but foolish. You must get out of here."

"Lord Goodman!" It was Slater.

"Into the Ashen, all of you!" Eamon yelled. "*Now!*"

The servants stared at him. They were pale-faced and wept.

"We can't go out there!" The voice was Callum's. "They'll kill us!"

"Would you rather roast like geese?" Eamon cried. "If you trust me, then do as I say, all of you!" Eamon seized Callum's quivering hand. "Follow me, *now!*"

He broke into a fit of coughing as the acrid smoke filled his lungs. Unable to speak another word, he strengthened his grip on Callum's hand and led the boy at a run from the hall. Timbers creaked all about them, weakened in the press of the flames. The servants, choking and crying, followed him as he charged down the college steps and into the May sunlight.

He brought the servants to a halt near the centre of the square.

"Slater, is this everyone you had with you? Have we lost anyone?"

Slater counted heads. "All of them, my lord. At least, all who were with us upon your arrival."

Too few. Far too few. Tears welled in Eamon's eyes.

"Lord Goodman," screamed Cara's voice, "behind you!"

He turned round. The Ashen teemed with Easters and King's men. For a moment, Eamon struggled to understand the girl's worry. A group of King's men approached from across the square. The servants cried out in terror.

Eamon did not have time to comfort them. He raised one hand to the nearest Easter.

"There may be others inside," he yelled, thrusting one hand back towards the burning hall. "This quarter belongs to Lord Anastasius. Douse the flames and find any who yet live."

A group of Easters charged towards the building. Anastasius's son, Ithel, reached Eamon's side. Callum still clung to Eamon's battle-worn hands. As the Easter halted, a look of amusement passed over his face.

"We must to the Four Quarters," Ithel said, looking to Eamon. "My men will see to the building."

Eamon nodded and turned to Slater. "Lead the house," he commanded. "Go and block yourselves into a building somewhere and wait for this to be over. If any men like these come against you, tell them that you are under the protection of the First Knight."

"The First Knight?" Slater stared. He repeated the word dumbly. "The First Knight? Who is that?"

"The King's second," Ithel told him.

Slater looked at Eamon in alarm. "But what if the First Knight were to come?" he asked. "How would we explain that we had used his name?"

Ithel laughed out loud. "If he were to come?" he cried.

Slater glanced at Eamon uncertainly. "What does he mean, my lord?"

It was then that Ithel forced mirth away from his lips. With utmost seriousness, he met Slater's gaze. "Your Lord Goodman is the First Knight."

For a moment Slater could not comprehend. His eyes slowly turned to Eamon, and his jaw dropped.

"Lord Goodman –"

"It is true," Eamon answered. A darkly confused look went over his servant's face. "We will speak," he said. "Please, Slater; lead the house."

Slater nodded in stunned silence.

Callum tugged at Eamon's gauntleted hand.

"Wouldn't we be safer if you stayed with us?" the boy whispered, quivering with fear.

"Maybe," Eamon told him, then smiled. "But only maybe. It seems to me that Mr Cook might make a more stalwart defender." He saw Cook turn red, and for a moment it distracted the servants from the Easters. He looked back down at Callum. "I have to go."

"Will you come back?"

Eamon matched the boy's gaze. "I will come back."

Callum clutched tighter at his hand and a tiny sob left his lips. Gently, Eamon leaned forward and kissed Callum's brow.

"You will be safe, and I will come back," he whispered. "I promise."

Nodding tearfully, the boy let go his hand.

Eamon turned again to Slater and touched his arm. "Take care of my house, Mr Slater."

"Yes, my lord," Slater replied.

"First Knight!" Leon returned from one of the side streets. "We must to the King!"

"We go," Eamon answered. The servants eyed him in awe and surprise. Though he wished he could stay to encourage them, Eamon turned and gathered his men to him. He led them on through the Ashen to its far end where a wide road led back down to Coronet Rise. Eamon cast one more look back at the Handquarters. Slater led the house away. Eamon felt a sudden doubt run through him.

The King's men had not reached the Ashen before him. Even if they had, they would not have set flame to the Handquarter. Who had done so?

CHAPTER XIX

Eamon and the King's men pressed on through the streets of Dunthruik. The thresholders hindered their passsage where they could, though it was never for long. Eamon lost many men in the time it took for them to cross the last stretch to the Four Quarters. Foul-reeking smoke billowed from the direction of the Blind Gate.

As they approached the Four Quarters, screams throbbed in the air. Straggles of Gauntlet on the road ran from hobilars and enthusiastic Easters. Eamon realized that the blockade on the Rise had been broken. The Four Quarters was ahead, and it sounded like the source of the fighting.

As Eamon pressed on to the end of the road, a cry sounded to his right. A javelin hurtled through the air and missed him by inches. A red-coated man followed close behind the javelin. He drew his sword. Before the guard could land a blow, the King's men were on him and he was down.

Eamon and his men poured out of the mouth of Coronet Rise and into the Four Quarters. The high stones and plinths where the statues stood caught the sunlight of the early afternoon. The great eagles seemed to be aflame as smoke and death wafted up about them.

In the quarters themselves, a group of thresholders and Gauntlet gathered about one man: General Cade. Cade led his last defence against the blue banners of the King. The King's men launched themselves against Cade from every side. Hughan's bodyguard was among those in the press from the south. To Eamon's left, a great group of Easters marched up the Coll from the Blind Gate. Eamon's heart swelled with elation: North, South, and Blind Gate were taken.

As he and his men came forward from the North, Hughan's party from the South, and Feltumadas's from the East, the thresholders realized that they could not hold. With cries of panic dozens of men tried to flee west along the Coll – many of them were cut down. As the thresholder lines crumpled and fell apart, Cade tried to rally his men before he fell beneath the blade of a King's man.

As the broken men ran, the King's scouts swift in their wake, Hughan himself came to Eamon's side.

"How is the North?" he called.

"There are barricades and some defenders still, but not many," Eamon answered. "The South?"

"Full of surrendering men," Hughan answered, his voice a mixture of relief and satisfaction. "I've left some groups to deal with them."

"As have I."

"The Hands and Gauntlet still fighting have fled west," Feltumadas said as he arrived. Eamon did not wonder how the Easter knew it. "For what little good it will do them!"

"They're trying to escape by the port," Eamon guessed.

"They will not pass the blockade even if they find a vessel," Hughan answered.

"They'll regroup for a last stand," Feltumadas added. "Likely at the palace."

"I would not make it the site of my last stand," Eamon gasped, appalled at the idea. Defence of the palace, even with its great gates, would be difficult and bloody, and there was nowhere to run to in the case of defeat.

"Yet that is where the Hands have been pressing the men to go," Feltumadas replied.

"And that is where we must go," Hughan told them.

"Many more flee south and west."

"They must be pursued and pinned down until they surrender." Hughan looked across at the Easter lord. "Detail more men to round up the defectors and stragglers and contain them. Then follow us to the palace."

Hughan raised his sword high. The King's men followed him as he turned from the circle of the Four Quarters and up along the Coll. The sun flashed on the King's helmet, a golden strike on a silver crown. Eamon followed.

They went up the Coll, past the gates of the Crown where more great stone eagles stood. Eamon's thought turned for a moment to Ilenia and the players. Did she, or any of them, live? Had they been drafted into the thresholders? He tried to imagine Shoreham wielding a blade against the blue banners, but could not.

Up the Coll advanced the men who fought beneath the banner of the King and his allies. The shrieks and cries of Dunthruik echoed all around. Eamon felt the fear of those who hid and those who ran, and the desperate courage of those men who were even then preparing their hands for their final stand. Perhaps the Gauntlet would, of their own accord, have surrendered, but those Hands that lived would rather drive them on to death for the Master.

As they passed the Brand and the West Quarter College, Eamon caught a glimpse of several men – evidently runners, for as soon as the King's banners came into sight they tore off towards the palace by ways known only to Dunthruik's men. Some of the Easters tried to take the runners down with their bows, but to no avail; the arrows split uselessly against the walls of the narrow streets. Eamon mused that it was hardly a secret that the King approached. What kind of last stand were the Hands preparing at the palace gates? What else lay in wait for them – for Hughan?

Where was the throned?

Hughan looked to the gates. For a moment Eamon thought that he discerned a troubled thought on Hughan's furrowed brow. A chill realization drenched him. The hardest battle would be fought not on Dunthruik's plains or in its streets, but rather in a room where King and throned would strive against each other for the right to claim the land.

Eamon shivered.

The palace walls came into sight before them, the gates firmly shut. Eamon knew that bolts and bars strengthened them from within. Behind them voices called to each other, the cries of Hands and Gauntlet. As they approached, defenders on the gates began a desperate volley of arrows. The King's men easily took cover, either at a safe distance or in the nearby streets, while they waited for the rest of their number to reach the palace. As they waited, Hughan stood watching the gates and its defenders, deep in thought. The arrows clattered harmlessly against the stones. Eamon wondered how many arrows the defenders could possibly have, and whether they realized that they used them on an enemy whom they could not hope to hit.

They waited on Hughan's command. Feltumadas paced impatiently for a time between the King and the men near him, then rounded on Hughan.

"Let us take them!" Feltumadas cried, slamming one palm against another. "We have taken the Blind Gate and the South and the North; Edelred's palace gates shall be no different."

"We can break these gates," Hughan agreed quietly, "but in so doing many men inside will lose their lives. There is enough blood on the streets of this city, Feltumadas, and I would not add to it where I have no need." Eamon was relieved to hear him say it.

Feltumadas sighed. "Yes, Star."

They all three looked to the palace gates again. The rain of arrows from the walls halted. For a moment all that could be heard was the sound of the men within.

"Regardless of bloodshed, we must do something," Feltumadas told Hughan fiercely. "They are doubtless preparing more trouble within, and the longer we leave them –"

"Let me speak to them," Eamon said suddenly.

Feltumadas gave him a strange, rolling look. "Do you think that men who barricade themselves behind palace gates and rain arrows down on those who come to them are willing to surrender?"

"I think that men with the throned's mark upon them and a Hand behind them will do many things that they would not do otherwise," Eamon answered, "even barricading themselves behind palace gates and loosing at kings."

Feltumadas snorted. "Then try to speak to them," he said, "but I hold little hope for your success."

Eamon looked across at Hughan. The King nodded to him. "Try, First Knight."

Eamon drew a deep breath and went firmly up to the gates. An eerie silence was behind them; a stinging, acrid smell emanated from there that Eamon could not place.

The gates were tall and strongly wrought. As he went to stand before them it occurred to him that, in all his long months in Dunthruik, he had rarely looked at them. They were broad and deep, painted red and gold, and bore two posterns, one to each side. Eamon knew the guardhouses to either side of the gates well. He remembered the first time he had taken his turn to watch them. It had been on that night that he had met Alessia.

He looked up at the gates. "Send forth a speaker!"

For a long moment there was no answer. Eamon stared up at the walls, willing someone to respond, wishing for the name of just one man inside on whom he could call.

His wish was granted.

"What would you, traitor?"

A darkly garbed figure stood on the wall. He knew the voice, though it took him a moment to remember the Hand's name.

"Lord Brettal," he called, "I am glad to see you."

"I cannot return the sentiment," Brettal replied. "If it lay within my power, both you and your Serpent would lie dead before me in an instant, and I would offer up your heads to the Master!"

"Yet you cannot," Eamon called. "Just as you cannot hold these gates, Lord Brettal." Eamon watched as an angry look passed over the Hand's face. "There is no need for you or the men with you to die. The King desires your surrender, not your lives."

"My orders come from the Right Hand," Brettal snapped, "and surrender does not form a part of them."

"I gave no such commands, Lord Brettal," Eamon answered, "and even had I, I would rescind them, and do so when I say to you: let you and your men come forth and live."

Brettal laughed. "Do not take airs to yourself," he spat. "My orders were not from you."

Eamon's blood chilled.

Arlaith.

"You need not follow his commands," Eamon said earnestly.

"Is that your counsel?" Brettal demanded. "That I play traitor with you?"

"Let the Gauntlet choose for themselves."

"The Gauntlet's choice is made by their duty," Brettal retorted, "and they will be constant in it – unlike you!"

"Then let the Gauntlet know," Eamon yelled, hoping that the men on the other side of the gate would hear him, "that the King does not consider them enemies, and that their oaths will not bar them from his service!"

Brettal's face waxed livid. "Go and counsel your hooded Serpent, Blight of Dunthruik!" He spat at Eamon with a hissing scowl, and left the wall.

Moments later the Hand howled words of threat and scorn at the men behind the gates with him.

Eamon returned to Hughan, downcast. "They cannot surrender," he said. He wondered how many of them wished to. "We must take the gates."

"Then we will take them," Hughan replied.

"We will not have to open them!" cried Feltumadas. He pointed ahead.

Eamon turned to see the palace gates yawn open. Ranks of Gauntlet were arrayed in the plaza. In the middle of the square sat a long, dark, raised metal tube. Eamon had never seen its like. He stared at it. As the gate opened wider, a second tube came into view. Behind both were lines of Hands, going back and forth between the tubes and great barrels. The Hands seemed to be feeding the tubes.

A Hand behind one of the strange tubes spread his palms – red light appeared. The Hand set fire in some part of the tube. The Gauntlet braced themselves.

"*This city has artillery…*"

Suddenly Eamon understood.

"Fire!" Eamon yelled. "*Fire!*"

And then it came: a great sweep of flame roared forward, fuelled by the red light. Smoke followed it in clouds as the ballast shot out of the gates and down the Coll.

The King's men fled to the side streets just before the metal beast gorged its mass of flame. As they sought refuge, the Gauntlet cheered and the Hands snapped further commands.

As another strike boomed over their heads and out of the gates, Eamon was flung back against a wall; the explosion reverberated through his armour and ears. A biting smell filled the air. Eamon suddenly realized he had smelled it before: standing by the burning remains of the Easter bridge that he had been accused of destroying.

He gagged on the stinging stench.

"They had the same kind of artillery at the Blind Gate," Feltumadas cried. The Easter was by Eamon's side.

"How did you get past it?" Eamon spluttered.

"With difficulty." Feltumadas's face was grim. "We shot the crew and charged it before they could reload. We cannot do the same here."

Eamon grimaced. He suspected the Hands were already reloading. Though some of the King's men tried shooting into the yard, he doubted they would have much success.

He glanced across the square and froze. "Where is the King?" he cried suddenly.

Feltumadas only looked at him. "I do not know."

Eamon looked in anguish across the square before the gates. The King's men were gathered together out of the line of fire, but a score had been hit in the blasts. Oddly twisted bodies lay on the stones and Eamon could not tell if any of them was Hughan's.

Then suddenly he saw him. The King stepped boldly back into the great gap before the gates.

"Hughan!" Eamon gasped.

"What is he doing?" Feltumadas hissed.

But Eamon had no breath to answer: he was in thrall to terror.

The King stood before the gates of the palace. He went alone, and a strange silence fell about him, for he looked back at the fire and might of Dunthruik with quiet assurance.

"Stay your fury, Hands of Edelred." His voice seemed as loud as thunder and as sweet as a summer rain. How could any man gainsay it?

"Fire!" yelled a voice within the yard.

Another heap of flame bounded from the gate towards the standing King. Horror etched the faces of the King's men. The King's name leapt to Eamon's lips. He started forward, but he knew that he could do nothing.

Hughan neither flinched nor moved as the flame howled towards him. He faced it silently. Suddenly the air about Hughan rippled. The King held the gazes of the Gauntlet and the Hands as the shot fire met a living, shimmering shield of blue light which flashed with fearsome brilliance, dousing the striking flames.

The fire was gone. The King stood untouched before the gates. All was silence.

Hughan drew a deep breath. "I will pass," he called.

In that moment Eamon's legs carried him to the King's side, though he scarcely knew how he could dare to stand there. None opposed him, and none spoke until he, reaching Hughan, called to them:

"King's men!"

They came to the King in silence, forming up behind him. The gaping Gauntlet were paralysed with awe and terror.

"Receive the King's mercy!" Eamon called.

"Never!" screeched Brettal. He stood by one of the great artillery machines; the Hand's contorted face was malice. His hands seared with red light that grew until it nigh engulfed him. Another Hand went up to him, adding more powder to the artillery and light to the gathering orb.

"*Never!*"

The Hands' motion freed the Gauntlet. They threw down their weapons and bolted forth from the gates, spreading in all directions. All the while, the light over the machine darkened. Some Gauntlet ran to the King's lines, their hands thrown up in surrender. Others disappeared into the city streets as the red light consumed the artillery.

"Stand, King's men!" Eamon cried. As if by premonition, he knew that their lives depended on it. "Stand for the King!"

As he cried, an arrow hissed by his ear as the King's men loosed arrows. The arrows flew with terrific accuracy through the air into the plaza. Brettal gave a choking screech and spun backwards, an arrow in his throat. As he fell, the light in his hands turned towards the great pile of ammunition behind him.

There was not even the time to scream; the light careered into the machine's food. Then a blast filled the air and a resounding crack shook the world. When next Eamon could see, it was through a veil of blue light which surrounded him and all the men who stood with the King. Gazing about himself in surprise, Eamon saw that the protective light emanated from Hughan. He looked back to the gates.

The machine and Hands were gone, replaced by a blackened husk of metal and charred flesh. Great swathes of the plaza's walls tumbled into cascades of broken, smoking stone. The stones of the great yard cracked. Debris hurtled in every direction and waves of fire went with it as the whole front of the palace collapsed, its gaudy innards revealed to every watching eye in spews of red, like the ribs and blood of a living man torn open. The towering arches crashed and tumbled, the great balcony was cast down, the stone turned black, and the halls filled with wolfish flames.

Eamon stared as Edelred's gates and walls fell, crushing the scores of screaming Hands beneath them. Destruction rained down in smoke and a hail of scathing stone. Yet apart from its entrance, the palace still stood. Though veiled by the falling rock, the West Wing was unscathed.

Still the stone and fire fell, but the King's men were untouched.

The fall of debris lessened into clouds of dust and the blue light fell away. Waves of heat engulfed Eamon. He choked on the air, which reeked of burnt and burning bodies and timbers. The remains of Hands and some Gauntlet men lay among the shattered gates and walls.

Hughan surveyed the destruction before him. Pity touched his face. "Lord Feltumadas."

The Easter came to him at once. "Star," he answered softly, his eyes wide.

"Take charge of those men surrendering here. Detail others to search the rubble for survivors. First Knight."

"Sire," Eamon breathed.

"We must enter the palace."

Eamon looked at the rubble of the broken gates, walls, and palace entrance, then back to Hughan.

"I will lead you," he answered.

Hughan gathered a group of King's men. When they had prepared themselves, they turned to Eamon.

"We are ready, First Knight."

Eamon clambered forward over the rubble of the gates. The ground was hot beneath him and his armour conducted that heat into his weary limbs. He picked his way through the Royal Plaza, followed by the King.

The palace's entrance hall and the corridors leading to the throne room had been destroyed when the balcony crashed down. As

Eamon threaded his way through the hot stones towards the East Wing, he prayed that the damage was not more extensive.

He hastened to the wall and to a broken arch. The palace's windows had shattered, spewing forth hundreds of grim shards which littered the ground like daggers. Carefully, Eamon crossed the glassy debris of talons and peered through the arch. There were shafts of light beyond it. His instinct told him that the hall was passable.

He pressed himself in through the narrow opening. The room beyond was dark and breathing was difficult; clods of dust and stone fell from the ceiling, but the doorway beyond was whole.

"This way!" he called.

The King and his men came one by one after him.

The great banners and emblems were scattered on the ground, torn down and crushed beneath fallen stones. Pillars and beams had boomed forward under the weight of what lay above them, and Eamon had to pick his way carefully to the end of the corridor.

They passed by several rooms in the gloomy darkness. In one, Eamon caught sight of the remains of an owl and ash painted on the wall. His heart stilled as he realized that it was the Hands' waiting hall – he remembered its splendour. But his vision of it faded away as he looked at it, for now it had been reduced to splintered stones. Of all the emblems in the room, only the Right Hand's black eagle survived, its face staring grimly down from the cracked ceiling.

They came to the throne room. The great doors stood intact. In the gloom of the dusty corridor a figure lay on the ground, crushed beneath a fallen beam. Edelred's doorkeeper. The man held a sword in his hand. His back was horribly arched, snapped in two where the beam had struck.

Eamon stepped back. The sight was loathsome to him.

Steps approached from behind. Hughan emerged through the darkness. He looked at the fallen man and sighed.

"This is the throne room," Eamon said, gesturing to the door. "There is a way into his quarters from within."

"Very well."

Eamon hesitated, remembering the many times he had knelt in the hall beyond before a false master. As he thought on it, he saw again with horrid clarity the paintings that hung on the walls.

His hand faltered at the door. He looked earnestly to the King. "I cannot go in there," he whispered. "Not with you."

Hughan laid his hand on Eamon's where it held the door. Eamon swallowed. He searched the King's eyes. "Hughan, the shame and guilt of Dunthruik is seen no more clearly than beyond these doors."

"I do not fear to see it."

The King set force against the door, and Eamon joined him in it. The great wooden panels opened, swinging back on damaged hinges to reveal the long, red floor of the throne room.

A rush of hot air struck them. Eamon keenly felt the sting of the Master's mark on his hand as he looked down the long hall. Though the floor was cracked and bent, large areas of it struck by falling debris from the ceiling and collapsing north balcony, the paintings of the flame-haired throned and the vile serpents still showed in dusty horror on the walls. Their forms grinned luridly at Eamon and mocked him. It turned his stomach.

Swallowing down his sorrowed anger, he stepped down from the doorway and crossed the hall. Hughan walked with him.

They crossed the shattered stones to the dais. As they approached, there was a shuddering lurch in the stones and a beam upon the platform struck downwards. As it went it caught the broad painting on the back wall. Stones, frame, and canvas were broken. The work crashed down in a flood of dust and stone. They fell heavily down upon the throne, which splintered into hundreds of glistening pieces. As the dust settled, all that remained of the painting was the flicker of a star.

"Which way?" the King quietly asked.

"There," Eamon answered, gesturing to the back wall and its torn curtains. He hesitated, watching in awe as Hughan ascended the dais and passed the broken throne.

They went to the back door, which led into the throned's own quarters. It too was sound. The red stone above it glinted threateningly in the light. Eamon wondered how they would pass it, but as the King approached, the crimson rock cracked and shattered.

Eamon stared. "Even the stones know you," he breathed.

The wall opened before them into a corridor and then a small hall. Eamon knew that from the hall they could climb the stairs up to the throned's chambers. He felt the Master's presence above him like a louring tempest.

They passed into the hall and Eamon stopped in alarm. The grand staircase was cracked and looked distinctly unstable. It might bear the weight of a man but it would not bear many, and perhaps not even just one dressed in armour.

The King and the King's men halted around him; there was no need of speech.

Hughan turned to him. "Is there another way?"

Eamon shook his head in disbelief. They might have used the south balcony but it was as likely to be unstable as the stairs before them. "I do not know."

There was a moment of silence. Then Hughan turned to the men. "Search this area. Go carefully."

Eamon felt the barb of failure in his breast. It brought a flush of horror to his stomach. "Hughan, I'm sorry. I…"

The King's gentle eyes fell on him. "Eamon," he laughed kindly, "that the stairway is impassable is not your doing."

Eamon glanced up again at the tall stairwell, remembering the time that he had climbed it and the crippling light that had awaited him in the Master's chamber. Would the King face that rending pain?

Would it break him?

He looked fearfully to Hughan. "You will fight him?"

"If he will not yield," Hughan answered, "yes."

"He is a terrible foe," Eamon breathed. How could the King stand against Edelred?

"Yet I will face him." As their gazes met, Eamon wondered how long Hughan had known that this day would come, and how much he had prepared for it.

"Are you afraid, Eamon?" Hughan asked.

"Yes." He would rather fight in a hundred battles than face the man who awaited the King. That same waiting man had known him and mocked him, had so often claimed his blood, kissing him one moment and striking him the next...

Driving back a shudder, Eamon silently searched the King's face.

"Are *you* afraid?" he whispered.

"I do not fear Edelred, nor what the outcome of this day may be." Hughan smiled gently at Eamon, a smile full of grace and courage. "And yet, I cannot say that I am not afraid."

Eamon nodded. Somehow the King's words strengthened him.

A group of the King's men returned through one of the hall's crumpled doorways. As they approached, they escorted a man between them. Eamon recognized him at once. He stared as Iulus Cartwright was brought before the King.

"Sire," said one of the men, "this man claimed to serve Lord Goodman."

"He does," Eamon confirmed. "Are you well, Mr Cartwright?" he asked, laying a hand on the man's shoulder.

"Yes, my lord," Cartwright answered. He was pale and covered with soot and dust. "I did as you ordered."

Eamon felt a wave of relief. He turned to Hughan. "This man has been a faithful servant to me. His name is Iulus Cartwright. Before he served in my house he served Lady Alessia."

"She speaks well of you, Mr Cartwright," Hughan said.

Cartwright's eyes widened. "You have seen Lady Turnholt?"

"Yes," Hughan answered with a smile. "She is safe and well."

"You bring me good news," Cartwright laughed, and then suddenly he took in the colours that Hughan wore. His face paled and he looked at Eamon in alarm. "My lord –"

"This man is the King." Eamon met the servant's gaze. "I serve him, Cartwright."

Cartwright stared at him for a moment then looked back to Hughan in astonishment.

"Cartwright," Eamon said gently, "you and the servants will be free to go, and you will be under no obligation to aid us." Cartwright nodded. "Do you know another way to the throned's chambers?"

Cartwright looked at the impassable stairs. "I know of one." He nodded slowly. "I will help you."

They called back the other King's men, and Cartwright led them from the hall into some of the narrower corridors. From there they went down into servants' corridors. The passageway was tight. Eamon had trouble passing in his armour; he had to edge along sideways in some places, and duck down in others. The passages were dark and claustrophobic, often set below the ground level of the palace. Eamon wondered how often the servants had passed through their like to move unseen according to the will of their masters.

The network of servants' tunnels opened into another small hall. There were dozens of doors leading from it. Eamon gazed at them. Small rooms lay beyond, filled with beds. Before Eamon had time to gather his bearings, Cartwright moved again into another corridor. Like the first, this passageway emerged in another tiny hall. It was dark, but a tall, narrow staircase led up at one side. It was whole and undamaged.

"It is one of the servants' stairways," Cartwright said quietly. He seemed reluctant to raise his voice. "It… it leads up to his chambers."

Hughan turned to him. "Your lady spoke truly of you, Mr Cartwright," he said. "I will send some of my men back with you. Please take yourself and the rest of the house safely from the palace."

Cartwright nodded. "Thank you," he said. "I will."

Some of the King's men went to the servant's side.

"Lord Goodman," Cartwright called as they prepared to leave.

"Mr Cartwright?"

The servant faltered for a moment. "Be careful, my lord."

"I will, Cartwright."

Hughan, Eamon, and the remaining dozen King's men slowly climbed the staircase. It was narrow, forcing them up one at a time. It led to a covered opening. Eamon pressed aside the heavy tapestry and stepped out into a broad corridor. They were not far from the throned's vault of treasures. The air was cool and dense. Eamon felt in his heart that the throned was near.

Hughan seemed to sense it, too. They both paused for a moment in the corridor and then the King stepped forward. Eamon followed him. They passed the throned's breakfast room on the right.

Then they came to the throned's chambers. Eamon knew the dark doorway; it filled his whole body with fear.

A group of the throned's guards and servants stood before the door. On seeing Hughan emerge from the shadows of the hall they froze. For a moment Eamon thought they would attack, but as Hughan stepped into the light, they only gazed at him in awe. The King seemed to be crowned with silver in the dim corridor.

"If you would live, lay down your arms," Hughan told them.

The guards looked at him for a long moment, then in absolute silence they set their weapons down on the floor.

"Go with these men of mine," Hughan said. "You will not be harmed."

The guards came away from the door and went to stand in the custody of Hughan's men. But the servants, who had had no arms to lay down, remained rooted by the threshold.

Eamon stepped forward. The servants were the men and women who had served him breakfast in the throned's own hall. One of them was the man who had brought him wine after he had endured the Master's fury, on the day that he had delivered the Nightholt to Edelred.

It was to that man that Eamon went. He could not remember the gesture Edelred used to dismiss his servants. Even had he been able to, he would not have wanted to mimic it.

Slowly, he reached out and took the servant's hand. The man gazed at him in astonishment and flinched. Eamon earnestly met the man's gaze.

"Please," he whispered, and pointed back at the King's men. "Go with them."

The servant searched his face before tilting his head towards Hughan's men. Pressing his hand once more, Eamon nodded.

The servant turned to those with him and made a couple of quick gestures. The other servants replied with movements of their own – one of them gestured wildly towards the Master's door – but the servant to whom Eamon had spoken shook his head. He turned his hand fluidly in Eamon's direction before gesturing to Hughan's men.

A moment later the King's men watched in silence as the servants stepped away from Edelred's door. Eamon lightly touched the leading servant's arm as he passed. Having attracted the man's attention, Eamon laid his right hand over his heart.

"Thank you."

The man bowed.

The guards and servants were escorted away by the King's men. As they disappeared into the dark, Eamon looked back to the throned's door. It stood before them, dark, unguarded, forbidding. The very silence of it crept into Eamon's blood.

In striking bound, Eben's son…

Hughan handed his shield to the man to his left. "Wait for me here."

"Yes, sire."

Hughan looked back to the door. Eamon felt ashamed. Was he to remain with the surviving bodyguard and accompanying King's men while the King fought against the throned? Yet why should he think himself worthy of going to that battle with the King? He was nothing but an encumbrance. If he went into that room with the King, he would fall, and the King would fall with him; they would both end in begging mercy from the Master while he tormented them.

Do you think yourself worthy, son of Eben, of begging before me? Do you believe that discarded colours loose you from me? A fool you remain.

Eamon swallowed in a parched throat. He had to be a fool if he thought that he could ever be the King's second in anything but name. He knew the voice was a liar's, but surely it was right now: Eben's blood was in his veins and Eben's son he remained, the traitor's heir, fit only for exile and works of blood…

"First Knight."

Hughan watched him. As he met the King's gaze, Eamon's dark thoughts passed from him, driven back by the King's clear eyes.

Eamon looked at him in awe. "My King," he breathed.

Hughan touched Eamon's shoulder. "Our houses will stand or fall this day. But they will stand or fall together." He touched Eamon's shoulder and smiled. Both gestures were as bright calls to courage and to hope.

"Come, Eamon Goodman. Stand with me."

Wordlessly, Eamon nodded.

So it was, in the heart of Dunthruik on a day of blood and smoke, the heir of Ede and the heir of Eben set their hands against a darkened door and passed together over the threshold of the throned.

CHAPTER XX

Eamon stood in the Star's wake as they passed through the doorway into a vale of shadow and flame. The darkness clawed at Eamon's skin and drove at his heart; fire stirred maliciously at his brow. It poured fear into his veins like poison.

But the King was there. The living shadows fell back before him.

Eamon knew the room into which they went. It was broad and high, built of red stones woven together like flame-threads. The May light fled from the shattered windows, as though even it dared not go where the King trod. The angled, unknown letters from the Nightholt glinted in the floor, casting back their glowers in a sea of shifting embers. Before them was a wide, dark table. The letters there moved in the wood like worms. Upon that table lay a tome darker than the blackened night; behind it stood its Master and Lord Arlaith, his last Hand. Edelred's grey eyes glinted. Eamon shuddered. They were eyes that had so often seen into his soul.

Despoiler of Allera and usurper of the River Realm, the Master smiled.

"And so the Serpent is led before me." Edelred's voice was thick with pleasure. "You have done well, my son."

Eamon recoiled.

Hughan strode through the darkness; it fell apart before him.

"Hear me, Edelred," he said. "This man is no son of yours, and I break any bond that you have laid on him by saying it."

Edelred regarded Hughan. He looked the King up and down with an amused glance before throwing back his head in a pounding laugh.

"Who are you, Serpent, to come into my hall and speak of loosing bonds? The man whom you so proudly bring by your side is mine." His gaze became eviscerating. "He knows it. Eben's son has been mine since before his days were writ."

Eamon trembled. His mind was filled with the hundred times he had knelt before the Master and received his kiss. Surely he could never be more than the Master's thrall?

The King stood, undaunted, before the throned. The sight called Eamon on to courage.

As sudden strength flooded him, Eamon met the gaze of the glowering man who had tormented him for so long.

"My father's name was Elior," he said fearlessly. "I am his son, and he was no man of yours."

For the briefest moment Edelred's face became so dire that it might have bansheed the very darkness.

"Miserable snake!" Edelred hissed. The words cut like knives. Then suddenly the long smile returned. "Never shall you be more than a worthless puppet."

"Edelred." Hughan spoke the name with such authority that a grey trace of fear passed across the throned's face. "You have harried my First Knight too long. You will no more."

Edelred laughed. "You cannot command me, Serpent!"

"Your tongue is false, as are the words you utter," Hughan answered. "No serpent am I: I am Hughan Brenuin, true beam of that house."

"What grand titles you take unto yourself, little upstart princeling," Edelred sneered. He leaned forward across the table, a grim light in his eyes. "Tell me, *Serpent*, what true beam is it that hails from the womb of a mere woman? Where is the kingliness, the authority of your line? In a woman?" Edelred laughed sharply. "Your line's authority lies crushed in the dust at Edesfield – never did you inherit it!" The throned looked at Hughan as though at an erring boy. "True beam! Nay, child of forked blood; the star of your house fell and died when Eben and I plunged our swords into Ede's heart."

Eamon gaped in horror. Hughan was not of Ede's line but of Elaina's. His ancient sire not a King but a duke. His heart quailed. How could he not have thought it before? Being but the son of a duke, how could Hughan's blood run pure?

The throned watched Hughan fiercely, with smile and gaze so condemning that Eamon wondered how Hughan could meet it. But the King met it without a trace of fear.

"Elaina's blood was no weaker than her brother's." Hughan grew in brightness as he spoke. "Through it many things will be undone.

"Aras, son of Amar, who named yourself Edelred," the King pronounced, "you have wrongfully striven in plots and wars against my house and against this land, turning fathers against their sons and daughters against their mothers. You cast down the high places of this city and realm, and laid your own in their stead, calling yourself Master and taking a hall which was never yours to claim. By your hands and your schemes this land has been filled with toil and blood, with shattered oaths and broken houses, with tear-strewn fields and brittle hearts. You have sown your power in a pestilence of violence and of hatred." Hughan's eyes never once left the throned's face. "I have come, Aras," he said, "to call you to account for all that you have done."

Edelred raised an incredulous eyebrow at him. "You are but a child, Serpent," he hissed. "You think to bring judgment on me? You may know my name, but I will not answer to you."

"You will answer. You will cede your wrongful hold over this land and you will render the Nightholt to me. Do so, and I will be merciful to you."

"What mercy would you give to me, Serpent?" Edelred sneered.

"I cannot offer you your life, for by that you must answer for your deeds. But you will have my pardon," Hughan added gently, and as he spoke the gaze with which he beheld the throned showed pity and kindness, "and the peace of my house."

Eamon's breath stole from him. Even after all that Edelred had done, Hughan was willing to forgive him.

Arlaith's face was a picture of astonishment. The Hand had not spoken a word. It was as if he and Eamon could do nothing but witness the words and deeds of the ones they served.

Edelred held Hughan's gaze in silence for a long time.

"I see that you took thought, Serpent, as to how you would defeat my Gauntlet in my realm and take my city. Even to the Source you went," he laughed, "and that was bold of you. In these matters you have been fortunate. I see also that you have pondered long, filling your mind with words too great for you, so that you might bring yourself before me in a manner suited to the lofty cause you claim."

Slowly Edelred came round the table to stand before the King. His armour glinted. Power shifted in the ground. The light in the dark letters eagerly moved to follow the wake of their Master. The throned's grey eyes passed over Eamon; they terrified him.

Edelred spoke again. "But, Serpent," he breathed, his voice thunderous in the hanging dark, "did you ever think what you would do should I refuse your spurious, ill-attempted grandiloquence?"

"Yes," Hughan answered evenly.

"And what then?" Edelred's face broke in a crushing laugh. "What then, Brenuin! What when you lose your life to me? What of your precious land and promise then, Serpent?"

Hughan remained silent. Eamon quivered. He wondered how long the King had grappled, in the countless long nights since he had learned of the right of his house, with the very fear that the throned now named.

Edelred peered at Hughan. "Have you no answer? Did it not come to you that, by your death, you would irrevocably commit all that is already mine to me?" Edelred laughed. "You have no heir, Serpent. You have no house, and without heir or house, this city and this land will have no other help. They will be mine." He fixed Hughan with a penetrating stare. "Will you risk that, Star of Brenuin?"

For a moment Eamon nearly warned Hughan against the folly, for confronting the throned was surely just that. His trembling lips parted to speak, but before he could, Hughan met his gaze. It stilled him.

The King's look, as he turned back to the throned, spoke of courage beyond measure.

"If you believe, Edelred, that this land's promise is ended when my house falls," he said, "then you know nothing."

Edelred was unperturbed. "Then leave with your scales, Serpent, and let another bear it."

"I will not."

Suddenly there was light about Edelred's palms. The same light flowed through him like blood. It pulsed crimson. As it grew, the walls and floors of the room flared with it until all was alight and the Nightholt blazed with wrath. All this fire Edelred raised into his hands and he looked hard at Hughan.

"Your blood will answer for your insolence."

With a gesture that seemed enough to strike down a mountain, Edelred cast the fire from his hands. It cracked and lurched toward Hughan with monstrous speed, blinding in its intensity.

In that terrible moment Eamon thought that all was lost; in that moment he did not remember how the King's voice had commanded Edelred's to depart, nor how the King had stood before the palace artillery. In his fear he remembered nothing of the King until he saw Hughan lift his left hand. The blue light danced forth from it.

The flames in the air and in Edelred's hands died at once, collapsed and dissipated in unearthly hisses and howls. Edelred flinched back with an angry cry.

As the light about Hughan grew, the floor of the room shook and the letters carved in it writhed and churned. The blue light washed over them and drove into them, binding them and breaking them until they fell still, never to glint more. The light ran on towards the Nightholt and engulfed it, dousing the hellish fire that lived on its pages.

Then, as suddenly as it had come, the blue light faded away.

Eamon's breath returned to him. He felt that something terrible had been forced from the room.

In the silence that followed, Edelred glared balefully at Hughan; even Arlaith's face was agog. The King stood calmly and lowered his hand.

"Edelred, once more I ask you," Hughan said. Eamon heard a patient earnestness in his voice that he had never before known. It was then that he understood that the King truly sought the throned's surrender. "Turn from your works and receive my mercy."

But the throned did not answer. Instead Edelred reached to his neck and unfastened his great cloak. He cast it aside with a grand gesture, revealing the glinting, gold-hued plate beneath. Then Edelred drew his sword. The blade was long and broad, riven with letters such as the Nightholt bore, and the weapon's gilded hilt was bejewelled and finely wrought. As Eamon looked at it the blade glistened red, as though it were already stained crimson by Hughan's blood.

Silently Hughan drew his own blade. The swordsong as it came from its scabbard was unlike anything Eamon had ever heard, filling his heart with wonder. The King's cross-guard had on it two unicorns, and a long shining snake had been crafted about the hilt. The blade itself shone like living silver.

The throned laughed. "Your light will not save you. Your blood will go down into the dust, Serpent," he snarled.

Suddenly Edelred turned the blade in his hands and stabbed for Hughan's face. The King parried the piercing blow at once, turned Edelred's sword away, and returned with a strike of his own. The throned blocked.

The two stepped back from each other. Edelred smiled softly as he prowled about the King, flexing his fingers on the hilt of his blade. Hughan moved with him, watching him carefully.

As the King and the throned clashed again, Eamon saw movement from the corner of his eye. He turned.

Now that his Master and the King fought, Arlaith seemed to have been loosed from whatever had held him still and silent so long. Eamon noticed that the Hand had dispensed with the yellow-trimmed cloak he had borne into battle, and his cloak now showed the red trim of the Right Hand.

For a moment Eamon felt a stab of envy, but it did not last. Arlaith took a step closer to the table. Though his face was turned to the duel between King and throned, Arlaith's eyes glanced every now and then to where the Nightholt lay.

Hating to take his eyes from the King, Eamon firmed his grip on his sword and swiftly stepped to the table. In his distraction, Arlaith did not see him coming until Eamon had reached his side. Hughan's First Knight halted there and turned the point of his sharp blade towards Edelred's Right Hand. Seeing the glint of the sword Arlaith looked at him, first in surprise and then in hatred. The Nightholt was but a hand away.

"Don't touch it," Eamon commanded grimly.

Arlaith fell back a pace from the table. Eamon glanced back at the King; he and the throned engaged in a series of feints, testing each other's skill. Neither man had yet been hit, though both came perilously close to receiving crippling wounds. Despite his armour and the fatigue of the morning's battle, Hughan moved agilely. Edelred seemed almost twice the King's strength but still he landed no blow – but neither did the King.

Trying to keep half an eye on Arlaith, Eamon watched the two opponents fall apart again. The hall rang with the sound of their swords.

Suddenly Edelred put all his force into a hacking blow aimed at Hughan's throat. The King quickly turned his own blade, blocking the blow with the flat of it. As he did so, Edelred tore back his sword and pivoted it round with terrifying speed and equal force to strike against the other side of the King's neck.

As the sword came round, Hughan brought his left arm up. There was a shrill ringing as Edelred's sword jarred against the King's gauntlet. The judder ran through Hughan's hand. A look of enraged surprise flashed across Edelred's face.

In that moment of surprise Hughan brought his sword down in a powerful stab towards Edelred's stomach. The throned twisted back and left with a furious cry, escaping the blow. But the motion forced him to withdraw his blade. As Edelred prepared to re-enter the fight, Hughan raised his sword from the stab, drawing the blade thickly across the throned's abdomen.

Edelred howled as tabard and flesh split before the blade, and blood issued from the wound. It ran in great gushes down the throned's side. Edelred drove his left hand over the gash.

Hughan returned with another blow. With a cry of humiliated rage, Edelred blocked it. He stepped back a pace. Hughan turned the blade in his hands and brought his sword back for another attack. He stabbed it across Edelred's left arm where the gilded vambrace ended.

The blade sheered across the throned's left hand. Blood thickened Edelred's armour.

Eamon gaped at the two men. Why did the throned not use the red light? Was he too afraid? – or unable?

Eamon's heart rose into his throat in fearful anticipation.

Would Edelred fall?

He glanced at Arlaith. The Right Hand's face was paler now than Eamon had ever seen it.

Edelred's calculated and confident style disappeared. With a thunderous cry – and slashes thick and furious enough to match it – the throned launched himself at Hughan. Hughan gave back before the sudden onslaught. The King's face set in hard concentration as he sought to deflect Edelred's rage.

The throned struck down powerfully for a cut at Hughan's left side; the King blocked. The two swords locked together. The force jarred through both men.

Edelred turned and drove the strength of his whole bloody body against Hughan. He jammed his left forearm up hard into Hughan's gorget. A series of unintelligible screams came from Edelred's lips. The King staggered. Edelred ground his armoured arm hard against the King's throat. Hughan's sword was still locked against Edelred's; he was pinned.

Edelred roared with vicious laughter. Hughan slammed his sword hard along the length of Edelred's blade until his own cross-guard hit the throned's steel. The King twisted the guard, wrenching the sword away from Edelred's hand. At the same time, the King took his free arm and brought his gauntleted hand down hard into Edelred's elbow.

Edelred's arm came away from the King's neck. The throned's sword spun across the floor. Eamon drew a gaping breath.

He should not have stared so long. As the sword clattered to the bloody floor, Arlaith dived forward. A second later the Right Hand dashed to the rear of the chamber at a break-neck speed. He tore aside one of the room's long drapes, revealing a door. Arlaith wrenched it open and disappeared down into darkness.

The Nightholt was in his hands.

For a second, Eamon froze in horror and surprise. Then he bolted towards the door.

"*Arlaith!*"

The door was narrow and opened into a stairwell crammed with darkness. As Eamon peered into it he heard Arlaith's mad clatter down the steps. Eamon heard cries behind him, heard the throned's voice caught in a great roar of agony, but he could not look back.

He rushed down the stairs in Arlaith's wake. The Right Hand's shadow, a tantalizing and fleeing shade, raced ahead of him. It goaded him on until Arlaith reached the foot of the stairs ahead of him. The Right Hand broke into a run down the ensuing corridor.

"*Arlaith!*" Eamon yelled again. He heard a distant cry behind him. A searing pain shot through his head and palm. It was pain wrought with a scream so piercing that he had to take his balance against the stairwell. Arlaith came to a staggering halt a short distance ahead of him. The Right Hand groped for a wall as he also clutched at his head.

Then, just as suddenly as it had come, the throbbing pain in his brow and hand vanished. Eamon felt a wash of release that left him with peace. Arlaith's face was greyed and sickened. As their eyes met across that long corridor, they both knew what had happened.

Edelred was dead.

For a moment as long as eternity they stared at each other. Eamon's heart pounded. Arlaith's swift breath resounded in the hall. He held the Right Hand's gaze, somehow also holding him still by it, and for a moment he believed that Arlaith would not flee further.

"It's over, Arlaith," he said, and laughed quietly. They were both free. "Over."

The Hand's fingers tightened on the Nightholt. A steely glint filled Arlaith's eyes.

"You're wrong," he answered, and took to his heels once more.

"Arlaith!" Eamon yelled, stunned, but the Hand was already a shrinking figure in the dim expanse of the corridor.

With a cry Eamon charged after him, his armour hampering his movement at every turn. "Arlaith, it's over! *Arlaith!*"

But the Right Hand did not heed him. He turned down another corridor. Forcing as much strength as he could into his limbs, Eamon pressed after him. Where did the Hand think he could go?

As he whirled into the next corridor, he saw something shining on the ground. He just had the time to realize that it was Arlaith's cloak clasp before he saw a puddle of darkness covering the floor. He vaulted the cloak, almost losing his footing as a fold of the garment tripped him. Eamon swore and looked up to see Arlaith pitch himself through a doorway into another room. He followed.

The room was broad but short. There was another doorway at the far side. The room's windows looked down across an interior garden. Dust caught in the streaks of sunlight that fell from the window.

Arlaith took to one side of the room by a long table. Eamon did not stop to wonder why the Hand did; he only cared that he had stopped.

"It's over," Eamon called again, coming to a breathless halt. "He's dead, Arlaith, and there is nowhere in this palace or this city that you can go."

Arlaith cast him a withering look. "You think you can outrun me?" he laughed. With horrid foreboding Eamon realized that the man was barely out of breath.

"You will not outrun me," he managed, "and you will not hide from me. I will follow you and I will find you, and I will fight you if I must. But before you run or fight, Arlaith, know that the King's mercy is also for you. Surrender yourself and the Nightholt, and receive it."

Arlaith smiled at him. Something about it rocked Eamon's very core.

"You would have me take the Serpent's mercy?" the Right Hand asked. "Why is that, Lord Goodman? Perhaps it is because you know that, if I fight you, the next your precious Serpent will find of you is a ruddy mulch in a dark corner?"

"I would have you take it for your own sake," Eamon answered earnestly.

"Oh, *for my own sake?*" Arlaith laughed again. "That's Lord Goodman all over! Always the altruist, always thinking of the other man, whatever his colour. Always trying to do good, always trying to save, always trying to salve his own conscience. It has entertained me," he added, and as he spoke he set the Nightholt down on the table. "The Raven's Bane, the Right Hand, the law-maker, the Quarter Hand, the Head-bringer, the Line-defier, the Hand, the first lieutenant, the sword-render, the lieutenant, the ensign, the cadet. That's my Goodman." He smiled delightedly and his eyes took on a vicious, sinister sheen. "That's my Ratbag."

Eamon's blood ran cold. He stared.

Arlaith's eyes fixed on him, smiling and goading. Horror and dread churned in every fibre of his being.

"What did you call me?" Eamon whispered.

Arlaith cocked his head pleasantly to one side. "Oh, I'm sorry –

perhaps you did not hear me properly? And who can blame you?" he cooed. "You've had a very difficult year."

As he spoke, Eamon recognized the strange familiarity that he had always seen in Arlaith's face. It twisted and shivered until it tore away. In its place appeared another face that was known to him. The dark eyes, the unkempt hair, the athletic build – but most of all, the smile.

Eamon lurched as that face smiled, and smiled, and smiled at him.

"*Poor* Eamon," it said. "Poor *Ratbag*."

Eamon stared at him. A torturous, cantankerous sickness coursed through his veins, devouring each, one by one. The man before him laughed.

It could not be.

"Did you honestly never figure it out?"

Eamon reeled. He scarcely registered the sword in the man's hand.

"But then, you always were a little dense." The man laughed again.

Ladomer laughed.

"You had better hope that you're as thick-skinned as you are headed!"

Ladomer lunged at him.

Eamon's shaking limbs struggled to respond. He brought his blade up, and barely managed to parry.

Ladomer struck and held the quivering blades together in a vicious and binding block.

"Well, Ratbag," Ladomer said cheerily, "isn't this fine?"

He tore his blade from the bind and stepped back a moment; the hilt slipped in Eamon's hands. He tried to strengthen his grip and his resolve.

"Ware left," Ladomer cried, stabbing for Eamon's left shoulder.

Eamon parried but knew that Ladomer toyed with him.

"Ware right!"

Another clash of blades as Ladomer thrust again. "Very good, Cadet Goodman," Ladomer crooned. "*So very good*. Have you been practising?"

"Stop!" Eamon's voice leapt suddenly to his throat in an angry, grief-fretted cry.

"Tired already?" Ladomer clucked his tongue disapprovingly. "Oh dear. Ware!" he cried, and came down hard for Eamon's face. Eamon blocked the blow, more forcefully this time.

"Stop!" he yelled. Tears burned deep in his eyes.

"Are you at all well read, Mr Goodman?" Ladomer came in with a sweep at Eamon's arms that forced him back a pace. "I've heard some say that you should have considered the university. Had you gone you might have read some of the early epics, or the great sagas out of the north, maybe even a little of the River Poet. I'm told that close reading of some of his tragedies will lead you to the conclusion that spurning the path laid out for you is somewhat arrogant – the erudite call it hubris – and leads to rather unfortunate consequences."

He laughed and swept down at Eamon's arm again – an easy parry. Eamon knew that Ladomer knew it. "Yet you have done it. Such hubris! What is it that your friend Anderas used to say?" he added thoughtfully. "Something about style? He forgot, I suppose, that there is only one viable end for a gentleman of such a calibre as yourself. It is so unfortunate that he won't ever hear how you matched it."

Eamon parried another blow and gaped. Ladomer feigned surprise.

"Oh, didn't you know?" he said. "I had your good captain shot this morning. It was a good deal easier than killing Greenwood, or your servants, or those infernal cadets of yours. An arrow loosed in battle strikes, as they say, where it strikes."

A horrific image leapt before Eamon's eyes, of Anderas impaled by a black feathered arrow and lying on the plain before Dunthruik in a pool of his own blood.

Ladomer came forward with a cutting blow aimed at Eamon's neck. Eamon stumbled back to avoid it. His limbs felt weary and his heart grossly weighted. He wanted to cry out his rage – but the face before him was the face of a man he loved.

Ladomer laughed grimly.

"Think of all that time I spent on you, Ratbag. Years and years! You think that the little fire that destroyed your miserable bookshop was an accident?" he asked pleasantly. "It was not. I joined you to the Gauntlet; I groomed you and prepared you to take your oath. Did you ever wonder why you were sent to Dunthruik, and under the auspices of lieutenant?" He eyed Eamon spitefully. "It was no merit of yours. A regional Hand and captain visited by the Right Hand do as they are told."

Eamon's face broke in enraged hurt; Ladomer grinned to see it. "Did you ever wonder why you became a first lieutenant, or were elected to the Hands?" Ladomer glared at him. "Oh, I had to spend *years*, Ratbag, telling you that you were good at the things you did, when you were not. Years listening to your woes." As they circled each other, Ladomer's face became a picture of pernicious pity. "Do you think that I didn't howl with laughter every time you came to me, your face filled with pious sorrow? But it was not so much your face," he spat, "it was you. You were utterly ridiculous then, and you have refused to grow out of it. Though perhaps you will shrink!" he added, swiping for Eamon's neck again.

Eamon blocked the blow and stared grimly into Ladomer's face. The dark eyes laughed at him even then. A hundred memories raced through Eamon, of words spoken and smiles given, of jokes and joys shared and comfort received. Every time Ladomer had sat with him in the Star, every time they had met in the streets of Dunthruik… when he had been counselled and questioned and surveyed…

It had been the Right Hand.

He looked uncomprehendingly back at him. "I only ever loved you, Ladomer, and to you, Arlaith, I was gracious."

"You were naive," Ladomer returned. "I had only to fawn and wail to overwhelm your little heart. It was not grace to let me live; it was stupidity – as only you can embody that virtue." He fixed

Eamon with a disparaging gaze. "I never despised you more than in that moment."

Eamon's mind turned back to Arlaith's apology, the look of awe on his face as he had spoken: *"I do not think that I would have said the same in your place."*

Eamon shook his head. "No, Ladomer; you despised me because I showed you grace. You despised me because you could not bind me." Angrily he matched the gaze that pinned him. "Now, you will despise me because you cannot break me."

Eamon turned the sword in his hand and struck at Ladomer's arm. It was a good strike. Ladomer had to work hard to block it. Pressing forward, Eamon arched his sword and swung again. Ladomer parried and stepped back. Eamon wondered what armour the man wore, and cursed himself for not taking better note of it earlier that day. The man had a thick black tabard, and Eamon could not tell if there was armour below it or not. Without armour, one good strike to the chest would kill him.

Did he mean to kill Ladomer?

In that moment Ladomer caught a weakness in his attack and countered an oncoming strike, turning it into a blow of his own. It was a strong one; Eamon felt it judder through his arm and remembered how tired he was. But he could not falter.

He came back from the blow, disengaging. His chest heaved under the wretched press of his armour. Ladomer also looked short of breath; it encouraged him. They both adjusted their grips on their swords. As Eamon watched, Ladomer reached to his belt and drew a dagger. The blade caught in the light and Eamon's eyes went wide.

"Recognize this?" Ladomer asked.

It was Eben's dagger. Eamon paled with anger.

Ladomer turned the blade in his hand as he prowled. "I'm a great appreciator of the arts, as you know. So I thought, wouldn't it be appropriate if I took your life with this? After all, this whole sorry story has been about poetry."

"*What?*" Eamon yelled, head spinning.

"Did you think that your blood truly had some extra special something, granting it greatness?" Ladomer spat. "No! It was Cathair who taught the throned a love of poetry. In time Edelred came to appreciate it. He thought that it would be appropriately poetic if he used you to strike down the Serpent."

Ladomer lunged for Eamon's thigh. Swift as lightning, Eamon dropped his sword down along the length of his limb, locking the two blades together in a shivering bind. Ladomer stabbed for his neck with the dagger; the letters along its length glinted wickedly in the light.

Eamon tore one hand from his sword hilt and seized Ladomer's wrist. Ladomer moved his hand to bring the crushing force of his vambrace around Eamon's fingers.

Never had Eamon been gladder of a gauntlet than in that moment.

He pressed all his strength against the dagger inching closer to his neck. He had to break free, but he did not know how.

Ladomer's dark eyes bore into him, more terrifying than any blow. "There was no grand design, Goodman, no fulfilment of prophecy. You were baited and trained for his amusement, and for mine." He pressed forward harder with the dagger. "You, Goodman," Ladomer sneered, "were nothing more than a poetic whim."

Eamon glared at him. "I like poetry," he retorted.

He forced his right hand up and launched the pommel of his sword towards Ladomer's face. The blade followed behind it in a broad arc.

Only Ladomer's considerable skill saved him. With a curse he leapt back from the sword-sweep – he had to either withdraw or lose his hand. Ladomer's hand straightened so as to pull from his grip; Eben's dagger was left behind. Eamon found it in his fingers as Ladomer pulled away.

As the dagger came to rest in the circle of his hand Eamon looked at its grim letters. In them – and the blade they tainted – the treachery of his house was commemorated and sealed. Eben had been killed with it, and, urged on by its grisly glint, Eamon had himself nearly been convinced to take his own life.

He felt something in his palm, but it was not the burn of the mark that he had borne so long. It was the steely shimmer of the King's grace.

It was as Eamon gazed at the blade then that the letters shivered and suddenly made sense to him, and for the first time he read what had so often been pronounced over him:

"*In striking bound.*"

A grim look passed over his face. Unless it was to Hughan, he would be bound no more.

Rejoicing at his resolve, the King's grace rushed into his hands. Suddenly the long blade of the dagger was aflame with blue light that danced through metal and letters, inflecting them with brilliance.

Ladomer fell still and stared in horror as the light penetrated deep into every part and pore of the blade and its hilt. There was a sharp crack and the blade split from hilt to point, shattering into dozens of pieces which scattered harmlessly to the ground. Then the hilt itself quivered until it too was rent in two by the power of the King's grace.

Eamon looked down at the sorry remains on his hand. A weight lifted from his chest.

Eben's dagger and its curse were gone.

"In breaking loosed." Letting the hilt drop from his hand, Eamon laughed.

For a moment Ladomer looked terrified, but the Right Hand swiftly changed his expression.

"You think that you can frighten me with your parlour tricks?" he snickered. "Do you honestly think that you can defeat me? Or kill me?"

A chill ran through Eamon.

Ladomer sneered at him. "You may fight me, Eamon," he said. "You may even draw blood. But you cannot kill me. How do I know that? Because I know you, better than you know yourself."

Smiling, Ladomer charged forward again, the shards of the dagger crunching beneath his feet. As he tore onwards, he launched a devastating cut towards Eamon's neck. Eamon swerved back from the attack and blocked it; again their blades locked together.

"You know, we have a lot in common," Ladomer told him. "But you are not half the man I am. You cannot ride, or fight, or speak, or strike, or act even a third as well as I." His smile turned into a hellish grin. "I'm even a better traitor than you are."

With a furious cry, Eamon slammed his sword down along the length of Ladomer's blade and knocked it away. The blade went spinning across the room. Before he could strike again, Eamon adjusted the awkward hold of his hilt.

But he was too slow. Ladomer hurled himself forward. Suddenly two flaming, gloved hands were at either side of Eamon's face; red light seared round them.

The Right Hand was not just a changer.

Eamon screamed as the red light cracked through his skull like knife-blows. The two hands clasped on his face like a vice and clawed mercilessly into his flesh and mind, rending him apart. He could not bear it much longer. Though he tried, he could not tear the burning hands off him.

Ladomer drove him up against the wall and fixed his head and neck against the stones as the reddened knives continued to strike. The pain was so great, Eamon could not keep hold of his sword.

"Save yourself, King's man!"

In his arching agony, Eamon heard Ladomer's mocking voice. The pain drove deeper into him, seeking that part of his mind where the whole could be broken.

Suddenly the blue light launched itself about him, setting itself ferociously against the red. Ladomer gave a cry of enraged surprise as the light erupted between them and threw him back. The Right Hand crashed heavily against the stony floor. Released, Eamon staggered, keeping himself upright only by merit of the wall behind him. He could not think and could barely see.

Suddenly Ladomer lunged away. Snatching up his sword, he lurched for the Nightholt.

Eamon wrenched himself from the wall, swept up his sword, and leapt towards him.

"Don't touch it!" he yelled, swiping down hard at Ladomer's outstretched arm. Ladomer flinched. Eamon followed up with a second blow. The Right Hand scowled viciously, turned, and bolted for the door.

For a moment Eamon only watched him run.

Fires, Gauntlet, marks, Nightholt. It had been Ladomer all along.

With a yell he charged after the Right Hand.

His quarry took to a stairwell, this one narrower than the first; Eamon turned sideways to run down it. He could not use his sword in so narrow a space. He whipped out his dagger and kept running.

As he raced down the spiralled corners of the tight stairs, a glow of red light rushed up the well towards him. An enormous sphere of angry flame followed it.

For a moment he froze with fear. Then he suddenly remembered standing against Cathair.

Hurriedly Eamon raised his hand and a wash of blue light struck out to shatter the red. But in his haste he lost his grip on his dagger. He became aware of it only when he heard the grim clatter of the blade running down the stairs before him. A second blast came at him. He was forced to block it. He still had no room to use his sword. As he pressed down the fire-beleaguered stairs after Ladomer, his only defence was his outstretched left hand and the grace that ran to his aid.

Ladomer sent another ball of light at him. Eamon raised his hand again, and an arc of blue light struck out to meet it; the two lights collided in the stairwell, blasting out a huge slab of the adjoining internal wall. As the stones and beams crumbled, Eamon could just about make out Ladomer's form as he plunged through the opening and into the dusty room beyond.

Eamon steadied himself on the crumbling wall of the stairway. Weariness flooded vengefully through his limbs and he knew far too well that he could not chase or fight much longer. For a moment he stared at the cavernous opening, which dribbled stone and dust like a bleeding wound; he hung back. But Ladomer's shadow and goading laugh spurred him on, and suddenly he burst through the crumbled opening into another room.

Ladomer had stopped just beyond the broken wall. Drawing up his sword again, Eamon launched himself at his enemy with a great cry, forcing the man to turn and parry the blow. Together they began another grim sword dance across the floor of the hall.

"It's over," Eamon yelled, his voice ragged and breathless. "Damn it, Ladomer!" Why couldn't he understand? "*Over!*"

"Damn you!" Ladomer returned caustically. He was panting. His parries and thrusts were slower than before. He hacked down at Eamon's neck. Eamon groggily blocked the blow and the blades jarred into another stalemate.

Ladomer drove forward his red-lit left hand. With an exhausted cry, Eamon brought up his own left hand from his hilt, and grabbed Ladomer's. He stopped the palm before the sparking flames reached his face. So they stood, blade locked against blade, hand against hand, in a long hall in Dunthruik.

"Perhaps you *want* to die," Ladomer mused, peering at his face past the long block. The man's dark eyes moved like shadows behind the sparring lights. "Perhaps you've realized that you have nothing left. Could that be it, Ratbag?" Ladomer laughed again. "Hughan doesn't need you any more, neither does the throned, neither does Dunthruik. What irony!"

Tears stung Eamon's eyes. "That's not true!" he yelled.

"Oh, but it is. You were always the pawn and the puppet," Ladomer spat, "whether Hughan's or Edelred's. They've both used you and now there's nothing of you left, and nothing left for you to do – except to seek a noble death, falling in battle against the Right Hand."

Ladomer pressed forward with blade and hand. Eamon's arms trembled with fatigue as the Right Hand fixed him in his gaze.

"Let me tell you something, Eamon," Ladomer hissed. "Death isn't noble – and yours won't be."

With a cry that was half a sob, Eamon wrenched himself back from the bind. Ladomer staggered forward, his sword coming down hard on his own outstretched arm. There was a ringing clang as the blade struck against the vambrace.

Eamon withdrew several paces across the room, panting, blood throbbing in his veins like fire. He knew that he needed to take better hold of his sword, to press against Ladomer and fight, to fight hard – even in that moment he should strike at the Right Hand while his foe was disadvantaged – but part of Eamon's ailing heart had heard a grain of what it feared was truth.

Why was he fighting Ladomer?

His eyes swam with exhaustion and he forced himself to focus on Ladomer's face.

"It's over, Ladomer," he tried again. "Stop this!"

Ladomer glared at him balefully. "Oh, I'll stop. I'll stop when you're dead and gutted, Goodman!"

He lunged.

There was fire in Ladomer's hands once more. It bit foully into Eamon as Ladomer lunged for him with the sword. The flame shivered along Ladomer's blade and arched across into Eamon's hands, penetrating deep into his armour and searing his weary flesh.

"You understand me?" Ladomer roared. "*When you're dead!*"

The flame was agonizing. Eamon tore away from it. As Ladomer's wild eyes and wilder hands came after him, Eamon's resolve was suddenly gone.

Turning, Eamon raced away down the long hall. In seconds Ladomer was behind him but Eamon's sudden fear drove him on faster. Ladomer's face was twisted with mocking hatred and rage as he followed.

Eamon ran from the corridor and up a small flight of stairs. A great blast of red light came up it behind him, followed by Ladomer's frenzied laughter. Eamon just managed to clear the path of the careering light. Stones shattered in his wake.

"Run, Ratbag!" Ladomer yelled. "*Run!* Run, like you've always done."

Tears burnt on Eamon's face. What could he do? He was exhausted, shattered, and broken, and Ladomer could not be stopped; he could not do it.

In a second his long months in Dunthruik passed through his mind, along with every moment of fear and self-loathing that he had borne in them. None of them were as strong as the torrent of emotion that drove him into the depths of the West Wing.

Would he let Ladomer shame him as well as betray him?

He turned into another room with long tapestries on its walls. Eamon recognized where he was: one of the long series of rooms that led to Ellenswell. Whether he had sought it purposefully or not, he did not know.

As he raced into the dark room, he saw a recess in the far wall and knew at once that the alcove led down into the well. How clearly he remembered that day when he had been there, with Mathaiah and Cathair, and how they had opened the well with the heart of the King. He remembered the blue light filling the well, driving into the stones and driving back shadow until the well had opened.

It was the place where, despite his treachery, blood, and fears, Eben had stood against Edelred and hidden the Nightholt.

Eamon's heart and sight returned to him. He looked about himself. The place where he stood was divided from the room that led into it by a thick wall with a curved ornamental doorway. He carefully pressed himself down to one side of it.

"Stand, King's man!" he whispered to himself. In moments Ladomer would charge into the room seeking him and would not see him. When the Right Hand passed through the doorway where Eamon hid, he would strike him.

For a few agonizing seconds Eamon heard nothing but his own breathing and his efforts to calm it. Then the pursuing footsteps burst into the room on the other side of the arch. They slowed.

Ladomer laughed loudly into the silence. "I cannot believe you, Eamon!" he cried. "Of all the places you could have chosen to die, you choose this?"

The footsteps circled the other room, but they were not close enough.

"I see that rats, when cornered, fight like rats," Ladomer continued. "I know you're here, Eamon. And I know that you won't leave alive."

There was a long silence.

"You know, your wench hid from me, too," Ladomer called. "It didn't save her – and it didn't save your child. It won't save you. What a happy family," he sneered. "I killed them all – your whore, your bastard, and your father."

Eamon bit down hard on his tongue to keep back the howl of rage that came into his throat, and waited. He knew what Ladomer did not: Alessia was alive.

He felt a throbbing in the air. He had waited too long. Too late he realized Ladomer's plan. Eamon moved back from the wall just as an enormous surge of red light struck it, smashing it to ruin.

Eamon staggered in the force of the blast. As he struggled to get his feet, Ladomer erupted through the smoking stones. Eamon blocked the first blow, but then Ladomer stabbed from the right for the inner part of his thigh. Eamon strained every muscle in his body to block it. It was almost more than he had in him. He coughed as smoke from the broken stones clawed at his eyes.

Ladomer brought his vambrace and blade hard against Eamon's sword, then pushed and twisted it from Eamon's grip. Eamon forced every tendon and fibre of muscle he possessed against the agonizing downward motion, but he could not stop it.

His sword fell to the ground. Ladomer's pommel – followed by his blade – struck dangerously near his head. Eamon leapt back.

Ladomer swung the pommel after him, almost hooking the blade-point under the edge of his armour. Eamon reeled back, his limbs aching and his armour like a dead weight upon him. His chest heaved with unimaginable exhaustion as he looked at his foe. His dagger was lost and his sword was far out of reach. As the Right Hand advanced on him, desperation filled Eamon's breast.

Ladomer raised his blade with a slow smile. "Things aren't looking so good for you just now, are they, Ratbag?"

"No," Eamon agreed, trying not to sound as terrified as he felt. There was only one thing left that he could do.

With a laugh Ladomer swung at him, driving at his groin and legs. With every ounce of his desperate courage, Eamon stepped forward into the blow, narrowly avoiding it, and took firm hold of Ladomer's face. He saw the dark eyes filling with rage before they both slipped onto the plain.

CHAPTER XXI

It was dark and the wind howled about them. Eamon felt the blue light near him.

"Please," he cried to it, "help me!"

The light grew bright and gathered about him.

"*Bastard!*" Ladomer yelled.

Eamon scarcely heard him. The King's grace went singing across the plain towards the Right Hand. It dropped and enveloped Ladomer like a cloak of water. With a foul cry he staggered back, clutching his head.

"No!" he roared.

Eamon gasped: though he was not breaching Arlaith, the skies around him were pierced with visions. Eamon saw the throne room, its dire paintings hideously bold in the light of a forgotten day. Arlaith knelt before the throned, shaking.

"Ashway was right, Master," Arlaith was saying. "The Serpent's heir was there."

"And you let him slip from your grasp." The throned spat thunder. Arlaith cowered. "You let snakes spirit him away from under your very eyes."

Arlaith's face was grim, set, pallid. He had failed the Master. His clenched eyes anticipated punishment.

In the agonizing silence, a sliver of a smile spread on the throned's face.

"Ashway spoke of the traitor's heir, as well as the Serpent's."

Arlaith could barely breathe. "Yes, Master."

"And so Eben's son is at Edesfield," the throned smiled. "Do you not find that poetic, Lord Arlaith?"

Arlaith grimaced. "Yes, Master."

"This Goodman you have found is little more than a boy. But he will be mine; it is in his blood. Already I know the feel of him." The throned's eyes fixed immutably on Arlaith's own. "You will atone for your failure. You will make him mine. He will finish what his line began for me."

Scarcely understanding what he saw, Eamon reeled.

"What would you have me do, Master?"

"Go to Edesfield," Edelred commanded, "and prepare him. Then, when he is ready, bring him to me. The Serpent's heir may be well hidden, but Eben's son will lead us to him, in time."

"I will go under my mother's name," Arlaith said. Arlaith's face changed until it became Ladomer's. "When you wish to send for me, Master, seek after the name of Kentigern…"

Ladomer hissed and cursed. The memory was torn away. Others took its place.

Eamon now saw wooded hills and valleys. He recognized them as the countryside surrounding Edesfield. Arlaith walked with another Hand, among fallen bodies left by a wayfarer skirmish. Arlaith examined them one by one then cast them aside in disgust.

"They aren't all here, my lord," the other Hand told him. "There are only six dead."

"Who is missing?" Arlaith demanded.

The other Hand paused. "One of the boys," he said at last. "Perhaps the snakes took him."

Arlaith snorted. "The Serpent is suffering indeed if he has taken to kidnapping children," he said. "They will not save him from the Master."

"They say that the Serpent is old and ailing," the other Hand answered, and laughed snidely. "Perhaps, my lord, he kidnaps children in the hope of passing one off as his own heir."

Arlaith fell very still and turned to him. "Who is missing?" he asked again.

The Hand looked at the bodies. "That lanky boy, my lord," he answered. "The one taken in by the miller just before the culls. Perhaps you've seen him?"

"Hughan." The name came as a dreadful sound from Arlaith's lips, filled with wrath and fear.

"Are you well, my lord?" the other Hand asked, looking at him with concern. The look swiftly turned to one of horror.

The Hand drew breath but he never spoke again. The next moment he lay dead on the ground, his throat slit by the Right Hand.

The next thing that Eamon saw was Ladomer taking Aeryn's hand in his own.

"It can't be true," Aeryn wept.

"Captain Belaal made me identify his body, Aeryn," Ladomer told her. "He's dead." He dashed false tears from his eyes. "It was terrible, I – I could barely recognize his face…" He shuddered with horror and then looked up. "Aeryn," he whispered, "where is Eamon?"

"I'll tell him." Aeryn drew a shuddering breath and pressed his hand. "I'll tell him, Ladomer."

The images changed again. Among them Eamon saw himself. Over and over he saw Ladomer speaking to him and encouraging him, while all along the Right Hand reviled him. He felt Arlaith's pride and elation as Eamon Goodman was finally convinced to join the Gauntlet and take his oath.

There was a shimmer. Eamon saw the Nightholt resting in Arlaith's hands. He was in a small room, which Eamon recognized to be the quarters of the Right Hand.

Arlaith rose and crossed his chambers to stand before a small mirror. There, the reflected face morphed into that of Lord Cathair. Arlaith inspected his new face, turning it from jowl to jowl, smoothing the pale skin, adjusting the intensity of the green eyes until he was satisfied with his imitation. Then, clutching the Nightholt beneath his robes – robes which bore the mark of the Raven – he left his eyrie, passing through a maze of dark corridors until he reached a vast hallway.

Cathair approached him from the far side. He too held the Nightholt.

Eamon gaped. How could there be two? And did Cathair not see that Arlaith wore his face? Why did the Raven permit Arlaith to go unchallenged?

Arlaith's vision focused in on the Master's tome in Cathair's hands. "What is that you've found in the crypts, Lord Cathair?" he asked.

Cathair's fingers drummed idly across the cover. "Oh, this?" He shrugged. "Nothing of any importance, my lord. It is merely an old book. I mean to add it to my library."

Arlaith looked at the Nightholt again. "Very well, Lord Cathair. You will, of course, inform me if you find anything of significance."

"Of course, my lord. Farewell."

Arlaith turned away to the left. In the same moment, Cathair turned to the right. The Raven did not bow – and Arlaith made no objection to this slight.

Why would Cathair not bow to the Right Hand? And why would Arlaith not protest?

Something about this memory rang false.

Arlaith returned to his eyrie. As he passed the mirror, his face was again his own. Without ever setting his eyes upon it, he dropped his Nightholt into a satchel and drew the bag shut.

He turned towards the mirror; his mirror image turned to meet him. His reflection grinned back at him.

The *reflection...*

Eamon reeled. Cathair had never held the Nightholt. The entire exchange had been a carefully orchestrated conversation between the Right Hand and his own reflection! Was this how Arlaith had convinced the Master of Cathair's treachery, and his own innocence? With a parlour trick?

Eamon knew the Master. Edelred would have been so enraged by the image of the Nightholt in Cathair's hands that he would never have paid heed to the memory's subtle inconsistencies.

Suddenly, Eamon saw Alessia.

"You will not show him!" Ladomer shrieked at the sapphire skies. "You will not!"

But Eamon saw. Alessia stood in the Hands' Hall and curtseyed low before Arlaith.

"You will pay court to Lieutenant Goodman."

Her face was faultlessly expressionless. "Yes, my lord…"

A hundred other moments flashed by; Eamon saw himself at the Crown, saw Arlaith leaning towards him and whispering: "Whatever its guise, Lord Goodman, treachery is a terrible thing. And those who betray those whom they claim to love?" The Right Hand shook his head before looking across the dark box to fix his eyes on Alessia's. "That, Lord Goodman, is most treacherous of all…"

He saw Alessia again, this time brought and cast to her knees before the Right Hand. Eamon gaped in horror.

"I was very clear with you, Lady Turnholt," Arlaith spat. "Very clear indeed, and yet you dared to go against me. Have no fear, you will be answered for your disobedience." Alessia was very still before him. "Where is the maid?" Arlaith demanded.

"Lillabeth?" Alessia whispered. Though her face was wracked with fear she shook her head. "Lillabeth? Please, my lord, she has no part in this –"

"Do you have an earnest desire to be breached again?" Arlaith snarled.

Alessia trembled. "No, my lord –"

"Then answer me," Arlaith hissed. "Where is your maid?"

Alessia shook her head again. "Please, my lord, I do not know. She was not at the house, I… she was not –"

"Do not lie to me!" Arlaith cried, striking her brutally across the face.

"Alessia!" Eamon cried.

Alessia had scarcely been thrown to the ground before the Right Hand snatched her throat and drove his hand viciously against her face.

"Please, my lord!" Alessia screamed. As red light grew about the Right Hand's fingers, she convulsed with anguish. "Eamon!" She sobbed his name as though it might bring him to her. Eamon recoiled. "Eamon!"

"He will not save you," Arlaith sneered. Alessia writhed beneath his burning fingers. "You were only ever his whore."

"No!"

Suddenly Arlaith stopped. With a livid roar he hurled the woman aside.

"Goodman." The word poured like a curse from his lip. "Summon Lord Cathair!" he yelled. Another Hand ran from the room. Arlaith rounded on Alessia. "Do not think that I have finished with you, Turnholt," he seethed. "I have not."

Arlaith stormed from the room, leaving the tormented woman in his wake.

"Alessia!" Eamon wept. He started forward, but he could not comfort her. The vision slipped away.

In its place came the Right Hand's eyrie. Arlaith paced it. Ashway stood before him.

"I tell you, Lord Arlaith, that I cannot make him read it. Nor can I prolong his life much longer. Cathair will execute the Master's command."

"He must not!" Arlaith stormed. "Fool! I need that boy alive. Everything depends on it! I *must* know how to change it."

"If we keep him alive much longer, Cathair will get suspicious," Ashway retorted. "His suspicions *will* reveal us. Is that what you want?"

Arlaith swore violently, then spun and seized Ashway by the throat. "You will find a way," he growled. "You will make him read it. *Understood?* You will do *whatever* is necessary."

Ashway's gagging face swirled away. Arlaith was now moving swiftly through the city streets towards the Brand, carrying a heavy satchel over his shoulder. As he hurried up the steps into the West Quarter College, Captain Waite stepped aside and bowed.

"Good evening, Lord Cathair," the captain said. "Forgive me; we did not expect your return so soon."

Arlaith waved his words away. "I wanted something to read on the road to Ravensill," he said. "One should never be without a good book, captain."

"Of course, Lord Cathair. By your leave, my lord."

"Do go about your business, captain."

Waite bowed again and returned to his office. Arlaith made his way through the college to the Raven's library. No dogs ran to greet him as he entered.

He strode purposefully to the case where Cathair's safe was hidden. A red light appeared in his hand, the shelves shimmered, and the safe opened. Arlaith lifted the satchel and drew out the Nightholt. He placed it into the alcove.

Cathair's library faded and became the East's Handquarter office. Tramist was there.

"His healing of the singer proves nothing," Tramist said. "Has not his house always carried both marks? Besides which, the Master is his keeper; does it truly matter whether he is a snake?"

"That the Master is blind to it suits me well enough, but this snivelling Goodman bastard is a thorn to me, Tramist, and one that I have endured too long," Arlaith retorted. "I mean to rid myself of him, and if you wish to be a friend to me you will do exactly as I say."

"I have always been a friend to you, my lord," Tramist answered.

"Ashway claimed the same," Arlaith snapped. "Do not make his mistakes."

Tramist looked pale. "Yes, my lord."

"Anderas knows something," Arlaith continued. "I am sending him to you with papers tonight. Find out what he knows – and then take care of him."

Tramist bowed. "Yes, Lord Arlaith," he answered.

As Eamon stared, Arlaith went to the throned. But now as Arlaith came striding before the Master, he bore the standard captured from the southern flank of the wayfarer line in one hand, and Eben's dagger in the other. The throned's face was full of wrath.

In rage, Arlaith hurled down the standard before the throned's feet. "Your precious project has gone awry," he yelled, "as I always told you it would."

"Do you dare to gainsay me?" the throned answered. Red light fretted his hands, but Arlaith disdained it.

"Ashway spoke too true, Master, and you were blind to it. Now Eben's bloody bastard son brings the Serpent into the city!"

"Why such fear, Left Hand?" the throned answered with a smile. "You know that I always meant for him to come." Suddenly his face turned bitter and angry, and he struck forward with his palm, sending cracking light all about Arlaith's form.

Suddenly the light ceased. Shuddering, Arlaith met the throned's gaze.

"If you want to live out this day," Edelred told him, "you will honour the oath that binds you, and you will stand with me."

The red light ran again from the throned's hands to Arlaith's. The Right Hand's face turned in pain as the light showed forth on his hands and brow.

"Yes, Master," Arlaith hissed. Though obedient, he was not cowed.

Ladomer screamed.

Eamon's eyes opened. The plain was gone – the Right Hand's face, lashed with red light, changed horribly between Arlaith's and Ladomer's.

After an ear-piercing cry, the Right Hand's knees buckled and he fell.

"Ladomer!" Eamon gasped.

"You blue bastard!" Ladomer yelled, and lashed at Eamon's face. Rather than touching flesh as he intended, Ladomer's hand caught hold of the broken strap of Eamon's helmet. He wrenched the helm from Eamon's head, blinding Eamon for a second.

As the helmet clattered away onto the ground, Eamon felt a

rush of cold air creep beneath his sweat-drenched hair. Ladomer straightened up. Suddenly the Right Hand turned and drove his rising pauldrons deep in Eamon's waistline, just below the breastplate of his armour.

Eamon felt the crushing force of the blow. His breath was torn from him as the shoulder plate impacted; the stomach-churning judder ran up and down his whole body.

He lost his grip on Ladomer's face. Ladomer staggered to his feet. Not a second later, Ladomer hurled Eamon over his back.

As Eamon fell down over Ladomer, he rolled into the fall. His gut ached and no amount of armour articulation could have spared him from the pain in every limb. His body slammed into the ground. He turned on to his back and for a second he lay stunned, seeing nothing but smoke and fire.

He heard Ladomer rise; Ladomer's feet appeared by his dazed head and Eamon saw him stooping for his blade.

Eamon flung out his left hand, grabbed his sword, and brought it over himself just in time to block the killing blow. The Right Hand tried to slip his blade over Eamon's sword.

With strength he had thought spent, Eamon rolled deftly out of the way. Using his left arm like a pivot, he brought himself up to his feet before casting a low lunge at Ladomer's lower legs.

They were both slow and tired, but Ladomer still managed to block the attack. Eamon's grip on the sword was weak. His arm pulsed with the wounds of Cathair's dog.

For a moment Eamon and Ladomer stared at each other and gasped for breath.

"Surrender," Eamon panted desperately.

"Who?" Ladomer asked sarcastically. "You or I?"

"You!" Eamon raged.

Ladomer looked wryly at him. "You know, I never understood why we adopted these clumsy, uncivilized things," he said, flexing his fingers about the hilt of Eamon's blade. "But you can be sure, Goodman, that I will wield it better than you."

Eamon recoiled with fatigue as Ladomer raised the blade and swung at him again. He had not the time to pass his sword into his strong hand. He twisted awkwardly round to take the blow. His right hand was free. He reached towards Ladomer. A huge spark of blue light left his palm and struck his foe.

The Right Hand yelled a vile curse as it touched him. He recoiled. Eamon turned Ladomer's sword back in his hands, and drew it up firmly across Ladomer's ribs and chest from right to left.

It was the sight of blood rather than Ladomer's irate scream that told him that he had landed a blow. As he continued with the strike the sword blade suddenly hit plate.

It was then that Eamon realized that, from the ribs up, the Right Hand wore no armour.

The sword was high in his hands. With a huge effort, Eamon turned to drive the blade deep into Ladomer's chest.

But Ladomer struck back with a powerful thrust. With horrific strength, the Right Hand's blade seared under the edge of Eamon's right pauldron and the rim of his back plate.

Eamon screamed as the blade drove into him. It smashed through his shoulder blade, cracking his ribs and finally puncturing through some channel that allowed air to pass into his lungs. As the shattering pain speared relentlessly through him, blood leapt up in great gushes into his throat and mouth.

In agony he spun away, a terrible weight in his back where Ladomer's sword still clawed through him. He fell heavily to the ground; his own blood spewed in waves beneath him. His gauntleted fingers slipped in it as he tried – and failed – to get a grip on the stones.

It was then that he knew he would die.

Blood cloyed in his throat. He choked violently on it as he turned, with starving lungs and swimming sight, to look back. Ladomer stood over him. The pain in his shoulder and lungs was nearly unbearable. Ladomer set his right hand to the top of the sword hilt, his left beneath it, and turned the point of the blade level with Eamon's gagging throat.

"So much for your house!" Ladomer hissed. "When they come seeking you they will learn at last that the only Goodman is a dead man!"

The bloodied point of the sword dripped gore onto Eamon's face. He tried to blink it from his eyes but it hardly seemed to matter. There was no fear in him as he saw that blade. He could only stare up at the man who had been his friend, and who, hissing and laughing, would kill him.

Ladomer straightened to plunge the blade down.

As the Right Hand raised his arms to lay the full weight of his body into the blow, a figure appeared behind him. Eamon's vision was fast fading, but he thought he saw a trace of blue.

The figure bolted forward, a great sword in his hands. As Ladomer plunged downwards the charging man turned his sword and swung it deep into the Right Hand's side. The long blade drove into unarmoured flesh and bone.

The plunging sword spun out of Ladomer's hands across the floor.

The newcomer tore his blade out of Ladomer. The force of the motion turned the Right Hand to face his unforeseen attacker. Ladomer's agonized face went wide with anger and with horror. He drew his lips open to speak, but no sound ever left them, for the man thrust his sword into Ladomer's undefended ribs and wrenched the blade in a lethal twist.

Ladomer crumpled to the floor, a mass of blood. His pale face came to rest near Eamon's own, the chilling, vacant eyes staring at him across the stones.

Eamon tried to speak, but blood slicked his throat like a choking mucous. It filled his lungs and poured away through the stones from the great gash in his back. With it, power over his limbs failed him.

He felt fear.

The newcomer knelt down by him. The great blue tabard was covered with blood and gore.

Tears ran down his clammy face, and sobs bubbled deep in his blood-filled throat. He did not know if the man near him was hurt and he knew that he would not live to know it.

With a gasping sob Eamon reached out with his failing hand to touch the face that he knew and loved. Darkness crept into his eyes as the one kneeling by him tore off his gauntlets and laid gentle, shining hands onto his face and over his heart.

"Hold on, Eamon," said Hughan.

It was the last thing that he knew before the darkness fell on him.

CHAPTER XXII

There was stillness. There were shadows, but there was also light. There was silence and then, both near and far, currents of music. It was the music that he followed.

He wandered long.

It was a place where he seemed neither waking nor sleeping, living nor dying. Often he did not understand where he went or what he saw, but it did not trouble him. Among those vales and dells trouble could not come.

The path he followed ran beside a river. It led him by crystal cliffs to a high place. There, wonder halted him. Shining gates stood before him, standing beneath a sky so clear that it pierced beyond all understanding. Unspeakable beauty dwelt in soaring towers. The river, streaming like silver, sprang from beneath the city's bright walls. As they ran by him and the path on which he stood, the waters danced with majestic delight.

It was from the city that the music came, drifting to him as a breeze in summer. He tarried at the riverside. Such loveliness dwelt in the city, such fearsome grace and wholeness, that he could not bear to go closer. And yet, even at such distance as he kept, all the griefs that he bore seemed to wash away.

There he stayed, for that place contented him beyond all measure. He closed his eyes and still the city's music filled him, gathering all that was broken in him and making it new. The river itself seemed to sing.

A figure further along the path came down from the city towards him. His face was radiance.

Seeing, the wanderer was undone by joy, for it was the face of a friend whom he loved.

Forward he went – forward to meet hale hands and shining eyes he had not thought to see again. Laughter and tears went with him, and wonder was with him as he laid his arms about the friend who had been a companion of joys and sorrows past. In love and with laughter the friend received him, and he knew then that there were joys, unimagined and uncounted, yet to come.

Long they spoke. Longer still they sang – he did not know how long – such songs as had rekindled hearts and shattered pits. They were that city's songs and part of its music.

As they sang, he heard other sounds. They came to him along the river, from the same way as he had come. He knew their speech and calls. They were well-loved voices, ones that had not yet followed the river to the bright city. They were voices from before.

He fell silent and turned to look back along the river's silver swell. The voices spoke and the city sang. The choice rested with him.

Quietly, he raised his head and looked again at the friend by him.

"I must go back," he whispered.

Smiles, richer and more loving than any earthly countenance might bear, touched his companion's face.

"There will be a day when your path brings you here," said the friend, "and on that day we shall meet again. Go with courage, hope, and peace, my friend."

The words filled the wanderer's heart. Tears – though not of grief – filled his eyes.

They embraced once more and then to the downward flow of the river the wanderer turned – for it showed the way.

Stars shone in the sky above him and stars shone in the river below, a mantel of brilliance over vale and dell. He followed the river, for he knew that he was called back and the waters would lead him safely there.

A high window looked down over him. Visions of the cloudless sky moved past, where high flocks of birds wheeled and soared, their voices raised in song. The sight and sound of them filled his heart, an achingly beautiful echo of the place where he had been.

He lay upon a wide, white bed. He felt cool linen soft around him, just as he felt his limbs, so long cased in heavy armour, now covered with a long, light shift. The room where he lay was tall and wide. Traces of faded paintings on the walls and ceilings danced as the sunlight played over them. A chair was set at the bedside, and by that a table on which stood a broad basin. The leaping light rippled on the water.

He saw and felt and, for a long moment, knew not who he was, where he lay, nor how he had come to be there. But it did not seem to matter.

He drew a deep breath. With wonder he felt that breath pass through him.

He could breathe!

It surprised and delighted him, though he did not know – or could not remember – why it seemed such a marvel. He felt the arch of his shoulders against the pillows; they were light and supple.

He had followed the river. He was alive, safe. Saved.

"Eamon."

Someone spoke a name. With a smile, he remembered that it was his.

Looking again, he saw that someone sat in the chair by him. How had he not seen her before? For a long time, he simply gazed, unlooked-for joy in his heart. He knew her.

"Aeryn," he breathed at last. As he spoke her name, she smiled. "Aeryn," he said again, overjoyed that he could speak, that he remembered her, and that she was there beside him.

"You're all right!" Reaching across, she took his hand, then her arms were about him and her face was next to his as she embraced him. He felt tears on her cheeks. "You're all right." Her voice shook.

"Yes," Eamon answered, deeply moved by the embrace that held him.

"I was so afraid for you. We all were."

"I'm sorry."

She pulled back and laughed. "Don't apologize!"

He gazed around the room. Memories quivered at the edges of his mind. As they returned, he felt the burdens that they carried: burdens of grief, sorrow and betrayal. They were burdens to which he had chosen to return.

"Where is Hughan?"

"Not far. He will come to you as soon as he can."

"And where is…"

Eamon stopped short of the name that came to his throat, his tongue becoming a dead weight as memory and pain – a terrible, driving pain in his shoulder – came back at him in a blow, stealing his breath. He gasped as it shot through him, for suddenly he saw blood and the pale face, and the sword raised above his own body, delivering the plunging blow…

A cry leapt to his lips and he shut his eyes in terror.

"Eamon."

He opened his eyes again. Aeryn was still there, her fingers clasped firmly about his own. For a moment he clung to her, shaking, and remembered.

"Ladomer," he whispered. His jaw trembled and he swallowed, hard. "Aeryn! He was… he was the Right Hand." He gripped her hand. Aeryn herself had so often been within Ladomer's grasp, so perilously close. "Oh, Aeryn!" he breathed. "All that time – *all* that time – he was…"

Words failed him. He looked up at her again, her face pale. Her eyes revealed unspoken grief. There was little that they could say. They had both been within the circle of the Right Hand; none more than they.

"What he would have done to you, if you had reached Dunthruik," Eamon whispered. The thought was horrific.

"Eamon," Aeryn whispered.

"He was a terrible foe, Aeryn."

He felt the stabbing anticipation of the sword-strike in every limb. He clenched his eyes shut again as it juddered through his shuddering flesh.

Aeryn pressed his hand. "He is gone," she said, "and you are safe. There will be a time to speak, but for now, you should concentrate on getting better."

Eamon drew a deep breath and looked up at her, tears burning in his eyes. As he trembled, he realized that he hardly knew what better was, or how he could ever reach it.

Aeryn's hand was smooth, gentle, soothing on his own. He held it – and realized then that he longed for the hand of another.

Alessia. His eyes closed. He saw her in his mind, prone before the Right Hand and yet made defiant by her love of him.

Love of him. His heart waxed with awe and shrivelled in shame. He had scorned her, rejected her. Reviled her. Believed the lies of a man who had degraded and abused her.

Traitor ever, he had betrayed her – a woman who had borne his love even against the wrath of a Right Hand.

Tears coursed down his face. He pressed at their streams with shaking hands, and shuddered into a sob.

With a mother's tenderness, Aeryn gathered him in her arms and hushed his tears.

"Is she here, Aeryn?" He didn't even know if she could understand his choked words. "Oh Aeryn! Please. Is she here?"

"Is who here, Eamon?"

"Alessia Turnholt."

His heart precipiced on her answer.

"Yes, Eamon."

He tried to rise from the bed, but the strength of grief in his limbs did not allow him the desire of his heart. Aeryn laid him back again.

"I must seek her –"

"Not now, Eamon."

"I must!"

"You are not strong enough," Aeryn told him. "There will be time yet."

Time! Already he had left it long, too long.

"Here; I've brought you something to eat." Aeryn laid a tray of bread and fruit on his lap. "There's drink, too. It will help you to feel stronger. When you are stronger, you may think of Lady Turnholt."

Eamon breathed deeply and relented. He nodded.

He ate and drank slowly. When at last he had finished and set the tray aside, Aeryn cocked her head at him.

"Can you walk?" she asked.

"I don't know," he answered truthfully.

"Would you like to try?"

Eamon watched her for a moment, shaking. What if he couldn't? But he raised his head.

"Yes, I'd like to try."

Aeryn smiled at him. "Good man."

An odd laugh bubbled up to his lips. "It seems that I am destined to bear that jest – and its tireless haunting – to the grave with me."

Aeryn looked at him. "It was no joke," she answered, fixing him with a sincere gaze. "And neither are you."

Eamon watched her for a moment, then sat up slowly. The lightness of his movement surprised him, as did its silence, for as he sat upright there was no chink of metal and no sliding of lame over lame. He flexed his fingers and they moved – and felt – all that was about them.

Aeryn stepped back and waited as he set his feet to the ground and stood. The light from the window flooded his face and poured over his hands and arms like an armour of living gold. For a moment he simply stood in it.

It was then that he heard steps in the antechamber. As he turned to them he heard a squeal of delight from the doorway.

"Mr Goodman!"

Eamon smiled. How long it had been since he had been addressed that way!

"I seem to be him," he answered.

Ma Mendel rushed forward towards him and, as she had done so long before at Hughan's camp, flung her arms about his neck. In the midst of her great laughter, she kissed his cheek.

"I'm so glad to see you awake!" she said. "Even with the King's grace, you didn't look at all well when they brought you."

"I expect I wasn't," Eamon answered quietly, and paused. He did not know what had happened to him.

Ma Mendel laughed. "The King will be glad to see you today!"

Eamon looked uncertainly across at Aeryn and was struck by a wave of shame.

"Today?" he whispered. Hughan had defeated both Edelred and Arlaith – what had his oft-trumpeted First Knight done? It seemed to Eamon that he had done woefully little. "I cannot…"

"Eamon," Aeryn said. As she spoke, Eamon's shame withered and his doubts fled. "If you had seen him, his thought turned towards this city and towards you while the lines of battle were yet being planned; if you had heard him, and how he spoke of you, after you came with Edelred's terms; if you had seen how he bore you back from where you fell, or how he – and many others – sat by you in that chair as often as they could spare… If you knew these things, then you would know that he is not ashamed of you."

Eamon tried to match her gaze. Aeryn laughed. "You are his First Knight and he loves you," she told him. "How can you say that you cannot go before him?"

"Perhaps, my lady," Ma Mendel put in gently, "he meant not dressed as he is."

"I'll confess readily enough that that was my very next concern," Eamon answered, offering Ma Mendel a grateful smile. He greatly valued her words, and she knew it.

Aeryn raised a wry eyebrow at him. "You're utterly incurable, Eamon."

Eamon spread his arms and gestured to himself. "The evidence speaks otherwise."

"Come with me," she returned, holding out her hand.

Eamon took it and rose. His limbs were weak with disuse, and even getting to his feet seemed to rob him of breath. His head first felt dull and then throbbed. But, gripping Aeryn's hands, he began to walk.

He was unsteady at first, but gained confidence. Each step seemed a marathon, and he wondered whether he might ever run or ride again. Aeryn helped him across the chamber to a small dressing room. Inside was a long couch. As his eyes adjusted to the light, he saw that clothes patiently awaited him there. Resting on the couch to touch them, tears stirred in his eyes – the cloak was blue, and a small sword and star were stitched upon it.

For a moment he simply held the garments and trembled with quiet joy.

"These are for me?" he whispered.

Aeryn nodded. "Yes."

Eamon laid his fingers against the sword and star on the cloak. Its design was very like the one that he had brazenly borne on his shirt to Edelred's ball, and yet it was unlike. This emblem was clear and pure, untrammelled and marvellous. It could not be hidden – nor did it need to be.

"He would not have cared if you had done so wearing the nightshift," Aeryn said with a smile, "but do you think that you could see Hughan in those?"

In silence, Eamon nodded. He thought he could.

As he gazed at the clothes, Aeryn left the room. Eamon scarcely noticed her go, so caught up was he in the things on his hands. They seemed finer than precious gems to him, and more dearly won than battles.

Ma Mendel helped him to dress; the clothes were smooth and gentle on his skin, so unlike the heavy feel of his Hand's cloak, or the robes that he had borne at Edelred's whim. At last she drew the cloak, as lithe and cool as a summer sea, gently over his shoulders, letting it fall about him. As he moved in the sunshine, it seemed to him almost as though he wore raiment woven from light.

Supported by Ma Mendel he stepped back into the chamber where he had woken. Aeryn awaited him. As he came forward, gowned in blue, Aeryn's face fill with wonder.

"That's your colour," she said quietly.

Eamon smiled fondly at her. "Good of you to tell me so."

With Ma Mendel to help him, he followed Aeryn from the room, marvelling anew at the long halls of the palace. He did not know where he was in comparison to the quarters of the Right Hand, but he knew that he was in a part of the palace that was distant from the gates. He wondered if he was in the area of the East Wing reserved for guests. Through some of the windows – many of them shattered – he caught glimpses of the sea and the roofs of the West Quarter. Somehow those images seemed clearer to him than before, yet as he saw them his heart grew heavy.

Dunthruik was changing. What place could it hold for him, now?

They went near to the heart of the palace, the sound of men working and singing in the morning light echoing down the corridors. Eamon supposed that they repaired the damage caused by the explosion.

"What day is it?" he asked, turning suddenly to Aeryn.

"The eighteenth of May," Aeryn answered.

Eamon stared at her for a moment.

"It was the sixteenth when we rode to war," he said. "Edelred was killed on the sixteenth…"

"It has been nearly two days since you fell," Aeryn told him quietly.

Eamon stared at her. Two days? His head swam. "A lot may happen in that time," he breathed.

Aeryn smiled softly. "It is time enough for a grand city to fall and be taken," she said, "but the aftermath of fallings and takings, it seems, happens much more slowly." She lightly touched his arm. "You have missed very little; Hughan will explain everything to you."

While the throne room was being repaired, the King and his counsellors had taken to meeting in a large hall in the East Wing. Eamon did not think that he had ever been in it, and realized that there was much of the palace he had never seen.

The doors to the great room were closed. As they approached, Eamon heard voices within, and made out that of Feltumadas among them. He was then not surprised to see that the two men guarding the doors were Easters, bearing the colours of Anastasius's house.

The guards came sharply to attention, then bowed. "My lady," one said. Eamon remembered that the woman before him would one day be Hughan's queen. He realized also that that day would come soon – for it could not be long before Hughan was crowned and made Aeryn his wife. The notion caused Eamon to look across at her with renewed awe.

Aeryn would be the mother of kings. The idea was as richly strange as it was breathtaking.

She cocked her head at him curiously. "Are you all right?"

He nodded dumbly.

"Please tell them that the First Knight is here," Aeryn said to the guards. One of the Easters stepped inside.

A moment later the doors opened wide into a circular room, rounded by tall windows that overlooked the palace gardens. Though now showing banners of blue and orange, the room still bore decorations in red. The colour did not terrify Eamon as it had once done. Glorious sunlight flooded the room, dazzling him for a moment as he entered.

His eyes adjusted swiftly to it. Many men were seated at the room's long table, which was spread with maps and papers. Some men he recognized, others he did not, but he saw many of the Easter lords – Anastasius, Feltumadas, Ithel, and Ylonous among them – as well as Easter banner commanders, Leon, several of the wayfarer generals, and of course the King. It was to Hughan that his gaze was drawn, for he was dressed all in blue and a small silver coronet rested on his brow.

Hughan met his gaze and smiled. "Welcome, First Knight."

"Thank you," Eamon answered, bowing low.

As he rose from his bow – steadied by the stalwart Ma Mendel – Feltumadas clapped, beating his palms so heartily that they might break. A second later Leon followed him, as did Anastasius and Ithel and all the others, until the whole room filled with mighty applause. His whole world was awash with it.

Blown away in astonishment, Eamon gazed at them.

"I do not deserve such welcome," he said, having to shout to make himself heard above the noise. His words were met with warm laughter, and contrary to his intent, an increase in jubilation.

As Eamon stared at them with an open mouth and a full heart, Hughan came down the room towards him. Suddenly Eamon remembered the sword-wielding figure that had cut through the dark hall to lay bright hands upon his breast.

Those same hands were laid then on Eamon's shoulders as the King looked at him.

"Sire," Eamon breathed. There were no words great enough to give the man before him. "Thank you."

"No, Eamon!" Hughan laughed gently. Eamon looked at him in amazement. "Thank *you*."

Smiling broadly, Hughan embraced him. The King's arms circled him and joy soared in his breast. He had never dared to dream that he would reach that moment. The fact that he had done so filled him with wonder and tears.

Applause rang in his ears as Hughan stepped back. The King's men and Easters came forward and clasped his hands, each with their words of congratulation and warm smiles. Eamon received them all in a daze.

"You wear good colours today," Anastasius told him.

"You are not the first to say so."

"The Star's faith in you proved good, and may yet prove more valuable than many swords. I am glad to have seen it – and this very fine cloak," Anastasius added with a smile.

Eamon bowed before the Easter lord. "I am glad also."

"This is a man who needs no colour to introduce him!" Feltumadas cried. "His fame will do that in all the years that follow us."

Eamon smiled at him, feeling his cheeks reddening with embarrassment. "If tales are told of me, Lord Feltumadas, the best I can hope is that they will be told truly."

"Indeed?" Ithel asked as he stepped up to take Eamon's hand. "And how would you mark the truthful telling of your tale, First Knight?"

"I would mark it true," Eamon answered quietly, "if the telling told that everything I sought to do was for the King – for only he brings sense and reason to what I have done. To speak my name without his, be it in song or story, is to tell a tale weighted with rage and sorrow. My name and doings should be as a banner, showing his."

Ithel smiled. "First Knight indeed, who keeps the Star first in his heart."

Eamon's cheeks flushed crimson; he clutched Ma Mendel's arm. She beamed at him.

The Easters stepped aside and when Eamon next looked up it was to find Leon standing before him. The man bowed.

"Well done, First Knight."

"I am sorry," Eamon replied. Leon looked surprised. "I have not forgotten how I used you, Leon," Eamon explained. "I could not offer a full apology to you then, but I would do so now. I ask for your pardon. You are brave and noble. I am glad that your fierceness did not quite spur you on to catch me that day when I took the head of an Easter lord. I am sorry that, for my purpose, I had to use you, insult you, and bind you, humiliating you before your enemies and your allies alike."

"I understand why you did," Leon answered quietly. He was silent for a moment but then drew a deep breath. "It was long before I was reconciled, and maybe I am still wary of you. But I know why you did as you did; and I forgive you for it."

Relief washed through Eamon. "There is no gift that I would rather have from you than that," he said, and clasped Leon's hand.

As the men around him fell back, Eamon surveyed them. In his time in Dunthruik he had been in many meetings and stood in the presence of the mighty, the terrible, and the powerful. But rarely had he stood surrounded by men as noble as those gathered round him. It astounded and thrilled him.

He looked back to the King. "Aeryn told me that I have been asleep for nearly two days," he said and then paused awkwardly, unsure of how to continue. As he met the King's gaze, his words failed him. There was so much that he had to ask…

Hughan looked at his gathered allies. "I would have a few moments with the First Knight."

The room resounded to sounds of agreement and the Easters and King's men left the room, each one smiling at Eamon as they departed. Aeryn took Hughan's hand for a moment and kissed his cheek before she too left. Ma Mendel brought Eamon to a chair before bowing and withdrawing.

Eamon sat before the King in the empty room. Hughan's joyful gaze grew more serious as it held him.

"How do you feel?" the King asked.

"I don't know," Eamon answered. "Strange." He touched once at his back, near where the blade had driven into him. "But I think everything is healed."

"Not everything," Hughan replied gently.

Eamon felt his gaze falling to the ground as he took the King's meaning. Somehow he could not answer.

Hughan's eyes searched his face. "Eamon, can you tell me what happened?"

There was a long silence. Then memories returned to him, groaning as they came.

"Arlaith took the Nightholt," Eamon answered at last. "I followed him. I asked him to surrender and put himself at your mercy. We knew Edelred was dead; we felt it, it must have been the moment that you…" He relived the fierce duel between King and throned. He could only imagine what the final blows had been like.

"It's all right," Hughan told him. "You can speak freely."

"I know that." Eamon's heart started to beat fast. "Just after you killed Edelred, Arlaith told me that he…" He faltered. "That he was Ladomer."

Hughan pressed his shoulder. Drawing a deep breath, Eamon met his gaze and spoke again. "We fought. He ran. He left the Nightholt and I followed…" Suddenly he realized what he had done and looked up in alarm.

The King saw the abject horror on his face. "Be at peace," Hughan told him. "It was recovered."

Eamon sighed with relief. "Thank goodness."

At Hughan's gesture, he took up his story again, telling it with the same heaviness with which he had wielded his sword against the Right Hand.

"We fought. He used the red light and he cast it at me, but the blue… The grace saved me. Then he said something to me, and… I lost my… no, I…" He drew a deep breath. "I ran…" he whispered. "But I recovered myself, and saw… inside his mind." He remembered Ladomer's shrieks, and shivered. "He did not want me to, but somehow I saw. I… I drew blood from him. He struck me. That was when you came." He looked earnestly into Hughan's deep gaze. "I would have died if you hadn't."

"You lay at the border of death when I found you," Hughan answered softly.

Eamon's heart filled with the shining river where he had walked, and the friend whom he had seen there. He remained silent for a long time.

At last, he looked up. "What has been done in Dunthruik while I was gone?"

"Much, and yet so very little," Hughan answered. "For the most part, we have grouped together and negotiated with those who surrendered or were captured. I've already set groups of men to work on repairing the South and Blind Gates, and the palace. Food and water are being distributed to the people, and news of Edelred's fall is going out to the regions. There's a lot of talk about how we're to restabilize the city, what messages we should give to Etraia and Edelred's other merchant allies – and our own. Above all, we have to decide how to handle the Gauntlet." Hughan looked keenly at Eamon. "Most external units have laid down their arms as, of course, have those still in the city. Now that we have a thorough tally of who has surrendered we must decide what to do with them. There was thought to meet on the matter this afternoon."

"May I attend?" Eamon asked at once.

"Will you promise to rest before then?" Hughan asked seriously.

"I will rest," Eamon answered with a small smile, "if you promise that I can come."

Hughan laughed. "Of course you can come! In part, the meeting has not yet been held because I wanted you to be present. Nobody understands the Gauntlet, and this city, better than you do, and nobody deserves to be present at a meeting which deals with both more than you."

Eamon stared at him incredulously. "You truly mean that?"

"Eamon," Hughan said, and as Eamon met his gaze he knew that the King would never speak words to him that he did not mean.

"I have detailed many men to burying the dead," Hughan said, his voice heavy. "I commanded separate graves on the field. Many lost their lives. I had no wish to devalue them, nor the colours under which they fought with all honour, by laying them together."

Eamon blinked back the sudden tears in his eyes. "You did wisely, sire," he whispered, "and well."

"Thank you," Hughan answered.

"How many surrendered?" Eamon asked at last.

"More than sixteen hundred infantry – including thresholders – five hundred and sixty-seven Gauntlet, and nearly fourteen hundred knights in the city, at the last count," Hughan replied. "A good portion were injured, and most of the city's Gauntlet facilities have been converted into hospitals. Overall, far more surrendered than we had hoped might do so. Giles tells me that surrendered men speak of a quarter captain who seems to have instructed his men that they would do better to surrender than fight to the death. His encouragement saved many men, if it is true."

Eamon knew at once that it was true, and knew also who had done it.

"Anderas." He spoke the name with sorrow. "He was my captain when I held the East Quarter," he said, answering Hughan's inquiring look. "When I asked him to, he willingly and joyfully took your colours over those he wore."

"It was brave of you to ask him," Hughan told him quietly.

"It was braver of him to accept. He was a true man of yours; truer at times than I." Eamon shook his head. "I wish that he could have lived to meet you, Hughan."

There was a long pause. In it, Hughan reached across to the table and took up one of the sheets of paper there, brow furrowed.

Eamon pressed his eyes shut. Anderas had been a dear friend.

It was Hughan's voice that stirred him. "Perhaps you shall have your wish," he said, looking up from the paper with a smile.

Eamon blinked hard. "What?"

"The overall surrender, treatment, and billeting of Gauntlet divisions is, if these notes are correct, being negotiated on the Gauntlet's behalf by one Captain Andreas Anderas," Hughan answered. A smile passed over his face. "A name like his is hard to forget. Feltumadas has been liaising with him and has noted that the man, though badly wounded, seems to 'both honour the Star and be stubborn enough to live to do so at length'." Hughan chuckled. "He adds that the captain is widely respected and that he has asked more than once for news of the Right Hand."

Eamon's jaw dropped. "I don't believe it."

"Is there more than one Captain Andreas Anderas?" Hughan asked.

"No…"

"Then I think that your captain lives, First Knight."

"But he was killed!"

"Who told you so?"

Eamon faltered. "Ladomer."

Hughan regarded him seriously. "Do not exchange the lies of one voice for another, Eamon," he cautioned. He put the paper down. "Feltumadas notes that the captain, like the majority of the Gauntlet wounded recovered from the field, is being treated in the West Quarter."

"Can I see him?"

"You're sure you do not need to rest?" Hughan asked. "I have no desire to completely exhaust you!"

"I will rest when we come back," Eamon promised.

Hughan smiled. "Then let us go and find him."

Chapter XXIII

Eamon and the King went together from the meeting room, Eamon in a daze. Arlaith's – Ladomer's – words had been undone before his eyes: Anderas lived. As he and Hughan left the meeting room, the two Easter guards dropped into step behind them.

Eamon and Hughan walked easily side by side through the palace. Eamon delighted in this: for months he had trod equal to no man, and he understood at last how that had weighed on him.

They came swiftly to one of the palace's side doors. Hughan advised him that the main hallway was still too badly damaged, though the masons and carpenters were optimistic that repair wouldn't be too difficult. Reserves of stone and timber were being used in the work both there and at the gates.

As they emerged into the Royal Plaza from the passages in the east wall, Eamon saw that the workers had not been idle – great scaffolds had been put up about the palace front. The men there worked hard. Only as they stepped outside did Eamon fully realize that it was mid-morning. He looked back at the palace and saw something unexpected.

Atop the West Wing, where Edelred had fought his final battle, flew a new banner. It was bright in the May light, showing forth blue and silver as it danced on the running wind.

Eamon stopped and gazed upwards in awe at the King's banner. He drank deeply of the sight.

"I never truly imagined that I would live to see that fly there," he said at last. "I was too afraid to dare as much. Your banner here

– and my life spared to see it – always seemed like things far beyond the horizon of my hope."

Hughan laughed quietly beside him. "You were not alone in that."

"There were days when you doubted it too?"

"Long days, Eamon; dark days." Hughan looked up at the banner, his face shaded by remembrances. "They were days when my judgments faltered, when all that I did seemed to fail and my hopes were weakened almost to their death. They were bloody days, filled with flames and cries and tears. After them came days of cowardice, folly, and blindness – for myself and for those who had pinned their hopes on me." Suddenly Hughan looked at him. "I did not always seek it – indeed, sometimes I sought to shun it – but grace always found me. On those days, Eamon – days where the whole wreck of the dark yoked me to despair – that grace pierced through all I thought I saw and called me by name, to courage and to account."

Eamon looked at him in silence for a moment. "Called you?" Hughan nodded. "You mean, like a voice?"

"Yes."

Eamon regarded him with amazement. "You hear it too," he breathed.

Hughan smiled. "I do," he answered.

For a moment Eamon could not speak. He glanced wordlessly back to the King's banner and then to the palace gates. He remembered how the King had stood before them – and the fury of the throned's artillery – alone.

"Did you doubt your hope when you went against the gates?"

"I have rarely done anything that seemed so reckless," Hughan laughed. "When I saw the weapons and men at the palace gates it was clear that we would not be helped by our own means; only a massacre would have seen us through. Such a thing would have been senseless – the day had already seen the shedding of too much blood." He paused. "The hope and courage that took me before these gates was born of my confidence that the King's grace went with me. I did not know for certain what would happen – and I am still not sure that I understand what *did* happen – I only felt sure that it would."

Eamon watched him uncertainly. "Then… the King's grace followed you?"

"No," Hughan answered quietly. He met Eamon's stunned gaze. "I do not know – and cannot command or contain – the full power of the grace that we both carry. What we call the King's grace is beyond my understanding, but even so, it is not beyond us. The hope that it had seeded in my heart told me that it would make a way against the gates. I followed it. I knew that we had not been brought so far only to fall there."

"That was conviction indeed," Eamon said. He paused. "Is that all it takes?" he asked, frowning. "Conviction?"

"No; Edelred was a man of conviction," Hughan told him. "So were his Hands. But they strove against the King's grace, against what is right and what is good."

"Then what of other men?" Eamon asked. "What of your men – men who held to you and to this grace with as much a heart and will as you? Why do so many who follow it, as you did at the gate, suffer? Why are they not aided?"

"Why are some healed, and not others?" Hughan added. "Why does the grace allow some to face death and yet delivers others from it with little but life? Why did it shield us at Edelred's gates but did not shield the countless men on the battlefield – or those who died in the culls?" Hughan looked at him compassionately. "I have asked myself the same questions, Eamon, and more than once. I do not know the answer to them. We often do not see – or cannot comprehend – what the King's grace does or doesn't do. I do not think that our own eyes and wits could ever be enough to search its deepest workings. We cannot always be answered, because this grace does not answer to us. But this I know: even when it does not answer, it serves and saves, and what it does is for good." He looked at Eamon. "I know," he said gently, "that it saved you."

Eamon drew a deep breath, remembering the agony of the blade that had driven into him, rupturing organ and vein to choke him with blood and steel. He remembered Ladomer's face, lifted first in an ecstasy of victory and then seized by the pallor of death, and how, as that face fell, the King's shining hands had come to rest upon his own brow...

Eamon tore open his eyes. He had begun shaking. "Yes," he whispered.

Hughan was watching him quietly.

"But... thousands of men fought with you, Hughan," Eamon said. As he spoke his mind filled with memories of the corpse-strewn battlefield where every colour was stained red. He remembered the injured men, the shattered limbs, and pale cadavers. His voice grew angry and he trembled. "Hundreds upon hundreds of them died – the King's grace did not save them."

"The cost of good is often a dear one," Hughan told him. "I do not rejoice at that, but I am comforted because I know what the price was paid for."

"Why had they to pay it?" In an agony of guilt Eamon sought the King's eyes. "Out of all the lives there were to save, Hughan, why was mine saved and not theirs? Why should I be worth more than they?"

Hughan looked gently at him. "You forget, Eamon, that thousands of men also live, and not just here but all over the River Realm. Those that died will be remembered and honoured, and those of us who live should do so with greater hearts, knowing what was paid for our freedom. As to your 'greater' worth, I know that did not save you. In the same way, those men who lost their lives did not do so because they were somehow of 'less' merit or distinction than you are. Whatever the colour they wore to battle, they were loved no less than you."

Eamon reeled. There would have been guilt enough in feeling that he had been saved for being worth more than another man – but at least such would have been a reason. That logic voided, he was left with nothing but the turmoil of the senseless fact. Agonized, Eamon stared at Hughan.

"Then why was I saved?"

"It is not that you were saved from death," Hughan answered quietly. "Death comes to all men in time. It is rather that, by grace, you were chosen on that day to live. Even so, that appointed way had to be of your choosing."

"I did choose," Eamon whispered. There were tears in his eyes. "I followed a river. It brought me back."

"And so you live." Smiling, Hughan touched Eamon's shoulder. "That you walk with me now is a gift to me and to this city. That you live, and that you chose to do so, are works of grace and goodness. Do not be ashamed of them."

Blinking back tears, Eamon nodded.

The First Knight and the King went together through the palace gates and onto the Coll. The long road was filled with men, many in the King's colours and some in the Easters'. Eamon heard working all over the city. In the distance, smoke rose from pyres. Eamon gazed at the billows.

"The bodies of many Hands were recovered from the palace rubble, and from the field," Hughan told him. "They have been sent on to the pyres. Edelred and Arlaith will also be taken to the pyres." A shiver ran down Eamon's spine. Hughan's eyes strayed down the Coll to the distant city gates. "Anastasius insists that they should both be displayed, stripped and upside down, at the Blind Gate. And I understand his reasoning."

Eamon could feel his face turning in disgust; he understood it, too. It was important to show Dunthruik and the River Realm that Edelred was truly dead. But the thought of the two pale bodies being shown at the gate brought bile into his throat.

"It is," he said, "what Edelred would have done to you, and most likely to me. Maybe it is what they do in the east, and maybe it has a place. But sire," Eamon added earnestly, "it has no place at your gates."

Hughan met his gaze and smiled gently. "That was my answer also," he said. "The bodies will be taken at the proper time in a formal procession to the pyres. Before that, the Nightholt must be destroyed and that, too, will be done publicly."

Eamon chilled; he had almost forgotten the Nightholt.

Hughan still held his gaze. "It holds only a little power now," he said, "but until it has been destroyed, its effects will linger. Even a surrendering Gauntlet soldier would find it difficult to take a new place in this city with that mark still on him."

Eamon glanced down at his palm. The mark had dwindled when Edelred was killed, but he knew Hughan was right; traces of the mark still remained in him.

It was an uncomfortable thought. "When will you destroy it?"

"When we have finalized the surrenders and disbanding of the Gauntlet."

"Did any Hands survive?"

"In the regions," Hughan returned, "but few in the city itself. Some who did not make a last stand at the palace gate fled the city. But they are few and scattered, and they will find themselves greatly impeded now that Edelred is dead; more so once we have destroyed the Nightholt."

Eamon breathed deeply, his mind awhirl with images of Hands escaping into the River Realm, only to be found and wrathfully killed.

He looked earnestly to Hughan. "The Hands must not become to us as the wayfarers were to them," he said. "Neither must the Gauntlet; their names must not become bywords for slaughter, or excuses to cull a man without due cause."

"I know," Hughan replied. "We will do everything we can to keep it from happening."

They walked a little further. Men paused and greeted the King warmly wherever he went, bowing and cheering. Hughan gracefully accepted their praise, greeting them in return. The domed roof of the Crown glinted ahead. The Brand and the West Quarter College were not far.

"There is one Hand being held," Hughan said. "Perhaps you know him?"

"It is more than likely."

"His name is Febian."

Eamon looked at him in surprise. "Febian? He was made the West Quarter Hand after Cathair's death."

"His is an interesting story," Hughan continued. "It seems that when Dunthruik's men retreated back into the city, Arlaith sent Febian down to the Pit to slaughter prisoners being held there."

Eamon blanched. "What happened?"

"He did not do it," Hughan answered simply. "I went to the Pit," he continued, "and I found him there. He gave himself, and the prisoners, over to me."

Eamon gazed at him silently, astonished. "Why?" he breathed, marvelling at what a sight it must have been when the King went down into the Pit.

"I do not know what moved Febian's mind to mercy," Hughan answered, "but the Pit is no more. For the present at least, it shall not be used."

"You closed it with the King's grace," Eamon guessed.

Hughan nodded. "I did. When a space of time has run its course, we may put it to some use, perhaps for storage. But it has been a place of ill and suffering too long. It, too, needs time to mourn what it has borne. When that time has passed, we will look to it again."

Eamon nodded. There seemed little that he could say.

They reached the West Quarter College and Eamon paused to look at it. Its doors were busy with men moving to and fro. As they approached the steps together, Eamon imagined that every room in the place – including those that had once been his own – had been made into a makeshift prison or infirmary.

The air cooled as they stepped into the hall, and as he had always done, Eamon glanced up at the wall.

Overbrook's map hung there still, but Waite's Hand name-board was gone. As he wondered on this, Eamon felt an odd grief.

Men bowed to the King as they went through the corridors. Eamon marvelled that their gestures of service were so freely given, accompanied by smiles and heartfelt words. None spoke to him, though he felt their eyes on him.

Hughan enquired after Anderas and received direction from one of the men stationed in the corridor. As they moved on, they passed the doors of the room which had been Eamon's own when he was a lieutenant; it now held a group of wounded men.

Anderas was in the officers' mess, which had been transformed into a large holding hospital. As they approached the doors, Eamon half expected to see Alben, or Fields, or Best inside.

They were not; the room was filled with men, some in the remains of their uniforms and others, from the thresholders and militia, without them. The place was busy and so few noticed them entering at first, but it was not easy to miss the King. As he entered the room, silence fell on those nearest the door, and whispers ran down the walls like wildfire.

Eamon stood by as Hughan spoke to those about him. He scanned the sea of faces around him on every side. He wanted to see Anderas.

He found the captain away to one side of the room. Though pale, he was standing and speaking to an Easter, perhaps one of Feltumadas's staff. A doctor was by him, wrapping a great swathe of bandage tightly about his shoulder and chest. Anderas winced as the material was drawn together. The doctor stepped aside and moved on.

Anderas, as though aware that someone watched him, looked up. His eyes searched the room for a moment and then alighted on Eamon. Anderas fell still and his jaw fell open.

With a great laugh, Eamon left Hughan's side. The hall was long, and he had to pick and weave his way around the men within it. He pressed onward, laughing still.

Anderas only closed his jaw after Eamon reached him.

"First Knight," he said, and moved to bow.

"Oh no you don't, Andreas!" Eamon cried, joyfully but gently embracing him.

"They said that the Right Hand was dead," Andreas whispered. His voice quivered.

"I was told the same about the captain of the East," Eamon replied. He laughed, and stepped back to look at his friend's face. "Do you like getting shot?" he added.

Anderas paused for a moment as though the matter necessitated some thought. "No."

"You seem to make rather a habit of it nonetheless!"

"And you seemed to make rather a good rider for someone who claims that he can't."

Eamon beamed. "Were you impressed?"

"I was," Anderas answered with a knowing smile. "Very."

They watched each other for a moment. Aware of the men about them, Eamon lowered his voice and drew the captain to a slightly quieter part of the room.

"Why did Arlaith have you shot?"

Anderas's face grew darker. "So they were Arlaith's orders," he murmured.

"They were." Eamon could not bring himself to say how he knew.

"I had been encouraging the men to fight bravely but surrender rather than throw away their lives," Anderas told him, pressing uncomfortably at the arrow wound on his shoulder. Though the bandage was fresh, traces of blood stained the fabric. "Not all the men were happy with my directive. Word must have reached Arlaith."

"What happened?" Eamon said quietly.

The captain looked up, his face both anxious and determined.

"That night before the battle, Arlaith asked me to take some papers to the South Quarter," he said. Eamon nodded; he remembered. "I was to meet one of the quarter officers. But it wasn't a Gauntlet officer who waited for me. It was Lord Tramist."

Eamon's blood curdled.

"He cornered me," Anderas continued somewhat haltingly. "He knew – about you. I think he was acting under Arlaith's orders…"

Arlaith's memory raced across Eamon's mind: *I am sending him to you with papers tonight. Find out what he knows – and then take care of him…*

"Tramist said that he knew whom you served, and he demanded to know what you meant to do under those colours. He intended to kill you."

Eamon stared at the captain in horror. "And you!"

Anderas blinked as though the thought had not really crossed his mind. He flexed his hand.

"It was a small room. He pinned me against the wall. He was going to breach me. I couldn't draw my sword. I…" He drew a deep breath. "My hands were all the weapon that I had. I killed him." He shuddered once and then, shaking, met Eamon's gaze again. "I'm a Gauntlet captain, and I have killed men before. But never like this. Never with such fear, or determination. Because I knew that he could not leave that room, or you would die."

Eamon looked at him with grief. While he delivered Edelred's terms to the King, Anderas had faced Tramist – alone and unaided – in the cramped dark of the South Quarter College. He shuddered.

"I had to hide the body," Anderas told him. "Fortunately, the South Quarter has a warren of rooms that I could use, and most men were occupied – or had gone to the walls to watch for your return from the parley. I was not discovered, but perhaps Lord Arlaith suspected what I had done." He paused for a moment. "I told the King's men where to find Lord Tramist's body as soon as I could. It was taken to the pyres, along with those of other Hands."

Eamon met the captain's gaze again. "I'm so sorry."

Anderas shook his head. "I do not regret killing Tramist, though it is true that I was, and am, afraid of what I did. But I have never felt more certain that the taking of a life was necessary than I did in that moment."

"You have done much, Andreas," Eamon breathed. Overcome with grief by what the captain had borne, and relief that he still lived, Eamon simply gazed at him. "Thank you."

"Lord Good…" Anderas stopped uncertainly. "I don't suppose they call you that much any more," he said with a quiet laugh. "What should I call you now?"

Eamon laughed. "You should call me as a friend would, Andreas – by my *name*."

"Eamon," Anderas said. As he spoke the name a smile broke on the captain's troubled face. "We said we would hold fast."

"And we did."

They clasped hands in a moment of silence.

"So, when they said that the Right Hand was dead…?"

"They were right: *Arlaith* is dead."

Anderas carefully surveyed his face. "Something tells me that there's a little more to it than that."

"There is," Eamon replied heavily. "And I will tell it to you, in every detail." He looked up at the injured and recovering men and the doctors that moved between them. "But not here," he added. "It is a tale that will take some telling. When the time for it comes, we will sit somewhere warm together and talk until long after the last star disappears."

"Yes…" The smile on Anderas's face became a look of awe.

Hughan approached them, and then Eamon understood the captain's expression. As Hughan walked across the hall, the glint of the silver coronet caught in his hair like starlight. The air of a King followed him.

As Hughan came to Eamon's side, he smiled at them both. "Captain Anderas?"

Anderas seemed unable to answer. With a look of utter amazement he sank down to one knee before the King. "Sire," he breathed.

Hughan smiled at him and gently touched his shoulder. "Rise, captain," he said, and Anderas rose. "I hear that you have charge of the negotiations for the Gauntlet surrender."

"Yes, sire," Anderas answered.

"I know that the surrender of so many is due, in no small part, to your great courage," Hughan told him. "It is a brave man who, for love of another, will go against the wisdom of the colours he wears. You have done me – and this city – great service. I thank you for it."

"Thank you, sire." For a long moment Anderas stood speechlessly before him. Then he found courage to speak again. "May I make a bold request?"

"You seem like a bold man," Hughan answered. "Could I gainsay you, if your request was good and you had set your heart on it?"

"You could not," Eamon told him.

Anderas looked up at them both. "It is my place, sire, to stay with the Gauntlet, and with the men from the East, until such a time as the Gauntlet is disbanded. It is not only my place; it is my duty and my choice. But if after that there is a chance," he whispered, "I would like to wear your colours openly, and serve you still."

Hughan pressed his shoulder once again. "At that time, captain, your service would honour me greatly. I would welcome you to it with open arms."

Anderas's eyes filled with tears. "Thank you, sire," he said.

As Hughan withdrew his hand, the captain winced and moved his injured shoulder.

"It hurts you?" Eamon asked.

"An arrow strike doesn't just disappear," Anderas answered.

"But it could," Eamon returned.

Anderas looked at him strangely. "You would heal me? Like you did at Pinewood?"

"Yes," Eamon answered, "but not I: the King's grace." He reached out with one hand but Anderas stopped him.

"Eamon," he said gently. "My arm will heal of its own accord, given time. Despite a raging battle and a plot against my life, I was brought alive from the field. Is that not also a grace?"

Eamon paused. "Yes."

"Then let us let the King's grace be a grace, and not a tool."

Slowly Eamon withdrew his hand, looked up, and smiled. "As is so very often the case, Andreas," he said, "I think you're right."

Anderas smiled wryly. "The question is: will you ever learn it?"

"Perhaps I never will," Eamon confessed with a grin.

With a laugh Anderas looked to Hughan again. "Sire," he said, "it is a rare man that serves as your First Knight."

"I know it well," Hughan replied.

Eamon turned to Hughan. "There is someone else you have to see," he said.

Hughan looked enquiringly at him. Eamon scanned the hall for a moment and then, unable to see the man he looked for, turned back to Anderas. "Is there a Lieutenant Manners here?"

Anderas looked blankly at him. "West Quarter?" he guessed.

"He was already in the infirmary before the battle," Eamon answered.

"Then you'd best ask the doctors."

Eamon turned and called to the nearest doctor. The man moved across to them and bowed deeply to Hughan as Eamon spoke. "I'm looking for a Gauntlet lieutenant," Eamon began. "He was here before."

The doctor, an Easter, paused thoughtfully for a moment. "Do you mean the 'sleeping one'?" he asked.

"'Sleeping one'?"

"He was in the infirmary already when we arrived. He has not once awakened in the time since – and it has not been for want of trying to wake him on our part."

Eamon nodded. "That's probably him."

"He is being kept separately from the wounded, in the third side room just off the corridor."

Eamon thanked him and turned to Hughan. The King watched him with a curious smile. "Will you come?" Eamon asked.

"I will."

Eamon looked back to Anderas. "You won't get shot again while I'm not looking, will you?"

Anderas rolled his eyes. "This is an infirmary, Eamon."

"Ah, but if anyone can get shot in an infirmary then I suspect that it is you."

A warm smile crept onto his friend's face. "Then I shall endeavour to be careful."

Eamon embraced Anderas once more. Parting from him, he went with Hughan into the corridor that led out of the hall.

They followed the corridor to the small room that the Easter doctor had spoken of. The room was unattended. Inside it was a small bed.

Manners lay on it, his still face peaceful in the light from the window. His chest steadily rose and fell to the pattern of his breathing and no noise or light seemed able to stir him. His wounds had been bound but his lieutenant's jacket, which was laid over him like a small blanket, was still marked with blood.

Hughan followed Eamon into the room and looked at Manners.

"This is Rory Manners. He was badly hurt when the port was attacked," Eamon explained, "and I could not heal him then. He also serves you."

"You won the hearts of many men for me," Hughan said, a proud smile on his face.

Eamon lowered his gaze, a little embarrassed. "Will you wake him?"

"Would you not do it?" Hughan asked him.

Eamon looked once at Manners' face, then slowly shook his head. "I am but the First Knight. He waits for you."

Hughan held his gaze a moment more, and Eamon nodded to him. Then the King stepped forward to the bed and knelt down by the low frame. He reached out and lightly touched Manners' brow. Light stirred between the King's fingers, and it threaded itself about the young man's face.

After what was both forever and no time at all, Hughan spoke. "Rory."

The lieutenant's eyes came slowly open. They rested on the King.

For a moment the young man simply watched him, a look of deep peace on his face.

Manners smiled a great smile. "You came."

"Yes," Hughan answered, "and so did my First Knight." As he spoke he turned a little so that the lieutenant could see Eamon. Manners beamed.

"Hello, sir," he said. His voice croaked from lack of use.

Eamon gazed at him speechlessly. "Hello, Rory," he answered at last. "It's good to see you."

"And you, sir," Manners replied. He looked back to Hughan. "You won?"

Hughan laughed gently. "Yes," he said. "But there is still much to do."

Manners nodded. "Yes, sire."

A moment later one of the doctors entered the room. The doctor took one look at Manners, awake and with the King kneeling next to him, and nearly fainted.

"Sire," the doctor said, bowing.

"Please make sure that good care is taken of this man," Hughan told him. "I suspect that something to eat and drink may be in order."

"Yes, sire," the doctor answered. He vanished from the room with a bow.

Hughan rose from the lieutenant's side. Eamon pressed Manners' hand.

"You're all right, sir?" Manners asked.

Eamon breathed deeply. "For the most part," he answered. "Yes." Manners smiled.

A moment later the doctor returned with a bowl of soup. Eamon nodded encouragement to Manners before he and Hughan left the room, leaving the lieutenant in the doctor's care.

Hughan and Eamon passed together into the college corridors. The sun was strong on Eamon's face as they returned to the hall.

"Thank you for going to him," he said quietly. "He is a good man, and will serve you heartily."

Hughan smiled at him. "Mathaiah always sent good words about Rory Manners," he said.

Eamon looked at him in surprise. "He did?"

"Always," Hughan repeated with a kind laugh. "I am glad to have met him at last."

As the words sank into Eamon, he almost glanced back over his shoulder towards where Manners lay. He wondered just how long Lieutenant Manners had been a King's man.

"Well done, Mathaiah," he whispered.

CHAPTER XXIV

I t was just after midday when they returned together to the palace. As they passed into the halls, weariness flooded through Eamon. He was overjoyed that Anderas and Manners both lived, but he knew that the King was right – there was still much to be done. The thought of it weighed strangely on him.

Hughan gazed at him. "Are you well, Eamon?"

Eamon blinked back an errant tear. "I am tired," he answered. He could put no other words to what he felt, and knew that those he spoke could not describe it.

Hughan touched his shoulder. "You should rest for a while."

"I promised that I would," Eamon answered. "I will return to my chamber and do so."

Hughan held his gaze for a moment. "Then I will send someone with food for you."

"Thank you."

They parted and Eamon made his way slowly to his room. To walk the corridors and see no flash of black, nor feel the creeping fear of the throned behind him, was strange. He walked lost in thought.

He was alive. It was the first thing he did not understand. He did not know how close to death he had come when Ladomer had struck him, or where he had wandered when the darkness fell over him. The thought of the silver river shivered through him and he tried to recapture the sounds of the songs that he had heard; they seemed beyond his grasp.

He had chosen to return from that place, and the King's grace had undone all that had been done to his body. To a looking eye he had to seem whole and well, healed and graced, and yet he did not feel it.

Did it matter how he felt? The King walked in Dunthruik. Had that not always been what he had dreamed of seeing? He thought once more of the blue banner caught atop the palace tower and of the blue that he himself now wore. Had that not been what he had always wanted? Had he not achieved what had been asked of him?

He had. And yet in his heart a brooding disquiet lingered, and to it he could give no name.

Wearily he paused in the corridor, catching his breath by a window. The air was filled with the sounds of the city – sounds different from any that he had heard before. The smell of the sea wafted towards him.

Hughan had spoken of the long way that they had yet to go. Victory was short, and as Eamon thought on it – on the dead who lay upon the field and in the city, and on Ladomer's bloodless face – he wondered whether it could ever be sweet.

He sighed and let the air from the window pass over him. Perhaps it was not Hughan's victory that was bitter; perhaps it was his own heart. But should he not be content? What cause had he, First Knight to the King, for bitterness?

More, his burdened heart answered him, than he would like to confess.

He shook the burgeoning thoughts from himself as a man might ward away a chill. Coming to the last stretch of corridor he stopped again.

Why should he not go to her?

He found himself retracing his steps along palace corridors, threading his way past servants and King's men and towards those quarters where he knew the women would be. Surely, if Alessia was anywhere, then she would be near Aeryn?

He stepped out into the last hall separating him from the women's rooms. Then he froze, slipping back into the shadows of the doorway.

A group of women spoke quietly to each other, encased in light from the tall embrasures. He could not hear what they said. Their voices melted into the warm air.

She was there. She was smiling.

His body froze, turning his limbs to those of a statue. What could he possibly say to her? And...

How was it that she smiled?

A deep ache seized him. Weary beyond his years, he left the hall.

He returned to his room and sank onto the bed, dazed. He didn't know how to approach her. What if she spurned him? What if, even after hearing him, she still would not allow him to make amends?

What if all he brought her was pain – how could he do that to her again? The thoughts stoked his sorrow.

Not long later there was a knock at his door. Ma Mendel came in, bringing food on a small wooden tray.

"Am I disturbing your rest, sir?"

"No," Eamon answered, grateful for the distraction. Ma Mendel set the tray down on the small table.

"It isn't much, I'm afraid."

"I'm sure it will be more than adequate," Eamon answered. He knew too well that the city's reserves were low following the blockade. He was impressed that Hughan had managed to get any kind of food distribution going at all.

"I'll leave you to eat and rest then," Ma Mendel said.

Eamon nodded. "Thank you, Mrs Mendel."

The smiling lady curtseyed to him and then left. Eamon gazed at the closed door for long moments in silence. He resolved that the best thing he could do was to press Alessia from his mind. He needed time to think.

It was when he looked down at the tray that he found that, in the silence, he had been rubbing the palm of his hand.

The palace halls were busy that afternoon when Eamon passed down them back towards the King's meeting room in the East Wing. He nervously resettled the cloak on his shoulders.

He was warmly greeted by the guards at the room's doors, and more heartily received by the men already gathered inside. The room was still in a state of movement as the King's advisors and allies arrived, a shifting sea of blue and orange and green, a universe of suns and stars. It stole his breath away.

As Eamon paused and looked at them, Ithel stepped over to him.

"It promises to be an interesting afternoon," the Easter told him.

"How so?"

Ithel tilted his head. "There are some differences in opinion," he answered, before excusing himself and going to take his place at the table.

Eamon frowned. Before he had time to ponder the Easter's words further, the King stood beside him. "Are you feeling better?"

"A little," Eamon replied. "Where would you have me sit?"

"Next to me," Hughan answered, gesturing to a place at the right of the table's head.

Eamon felt a terrible press in his heart as he looked at the empty seat. Part of him, being commanded by the King, would take it and sit for the sake of the command, without accepting the honour and love of him who gave it. Part of him looked at the place, and while asking whether he could dare sit in it, also asked another question: Was he now simply Hughan's right hand, to be used no differently to Edelred's?

"Eamon?" Hughan watched him intently.

He blinked and met the King's gaze.

"Are you well?"

"Sire," Eamon answered uneasily, "I don't feel that I can…" he trailed off then shook his head angrily. "This is ridiculous, Hughan," he whispered, turning so that the others in the room could not see the anguish on his face. "I have every reason for joy. Why is it that I am plagued with fear? How can I sit at your right hand when these…" his words failed him and he spread his hands in frustration, "these *thoughts* will not permit me to do so with a clear heart?"

Hughan flinched neither from his tone nor his words. He touched his shoulder.

"The battle for the heart of Dunthruik begins here, in this room, on this day," he said quietly. "It will be a more difficult battle than any fought upon a plain, or in a city, or in the passages of a darkened wing. When men march to battle on a field, they have swords in their hands and banners to fly above their heads; they know their enemy and they know what they must do. When the field becomes a room of men, when the banners are hung on the walls and the swords are sheathed, knowing what to do – having a clear heart – is more difficult. But, perhaps more than the first, it is also a place for courage."

The King's gaze held Eamon. "First Knight," Hughan told him, "the seat I offer you is a place of honour, but it is no place of rest. There may come times when speaking from it is more difficult than anything you have ever done for me. Yet be encouraged; there is no man more clear-hearted to whom I would rather entrust it."

Eamon watched him for a long moment. To stand for Hughan had taken almost every part of his courage; to sit for him would take as much, and maybe more.

Nodding once, he quietly moved to take his place at the King's right, men watching him as he did. The other Easter lords and King's men stood behind their chairs. Five, set at the far end of the table, stood empty. Eamon realized that they were reserved for the Gauntlet's representatives.

Hughan lifted his voice towards the guards posted just inside the door. "Call in the Gauntlet speakers."

Moments later they came. Eamon turned to see them – five men, each of them wearing the Gauntlet's full insignia. He recognized all of them. The five men stood behind the empty seats.

"Would you give your names?" Hughan asked. One of the notaries at the table began to write.

"Captain Andreas Anderas of the East Quarter," said Anderas, the first in the line. "I speak for the East and for each regional division stationed in it prior to the battle."

"Captain Tomas Longroad of the North Quarter," spoke the second. Eamon was glad to see him alive. "I speak for the North and each regional division stationed in it prior to the battle."

"First Lieutenant Ronnel Fletcher," spoke the third, "former lieutenant to the Right Hand. I speak for the South Quarter, from which I came, for each division stationed there prior to the battle, and for those who served in the palace guard." Eamon wondered whether the man had been promoted on the field. He remembered the way that Fletcher had armed him for battle. The man could never have imagined whom he armed, or for what purpose.

"General Sir Enbern Rocell," spoke the fourth. "I speak for the knights and nobles at arms of this city."

"General Alduin Waite," spoke the last. He stood proudly, his head raised. His arm hung in a sling and his determined face looked pale. "I speak for the West Quarter, and for any division stationed there prior to the battle. As commander of the Gauntlet, I also speak for any divisions not present in the city at this time." Waite did not meet Eamon's gaze. It turned his heart with sadness.

Hughan gestured to his own men: Alnos and Leon. Both men had several aides with them. The Easters were also a formidable presence at the table: Anastasius, Feltumadas, Ithel, and Ylonous. Last of all was Eamon himself. He tried to keep his voice steady as he gave his name:

"Eamon Goodman, First Knight to Hughan Brenuin." The Gauntlet officers stared at him as he said it.

"Thank you all, and welcome," Hughan said. He gestured to the chairs about the table. "Please be seated."

As with one motion, all those in the room sat. A couple of the Easters – Feltumadas in particular – eyed the Gauntlet officers with distrust.

"Let the council be advised," Hughan began, "that these officers have come on behalf of many, and that their surrenders have already been accepted. As such, they will be treated with respect." The King's gaze took in the whole table. "This meeting," he added, "will discuss the expiating of guilt and disbanding of the Gauntlet."

A heavy silence fell on the room. Disbanding the Gauntlet was necessary – Eamon knew that perhaps better than any of them – but as the words were spoken, he looked at the red uniforms that the officers bore, and the thought saddened him. In that moment the red jackets had about them a tragic grandeur.

"The Gauntlet is guilty of nothing more than following its orders," Waite said. His voice was firm but tired.

"The Gauntlet was bound to Edelred in foul oaths," Leon countered. "It bears his mark and his guilt, and killed all those who stood against it."

"Haven't you done the same?" Waite asked, his eyes flashing angrily. "More men of ours than yours lie dead upon the field."

"Any of your men would have been better left to the dogs than the earth's embraces," Feltumadas retorted. "And so they would have been, had matters been left in my hands."

"Then I thank the house of Brenuin that it saw fitter than to follow your suggestion," Waite replied, his eyes passing to the King. "But I shall thank it for little else."

Eamon's heart churned. Could the general not see that the King was true, truer than any other man?

Waite's gaze passed over his. The general's expression grew harder. It was an unpleasant blow and Eamon bore it in silence.

"The Gauntlet and the knights committed atrocities in Edelred's name," Hughan said quietly, "and not only in times of war. They have long been agents of torment and oppression against the people of this realm. The blood that has been spilled must be answered for."

"Did you not guarantee us our lives, Star of Brenuin?" Waite asked. "Or is your mercy in going back on your word?"

"My word holds. This city has seen too many culls and too much bloodshed," Hughan continued, squarely matching Waite's gaze. "In place of blood for blood, I would have the Gauntlet answer for what has been done in coin, as was done in times long before Edelred took the throne. The Gauntlet's payment will be used to repair the city and to assist the people of the River Realm. Some will go to the Easter lords."

"Blood money," Waite said quietly. For a moment his face was caught between an expression of disgust and relief. "Tell me, O Star: how much are we to pay?"

"Each serving man shall pay sixty crowns."

Eamon blinked – it was half a year's wages for most Gauntlet. Though it would not be impossible for them to pay, it would be difficult.

"That is a harsh sum," Waite replied.

"It is no recompense for the sons of my land that have been slain," Anastasius answered grimly, "nor can it ever answer for those lives lost in the Pit, or the lives of your own people."

"Not every life lost to the hands of the Gauntlet was lost unfairly." It was Anderas who spoke. "Not every man killed by the Gauntlet was a servant of the King, and not every man killed was innocent. Some were thieves and murderers who cared nothing either for Edelred or for the house of Brenuin. Those men we dealt with also. Do not forget that the Gauntlet has been an instrument of the law."

"Edelred's law," Leon replied.

"Apart from money to acquit our so-called guilt," Waite said, "what else will this council require of us?"

"Nothing," Hughan answered, "bar the laying down of arms. The Gauntlet will be disbanded, its insignia burnt, its men released from their oaths. They shall then be free to establish themselves in this land as men renewed, settling according to their desires and with my blessing."

"Will your blessing protect a man who once wore red from a knife in the dark?" Fletcher asked.

"Ungrateful cur," Feltumadas spat, almost rising from the table. "He has already offered you more than you deserve."

"Lord Feltumadas," Hughan cautioned. His voice gripped the

hall at once. "These men have come in peace and at my bidding."

"Yes, Star," Feltumadas answered, casting a final glower at Fletcher.

Hughan looked back to Fletcher. "I will do everything in my power to protect those who once wore red."

"The Gauntlet cannot idyllically return to hoes and fields," Waite said, "nor even to trades, even if they knew them before."

"Not all of them," Hughan agreed. "It is my hope, general, that after a time some of them may take another colour."

A shocked silence fell.

It was Anastasius who first spoke. "With due reverence, Star," he said, turning quietly to Hughan, "these men were bound to Edelred. How can you propose binding them to yourself?"

"They are fit for the gallows and precious little else," Feltumadas fumed. "There is not a man among them who can truly clear his name or hands by paying. Their guilt cannot be expunged so easily and it is no mercy to pretend that it can."

Suddenly Eamon found his voice on his lips. "You cannot know, Lord Feltumadas, what these men have endured." All the eyes in the room turned to him and his voice grew in anger as he spoke. "How many of these men knew what it meant to bend their knee to Edelred when they received marks on their palms? How many of them understood, when they strove against wayfarers or Easters, the battles that they fought? How many of them ever thought of a King, a true King, as more than a figment of a childhood imagining or a diseased mind? Maybe none of them. Should they be outcast and hounded for that, or for a colour that they donned when they knew no better?"

Feltumadas looked grimly at him. "I think you paint them with too simple a brush, First Knight."

Eamon saw Hughan raise an eyebrow. As their gazes met, the King nodded. Eamon turned to answer Feltumadas.

"Only one thing about the Gauntlet is simple, Lord Feltumadas: they are men. They gave service, unto their lives, for Edelred. Is it wrong that they should be afforded the chance to do the same for the King, and in better heart? There is honour, courage, and loyalty among them no less than among the King's own. You do these men wrong to call down curses on them, to denounce them and revile them. I have walked where these men walk. I know what they know and I tell you, Feltumadas, that red is also a noble colour."

"Red is no more noble than black," Feltumadas said spitefully. Then his face suddenly grew grey as he realized what he had said, and to whom.

Eamon looked at him with anger. "Both are noble."

There was a pause in which Eamon felt the room stare at him. Perhaps the greyest faces of all were those of the Gauntlet, who could not comprehend that the man who wore blue and sat beside the King spoke for them.

Hughan's hand alighted on his shoulder.

Drawing a deep breath, Eamon tried to calm himself. "I say to the council that many of the Gauntlet are noble men, with skilled hands and able hearts. If a man turns to the King he should be welcomed with joy. Why should it matter, when he turns, whether that man once wore red, or black?"

"Of course it matters!" Feltumadas answered.

Eamon looked at him. "If you would cast out a man that has worn red or black then you must cast me out also," he returned fiercely, "for I have worn them both."

"I know you to be the Star's from what you have done," Feltumadas answered, looking only a little cowed. "These men will have done nothing."

"Except turn to me," Hughan interjected calmly.

The Easter seemed taken aback. "Forgive me, Star. But if they do not turn?"

Caught up in his fury, Eamon did not allow Hughan to answer. "They are still men enough to take up arms!" he cried. "You demean them and slander them, and yourself, to make that worthless, which you do when you speak of sending them to the dogs like…"

"Like a Hand?" Feltumadas snorted and shook his head.

"Hands are a different case to the Gauntlet, First Knight," Ithel put in quietly, leaning slightly across the table towards him.

"I would agree, Lord Ithel," affirmed Hughan. Their eyes turned to Feltumadas.

The incensed Easter gave Eamon a curt look. "You may speak for the Gauntlet as much as you like, First Knight, and perhaps I shall cede to you, but you cannot speak for the Hands, nor can you claim suffrage with them or intercede for them."

"The Hands are not beyond the King's mercy," Eamon told him. "Have you not heard what Febian did, or of the lives that he saved?"

"We know of the lives he took," Leon put in.

"That was long before those he saved," Eamon replied. "Why is it so hard to believe that a Hand might change? Did you never hear of Lord Ashway?"

"Lord Ashway?" Feltumadas gaped. Confused looks passed about the table. Feltumadas laughed unpleasantly.

Hughan watched him appraisingly. "Why do you laugh, Lord Feltumadas?" he asked. His voice was calm, but Eamon guessed that the King's patience for the Easter's outbursts was practised, and perhaps waning.

"Star, even I know that he was there at the beginning, when Ede was slain! His hands were steeped in blood from the beginning. *From the beginning!*" Feltumadas shook his head bitterly. "Never could Ashway have been received by you."

"Were you with him at the end?" Eamon retorted. In his mind, Eamon saw the Hand, bound and weeping: "*I will say nothing to him of you…*"

Eamon glared at the Easter, tears in his own eyes. "At his end Ashway knowingly defended a King's man from Edelred, at the cost of his life."

"How would you know that?" Feltumadas demanded.

Eamon looked straight at him. "Because I was with him at the end, and I am the man that he saved."

There was a long silence. Apart from the King every man in the room gaped like a fish out of water. Anderas's face went wide with realization, as if he finally understood what he had witnessed in the East Quarter the night that Ashway had lost his life. Longroad and Fletcher both stared at him. Rocell's face was twisted in an odd mixture of awe and fear. Only Waite seemed little moved.

Eamon drew a deep breath. When he spoke again, his voice was quieter. "Neither you nor I, Lord Feltumadas, can speak as to whether the King will accept a man into his service. But I do not believe that any man, if he truly turns, is beyond it."

Quelled at last, Feltumadas sat back in his chair. "Of the former you have the right of the matter, First Knight," he said. "I earnestly hope that I shall live to say the same of the latter."

Eamon felt a light touch on his arm. He turned and Hughan nodded to him. Silent and shaking, Eamon sat.

"I will welcome any man who would serve me," Hughan said firmly, looking at the men before him. "Any man, be he Gauntlet or Hand, thresholder or knight. But let him first wrest his heart from old oaths."

"What of the knights?" Rocell asked. "Are they to be stripped of their titles and their lands?"

"No," Hughan answered. "Any man still living who held land will hold some still, though in the months to come what they hold will change. The knights and nobles will be required to pay, just as the Gauntlet – they too took oaths to Edelred, although not as binding. From them the sum shall be fifty crowns."

Rocell nodded quietly then looked up. "It will be done," he said.

"Thank you, General Sir Rocell," Hughan answered him, then looked to Waite. "Will the Gauntlet accept also?"

Waite sat silent for a long moment. Eamon felt the general's eyes on him, and perhaps he saw a look of pride touch the general's face.

"We have laid down our arms. These terms also will we accept," Waite said. "We will pay, and we will disband."

"Are you all in agreement?" Hughan asked, looking at the others.

"Yes," the captains and lieutenants answered in turn.

"Thank you," Hughan answered.

They proceeded to discuss the arrangements as to how the money was to be gathered and paid, but Eamon heard only parts of it. His blood still pounded with his stirred passion.

Shortly the meeting concluded. The Gauntlet officers were escorted from the room. At the King's dismissal, men rose from the table all around Eamon. Standing himself, if somewhat unsteadily, he crossed the room to Feltumadas. The Easter lord finished exchanging a few quiet words with Ithel. He laughed a little as Eamon approached.

"The Gauntlet has a fierce champion."

"Lord Feltumadas –" Eamon began, but Feltumadas stopped him.

"I must ask your pardon, First Knight," he said. "This is not my court and I should not have spoken to you as I did."

Eamon looked at him in surprise. "I will be frank, Lord Feltumadas: I did not expect an apology from you." Feltumadas laughed. "I wanted to offer you an apology of my own."

Now it was the Easter's turn to look surprised. "I shall hear it, but only out of curiosity."

"I do not retract a word of what I said," Eamon told him, "but I perhaps could have expressed myself more calmly. Like me, you spoke out of the heat of your heart, and it was not wrong of you to do so."

"The Gauntlet and the Hands will be the object of much hatred and scorn in the months and years to come," Feltumadas answered. "Many will speak against them as I do; it is right that someone should also speak for them." He smiled. "They could not have chosen a better defender."

"Thank you," Eamon replied. Feltumadas bowed once to him and took his leave. Eamon gazed after him.

As men left the room Eamon found the King at his side. "Did I dishonour you?" he asked.

"Dishonour me?" Hughan repeated. He seemed surprised.

"I grew angry."

"With reason," Hughan replied. "You spoke fearlessly and well. The Gauntlet have long been the arm of a man who cared nothing for them. To know that the First Knight himself pleads for them, braving the wrath of the Easters and many wayfarers, will give them hope."

Eamon paused before he spoke.

"I too will pay," he said. "I should pay more than any other man – I was Gauntlet, and a Hand, and a Right Hand, and many were the times that I shed blood that should not have been shed. Worse than that, I shed it having given my oath to you."

Hughan nodded. "It would be a valiant act – and a right one."

They stood together for a moment, the silence of the hall all around them.

"What happens now?" Eamon asked quietly.

"The Gauntlet will disband, renouncing their oaths," Hughan answered. "We will destroy the Nightholt, committing it and its Master to the flames. There will be a procession in two days' time; the announcements have already gone forth." He paused and looked up. "When that is done, First Knight, we can set this city and this land on the long road to peace."

Peace. The word hung in the air like longed-for birdsong on a distant hill. The battles had been fought, and won, but peace was still far away. It would have to be made, and kept. Eamon's heart shrank before the thought of the countless meetings, the petty wars and trade disputes, the rebuilding of cities and towns, and strengthening of infrastructure, the swaying of men's hearts… These things and many more lay on the road about which the King spoke.

And then there was Alessia.

"Neither peace nor righteousness can be yours, Eben's son."

The voice had died with Edelred, but the remembered words shocked through him like a blow. Pain drove through his shoulder and he drew a sharp breath.

"Eamon."

Blinking hard, he looked up. His mind whirled. How could he ever be a man of peace? He could not even make peace with the woman he loved. How could he then serve the King?

Hughan's keen eyes watched Eamon's face with concern, but Eamon resisted his desire to speak aloud what troubled him. Had the King not been burdened enough with his First Knight for one day?

"It is nothing," he said distractedly.

Hughan looked long and hard at him. "Lying will never protect me, Eamon," he said, "and it will not help you."

Eamon was horrified. "Hughan, I never meant to…" he faltered.

"Then do not," Hughan replied simply. His gaze softened. "What ails you is not nothing. You have borne much, First Knight, and there is much still to bear. You see the days of mourning, you carry the burden alone, and you ask, when will comfort come? For you do not see it."

Eamon felt as though he gazed upon the radiance of a living star. The King's face was loving and resolute, undaunted by the road ahead.

"But comfort will come. Courage, Eamon," Hughan told him, "for you will know peace, and you will live to see peace restored, and I tell you that you will live to see it become an inheritance even of your own house. Look to that, Eamon, and take heart."

Eamon met the King's gaze and his courage returned to him. He knew that the King spoke the truth. He knew also that though the road ahead was long, he had chosen to return so that he might walk it.

"I followed you to war, Hughan," he whispered at last. "I will follow you to peace."

CHAPTER XXV

Though the stones and streets of Dunthruik rang to the beat of rain during the next day and all of its night, the early hours that followed brought with them fresh skies and birdsong that reached up towards fading stars. It was the twentieth of May.

In those grey hours before the dawn, the city stirred. From every street and every house, the men and women of Dunthruik came forth, their shoulders covered against the pre-dawn chill with cloaks or shawls. In the quiet, each one turned their steps through the streets towards the Four Quarters. From the colleges and from buildings made into hospitals or holding areas, from every quarter and every gate came the Gauntlet and the knights, the thresholders and the militia. Like the people of Dunthruik, they too turned towards the city's heart.

Even as they walked, a procession left the palace. It passed quietly from the gates, bearing no torch in the grey light, and went silently along the Coll. It was formed of sombre men in blue. The King went at its head and before its load.

Eamon went at his side, feeling the stillness and quiet of the city all around them. He thought of the hundreds of times that he had walked the Coll or seen the streets and alleys of Dunthruik. Long before the grey light revealed them, he knew the roof of the theatre and the shapes of the houses running along to the gates, and he knew also the Blind Gate and the mountains which loomed behind them, masses on the horizon cloaked by the half-light.

He had walked the Coll as a lieutenant, a first lieutenant, a Hand, a Right Hand, a King's man, and even a First Knight. That day he walked it as a witness – one who went with the great palls being brought down from the palace gates.

The procession wound down the road towards the Four Quarters. Eamon saw the tall statues up ahead, and between each quarter the shape of the buildings and roads. Gaps in the buildings looked east to the plain, north to the hills, west to the sea, and south to the River. The Four Quarters were the heart of the city. Eamon wondered whether the whole of the River Realm might not have its heart there.

Traffic did not move through the quarters that day, nor did battle roll across its stones. That day the Four Quarters were filled with people – men and women, young and old, noble and servant, Gauntlet and King's man. The procession came before them into the quarters and they watched it in silence and in awe.

A platform had been raised in the centre of the quarters. To this Hughan made his way. The two long palls borne by the procession came after him. A great red banner covered one; the other was shrouded in black. Dunthruik saw them, and was silent.

Eamon watched as the palls were set upon the platform and the King stepped up between them. With the still twilight all about him and the silver coronet on his head, the King stood upon the bank of an ancient shore, like a man from time forgotten.

Hughan Brenuin looked towards the east, and towards the watching city.

"People of Dunthruik," he said, "the city in which you live, which you have served and which you love, had of old another name. Its name was Allera, a name given to it by the first of the house of Kings. To that same house, the people of the River and of this city gave loving allegiance.

"That house was the house of Brenuin, a house of stars, of swords undrawn, and promise. To it had been given the kingship of the River and its lands. The house pledged itself to keep them in prosperity and peace. That pledge was made by the first Brenuin, between himself and the people of the River; in return, the people swore service to his house. He was given lordship over the land, as had been promised to him, and the pledge that he made became known as the King's Covenant. For many years it was kept and this land prevailed against many evils.

"Becoming sure and reckless in their strength and in the Kings who governed them, the hearts of the people of the River Realm changed, and the promises made to them, promises bound in the King's Covenant, were forgotten or abused. In place of courage and goodness came arrogance, weakness, and oath-breaking."

The crowd fell utterly still.

"It was in that time that an Easter, Aras, son of Amar, learned of the King's Covenant. He was a learned man and he was keen of wit. He understood that the protection over the River Realm had grown weak, as the laws on which it was founded had fallen by the wayside, and he understood also how he might gain from that weakness.

"He came to the River Realm's borders openly, but with a hidden heart. Into Allera he came, and by deceit he took the King's Covenant and in its place he wrote his own, seeking to bind land and people to his will by words of his own devising. No promise had been made to him; he had made no pledge with the people nor had any lands been given into his hands, and yet he desired them. So he claimed that by the ending of the house of Kings, and the destruction of the King's Covenant, his own house would take their place.

"He drew men away from the King, making them his servants, promising them strength and power, and binding them to him. Among these men he also drew the King's First Knight, through treachery and deceit. When the last battle between Aras and King Ede was joined, it was the First Knight who brought the first strike against his King. Betrayed, King Ede was killed."

Some gasped – perhaps they had not known the story. Eamon inhaled deeply, wondering if their eyes turned to him. Then he exhaled: he was no longer bound by the fate of his forebears.

The King once more took up his tale: "The King's Covenant was destroyed and the King lay dead. Aras took another name – Edelred – and Ede's First Knight became Edelred's Right Hand.

Those men who had followed Edelred witnessed the raising of the tome in which Edelred had set his will for the land. He deemed that it should serve him in body and in blood, receiving nothing in return. This covenant was one of blood and suffering, holding dark and hidden things, the fruit of Edelred's own thought. He called it the *tierrascuro*; his closest, who would be called his Hands, named it the Nightholt, and none could see it or change it but he alone.

"Edelred marched to Allera in the power of his will and waged war against the city until it was taken and its people were laid to waste. Edelred claimed sole hold of the city, renaming it Dunthruik, and an eagle was set over the River Realm.

"The men who had served Edelred on the field of battle became known as the Gauntlet. Along with the Hands, they received the power which had been promised to them, for it was marked into their flesh with fire." In the crowd, some rubbed at palms or tucked hands away. "By that mark they worked Edelred's will, and receiving it, they feared him, for he bound their own blood to his power. The River bowed, and trembled.

"Edelred's power was in the Nightholt, and Edelred was secure as long as none could gainsay him. To this end he sought to blot out the last of the royal line. But the First Knight remembered his vow and saved Elaina Brenuin, last of her house, from the Eagle's grasp.

"It is from that last daughter of the house of Brenuin that I descend. I have come to take up again the rights of my house and to undo the bonds of the Nightholt, to which this land and its people have been unlawfully bound."

Eamon listened to the King's words as though under a spell. Suddenly Hughan's eyes were upon him.

Gathering all his courage, he stepped out from among the King's men. The men and women in the quarters stared at him as he moved like a shadow across the square. He knew that many of them would recognize him; they knew who he had been, and now they knew the story of his house. As he went forward, garbed in the cloth of a King's man, they could also see who he had become.

Slowly he climbed the steps of the platform where the King stood. Behind him the long swell of the Coll led west to the sea caught up between the tall posts of the Sea Gate. To either side of the King lay the two draped hearses; the sight of them cooled Eamon's blood.

There was a bag in his hands – his blood money. In the moment of silence as he met Hughan's gaze, it felt heavy.

"Let this stand against the blood that I have unjustly shed," Eamon said. He pronounced the words loudly, though his voice shook. "By it, let peace come between me and the people of the River Realm."

In silence he held the bag out towards Hughan. It was everything he had, but he relinquished it into the King's hands without a second thought. The King set the bag aside on a broad dish. By it was another, filled with water.

Hughan looked back to Eamon. As he did so, Eamon spoke again.

"I, Eamon Goodman, who was Lord of the East and Right Hand to Edelred, do hereby renounce all bonds between himself and me. His will is not my own, and shall no longer hold over mine." He struggled to keep his voice steady. "As it is for me," he said at last, "so let it be for the Hands."

Looking up he found that the King watched him keenly.

"Hold up your hand, Eamon."

For a moment Eamon looked at him in confusion. Then, not daring to guess or to hope at what might follow, he silently lifted his right hand and held it out towards Hughan. It shook in the growing light. Hughan took hold of his palm. The King gently pressed his own fingers against Eamon's hand. Light appeared about them – light that felt as cool and clear as a mountain spring. Eamon gazed on in wonder. Hughan drew his finger in a firm gesture over Eamon's palm, striking through the mark of Edelred. Then he took Eamon's hand and gently set it in the basin of water. The King cupped water in his own hand, and with it he washed Eamon's forehead. Eamon was unable to breathe for sheer wonder.

The King raised Eamon's hands from the basin and brushed the last drops of water from his brow. The mark of Edelred, and all its lingering fire, went with them.

Tears ran freely down Eamon's face as the King stepped back from him.

"Thus are you released from all oaths to Edelred," Hughan said. "As it is with you, so may it be with every Hand."

"Thank you," Eamon whispered.

Hughan smiled at him. "Stay here with me."

Shaking still, Eamon stepped back to one side of the platform. Blinking tears from his eyes, he watched as Waite came forward from the gathered Gauntlet. The general also bore a bag in his hand: coins chinked inside it as the man climbed the platform.

Waite held the King's gaze for a long moment.

"Let this stand against the blood which I have unjustly shed," he said at last. "As it is with me, so shall it be with the Gauntlet. Let there be peace between the Gauntlet and the people of the River Realm." Wordlessly, Waite handed the bag to Hughan. The King nodded to him and set it aside. Waite paused for a long moment, and Eamon felt the man's eyes meet his across the platform.

At last Waite spoke. "I, Alduin Waite, who was general of the Gauntlet, do renounce all bonds between Edelred and myself. As it is with me, so let it be for the men under me."

Hughan reached out and gently touched Waite's hand; light flickered on the King's fingers. Astonished fear swept across Waite's face as the King laid the general's hand in the water and washed it. Eamon understood the man's look: Waite had joined the Gauntlet in his youth and he had borne the throned's mark upon his palm through all the long seasons of his life. Now, the light in Hughan removed it in a moment.

Waite shook as Hughan let go his hand. The King smiled kindly at the trembling man.

"Thus are you, Alduin Waite, released from all oaths to Edelred," he said. "As it is with you, so let it be with the Gauntlet."

As he said it, sounds of surprise erupted from the men that watched. Many touched their hands in alarm or astonishment. Some had tears on their faces; others merely stared.

Eamon looked back to Hughan with renewed amazement. At Hughan's words and gestures, the mark had been lifted from the Gauntlet.

Waite stepped back and descended the platform. As he did so, Eamon saw more movement among the King's men. Leon came forward. The King's man also held a bag in his hands.

"Let this stand against the blood which I have unjustly shed," he said, his voice firm and clear in the morning light. "As it is with me, so shall it be with those who served the King in the long months before open battle. Thus let there be peace between the wayfarers and the people of the River Realm."

Dunthruik watched in amazement as Leon solemnly handed the bag to the King then bowed low and left the platform.

At a look from Hughan, Eamon went and stood by the King's side. It was then that Anastasius climbed the platform towards them. The Easter had something spread across his hands – a black cloth lay over it. Anastasius halted before the King. Hughan slowly uncovered what the Easter bore.

Eamon's blood chilled as he saw what lay beneath the dark fabric, for he knew it at once. He knew its touch, its feel, its bitter darkness, and the writhing letters wrought upon it.

On the Easter's hands, fell but still in the grey light, lay the Nightholt.

For a moment Eamon could only stare at it, but then he felt Hughan's eyes on him. He understood why the King had asked him to stay.

In silence, Eamon stepped across to Anastasius and took up the book from his outstretched palms. The Easter gave a small sigh of relief as Eamon held the tome in his own hands. Eamon had drawn it out of Ellenswell, he had taken it from Arlaith's treacherous grasp, and he had rendered it into the hands of Edelred himself. Now

Eamon turned, and before the gaze of the whole of Dunthruik, he carried the Nightholt to Hughan.

With the book in his hands, he stood before the King. Then he opened it across his palms so that the tome's very heart and spine lay exposed to Hughan. The weight of the pages writhed against his hands, but Eamon held it resolutely. Though the pages strove against him, there was no longer any mark upon him, and they could harm him no more.

"This is the Nightholt of Edelred," Eamon said, his voice ringing clearly between the stones of the city's heart. "Hands and Gauntlet both have renounced its bindings as unlawful. To the King we commit it, hoping in the line of Brenuin, and trusting to the grace vested in that house. O King," he said, going down onto one knee, "let the Nightholt be unbound, and its hold undone."

A terrible and breathless silence fell over the watching men and women. Eamon's hands trembled.

Hughan Brenuin laid his hand upon the pages of the Nightholt. The letters on those pages tried to flee before the King's fingers, yet they could not.

"For this land and for its people I speak," Hughan said. "We have seen the ill that has been done through the will of Edelred; we have renounced it and its works. We will not be beholden to a false covenant. Let us, then, be loosed from it, and return to the first things of this land, in full and lawful hearts." He looked at the book and the silence deepened.

Eamon's heart and breath fell still. The King's bare palm was set against the pages, and the presence of the King's grace thrilled through Eamon's every pore and stirred the air all around him, like the thousand singing voices in the faraway city he had once seen.

"In the power of the promise and grace given to my house, and sealed still in the King's Covenant," Hughan said, "I declare this work undone."

Suddenly the light came. It erupted about the King's palms like a cascade of streaming, living water, filling the air and covering the

Nightholt with its brilliance. In the midst of the rushing splendour, the tangled letters on the Nightholt's pages grew disfigured, distorting under the inundation of light. For a moment, as the light soared and danced over and about him, the King shadowed forth in fearsome brilliance, a mirror to a King of old, a glimmer of a King to come.

The light and vision faded. As Hughan withdrew his hand, Eamon felt again the weight of the book in his hands – but now that weight was dull and lifeless. The pages lay limp. The letters, and all they had held, were gone.

Hughan slowly took the book from Eamon's hands and raised it high, showing the now blank pages to the staring city.

"People and realm of the River," he called, "you are beholden to Edelred no more."

Lowering the book, the King took the cloth that Anastasius still held. He carefully wrapped the Nightholt in it once more. Then, turning, he laid the black-bound book down on the breast of the red-clothed hearse. So doing, Hughan slowly drew back the pall from the face below. Eamon looked at what it revealed, part in fear and part in hope.

The pale face beneath was Edelred's. Red hair lay about it like a pool of frozen fire, the grey eyes closed forever.

Hughan stepped across to the black hearse and also pulled back the cloth. Eamon stared in surprise. The face that lay beneath the black shroud was Arlaith's. It was as though Ladomer had never existed.

As the King stepped back a pace, a group of Easter drummers in the quarters beat a solemn march. Each long hearse needed six men to bear it. The King, Anastasius, and Waite went to Edelred's; each of them was matched by a wayfarer, an Easter, and a former Gauntlet. Eamon himself went to Arlaith's pall; Feltumadas and Rocell did the same, and men of their colours matched them.

As the drums beat on, the palls were lifted. Eamon felt the weight of the wooden frame and the body upon it as it bore down on his shoulder. The King led Edelred's pall down from the platform and towards the Coll. The men and women of Dunthruik fell back before it.

Drawing a deep breath, Eamon set his steps to the beat of the drums and led the Right Hand, in Edelred's wake, from the Four Quarters towards the East Gate.

The march went slowly down the Coll. Eamon's world shrank to the weight on his shoulder, to the beat of the drums, to the gate before him. The long road was lined with people, with faces pale and staring in the half-light, who stood in silence, watching Edelred and his Right Hand pass by. Marching feet, like the beat of a thousand drums, followed behind the procession. No word was said, no song was sung. Dunthruik watched its fallen Master as he passed.

The procession came steadily to the Blind Gate. That morning the damaged gate stood open, its broad expanse looking out towards distant mountains where the hidden sun climbed.

Through the gates they passed, going on from the city to the plain where pyres once burned. The city's plain was marked with hundreds upon hundreds of graves on either side of the East Road. A small group of standards marked them. To the north stood red banners for the Gauntlet and the knights, while to the south stood blue and orange for the King's men and Easters.

The pyres had grown still in the days leading up to the battle, but they had also grown after it. A great mound of kindling had been set before them.

It was to this mound that the procession headed. Hughan and his group laid Edelred's pall down upon the kindling; Eamon and his men set Arlaith's hearse down at its side. Eamon's hands trembled as he came down from the mound.

The Gauntlet marched from the city, each man bearing his red jacket and banners. One by one, the captains and first lieutenants brought forth their standards and laid them on the great mound, forming a sea of red about the hearses.

As Eamon stood and watched them, Feltumadas stepped quietly to his side.

"First Knight," he whispered. The Easter lord held in his hands a spread of black. At once Eamon recognized it – the torn tabard that had been bestowed upon him by the throned.

In silence Eamon took it from the Easter. As the last of the Gauntlet laid down their colours, he stepped forward. The mass of red before him was overwhelming. The river of emblems flowed ceaselessly about the mound where throned, Nightholt, and Right Hand lay.

Eamon carefully set his tabard down over the colours then stepped back to join the ranks. The whole of Dunthruik had followed them.

Hughan took a torch from one of the King's men and carried it to the sea of red.

"In flame did Edelred come to Allera." Hughan's voice carried across the plain. Eamon felt as though the whole world might hear it. "In flame does he depart."

The King turned to the pyre. For a moment he stood and watched it. Then he leaned the torch forward against the tabards and the banners.

It was not long before the flames caught. Hughan stepped back as the great ribbons of fire streaked upwards, reaching for the two hearses.

As he watched the flames, tears stung Eamon's eyes. Since he had first come to Dunthruik his fate had been bound to the throned and to the Right Hand. Now their hold had been loosed, their power renounced, and both men were circled with fire. Memories of Edelred's affections, Ladomer's laughter, and Arlaith's cruelty danced in the flames.

With the hearses went a part of Eamon also. Though it had been tainted – by treachery, by lies, by wiles, by hurt, by anger, by pain, by abuse, by words and deeds wrought against him and against those whom he loved and served – he realized that he had at times loved both men; and he had loved Ladomer most of all.

Hughan came to his side. Though they exchanged no words, the King met his gaze with compassion.

As the sun struck over the crests of the mountain, flooding Dunthruik with light, and the flames slipped up towards Arlaith's still form, Eamon knew that he would never see Ladomer again. Edelred's pyre would burn long, and many would stay to watch it die in dark embers on Dunthruik's plain. Some would stay until nothing could be recognized of either throned or his Right Hand before they returned to the city.

But Ladomer Kentigern's was a lost face, not even to be consumed by fire. None would give it vigil.

The smoke stung at his eyes and the pain at his heart. Bravely, and with the King at his side, he forced himself to face the pyre. But as he did so, Eamon wept.

Later that day Hughan assigned groups of men to take responsibility for the quarters. Still in a daze, Eamon stood and listened as Hughan directed Feltumadas and a mixed group of Easters and wayfarers to the North, while Leon and a similar group took charge of the South.

"Lord Anastasius," Hughan said, "I would have you take the East; it was ever the place of your people in this city."

Eamon's heart sank as the words were spoken. He had hoped to be assigned there, for the East was the nearest place to a home he had in Dunthruik.

"I will take it, Star," Anastasius answered.

"First Knight, I would have you take the West," Hughan said.

"Yes, sire," he answered. The smell of smoke clung to him.

"There are some who would serve you," Hughan added. "I will take you to them in a moment."

Eamon nodded silently. After a few more minutes the King dismissed the others. "I know that the North shares responsibility with the West in the matter of the port," he said. "The port is going to need particular attention. Zharam says that the damage is still severe, and that we will have trouble getting food to the city and out into the rest of the realm until that is handled."

"Who is Zharam?" Eamon asked, struggling with the pronunciation of the strange name.

"He was in charge of the fleet that attacked the port," Hughan answered. Eamon's heart filled with his memory of that day, of the smoke in the air… "He's an ally from the southern merchant states."

"It was a violent attack," Eamon told him. "We lost many men that day." The image of burning ships and quaysides, of Manners being brought down from the wall, of the pile of bodies lying desolate on the wharf lingered with Eamon still. "Including Lord Dehelt," he whispered, and his heart churned. He looked up, feeling a touch of anger. "Did Zharam order that?"

"The order was to attack the port," Hughan answered gently, "not to kill particular men."

"Why did Dehelt have to be killed?" Eamon retorted.

"Men are killed in battles, Eamon," Hughan replied quietly.

Eamon remembered the Hand's face and supportive words… "But Dehelt might have turned!" he cried.

Hughan's face softened. "Eamon," he said, "Dehelt had been a Hand for a long time. He had long years in which to turn, yet he did not."

"But he might have done, had he lived," Eamon answered angrily.

"He might have done," Hughan conceded, "but in his long years in Edelred's service he did not. You may have been the last reminder of that sent to him, but still he did not turn." Eamon sighed. Hughan looked carefully at him. "His death does not lie on you," he said, "and that he did not serve me when he died does not make it wrong to mourn him."

The King took him from that room to another. Quiet voices filtered through the doors as they approached.

"There will be a lot to do in the next few days," Hughan told him, "and a lot of it will need to be done in the West. I am afraid that you will be very busy."

Eamon nodded. "I don't mind it, sire," he said. He knew full well that running a city was hard work at the best of times. When that city had also to prepare for a coronation and wedding, and adjust to regime change, as well as feed and protect itself while power changed hands, that work would be nearly doubled.

It would keep his mind from other matters, and that was not unwelcome.

The doors opened before them.

"These are some of the men who will help you with the West Quarter," Hughan said with a smile.

Surprise washed over Eamon. A number of King's men stood to one side, most of whom he recognized from the storming of the North Gate. Giles was among them. But it was not the King's men that surprised him; rather, it was the group of plainly dressed men who stood on the other side of the room.

One was Anderas. The second was Manners. And by them stood the man who had been Edelred's doctor. Beyond them stood three other men who had once been Edelred's servants.

Eamon gaped in amazement, then looked back to Hughan.

"They all asked to serve with you," Hughan told him. "I granted them their requests."

In a daze, Eamon greeted each of the two dozen men in the room. Giles was gruffly pleased to see him. Eamon embraced Anderas and Manners fondly. When he came to the doctor he felt a wry smile coming over his face.

"You asked to serve with me?"

"Yes, sir," the doctor answered. "I surrendered with the palace servants. They offered me a choice."

"Did they offer your leeches a choice, too?"

"I am afraid they were pressed into service before then," the doctor answered with a small smile.

"I'm sorry if this next question seems rude or blunt," Eamon told him, "but... why did you ask to serve me?"

The doctor watched him quietly for a moment. "I was no less

shocked than any other man to discover who you were," the doctor replied, "but you were kind to me those few times that we met. Kindness was a rare thing among the hearts of the men whom I served," he added quietly, "and so your kindness stuck with me."

Eamon smiled. "I am sorry to have forgotten it," he said, "but I hope you will answer when I ask… what is your name, doctor?"

"Leander Doveton," the doctor answered.

"Then I thank you, Dr Doveton, for asking for me," Eamon told him. "I must introduce you first of all to Andreas Anderas. He has the habit of getting stuck with arrows, and so I must ask you to keep him under your particular notice."

Anderas pulled a face but clasped hands warmly with the doctor.

Last of all, Eamon went to Edelred's former servants. One of them was the man who had first served him breakfast, and all three of them smiled. Eamon clasped each of their hands in turn.

"Welcome," he said. "I do not know how to say it with my hands," he added, "but I will learn."

The first servant smiled. "You will gesture well," he said.

Eamon's jaw dropped. "You can hear – and speak!"

The servant nodded. "I can now," he said. His voice was thick, as though he had to concentrate on forming the words. "Some could not speak," he added, gesturing to the third servant with him as an example, "but many of us were silenced by the red light. It does not silence us now."

"This man never spoke, even before?" Eamon asked, looking to the third servant.

"No."

Eamon paused. "How may I thank him?"

"The Master did not thank us," the servant explained slowly, "but we always touch our hearts – as you did, before."

Eamon turned to the third servant. The man looked attentive, his eyes wide as they darted around the room. Eamon stepped towards him, touched his hand to his heart, and bowed low.

"Thank you," he said.

The servant stood uncertainly for a moment. Then he echoed the gesture, and bowed. It filled Eamon's heart with joy.

As Eamon stepped back he looked to the first servant again. "Will you teach me to speak with him, and the others?"

The servant nodded. "I will," he said. Then he stood for a moment, simply watching Eamon. When Eamon offered him a quizzical look, the servant smiled. "You have a wonderful voice," the servant told him. "It is good to hear it."

"It is better to hear yours," Eamon answered, laughing.

Eamon proceeded to introduce each of the men in the room to all the others, and was pleased to see that there seemed to be no animosity between any of them. Giles was a little reserved but hid it well for a man of his bluntness. Eamon dared to hope that the formal show of reconciliation at the Four Quarters, the paying of blood money and renouncing of oaths, was already having some effect.

As the men gathered their things together and prepared to go with Eamon to the West Quarter, Eamon looked to Hughan again. The King had stood quietly to the side, a smile on his face. The King laughed.

"There is a lot of work to do," Hughan replied. "You deserve to work with men you love."

Eamon looked back at the men in the room and smiled. In that moment, the morning's pyre was forgotten.

The days that followed were perhaps the busiest of his life and Eamon was swiftly glad of the number of men Hughan had assigned to help him. The wayfarers were divided among the quarters, and Eamon oversaw repairs to the port, as well as the feeding and re-housing of many of Dunthruik's people, some of whom returned to the city from their places of exile as news of the throned's fall spread.

Eamon was glad that the work kept him occupied, for when the darker hours came, his thoughts grew dark with them. Working hard all day ensured that he fell asleep swiftly at night.

Having Manners and Anderas, even Doveton and Giles, with him was a constant joy, and he delighted in their company and passion for the work, even the most menial things, that needed to be done. Eamon slowly learned how to communicate with those who could not speak. Some of the wayfarers outside Eamon's immediate staff were suspicious of the former Gauntlet officers – and more so of Doveton – but most seemed content to let their suspicions be overridden by Eamon's own confidence in the men.

It was from the doctor that Eamon first learned that although the vast majority of the palace's servants had surrendered, the most senior had all been killed. The doorkeeper, as Eamon had seen himself, had died when the palace fell. He learned that the taster had been struck down shortly after Edelred's death by one of Hughan's own guard, and that the throned's secretary had been caught among fleeing Hands at the port.

Hughan sent messengers out to every part of the River Realm speaking of Edelred's fall. Word slowly trickled back from the provinces and regions of the land, from distant towns and Gauntlet divisions; each sent tokens of their surrender and gave their allegiance to the King. Most advised that they would send men to witness the forthcoming coronation, and as news of that event spread, work for the coronation quickened its pace.

Four days after Edelred's pyre, a group of men arrived at the palace, carrying a simple but broad casket. When he later spoke to Hughan on the matter, the King told Eamon that the men were the last of the bookkeepers. They had brought with them the surviving copy of the King's Covenant and were to preside over the coronation.

Though word of the surrender and disbanding of the Gauntlet arrived in a steady stream to the palace, news also reached the city of a particular Gauntlet captain in the northern borders. The man had not believed news of Edelred's fall, had refused to surrender, and having fought his way out of Galithia against enormous odds, had led his men to a fortress near Dunway, north of the city. The group held there.

"They're saying now that the captain won't give his surrender until he has seen the King himself," Anderas told Eamon. They walked back to the palace together after a long afternoon at the port, and the story, as it grew day by day, was a welcome distraction. "He seems to be awaiting further instructions."

"He certainly has courage," Eamon granted.

"His name is Roe."

Eamon looked across at him, startled. "Roe?" he repeated.

"Yes. By all accounts a most tenacious man," Anderas said, smiling. He looked back to Eamon. "I think you'd like him, if you met him."

"We've met his wife," Eamon answered.

Anderas looked at him in surprise. "Oh?"

"The singer from the Crown." As Eamon thought of Ilenia he wondered how she fared. He had not yet had the time to go and find her, or Shoreham, or any of his servants in the East Quarter. "Hughan will send someone to parley with Captain Roe. Probably someone formerly of the Gauntlet, whose word he may trust."

"We must only hope it isn't me," Anderas jibed.

"Because he'd shoot you?"

Anderas grinned. "Something like that," he said.

That afternoon Eamon went to see Hughan. As he gave his report on the work at the port, the King followed him attentively.

"If the wind holds fair, the first grain ship should come tomorrow," he finished at last.

"We shall have need of it," Hughan answered.

"We still have quite a broad store of the Ravensill wines," Eamon added. "Giles was taking stock of them this morning. They will set us in good stead for trade for a little while yet." He flicked through his notes. "A few more former Gauntlet came in as well, about half a dozen of them, asking for service. Manners and Anderas are vetting them." He looked up. "I heard that Leon had some news on Captain Roe?"

"Captain Roe," Hughan said with a smile. "His is becoming a good story indeed. Leon tells me that the captain has sent a delegation – one in which he includes himself – to come and see if Edelred has fallen. They are likely to arrive in two days. When the hobilars advise that the delegation is close enough, I will send Anderas to meet it."

"Not Waite?" It seemed to Eamon that Waite would be the obvious choice of ambassador.

"No. Waite did not feel ready to serve me in such a way."

The news saddened Eamon.

"I know Roe's wife, sire," Eamon added at last. "If we were to send for her when he comes, I think he may more swiftly give his surrender. It would also ease her heart."

Hughan nodded. "Thank you for everything you're doing, Eamon."

Eamon received the thanks with a tired smile. "Is there a date set for the coronation yet?"

"Oh that I might enact a tax upon every man who asks that question, the city's repairs would already be paid." Hughan smiled. "Maybe when we have cleared this situation with Roe," he answered at last.

"This city has awaited you for a long time," Eamon told him. "It will wait a day or two more."

"Waite has asked for leave to go from the city," Hughan told him. Eamon looked up in surprise.

"He's leaving before the coronation?"

"I will not make him stay."

Eamon pursed his lips together and looked up. "I will speak to him."

"You may," Hughan told him, "but I do not think that he will change his mind."

"He's a good man, Hughan," Eamon persisted.

"I know. But he is also a weary one, and he has borne much." Hughan paused for a moment. "They've finished clearing much of the rubble from the palace corridors. I've been told that the way to your old quarters is passable again. You may wish to go and recover some of your things when they clear the rooms."

"When do they mean to do that?" Eamon asked.

"Tomorrow morning. The carpenters will probably go up very early, but I'll ask the men to wait for you in the Round Hall."

"Thank you." Eamon drew a deep breath. "Where is Febian being held?"

"When I was last informed, he was being held with the last of the belligerent knights, in the lower East Wing corridors."

Eamon frowned. "But he surrendered," he said. Following the dissolution of their oaths, many of the Gauntlet and infantry had been given leave to go. Some had returned to their own regions, though many waited in the city to see Hughan crowned before starting the long journey home. If Febian had surrendered, he was entitled to that. "Isn't he as free as any other man?"

"Yes," Hughan replied, "but he has so far refused to come out of holding. He is one of the few Hands in the realm – and the only Hand in the entire city – that surrendered," he added.

"He must be afraid. May I speak with him?"

"Whenever you wish," Hughan answered.

CHAPTER XXVI

That evening Eamon left the palace. He returned to the West Quarter College, where his officers were based, to brief them on the latest news from the other quarters. After dismissing them, he called for Manners.

"Mr Manners?"

"Sir," Manners answered. The young man had proved himself a very able hand in the quarter's affairs, and had swiftly won the approval of the King's men with whom he worked.

"I understand from Giles that you are the fount of all West Quarter knowledge," Eamon began.

Manners smiled. "So he calls me, sir, in moments of what I am sure are utmost sincerity."

Eamon laughed. "Can you tell me where Waite resides?"

"With his sister, Lady Alben," Manners answered. "She has a house not far from here – Caulders' Way, I think." Manners looked at Eamon carefully. "You're going to see him, sir?"

"Yes."

"Would you give him my best?"

"Of course."

Eamon left the college and took himself out onto the Coll. The scent of high summer was all about him.

The house was down a quiet cobbled side street, which led south from the Coll. Grateful for the evening light, Eamon threaded his way past the doorways, and under the hanging balconies. He had done the same on that bright morning when he and the hobilars had come through the city, claiming the streets for the King.

Now he walked alone, and though he knew that many people still had much to mourn, the air about him seemed at peace. It was a feeling he had not often felt in Dunthruik, and for a long moment he stopped to let it fill his senses.

The Albens' house was well sized and well kept. A small flight of steps led from the street up to its door. Lights shone within. He knocked.

For a long moment there was no answer. Then he heard a voice on the other side of the door.

"Who is there?" it called.

"Eamon Goodman."

The door drew open and the light fell on Eamon's face. Waite stood in the threshold, keeping the door only narrowly open. Lady Alben stood behind him, her face pale and worry-creased.

"What would you, First Knight?" Waite asked, his voice crushingly formal. His limp right arm was still bound in a sling.

"I have not come as the First Knight," Eamon answered quietly. "I am sorry, Lady Alben, to intrude on your house. I hope you and your husband are well."

"Her husband fell on the field," Waite replied harshly.

Eamon looked at the frightened lady and his heart turned in remorse. "I am so sorry, Lady Alben."

"It was not your doing, sir, any more than my son's death was," the woman answered.

Waite looked at Eamon but Eamon did not meet the gaze.

Lady Alben drew a shuddering breath and looked at him again. "I thank you for your kind words," she said, "but I am sure you did not come to speak with me."

"In truth, I came to speak with your brother," Eamon replied, then met her gaze again. "I am sorry, Lady Alben, for what you have suffered, and hope that you may find comfort and kindness in the days ahead."

The lady watched him for a moment, then bowed her head. "Thank you," she said, then looked at Waite. The man still held the door defensively in one hand. His gaze was filled with anger. "Let him in, Alduin," Lady Alben said quietly.

Silently Waite drew back the door and stepped aside, leaving just enough room for Eamon to pass. Climbing the last of the steps, Eamon did so. The door closed heavily behind him.

Lady Alben led them both to a small side room. There were some chairs in it on a broad, faded carpet.

"You may speak in here. You will not be disturbed."

"Thank you for your kindness, Lady Alben," Eamon told her.

A faint smile passed over her face. She looked once to her brother and then withdrew, closing the door.

For a moment, Waite and Eamon stood and watched each other. The piercing quality of Waite's gaze pricked at Eamon, and in it he felt the hurt that the man bore.

"Mr Manners asked me to convey to you his best and warmest wishes."

At last, the former general drew breath. "Please thank him." He looked at Eamon with a guarded gaze. "You have come as a guest into my sister's house. Do sit, First Knight."

Feeling awkward, Eamon took the chair offered to him. Waite sat heavily down across from him, and held his gaze in the long silence. Eamon found that he could not speak.

After a time Waite gave a snapping laugh. "Is it possible that the Star's First Knight has become dumb since he entered this room? You have been many things, Eamon Goodman, but you have never been dumb, nor have you yet borne the appearance of it."

"The King told me that you mean to leave the city."

Waite bitterly threw back his head. "I cannot believe that you would come here about that!"

"Of course you can."

Waite stared at him. "My sister doesn't believe that you had any part in her husband's death," he said, an unpleasant glint to his eye.

"I didn't," Eamon answered levelly. "Lives slain on the battlefield cannot be counted in the same way as lives lost away from it. You know that."

"And her son?" Waite countered viciously.

Eamon looked at him through pained eyes. "For that I have paid," he replied. "His was not the only life I regret taking."

Waite looked at him silently, then shook his head in disgust. "He was sent against you," he said, the bitterness in his voice increasing. "For that – for you – he lost his life."

"I know. I regret that many who were dear to you have died because of me," Eamon told him.

Waite looked at him suspiciously for a moment. "My cadets." Waite bore the look of an outraged father on his face. "Long before the battle many of my boys lost their lives because of you."

"The deaths of 'the good men' was Arlaith's doing."

Waite stared at him. "You implied, after you killed him, that Lord Cathair was the author of those deaths."

"I believe that he was," Eamon answered, "and that he was working with Arlaith. Both of them hated me."

"Why would Arlaith –?" Waite began.

"I had taken his place," Eamon answered.

"They were not men as petty as that," Waite answered, shaking his head.

"Not as petty?" Eamon had to take a moment to recover himself. "Don't you remember when they meant to decimate my men after Pinewood? They did that to strike at me. They would willingly have killed every single man." Waite remained silent. "But they were not just petty. Though Cathair did not know it, Arlaith meant to challenge Edelred."

Waite laughed. "Don't be absurd!"

"Arlaith took the Nightholt and withheld it from Edelred because he wanted it for himself," Eamon told him. "Tramist was a conspirator with him, and Ashway, too. When I became Right Hand I became a threat to him and his plans." Eamon paused. "It was not the only reason he had to revile me."

"Knew about your Star, did he?" Waite griped angrily.

"Whether he knew or not, he killed your cadets to strike me."

"He killed them?" Waite shook his head with a snarl. "No,

Goodman, you did. You betrayed the Gauntlet: *you* killed them."

Eamon stared. "I never betrayed the Gauntlet."

"How was it not betrayal," Waite yelled, "to lead them onto the field and then leave them there?"

"I did not leave you," Eamon answered. "I did everything that I could to save you."

"Is that what Anderas thought he was doing?" Waite asked, his voice quieter but bitter still. "Is that why you've come now?" He laughed. "To save me?"

Eamon measured his gaze unhappily. "I came to ask you to change your mind, and stay."

Waite gave a grunting, resentful laugh. "Stay? For what?" he asked. "To kneel before Hughan Brenuin?" He spat the name viciously.

"He is the King," Eamon replied.

"And I am an old man," Waite replied, his voice growing louder and more wrathful as he went on. "My years of service were spent beneath your King's enemy. Your Star has taken every badge of my honour and burnt it, on a pyre, as though it were testimony of felony and I were worth little more than a dog!"

Eamon stared at him. "The King has never treated you as less than the man of honour and worth that you are. The Gauntlet was never ignoble for serving Edelred. All the same, it is now that the Gauntlet has its nobility to win."

"I heard you speak at the meeting," Waite interrupted. Eamon fell silent and watched as the former general sat, touching at the palm of his limp right hand with his left. "I know your view. You spoke well." He looked up suddenly, and laughed. "Since you first came to Dunthruik, Mr Goodman, you have spoken well, and men have spoken well of you. Sometimes I wondered why there were so many snakes in the West, in my quarter. There were many – Grahaven, Manners, probably half of the cadets who died were, too."

"They were not," Eamon answered, "but, whatever their colour, I loved each of them no less than you."

Waite paused for a long moment, pressing at his mark-less hand. "On the battlefield I understood that the number of snakes was not my doing; it was yours. You were always a King's man, but I never saw it and I never stopped you. That shames me, Mr Goodman. Because had I seen and stopped you, this story would have been very different."

"You would not have turned me," Eamon told him quietly.

"Maybe not," Waite answered ambivalently. "I always liked you and have been at times prouder of you than of any other man." His gaze hardened. "But, for all my fondness, I would have struck you down had I known what you meant for this city. It is only my shame, and that old care, which keeps me from doing so even now."

Eamon measured his gaze. "And your arm," he said quietly.

Waite arranged how the limp limb hung in the bandage. "It might have been better if it had been amputated," he mused. "I shall not use it again."

"Will you…" Eamon faltered. "Would you let me heal it?"

Waite drew a deep breath and laughed bitterly. "No, Mr Goodman," he said. "I shall bear this arm away with me and retire with my shame. Both shall be the prizes of my stupidity, the fruit of my service."

"You bear no shame."

There was a long silence. Waite held his gaze. "You would have me go and bend my knee to your King? You would have me add that to what already lies on me? I will not; I cannot. Do not look so alarmed," he said, laughing at the expression on Eamon's face. "Be assured that I will do as I have promised and has been commanded of me. I will take up no arms against your Star and I will advise any who ask me that they would do well to pay their blood money and go free. These things I will do; but I will not humble or humiliate myself before your King. I did not turn you," he said, "and you shall not turn me."

Eamon watched him for a moment. Waite matched his gaze evenly, and Eamon understood at last that he could not be swayed.

Slowly he rose to his feet. "I am sorry to have troubled you, and your sister, with my coming," he said. "I would say but one thing more." Waite raised a derisive eyebrow at him. Eamon steeled himself against it. All the words that he had hoped he might say to the man before him – a man whom he had served and loved – he now knew would likely always go unsaid. But still, he spoke.

"It was an honour to serve under you, sir."

Waite's gaze seemed to soften a little. "I mean you very little offence, Mr Goodman," he said, "when I ask you to go."

Eamon left.

Eamon lay awake for a long time that night. His dreams, when he slept, came upon him like blows. But he could not remember them when he started awake, searching for her hand; all he felt then was the moonlight streaming through the window onto his clammy face.

When the morning came at last he took himself down through the palace to the East Wing holding areas. They had been designated as detention rooms for some of the higher-ranking knights and officers. A series of storerooms had been converted for the purpose. In one such room Febian was kept.

The guards at the door bowed to Eamon.

"Good morning, First Knight," one said as he rose.

"I've come to speak with Febian."

The guard raised an eyebrow. "He is no longer here, sir."

"Oh. Can you tell me where he is?"

"No, sir. When the duty went down to deliver him food this morning, they found him fled."

Eamon couldn't mask his surprise. "I thought he was refusing to come out?"

"Yes, sir. He did leave a letter, sir; it's addressed to you."

Astonished, Eamon took the guard's direction to Febian's former quarters. He found a small but reasonable room, well tended and lit.

The letter lay on the bed, its markings those of a man who had written in a hurry. As Eamon unfolded it, something chinked to the ground. Light from the high windows helped him to locate its whereabouts: a small silver ring.

Eamon tightened his hand about it. He knew the ring. He had once taken it from under the eyes of the throned himself to return it to its keeper. He had last held it in the Pit. Had Febian come by it there?

He looked then to the letter. Its lines were rushed, but their fluidity marked a man of no little learning:

> Lord Goodman,
>
> *I know the price that will be demanded of me for my service now that your colours hold sway: I cannot pay it. That I leave this city with my life is all I can hope for.*
>
>   *This ring was given to me by one in the Pit – he asked me to give it to you. I trust that you know its meaning.*
>
> *Febian.*

Eamon sighed. He had hoped to come to Febian and be reconciled, perhaps even to call the man who might be Dunthruik's last Hand to serve the King. He did not know what haven the man would find outside the city.

He tucked the letter inside his jacket. Perhaps once coronation and wedding had been solemnized and the city set back in order, he would look for Febian. And then they could have peace.

CHAPTER XXVII

Passing through palace corridors, Eamon found his heart darkened. Waite was still a shadow, fluttering darkly at the back of his mind. Like Febian, he had made Waite a pawn.

He, too, knew that pain.

He drove the thought of Arlaith down deep into the pit of his mind, hoping to cage it there. He would never have had Ladomer's apology even if he had lived; Ladomer had meant every part of what he had done.

They could never have had peace.

Would he ever have peace with Alessia?

He walked swiftly to the Round Hall. The hall had many passages leading from it, and a group of men waited at its centre, Anderas and Giles among them. Anderas's head was tilted back as he gazed at the ceiling and its paintings. As Eamon approached, Anderas gestured to a part of the painting up in a distant corner of the ceiling, a smile on his face. The wayfarers about him, however, looked no more enlightened.

Eamon threaded his way past the other moving people to reach those that waited for him. He was glad to see that Anderas could still be relied upon for interesting architectural and artistic comment.

"What am I missing?" he asked, turning his own gaze upwards for a moment.

"Not much," Anderas answered brightly. "Just an example of an oft-maligned style of –"

"Good morning, First Knight," interjected a wayfarer.

"Good morning each," Eamon replied, looking at the men in turn. "I'm sorry to have kept you waiting."

"We weren't waiting long," Giles answered.

"I am glad of it, else you would all have been experts in oft-maligned art styles long before me," Eamon replied. "Shall we go up?"

The group moved across the hall. Eamon looked about the palace again: it chimed to the melody of King's men working. His heart cheered to witness it.

As they made to leave the hall, Eamon caught sight of a group of women passing along its far side. He paused for a moment, for a group of women in the palace was a strange and delightful sight. Aeryn walked at the head of the group; a few of Hughan's guards followed her. She spoke with a woman to her right, and then the group stopped for a moment while Aeryn spoke to one of the guards.

It was then Eamon noticed another face that he knew – how well he knew it! He knew its every contour, knew how a hundred shades of joy, sorrow, kindness and fear could move across the fair skin. That face looked up and caught his gaze across the crowded hall, and pierced through him like a blade.

It was Alessia.

For the briefest of moments what he had seen in Arlaith's mind flashed before him – Alessia, kneeling and weeping wretchedly before the Right Hand – and grief and remorse welled in him. Had he not seen what Arlaith had done to her – what she had endured for him?

He longed then to race across the hall, to wrap her in his embrace. Whatever else might pass between them, she needed to know that he knew everything she had done for him.

Their eyes met. The look froze him. He felt himself flush red with shame. How could he have treated her as he had done?

She lowered her eyes; her face darkened. It was as if she could not bear to look at him. The injury he took from it was keener than any he had received from Ladomer.

Would she not even give him a chance?

He began to quake. Haltingly, almost imperceptibly, he tried to step towards her. Surely she would at least hear him, even if she could not look at him? Her name bubbled to his lips.

"Alessia –"

Without even a glance at him, she swept from the hall. It seared him in two.

Would she not even –?

There was a light touch at his shoulder. "Eamon?" Anderas said quietly.

Eamon realized that he stood in the hall, gaping. The others waited for him.

Eamon shook. Anger began seeping into him – it was his only defence against his sorrow. He shook off Anderas's hand.

"I'm coming," he said.

The climb up to the Right Hand's quarters seemed long to him, and fraught with memories he could not shake. Almost, when he looked up, he saw Arlaith going before him, howling vicious taunts.

The doors to the quarters stood open. The rooms rang to the sound of voices and a small pile of things lay to one side. The black bedcovers lay in a crumpled mess on top of it.

Eamon's heart was heavy as he stepped through the doors into the chamber. Many of its decorations, such as its tapestries and hangings, had already been taken down, and some of the eagles had been brought down too; the stones were marked where the chisels had been employed against them. Some of the furniture had been gathered into the main hall and a couple of men carried one of the smaller tables across to stand it by the chaise longue.

"These were your quarters?" Anderas whispered. His eyes were wide with awe.

"Yes," Eamon answered. There was a touch of grief to his voice, for all about him the emblems of the Right Hand fell away from the walls in a wash of noise.

"Perhaps being Right Hand was not as terrible as it appeared," one of the wayfarers commented lightly.

Eamon rounded on him. "Not as terrible?"

Hearing latent anger in his voice, the wayfarer looked at him in confusion. "I meant, sir, that the quarters were comfortable –"

Eamon did not hear him. The grief that had been building in him since he left the hall erupted. "Not as terrible? Do you think that being Edelred's Right Hand, or the road that led there, was easy, or comfortable?"

The wayfarer didn't answer him.

"I took oaths that could never be reconciled, I was the pawn and prodigy of the Hands, who groomed me to evil. Those closest to me were killed, tormented in the Pit, or pierced by the rage of my enemies. This I had to suffer, never grieving or mourning, else I would have been discovered." His hands shook. "When I tried to feed the city I was ridiculed, when I tried to save innocent men I was reviled; I was baited and caged and made a fool; I was made Right Hand and dressed at Edelred's whim like a doll, watched and steered and touched by him. Whether he chose to love me or to hate me, I bore it, and at the end I was betrayed nigh to death." His voice had grown to a raging volume and the whole room stared at him. "Not as terrible?" he laughed bitterly. "I know terror when I see it and I tell you, King's man, that this is the most terrible room you have ever seen."

The wayfarer met his gaze fearfully. "Yes, sir."

Regret flooded through Eamon at an instant, but no more words came to his mouth. His anger had taken all his speech.

Giles and Anderas exchanged glances.

"There's work to do," Giles said, leading the other men away.

Eamon watched them go in a daze.

"Eamon," said Anderas.

"Andreas," he began, "I didn't mean to…"

"I know," his friend answered. There was a brief pause. "What happened in the hall?"

"Nothing."

"I don't think you would have spoken to him like that if that were true," Anderas replied firmly.

Eamon fell silent.

"You were looking at the women in the hall. Was one of them... her?" Anderas asked more quietly.

"Yes," he whispered.

Anderas laid a hand on his arm. "Perhaps you should let us deal with this," he said, gesturing to the room.

"There's only a small wooden trunk of my things," Eamon told him. "It was in the bedchamber."

"I'll recover it for you."

"I should apologize to that man," Eamon began.

"Yes, you should, but I think you must have other priorities to deal with first," Anderas told him. "I will speak to him for now."

Eamon looked at him sorrowfully. "You shouldn't have to do that for me –"

"But I will."

The gaze of his friend comforted him.

"Eamon – go and find her."

Anderas was right. Nodding silently, Eamon left the room.

He went slowly back down to the hall, his head spinning. The place was filled with people going about their business. Eamon's eyes wandered back to the place where he had seen Alessia, and he stared as though he saw her still.

Without the shelter of his anger, he felt only pain – pain that she would not hear him, that she would not let him seek her forgiveness. How could he forgive himself without it?

He took the door that she had taken from the hall. He followed the sound of women's voices, thirsting after the sound of hers. He did not hear it. When he found the women, she was no longer among them.

He asked the women as to Alessia's whereabouts, but they could not tell him: she had taken her leave without giving any indication as to her destination. He combed the palace, searching through nearly every room and hall without success. He realized that she might not even remain in the palace. And if she had chosen to retreat to the streets of Dunthruik?

Then he would never find her.

In desperation, he went to Aeryn.

His old friend was enjoying some moments of quiet in her chambers – to which he was readily admitted.

"Eamon," she smiled, "it's good to see you."

"Thank you." He bit his lip. "Aeryn, have you... can you... do you know where I can find Lady Turnholt?"

Aeryn looked at him in surprise. "Perhaps," she said.

"Please... I need to speak to her."

"You haven't yet?"

Shame rushed through him. "No."

"When exactly were you planning to make time for her?" Her face was inscrutable.

Eamon's mind whirled. So much time had already passed since he woke... how could he not have sought Alessia already? She was the one thing that could not wait, and he had allowed himself to be led from distraction to distraction. What reception could she give him, after so long?

"Aeryn, I..." He pressed his hands over his face.

Ladomer was right: he had always been a fool. "I'm sorry, Aeryn," he said.

"You shouldn't be apologizing to me!"

"You must have other business to attend to –"

"She's here, Eamon."

His heart stopped.

"What?"

Aeryn gestured to the adjoining room. She looked to him again, her face unreadable. "I've just remembered some business I must attend elsewhere," she said softly. "You may remain here if you wish." Without another word, she slipped from the quarters.

Eamon gazed at the door, felt the stillness of the air. He heard the stifling of breath in the silence.

He moved towards the room. His search ended.

She was there.

Their eyes met. They were trapped, suspended in each other's gazes.

A shiver ran through his spine – his fear, his shame; his memory of her touch, gentle as the petals of a rose – and sweat pricked his brow.

"A... Alessia?"

She flushed scarlet, her eyes dropping to the floor. She neither stepped towards him nor moved away. He watched the fall of her hair about her face, ached to gather her to him. Ached at what he had done to her.

Ached at what they had lost.

He did not dare to move lest she dart away. He had longed to seek her out, to tell her –

What?

That he was sorry? That he had wronged her? That he had answered love with wrath – unjustly? That he had been a fool?

That he loved her? Yes, despite all the lies and anger he had harboured in his heart, he loved her. His passion for her had stoked his hurt. Anger had been his only defence against despair. Perhaps she would understand that, perhaps –

And if she should scorn him?

Slowly, so very slowly, he walked towards her. They scarcely breathed. She held still, like a doe in the dew. He stopped. She was an embrace away.

For what had passed between them, it might have been the universe.

"Alessia." He breathed her name – for it was as vital to him as breath itself. How could he have forgotten that?

She shuddered. Tears appeared on her cheeks. He reached out to comfort one he knew more intimately than any.

She slapped his hand away. "Don't touch me."

"Alessia?" He ached to hold her. "Alessia, I –"

"How dare you." She looked at him now, eyes darkened with grief and anger. "Did you once seek me, Eamon? Even once?" She trembled, as if neither her body nor her words were able to contain what she felt. "Did you even once think of what I bore for you? You knew how the Hands used me. Did you even know what I carried – what *he* took from me? Can you imagine that grief?"

He could not. Stunned, he could only be silent.

His silence was damning.

She shook her head in anger and in sorrow. "I knew that you would not be able to seek me until after the city was taken... I waited. I waited and waited for you. Still you did not come. I was forgotten, ignored, spurned. It hurt me more than everything I suffered at Arlaith's hands, for I realized then what worth I was to the man whom I had suffered to protect."

She bit her lip hard. "I don't even know why I should say this to you. I don't know what I can expect of you now."

He prayed that she spoke because she loved him still. "Alessia, please –"

"You did not hear me when I pleaded."

It cut him to the heart. It was true. It shamed him.

"Will you not even let me say –"

"There's nothing you can say, Eamon," she sobbed. "I loved you, I gave everything for you. You left me." Her sobbing became anguished cries. "Your time to speak and do has passed. You should have protected me, us. You did nothing. So there is nothing left that you can say. Do you understand? *Nothing.*"

He reached out to her again. She inclined towards him – almost she let him take her in his arms. But with a cry she snatched herself away.

"*I said don't touch me!*"

She turned and ran, weeping, from the room.

Eamon gaped after her, everything he longed to say burning in his heart. Anger and sorrow flooded him. He could not bear it.

There was only one to whom he could go.

He staggered dizzily through the palace to find Hughan.

Hughan's meeting room was guarded by two grim-faced Easters; they fell back before Eamon as he burst into the chamber.

Hughan stood alone at the long table, gazing thoughtfully at a map of the River Realm. There was a collection of papers in his hands. He looked up and cast the papers down at once.

"Eamon," he breathed. He swiftly crossed the hallway to him. Eamon could not breathe, could barely think, and did not feel the King's hands as they set themselves to his arms. "Eamon, what has happened?"

Eamon stared at the King for a long moment. His voice and sobs loosed in his throat.

"Why didn't you tell me?" he roared. "When I came with Edelred's terms before the battle and you told me she was alive – that she loved me! – why didn't you tell me what Arlaith had done to her?"

Hughan looked on Eamon with compassion. Eamon was vaguely aware of the gentle pressure of the King's hand on his arm.

"How would it have served you to know all of it on the eve of battle?" Hughan asked gently.

"I would have hurled Arlaith's bloody, lying, murderous corpse over the walls!" Eamon spat, screaming with fury.

"Yours would have been next."

"You kept this from me!" Eamon yelled.

"Yes," Hughan replied evenly. "All you needed to know then was that she was safe."

Eamon tore himself away from Hughan, his mind filled with fury. "But she wasn't!" he howled. "She was in his hands the whole time! The whole time!"

"She was not in his hands, Eamon, when you came to me," Hughan answered, "nor is she now, nor will she be again."

"Bloody bastard!" Eamon cried. He stared at Hughan. "While he lied, and fawned to me, *me and my little heart*, he was..." A wordless sob leapt out of his throat. Had he chosen to return to this? "She won't let me speak to her! I wish he'd killed me, Hughan!"

Hughan fixed him with a firm gaze. "Do not speak such things over yourself, Eamon."

"He might as well have killed me!" Eamon cried. "Look at me, Hughan!" he howled. "Look at me! Even dead he webs me in his schemes!"

His words struck up at the ceiling of the hall as though they might shatter it.

"He will have no victory over you, Eamon," he said.

"No victory?" Eamon stared at him in outrage. "Will you mock me too?" he cried. "No victory? He beat her, breached her…" The word came in disgust from his mouth, for suddenly he knew that in breaching Alessia, Arlaith would have sought and seen anything that she and Eamon had ever shared. It filled him with horror that threatened to make his knees buckle. He imagined Arlaith's snide, laughing face, a voyeur of his every moment with the woman he had loved.

"He killed my child!" he cried. "And he stoked my hatred of her. And now she and I will never have peace. I should rather be dead than bear this. No victory? He has destroyed me, Hughan!" he howled. "He knew what he had done and knew even as he died that I could never undo it. There is his victory!"

"It is not his victory until you are defeated," Hughan answered.

Eamon laughed bitterly. "Do I not look defeated to you?"

"Angry, grieved, anguished – yes. Defeated?" Hughan shook his head. "You are not that."

Eamon stared at him, then gave another clipped laugh. "You don't understand," he snarled. "How could you? I was a fool to come to you."

"Those are his words you speak, Eamon," Hughan told him, "and not your own."

"Words? Words!" Eamon yelled. "You don't understand what he *did* to me!" A sob caught in his throat. "After all he had done to me, I couldn't even kill him –"

"How old are you, Eamon?" Hughan asked quietly.

Eamon stared at him. "You know how old I am," he said.

"I think you may have forgotten it," Hughan answered. "How old are you?"

"I will be twenty-four in the summer," Eamon replied.

"And how long did you train with the Gauntlet before coming to Dunthruik?"

"Three years," Eamon answered belligerently. He had been more than three years under Ladomer's watchful eye. "You know that, too!"

The King looked at him firmly. "Lord Arlaith had the experience and strength of long years, beyond the lifespan of men, and Edelred's mark," he returned. "He was trained, and he was deft and sly, and he was swift and powerful. He had defeated many and his hands were well versed in battle." The King's gaze searched Eamon's face. "And yet in you he met his match, because unlike any foe before you, Eamon, you held against him with your whole strength. That is no defeat! Your hope he never touched. He sought your life and you withheld it to the very last. He sought your courage and you held that, too. If he sought or took your heart, you may yet reclaim it."

"How can I?" Eamon cried in anguish. There could be no words of apology and no forgiveness. There could be no undoing of the years of scheming and treachery wrought against him, no bringing back of dead babes or murdered fathers, nor any unweeping of tears. Eamon shook his head. "He took me to the grave with him. A dead man cannot serve you."

Hughan watched him, then reached out and touched his shoulder. "Do you remember what I said to you, before we went into Edelred's chamber?"

Eamon swallowed. "That our houses... would stand or fall together."

"We stood," Hughan told him, "and I tell you, Eamon Goodman, that neither Edelred's power nor Arlaith's schemes have conquered you. To choose another First Knight would be to disown you – that I will not do, nor will I let you disown yourself by bowing to Arlaith's curses and treacheries. He will have no hold over you."

"But he does," Eamon sobbed, his aching voice a whisper.

"No hold but what you grant him."

Eamon stared at him uncomprehendingly for a moment. "What?" he whispered.

"This is Arlaith's last trap for you," Hughan told him gently. "He knew you, and he hoped that when you learned what he had done, the depth of your great heart would undo you. That is why he did not want you to see his memories."

Remembering Arlaith's shrieks, Eamon shivered. "I don't understand."

"At the end, Arlaith realized that the truth could also set you free. And it will."

Eamon began to shake. "How can it?"

"Truth in a loving heart is more powerful than curses or death." Hughan took him by the shoulders and looked deeply into his eyes. "Dear and beloved friend," he said, "if you think that I will stand and let you fall into the jaws of this, then you know me not at all."

Eamon shuddered tearfully. Hughan steadied him.

"You will overcome this," he said. "You are my First Knight, Eamon, and I need you more now than ever. So does this city. Who would speak for the Gauntlet or defend the Hands? Who would set his whole heart with mine on the long and difficult road to peace that we now must face? Arlaith knew that it would be you. I say to you, arm your courage with the truth, and stand against him. Then you can make your house a house of peace."

"I have no house!" Eamon cried, and he wept bitterly.

Gently Hughan reached out and drew Eamon into his arms, embracing him as he quaked and sobbed.

"Eamon," he said gently, "speak to her."

"I have tried. She will have none of me!"

"She was angry, as you have been angry. Anger ebbs. You cannot abandon hope."

Eamon fell back and stared at him. "And what would I say to her? What words of mine can undo what she bore for me, or what I have done to her?"

"Would you have it undone?" Hughan asked.

"Yes," Eamon wept.

"Then you will find the words – and she will come to a place where she is able to hear you. You will win each other again. And even at that time will you both go free of Arlaith's curse."

Eamon looked at him and his grief subsided. He knew that the King spoke the truth.

"I will try again," he whispered at last. "Though I do not know what I can say."

"Your heart will lead you," Hughan replied. "Words are not the only way."

Eamon nodded and met the King's gaze again. They watched each other in silence for a long time. Birdsong echoed beyond the walls of the room.

"Thank you, Hughan," he said at last.

"You have been hurt, and the road to undoing it is long, but you will be healed," Hughan told him. "Do not lose hope in that." Hughan watched Eamon a moment longer, then spoke again. "There was something I wanted to ask you, First Knight," he said. "Indeed, I was about to send after you, but you have removed my need of that."

"How may I serve you?" Eamon asked, looking at him curiously.

"I wanted to ask you if you would show me this city," Hughan answered. "But not for politics or negotiations or food – I know far too much about those! Many have told me about the things you have done in Dunthruik for me," he added, "but I want to hear your story, and see what you have seen. I wanted to ask you if you would show me the places you have lived and loved."

A smile crept to Eamon's tear-stained face. "I would love to," he whispered.

CHAPTER XXVIII

Eamon led the King through Dunthruik. To each quarter they went, along the roads and alleys that Eamon had known. He pointed out the places he had been. He told Hughan the long story of the rebuilding work to the quayside of the port, and of how the cadets and sailors had worked tirelessly to reset the stones to irk Cathair. He described the attack on the port, and its impact on the shops and vessels. He spoke about the grain hoarding, and showed Hughan the secret places where it had been stored. Eamon spoke also about the morning when the men whom he had saved from the Right Hand gave him a coin. Tears flooded his eyes as he remembered.

They went through the West, through the college and the roads. Eamon described the course and the bitter feuds between the groups of cadets who trained there. He spoke of his first meeting with Manners, of Alben, of Waite's scoreboard, of the Handbook classes. He talked at length about the majesties, gesturing with his hands to give a sense of how the people of Dunthruik processed up the Coll into the Royal Plaza. He spoke shyly of his amazement when he had been nominated as a Hand, and vividly about the long day that he and Mathaiah had spent scouring Dunthruik for a costume he could wear to the ball. He looked for the draper's shop where he had found the sword and star, but was not able to find it.

At the Four Quarters he paused for a long time, gazing down into the city. He described his first meeting with Anderas, and how he had seen Cartwright in the line of exiles, and he remembered the cart that bore Mathaiah away to the pyres. As he stood and looked at the tall sides of the quarters, he remembered also that it was there the King had unbound the Nightholt.

Eamon took Hughan to the Crown and showed him every inch of the place of which he had been patron. He talked about the singers at length, and Ilenia in particular, and made special note of her song that had so struck him. He felt embarrassed to mention it, but Hughan encouraged him and nodded as he listened to Eamon recount the lyrics. They searched the Crown for Ilenia. Though they did not find her, they were told that she was well. Eamon introduced Hughan to Shoreham, who was still the theatre's director, and they spoke about the possibility of celebrations at the theatre after the coronation.

It was to the East Quarter that they went last of all. Eamon showed Hughan every street that he knew, the Grennils' home, the site of the ill-named "Goodman" inn, the fruit vendor's shop, the Crown office, and the house where the Lorentides had lived. They went to Tailor's Turn; some of the men and women whom Eamon had helped save were there. Eamon had great joy in introducing them to Hughan. The people spoke unreservedly about Eamon's courage until Eamon became red in the face with sheer embarrassment; but Hughan beamed to hear the stories of Lord Goodman, and all that he had done.

Lastly they went to the Ashen. As they arrived Eamon remembered his reception as a Quarter Hand, and recalled the day Cara had been flogged, and when Marilio had been taken to the pyres. He remembered bringing Arlaith to the quarter, the secret consignments of grain, the faces of the ensigns, the Hands, Ashway, and Anderas. He told Hughan about them all, and looked about the Ashen with clear sight.

"You love the East," Hughan said with a smile.

"Yes," Eamon answered. It had always been home to him. But the Ashen now belonged to the Easters. Indeed, Anastasius's men filled it. It was his home no longer.

Shaking off his sadness, he took Hughan through the square towards the Handquarter; large scaffolds had been set up around it. Easters busily repaired the damage done to it and the college in the fire. Anastasius stood before the Handquarter steps in the Ashen, surveying the work. As Eamon and Hughan approached, he greeted them.

"The East welcomes you," he said with a smile.

The comment stirred Eamon's memory further. For a moment he remembered the Gauntlet lined up in the square, receiving him. But when he looked up, only Anastasius stood before him.

"Repair work is coming on well," Eamon commented.

"It is," Anastasius replied. "The people of this quarter have much hope."

Eamon smiled. "They always did."

"I have been asked especially to preserve the dining room," Anastasius told him with a wry smile. "It seems to be a location of some local interest. I am told that you once served a two-crown dinner there?"

"That was bold!" Hughan laughed.

Eamon flushed. "Everybody seems to know what a *faux pas* it was except for me. It was foolhardy," he answered, "and I knew not my peril. But I had good men and fine servants to defend me from myself."

"Your old household is here still," Anastasius told him. Before Eamon could say another word, Anastasius turned to an aide and asked for the household to be summoned.

Those who had served Eamon in the East emerged from the building works: Slater, Cook, Cara, Callum, and a collection of stablehands. They looked confused at first. When they saw Eamon dressed in blue they paused uncertainly. Callum turned his head and peered across the distance, as if unsure of whom he saw.

Suddenly the boy gave a little squeal of delight and hurtled forward.

"You came back!" he cried. Eamon dropped to one knee to receive the child's overjoyed embrace.

"I promised I would," he answered, and laughed as Callum's

small arms fixed about his neck with almost enough strength to throttle him. Anastasius arched an eyebrow, but said nothing.

The other servants came forward more cautiously. As Eamon rose to his feet with Callum still tangled about him, the child frowned at Hughan.

"Are you the King, sir?" Callum asked.

Hughan smiled kindly. "I am."

"And you're his First Knight," Callum said, looking back to Eamon.

Eamon smiled.

"I am," he answered.

"Everyone's been talking about you!" Callum continued. "Can I ask you something?"

Eamon smiled broadly as he set Callum down again. "You can."

"I was thinking about it the other day – it might have been yesterday, but I'm not sure…" He trailed off. "It doesn't really matter when it was. I asked Cara, and I asked Mr Cook, but they couldn't tell me the answer. Perhaps you can."

"Perhaps I can," Eamon grinned, "provided you ask me the question."

Callum smiled sheepishly. "Is being the First Knight like being the Right Hand?"

An odd quiet fell. Eamon realized that he was not certain of the answer.

Hughan stepped forward and matched Callum's gaze with his own. "It is not," he said.

"Oh," Callum murmured. He frowned. "I don't understand."

Hughan held Callum's gaze for a long time. "When Edelred appointed a Right Hand," Hughan said, "he did so on a whim, and on a whim he was dismissed – usually by death – whenever it pleased Edelred." Hughan looked for a moment at Eamon. "The King's First Knight is always the First Knight as long as he lives. His duty is to speak truly and freely; in doing so he will serve the freedom of this city, this land, and our people."

Callum beamed a great, satisfied smile and looked at Eamon. "That sounds better than being Right Hand, sir."

Eamon laughed – a long, clear laugh, such as he had not laughed in many months.

"Yes, it does!" he said.

Anastasius stepped forward. "Star, there are a couple of matters on which I would speak to you," he said, "and perhaps the First Knight would like to speak with his former servants?"

"Of course," Hughan said. "If you will excuse me, gentlemen." He smiled at Eamon and Callum. Each of them nodded and bowed.

Hughan and Anastasius walked into the Handquarter; Eamon looked to the servants. Laughing still, he greeted each of them fondly by name. As he made his way through the gathered throng, he was surprised to find Wilhelm Bellis standing next to Cara.

"Mr Bellis!" Eamon said, joyfully taking the young man's hand. "Are you well?"

"Recovering still, sir," Wilhelm answered, gesturing to his arm, "but well for that."

"I almost didn't recognize you without the uniform."

"I mean to take the King's blue," Wilhelm answered, "and maybe become a doctor, but I thought I might be able to serve Lord Anastasius here for a while first." As he spoke, Cara slipped her hand into his.

Eamon smiled. "I am sure you can," he said. Cara blushed.

"That was a spectacular ride that you made, sir," Wilhelm told him.

"Thank you," Eamon answered. "You didn't ride badly yourself."

"Thank you, sir," Wilhelm replied. "I've meant to speak to you about that, but…" He looked around and gestured at the general chaos. "As you can see, it's been busy."

Eamon furrowed his brow. His ride across the field seemed like a lifetime ago. "Yes. I've wondered about it myself. Why did you follow me?"

Wilhelm shrugged. "You were different from the other Hands. I always knew that, but could never figure out why. When you gave that speech on the field, suddenly it all made sense."

Eamon set his hand on Wilhelm's shoulder. "Thank you," he said quietly. "That took courage."

"Even so, I'm not sure I'd have had the courage to follow you if I'd not seen Lonnam and Heathlode chase after you."

Lonnam and Heathlode. Eamon had nearly forgotten about the two Hands who followed him across the field. He pursed his lips at the recollection.

Wilhelm continued, "Even if Heathlode was only trying to kill you – I didn't realize it at the time."

"Heathlode and Lonnam, you mean," said Eamon.

Wilhelm looked confused. "I beg your pardon?"

"You meant to say 'Heathlode and Lonnam' tried to kill me as I rode across the field."

"Oh! By no means! Don't you know? Lonnam saved your life!"

Eamon stared. "What?"

"When Heathlode drew his sword and swung at you, I was riding too far back to stop him. It was Lonnam who rode up behind him and cut him down off his horse. Lonnam was struck by a Gauntlet arrow after that – probably after they saw what he did to Heathlode."

Eamon suddenly felt very small and vulnerable. He swallowed heavily. "He sacrificed himself for me, and I never knew…"

"Don't blame yourself for that, sir. I'd have said something sooner if I'd known you weren't aware."

"I shall speak to Hughan – it wouldn't be right to bury him with the other Hands. His heroism should be given fitting recognition. Thank you for bringing this to my attention, Wilhelm."

The young man nodded.

"Wilhelm," Eamon spoke again, "there was another matter I wished to discuss with you. May I speak with you about your father?"

Wilhelm stiffened. "Yes."

"I have learned that it was Lord Arlaith who had him murdered," Eamon said gently. "He did so to strike at me."

Wilhelm nodded. Cara pressed his hand. Callum shuffled away from Eamon's side and took Wilhelm's other arm. The sight of the three of them together warmed Eamon's heart.

"Arlaith has answered for your father's death," Eamon said, "and many other crimes, with his life. It may not bring you comfort, but I hope that it will bring you peace."

"Thank you, sir," Wilhelm answered.

After a little while the servants dispersed. As they did so Eamon stepped up to Slater.

"Mr Slater?" he said.

"Sir," Slater answered formally, bowing low.

Eamon watched the man for a few moments. "I wanted to speak with you in particular," he said. "I am sorry that it has taken so long for me to find time to see you."

"You are a busy man, sir, as always," Slater answered. "I understand."

"Many men died in this quarter, and in your household, because of me," Eamon added quietly. He looked over his shoulder to where Wilhelm, Cara, and Callum started to move back towards the Handquarter. "Marilio was one of them. Cara was flogged for me. Greenwood lost his life on my account. So did Lorentide." It was a painful list and he paused. Slater watched him with a gentle gaze. "I am sorry, Slater, that you and so many others stood in danger, or bore Arlaith's wrath, and never knew why."

After a long breath, Slater looked up. "I wish that death had not followed on you so surely," he answered quietly. "But I also know that you did good things for this quarter, and for us, and I know that, through you, this city received the King's blessing before he came. In the end," he said, "I think more of us would have died if you had not held to the King, so I take comfort in the lives that have been saved, and the good that was done."

Eamon looked at him for a long moment. "Thank you, Mr Slater."

Slater smiled. "You're welcome, sir," he answered. "If you'll excuse me," he added.

"Of course."

Slater returned to his work. Eamon watched him go. His step seemed lighter and his head higher as he caught up with the other servants. They went back to work together. Callum turned and waved heartily from the door of the Handquarter. Eamon smiled and waved back.

He suddenly remembered the charge delivered to him that morning by Febian's letter. If that morning seemed long ago, then the day when Mathaiah had charged him with delivering a message to one he loved was like an ancient and half-forgotten song. But in that moment it returned to Eamon's mind as clear as the dawn. Reaching into his pouch, he quietly drew out the small silver ring that Febian had given him. He held it for a long moment, remembering Mathaiah's last words to him and wondering if he would dare to deliver them.

Whether he spoke those words or not, of one thing he was certain: the ring had to go to Lillabeth.

CHAPTER XXIX

Eamon found a servant and left a message for Hughan as to his whereabouts, then left the Ashen. All his senses were heightened, as though he were seeing things for the first time. The tones and colours of the streets and their stones came alive before his eyes. The wind from the sea brought with it the smell of the approaching summer, as light touched each arch and wall along the Coll. The Four Quarters flooded with radiance as Eamon passed. At their centre he stood and turned, looking at the face of each wall in delight. It was with renewed heart that he went seeking Lillabeth.

He arrived at the palace. It was early afternoon when he reached the women's quarters.

"Good afternoon, sir!"

"Good afternoon, Mrs Mendel," Eamon answered, delighted, as always, to see her. "I need to find Mrs Lillabeth Grahaven." He was struck by a blow of guilt as he said her name aloud, but he held his nerve. "Do you know where I might find her?"

Ma Mendel smiled kindly at him. "I do," she said. "Would you like me to take you to her?"

"Yes," Eamon replied, "thank you."

Ma Mendel set herself to her new task with inspiring ease and merriness, leading Eamon from the quarters and into the corridors of the East Wing. Her chatter reminded him of that September day when the same lady had led him to the Hidden Hall to meet the King. He saw it in his mind as clearly as he had seen it then, and remembered the way that those around him had stared at him as he passed.

533

None stared at him now, and Ma Mendel's talk was not about plants or the weather, nor was it of gloves, as it had been when he had walked through the King's camp in February. Instead, the smile on her face grew broader as she spoke of the forthcoming – and eagerly awaited – celebrations.

"The word is that the coronation is set to take place before the end of the month, and that the King means to announce its proper date tomorrow morning," she beamed, and turned to look at him. "I shouldn't ask, sir, but do you know if it is true? Will he announce the coronation?"

"The King has asked most people not to mention that particular word too lightly," Eamon answered with a wry smile. "This being the case, I can hardly comment. But I am sure that it will be soon."

"What a day it will be!" Ma Mendel enthused. She skipped down the corridor as though she were a young girl, but stopped short of clapping her hands for joy. "What a day! This city and this land shall have a King again – and a queen! – for he will take Lady Aeryn's hand that same day. And the long years of waiting, and hoping, will have a glorious end. Is that not marvellous?"

Eamon laughed, for her delight was infectious. "It is."

They came into some of the palace's broader halls. Ma Mendel led him through one to a corridor and then to a low archway which led into a series of small rooms. Voices inside, mostly of women, spoke quietly, sometimes laughing. Through the curve of the entrance arch, great rolls of thread and reams of cloth in varying colours were laid out. Eamon was surprised to see traces of black among them. It reminded him for an awful moment of Edelred's tailors.

The moment passed. A servant went and took up a great spiral of blue cloth, then carried it to the speaking women.

Ma Mendel paused in the doorway as though remembering something, and looked to him.

"If you will wait here a moment, sir, I'll just see if she's here."

"Of course," Eamon answered. Although he had seen women in the palace during the last few days the sight and sound of them still astonished him; never as a Hand had he heard it. He was content merely to listen to their voices as Ma Mendel disappeared through the arch into the curved room beyond. Eamon stared after her for a moment, and then stepped to one side as a young woman carrying a wide collection of coloured threads passed within. The room felt curiously off-limits to him and he resisted the urge to sneak a quick look past the arch into the strange world beyond.

He was on the verge of yielding to his curiosity when Ma Mendel reappeared. "She's just coming, sir."

"Thank you," Eamon answered. Ma Mendel had an even broader smile on her face, and he frowned to see it. "I'm curious, Mrs Mendel," he began. "What is it that delights you so?"

"I'm sorry, sir, but I can't tell you!"

Eamon laughed. "I shall resign myself to it nobly."

"I knew that you would, sir."

Lillabeth came out from the room. An odd wash of emotion ran through Eamon at the sight of her, one made up of grief, joy, hope, and sorrow all intertwined. She seemed somehow greater, in courage and in years, than when he had last seen her, on that night when he had led her from the city to the safety of the King's men. He remembered the tunnel down which they had struggled and the terrible darkness within it, and how she had spoken for him, a Hand, against those same King's men.

All this he thought as he bowed low to Mathaiah's wife. "Mrs Grahaven," he said.

Lillabeth smiled at him. "First Knight," she said. The title came joyously from her lips and she laughed as she stepped forward and embraced him briefly. It astounded him, and he gazed at her in amazement as she stepped back again. "You'll forgive me if I do not curtsey," she added, setting one hand apologetically over her swollen belly.

"I would not ask you to," Eamon answered. He realized that though he had learned much about death and destruction in Dunthruik he understood little about life and restoration. Somehow the sight of Lillabeth – and the knowledge that she bore a child that he might one day live to see grow into a man – filled him with awe.

"I am sorry that I have not come before," he began. "I have wanted to speak with you. Would you mind walking with me for a short while?"

"Or perhaps sitting?" Lillabeth asked. Eamon blushed, and was about to apologize to the smiling lady when Ma Mendel stepped forward.

"There're some benches in the garden just here," she said, gesturing to an arched doorway which led from the passage where they stood out into the bright afternoon light.

"Then, Mrs Grahaven, would you sit with me for a few minutes there?" Eamon asked.

"Of course," Lillabeth answered.

Eamon looked to Ma Mendel. "Thank you, Mrs Mendel."

"Sir." Curtseying low and smiling at Lillabeth, she turned and returned to the palace corridors.

Eamon and Lillabeth went together into the shady courtyard across the hall. As they left the cool stone walls the heat beat down on them. Eamon was glad to see that the stone benches were shaded.

It was to one of these that he led Lillabeth, lending her his arm despite her quiet protests, so that she would not slip and fall on any of the stones. When they reached the bench he helped her sit, and then stood, watching, for a moment. As she expectantly met his gaze he suddenly felt awkward.

Lillabeth touched his hand, calling his mind back from where it wandered. "It's good to see you, Eamon," she said, smiling at him, "and it is better still to see you safe."

"Thank you," Eamon answered. "Were you doing something important?"

"A little sewing," Lillabeth answered, and suddenly the smile on her face was brilliant. "I am afraid that I can't tell you anything else," she added with an enigmatic curve of her mouth.

"But I'll know it when I see it?" Eamon guessed. He imagined that the sewing involved a wedding dress for Aeryn, though that did not explain the black he had seen among the cloth and thread.

"You will," Lillabeth encouraged him. Her hand was still on his, and as she smiled at him he drew a deep breath.

"You wanted to speak to me?"

At last Eamon sat down beside her. "I received something this morning," he said. "I knew it at once…"

He trailed off but knew that he could delay no longer. Lillabeth watched him curiously as he drew out the ring. For a long moment he held it, hidden, in the palm of his hand, but then at last he matched her gaze again. "I knew it," he whispered, "and I knew also that it had to go to you."

Silently he opened his hand before her. Her eyes fell to what he held, then astonishment and sorrow crossed her face. Reaching out, Lillabeth laid one finger to the band, tracing it in disbelief, then looked at him.

"How did you find this?" she whispered.

"It has passed my hand several times," Eamon answered. "Even so, I can only tell you a little of its story." He met her gaze, assessing her face and grief, and knew then that he had to tell her as much as he knew.

"I know that it was taken from your husband when he was imprisoned. I then took it from his keepers, and when I went into the Pit I returned it to him." He paused, remembering how he had embraced Mathaiah and the song that had shaken down the walls of the Pit. "I can only think," he whispered, "that he somehow knew which ascent from the Pit would be his last and that, to defend us both, he gave this ring into the hands of one whom he trusted.

"Where it was then held and hidden, I do not know. This morning I received it with a letter from Lord Febian, who surrendered in the Pit on the day this city was taken. Febian's letter told me that it came from the hand of a prisoner, with instruction that it should be given to me." He swallowed, feeling a horrid grief in his throat. "That instruction must have come from your husband, and I am sure that he meant for me to bring it to you." He paused, trying to hold her gaze steadily, but his strength failed him and he looked away.

"I promised you once that I would return him to you," he whispered. "It was a foolish promise to make, and it grieves me to have broken it. Your husband was dear to me, and I would have given my life to save him. Yet he is gone, and this," he said, looking at the ring on his palm, "is all of him that I can bring."

Lillabeth's eyes misted with tears as they followed his own to the ring. Gently she then took it from his hand and weighed it in hers. She wore her wedding ring openly now. The two silver bands glinted together in the light.

Lillabeth suddenly looked up at him. "What happened to him, Eamon?"

Eamon paled.

"I don't think I…" He faltered and met her gaze. She was the one with the most right to know what had befallen Mathaiah, but as he looked at her he feared for her, and for the child that she carried. If he had scarcely been able to bear the news, how could she?

"Lillabeth," he said gently, "you deserve to know, and know in full, yet I am afraid of what might happen to you should I tell it."

Lillabeth looked down at the ring in her hand for a long moment, then back at Eamon. "The King's grace was with him to the very end," she said. "It will also be with me as I listen."

Eamon measured her gaze. It was stalwart, though afraid.

"You know of the Nightholt?" he asked at last. Lillabeth nodded. Eamon belatedly realized that she would have seen it on the day that it was destroyed.

"When Mathaiah and I first came to Dunthruik we were sent to find it," he said. "We had no idea what it was. I knew that it was evil – I could hardly hold it. But Mathaiah could read it."

Lillabeth nodded again. "He spoke of it," she said.

The news did not surprise Eamon.

"They took him because he could read it."

"Why should they have needed him to read it?" Lillabeth asked. "Surely Edelred could read it himself?"

"It was not Edelred who took him," Eamon answered. "It was Arlaith."

Lillabeth's eyes widened in surprise.

"One of the Right Hand's chief responsibilities was to find the Nightholt. At Arlaith's command, it had been found." Eamon's heart grew heavy as he saw another facet of how deeply Ladomer had used him. "But Arlaith did not give it to Edelred; he kept it for himself. He conspired to overthrow Edelred, and the only way he could do so was by tampering with the Nightholt. But Arlaith could not read it. Neither could the other Hands, and when he learned that Mathaiah could, Arlaith took him and tried to force him to do it."

Lillabeth's face grew pale and Eamon trembled. Suddenly it was all so clear to him: Cathair, and maybe even Ashway, had thought all along that Arlaith's commands about Mathaiah and the Nightholt had come from the throned, but they had not. Arlaith had put all the blame of his backfired scheme onto Cathair, the only one left who could have gainsaid him. It was why the Left Hand had been so keen to see Eamon return in victory from the Raven's nest.

How could he not have understood it sooner?

"Did they torture him?" Lillabeth asked.

"He was held in the Pit, which was torture enough for most men. While they hoped that he might be made to read, the worst they did was beat him and lie to him that they held you and tortured you, Lillabeth. You must know that he did not fear the former and never believed the latter. They tried to breach him but they could not, and when they could not breach him they tried all that they could to break him." He fell quiet. "I do not know whether they then killed him because he would not surrender to them what they wanted, or whether Arlaith feared that he would be discovered, or whether Cathair killed him to strike at me and unwittingly worked against Arlaith. Your husband was blinded." Suddenly he was in the

Four Quarters as the cart moved past him in the chill night. "He was blinded and they took his hands. But they never took his hope."

"You saw him," Lillabeth breathed. Perhaps she saw in his face a ghost of what he had seen.

"I saw his body," Eamon answered. "And I am glad, Lillabeth, I cannot tell you how glad, that you did not. As for him…"

It was then that his heart was filled with singing, and he remembered – with clarity that his mind could scarcely contain – the river and the city where he had tarried, and the one who had met him there.

He looked back to Lillabeth and a smile filled his face. "I saw him again."

Lillabeth looked at him in amazement. "What do you mean?"

"There was a place," Eamon began, "a place I went to, after I fell. I cannot describe it! It was bright, Lillabeth, and it was beautiful and radiant… and so was he. He was there – whole and full of joy."

Tears filled Lillabeth's eyes and she shook. Eamon reached across and took her hand.

"I know that he loved you," he said.

There were tears on Lillabeth's face. She closed her hand about the ring and pressed it close to her lips in sorrow.

Eamon gently touched her shoulder. "Lillabeth," he whispered. "Mathaiah gave his life for the King, for this land, for this city, for me and for you and for your child; peace is his prize. And you and I will both see him again."

Swallowing back her tears, she looked up. "Thank you for telling me all of this," she said. "The news is grievous, Eamon, but knowing what happened comforts me, and knowing that he…" Dashing a tear from her eyes she looked up at him, and pressed his hand. "I am sorry that you had to bear it, in the fullness of its horror, and with none to comfort you. I know you loved him."

"I have been comforted," Eamon answered. "I love him still."

They sat together in silence for a long moment. A flight of birds winged past. The sun struck the underside of their wings with silver.

For a moment Eamon was lost in it. Suddenly, he remembered that he had not said everything that he had come to say.

He looked at Lillabeth. Her own face was pale and tear-marked, and Mathaiah's ring was held tightly in her hand. Eamon's breathing quickened. Mathaiah's voice filled his mind as clearly and freely as the soaring birds:

"Then she shall name him…"

He closed his eyes.

Lillabeth's eyes came to rest on his face. "Is something the matter?"

Eamon realized that he had been biting his lip and drew a deep breath. "I have not yet told you everything," he said quietly. He swallowed hard and folded his hands together to keep them from shaking. "Mathaiah was sent down into the Pit because of me…"

"I – I know. If it is forgiveness you seek, know that you already have it. I do not blame you for whatever part you feel you played. Mathaiah only ever spoke well of you."

At last he matched her gaze. "Thank you. That means much to me, but there is more. The last time I saw Mathaiah alive," he said, "I took him news that I had seen you; I told him that you bore his child."

Lillabeth's face opened with surprise. "You told him?"

"Yes," Eamon nodded.

Lillabeth gazed at him in joyous wonder. "Thank you."

"Lillabeth, when I took him news he told me…" He faltered. "He asked me to bring you a message."

"What message?" Lillabeth asked gently.

Eamon knew that he could delay no longer. Drawing all his courage he forced himself to look at her, and not to shy from her gaze as he spoke.

"Mathaiah said that his child… should bear my name."

Shame flushed through him as soon as he said it. Lillabeth looked surprised, and for a moment he feared that her face would turn to outrage or to hatred. He drew breath at once to apologize, to tell her that she need not do it and that he was sorry he had mentioned it at all.

"Lillabeth –" he began.

Lillabeth's still eyes silenced him. "Mathaiah loved you," she gently told him. "He would be proud of you and of what you've done."

"Lillabeth –"

"If my child's father was a righteous man, and his namesake were to be that of a good man…" She paused, and then smiled. "Then I do not think that I could give him a better legacy or hope than to give him the name chosen by his father. Yours is a good name, Eamon, and – assuming it's a boy – my son's will be a good name, too."

Eamon gazed at her in wonder and tears stung his eyes.

"You have amazed me since the very first day I met you."

"You have amazed us all," Lillabeth replied.

They sat together for a moment, letting the breeze run past them. Eamon breathed deeply.

He sat silently for a long time. His thoughts stilled. Suddenly he looked at her. "How is she?" he asked quietly.

Lillabeth looked at him with a small frown. "You mean…?"

"I'm sorry," he said quickly, and rubbed a hand across his face. "Forgive me, I… I think of her often."

"As does she of you."

His heart leapt. Could it be true? Lillabeth's steady face told him that it could. He forced down a tremor in his hands. "Lillabeth, could you… could you take her a message from me?"

"You would not rather take one yourself?"

"I would. But I have left things too long, and now… now I do not know what I must do before I can go to her again."

Lillabeth nodded. Perhaps Alessia had already confided in her the entire conversation he had tried to have with her before. "I will take her a message from you," she promised.

"Then, could you tell her…" He pursed his lips in thought. What was the one thing that he most wished he could say to her?

He knew it at once. "Lillabeth, would you tell Alessia that I know now that I wronged her, and that I am sorry. I hope, one day, to say as much to her myself."

Slowly, Lillabeth nodded. "I will tell her."

It was more than he could have hoped for. "Thank you."

They were interrupted by the sound of approaching footsteps. Manners walked briskly down the path. The young man looked satisfied to see Eamon and smiled as he stopped near them.

"I've found you, sir," he said. "Anderas said that you weren't well."

"I'm a little better now," Eamon answered.

"I didn't expect to find you here," Manners added, "but I was assured…" He suddenly started in surprise. "Lillabeth!"

"Rory," Lillabeth answered, rising to her feet and embracing the astonished young man. "It's good to see you."

"And you," Manners answered, stepping back with a laugh. "I didn't know you were in the city, Mrs Grahaven, else I would have…" He shook his head in delight. "How are you?" he finished.

"Well," Lillabeth replied. Manners still stared at her and his eyes then fell to her belly.

"Lillabeth," he stammered, "are you…?"

"Yes," Lillabeth replied, then smiled at the First Knight. "Mathaiah's child. If it is a son, his name will be Eamon Grahaven."

Manners blinked, stared at Eamon for a second, then looked back to Lillabeth, then shook his head in bemusement.

"I… What can I say? That's wonderful."

Lillabeth looked at Eamon again. "Thank you for everything you've told me."

"You're welcome," Eamon answered dumbly. He realized that there was much about Manners that he had not understood.

Lillabeth bade farewell to them both and returned inside. Together, Eamon and Manners watched her go, then looked at one another.

"You must be honoured, sir," Manners said.

"Sorry?" Eamon answered distractedly.

Manners smiled at him. "She means to name her son after you. Then again," he laughed, "I suspect that there will be quite a number of Eamons in this city over the next few years."

Eamon blinked hard. "That's a bizarre thought, Mr Manners," he answered, "and I thank you for befuddling me with it."

"My pleasure, sir," Manners replied brightly.

They moved back towards the palace, and walked in silence for a few moments.

"I didn't know that you knew Lillabeth," Eamon said at last.

The young man looked apologetically at him. "Mathaiah asked me to go with him on the day they made their pledges," he replied. "I'm sorry, sir," he added, "those were strange days. It should have been your place…"

Eamon shook his head. "I had forfeited that right, Rory," he answered. "I am glad that Mathaiah had you by him, and I know he would be glad to know that you are near Lillabeth now."

"Thank you, sir," Manners answered, looking quietly to where Lillabeth had gone. His face had an odd look to it as he did so.

"Are you well?" Eamon asked.

Manners looked up with half a smile. "Yes, sir."

They moved back into the palace together, as Manners explained that he had come on Feltumadas's behalf.

"He said that he wanted to speak to you about Etraia," Manners told him. "He declined to mention much more. He is a fearsome fellow," he added.

"He is," Eamon answered.

"The voice of experience?" Manners asked.

"I'm afraid so," Eamon laughed.

Feltumadas awaited Eamon in one of the palace's many halls. When Eamon and Manners arrived, they found the Easter lord passing the time by looking at the paintings and decorations, with his hands clasped behind his back. He looked up as Eamon drew near and smiled.

"First Knight," he greeted.

"Lord Feltumadas," Eamon replied.

"I understand that you will be meeting a grain ship from Lamiglia tomorrow?"

"That is my hope," Eamon answered. Lamiglia was one of the northern merchant states and had maintained a broad loyalty to Hughan, often by setting itself in direct opposition to its neighbours, over the past year or so.

"I would go myself, but have a couple of matters to attend to," Feltumadas continued. "I wanted you to know: I've heard that the word on the water before the fall of Dunthruik was that Etraia and her allies would not have peace with this city should the Star take it. Many Gauntlet are still there."

Eamon's heart sank. "She would not dare go to war with us?"

"Etraia is large and strong. She was a staunch supporter of Edelred, is likely the place where any escaping Hands fled to, and has been trading wood, weapons, and wines with the River Realm in exchange for grain for many years," Feltumadas replied. "She is grim and powerful. Tell me, First Knight, whether you think she will have peace with the Star?"

Eamon's face blanched grey.

Feltumadas nodded. "It is as I feared. It may not be today, nor even tomorrow," he said, shaking his head, "and perhaps Etraia will not come against the Star for many months, perhaps not for a year or more. But such is the rumour. You will have an opportunity tomorrow to ascertain whether the rumour holds any truth, or was just water-talk."

Eamon sighed. "Thank you, Lord Feltumadas."

"I heard that you spoke with General Waite? What of him?"

Eamon became suddenly and inexplicably conscious of Manners, waiting for him in the hallway behind.

"He is embittered," he said quietly. He did not add that he felt himself to be the root of the man's hatred.

"I would not have *spoken* to him," Feltumadas mused.

"You would have found no weapon to hand by which to strike him," Eamon countered, catching his implied meaning at once.

Feltumadas gave him an ironic smile. "We have a proverb in the east, First Knight: 'When swords are broken there are still rocks' – I'm afraid that it translates badly," he said. "I am, however, glad that *you* spoke to him; I would have found a rock to throw."

Eamon laughed a little. "Are there many rocks in Istanaria?"

"In abundance," Feltumadas answered. "And a multitude of men at which to throw them. Siblings frequently argue, First Knight, and the Land of the Seven Sons has many siblings." He smiled. "But it has great cities, and lakes, and forests and mountains, and deserts. Perhaps, one day, you will see them, and perhaps you will walk in Istanaria, the city of the sun. Perhaps," he added with an amused smile, "we will go together."

"Perhaps we shall," Eamon answered. "But before I venture into the east, I would see peace in my own land."

Feltumadas nodded. "You have the right of that, First Knight."

CHAPTER XXX

The day was long, and Eamon was glad when it drew to its end. He moved through the corridors of the palace back to his own room, passing between the shadows and the starlight with a strange uneasiness. News of potential unrest in the merchant states disturbed him, and ever at the back of his mind was a thought he tried not to face. But it remained, and so did she.

He paused at last before a great arch that looked out to the star-marked sea. The clear light glistened on the waves, making them like a thousand shifting candles. His thought drifted back to Lillabeth, to her words and look, and he drew a deep breath.

Eamon Grahaven. A child was to be born that would bear his name. It was a thought as terrifying as it was awesome.

There should have been another child bearing his name... And as he tried to drive Ladomer's face from his mind, he laid his hands against the frame of the window, letting the feel of the cool stone fill him.

Footsteps sounded in the passage behind him. A glimmer of light was followed soon after by a lamp-bearer. Eamon turned his head from the still sea.

A man approached him and bowed. "First Knight."

"Mr Cartwright," Eamon breathed. For a moment he almost embraced the man in his joy but an odd awkwardness held him back.

"You are well, sir?" Cartwright asked. The lamplight showed flickers of concern on his face.

"Yes," Eamon answered. "For the most part," he then added. "Yourself?"

"I am well, thank you," Cartwright answered. There was a silence, then he looked up. "I sought you, sir, to apologize."

"You have no apology to make to me, Cartwright," Eamon said kindly.

"You did not find me serving you when you first recovered, sir," Cartwright answered. Eamon had to think for a moment before he understood the servant's meaning. "I am sorry for it. I meant no slight to you, sir,"

"I bear you no ill will for it," Eamon answered. "So much has happened since I woke that, in truth, I must say that I scarcely had a thought to spare you. But I thank you for your concern," he said with a small smile, "and forgive you quite completely. Being the Right Hand was perhaps the most difficult thing that I had to do. Your service to me was invaluable and I wonder sometimes whether I should be standing here today if you had not passed me in the Four Quarters that day."

"Thank you, sir," Cartwright answered. He paused, then looked at Eamon a little uncertainly. "I wanted to tell you, sir... I mean no offence by it, but I have returned in these days to the service of Lady Turnholt."

The words brought an ache to Eamon's heart.

"I am sure that she finds comfort in your presence," he said at last. He remained silent for a long time, then turned to look at Cartwright. "You may not be able to answer me," he whispered, "but do you know if Mrs Grahaven has spoken to her?"

Cartwright frowned, puzzled. "I am sure that she has, sir."

"Please... wish Lady Turnholt a good night on my behalf."

Cartwright looked as a man stunned with a blunt instrument. Eamon nodded to him. At last, Cartwright bowed. "I have some duties to which I should attend, if you will forgive me."

"And I keep you from them. I am sorry," Eamon answered. "Please do not let me keep you further."

Cartwright seemed to measure him for a long moment. "Good night, sir," he said at last.

"Good night, Mr Cartwright."

The servant bowed and continued along the passage.

Eamon looked back out to the sea, his eyes heavy with sudden tears. In that moment he suddenly longed for Alessia beside him, for her hand in his own or her kiss on his cheek. He longed for her touch at his brow, for the lightness of her fingers to brush his hair and his weariness from his face, and he longed for her voice, for the feel of her heart beating near his own.

Above all, as he watched the sea, he longed for words that would set peace between them. He fixed his eyes upon the distant waters, where the furthest waves rolled and the deep mirrored the deeper sky. Tears slipped down his cheeks. His hands tightened together. He leaned against the stone embrasure.

The city lay peacefully beneath the night, the pyres still; ships waited in the port and the streets stood beneath the banner of the King. Somewhere just beyond the city's walls, Roe – the last Gauntlet captain – was being escorted to Dunthruik by Anderas. After Waite's refusal Anderas had been sent out to meet the delegation coming from the north. But within the walls, General Waite prepared to leave his shattered city and devastated house, burdened with shame and despair. Febian had fled in fear – certainly of Hughan, perhaps of him. Somewhere within the city walls lay Alessia, and he did not know whether she slept or wept; he knew only that she who should have nursed his child now nursed grief.

He longed to go to her. He could not. He did not know if she would receive his messages – let alone him.

As he stood in thought, he realized that he could not be a man of inaction. If he wanted things to be right with Alessia – and he wanted that with all his heart – then he had to show her that he understood, and that he had changed.

Courage, Eamon.

A field of stars shimmered in the deep dark far across the sea. He pressed the tears from his cheeks.

Returning to his room he went at once to the desk. A candle

glimmered there. He searched the drawers for parchment and ink, which he set in front of him. For long moments he gazed vacantly ahead, sorting through his whirling thoughts until they settled. Then he took the quill, dipped it with exaggerated care into the inkwell, and began to write.

Dearest Alessia... No; *Dear Alessia...*

He wrote at length, disdained it, began again, hurled it into the fire.

He did not know how much later it was that he leaned back, sighed, and watched the candlelight glimmer on the drying ink of his name. No signature of his had ever marked a paper so important.

He sealed the letter with a single globule of wax that he pressed flat with inky fingers. He watched the parchment as it rested, trying not to weigh its significance. He could do no more – at least, not for tonight.

With an eased mind, he retired.

The following morning he sought out Cartwright, letter in hand. The servant eyed him curiously when he asked if it could be delivered to Lady Turnholt, but he bowed, assuring it would be done.

Eamon went early to the port and watched the first merchant ship come into the harbour. As Feltumadas had surmised, it came from the province of Lamiglia and proudly flew a blue flag on its mast beneath its own colours. The stalwart vessel glided in across the calm waters. Eamon smiled to hear the applause running across the quays as the craft's moorings were fixed. The vessel's captain descended and Eamon went forward to meet him.

"Welcome to the city of the King," he said. "Warmly it welcomes you."

"I thank you." The captain – a tall, willowish man – looked as though he might be better suited to sewing than sailing, but there was a keen glint to his eyes and a chiselled look to his face that spoke of long years at sea. "I am Petreus, captain of the *Wave-Rider*. On behalf of my liege, I convey congratulation and honour to the Star of this city."

"My name is Goodman," Eamon answered. He saw the captain's eyes widen as he continued. "I am First Knight to the King."

"This is an unexpected pleasure," the captain replied. "May I clasp your hand, sir?"

"Yes," Eamon replied. He almost laughed at the seeming absurdity of the question, but felt too astonished to do so. The captain reached out and fervently took his hand.

"There have been stories of you in every port recently," he said, "some of them so exaggerated that they could only have been true."

Eamon smiled, unsure how to react. "Thank you. If I may direct your boatswain to the harbour master, we can unload your cargo."

"Of course," Petreus said, nodding. "You must have need of grain."

"We do," Eamon replied. "Likely far more than you shall have need of wine."

"With the throned fallen and his Hands felled, First Knight, the Raven's Brew will sell well indeed," the captain laughed with a broad smile. "The elite will clamour to have it in their cellars, that they may boast to their peers that they have bottles laid down in the last days of Edelred."

Eamon blinked; the idea surprised him. "Well, I am glad if it will do you good business."

"It will," the captain replied, "and you shall need it! Etraia won't be sending any of her ships in the near future."

"I have heard this rumour," Eamon answered quietly, "and perhaps you can clarify it for me a little. Do you think Etraia's discontent will continue?"

Petreus shrugged. "Popular opinion over the water, First Knight, is that your King will have to strike her," the captain answered simply. "Etraia is not known for letting grievances go quietly to dust. But it will be some time," he added, "before she can challenge you."

Eamon nodded with a sigh; at least there was that comfort.

The captain called his boatswain and Eamon directed them both to the harbour master's offices. Tomas Longroad, who had donned the King's blue in the days following the destruction of the Nightholt, received them. He was as invaluable to those managing the North as Anderas and Manners were to Eamon, for the man knew the ins and outs of the port as no other.

Longroad greeted both captain and his boatswain before politely enquiring after their crossing.

"The summer does improve matters," Petreus said, "but ah! The straits, good sir; even in the gentle sway of the fairer tides, the straits remain lamentable and treacherous."

A small grin broke out on Eamon's face as he remembered Fletcher's desperate warning not to ask a captain about his crossing. Longroad had perhaps stepped willingly into the terrible monologue, and he bore it well, but Eamon reminded himself to mention the matter to Feltumadas, in case the Easter ever chose to receive one of their merchant allies.

It was as he left the offices that he met Manners. The young man was breathless with running.

"Sir!" he called.

"Mr Manners?"

"He's here, sir!" Manners panted, drawing himself to a halt before Eamon.

Eamon frowned. "Who is?" he asked.

Manners thrust a hand back over his shoulder towards the palace. "Anderas is back," he said, "and he's brought Captain Roe."

"They're going to the palace now?" Eamon asked.

"Yes, sir, to see the King."

"Manners, I'd like you to go to the Crown," Eamon told him. Part of him wondered whether the theatre's name would change, but it was only a fleeting thought. He strode towards the Coll, Manners matching his pace faithfully. "There is a player there, Madam Ilenia by name. Please find her and bring her to the palace."

"Who is she, sir?" Manners asked.

"Roe's wife."

They went together down the Coll a fair way then parted company as they reached the palace gates. Eamon passed through the gates, swiftly climbed the steps, and made his way to the King's meeting room.

Hughan and Feltumadas were already there with several others. Eamon suspected that many of them had come, much as he had, to see the infamous captain.

"Sire," Eamon said, bowing as he entered. "Is he here?"

"He is," Hughan answered, and gestured to one of the men at the door. "Send word to Anderas."

"Will you be disappointed, Star, if you find this man to be a petty, thieving soul?" Feltumadas asked. He sounded haughty, as though the expectancy with which the captain was awaited was a ridiculous thing.

"We will see what kind of man he is, Lord Feltumadas," Hughan replied.

Not long later the doors opened and Anderas entered. With him walked a couple of men in Gauntlet uniform. One came firmly at Anderas's side. He was tall and dark haired, though threads of grey showed at his brow. His uniform was stained and worn. He had the look of a shrewd and thinking man; his face grew grim as he measured those gathered before him.

"Sire," Anderas said, bowing before them, "this is Captain Roe."

"Welcome, captain," Hughan said.

Roe watched him for a moment. The men who had come with him, their faces pale with toil, stood nervously behind him.

"You are the Lord of Dunthruik?" Roe asked quietly. He sounded as though he had not slept properly for some nights.

"I am," Hughan replied gently.

"In what manner do we stand with you?"

"You need not stand against me, captain," Hughan told him. "I hold you in as much esteem as all those who have borne your colours. The terms of the Gauntlet surrender hold good for you, and for your men – and all of you are welcome here."

Roe looked at him in surprise. "We have persisted in hostility towards you."

"You have done everything that you could to preserve the lives of the men with you," Hughan answered. "You, and they, are free, upon the disbanding of colour and payment of blood money, to do as you will, as long as you do not bear arms against me."

"We will not come to harm?" Roe repeated.

"You will not," Hughan answered.

The captain looked at him for a moment. "I have heard many rumours about things that you have done, and about who you are claimed to be," he answered. "If I asked you if you were truly the heir of Brenuin, what would your answer be?"

Hughan met his gaze firmly. "That I am."

"And is it true that of the men who have surrendered to you, not one has been killed?"

"It is true," Hughan answered. "Many of them now serve me."

Roe held his gaze a moment more, then his quick eyes darted from face to face. Eamon watched with bated breath as the captain stepped forward.

"What proof do I have of your words?"

"Ask. Seek. Look. The truth attends to itself throughout the city," replied the King. "Edelred's former Right Hand himself stands here among us as my First Knight." Hughan gestured to Eamon and Eamon bowed.

"I do not recognize this face as that of the Right Hand," said Roe. "Arlaith's countenance was known to me, and this man is not he."

"I make no claim to be Arlaith," said Eamon, "but I served as Edelred's Right Hand nonetheless when Arlaith was stripped of his rank and made Lord of the East Quarter."

"A convenient narrative indeed, but not what I should count as proof."

"You will find proof enough when you wander the city."

"But I cannot wander the city freely until I have renounced my colours?"

"I'm afraid not. As a military man, I'm sure you can appreciate that I cannot allow that until I am certain of your loyalty."

"But without wandering the city I shall not gain the proof I require to renounce my colours."

"I agree that it does require some measure of faith on your part," said Hughan. "You must first take the step. Freedom will follow. You have my word."

"But only your word."

Hughan nodded.

"Then we are at an impasse," said Roe, "for I shall not renounce my colours without first having proof."

Then the doors opened again. A moment later Manners and Ilenia entered. Eamon felt awash with delight at the sight of her. He remembered her voice and song, her kind words when they had shared breakfast, her blood on his hands… and wondered whether she knew of the latter. He imagined that she must have seen him at Hughan's side when the Nightholt was destroyed, for as she came forward she did not seem at all surprised to see him in blue. She glanced briefly at Eamon. With a great smile, Eamon turned to Hughan.

"Sire," he said, "may I present to you the Lady Ilenia, wife of Captain Roe."

Ilenia curtseyed low. "You asked for me, sire?" she said.

A look of astonishment pierced the captain's face.

"It was the First Knight who sent for you, Mrs Roe," Hughan replied gently.

Rising from her delicate curtsey, Ilenia looked up and then finally saw her husband. Tears leapt to her eyes and a gasp to her throat. She trembled. She looked at Eamon as though she wished to speak, but could not.

Slowly, Eamon stepped forward and led her gently by the hand to where her husband stood.

"It has long been my hope to see your husband returned to you," he said. Smiling, he set her hand in Roe's. The weary and astonished captain reached out to touch her face before embracing her with a cry of joy.

"Ilenia! You are well. This is more than I could have hoped for!"

Ilenia smiled through her tears. "The King and his men have kept me safe from harm. They are good men. This one especially." She gestured towards Eamon. "You can trust them."

"Then it is true," said Roe. He turned to the King with tears in his eyes. "You have returned my Ilenia to me. I require no further proof. I will trust myself and my men to your mercy." He sank down to one knee before Hughan. "With me those divisions of the Gauntlet who were stationed in Galithia also give their belated surrender."

"I accept it, with wholehearted joy," Hughan answered. "And I congratulate you again on your wholehearted courage. This city will have need of such men as you in the years ahead."

"I thank you," Roe said.

At Hughan's gesture Roe rose to his feet. Eamon nearly laughed to see the odd expression on the man's face.

"You will be tired from long miles made in haste," Hughan said, looking at the overjoyed Roe. "You and your men will be my guests and rest here tonight. Tomorrow you may return to your outstanding men in the north, so as to bring them here."

Roe, his arms still clasped tightly about his wife, breathed his thanks. Then with a single graceful gesture, Ilenia drew back from her husband's embrace and curtsied low before them. Her husband bowed with her.

"Long life to you, sire," she said, "and to your house."

Eamon gaped at her, stunned speechless with awe, for her words seemed to undo a thousand cries to Edelred's glory.

"Thank you, Mrs Roe," Hughan answered. "May your kindness return to your own house. Mr Manners," he added, "would you kindly take Mr and Mrs Roe, and these good men of his, to quarters where they may rest?"

"Of course, sire. If you would come with me, captain," Manners said, gesturing to the doors.

Roe nodded. He took his wife's hand firmly in his own and went, together with wife and men, from the hall.

Eamon watched them go with deep fondness. He was vaguely aware of Feltumadas nodding at Hughan.

"First Knight," Hughan said.

Eamon looked up from his thought. "Sire?"

"Would you come with us to the East Quarter? Lord Anastasius has a matter he wishes to discuss."

"Yes, sire," Eamon answered. He half-wondered why Anastasius had not come to the palace, but the thought left him as swiftly as it had occurred. The King finished his dealings with the others, and then dismissed those in attendance.

Together with Feltumadas and Anderas, King and First Knight left the palace.

"What is it that Anastasius needs to discuss?" Eamon asked as he went at Hughan's side.

"Something regarding the East," Hughan answered. "He thought it would be appropriate to discuss it there with us, and I agreed with him."

They trod swiftly through the sunlit streets to the Ashen. The reconstruction work was going well, and a great deal of the building's façade had been reworked already.

Anastasius awaited them at the Handquarter steps. He greeted them, his brow knit with concentration. Ithel, Ylonous, and several other Easter lords stood nearby. Slater appeared briefly in the doorway, but disappeared inside when he saw Eamon.

"Good morning and welcome," Anastasius said. His greeting was variously returned. "Would you all come with me into the hall?"

"Of course," Hughan answered. He followed Anastasius through the partially scaffolded doorway. Eamon followed, allowing his eyes to adjust to the light.

Many of the ceiling paintings – those so beloved by Anderas when he had been the quarter's captain – had been smoke-stained by the fire, but now, to Eamon's delight, they showed fresh in the morning light. Eamon gazed up at them, admiring the long mountains, valleys, and glimpses of towers between the lower passes.

"They're marvellous!" Anderas breathed.

"They are," Eamon agreed. He had to gaze straight up at them, turning in the centre of the hall so that he could admire them each in turn.

"I am glad that you approve, First Knight," Anastasius answered. "I wished in particular to seek your opinion on this banner," he added, touching Eamon's arm to draw his attention to the wall opposite the entry door.

He was not sure how he could not have looked that way when he entered, but, at Anastasius's gesture, Eamon turned to look. What he saw stunned him.

The wall was draped with a long banner, a streak of mid-blue framed with black, that hung delicately where once the owl and ash had been. The great banner bore a bold, rearing black horse; it looked to the left and its mane was tossed back as it gazed undauntedly ahead. At the horse's breast flamed a silver star.

It was a stunning emblem. Eamon stared at it in wonder.

"It is beautiful," he said, "but I do not recognize it. Whose is it?" He had never seen black employed in any of the banners born by Hughan's men.

A smile crept onto Anastasius's face. Eamon thought suddenly of Ma Mendel and of Lillabeth, and the women who had needed black cloth for their work...

"Whose is it?" he asked again, his voice scarcely audible even to himself.

"By the Star's will, it is yours," Anastasius replied.

Eamon gaped at him, agog. "Mine?"

Hughan touched his shoulder. "If you will have it, it shall be the emblem of you and of your house."

"I can't even ride!" Eamon spluttered. He laughed as he gazed up at the horse in surprise and joy.

"Despite your best efforts," Anderas told him, "the evidence is to the contrary."

The banner filled Eamon's eyes; tears touched his face. A horse, black as the Hand who had ridden it, with a star over its heart. The emblem honoured him yet did not deny what he had done.

Suddenly he laughed. "Thank you," he said, and then he looked to Hughan as another thought struck him. "Why does it hang here?"

"Because this hall also belongs to you," Hughan answered.

"What?" Eamon bleated, feeling faint. "Surely, Lord Anastasius, this hall is yours –?"

"And I give it to you," Anastasius answered. Eamon stared at him and the Easter laughed. "It is true that this quarter belonged to the east of old, but this realm, this city, and all that is in both, have been set under the Star." He smiled kindly. "It had long been my desire and design that, should the Star take his victory from Edelred, this quarter should be rendered unto another. I have seen your heart for it, First Knight, and its heart for you. So it is my desire to set this quarter in your hands."

Tears streamed down Eamon's face as the words washed over him.

"You have done much, First Knight. In honour of your great service there is one more thing I would bequeath to you and to your house: the highest title of our land."

The Easter stepped forward and reached for the neck of Eamon's cloak. There, the Easter lord pinned a small golden sun. Anastasius stepped back.

"Istanaria and its sons honour you, Lord Goodman, Lord of the East," he said. "May the sun and Star be ever over you and your house."

The men around him applauded – it was hard to tell whose beating hands clapped loudest. Eamon gazed back at Hughan.

"Sire," he whispered.

"It was a title borne long before the Hands took it," Hughan told him. "Many things of worth and goodness were taken and warped by Edelred. It is our task to restore those things."

"You are a bridge, First Knight," Anastasius added, "between the Gauntlet and the Star's men, between Istanaria and this city, between what has gone before and what will come after."

"Thank you," Eamon breathed. He shook his head in amazement. "These honours seem beyond me," he said, and looked at their smiling faces. "You all knew of this?"

"Our shameless grins don't answer that?" Anderas returned.

"I suppose that they do," Eamon conceded with a laugh.

"There will be a formal ceremony after the coronation," Anastasius told him. "I will hold the quarter until then, but you may wish to make preparations to transfer here nonetheless."

"When is the coronation?" Eamon asked, looking once to Hughan.

"It will be held on the thirty-first," Hughan answered. "It is a date which I mean to announce tomorrow."

It would be a long-awaited day.

Fired with infectious joy, Eamon spent a little time in the East Quarter – as familiar to him as the beat of his heart – speaking to his former servants, working through some arrangements with Anastasius, and gazing in awe at the banner that had been created for him. It was a badge of all that he had suffered and achieved, and moved him deeply.

Before he left, he took the time to walk in the gardens, marvelling at the curious elegance of vine and leaf, drawing in deep lungfuls of the heady scent of the tended blooms. The array of colours was startling, richer than the prizes of any treasure horde.

He found his thoughts turning to Alessia. He realized that what he longed for then was her beside him – to share his delight as once she had shared his sorrows.

Perhaps she had received and read his letter, perhaps she had not. But there was more to be done than simply to entreat her. She was worth so much more than that.

With a smile, Eamon moved about the garden, taking examples of the choicest blooms. He gathered them together into a luxurious bouquet, binding them with a ribbon he sought of Slater, and among the reds, fuschias, and gold, he set a single white rose. He carried the flowers with him as he returned through the city to the palace, emboldened by their beauty.

He came at last to the part of the palace where many of the women stayed. He found Aeryn there, making arrangements that he was sure pertained to the forthcoming wedding.

"Could I trouble you a moment, Aeryn?"

Despite the bustle of chatting women and quick-moving scribes, Aeryn turned to him with a smile. "Of course, Eamon."

"Is Lady Turnholt here with you?"

"She is."

Eamon's heart soared. "I am not sure she would accept them from me in person," he said, "but would you be willing to give these to her, from me?"

Aeryn's eyes fell to the dazzling bouquet. Entrusting the flowers to her, Eamon added: "Please tell Lady Turnholt that these flowers are no match to her, but I hope they will give her some joy today."

With a gentle smile, Aeryn nodded. "I will," she replied.

Eamon continued diligently for much of the rest of the day at his own tasks, spending time between the West Quarter and the port. But whenever he paused, his mind returned in delight to the banner that hung in the East and the promises and title that had been given to him there. They amazed him.

He knew also that not every man with him in the West would go with him to the East. He felt sure that Anderas would follow him; indeed, his certainty was confirmed when he spoke to the man later that afternoon.

"Anderas, when I take up the East Quarter, will you –?"

"Do you even have to ask?" his friend grinned.

In the early evening he gathered his men together in the West Quarter and explained the situation to them. He offered them each time to think on whether they would prefer to remain in the West or follow him to the East. Like Anderas, Manners threw his lot in with Eamon's at once. Doveton and Edelred's former servants expressed similar intent.

The meeting was a brief one, and, as the men returned each to their tasks, Eamon saw Giles.

"Giles," he said, "could you stay a moment?"

The man met his gaze and nodded. "Yes, First Knight."

Eamon waited while the others left the room.

"How can I serve you, First Knight?" Giles asked.

"Before you make your decision about the East or West, I need to speak to you," Eamon began. "About what happened between you and me when I entered your camp many months ago," he added quietly.

Giles frowned. "Do I need to know?"

"I think it right that you do," Eamon answered. He drew a deep breath. "I told you once that I would forget all enmity between you and me, and to that I hold. I also told you that the reason for your remembering so little about before is of my doing."

"I remember nothing of it," Giles answered. "It matters very little to me – what I have now is more important."

"Before you make a decision about whether or not to follow me, I want you to know the truth."

Giles measured his gaze for a moment. "If you insist upon it, then I will hear it."

"I was with a group of Hands," Eamon began. "We had been sent to scout the King's camp and draw up details as to its logistics. There was a cadet with us," he said gently, "a skilled cartographer. He was killed."

"I killed him?" Giles guessed.

"Yes," Eamon answered. He forced himself to meet Giles's gaze unflinchingly. "I loved this man," he said, "and, at that time, I hated you. You spoke the truth, and I hated you for it. I had betrayed the King and so you attacked me. I cannot claim that my manner of answering you was one of self-defence; it was not. I retaliated with all my power. I meant to strike you down."

Giles watched him carefully. "Sir –"

"You have heard of breachers," Eamon told him quietly. "I was one, and I opened your mind, Giles, but I did not mean to breach it; I meant to break it." Giles looked hard at him, surprised, and gave a low breath. "Where there is something that you do not recall, you do not recall it because I took it from you," Eamon said. It seemed long ago and yet so very vivid still before his mind. "I am sorry for what I did. You must know also," he added at last, "that I knew I had done wrong, and that I had no peace thereafter. When I destroyed your mind I saw how much I had become Edelred's servant. It was then that I resolved to turn back to the King."

"Then good came from it," Giles said simply.

"That still does not excuse what I did to you," Eamon replied. "I am sorry, Giles. Whatever wrongs you had done me…" He trailed off. "I should not have done it to you. But I was angry, and I was blinded, and I hated you. I do not now."

"I have no reason to disbelieve you," Giles told him. "Since I woke, sir, you have never spoken an unkind word to me, nor have you ever treated me with hatred or disdain. And all I have seen of you is courage." He watched Eamon for a long moment. "Thank you for telling me what happened," he said, "but I do not remember it. Why should I want to hold it against you?"

"Because I did it, and one day you may remember it," Eamon replied. "You may also remember the wilfulness and hatred with which I did it."

Giles laughed kindly. "You do not seem to be a man who does anything unless he does it wilfully," he replied. A small smile came onto his face. "That is how I know I don't need to hold it against you: wilfully you broke my mind, and wholeheartedly you spoke to me of it so that I would know of it before I remembered it. The latter far outweighs the former."

Eamon felt relieved. "Thank you," he said. "You are a good man, Giles. I am glad to have come to see that in you, and to have peace with you."

"Then we are both content," Giles smiled. "I will think on the matter with the East," he added.

"Thank you."

Giles bowed and left; Eamon watched him go. Could forgiveness – even where bitterness and hurt and wrath had passed between two men – be so simply and deeply given?

But Giles had forgiven him knowing what he had done – not remembering it, nor the agony which Eamon had caused. Did that undo the worth of the man's gesture?

Perhaps she would forgive him, too.

He gathered his things and returned to the palace.

As Eamon went through the Round Hall, a man called to him.

"First Knight?"

Eamon turned and stopped in surprise to see Captain Roe with a couple of King's men.

The captain sauntered up to him and bowed. "Good evening. I hope I'm not disturbing you."

"Not at all," Eamon answered, extending his hand. "Let me add my own words to the King's and say that it is a pleasure to have you in the city, captain."

Roe clasped his hand with a friendly smile. "Thank you."

"Are you seeing the palace?" Eamon asked.

"Yes. My wife needed to return to the theatre for a few things," Roe told him, "and the guards told me that I was welcome to walk while I waited for her return."

"It is a magnificent building," Eamon nodded.

"So Anderas explained to me," Roe smiled.

Eamon laughed. "Few escape him in such matters, I fear," Eamon replied. "I am sorry that he cornered you!"

"He served very briefly under me some years ago. Perhaps, on account of the old respect of an ensign for a commanding officer, he was lenient with me," Roe replied. He was quiet for a moment and then met Eamon's gaze again. "To tell the truth, sir, I hoped that I might find you. It may seem bold, but I wanted to thank you."

Eamon frowned in surprise. "Thank me?"

"My wife and I have spoken much today," Roe returned, and a smile grew on his face. "As perhaps you might imagine! She told me many things – I have been out of the city for a number of years – and she spoke to me of many people. She spoke of you in particular." The captain met his gaze. His eyes were creased with the passing of years. "You were the Right Hand," Roe said, "a man with many worries and troubles of his own. Even so, and at your own peril, you took my wife under your wing."

"I did," Eamon answered, "but, captain, you must know that never did I –"

"I know," Roe nodded. "Ilenia told me."

"I am sorry that I was only able to protect her for so short a time," Eamon answered.

"It seems to me that you were there to shield her when she was in the greatest danger," Roe replied.

"She would not have been in peril but for me..."

"But you saved her as a King's man."

Eamon blinked hard. "How do you know about that?"

Roe smiled. "In truth I merely suspected until you confirmed it just now. Ilenia suspected as well."

"It is true," Eamon answered.

"Then for that I thank you more than all the rest," Roe said. "Mine would have been a bitter homecoming, First Knight, to return to my city and to find her gone. The mark I bore on my palm is gone – I felt it go days ago. When it went I decided that I had to come to the city, to see if what we had heard was true." The captain touched his hand once, and smiled. "I had forgotten what it was to be without it. Perhaps you understand how free I feel to have lost it."

Eamon smiled. "I do," he answered. He measured the man's gaze, feeling a deep respect for him, then held out his hand and clasped Roe's once more. "This city has been mesmerized by your courage in returning to it, captain," he added. "If freedom from Edelred moves you as I feel it does, and you feel that it would be right, there is a place for you beneath the King's colours."

Roe's eyes widened. "Thank you, First Knight."

"Please give my kindest regards to your wife," Eamon said. "She is a noble woman, and I see that she is matched in that by her husband."

Roe thanked him again, and returned to his tour through the halls. Eamon watched him go. Then his eyes were drawn by a group of women passing through the far side of the hall. His pulse quickened. She walked with them.

The women moved purposefully – he knew they were deep in preparations for the marriage – but their eyes met. Her face was different, softer. Unable to contain it, a great smile spread across his face – a smile for her. Across the expanse of the hall, he bowed to her.

A flush of red, a demure gaze, and... the glimmer of a smile?

To him, it was as radiant as dawn.

The women passed from the hall.

CHAPTER XXXI

On the twenty-eighth of May the city woke to the proclamation that the King would be crowned three days thence. Dunthruik became a buzz of activity such as Eamon had never seen. The Coll was strung with jubilant blue banners and stars, while every house and every street was filled with flowers and with colour. At the Four Quarters great banners were hung. There was not a man about town who did not apply himself with gladness to his duties; and so anticipation heightened as the preparations continued.

Roe left the city to return to his men. Their surrender would be formally welcomed when they returned.

Work on the East Gate continued at a frenetic pace so that it might be as close as possible to ready for the coronation. But it was the Royal Plaza – the enormous square that had seen so many of Edelred's majesties – which became the most frenzied hive of activity. Though its walls and gates were still damaged from the explosion of the throned's artillery, Hughan chose it as the place for the coronation ceremony itself, as it was a space big enough to hold a large number of the city's people. The inns all over Dunthruik filled with guests. Eamon had never seen such a variety of people going through the city streets.

On the twenty-ninth Eamon received word that General Waite had departed Dunthruik. The news weighed on him but he had little time to think upon it.

In the days leading up to the coronation Eamon made several visits to the East Quarter and took careful note of the progress of reconstruction with Anastasius. He oversaw the unloading of another ship from Lamiglia.

Thanks to the returning ships, the air up and down the Coll was filled again with the smell of freshly baked bread. It was something that had long been missing from the city. A baker in the West Quarter baked star-shaped breads, in celebration of the forthcoming coronation. It was not long before bakers all over the city got wind of the idea and by the thirtieth of May the city was filled with "Brenuin" breads, as they soon became called. Eamon tried several different kinds and was surprised at the ingenuity with which the bakers vied, varying all manner of ingredients to produce sweet and savoury loaves.

It was as he was sampling some of these breads that Cartwright came to him. The man bowed low.

"Sir."

"Mr Cartwright, you catch me with my mouth full," Eamon mumbled, offering an apologetic smile.

"I am not offended, sir."

"I accept your indulgence with thanks!"

"I bring a message, sir, from Lady Turnholt."

Eamon fell still.

"She asked me to thank you, sir, for your letter and the flowers."

Though his feet remained firmly fixed on the ground, he felt his spirits soar heavenward.

"Mr Cartwright, your message is as joyous to me as the coming of the King himself!"

As darkness fell on the evening of the thirtieth, Eamon stood in the door of the West Quarter College, looking down through the Brand to the Coll.

Anderas came to his side. "Good evening, First Knight."

"The city, the River…" Eamon whispered. "It's almost as if everything quivers as it waits for the morning." He shook his head in amazement and drew his gaze from the city to look at Anderas. "Have you ever felt anything like this before, Andreas?"

"I have seen, and felt, many things in these walls," Anderas replied, "but never such a thing as this."

"Neither have I," Eamon breathed.

"Perhaps we never will again," Anderas mused, "and perhaps our children will gaze at us in awe when we tell them that we stood here, on this night, waiting for tomorrow."

Eamon sighed. "Perhaps they will," he answered quietly.

They stood in silence for a long time. It was as Eamon looked out over the star-struck city that long-buried words came to him:

> *"The dawn has come. The River sings*
> *To see the crowning of her King."*

Anderas looked at him in quiet amazement; there was no further word to be said.

The sun rose and the thirty-first of May soared in golden glory to the skies over the River Realm. The River was a running flood of silver and gold. The city stood, like a star, at its mouth.

The East Gate cast its doors open towards the dawn. It was in the gate, before the very threshold of the city, that Eamon waited. His whole heart was turned in wonder towards the one who rode in from the dawn-struck plain. The whole of Dunthruik lined the streets behind him, their breath still on their lips as they too watched.

From the east towards the blue-bannered city came the King. He rode on a great white horse whose mane was like silver fire, and he was dressed in blue. He bore no banner, but the silver circlet of stars resting on his brow was as bright as the sun.

The King halted before the gate and looked into the heart of the city.

"In the authority of the first promise I come," he said, his voice truer and finer than a joyous trumpet call. "I have followed the River from its source to its mouth; I have stayed the course. As

Brenuin I come, to uphold the pledge of my house with the River's Realm, until the stars go out."

The King's voice carried across the gates, washing over the stones so that they answered him. Light shivered in the stones all around him, singing the King's words back to him; the light shimmered and then grew faint.

Hughan met Eamon's gaze and the First Knight drew his sword. He had not held a sword since he had charged after Arlaith through the bowels of the palace, and for a moment he felt the fear and the terror of that chase fill him. But as the steel glinted before his eyes, it came to him that though it was a token of war it was also a symbol of justice, and a prize of peace.

Taking his sword firmly between his hands and raising it before him, Eamon turned from the plain to look down the Coll. It and the whole city were stretched out before him in the light – the Four Quarters, and beyond them the wash of the sea.

In the crystal silence of that moment, the Blind Gate saw the First Knight step across the threshold into the city. The King followed after him.

So it was that the sword heralded the star through the gate and down the streets of Dunthruik, before the watching gazes of the men and women of the River Realm. As they passed, reams of King's men stepped into formation behind them, each proudly holding aloft the banners of the King and the house of Brenuin. Banners showing the joined colours of all those who had been the King's allies against Edelred were there also.

The procession went down the Coll. At first many watched in silence, stunned still by the vision of the King coming through the gate and reclaiming the city as it had been usurped. Yet as they came under the great blue banners to the Four Quarters, applause erupted to north and south.

"Long live the King!" cried a voice. Suddenly the Four Quarters reverberated with it, North, South, East, and West. Men and women from every quarter were there. Some of them Eamon recognized, and scores upon scores of faces he did not know; but they knew him, and they cheered and sang as the procession went by.

"*Long live the King!*"

On they went, past the calling sea of faces, drawing ever closer to the Royal Plaza. Those who had cheered them joined the tail of the procession until the whole Coll became a river of living joy, singing the praise and life of its King.

They went to the Royal Plaza. There many were arrayed in waiting. The Easters and other men who served the King stood in formal lines. Those men turned to look at the arriving procession and stared in awe, for the King seemed like a bright rider come down from a distant age, and his face radiated the kindness and grace within him.

A platform had been set at the end of the square. Tall banners hung by it and at its centre stood a throne carved from light wood. A star was marked high on it, and the beams that stuck out from it were like sun-rays forming a living crown.

At the throne's side stood several figures cloaked in grey. The first among these was tall and grey haired, like a crested wave made man. His look was solemn but he seemed good. The man at his side held in his hands something covered with a blue cloth.

As the grey man stepped forward and stood before the throne, the whole square fell silent. His voice as he spoke was like the roll of the sea.

"Son of Elior," he called, "whom do you herald?"

Joy ran through Eamon's veins. "I herald Hughan," he called, "heir to the house of Brenuin and our undoubted King." So saying, he sheathed his sword and stepped aside, bowing before Hughan.

It was then that the King dismounted. He seemed to grow in greatness. He stepped forward before the grey-garbed bookkeepers, and stood unfalteringly before the first of them. That man then spoke again.

"Are you, Hughan Brenuin, the King of this River and its realm?"

"By promise and by blood," Hughan replied, "it is as you say."

"And are you, Hughan Brenuin, willing to take oaths before these, your people?"

The question hung in the air, and Eamon shook. Never would Edelred have answered such a demand, never would he have taken oaths; he had only commanded them. The watching city knew it as well as did the First Knight.

"I am willing," Hughan answered.

"Then come hither, Star of Brenuin."

Every eye was on the King as he went forward. As Hughan stepped onto the platform he bowed down to one knee before the grey-garbed man. The man turned to one of his fellows and drew away the cloth that covered what he bore. The gesture revealed a great book.

Eamon gasped as he saw it, understanding at once what it was: the surviving copy of the King's Covenant, made by the first of the Brenuin Kings long years before.

The bookkeeper held the book up to show it to the city, then turned to Hughan with it still in his hands. After Hughan had reached out and laid one hand upon it the bookkeeper spoke again.

"Will you solemnly promise and swear to govern the people of the River Realm according to its laws?"

"I will," Hughan answered.

"Will you, to the utmost of your power, cause law and mercy to be executed in all your judgments?"

"I will."

"Will you, to the utmost of your power, maintain this land in goodness and in hope, punishing the wicked, protecting and cherishing the just, maintaining the promise by which this land was founded, and leading your people by the way that they should go?"

"All these I promise to do," Hughan answered.

There was a moment of silence while the King's oaths filled the square and the city. Then Hughan rose to his feet before the bookkeeper. The man held his gaze for a moment before speaking again.

"In this book is held promise and wisdom and hope. Receive it, gracious King, and let it be in your heart and in your land."

He set the book into Hughan's hands; Eamon saw a flicker of blue about its pages, and he knew that all about him the world seemed silent.

The man in grey smiled as he looked on the King. "May your throne, delivered to you by those who have held the River's book and memory of the first promise, be established in righteousness. May peace be yours, and wisdom of governance. May you be strengthened, comforted, confirmed, and counselled, in knowledge and goodness, in reverence and hope, until the stars go out."

So saying, the bookkeeper stepped aside.

Hughan walked slowly forwards and then sat formally in the wooden throne. A scarcely audible, but keenly felt, gasp filled the square. As Hughan sat, the bookkeeper took a small blue flask from another of his fellows. Eamon did not know what it held but he watched as the keeper dipped his fingers into the flask and turned again to the King. He reached forward and, taking Hughan's hands, marked the shape of the star upon his palms.

"May your hands be anointed with oil of the promise," he said. "May your breast and brow be anointed with it also. May the promise live truly in your heart and in your house; may the work of your hands prosper; may you govern and preserve the lands and people given into your charge in wisdom, justice, and temperance. May you restore the things that have gone to decay and maintain the things that are restored. May you not forget your people, to whom your pledges are made, nor they you."

A crown was solemnly brought forth – it was tall, silver, and wrought about with bright stones as though with the twinkling stars of a silver sky.

The bookkeeper stepped behind the throne and raised the crown high in his hands over the King's head.

"This is a crown of faith, a symbol of majesty. With it may this, our King, be filled with grace and all princely virtues; may he be held in righteousness until the stars go out."

For a moment more he held the crown aloft and then, before the city and the River, he set it upon Hughan's head.

Cries of joy pealed in Eamon's heart, and there were tears in his eyes. Yet he remained in silence a moment more.

The bookkeeper stood before Hughan again. "May you have faithful councils and quiet realms," he said. "May you have sure defence against enemies, a prosperous land, wise counsellors, and honest, peaceable, and dutiful people. May the promise which has made you King over them give you increase of grace, honour and happiness, vigilance and valour, until the stars go out."

The bookkeeper stepped back and bowed down once to his knees before rising to his feet and turning to the watching people. "A star over his house," he called. "Long live the King!"

With one cheering and jubilant voice the River Realm answered him:

"Long live the King!"

When the shout quieted, the bookkeeper looked kindly to Eamon. "Let the King's First Knight come forth."

Eamon went forward up onto the platform. In a daze of joy he knelt before the starry throne. Hughan was before him. As he knelt there, Eamon held forth his hands; Hughan placed his own about them. Eamon took a deep breath as he declared his fealty to Hughan in words he never dreamt would escape his lips.

"I, Eamon Goodman, will be faithful and true," he said. His hands shook but he felt the press of the King's palms about his own, holding him and calling him on to courage. "Faith and truth will I bear unto you," he said, "and unto the heirs of your house, as long as I live, until the stars go out." So saying Eamon bent his head forward and joyfully kissed Hughan's hand.

The King smiled at him. "Your faith I receive, Eamon Goodman," he said, "proclaiming you First Knight of this realm, first defender of my house, and first voice of my people."

Two bookkeepers came forward, carrying between their hands a long, dark blue cloak. For a moment Eamon noticed nothing else about it, but then he couldn't believe what he saw.

At its bold heart stood the sword and star. The emblem had been sewn in silver and edged in black. The eight slim beams of the star reached out to the cloak's black edge, the downward beam behind the blade of the sword. In the two top corners of the cloak two black horses reared, stars shining brightly at their breasts.

Tears of amazement filled Eamon's eyes as the bookkeepers came forward. The cloak he wore was taken from off his shoulders, and then the cloak of the First Knight was laid upon him.

As the bookkeepers fell back a pace, the King rose, bidding Eamon to do the same.

"Draw your sword, First Knight."

Eamon did so, laying his blade across his hands before kneeling again to Hughan. The King laid his hands on the blade of Eamon's sword.

"Bear not, First Knight, this sword in vain," he said. "Bear it for the protection and encouragement of those who do good, and for the terror of those who knowingly do evil. With it, protect my house and all in this land, from the greatest to the least. May your promise and service to me be of comfort and of hope, to you and to all those who serve me, and may you strike in goodness, in truth, and in courage always."

Hughan leaned forward and kissed his brow. Eamon felt the strength and loving wholeness of that gesture, knowing at last what Edelred had always meant to claim for his own, and knowing that the King had restored it to its proper place.

"Rise, First Knight," Hughan said. "May courage always be first in your heart."

Eamon rose. Hughan turned with him to look at the people.

"This man is Eamon Goodman," the King said. "He is the First Knight and witness of my house, of my realm, and of this city.

"But not to Dunthruik do I present him, for this city shall be called Dunthruik no more. The name of this city shall henceforth be Eldaran – a city of promise shall it be.

"Eldaran, here is your knight."

There was an awe-stricken silence. And the city rejoiced.

"Eldaran for the King! Eldaran for the First Knight!"

The calls shivered through Eamon. He remembered the prophecy delivered, what seemed so long ago, by Ashway: *The city rises with a new name...*

Tears struck his eyes. He had lived to hear that name. Eldaran would be a city of Kings and promise, and he was its First Knight.

As the applause quieted again, Eamon, shaking from the city's praise, stepped to one side. The bookkeeper's voice stilled the air.

"On this day that the River's realm takes a King and a First Knight, a queen shall it take also," he said, and he smiled. "Let her come forth!"

There was a stir of music and then a group of women proceeded with solemn joy through the square. Aeryn walked at their head. Eamon stared at her in awe, for she was dressed in purest white. Her hair was caught back with bright flowers, and her eyes shone. Behind her walked six women, each dressed in the King's blue and each bearing a part of her train. Leon walked at her side, his arm looped through her own.

Among the bridesmaids went Alessia. She wore a single white rose in her hair and, as the bridal party came forward, her eyes sought his. Her tender look was for him.

Leon led Aeryn to the platform and up the steps to where Hughan stood. The King's face filled with unspeakable pride and joy as Aeryn came before him.

Eamon, Leon, and the bridesmaids stepped formally down from the platform. As they did so, Eamon saw Hughan and Aeryn standing, hand in hand, before the bookkeeper.

"As is the pledge between the King and the River Realm, so it is between a man and his wife," the bookkeeper said, looking sincerely to the King. "Hughan Brenuin, do you mean to hold to this woman in the fullness of that promise, doing her love and honour, rendering comfort in adversity and song in joy, protecting her and serving her, until your days are ended?"

"So mean I," Hughan answered.

"Aeryn Connara, lady of Edesfield, do you mean to hold to this man in the fullness of that same promise, doing him love and honour, rendering comfort in adversity and song in joy, protecting him and serving him, until your days are ended?"

"So mean I," Aeryn said. A thrilling quiet followed her words.

"Take, then, these rings," the bookkeeper told them. Eamon saw two rings being set before the King and his queen. "And with them speak your pledges."

Hughan and Aeryn turned to face each other. Eamon watched in amazement as they then knelt down together.

Taking up a ring, Hughan gently took Aeryn's hand. His voice was deep and loving. "With this ring I wed you, and with it I make my promise," he said, "to cherish you in all seasons, forsaking all others, until my days are ended. You shall be the crown of my joy, this day and all days. In love shall I serve you and honour you, dear queen and dearer wife."

"With this ring I wed you," Aeryn answered, setting a ring on Hughan's hand, "and with it I make my promise to cherish you in all seasons, forsaking all others, until my days are ended. You shall be the lord of my heart, this day and all days. In love shall I serve you and honour you, dear King and dearer husband."

They clasped together their ringed hands as the bookkeeper spoke again.

"River's Realm and city," he said, "behold here your King and queen, remembering that as a lord he will serve and save you, and as a bride you may rejoice in him and honour him." He turned to Hughan and Aeryn, a great smile on his face. "Your pledges made, honour your bride, O King, and welcome her with a loving kiss."

There, before the watching eyes of the city, the kneeling King joyfully kissed his wife. As he did so the square erupted into applause and overwhelming cheers. They were cheers that only grew as the King and queen then rose to their feet, hand in hand.

"Long live the King! Long live the queen! Long live the house of Brenuin!"

Eamon was on his feet with the whole city, his being overwhelmed as the King and queen received the hearts of their people. He watched with tears streaming down his face as he beat his hands together with the force of his rejoicing soul. It was a joy made keener by the long, dark road that he had followed to reach that day.

So Eldaran rejoiced.

The King and queen came down from the platform in procession, the bookkeepers behind them, towards the palace. It was there that the day's ceremonies were to be feasted. Great banqueting tables had been laid throughout the palace halls.

As Eamon followed the procession into the palace, music began in every quarter of the city, rising with the people's cheers.

The King and queen went to the throne room. Long tables had been set there and Eamon was amazed to see their bounty and their beauty. There were musicians robed in blue, and as the King and queen arrived, they played, strumming and singing with the same infectious joy found throughout the whole of the city.

The hall filled with guests: Anderas and Giles, then Feltumadas, Ithel, Anastasius, and the other Easters. Each one spoke to the King, congratulating him and the smiling queen. Servants, lords, wayfarers, and ex-Gauntlet alike soon joined them. Eamon knew that the palace was filled with dozens of the same. Anderas was carried away in conversation with Leon. Manners and Lillabeth sat together at another table. Doveton and Giles raised glasses to him in tacit celebration. There were men and women in the room whom Eamon loved, and Eamon knew as he looked that all that he had done in Dunthruik had been for this day, and for this joy. He wondered, as he watched, what Mathaiah would have thought to see it.

The throne room had been cast with great blue banners. Where

Edelred's throne had once stood, where Eamon had knelt countless times – in fear, in terror, in loathing, and in shame – there now stood a tall wooden throne on which was carved a star. As he looked at it, Eamon's heart grew light. Never would he kneel before that throne, or the one to whom it belonged, in fear.

As the music continued, he made his way to Aeryn's side. She was speaking to Ithel, but as he approached, the Easter lord bowed to him.

"First Knight," he said, "or Lord Goodman, as you shall soon be called again."

"Lord Ithel," Eamon answered.

"I am very glad that I spared you at Pinewood," Ithel smiled, and clasped his hand. "May a star be over your house, and yours, my lady." He bowed again to Aeryn.

"Thank you," Aeryn answered with a smile.

Ithel took his leave and went on. Eamon turned to Aeryn.

"Congratulations." He looked at her, at her smiling face and at the flowers caught up in her hair, and smiled, taking her hands in his as he had done at the Hidden Hall long months before. "You look wonderful."

Aeryn blushed. "Thank you."

Eamon smiled at her – and his mind was filled with thoughts of the one who had worn a white rose in her hair.

"Aeryn, I would like to speak to Lady Turnholt. Perhaps you have heard her thoughts of late. Do you think that she would welcome me?"

With a smile, Aeryn lightly kissed his cheek. "I think she would."

"I saw her among your ladies before. Do you know where I might find her?"

"I was just speaking to her. She wanted to walk in the gardens."

Eamon nodded silently.

Aeryn pressed his hand. "You are a man of promise and of courage," she said, "and I am glad, Eamon, that you will be a guardian of my husband, and of my house."

Aeryn embraced him. As he stepped back he saw that Hughan watched him from across the hall. As Eamon met his gaze the King nodded to him with a gentle, and encouraging, smile.

"Courage." Eamon whispered the word to himself. Aeryn smiled.

"Courage," she agreed.

The sound of the musicians was on the air as Eamon stepped from the great corridors of the palace and into the gardens. Spring blossomed into summer about him, a wash of life and hope. He felt the sun on his face.

For a short time he followed the garden path, lost in the sights and sounds and smells of the garden. His feet took him on, and he knew not where he went in the wide garden; he knew only that he would find the one whom he sought.

He came at last to the heart of the gardens and stood still for a moment in the sun. As he surveyed the leafy, radiant world about him he remembered, as though in a living memory, the song that had so captivated him at the Crown:

"As roses smell their sweetest after rain…"

It had brought him hope then, and did so again in that moment.

Before him was the fountain, its great eagles gone. Beyond it the hidden path led to the garden of roses and the basin of stars. Looking at the twining path of petals and of thorns, he knew that it was the path to follow.

It led him truly. The white wooden frames stood still, rose-twined.

The garden was sheltered and quiet; peace dwelt there. Like a wanderer from a distant land reaching home at last, he was filled with wonder.

He saw the basin. The pool of clear water caught in the stones reflected the highest reaches of the sky. The tall pedestal was wound about with carved flowers that blossomed like stars, and at the steps of the pedestal, with her head leant gracefully against its stem, sat the one he sought.

Eamon paused. Her back was almost to him and her long, beautiful hair tressed the stones against which she leant. In silence she sat, lost in all her own thought; and as Eamon watched her he felt his resolve strengthening.

Quietly he stepped forward and crossed the small courtyard. The breeze whispered through the roses.

Her eyes were closed. Eamon paused by her, watching the wind stir in her star-woven hair, and as he gazed at her, he saw how fair she was.

"My lady."

Her eyes – eyes where he had so often seen himself – looked up at him. They rimmed with tears.

"You came," she breathed.

"Yes. Too late, I know; but I have come."

She lowered her gaze, seeming not to know what to say. "Thank you for your messages."

"Thank you for receiving them." He watched as she turned a white rose in her hands. "My lady, might I sit with you a while?"

"Yes."

Quietly Eamon sat beside her. The stone was cool.

"I spoke out of turn to you when last we met," she told him. "I was hurt, and angry."

"Lady, you had every reason to be both," he answered. "I did you great wrong."

There was silence. Biting her lip, Alessia fingered the rose petals. Tears stung his eyes, for as he looked at her he saw her as he had never seen her before: fair she was, bright and noble as a star before him.

"Great wrong you bore for me," he said. "I did not deserve your faith, and yet you still kept it for me."

"Yes." Fresh tears touched her face. Eamon longed to brush them away.

"I am sorry for all that was done to you on account of me," he told her. "I wish that I could undo it. I wish that I could have understood the truth. I wish I could have seen clearly when you first spoke to me. I wish I had protected you, as you deserved. I am sorry for what I did to you. I am sorry for speaking ill of you, for harbouring hatred against you in my heart. I know now that I was at fault, and that I poured sorrow, in the full strength of my will, upon you. And yet… you bore it. After all that I did, and all I said? I do not know how you saw to keep your faith with me. I know only that you did." He gazed at her in awe. "Why did you, and for so worthless a man as I?"

Alessia was silent for a long time. When at last she spoke, her voice was scarcely audible above the singing roses.

"Because I loved you," she whispered.

There was quiet between them. As he looked at her then Eamon knew that, despite all that had passed between them, he loved her still.

"I have come to seek your forgiveness."

"Forgiveness?" she breathed.

"I cannot undo what you endured for me," Eamon answered. "I cannot undo the darkness, the tears and lies, the life and love lost. I will not ask if you love me still, or whether you may yet love me again. Rather, I here confess my wrongs to you. I treated ill with you, and in my anger and my hurt I forgot all that I loved, and all that I had promised to be. Forgive me."

Alessia held him in her gaze for long moments. "It is a difficult thing you ask of me, Eamon."

He swallowed. "I understand."

She drew a deep breath and closed her eyes for a moment. "But it is my choice. Eamon… I forgive you."

The weight of a universe lifted from him. Eamon gazed back at her with compassion and joy and wonder. "It is more than I deserve. Thank you, Alessia."

Then her face softened. His voice empassioned, he whispered, "I cannot imagine what paths of grief and torment you have trodden since those dark days when we parted, nor what rage and suffering you bear still. But I know that you have set your heart on peace, and on life in hope. If... if you would be willing, I would walk with you along that way to peace. And I would have peace with you." He laughed gently. "Dear Alessia," he said, and it was as her name came from his lips that he reached across and earnestly took her gentle hand in his own. "I would have peace with you, for all the days of my life."

For a moment she watched him, and for a moment he feared that she would not speak. Then her fingers pressed his.

"And I with you," she answered. "Until the stars go out."

They watched each other. A smile, such as Eamon had always loved, touched her face.

She laid her head then against his shoulder and spoke his name to him. The music of Eldaran and of the King danced all about them. The roses swayed to it.

Gently he turned and kissed her forehead. "Until the stars go out," he whispered.

So they sat together, hand in hand and brow against brow, until the twilight high above them brought forth the long-awaited evening stars.

EPILOGUE

Hughan Brenuin was crowned King over the River Realm five hundred and thirty-three years after the battle of Edesfield. How long it had been since the promise that had first brought the house of Stars to the River had long since been forgotten.

Following the crowning of the King, the First Knight was set over the East Quarter, which he loved as dearly as he had ever done. Many of his men, including Giles, followed him, and the East was proud ever after of the First Knight's special history with the quarter. Wilhelm Bellis took up the King's colours shortly after the First Knight came to the East. As he had been at the battle of Dunthruik, he was made the First Knight's standard bearer.

The doors of the city's university were opened and the bookkeepers kept the newly scribed people's copy of the King's Covenant there. The folk of the River Realm came to see it and read the promises joining them and their King.

The Coll was renamed the King's Way, remembering always the first entry that Hughan Brenuin had made into the city, and the Four Quarters were often strung with stars. The Crown Theatre retained its name. On Shoreham's death, Ilenia Roe was made the theatre's director. She commissioned the writing of many new works and took dozens of writers under her wing. The theatre's inaugural performance following the coronation, *Brothers in Law*, was remembered in later years as one of the most loved pieces of theatre that the city had ever seen.

Shortly after his coronation, Hughan formed an order of knights, known as the Knights of the Star, to serve him under the

First Knight. It was not an order of wealth or lands but rather of heart. Many were those who sought to join it. General Rocell took the King's colours and devoted much of his time to liaising with the realm's knights and nobles. Febian, returned at length from his flight, also became a King's man; he worked with the King's riders, helping to form a unit of horse-archers to serve the King's banner.

In early June Captain Roe and his men were welcomed into the city and gave their formal surrender. Many of them took the King's colours and their captain was made one of the King's own generals. It was a title additionally granted to Andreas Anderas, who later also became a Knight of the Star.

Callum Tenent was admitted to this order some years later. His sister, her husband, and their daughter were there to witness the giving of his promises to the First Knight and the King.

In September of 533 Rory Manners married Lillabeth Grahaven, meaning to provide for her and for her child. Eamon Grahaven was born in October and was visited by his father's father. Upon the young child were formally bestowed the lands and titles of the Grahavens, to be kept in trust until his coming of age.

In August of 534 Queen Aeryn gave birth to her first child and heir of her husband's house. Two more children of royal blood came in the years that followed, and all three grew strong and bright, showing their parents' courage and hope.

Not long after the birth of Hughan's first-born son, Eamon Goodman took the hand of Alessia Turnholt in marriage.

Three years after Hughan's coronation an alliance of merchants, assisted by rebels and led by the Etraian princes, led a great force towards Hughan's city. It was a mission undertaken partly in vengeance and partly in pride. Leaving Queen Aeryn to govern in his stead and General Alnos to assist her, the King went to meet the invaders. Many King's men and former Gauntlet took anew his colours and went with him to battle. Both King and First Knight fought at the battle of Brightwood, where the merchants were at last decisively defeated. It was a fiercer, bloodier field than that of Dunthruik, and was the place where Giles and Sir Rocell both lost their lives, to the great sorrow of those who knew them. Thousands of men were injured, including General Anderas, who returned to Eldaran with no fewer than two arrow wounds. The King's victory at Brightwood marked the beginning of a flourishing peace for the River Realm.

Anastasius and the Easter lords returned each to their own country. The Land of the Seven Sons rejoiced at the return of its masters, but bitter feuds followed in those years as the cities and their lordlings quarrelled over successions. Lord Anastasius did bring those under him to peace, though it took several years, and the lives of both Lord Ithel and Lord Ylonous were lost before peace was restored.

Of the Easters only Lord Feltumadas remained in Eldaran. He had learned much of the ways of war. He stayed then in the King's city to learn the ways of peace and prove himself a worthy heir to his father. He was a trusted advisor at the King's court, and his wife, Aiday, soon joined him there. When Lord Feltumadas learned of his half-brother Ithel's death, it was the King's First Knight who sat with him through his grief and rage, and calmed him. Over time, Lord Feltumadas and the First Knight became firm friends, though they still fiercely – and sometimes angrily – debated many matters.

In 547 Lord Feltumadas at last returned to Istanaria, to be formally recognized as heir to the Land of the Seven Sons, arriving there shortly before his father's death. At Feltumadas's request, and remembering a wish expressed long before, the First Knight went with him to the sun-struck halls of the Easter princes. He returned to Eldaran after long months and was received home with joy.

Lady Alben lived for a number of years and, upon her death, bequeathed all her family's holdings to the King. At her death Alduin Waite reluctantly returned to the city and there, but a short time later, he also died. The First Knight sat as his sole companion as he lay upon his deathbed.

In 550 Hughan's eldest son came of age. Prince Edwin, a bold and fiery young man, was made a Knight of the Star, and in that order he spent much time with his father's First Knight. At that time the duchy of the West Bank, lost long years before on the death of Elaina's husband, was restored, to be held in regency until Hughan's second son was old enough to claim it for himself.

The First Knight remained faithful to his King all his days. In 551, long after he and his wife had thought it lost to them, Alessia conceived a child. Mathaias Goodman was born in the spring of 552, to the delight and joy of the whole city.

So it was that on the day when Prince Edwin took his father's throne, the house of Brenuin was served still by the house of Goodman.